Elizabeth George's first novel, *A Great Deliverance*, was honoured with the Anthony and Agatha Best First Novel awards in America and received the Grand Prix de Littérature Policière in France. The critically acclaimed *Payment in Blood* followed, and *Well-Schooled in Murder*, which was awarded the prestigious German prize for international mystery fiction, the MIMI, in 1990. *A Suitable Vengeance, For the Sake of Elena, Missing Joseph, Playing for the Ashes, In the Presence of the Enemy, Deception on his Mind, In Pursuit of the Proper Sinner, A Traitor to Memory, A Place of Hiding, With No One as Witness* and most recently *Careless in Red*, were also highly acclaimed by critics. Her novels have now been adapted for television by BBC TV. Elizabeth George lives on Whidbey Island, in the state of Washington. Visit her website at www.elizabeth-georgeonline.com.

Praise for Elizabeth George and *This Body of Death*:

'Terrific as always – and how great to have Lynley back on the force.'
Time Out

'Dark, unrelenting and powerful'   *Kirkus Reviews*

'An intelligent book, clipped and precise, every word chosen with care . . . a cool, clever book that needs concentration and a sharp brain to unravel . . . Along the way to solving the crime we meet some finely drawn characters who emerge as real people with faults and frailties. Ms George is the connoisseur's crime writer. Like fine wine, her words need to be savoured . . . Lynley is a policeman with a gentle touch and it is good to have him back on such brilliant form.'   *Sunday Express*

'The author writes brilliantly and has an incredible ability to set a scene and create characters you want to know more about.'   *Sun*

'This is crime writing at its finest. George's books are long, solid and wonderfully crafted; she is a modern Dorothy L Sayers.'   *Saga*

Also by Elizabeth George

Fiction
A Great Deliverance
Payment in Blood
Well-Schooled in Murder
A Suitable Vengeance
For the Sake of Elena
Missing Joseph
Playing for the Ashes
In the Presence of the Enemy
Deception on His Mind
In Pursuit of the Proper Sinner
A Traitor to Memory
A Place of Hiding
With No One as Witness
What Came Before He Shot Her
Careless in Red

Short Stories
The Evidence Exposed
I, Richard

Anthology
Crime From the Mind of A Woman (Ed.)
Two of the Deadliest (Ed.)

Non-Fiction
Write Away: One Novelist's Approach to Fiction and the
Writing Life

ELIZABETH GEORGE

This Body of Death

HODDER

First published in Great Britain in 2010 by Hodder & Stoughton
An Hachette UK company

First published in paperback in 2011

1

Copyright © Susan Elizabeth George 2010

A CIP catalogue record for this title is available from
the British Library

ISBN 978 1 444 71119 6 (B format)
ISBN 978 0 340 92302 3 (A format)

Typeset in Plantin Light by
Palimpsest Book Production Limited, Falkirk, Stirlingshire

Printed and bound by CPI Mackays,
Chatham, Kent

Hodder & Stoughton policy is to use papers that are natural, renewable
and recyclable products and made from wood grown in sustainable
forests. The logging and manufacturing processes are expected to
conform to the environmental regulations of the country of origin.

Hodder & Stoughton Ltd
338 Euston Road
London NW1 3BH

www.hodder.co.uk

What a wretched man I am! Who will rescue me
from this body of death?

Romans, 7:24

For Gaylynnie

BEGINNINGS

Reports from the investigating officers who interviewed both Michael Spargo and his mother prior to charges being filed against him all suggest that the morning of the boy's tenth birthday began badly. While such reports might well be deemed suspect, considering the nature of Michael's crime and the strength of the antipathy felt towards him by police and by members of his community, one cannot ignore the fact that the extensive document written by the social worker who sat with him during his interrogations and his subsequent trial reveals the same information. There will always be details that remain unavailable to the student of childhood abuse, family dysfunction, and the psychopathology that such abuse and dysfunction ultimately engender, but major facts cannot be hidden because they will necessarily be witnessed or directly experienced by those who come into contact with individuals in the midst of displaying – whether consciously or unconsciously – their mental, psychological and emotional disturbances. Such was the case with Michael Spargo and his family.

As one of nine boys, Michael had five older brothers. Two of these boys (Richard and Pete, aged eighteen and fifteen at the time) as well as their mother Sue each had supervision orders filed against them as a result of ongoing disputes with their neighbours, harassment of pensioners living on the council estate, public drunkenness and destruction of public and private property. There was no father present in the home. Four years prior to Michael's tenth birthday, Donovan Spargo had deserted wife and children and taken up life in Portugal with a widow fifteen years his senior, leaving a note of farewell and five pounds in coins on the kitchen table. He had not been seen or heard of since. He made no appearance at Michael's trial.

Sue Spargo, whose employment skills were minimal and whose education was limited to a failure to pass any one of her GCSEs, readily admits that she 'took to the drink a bit too hard' as a result of this desertion and was consequently largely unavailable to any of her boys from that time forward. Prior to Donovan Spargo's desertion, it seems that the family maintained some degree of external stability (as indicated both by school reports and by anecdotal evidence from neighbours and the local police), but once the head of household departed, whatever dysfunction had been hidden from the community came spilling out.

The family lived on the Buchanan Estate, a dreary sprawl of grey concrete-and-steel tower blocks and unappealing terrace houses in a section of town fittingly called the Gallows, which was known for street fights, muggings, car jackings and burglaries. Murder was rare here, but violence was common. The Spargos were among the luckier inhabitants. Because of the size of the family, they lived in one of the terrace houses and not in one of the tower blocks. They had a garden at the back of their house and a square of earth at the front although neither of these was kept up for planting. The house contained a sitting room and kitchen, four bedrooms and one bathroom. Michael shared a room with the younger boys. There were five of them in all, distributed in two sets of bunk beds. Three of the older boys shared an adjoining bedroom. Only Richard, the eldest, had his own room, a privilege apparently having to do with Richard's propensity for committing acts of violence upon his younger brothers. Sue Spargo had a separate bedroom as well. Curiously, in interviews she repeated several times that when any of the boys became ill, they slept with her and 'not with that lout Richard.'

On Michael's tenth birthday, the local police were called shortly after seven in the morning. A family dispute had escalated to the point of causing a disturbance in the immediate neighbourhood when the occupants of the house adjoining the Spargos' dwelling had attempted to intervene. Their later claim was that they were merely seeking peace and quiet. This is in opposition to Sue Spargo's allegation that they attacked her boys. However, a careful reading of everyone's ensuing interview with the police shows that a brawl between Richard and Pete Spargo began in the upstairs corridor of the Spargo house and grew from the latter boy's unhurried vacating of the bathroom. Richard's subsequent attack upon Pete was brutal, as he was much larger and stronger than his fifteen-year-old brother. It brought sixteen-year-old Doug to his assistance, which seems to have turned Richard and Pete into allies, who then attacked Doug. By the time Sue Spargo waded into the fray, it had spilled down the stairs. When it appeared that she, too, was going to come under attack from Richard and Pete, twelve-year-old David sought to protect her with a knife from the kitchen, where he'd gone allegedly to make his breakfast.

It was at this point that the neighbours became involved, roused by the noise, which they could hear through the badly insulated walls of the adjoining houses. Unfortunately, the neighbours – three in all – came to the Spargo residence armed with a cricket bat, a tyre iron and a hammer, and according to his account it was the sight of these that inflamed Richard Spargo. 'Going after the family, they were,' was his direct statement, the words of a boy who saw himself as the man of the house whose duty it was to protect his mother and siblings.

Into this developing imbroglio, Michael Spargo awakened. 'Richard and Pete was going at it with Mum,' his statement recounts. 'We could hear them, me and the little ones, but we didn't want nothing to do with it.' He indicates that he wasn't frightened, but when probed for more information it's clear that Michael did his best to give his older brothers a wide berth so as to avoid 'a thumping if I looked at them crosswise'. That he wasn't always able to avoid the thumping is a fact attested to by his teachers, three of whom reported to social workers bruises, scratches, burns and at least one black eye seen on Michael's body. Other than a single visit to the home, however, nothing more came of these reports. The system, it seems, was overburdened.

There is some suggestion that Michael passed on this abuse to his younger brothers. Indeed, from accounts gathered once four of the children went into care, it seems that Michael was given the responsibility of seeing to it that his sibling Stevie did not 'wee the sheets'. Without resources as to how this was supposed to be accomplished, he apparently administered regular thrashings to the seven-year-old, who in turn took out his own rage on the other boys further down the line.

Whether Michael abused any of the littler boys that morning is not known. He reports only that once the police arrived, he got out of bed, dressed in his school uniform and went down to the kitchen with the intention of having his breakfast. He knew it was his birthday, but he had no expectation of the day being acknowledged. 'Didn't care, did I?' was how he later put it to the police.

Breakfast consisted of frosted flakes and jam rolls. There was no milk for the cereal – Michael brings up this point twice in his initial interviews – so Michael ate the frosted flakes dry, leaving most of the jam rolls for his younger brothers. He put one of these into the pocket of his mustard-coloured anorak (both the jam roll and the anorak becoming crucial details as things developed) and he left the house through the back garden.

He said his intention was to go directly to school, and in his first interview with the police he claims he did go there. This was a story he did not change until he was read the statement made by his teacher attesting to his truancy that day, at which point he changed his story to confess that he went into the allotments, which were a feature of the Buchanan Estate and which were positioned behind the terrace where the Spargos lived. There, he 'might've give a bit of aggro to an old bugger working in a patch of veg' and he 'might've bashed in some shed door or something' where he 'could've nicked some secateurs maybe only I didn't keep them, I never kept them'. The 'old bugger' in question does verify Michael's presence in the allotment at eight in the morning, although it's doubtful that the small enclosures of raised beds held much attraction for the boy, who seems to have spent some fifteen minutes 'tramping them about' according to the pensioner, until 'I gave him a right proper talking to. He swore like a little thug and scarpered.'

It seems at this point that Michael headed in the general direction of his school, some half mile from the Buchanan Estate. It was somewhere on this route, however, that he encountered Reggie Arnold.

*   *   *

Reggie Arnold was quite a contrast to Michael Spargo. Where Michael was tall for his age and rake thin, Reggie was squat and had carried baby fat well beyond babyhood. His head was regularly shaved to the skull, which made him the subject of considerable teasing at school (he was generally referred to as 'that slaphead Charlie Brown wanker') but, unlike Michael's, his clothing was usually neat and clean. His teachers report that Reggie was a 'good boy but with a short fuse' and when pressed they tend to identify the cause of this short fuse as 'Dad and Mum's troubles and then there's the trouble with his sis and brother'. From this, it is probably safe to assume that the unusual nature of the Arnold marriage in addition to the disability of an older brother and the mental incapacity of a younger sister put Reggie into a position of getting lost in the shuffle of daily life.

Rudy and Laura Arnold, it must be said, had been dealt a difficult hand of cards. Their older son was permanently wheelchair bound from severe cerebral palsy and their daughter had been deemed unfit for a normal classroom education. These two elements of the Arnolds' life had the effect of simultaneously focusing nearly all parental attention on the two problematical children and burdening what was already a rather fragile marriage in which Rudy and Laura Arnold had separated time and again, putting Laura into the position of coping on her own.

Caught up in the middle of trying familial circumstances, Reggie was unlikely to receive much attention. Laura readily confesses that she 'didn't do right by the boy', but his father claims that he 'had him over the flat five or six times', in apparent reference to meeting his paternal obligations during those periods when he and his wife were living apart. As can be imagined, Reggie's unmet need for nurturing metamorphosed into common attempts at gaining adult attention. In the streets, he evidenced this through petty thievery and the occasional bullying of younger children; in the classroom, he acted up. This acting up was seen by his teachers, unfortunately, as the aforementioned 'short fuse' and not as the cry for help it actually was. When thwarted, he was given to throwing his desk, beating his head upon it and upon the walls and falling to the floor in a tantrum.

On the day of the crime, accounts have it – and CCTV films confirm – that Michael Spargo and Reggie Arnold encountered each other at the corner shop nearest the Arnold home and on Michael's route to school. The boys were acquainted and had evidently played together in the past but were as yet unknown to each other's parents. Laura Arnold reports that she'd sent Reggie to the shops for milk, and the shopkeeper confirms that Reggie purchased a half litre of semi-skimmed. He also apparently stole two Mars bars 'for a bit of a laugh,' according to Michael.

Michael attached himself to Reggie. Along the route back to the Arnold house, the boys extended their enjoyment of Reggie's errand by opening the milk and dumping its contents into the petrol tank of a Harley-Davidson motorcycle, an act of mischief witnessed by the motorcycle's owner, who chased them unsuccessfully afterwards. He was later to remember the mustard-coloured anorak that Michael Spargo was wearing, and although he was not able to identify either boy by name, he recognised a photo of Reggie Arnold when the police presented it to him, along with other faces.

Reaching home without the milk he'd been sent out to fetch, Reggie reported to his mother – with Michael Spargo as putative witness – that he'd been bullied by two boys who took the money intended for the milk. 'He cried and was getting himself into one of his states,' Laura Arnold reports. 'And I believed him. What else was there to do?' This is indeed a relevant question, for without her husband in the home and considering that she was attempting alone to care for two disabled children, a missing carton of milk, no matter how needed it might have been that morning, would have seemed a very small matter to her. She did, however, want to know who Michael Spargo was, and she asked her son that question. Reggie identified him as a 'mate from school', and he took Michael along to do his mother's next bidding, which was evidently to get his sister out of bed. By now, it was in the vicinity of eight forty-five and, if the boys planned to go to school that day, they were going to be late. Doubtless, they knew this, as Michael's interview details an argument that Reggie had with his mother following her instructions to him: 'Reggie started whingeing about how it would make him late, but she didn't care. She told him to get his bum upstairs and fetch his sister. She said he was to pray to God and say thanks that he wasn't 'like the other two', by which she likely was referring to the disabilities of his brother and sister. This last remark from Laura Arnold appears to have been a common refrain.

Despite the command, Reggie did not fetch his sister. Rather, he told his mother to 'do the bad thing to herself' (these are Michael's words as Reggie seems to have been more direct) and the boys left the house. Back in the street, however, they saw Rudy Arnold who, during the time they'd spent in the kitchen with Laura, had arrived by car and was 'hanging 'bout outside, like he was afraid to come in'. He and Reggie exchanged a few words, which seem to have been largely unpleasant, at least on Reggie's part. Michael claims he asked who the man was, assuming it was 'his mum's boyfriend or something', and Reggie told him 'the stupid git' was his father and followed this declaration with a minor act of vandalism: he took a milk basket from a neighbour's front step and threw it into the street, where he jumped upon it and crushed it.

According to Michael, he took no part in this. His statement asserts that at this point he had every intention of going to school, but that Reggie announced he was 'doing a bunk' and 'having some bloody fun for once'. It was Reggie, Michael says, and not Michael himself who came up with the idea of including Ian Barker in what was to follow.

At eleven years old, Ian Barker had already been labelled as damaged, difficult, troubled, dangerous, borderline, angry and psychopathic, depending upon whose report is read. He was, at this time, the only child of a twenty-four-year-old mother (his paternity remains unknown to this day), but he'd been brought up to believe that this young woman was his older sister. He seems to have been quite fond of his grandmother, who he naturally assumed was his mother, but he apparently loathed the girl he'd been taught to believe was his sister. At the age of nine, he was considered old enough to learn the truth. However, it was a truth he did not take well to hearing, especially as it came hard on the heels of Tricia Barker's being asked to leave her mother's house and being told to take her son with her. In this, Ian's grandmother now says she was doing her best to 'practise the tough love. I was willing to keep both of them – the lad and Tricia too – as long as the girl worked, but she wouldn't hold onto a job and she wanted parties and friends and staying out all hours and I reckoned if she had to bring up the boy on her own, she'd change her ways'.

She didn't. Courtesy of the government, Tricia Barker was given accommodation, although the flat was small and she was forced to share a bedroom with her son. It was evidently in this room that Ian began to witness his mother engaging in sexual acts with a variety of men and, on at least four occasions, with more than one man. It's worthy of note that Ian consistently refers to her neither as his mother nor as Tricia, but rather through the use of pejorative terms such as slag, cunt, gash, tart and minge bag. His grandmother he doesn't refer to at all.

Michael and Reggie seem to have had no trouble locating Ian Barker that morning. They did not go to his house – according to Reggie 'his mum was pissed most of the time and she yelled abuse out the door' – but rather they came upon him in the act of shaking down a younger boy on the route to school. Ian had 'dumped the kid's rucksack out on the pavement' and was in the process of going through its contents to find anything of value but most particularly money. There being nothing of value for him to take from the child, Ian 'shoved him meanlike against the side of a house', in Michael's words, 'and started going at him'.

Neither Reggie nor Michael attempted to stop the harassment. Reggie says that 'it were only a bit of fun. I could see he weren't going to hurt him', while Michael claims he 'couldn't see 'xackly what he was up to', a rather doubtful claim as all of the boys were in plain sight on the pavement. Nonetheless, whatever Ian's full intentions were, they came to nothing further. A motorist stopped and demanded to know what they were doing, and the boys ran off.

There have been suggestions that Ian's desire to hurt something that day, having been thwarted, became the root of what occurred later. Indeed, under questioning, Reggie Arnold seems only too eager to point the finger in Ian's direction. But while Ian's anger had in the past certainly led him to commit acts the reprehensible nature of which caused him to be hated even more than the other two boys when the truth came out, the evidence ultimately shows that he was an *equal participant* (emphasis mine) in what followed.

JUNE
THE NEW FOREST
HAMPSHIRE

Chance alone brought her into his orbit. Later he would think that had he not looked down from the scaffolding at that precise moment, had he taken Tess directly home and not to the wood that afternoon, she might not have come into his life. But that idea comprised the very substance of what he was supposed to think, which was a realisation he would only come to once it was far too late.

The time was mid-afternoon, and the day was hot. June generally prompted torrents of rain, mocking anyone's hope for summer. But this year, the weather was setting itself up to be different. Days of sun in a cloudless sky made the promise of a July and an August during which the ground would bake, and the vast lawns within the Perambulation would brown over, sending the New Forest ponies deep within the woodlands to forage.

He was high up on the scaffolding, getting ready to climb to the peak of the roof where he'd begun to apply the straw. Far more pliable than the reeds that comprised the rest of the materials, the straw could be bent to form the ridge. Some people thought of this as the 'pretty bit' on a thatched roof, the scalloped pattern crisscrossed with spars in a decorative fashion. But he thought of it as what it was: that which protected the top layer of reeds from weather and avian damage.

He'd got to the knuckle. He was feeling impatient. They'd been working on the enormous project for three months, and he'd promised to begin another in two weeks' time. The finishing work still needed doing, and he could not hand off that part of the job to his apprentice. Cliff Coward was not ready to use the leggett on the thatch. That work was crucial to the overall look of the roof, and it required both skill and a properly honed eye. But Cliff could hardly be trusted to do this level of work when so far he hadn't managed to stay on task with even the simplest job, like the one he was meant to be doing just now, which was hauling another two bundles of straw up to the ridge as he'd been instructed. And why had he not managed this most mundane of tasks?

Seeking an answer to that question was what altered Gordon Jossie's life. He turned from the ridge, calling sharply, 'Cliff! What the bloody hell's happened to you?' and he saw below him that his apprentice was no longer standing by the bundles of straw where he was supposed to be, anticipating the needs of the master thatcher above him. Rather he'd gone over to Gordon's dusty pickup some yards away. There Tess sat at attention, happily wagging her bush-like tail while a woman – a stranger and clearly a visitor to the gardens if the map she held and the clothing she wore were anything to go by – patted her golden head.

'Oy! Cliff!' Gordon Jossie shouted. Both the apprentice and the woman looked up.

Gordon couldn't see her face clearly because of her hat, which was broad-brimmed and fashioned from straw with a fuchsia scarf tied round it as a band. This same colour was in her dress as well, and the dress was summery, showing off tanned arms and long tanned legs. She wore a gold bracelet round her wrist and sandals on her feet, and she carried a straw handbag tucked under her arm, its strap looped over her shoulder.

Cliff called out, 'Sorry! I was helping this lady—' as the woman called, 'I've got myself completely lost,' with a laugh. She went on with, 'I'm awfully sorry. He offered . . .' She gestured with a map she was holding, as if to explain what was patently obvious: she'd somehow wandered from the public gardens to the administrative building, which Gordon was re-roofing. 'I've never actually seen someone thatch a roof before,' she added, perhaps in an effort to be friendly.

Gordon, however, wasn't feeling friendly. He was feeling sharp, all edges and most of them needing to be smoothed. He had no time for tourists.

'She's trying to get to Monet's pond,' Cliff called out.

'And I'm trying to get a bloody ridge put onto this roof,' was Gordon's reply, although he made it in an undertone. He gestured northwest. 'There's a path up by the fountain. The nymphs and fauns fountain. You're meant to turn left there. You turned right.'

'Did I?' the woman called back. 'Well . . . that's typical, I s'pose.' She stood there for a moment, as if anticipating further conversation. She was wearing dark glasses and it came to Gordon that the entire effect of her was as if she was a celebrity, a Marilyn Monroe type because she was shapely like Marilyn Monroe, not like the pin thin girls one generally saw. Indeed, he actually thought she might be a celebrity at first. She rather dressed like one, and her expectation that a man would be willing to stop what he was doing and eagerly converse with her suggested it as well. He replied briefly to the woman with, 'You should find your way easy enough now.'

'Were that only the truth,' she said. She added, rather ridiculously, he thought, 'There won't be any . . . well, any horses up there, will there?'

He thought, What the hell . . . ? and she added, 'It's only . . . I'm actually rather afraid of horses.'

'Ponies won't hurt you,' he replied. 'They'll keep their distance 'less you try to feed them.'

'Oh, I wouldn't do that.' She waited for a moment as if expecting him to say more, which he was not inclined to do. Finally she said, 'Anyway, thank you,' and that was the end of her.

She set off on the route that Gordon had indicated, and she removed her hat as she went and swung it from her fingertips. Her hair was blonde, cut like a cap round her head, and when she shook it, it fell neatly back into place with a shimmer, as if knowing what it was supposed to do. Gordon wasn't immune to women, so he could see she had a graceful walk. But he felt no stirring in his groin or in his heart, and he was glad of this. Untouched by women was how he liked it.

Cliff joined him on the scaffolding, two bundles of straw on his back. He said, 'Tess quite liked her,' as if in explanation of something or perhaps in the woman's defence, and he added, 'Could be time for another go, mate,' as Gordon watched the woman gain distance from them.

But Gordon wasn't watching her out of fascination or attraction. He was watching to see if she made the correct turn at the fountain of nymphs and fauns. She did not. He shook his head. Hopeless, he thought. She'd be in the cow pasture before she knew it, but he fully expected she would also be able to find someone else to help her there.

Cliff wanted to go for a drink at the end of the day. Gordon did not. He did not drink at all. He also never liked the idea of becoming chummy with his apprentices. Beyond that, the fact that Cliff was only eighteen made Gordon thirteen years his senior and most of the time he felt like his father. Or he felt the way a father *might* feel, he supposed, as he had no children and possessed neither the desire nor the expectation of having them.

He said to Cliff, 'Got to give Tess a run. She won't settle tonight if she doesn't work off some energy.'

Cliff said, 'You sure, then, mate?'

Gordon said, 'Reckon I know my dog.' He knew that Cliff hadn't been talking about Tess, but he liked the way his remark served to cut off conversation. Cliff enjoyed talking far too much.

Gordon dropped him at the pub in Minstead, a hamlet tucked into a fold of land, consisting of a church, a graveyard, a shop, the pub and a cluster of old cob cottages gathered round a small green. This was shaded by an ancient oak and near it a piebald pony grazed, its clipped tail grown out in the time that had passed since the last autumn drift when it had been marked. The pony didn't look up as the pickup rumbled to a stop not terribly far from its hind legs. Longtime denizen of the New Forest, the animal likely knew that its right to graze wherever it wished long preceded the pickup's right to travel the Hampshire roads.

Cliff said, ''Morrow, then,' and went off to join his mates in the pub. Gordon watched him go and, for no particular reason, waited till the door closed behind him. Then he put the pickup into gear once more.

He went, as always, to Longslade Bottom. Over time, he'd learned there was security in being a creature of habit. At the weekend he might well choose another spot to exercise Tess, but during the week at the end of his workday, he liked a place that was closer to where he lived. He also liked the openness of Longslade Bottom. And in moments when he felt a need for seclusion, he liked the fact that Hinchelsea Wood climbed the hillside just above it.

The lawn stretched out from an uneven car park over which Gordon jounced, with Tess in the back of the pickup yelping happily in anticipation of a run. On a fine day like this, Gordon's wasn't the only vehicle nosing the edge of the lawn: six cars lined up like nursing kittens against the sprawl of open land upon which in the distance a herd of ponies grazed, five foals among them. Used to both people and the presence of other animals, the ponies remained undisturbed by the barking of the dogs already at play on the lawn, but when Gordon saw them some hundred yards away, he knew that a free run on the closely cropped grass was not on the cards for his own dog. Tess had a thing about the wild New Forest ponies, and despite having been kicked by one, nipped by another and thoroughly scolded by Gordon time and again, she refused to understand that she had not been created for the purpose of chasing them.

Already she was itching to do so. She was whining and licking her chops as if in anticipation of a challenge that she assumed lay before her. Gordon could almost read her canine mind: *And foals as well! Wicked! What fun!*

He said, 'Don't even think about it,' and he reached inside the pickup bed for her lead. He clipped it on and then released her. She made a hopeful lunge. When he brought her up short, heavy drama ensued as she coughed and gagged. It was, he thought with resignation, a typical late afternoon with his dog.

'Don't have the brains God gave you, do you?' he asked her. Tess looked at him, wagged her tail and dog-smiled. 'That may have worked at one time,' he went on, 'but it won't work now. We're not going that direction.' He led the Golden Retriever northeast, determinedly away from the ponies and their offspring. She went but she was not averse to what manipulation she could manage: she looked repeatedly over her shoulder and whined, obviously in the hope that this would move him to change his mind. It did not.

Longslade Bottom comprised three areas: the lawn upon which the ponies were grazing, a heath to the northwest that budded with cross-leaved heather and purple moorgrass, and a central bog between the two, where amorphous cushions of sphagnum moss soaked up moving water while bogbean flowers grew in pink and white bursts from rhizomes that rose from shallow pools. A path from the carpark led walkers on the safest route through the bog, and along this route the feathery seed heads of cotton grass formed great white tussocks in the peaty soil.

Gordon headed in this last direction, for the path across the bog would take them up the slope to Hinchelsea Wood. In the wood he could release the dog. The ponies would be out of sight and, for Tess, out of sight was decidedly out of mind. She possessed that most admirable of qualities: she could live entirely in the moment.

Summer solstice was not far off, so the sun was still high in the cloudless sky despite the hour of the day. Its light flashed against the iridescent bodies of dragonflies and upon the bright plumage of lapwings taking to the air as Gordon and the dog passed by. A slight breeze bore the rich scent of peat and the decomposing vegetation that had created it. The entire atmosphere was alive with sounds: from the gravelly *cour-lee* call of curlews to the cries of dog owners out on the lawn.

Gordon kept Tess close. They began the ascent towards Hinchelsea Wood and left both bog and lawn behind them. When he thought about it, Gordon decided the wood was better for an afternoon walk anyway. With the beeches and oaks in full summer leaf and the birches and sweet chestnuts providing additional cover, it would be cool on the paths beneath the trees. After a day in the heat, hauling about reeds and straw on a rooftop, Gordon was ready for a respite from the sun.

He released the dog when they reached the two cypresses that marked the official entrance to the wood and watched her till she disappeared entirely into the trees. He knew that she'd return eventually. Dinner wasn't far off, and Tess wasn't a dog to miss her meals.

He himself walked along and kept his mind occupied. Here in the wood, he named the trees. He'd been a student of the New Forest since coming to Hampshire, and after a decade he knew the Perambulation, its character and its heritage better than most natives.

After a bit, he sat on the trunk of a downed alder, not far from a grove of holly. Sunlight filtered through the tree branches here, dappling ground that was spongy with years of natural composting. Gordon continued to name the trees as he saw them and went on to the plants. But there were few of these as the wood was part of the grazing land and as such was fed upon by ponies, donkeys and fallow deer. In April and May they would have made a feast of the tender spring growth of ferns, happily moving on from these to wild flowers, juvenile alders and the shoots of new brambles. The animals thus made Gordon's occupation of mind a challenge, even as they sculpted the landscape in such a way that walking beneath the trees in the wood was a simple thing and not a challenge described by beating a path through undergrowth.

He heard the dog bark and roused himself. He wasn't worried, for he recognised the different kinds of barks that Tess produced. This was her happy bark, the one she used to greet a friend or a stick thrown into Hatchet Pond. He rose and looked in the direction from which the barking continued. It came nearer and as it did so he heard a voice accompanying it: a woman's voice. Soon enough he saw her emerge from beneath the trees.

He did not recognise her at first, for she'd changed her clothes. From the summer frock, the sunhat and the sandals, she'd altered her get-up to khaki trousers and a short-sleeved shirt. She still had on her sunglasses – so did he for that matter, for the day continued bright – and her footwear was again largely inappropriate for what she was doing. While she'd given up the sandals, she'd replaced them with Wellingtons, a very odd choice for a summer stroll unless she intended to trek through the bog.

She spoke first, saying, 'I *thought* this was the same dog. She's the sweetest thing.'

He might have thought she'd followed him to Longslade Bottom and Hinchelsea Wood, save for the obvious fact that she'd got there before him. She was on her way out; he was on his way in. He was leery of people, but he refused to be paranoid. He said, 'You're the woman looking for Monet's Pond.'

'I did find it,' she replied. 'Though not without ending in a cow pasture first.'

'Yes,' he said.

She tilted her head. Her hair caught the light again, just as it had done at Boldre Gardens. He wondered, stupidly, if she put sparkles in it. He'd never seen hair with such a sheen. '"Yes"?' she repeated.

He stammered, 'I know. I mean yes I know. I could tell. From how you were going.'

'Oh. You were watching me from the rooftop, were you? I hope you didn't laugh. That would be too cruel.'

'No,' he said.

'Well, I'm wretched at map reading and not much better with verbal directions, so it's no surprise I got lost again. At least I didn't run into any horses.'

He looked round them. 'Not a good place to be, this, is it? If you're bad with maps and directions?'

'In the wood, you mean? But I've had help.' She gestured to the south and he saw she was pointing to a distant knoll where an enormous oak stood beyond the wood itself. 'I very carefully kept that tree in sight and on my right as I came into the wood and now that it's on my left, I feel fairly sure I'm heading in the direction of the carpark. So you see despite stumbling onto a thatching site and into a cow pasture, I'm not entirely hopeless.'

'That's Nelson's,' he said.

'What? D'you mean someone owns the tree? It's on private property?'

'No. It's on crown land, all right. It's called Nelson's Oak. Supposedly he planted it. Lord Nelson, that is.'

'Ah. I see.'

He looked at her more closely. She'd sucked in on her lip, and it came to him that she might not actually know who Lord Nelson was. Some people didn't in this day and age. To help her out while not embarrassing her, he said, 'Admiral Nelson had his ships built over Buckler's Hard. Beyond Beaulieu. You know the place? On the estuary? They were using up a hell of a lot of timber, so they had to start replanting. Nelson probably didn't put any acorns in the ground himself but the tree's associated with him anyway.'

'I'm not from around here,' she told him. 'But I expect you worked that out yourself.' She extended her hand. 'Gina Dickens,' she said. 'No relation. I know this is Tess –' with a nod at the dog who'd settled herself happily at Gina's side – 'but I don't know you.'

'Gordon Jossie,' he told her and clasped her hand. The soft touch of it brought to mind how work roughened he himself was. How filthy as well, considering he'd spent all day on a rooftop. 'I reckoned as much.'

'What?'

'That you weren't local.'

'Yes. Well, I suppose the natives don't get lost as easily as I do, do they?'

'Not that. Your feet.'

She looked down. 'What's wrong with them?'

'The sandals you were wearing at Boldre Gardens and now those,' he said. 'Why've you got on wellies? You going into the bog or something?'

She did that bit with her mouth again. He wondered if it meant she was trying not to laugh. 'You're a country person, aren't you, so you'll think I'm foolish. It's the adders,' she said. 'I've read they're in the New Forest and I didn't want to run into one. Now you *are* going to laugh at me, aren't you?'

He did have to smile. 'Expect to run into snakes in the forest, then?' He didn't wait for an answer. 'They're out on the heath. They'll be where there's more sun. Could be you might run into one on the path as you cross the bog, but it's not very likely.'

'I can see I should have consulted with you before I changed my clothes. Have you lived here forever?'

'Ten years. I came down from Winchester.'

'But so have I!' She gave a look to the direction she'd come from and said, 'Shall I walk with you for a while, Gordon Jossie? I know no one in the area and I'd love to chat and as you look harmless and you're out here with the sweetest dog . . . ?'

He shrugged. 'Suit yourself. But I'm just following Tess. We don't need to walk at all. She'll take herself into the wood and come back when she's ready . . . I mean if you'd rather sit instead of walk.'

'Oh, I would actually. Truth to tell, I've had quite a ramble already.'

He nodded to the log on which he himself had been seated when she'd first emerged from the trees. They sat a careful few feet from each other, but Tess didn't leave them as he thought she would. Rather, she settled next to Gina. She sighed and put her head on her paws.

'Likes you,' he noted. 'Empty places need filling.'

'How true,' she said.

She sounded regretful, so he asked her the obvious. It was unusual for someone her age to move into the country. Young adults generally migrated in the other direction. She said, 'Well, yes. It was a relationship gone *very* bad,' but she said it with a smile. 'So here I am. I'm hoping to work with pregnant teenagers. That's what I did in Winchester.'

'Did you?'

'You sound surprised. Why?'

'You don't look much more'n a teenager yourself.'

She lowered her sunglasses down her nose and looked at him over their tops. 'Are you flirting with me, Mr Jossie?' she asked.

He felt a rush of heat in his face. 'Sorry. Didn't mean to. If that's what it was.'

'Oh. Pooh. I rather thought you might.' She shoved her sunglasses to the top of her head and looked at him frankly. Her eyes, he saw, were neither blue nor green but something in between, indefinable and interesting. She said, 'You're blushing. I've never made a man blush before. It's rather sweet. Do you blush often?'

He grew hotter still. He didn't *have* these sorts of conversations with women. He didn't know what to make of them: the women *or* the conversations.

'I'm embarrassing you. I'm sorry. I didn't intend to. I tease sometimes. It's a bad habit. Perhaps you can help me break it.'

'Teasing's all right,' he said. 'I'm more . . . I'm a bit at sixes and sevens. Mostly, well . . . I thatch roofs.'

'Day in and day out?'

'That's 'bout it.'

'And for entertainment? For relaxation?'

He tilted his chin to indicate the dog. 'That's what she's for.'

'Hmmm. I see.' She bent to Tess and petted the dog where she liked it best, just outside her ears. If the retriever could have purred, she would have done so. Gina seemed to reach a decision, for when she looked up, her expression was thoughtful. 'Would you like to come out for a drink with me? As I said, I know no one in the area and as you *do* continue to seem quite harmless and as *I'm* harmless and as you have a lovely dog . . . Would you like to?'

'I don't drink, actually.'

She raised her eyebrows. 'You take in no liquids at all? That can't be the case.'

He smiled, in spite of himself, but he made no reply.

'I was going to have a lemonade,' she said. 'I don't drink, either. My dad . . . He hit it rather hard, so I stay away from stuff. It made me a misfit in school but in a good way, I think. I've always liked to be different.' She rose then and brushed off the seat of her trousers. Tess rose as well and wagged her tail. It was clear that the dog had accepted Gina Dickens' impulsive invitation. What was left for Gordon was simply to do likewise.

Still, he hesitated. He preferred to keep himself distant from women, but she wasn't proposing involvement, was she? And, for God's sake, she looked safe enough. Her gaze was frank and friendly.

He said, 'There's a hotel in Sway.' She looked startled, and he realised how that declaration had sounded. Ears burning, he hastened to add, 'I mean Sway's closest to here and they've got no pub in the village. Everyone uses the hotel bar. You can follow me there. We can have that drink.'

Her expression softened. 'You are the loveliest-seeming man.'

'Oh, I don't expect that's true.'

'It is, really.' They began to walk. Tess loped ahead and then, in a marvel that Gordon would not soon forget, the dog waited at the edge of the wood where the path curved down the hill in the direction of the bog. She was, he saw, pausing to have the lead attached to her collar. That was a first. He wasn't a man to look for signs, but this seemed to be yet another indication of what he was meant to do next.

When they reached the dog, he attached her to her lead and handed it over to Gina. He said to her, 'What did you mean: no relation?' She drew her eyebrows together. He went on. 'No relation. That's what you said when you told me your name.'

Again that expression. It was softness and something more and it made him wary even as he wanted to approach it. 'Charles Dickens,' she said. 'The writer? I'm no relation to him.'

'Oh,' he said. 'I don't . . . I never read much.'

'Do you not?' she asked as they set off down the hillside. She put her hand through his arm as Tess led them on their way. 'I expect we'll have to do something about that.'

JULY

I

When Meredith Powell awakened and saw the date on her digital alarm clock, she absorbed four facts in a matter of seconds: it was her twenty-sixth birthday; it was her day off from work; it was the day for which her mum had suggested a gran-spoils-the-only-grandchild adventure; and it was the perfect opportunity for apologising to her best and oldest friend for a row that had kept them from being best and oldest friends for nearly a year. This last realisation came about because Meredith shared her birthday with that best and oldest of friends. She and Jemima Hastings had been thick as thieves from the time they were six years old, and they'd celebrated their birthdays together from their eighth one on. Meredith knew that if she didn't make things right with Jemima today, she probably wouldn't ever do it, and if that happened, a tradition that she'd long held dear was going to be destroyed. She didn't want that. Dear friends weren't easy to come by.

The *how* of the apology took a little thought, which Meredith engaged in as she showered. She settled on a birthday cake. She would bake it herself, take it to Ringwood, and present it to Jemima along with her heartfelt apology and her admission of wrong-doing. What she would not include in the apology and the admission was any mention of Jemima's partner, who'd been the source of their row in the first place. For Meredith now understood that would be pointless. One simply *had* to face the fact that Jemima had always been a romantic when it came to blokes, whereas she, Meredith, had the complete and utterly undeniable experience of knowing men were essentially animals in human clothing. They wanted women for sex, child-bearing and housewiving. If they could just *say* that instead of pretending they were desperate for something else, women who involved themselves with them could then make an informed choice about how they wanted to live their lives instead of believing they were 'in love'.

Meredith pooh-poohed the entire idea of love. Been there, done that, and Cammie Powell was the result: five years old, the light of her mother's life, fatherless and likely to remain that way.

Cammie was, at that moment, bashing away on the bathroom door, calling, 'Mummy! Mummmmmmmm-eeeeeee! Gran says we're going to see the otters today 'n' we'll have ice lollies 'n' beef burgers. Will you come 's well? Cos there's owls, too. She says someday we'll go to the hedgehog hospital but that's for an overnight trip and she says I got to be older for that. *She* thinks I'll miss you, that's what she says, but you could come, couldn't you? Couldn't you, Mummy? Mummmmmmeeeee?'

Meredith chuckled. Cammie awakened every morning in full monologue-mode, and she generally did not cease talking until it was time to go to bed. Meredith said as she towelled herself off, 'Have you had your breakfast already, luv?'

'I forgot,' Cammie informed her. Meredith could hear some scuffling and knew her daughter was shuffling her slippered feet on the floor. 'But anyway, Gran says they've got babies. *Baby* otters. She says when their mums die or when they get eaten their babies need someone to look after them properly and they do that at the park. The otter park. What eats an otter, Mummy?'

'Don't know, Cam.'

'Something *has* to. Everything eats everything. Or something. Mummy? Mummmeee?'

Meredith shrugged into her dressing gown and pulled the door open. Cammie stood there, mirror image of Meredith at the very same age: too tall for five and, like Meredith, far too thin. It was a real gift, Meredith thought, that Cammie did not resemble her worthless father in the slightest. This was beyond good, since her father had sworn he would never see her should Meredith 'be pig-headed and carry on with this pregnancy because, for God's sake, I've a *wife*, you little fool. *And* two children. *And* you bloody well *knew* that, Meredith.'

'Give us our morning hug, Cam,' Meredith said to her daughter. 'Then wait for me in the kitchen. I've a cake to bake. D'you want to help?'

'Gran's making breakfast in the kitchen.'

'I expect there's room for another two cooks.'

That turned out to be the case. While Meredith's mother worked at the cooker, turning eggs and overseeing bacon, Meredith herself began the cake. It was simple enough as she used a boxed mix, which her mother tut-tutted as Meredith emptied its contents into a bowl.

'It's for Jemima,' Meredith told her.

'Bit like taking you-know-what to Newcastle,' Janet Powell noted.

Well, of course, it was but that couldn't be helped. Besides it was the thought that mattered, not the cake itself. Beyond that, even working from scratch with ingredients provided by some goddess of the pantry, Meredith would never have been able to match what Jemima could fashion out of flour, eggs and all the rest. So why try? It wasn't a contest, after all. It was a friendship in need of rescue.

Gran and granddaughter were off on their adventure with the otters and granddad had taken himself to work when Meredith finally had the cake completed. She'd chosen chocolate with chocolate icing and if it was just a *tiny* bit lopsided and a tinier bit sunken in the middle . . . well, that was what icing was for, wasn't it? Copiously used and with plenty of flourish, it covered a host of errors.

The heat of the oven had raised the temperature in the kitchen, so Meredith found she had to shower another time before she could set off to Ringwood. Then, as was her habit, she covered herself shoulders to toe in a caftan to disguise the beanpole nature of her body and she carried the chocolate cake to her car. She placed it carefully on the passenger seat.

God, it was hot, she thought. It was absolutely boiling and it wasn't even ten a.m. She'd thought the day's heat had been all about having the oven blasting away in the kitchen, but that was clearly not the case. She lowered the windows in the car, eased herself onto the sizzling seat, and set out on her journey. She'd have to get the cake out of the car as soon as possible or she'd have a nothing but a pool of chocolate left.

The trip to Ringwood wasn't overly long, just a dash down the A31 with the wind blowing in through the windows and her affirmation tape playing at high volume. A voice was intoning, 'I am and I can, I am and I can,' and Meredith concentrated on this mantra. She didn't actually believe this sort of thing really worked, but she was determined to leave no stone unturned in the pursuit of her career.

A tailback at the Ringwood exit reminded her it was market day. The town centre was going to be jammed, with shoppers surging towards the market square where once each week stalls spread out colourfully beneath the neo-Norman tower of St Peter and Paul's parish church. In addition to the shoppers there would be the tourists, for at this time of year the New Forest was teeming with them like crows on road kill: campers, walkers, cyclists, amateur photographers and all forms of outdoor enthusiasts.

Meredith gave a glance to her chocolate cake. It had been a mistake to place it on the seat and not on the floor. The sun was blasting fully upon it, and the chocolate icing wasn't benefitting from the experience.

Meredith had to admit that her mother had been right: what on *earth* was she thinking, bringing Jemima a cake? Well, it was too late now to change her plans. Perhaps they could laugh about it together when she finally managed to get herself and her cake to Jemima's shop. This was the Cupcake Queen, located in Hightown Road, and Meredith herself had been instrumental in Jemima's finding the vacant space.

Hightown Road was a bit of a mixed bag, which made it perfect for the Cupcake Queen. On one side of the street, red-brick residences took the form of terraces and semis that curved along in a pleasant bow of arched porches, bay windows and dormer windows with white gingerbread woodwork forming their lacy peaks. An old inn called the Railway Hotel stood further along this side of the street, with plants tumbling from wrought iron containers that hung above its windows, spilling colour towards the pavement below. On the other side things automotive offered services from car repair to four-by-four sales. A hair salon occupied space next to a launderette, and when Meredith had first seen, adjacent to this, an empty establishment with a dusty To Let sign in the window, she'd thought at once of Jemima's cupcake business which had been going great guns from her cottage near Sway but was in need of expansion. She'd said to her, 'Jem, it'll be grand. I can walk over in my lunch hour and we can have a sandwich or something.' Besides, it was time, she'd told her friend. Did she want to operate her fledgling business out of a cottage kitchen forever or did she want to take the leap? 'You can do this, Jem. I have faith in you.' Faith with regard to business matters, was what she didn't add. When it came to personal matters, she had no faith in Jemima at all.

It hadn't taken much convincing, and Jemima's brother had provided part of the cash, as Meredith had known he would. But soon after Jemima had signed the lease, Meredith and she had parted ways in their friendship because of a hot and frankly stupid discussion about what Meredith saw as Jemima's eternal need for a man. 'You'll love anyone who'll love you back,' had been the way Meredith had concluded her passionate denunciation of Jemima's most recent partner, one in a long line of men who'd come into and gone out of her life. 'Come on, Jem. *Anyone* with eyes and half a brain can see there's something off about him.' Not the best way to assess a man whom one's best friend declares she's determined to marry. Living with him was bad enough, as far as Meredith was concerned. Hooking up permanently was another matter.

So it had been a double insult: to Jemima and to the man she ostensibly loved. Thus Meredith had never seen the fruits of Jemima's labours when it came to launching the Cupcake Queen.

Unfortunately, she didn't see the fruits of those labours now, either. When Meredith parked, scooped up the chocolate cake – it was looking ever more as if the chocolate itself were actually *perspiring*, she thought, which could not have been a very good sign – and carried her offering to the door of the Cupcake Queen, she found the shop locked tightly, its window sills grimy, and its interior speaking of a business failed. Meredith could see an empty display case, along with a dusty sales counter and an old-fashioned baker's étagère showing off neither utensils nor baked goods. And this was . . . what? Ten months after she'd opened? Six months after? Eight? Meredith couldn't remember exactly, but she certainly didn't like what she saw, and she had difficulty believing that Jemima's business could have gone under so quickly. She'd had more than a score of regular customers she had served from her cottage alone, and they would have followed her to Ringwood. So what had happened?

Meredith decided she would seek the one person who could probably explain. She had her own, immediate theory about matters, but she wanted to be forearmed when she finally saw Jemima herself.

Ultimately, Meredith found Lexie Streener at Jean Michel Hair Styling, in the High Street. She went first to the teenager's home where the girl's mother stopped what she was doing – typing a lengthy tract on the Third Beatitude – to expound in some tedious detail what it truly meant to be among the meek. When pressed for information, she revealed that Lexie was washing hair at Jean Michel's. ('There's *no* Jean Michel,' she pointed out sharply. 'That's a lie, that is, which is against God's law.')

At Jean Michel's Hair Styling, Meredith had to wait for

Lexie Streener to finish scrubbing energetically at the scalp of a heavy set lady who'd already had more than enough summer sun and was currently showing far too much flesh as an illustration of this troubling fact. Meredith wondered if Lexie was planning on a career of styling hair. She hoped not, for if the girl's own head was any indication of her talents in this area, no one with any sense would allow her near them as long as she had either scissors or dye in hand. Her locks were pink, blonde, and blue. They'd either been cropped to a punitive length – one thought at once of head lice – or they'd broken off, incapable of anything else after repeated exposures to bleach and to colour.

'She just phoned up one day,' Lexie said when Meredith had the girl to herself. She'd had to wait for Lexie's break and it had cost her a Coke, but that was fine by her if the minimal expense provided her with maximum details. 'I reckoned I'd been doing a good job wif ever'thing, but all's of a sudden, she phones me up and she says not to come to work tomorrow. I aksed her was it summick I done, like smoke a fag too close to the door like I might of done, you know, or what have you but all she says is . . . like . . . "No, it's not you." So I reckon it's my mum or dad with all their Bible stuff and I reckon they been preaching at her or leaving, you know, those tracks Mum writes? Like, under her windscreen wipers? But she says, "It's me. It's not you. It's not them. Things's changed." I say what things but she won't tell me. She says she's sorry and not to aks her nuffink else.'

'Was business bad?' Meredith asked.

'Don't think so. There's *always* people were there, buying stuff. You aks me, it was weird she wanted to close up, and I knew that, innit. So I rang her 'bout a week after she talked to me. Maybe more. Dunno exactly. I ring her on her mobile to find out what's what, but all's I just get is just her voicemail. I leave a message. At least twice, this was. But she never rang me back and when I tried another time, the phone was . . . There was nothing. Like she lost it or summick.'

'Did you phone her at home?'

Lexie shook her head. She picked at a healing cut on her arm. It was what she did – cutting herself – and Meredith knew this, for Lexie's aunt owned the graphic design company where Meredith worked while she waited to break into what she really wanted to do, which was fabric design, and as Meredith greatly admired Lexie's aunt and as Lexie's aunt worried about the girl and talked about her and wondered wasn't there *something* that could get her out of the house and away from her half-mad parents for a few hours each day . . . Meredith had suggested Lexie to Jemima as the Cupcake Queen's first employee. The plan had been for her to help Jemima in setting up the shop first and then behind the counter second. Jemima couldn't do everything herself and Lexie needed the job and Meredith wanted to score points with her employer. It had all seemed perfect.

But something clearly had not worked out right. Meredith said, 'So you didn't talk to . . . well, to him? She didn't say anything about what might have been going on at home? And you didn't ring her there?'

Lexie shook her head. 'Just reckoned she di'n't want me,' the girl replied. 'No one gen'rally does.'

So, really, she had to go to Jemima's home. There was nothing else for it. Meredith didn't actually like this idea because she felt it gave Jemima a sort of advantage over her in the conversation that was to come. But she knew that if she was going to be serious about making up with her friend, then she was going to have to do what it took.

Jemima lived with her partner between Sway and Mount Pleasant. There, she and Gordon Jossie had somehow lucked their way into the rights of a commoner, so there was land attached to the holding. True there was not a *lot* of it but, still, twelve acres were nothing to sniff at. There were buildings as well: an old cob cottage, a barn and a shed. Part of the land comprised ancient paddocks to serve the needs of the holding's ponies should they get out of condition during the winter. The rest of it was vacant land, characterised largely by a heath which, in the distance, gave way to woodland, which was not part of the holding.

The buildings on the property were shaded by sweet chestnut trees, all of them pollarded long ago so that now their branches grew above head height from the bulbous remains of those early amputations, which had saved the trees in their youth from the hungry mouths of animals. They were huge, those chestnuts. In summer, they lowered the temperature around the cottage and they scented the air with a heady fragrance.

As she pulled past the tall hawthorn hedge and into the drive that sketched a pebbled line between the cottage and the west paddock, Meredith saw that beneath one of the chestnut trees in front of the house, a rusty iron table, four chairs and a wheeled tea trolley formed a picturesque summer dining area, complete with potted ferns, candles on the table, colourful cushions on the chairs and three ornate torchères, all of it giving the place the look of a photo from a home living magazine. *This* was not like Jemima at all, Meredith thought. She wondered how else her friend had changed in the months that had passed since they'd last seen each other.

She pulled to a stop not far from the cottage, just behind the second sign of change. This constituted a late model Mini Cooper, bright red with white striping, newly polished, its chrome agleam and its convertible top lowered. Meredith stirred a bit in her seat when she saw this vehicle. It brought home to her what she'd arrived in: an old Polo held together by duct tape and dreams, the passenger's seat of which was currently beginning to accept an ooze of melted chocolate from the cake that sat upon it.

The cake seemed like a truly ridiculous offering now, Meredith thought. She should have listened to her mother. Not that she'd ever listened to her mother before. Which in itself was a thought that brought Jemima even more firmly into her mind, how she'd always said, 'At least you *have* a mum,' whenever Meredith complained about the good woman. And that made her miss Jemima with a stab of the heart, so she gathered her courage and her lopsided cake, and she made her way to the cottage door. Not the front door, which she'd never used, but the door at the back, the one that led out from a lean-to laundry room into an open space edged by the cottage, the barn, the shed, a little farm lane and the east paddock.

There was no answer to her knock; there was no reply to her call of, 'Jem? Hey? Hullo? Birthday girl, where are you?' She was thinking of letting herself inside – no one locked doors in this part of the world – and leaving the cake along with a note when she heard someone call in return, 'Hullo? C'n I help you? I'm over here.'

It was not Jemima. Meredith knew that at once from the voice, without having to turn from the door. But turn she did, and it was to see a young blonde coming round the side of the barn, shaking off a straw sunhat, which she put on her head as she drew near. She was saying, 'Sorry. I was having a go with the horses. It's the oddest thing. For some reason this hat seems to frighten them, so I take it off when I go near the paddock.'

Perhaps, Meredith thought, she was someone they'd hired, Gordon and Jemima. With common rights, they were allowed to keep wild ponies, and they were also required to care for them if the animals weren't able to graze freely on the Forest for some reason. With Gordon's work and Jemima's work keeping them busy, it wasn't completely out of the question that they'd had to bring along someone in the event they were forced to keep ponies on the holding. Except . . . This woman didn't look like a caregiver to ponies. True, she wore blue jeans, but they were of the designer sort one saw on celebrities: hugging her curves. She wore boots, but they were polished leather and very stylish, not boots for mucking out in. She wore a work shirt, but its sleeves were rolled to show tanned arms and its collar stood up to frame her face. She looked like someone's *image* of a countrywoman, not like an actual countrywoman at all.

'Hullo.' Meredith felt awkward and ungainly. She and the other woman were of similar height, but that was the extent of their similarities. Meredith wasn't put together like this vision of life-in-Hampshire approaching her. In her body-shrouding caftan, she felt like a giraffe in draperies. 'Sorry. I think I've blocked you in.' She tilted her head in the direction of her car.

'No worries,' the woman replied. 'I'm not going anywhere.'

'Not . . . ?' Meredith hadn't thought that Jemima and Gordon might have moved house, but that seemed to be the case. She said, 'Do Gordon and Jemima not live here any longer?'

'Gordon certainly does,' the other replied. 'But who's Jemima?'

In looking at everything that happened to John Dresser, one must begin with the canal. Part of the nineteenth century's means of transporting goods from one area of the UK to another, the particular section of the Midlands Trans-Country Canal that concerns us bisects the city in such a way as to create a divide between socioeconomic areas. Three-quarters of a mile of its length runs along the north boundary of the Gallows. As is the case with most of the canals in Great Britain, a towpath gives walkers and cyclists access to the canal, and various types of housing back onto the waterway.

One might harbour romantic images invoked by the word *canal* or by canal life, but there is little romantic about the length of the Midlands Trans-Country Canal that flows just north of the Gallows. It's a greasy strip of water uninhabited by ducks, swans, or any other sort of aquatic life, and there are no reeds, willow trees, wildflowers or grasses growing along the towpath. What bobs at the canal's edges is usually rubbish, and its water carries a putrid odour suggestive of faulty sewer pipes.

The canal has long been used by residents of the Gallows as a dumping ground for items too bulky to be taken away by the rubbish collectors. When Michael Spargo, Reggie Arnold and Ian Barker arrived there at roughly 9:30 a.m., they found a shopping trolley in the water and they commenced using it as a target at which they threw rocks, bottles and bricks found along the towpath. Going to the canal appears to have been Reggie's idea, one initially rejected by Ian who accused the other two boys of wanting to go there 'to wank each other or do it like doggies', which can be seen as an apparent reference to what he himself had witnessed in the bedroom he was forced to share with his mother. He also seems to have harassed Michael about his right eye, as reported by

Reggie. (The nerves of his cheek having been damaged during a forceps delivery at his birth, Michael's right eye drooped and did not blink in concert with his left eye.) But Reggie indicates he himself 'sorted Ian proper', and the boys went on to other things.

As the back gardens of the houses along the towpath are separated from it only by wooden fences, the boys had easy access to properties where the wooden fences were in disrepair. Once they exhausted the possibilities presented by throwing things at and into the shopping trolley, they wandered along the towpath and found mischief where they were able: they removed fresh washing from a line behind one house and dumped this in the canal; at another they found a lawn mower ('But it were rusty,' Michael explains) and did the same with it.

Perhaps the perambulator gave them the ultimate idea. They found this object sitting next to the back door of yet another of the houses. Unlike the lawn mower, the perambulator was not only new, but it also had a metallic blue helium balloon attached to it. On this balloon was printed 'It's a Boy!' and the boys knew the words referred to a brand new baby.

The perambulator was more difficult to get their hands on because the fence here was not in bad condition. Thus it is suggestive of a sort of escalation of intent that two of the boys (Ian and Reggie, according to Michael; Ian and Michael, according to Reggie; Reggie and Michael, according to Ian) climbed over the fence, stole the perambulator and hoisted it over and onto the towpath. There the boys pushed each other for perhaps one hundred yards before tiring of this game and shoving the perambulator into the canal.

Michael Spargo's interview indicates that, at this point, Ian Barker said, 'Too bad it weren't a baby inside. That'd make a lovely splash, eh?' Ian Barker denies this, and when questioned, Reggie Arnold becomes hysterical, shrieking 'There weren't no baby, ever! Mum, there weren't no baby!'

According to Michael, Ian went on to talk about 'how wicked it'd be to get a baby from somewheres'. They could, he suggested, take it to 'that bridge over West Town Road and we could drop it on its head and see it splat. Blood and brains'd come out. That's what he said,' Michael reports. Michael goes on to insist that he spoke hotly against this idea, as if he knows where his interview with the police is heading when they get to this topic. Ultimately the boys grew tired of playing in the environs of the canal, Michael reports. Ian Barker, he tells the police, was the one to suggest they 'clear out of here' and go to the Barriers.

It should be noted that not one of the boys denies being in the Barriers that day, although all of them repeatedly change their stories when it comes to what they did when they got there.

West Town Road Arcade has been known as the Barriers for such a length of time that most people have no idea that the shopping arcade actually has another name. Early in its commercial lifetime, it developed this appellation because it sprawls neatly between the bleak world of the Gallows and an orderly grid of semi-detached and detached houses occupied by middle class working families. These buildings comprise the Windsor, Mountbatten and Lyon Housing Estates.

While there are four distinct entrances to the Barriers, the two most commonly used are those giving access to residents of the Gallows and to residents of the Windsor Estate. The shops at these entrances are rather depressingly indicative of the expected clientele. For example, at the Gallows entrance, one finds a William Hill betting lounge, two off-licences, a tobacconist, an Items-for-a-Pound shop and several take-away food enterprises featuring fish and chips, jacket potatoes and pizza. At the Windsor Estate entrance, on the other hand, one can shop in Marks & Spencer, Boots, Russell and Bromley, Accessorize, Ryman's and independent shops offering lingerie, chocolates, tea and clothing. While it's true that nothing stops someone from entering at the Gallows and traversing the arcade to shop where she pleases, the implication is clear: if you are poor, on benefits or working class, you're likely to be interested in spending your money on cholesterol-laden food, tobacco, alcohol or gambling.

All three of the boys agree that when they entered the Barriers, they went into the video arcade at the centre of the place. They had no money, but this did not stop them from 'driving' the jeep in the Let's Go Jungle video game, or 'piloting' the Ocean Hunter on a search for sharks. It's an interesting fact that the participatory video games allowed for only two players at one time. Although, as previously noted, they had no money, when they pretended to play it was Michael and Reggie who manned the controls, leaving Ian the odd man out. He claims he was not bothered by this exclusion, and all the boys declare themselves unbothered by the fact that they had no money to spend in the video arcade, but one cannot help speculating if the day would have turned out differently had the boys been able to sublimate pathological tendencies through engaging in some of the bellicose activities provided by the video games they encountered but were not able to use. (I don't mean to imply here that video games can or should take the place of parenting, but as an outlet for young boys with limited resources and even less insight into their individual dysfunction, they might have been helpful.)

Unfortunately, their time in the video arcade came to a precipitate end when a security guard noticed them and shooed them on their way. It was still school hours (the CCTV film has it at half-past ten), and he told them he would phone the police, the schools or the truant officer if he saw them again on the premises. His interview with the police has him claiming that he 'never saw the little yobs again', but this seems more like an effort to relieve himself of guilt and responsibility than the truth. The boys did nothing to hide from him once they left the video arcade, and had he only made good on his threat, the boys would never have encountered little John Dresser.

John Dresser – or Johnny, as he was termed by the tabloid press – was twenty-nine months old. He was the only child of Alan and Donna Dresser, and on a working day he was normally taken care of by his fifty-eight-year-old grandmother. He walked perfectly well, but like many toddler boys, he was slow to develop language. His vocabulary at twenty-nine months consisted of *Mummy*, *Da*, and *Lolly* (this last referring to the family dog). He could not say his name.

On this particular day, his grandmother had gone to Liverpool for an appointment with a specialist, to discuss her failing vision. As she could not drive herself, her husband took her. This placed Alan and Donna Dresser in the position of having no child care, and when this occurred (as it did occasionally), it was their habit to take turns minding John since neither of them found it easy to take time off work. (Donna Dresser was at this time a secondary school chemistry teacher and her husband a solicitor specialising in property sales.) By all accounts, they were excellent parents, and John had been a much-anticipated addition to their lives. Donna Dresser had not found it easy to become pregnant in the first place and had taken great care during her pregnancy to ensure the birth of a healthy baby. While she came under scrutiny and criticism for being a working mother who allowed her husband to care for their child on this particular day, it should not be assumed that she was anything other than a devoted mother to John.

Alan Dresser took the toddler to the Barriers at midday. He used the little boy's pushchair, and he walked the half mile from their home to get there. The Dressers lived on the Mountbatten Housing Estate, the most upmarket of the three neighbourhoods that touched on the Barriers and the one farthest from that shopping arcade. Prior to John's birth, his parents had purchased a detached three-bedroom home there, and on the day of John's disappearance they were still in the process of renovating one of the two bathrooms. In his statement to the police, Alan Dresser explains that he went to the Barriers at his wife's request to fetch paint samples from Stanley Wallingford's, an independent DIY shop not far from the Gallows end of the shopping arcade. He also goes on to say that he wanted a 'bit of air for me and the boy', a reasonable desire considering the thirteen days of bad weather that had preceded this outing.

Evidently, at some point while in Stanley Wallingford's, Alan Dresser promised John the treat of a McDonald's lunch. This seems to have been at least partially an attempt to settle the child, a fact which the shop assistant later verified to the police, for John was restless, unhappy in his pushchair, and difficult to keep occupied while his father chose the paint samples and made purchases relevant to the bathroom renovation. By the time Dresser got his son to McDonald's, John was irritable and hungry and Dresser himself was annoyed. Parenting did not come naturally to him, and he was not averse to 'swatting a bum' when his son did not behave appropriately in public. The fact that he was indeed seen just outside McDonald's giving John a sharp smack on his bottom ultimately caused a delay in the investigation once John disappeared although it's unlikely that even an immediate search for the boy would have altered the outcome of the day.

While Ian Barker's interview has him claiming that he didn't care about being excluded from the imaginary playing of video games, Michael Spargo evidently assumed that this exclusion prompted Ian to 'grass me and Reg to the security guard', an accusation that Ian hotly denied. However, they came to the guard's attention, though they escaped his further attention when they next went into the Items-for-a-Pound shop.

Even today, this establishment is chock-a-block with goods, offering everything from clothing to tea. Its aisles are narrow, its shelves are tall, its bins are a jumble of socks, scarves, gloves and knickers. It sells overruns, knockoffs, seconds, mislabelled items and Chinese imports, and it's impossible to see how stock control is managed although the shop's proprietor seems to have perfected a mental system that takes all items into account.

Michael, Ian, and Reggie entered the shop with the intent to steal, arguably as an outlet for the displeasure they felt at having been told to leave the video arcade. While the shop had two CCTV cameras, on this day they were not operational and had not been for at least two years. This was widely known to the neighbourhood children, who evidently made Items-for-a-Pound a frequent haunt. Ian Barker was among the most regular visitors to the shop, as its owner was able to name him although he was unfamiliar with Ian's surname.

While in the shop, the boys managed to steal a hairbrush, a bag of Christmas poppers and a package of felt-tip marking pens, but the ease of this activity either did not satisfy their need for anti-social behaviour or lacked a suitable frisson of excitement, so upon leaving they went next to a snack kiosk in the arcade's centre, where Reggie Arnold was quite well known to the proprietor, a fifty-seven-year-old Sikh called Wallace Gupta. Mr Gupta's interview – taken two days after the fact and consequently at least somewhat suspect – indicates that he told the boys to clear off at once, threatening them with the security guard and being labelled in turn 'Paki,' 'wanker,' 'bumboy,' 'fucker' and 'towelhead'. When the boys did not move away from the kiosk with the alacrity he desired, Mr Gupta pulled from beneath the cash till a spray bottle in which he kept bleach, the only weapon he had with which to defend himself or to urge their cooperation. The boys' reaction, reported by Ian Barker with a fair degree of pride, was laughter, followed by the appropriation of five bags of crisps (one of which was later found at the Dawkins building site), which prompted Mr Gupta to make good on his threat. He sprayed them with the bleach, hitting Ian Barker on the cheek and in the eye, Reggie Arnold on the trousers, and Michael Spargo on both trousers and anorak.

While both Michael and Reggie understood quickly that their school trousers were as good as ruined, their reaction to Mr Gupta's attack upon them was not as fierce as Ian's reportedly was. 'He wanted to get that Paki,' Reggie Arnold declared when questioned by the police. 'He went mental. He wanted to rubbish the kiosk, but I stopped him, I did,' an assertion unsupported by any facts that followed.

It's likely, however, that Ian was in pain and, lacking any socially acceptable response to pain (it appears unlikely that the boys sought out a public lavatory in which to wash the bleach from Ian's face), Ian reacted by blaming both Reggie and Michael for his situation.

Perhaps as a means of deflecting Ian's anger and avoiding a thrashing, Reggie pointed out Jones-Carver Pets and Supplies, in the window of which three Persian kittens played on a carpet-covered set of platforms. Reggie becomes vague at this point, when asked by the police what attracted him to the kittens, but he later accuses Ian of suggesting they steal one of the animals 'for a bit of fun'. Ian denied this during his questioning, but Michael Spargo has the other boy saying that they could cut off the cat's tail or 'nail it to a board like Jesus' and 'he thought that'd be wicked, that's what he said'. Naturally, it's difficult to know who was suggesting what at this point, for as the boys' stories take them closer and closer to John Dresser, they become less and less forthright.

What is known is this: the kittens in question were not readily available to anyone, being locked inside the window display cage because of their value. But standing in front of the cage was Tenille Cooper, four years old, who was watching the kittens as her mother made a purchase of dog food some six yards away. Both Reggie and Michael – interviewed independently and in the presence of a parent and a social worker – agree that Ian Barker grabbed little Tenille by the hand and announced 'This is better than a cat, innit,' with the clear intention of walking off with her. In this he was thwarted by the child's mother, Adrienne, who stopped the boys and, in some outrage, began to question them, to demand why they weren't at school and to threaten them with not only the security guard but also with the truant officer and the police. She was, of course, crucial in identifying them later, managing to pick photographs of all three of them from sixty pictures that were presented to her at the police station.

It must be said that had Adrienne Cooper gone for the security guard at once, John Dresser might never have come to the attention of the boys. But her failure – if it can even be called a failure because how, indeed, was she even to imagine the horrors to follow? – is minor compared to the failure of those individuals who later saw a progressively more and more distressed John Dresser in the company of the three boys and yet made no move either to alert the police or to take him from them.

2

'You're up to speed about what happened to DI Lynley, I take it?' Hillier asked, and Isabelle Ardery considered the man as well as the question before she replied. They were in his office at New Scotland Yard, where banks of windows looked out upon the rooftops of Westminster and some of the costliest real estate in the country. Sir David Hillier was standing behind his oceanic desk, looking crisp and clean and remarkably fit for a man his age. He had to be somewhere in his middle sixties, she decided.

At his insistence, she herself was seated, which she thought quite clever of him. He wanted her to feel his dominance on the chance that she might think herself his superior. This would be physically, of course. She was unlikely to conclude that she had some other sort of ascendancy over the Assistant Commissioner of the Metropolitan Police. She was taller than he by a full three inches – even more if she wore higher heels – however there her advantage ended.

She said, 'You're referring to Inspector Lynley's wife? Yes. I know what happened to her. I daresay everyone in the force knows what happened. How is he? Where is he?'

'Still in Cornwall, as far as I know. But the team want him back, and you're going to feel it. Havers, Nkata, Hale . . . All of them. Even John Stewart. From detectives to filing clerks. The lot. Custodians as well, I have no doubt. He's a popular figure.'

'I know. I've met him. He's quite the gent. That would be the word, wouldn't it? *Gent*.'

Hillier eyed her in a way she didn't much like, suggesting he had some thoughts on the wheres and hows of her acquaintance with Detective Inspector Thomas Lynley. She considered an elucidation on the subject, but she rejected the idea. Let the man think what the man would think. She had her chance to capture the job she wanted, and all that mattered was proving to him that she was worthy to be named *permanent* and not just *acting* detective superintendent.

'They're professionals, the lot of them. They won't make your life a misery,' Hillier said. 'Still, there're strong loyalties among them. Some things die hard.'

And some don't die at all, she thought. She wondered if Hillier intended to sit or whether this interview was going to be conducted entirely in the headmaster/recalcitrant pupil mode that his present position seemed to indicate. She also wondered if she'd made some sort of professional faux pas in sitting herself, but it seemed to her that he *had* made an unambiguous gesture towards one of the two chairs that were positioned in front of his desk, hadn't he?

'. . . won't give you a problem. Good man,' Hillier was saying. 'But John Stewart's another matter. He still wants the superintendent's position, and he didn't take it well when he wasn't named permanent superintendent at the end of his trial period.'

Isabelle brought herself round with a mental jolt. The mention of DI John Stewart's name told her that Hillier had been speaking of the others who had worked temporarily in the detective superintendent's job. He'd have been talking about the in-house officers, she concluded. Mentioning those who, like her, had auditioned – there was no other word for it – from outside the Met would have been pointless as she was unlikely to run into them in one or another of the endless, lino-floored corridors in Tower Block or Victoria Block. DI John Stewart, on the other hand, would be part of her team. His feathers were going to need smoothing out. This wasn't one of her strengths, but she would do what she could.

'I understand,' she told Hillier. 'I'll tread carefully with him. I'll tread carefully with them all.'

'Very good. How are you settling in? How are the boys? Twins, aren't they?'

She made her lips curve as one would normally do when 'the children' were mentioned, and she forced herself to think about them exactly like that, in inverted commas. The inverted commas kept them at a distance from her emotions, which was where she needed them. She said, 'We've decided – their father and I – that they're better off remaining with him for now, since I'm only here on trial. Bob's not far from Maidstone, he has a lovely property in the countryside, and as it's their summer holidays, it seemed wisest to have them live with their father for a while.'

'Not easy for you, I expect,' Hillier noted. 'You'll be missing them.'

'I'll be busy,' she said. 'And you know what boys are like. Eight years old? They need supervising and plenty of it. As both Bob and his wife are at home, they're in a good position to keep them on the straight and narrow, a far better position than I'll be in, I dare say. It should be fine.' She made the situation sound ideal: herself hard at work in London, nose to the metaphorical grindstone, while Bob and Sandra breathed copious amounts of fresh air in the countryside, all the time doting on the boys and feeding them home-cooked chicken pies filled with everything organic and served with ice cold milk. And, truth told, that wasn't too far from how it likely would be. Bob, after all, adored his sons and Sandra was perfectly lovely in her own way, if a bit too schoolmarmish for Isabelle's taste. She had her own two children, but that hadn't meant she had no room in her home and her heart for Isabelle's boys. For Isabelle's boys were Bob's boys as well, and he was a good dad and always had been. He kept his eye on the ball, did Robert Ardery. He asked the right questions at just the right time, and he never made a threat that didn't sound like an inspiration he'd just been struck by.

Hillier seemed to be reading her, or at least attempting to, but Isabelle knew she was more than a match for anyone's effort to see beyond the role she played. She'd made a virtual art of appearing cool, controlled and completely competent, and this façade had served her so well for so many years that it was second nature by now to wear her professional persona like chain mail. Such was the result of having ambition in a world dominated by men.

'Yes.' Hillier drew out the word, making it less confirmation than calculation. 'You're right, of course. Good that you have a civilised relationship with the ex, as well. High marks for that. It can't be easy.'

'We're tried to remain friendly throughout the years,' Isabelle told him, again with that curve of her lips. 'It seemed best for the boys. Warring parents? That's never good for anyone, is it.'

'Glad to hear it, glad to hear it.' Hillier looked towards the doorway as if expecting someone to enter, perhaps in order to come to his rescue. No one did. He seemed ill at ease, and Isabelle didn't consider this a bad thing. Ill-at-ease could work to her advantage. It suggested that the AC wasn't as dominant a male as he thought he was. 'I expect,' he said, in the tone of a man concluding their interview, 'you'd like to get to know the team. Be introduced formally. Get down to work.'

'I would,' she said. 'I'm going to want individual conversations with them.'

'No time like the present,' Hillier said with a smile. 'Shall I take you down to them?'

'Brilliant.' She smiled back and held his gaze long enough to see him colour. He was a florid man already, so he coloured easily. She wondered what he looked like in a rage. 'If I can just pop into the Ladies, sir . . . ?'

'Of course,' he said. 'Take your time.'

Which, naturally, was the very last thing he actually wanted her to do. She wondered if he did that often, making remarks he didn't mean. Not that it mattered as it wasn't her intention to spend a great deal of time with the man. But it was always helpful to know how people operated.

Hillier's secretary – a severe looking woman with five unfortunate facial warts in need of dermatological exploration – directed Isabelle towards the Ladies. Once inside, she checked carefully to ensure that she had the room to herself. She ducked into the stall farthest from the door and there she did her business. But this was merely for effect. Her real purpose lay within her shoulder bag.

She found the airline bottle where she'd earlier stowed it, and she opened it, drinking down the contents in two swift gulps. Vodka. Yes. It had long been just the ticket. She waited a few moments till she felt it take hold.

Then she left the stall and went to the basin, where she fished in her bag for her toothbrush and toothpaste. She brushed thoroughly, her teeth and her tongue.

She was ready to face the world.

The team of detectives she'd be supervising worked in close confines, so Isabelle met them together first. They were wary of her; she was wary of them. This was natural, and she wasn't bothered by it. Introductions were made by Hillier and he offered them her background chronologically: community liaison officer, burglary, vice, arson investigation and more recently MCIT. He didn't add the period of time she'd spent in each of her positions. She was on the fast track, and they would know it by reckoning her age, which was thirty-eight although she liked to think she looked younger, the result of wisely having stayed away from cigarettes and out of the sun for most of her life.

The only one of them who looked impressed with her background was the departmental secretary, a princess-in-waiting type called Dorothea Harriman. Isabelle wondered how any young woman could look so put together on what her salary had to be. She reckoned Dorothea found her clothing in charity shops, of the type where one could dig out timeless treasures if one was persistent, had an eye for quality and looked hard enough.

She told the team she would like to have a word with each of them. In her office, she said. Today. She would want to know what each of them was working on at present, she added, so do bring your notes.

It went much as she expected. DI Philip Hale was cooperative and professional, possessing a wait-and-see attitude that Isabelle could not fault, his notes at the ready, currently at work with the CPS preparing a case involving the serial killing of adolescent boys. She'd have no trouble with him. He hadn't applied for the superintendent's position and he seemed quite happy with his place on the team.

DI John Stewart was another matter. He was a nervy man if his bitten fingernails were anything to go by, and his focus on her breasts seemed to indicate a form of misogyny that she particularly detested. But she could handle him. He called her *ma'am*. She said *guv* would do. He let a marked moment pass before he made the switch. She said, I don't plan to have difficulty with you, John. Do you plan to have difficulty with me? He said, No, not at all, guv. But she knew he didn't mean it.

She met DS Winston Nkata next. He was a curiosity to her. Very tall, very black, scarred on the face from an adolescent street fight, he was all West Indies via South London. Tough exterior but something about the eyes suggested that inside the man a soft heart waited to be touched. She didn't ask him his age, but she put him somewhere in his twenties. He was one of two children who were yin and yang: his older brother was in prison for murder. This fact would, she decided, make the DS a motivated cop with something to prove. She liked that.

This was not the case for DS Barbara Havers, the last of the team. Havers slouched into the office – there could, Isabelle decided, be absolutely no other word for how the woman presented herself – reeking of cigarette smoke and carrying a chip on her shoulder the size of a lorry. Isabelle knew that Havers had been DI Lynley's partner for several years preceding the death of Lynley's wife. She'd met the sergeant before, and she wondered if Havers remembered.

She did. 'The Fleming murder,' were Havers' first words to her when they were alone. 'Out in Kent. You did the arson investigation on it.'

'Good memory, Sergeant,' Isabelle said to her. 'May I ask what happened to your teeth? I don't recall them like this.'

Havers shrugged. She said, 'C'n I sit or what?' and Isabelle said, 'Please.' She'd been conducting these interviews in AC Hillier mode – although she was seated, not standing, behind her desk – but in this case she rose and moved over to a small conference table where she indicated DS Havers should join her. She didn't want to bond with the sergeant, but she knew the importance of having with her a relationship rather different from the relationship she had with the others. This had more to do with the sergeant's partnership with Lynley than with the fact that they were both women.

'Your teeth?' Isabelle said again.

'Got in something of a conflict,' Havers told her.

'Really? You don't look the sort to brawl,' Isabelle noted and while this was true, it was also true that Havers looked *exactly* the sort to defend herself if push came to shove, which was apparently how her front teeth had come to be in the condition they were in, which was badly broken.

'Bloke didn't like the idea of my spoiling his kidnap of a kid,' Havers said. 'We got into it, him and me. A bit of this with the fists, a bit of that with the feet, and my face hit the stone floor.'

'This happened in the past year? While you were at work? Why've you not had them fixed? There haven't been problems about the Met paying, have there?'

'I've been thinking they give my face character.'

'Ah. By which I take it you're opposed to modern dentistry? Or are you afraid of dentists, Sergeant?'

Havers shook her head. 'I'm afraid of turning myself into a beauty as I don't much like the idea of fighting off hordes of admirers. 'Sides, world's full of people with perfect teeth. I like to be different.'

'Do you indeed?' Isabelle decided to be rather more direct with Havers. 'That must explain your clothing, then. Has no one ever remarked upon it, Sergeant?'

Havers adjusted her position in her seat. She crossed a leg over her knee, showing – God help us, Isabelle thought – a red high top trainer and an inch of purple sock. Despite the hideous heat of summer, she'd combined this fashionable use of colour with olive corduroy trousers and a brown pullover. This last was decorated with specks of lint. She looked like someone involved in an undercover investigation into the horrors of life as a refugee. 'Due respect, guv,' Havers said although her tone suggested there was something of grievance attached to her words, ''sides the fact that regulations don't allow you to give me aggro about the clothes, I don't think my appearance has much to do with how I—'

'Agreed. But your appearance has to do with your looking professional,' Isabelle cut in, 'which you don't at the moment. Let me be frank, regulations or not, professional is how I expect my team to look. I advise you to have your teeth fixed.'

'What, today?' Havers asked.

Did she sound borderline insolent? Isabelle narrowed her eyes. She responded with, 'Please don't make light of this, Sergeant. I also recommend you alter your manner of dress to something more appropriate.'

'Respect again, but you can't ask me—'

'True enough. Very true. But I'm not asking, am I? I'm advising. I'm suggesting. I'm instructing. All of which, I expect, you've heard before.'

'Not in so many words.'

'No? Well, you're hearing them now. And can you honestly tell me that DI Lynley *never* took note of your overall appearance?'

Havers was silent. Isabelle could tell that the mention of Lynley had struck home. She wondered idly if Havers had been – or was – in love with the man. It seemed wildly improbable, ludicrous actually. On the other hand, if opposites did indeed attract, there could not have been two people more dissimilar than Barbara Havers and Thomas Lynley, whom Isabelle remembered as gracious, educated, plummy voiced and exceedingly well dressed.

She said, 'Sergeant? Am I the only—'

'Look. I'm not much of a one for shopping,' Havers told her.

'Ah. Then let me give you some pointers,' Isabelle said. 'First of all, you need a skirt or trousers that fit, are ironed, and have the proper length. Then a jacket that is capable of being buttoned in the front. After that, an unwrinkled blouse, tights and a pair of pumps, court shoes or brogues that are polished. This isn't exactly brain surgery, Barbara.'

Havers had been gazing at her ankle – hidden though it was by the top of her trainer – but now she looked up at the use of her Christian name. 'Where?' she asked.

'Where what?'

'Where 'm I s'posed to do this shopping?' She made the final word sound as if Isabelle had been recommending she lick the pavement.

'Selfridge's,' Isabelle said. 'Debenham's. And if it's too daunting a prospect to do this alone, take someone with you. Surely you've a friend or two who know how to put together something suitable to wear to work. If no one's available, then browse through a magazine for inspiration. *Vogue. Elle.*'

Havers didn't look pleased, relieved or anything close to accepting. Instead, she looked miserable. Well, it couldn't be helped, Isabelle thought. The entire conversation could have been construed as sexist, but for heaven's sake, she was trying to *help* the woman. With that in mind, she decided to go the rest of the way: 'And while you're at it, may I suggest you do something about your hair as well?'

Havers bristled but said calmly enough, 'Never been able to do much with it.'

'Then perhaps someone else can. Do you have a regular hairdresser, Sergeant?'

Havers put a hand to her chopped up locks. They were a decent colour: pine would come closest to describing it, Isabelle decided. But they appeared completely unstyled. Obviously, the sergeant had been cutting her hair herself. God only knew how, although Isabelle reckoned it involved the use of secateurs.

'Well, have you?' Isabelle asked her.

'Not as such,' Havers said.

'You need to find one.'

Havers moved her fingers in a way that suggested she wanted a smoke: rolling a fantasy fag between them. 'When, then?' she asked.

'When then what?'

'When am I s'posed to take all of your . . . suggestions to heart?'

'Yesterday. Not to put too fine a point on it.'

'Straight away, you mean?'

Isabelle smiled. 'I see you're going to be good at reading my every nuance. Now,' and here they were at the real point, the reason that Isabelle had moved them from the desk to the conference table, 'tell me. What do you hear from Inspector Lynley?'

'Nothing much.' Havers looked and sounded immediately cagey. 'Talked to him a couple times is all.'

'Where is he?'

'Don't know, do I,' Havers told her. 'I expect he's still in Cornwall. He was walking the coast last I heard. All of it.'

'Quite a hike. How did he seem when you spoke to him?'

Havers knotted her unplucked eyebrows, clearly wondering about the line of questioning upon which Isabelle had embarked. She said, 'Like you'd expect someone to seem when he's had to pull the plug on his wife's life support. I wouldn't call him chipper. He was coping, guv. That's about all.'

'Will he be returning to us?'

'Here? London? The Met?' Havers considered this. She considered Isabelle as well, obviously with her mind clicking away with all the possibilities that might explain why the new acting detective superintendent wanted to know about the former acting detective superintendent. Havers said, 'He didn't want the job. He was just doing it temporarily. He's not into promotion or anything. It's not who he is.'

Isabelle didn't like being read. Least of all did she like being read by another woman. Thomas Lynley was indeed one of her worries. She wasn't averse to having him back on the team, but if that was going to happen, she wanted it to be with her prior knowledge and on her terms. The last thing she desired was his sudden appearance and everyone welcoming him with religious fervour.

She said to Havers, 'I'm concerned about his well-being, Sergeant. If you hear from him, I'd like to know. Just how he is. Not what he says. May I rely on you for that?'

'I suppose,' Havers said. 'But I won't be hearing from him, guv.'

Isabelle reckoned she was lying on both accounts.

Music made the ride bearable. The heat was intense because, while windows nearly the size of cinema screens lined both sides of the vehicle, they did not open. Each of them had a narrow, tilt-in pane of glass at the top, and all of *these* were open, but that did nothing to relieve what sunlight, weather and restless human bodies effected within the rolling tube of steel.

At least it was a bendy bus and not one of the double-deckers. Whenever it stopped, both its front door and its back door opened and a gust of air – hot and nasty but still *new* air – allowed him to breathe deeply and believe he could survive the ride. The voices in his head kept declaring otherwise, telling him that he needed to get out and get out *soon* because there was work to do and it was God's mighty work. But he couldn't get out, so he was using the music. When he had it coming through his earphones loud enough, it drowned out everything else, voices included.

He would have closed his eyes to lose himself in it: the sweep of the cello and its mournful tone. But he had to watch her and he had to be ready. When she made a move to debark, so would he.

They'd been riding for over an hour. Neither of them should have been there. He had his work, as did she, and when people didn't do what they were meant to do, the world went amiss and he had to heal it. He was *told* to heal it, in fact. So he'd followed her, careful not to be seen.

She'd got onto one bus and then onto another and now he could see she was using an *A to Z* in order to follow the route. This told him that she was unfamiliar with the area through which they were riding, an area that looked to him like much of the rest of London. Terraces of houses, shops with grimy plastic signs above their front windows, graffiti looping letters into meaningless words like *killdick boyz, chackers* and *porp*.

As they wound through town, on the pavements tourists morphed into students with backpacks who themselves became women in black from head to toe, slits for their eyes, in the company of men comfortably dressed in jeans and white T-shirts. And these became African children at play, running circles beneath the trees in a park. And then for a time, blocks of flats blended into a school, and this in turn dissolved to a collection of institutional looking buildings from which he turned his gaze. Finally, a narrowing of the street occurred and it then curved and they came into what looked like a village, although he knew it was not a village at all but rather a place that had been a village once. It was another of the multitude of communities consumed over time by the creeping mass of London.

The street climbed a modest hill and then they were among the shops. Mothers pushed prams here, and people mixed. Africans talked to whites. Asians shopped for *halal* meats. Old men sipped Turkish coffee in a café advertising pastries from France. It was a pleasant place. It made him relax, and it almost made him turn his music off.

Up ahead, he saw her begin to stir. She closed her *A to Z* after carefully turning down the corner of a page. She had nothing with her but her shoulder bag, and she tucked the *A to Z* into this as she made for the door. He noticed they were coming to the end of the high street and its shops. A wrought iron railing atop a brick revetment suggested they had reached a park.

It seemed odd to him that she'd come all this way by bus in order to visit a park, when there was a park – or perhaps more accurately a *garden* – not two hundred metres from where she worked. True, the day was wretchedly hot and beneath the trees it would be cool and even he looked forward to cool after that ride in the moving furnace. But if cool had been her intention all along, she could merely have gone into St Paul's parish church, which she sometimes did in her lunch hour, reading the tablets on the walls or just sitting near the communion rail to gaze at the altar and the painting above it. Madonna and child, this painting was. He knew that much although – despite the voices – he did not think himself a religious man.

He waited until the last moment to get off the bus. He'd placed his instrument on the floor between his feet and because he'd watched her so closely as she headed in the direction of the park, he nearly forgot to take it along. That would have been a disastrous mistake, and because he'd come so close to making it, he removed his headphones to silence the music. *The flame is come is come is here* went round in his head immediately when the music ceased. *I call on the birds to feast on the fallen.* He blinked hard and shook his head roughly.

There was a gate of wrought iron fully open at the top of four steps leading into the park. Before mounting these, she approached a notice board. Behind glass, a map of the place was posted. She studied this, but only briefly, as if verifying something that she already knew. Then she went inside the gate and in an instant she was swallowed up by the leafy trees.

He hurried to follow. He glanced at the notice board – paths wandering hither and yon, a building indicated, words, a monument – but he did not see the name of this park so it was only when he was on the trail leading into its depths that he first realised he was in a cemetery. It was unlike any cemetery he'd ever seen, for ivy and creepers choked its gravestones and cloaked its monuments at the base of which brambles and campion offered fruit and flowers. People buried here had been long forgotten, as had been the cemetery itself. If the tombstones had once been incised with the names of the dead, the carving had been worn away by weather and by the encroachment of nature, seeking to reclaim what had been in this spot long before any man had contemplated burying his dead here.

He didn't like the place but that couldn't be helped. He was her guardian – *yes, yes, you begin to understand!* – and she was his to protect and that meant he had a duty to perform. But he could hear the beginning of a wind howling in his head and *I am in charge of Tartarus* emerged from the gale. Then *listen just listen* and *We are seven* and *We stand at his feet,* and that was when he fumbled about, shoved the earphones back on, and raised the volume as high as it would go until he could hear nothing but the cello again and then the violins.

The path he walked on was studded with stones, uneven and dusty, and along its edges the crust of last year's leaves still lay, less thick here than upon the ground beneath the trees that towered over his head. These made the cemetery cool and its atmosphere fragrant and he thought if he could concentrate on that – the feel of the air and the scent of green growth – the voices wouldn't matter so much. So he breathed in deep and he loosened the collar of his shirt. The path curved and he saw her ahead of him; she had paused to gaze at a monument.

This one was different: it was weather-streaked but otherwise undamaged and clean of undergrowth; it was proud and unforgotten. It formed a sleeping lion atop a marble plinth. The lion was life-size, so the plinth was large. It accommodated inscriptions and family names, and these too had not been left to wear away.

He saw her raise a hand to caress the stone animal, his broad paws first and then beneath his closed eyes. It looked to him like a gesture made for luck, so when she walked on and he passed the monument, he touched his fingers to the lion as well.

She took a second, narrower path that veered to the right. A cyclist came towards her, and she stepped to one side, into a mantle of ivy and sorrel, where a dog rose twisted round the wings of a praying angel. Further along, she made way for a couple who walked arm in arm behind a pushchair that each of them guided with one hand. No child was within, but rather a picnic basket and bottles that shimmered when he passed them as well. She came across a bench round which a group of men were gathered. They smoked and listened to music coming from a boom box. The music was Asian as were they, and it was turned so loud that he could hear it even above the cello and the violins.

He realised suddenly that she was the only woman he'd seen who was walking in this place alone. It came to him that this meant danger, and this danger was underscored when the heads of the Asian men turned to watch her. They didn't move to follow her, but he knew they wanted to. A woman alone meant either an offering to a man or a female in need of discipline.

She was very foolish to have come here, he thought. Stone angels and sleeping lions could not protect her from what might roam in this place. It was broad daylight in the middle of summer but trees loomed everywhere, the undergrowth was thick and it would be a small matter to surprise her, to drag her off and to do to her the worst that could be done.

She needed protection in a world where there was none. He wondered why she did not seem to know it.

Ahead, the path opened into a clearing where uncut grass – browning with the lack of summer rain – had been beaten down as walkers sought a means to get to a chapel. This was brick, with a steeple that soared into the sky, with round rose windows marking both arms of the cross that the building formed. But the chapel itself was not accessible. It stood as a ruin. Only when one approached it could one see that iron bars fronted what had once been its door, that sheets of metal covered its windows, and that where there should have been stained glass between the tracery of the roundels at each end of its transept, dead ivy clung like a grim reminder of what lay at the end of every life.

Although he was surprised to see that the chapel was not as it had seemed from even so short a distance away as the path, she did not appear to be. She approached the ruin and made her way towards a backless stone bench across the uncut grass. He realised she would likely turn and sit here, which would make him immediately visible to her, so he dashed at once for one side of the clearing, where a seraph that was green with lichen curved one arm round a towering cross. This provided him with the cover he required, and he ducked behind it as she settled herself upon the stone bench. She opened her shoulder bag and brought out a book, not the *A to Z* surely, for at this point she must have known where she was. So this would be a novel, perhaps, or a volume of poetry, or the Book of Common Prayer. She began to read and he saw within moments that she was lost within its contents. Foolish, he thought. *She calls for Remiel,* the voices said. Over the cello and above the violins. How had they ever become so strong?

She needs a guardian, he told himself in answer to the voices. She needed to be *on* her guard.

Since she was not, he would be on guard for her. That and no other would be the duty which he would embrace.

3

Her name was Gina Dickens, Meredith learned, and it seemed that she was Gordon Jossie's new partner, although she didn't actually refer to herself as that. She didn't use *new* because, as things turned out, she had no idea there was an *old* partner or a *former* partner or whatever one wanted to call Jemima Hastings. She also didn't use *partner* as such, as she didn't quite live there in the cottage although she 'had hopes', she said with a smile. She was there on the holding more than she was at her own place, she confided, which was a tiny bed-sit above the Mad Hatter Tea Rooms. They were in Lyndhurst High Street, she said, where, frankly, the noise from dawn to dusk was appalling. And, come to think of it, the noise went on far *beyond* dusk because it was summer and there were several hotels, a pub, restaurants . . . and with all the tourists at this time of year . . . She was lucky to average four hours sleep a night when she was there. Which, to be honest, she tried not to be.

They'd gone inside the cottage. It had, Meredith quickly saw, been stripped of all things Jemima, at least as far as the kitchen went, which was as far as Meredith herself went and was as far as she wanted to go. Alarm bells were ringing in her head, her palms were wet and her underarms were dripping straight down her sides. Part of this was due to the day's ever increasing heat, but the rest was due to everything being absolutely *wrong*.

Outside the cottage, Meredith's throat had instantly dried to a desert. As if knowing this, Gina Dickens had ushered her within, sat her down at the old oak table and brought from the fridge designer water in a frosty bottle, just the sort of thing Jemima would have scoffed at. She poured them both a glass. She said, 'You look as if you've . . . I don't know what to call it.'

Meredith said stupidly, 'It's our birthday.'

'Yours and Jemima's? Who is she?'

Meredith couldn't believe at first that Gina Dickens didn't know a thing about Jemima. How could one live with a woman for as long as Gordon had lived with Jemima and somehow manage to keep the knowledge of her existence from his . . . Was Gina his *next* lover? Or was she one in a *line* of his lovers? And where were the rest of them? Where was Jemima? Oh, Meredith had *known* from the first that Gordon Jossie was bad news on legs.

'. . . at Boldre Gardens,' Gina was saying. 'Near Minstead? D'you know it? He was thatching a cottage there and I'd got myself lost. I *had* a map, but I'm completely useless even with a map. Spatially hopeless. North, west, whatever. None of them mean a thing to me.'

Meredith roused herself. Gina was telling her how she and Gordon Jossie had met, but she didn't *care* about that. She cared about Jemima Hastings. She said, 'He never mentioned Jemima? Or the Cupcake Queen? The shop she opened in Ringwood?'

'*Cup*cakes?'

'It's what she does. She had a business she ran from this cottage and it'd grown so much and . . . bakeries and hotels and catering for parties like children's birthdays and . . . he never mentioned . . . ?'

'I'm afraid he didn't. He hasn't.'

'What about her brother? Robbie Hastings? He's an agister. This—' She waved her arm to indicate the entire holding. 'This is part of his area. It was part of his father's area as well. And his grandfather's. And his great-grandfather's. There've been agisters in their family so long that all this part of the New Forest is actually called the Hastings. You didn't know that?'

Gina shook her head. She looked mystified and, now, a little bit frightened. She moved her chair a few inches away from the table and she glanced from Meredith to the cake she'd brought, which, ridiculously, she'd carried into the cottage. Seeing this, it came to Meredith that Gina wasn't afraid of Gordon Jossie – as she damn well should have been – but of Meredith herself who was talking rather like a mad woman.

'You must think I'm barking,' Meredith said.

'No, no. I don't. It's just . . .' Gina's words were quick, marginally breathless, and she seemed to stop herself from going on.

They were silent together. A whinnying came from outside. 'The ponies!' Meredith said. 'If you've got ponies here, Robbie Hastings would likely have brought them in off the Forest. Or he would have arranged with Gordon to fetch them. But in either case, he would have come by at some point to check on them. Why d'you have ponies here, anyway?'

If anything, Gina looked more concerned than before at this ping-ponging of Meredith's conversation. She clasped both hands round her water glass and said to it rather than to Meredith, 'Something about . . . I don't exactly know.'

'Are they hurt? Lame? Off their feed?'

'Yes. That's it, isn't it. Gordon said they were lame. He brought them in off the forest . . . three weeks ago? Something like that. I'm not sure, actually. I don't care for horses.'

'Ponies,' Meredith corrected her. 'They're ponies.'

'Oh, yes. I suppose. I've never quite seen the difference.' She hesitated, as if considering something. 'He did say . . .' She took a sip of the water, lifting the glass with both hands as if she'd not have been able to get it to her mouth otherwise.

'What? What did he say? Did he tell you—'

'Of course one *asks* eventually, doesn't one?' Gina said. 'I mean, here's a lovely man living on his own: good-hearted, gentle, passionate when passion's called for if you know what I mean.'

Meredith blinked. She didn't *want* to know.

'So I did ask how he happened to be alone: no girlfriend,

no partner, no wife. No one's snapped you up? That sort of thing. Over dinner.'

Yes, Meredith thought. Outside in the garden, sitting at the wrought iron table with the candles lit and the torchères blazing. She said stiffly, 'And what did he say?'

'That he'd been involved once and he'd been quite badly hurt and he didn't like to talk about it. So I didn't want to intrude. I assumed he'd tell me when he was ready.'

'That's Jemima,' Meredith said. 'Jemima Hastings. And she's . . .' She didn't want to put it into words. Putting it into words might make it true and for all she knew it wasn't true at all. She assessed her facts, for they were few enough. The Cupcake Queen was closed up. Lexie Streener had made phone calls that had gone unreturned. This cottage was semi-occupied by another woman. She said, 'How long have you and Gordon known each other? Been involved? Whatever?'

'We met early last month. At Boldre—'

'Yes. At Boldre Gardens. What were you doing there?'

Gina looked startled. Clearly, she hadn't expected the question and even more clearly, she didn't much like it. She said, 'I was having a walk, actually. I've not lived in the New Forest long and I like to explore.' She offered a smile as if to take the sting out of what she said next. 'You know, I'm not sure why you're asking me this. D'you think something's happened to Jemima Hastings? That Gordon *did* something to her? Or that I did something? Or that Gordon and I together did something? Because I want you to know that when I got here, to this cottage, there wasn't a sign that *anyone*—'

She'd stopped abruptly. Meredith saw that Gina's eyes were still fixed on hers, but they'd lost their focus, as if she was seeing something else entirely. Meredith said, 'What? What is it?'

Gina dropped her gaze. A moment passed. The ponies whinnied outside once again and the excited warbling of pied wagtails broke into the air, as if warning one another that a predator was approaching. 'Perhaps,' Gina finally said, 'you ought to come with me.'

When Meredith finally found Robbie Hastings, he was standing in the car park behind the Queen's Head in Burley. This was a village at the junction of three roads, arranged in a line of buildings undecided between cob, half-timber and red brick, all of them possessing roofs that were equally undecided between thatch and slate. Midsummer, there were vehicles everywhere, including six tour coaches that had brought visitors to this place for what would likely be their only New Forest experience outside of riding through the lanes and seeing it in air conditioned comfort from well-padded coach seats. This experience would consist of snapping photos of the ponies that wandered freely through the area, of having an expensive bar meal in the pub or in one of the picturesque cafés, and of making purchases in one or more of the tourist shops. These last largely defined the village: they comprised everything from the Coven of Witches – proudly the former home of a bonafide witch who'd had to leave the area when her fame exceeded her willingness to have her privacy invaded – to Burley Fudge Shop and everything in between. The Queen's Head presided over all of this, the largest structure in the village and the off-season gathering place for those who lived in the area and who wisely avoided both it and Burley itself during the summer.

Meredith had phoned Robbie's home first, although she knew how unlikely it was that he'd be there in the middle of the day. As an agister, he was responsible for the well-being of all the free-roaming animals in his assigned area – the area that she'd told Gina Dickens was referred to as the Hastings – and he'd be out in the Forest either in his vehicle or on horseback making sure that the donkeys, ponies, cows and the occasional sheep were being left in peace. For this was the biggest challenge that faced anyone who worked in the Forest, especially during the summer months. It was appealing to see animals so unrestricted by fences, walls and hedges. It was even more appealing to feed them. People meant well but they were, alas, congenitally stupid. They did not understand that to feed a sweet little pony in summer conditioned the animal to think that someone was likely to be standing in the car park of the Queen's Head ready to feed him in the dead of winter as well. Robbie Hastings was apparently explaining this to a throng of camera-wielding pensioners in Bermuda shorts and lace-up shoes.

Meredith gave a glance to her chocolate cake as she climbed out of her car. Its icing had begun to pool viscously at its base. Several flies had managed to find it, but it was like one of those insect-eating plants: Whatever landed upon it was becoming mired in sugar and cocoa. Death by delight. The cake was done for.

It no longer mattered. Things were wildly out of joint, and Robbie Hastings had to be informed. For he'd been his sister's sole parent from her tenth year onward, a car crash catapulting him into this position when he was twenty-five. That same car crash had also catapulted him into the career he had thought never to attain: one of only five agisters in the New Forest, replacing his own father.

'. . . for what we mustn't have is the ponies hanging about one spot.' Robbie seemed to be completing his remarks to an audience looking rather guilty for what they apparently had stowed about their persons: apples, carrots, sugar and whatever else might appeal to a pony otherwise meant to forage. When Robbie was finished with his remarks – made patiently while visitors continually snapped his picture although he wasn't wearing his formal attire but rather jeans, T-shirt and a baseball cap – he gave a sharp nod and opened his Land Rover's door, preparatory to driving off. The tourists drifted towards the village proper and towards the pub, and Meredith worked her way through them, calling Robbie's name.

He turned. Meredith felt the way she'd always felt when she saw him: warmly fond but nonetheless terribly sorry for what he looked like with those huge front teeth of his. They made his mouth the only thing one noticed about him, which was a shame, really. He was very well built, tough and masculine, and his eyes were highly unusual – one brown and one green, just like Jemima's.

His face brightened. He said, 'Merry Contrary. It's been donkey's years, girl. What're you up to in this part of the world?' He was wearing gloves, but he removed them and spontaneously held out his arms to her, as he'd always done.

She embraced him. They were both hot and sweaty, and he was acrid with the mixed odours of horse and man. 'What a day, eh?' He took off his baseball cap, revealing hair that would have been thick and wavy had he not kept it shorn close to his skull. It was brown flecked with grey, and this served as a reminder of Meredith's estrangement from Jemima. For it seemed to Meredith that his hair had been completely brown the last time she had seen him.

She said, 'I phoned the verderers' office. They said you'd be here.'

He wiped his forehead on his arm, replaced the cap and tugged it down. 'Did you, now? What's up?' He glanced over his shoulder as the pony apparently within the horse trailer clomped restlessly and bumped against its side. The trailer shuddered. Robbie said, 'Hey now,' and he made a clucking sound. 'You know you can't stay here at the Queen's Head, mate. Settle. Settle.'

'Jemima,' Meredith said. 'It's her birthday, Robbie.'

'So it is. Which makes it yours as well. Which means you're twenty-six years old and *that* means I'm . . . Blimey, I'm forty-one. You'd think by now I would've found a lass willing to marry this heap of manhood, eh?'

'No one's snapped you up?' Meredith said. 'The women of Hampshire are half mad then, Rob.'

He smiled. 'You?'

'Oh, I'm full mad. I've had my one man, thank you very much. Not about to repeat the experience.'

He chuckled. 'Damn, then, Merry. You've no idea how often

I've heard that said. So why're you looking for me since it's not to offer your hand in marriage?'

'It's Jemima. Robbie, I went to the Cupcake Queen and saw it was closed. Then I talked to Lexie Streener and then I went to their place – Gordon's and Jemima's – and there's this woman Gina Dickens there. She's not exactly living there or anything but she's . . . I s'pose you'd call it established. And she didn't know the first thing about Jemima.'

'You haven't heard from her, then?'

'From Jemima? No.' Meredith hesitated. She felt dead awkward. She looked at him earnestly, trying to read him. 'Well, she must have told you . . .'

''Bout what happened 'tween the two of you?' he asked. 'Oh, aye. She told me you had a falling out some time back. Didn't think it was permanent, though.'

'Well, I *had* to tell her I had doubts about Gordon. Aren't friends meant to do that?'

'I'd say they are.'

'But all she'd say in return is "Robbie doesn't have doubts about him, so why do you?"'

'Said that, did she?'

'*Did* you have doubts? Like me? Did you?'

'Oh, that I did. Something about the bloke. I didn't dislike him 'xactly, but if she was going to have a partner, I would've liked it to be someone I knew through and through. I didn't know Gordon Jossie like that, and that bothered me. But as things turned out, I needn't have worried – same applies to you – because Jemima found out whatever she needed to find out when she hooked up with him and she was clever enough to end it when it needed to be ended.'

'What's that mean, exactly?' Meredith shifted. She was absolutely baking in the heat. At this point she felt as if her entire body were melting like her poor chocolate cake in the car. 'Look, can we get out of the sun?' she asked. 'Can we get a drink? Have you the time? We need to talk. I think . . . There's something not quite right.'

Robbie gave a look to the pony and then a look to Meredith. He nodded and said, 'Not the pub, though,' and he led them across the car park to a little arcade of shops, one of which offered sandwiches and drinks. They took theirs to a sweet chestnut that spread its leafy branches on the edge of the car park, where a bench faced a lawn opening out in the shape of a fan.

A smattering of tourists were taking photos of ponies that grazed with their foals nearby. The foals were especially appealing, but they were also skittish which made approaching them and their dams more dangerous than usual. Robbie watched the action. 'One damn well wonders,' he said darkly. 'That bloke over there? He's likely to be bit. And then he'll want the pony put down or he'll want to sue God knows who. Not that the wanting is going to get him anywhere. Still, I always think there's some kinds need to be permanently removed from the gene pool.'

'Do you?'

He coloured slightly at the question, then he looked at her. 'S'pose not,' he said. And then, 'She's gone to London, Merry. She phoned me up one day, somewhere near end of October this was, and she announced she was going to London. I thought she meant for the day, for supplies or something for the shop. But she says No, no, it's not the shop. I need time to think, she says. And she's still there.'

'But what about the Cupcake Queen?'

'Yeah. Bit odd that, eh? I tried to talk to her about that, but she wasn't having any. All she would say is the bit about needing to think.'

'London.' Meredith worked on the word. She tried to relate it to her friend. 'Think about what?'

'She wouldn't say, Merry. She still won't say.'

'You talk to her?'

'Oh, aye. 'Course I do. Once a week or more. She's that good about ringing me. Well, she would be. You know Jemima. She worries a bit: how I'm doing without her coming round like she did. So she stays in touch.'

'Lexie told me she tried to ring Jemima. First she left messages and then the calls didn't go through. So how're you talking to her once—'

'New mobile,' Robbie said. 'She didn't want Gordon to have the number. He kept ringing her. She doesn't want him to know where she is.'

'What on earth happened between them?'

'That I don't know, and she won't say. I went over there once she'd gone 'cause she'd been in a right royal state and I thought to have a word with Gordon.'

'And?'

He shook his head. 'Nothing. Gordon says, "You know what I know, mate. I still feel the same as always. She's the one whose feelings changed."'

'Someone else?'

'On Jemima's part?' Robbie lifted his can of Coke and downed most of it. 'Wasn't someone when she left. I asked her that. You know Jemima. Hard to think she'd leave Gordon without having someone ready to partner up with.'

'Yes. I know. That "being alone" business. She can't cope, can she?'

'Who's to blame her, really? After Mum and Dad.'

They were both silent, considering this: what fears that losing her parents in childhood had wrought in Jemima and how those fears had played out in her life.

Across the lawn from them, an elderly man with a zimmer frame was getting too close to one of the foals. Its dam's head snapped up but then, no worries. The foal scampered off and the small herd moved as well. They were more than a match for a bloke with a zimmer. He called out to them, a carrot extended.

Robbie sighed. 'Should have saved my breath for the porridge, all the good it does to tell them, eh? Reckon some people have cotton wool up there 'stead of brains. Look at him, Merry.'

'You need a loud hailer,' she told him.

'I need my shotgun.' Robbie rose. He would confront the man as indeed he must. But there was something more that Meredith wanted him to know. Things might have been explained with regard to Jemima, but things were still not right.

She said, 'Rob, how did Jemima get up to London?'

'I expect she drove.'

And this was the crux of the matter. It was the answer she feared. It constituted the bells and whistles, and it became the alarm. Meredith felt it in the tingling of her arms and the shiver – despite the heat – that went up her spine. 'No,' she said. 'She didn't do that.'

'What?' Robbie turned to look at her.

'She didn't drive up there.' Meredith rose as well. 'That's just it. That's why I've come. Her car's in the barn at Gordon's, Robbie. Gina Dickens showed it to me. It was under a tarp like he was hiding it.'

'You're joking.'

'Why would I joke? She'd asked him about it, Gina Dickens. He said it was his. But he hasn't ever driven it which made her think . . .' Meredith's throat was dry once more, desert-like as it had been during her conversation with Gina.

Robbie was frowning. 'It made her think what? What's going on, Merry?'

'That's what I want to know.' She curved her hand round his work-muscled arm. 'Because, Rob, there's more.'

Robbie Hastings tried not to be concerned. He had obligations – the most important at the moment being the transport of the pony in the horse trailer – and he needed to keep his mind on his duty. But Jemima was a large part of that duty, despite the fact that she was now an adult. For Jemima's becoming an adult hadn't changed things between them. He was still her father figure while to Robbie she'd always be his sister-child, the waif who'd lost her parents after a late night dinner on holiday in Spain: too much to drink, confusion over which side of the road to be driving on, and that had been that, gone in an instant, mown down by a lorry. Jemima hadn't been with them, and thank God for that. For had she been, everyone he'd known as family would have been wiped out. Instead, he'd been staying with her in the family home, and so his stay had become permanent.

Thus even as Robbie delivered the pony to the commoner who owned her and even as he had a talk with that gentleman about what ailed the animal – Robbie reckoned it was cancer, sir, and the pony was going to have to be put down although you might want to phone the vet for a second opinion – he still thought about Jemima. He'd phoned her upon waking that morning because it was her birthday, and he phoned her again along the road back to Burley after leaving the pony with its owner. But he got this second time what he'd got when he phoned the first time: his sister's cheerful voice on her voicemail.

He hadn't given that a thought when he'd first phoned, for it had been early in the day and he reckoned she'd switched the mobile off if she wanted a lie-in on her birthday. But she generally phoned right back when she got a message from him, so when he left a second message, he became concerned. He phoned her place of employment after that, but he learned that she'd taken a half day off on the previous day and today was not a workday for her. Did he want to leave a message, sir? He didn't.

He rang off and worried the tattered leather cover on his steering wheel. All right, he told himself, Meredith's concerns aside, it was Jemima's birthday and likely she was merely having a bit of fun. And she *would* do that, wouldn't she? As he recalled, she'd enthused about ice skating recently. Lessons or something. So she *could* be off doing that. It would be exactly like Jemima.

Truth of the matter was that Robbie hadn't told Meredith everything beneath the sweet chestnut tree in Burley. There hadn't seemed to be a point, mostly because Jemima had a history of attachments to men while Meredith – bless her heart – definitely had not. He hadn't wanted to rub Meredith's face in this fact, her being a single mum as the result of the only disastrous relationship she'd managed. Besides, Robbie respected Meredith Powell: how she'd stepped up to the plate of motherhood and was making a proper job of it. And anyway, Jemima *hadn't* left Gordon Jossie for another man, so that much of what Robbie had told Meredith had been true. But, exactly in character, she'd found another man quickly enough. Robbie hadn't told Meredith that. Afterwards, he wondered if he should have.

'He's very special, Rob,' Jemima had burbled in that way she had. 'Oh, I'm *madly* in love with him.'

That's what she always was: madly in love. No point in like or interest or curiosity or friendship when one could be madly in love. For *madly in love* equated to warding off solitude. She'd gone to London to think, but thinking was something that led Jemima to fear and God knew she'd far rather run from fear than face it head on. Well, didn't everyone? Wouldn't he if he could?

Robbie wound up the hill that was Honey Lane, a short distance outside of Burley. In midsummer it was a lush green tunnel, sided by holly and arced by beech and oak. It was packed earth only – no paving here – and he passed along it with care, doing his best to avoid the occasional pothole that made the going rough. He was less than a mile outside the village, but one stepped back in time in this area. The trees sheltered paddocks and beyond them ancient buildings marked both common holdings and farms. These were backed by a wood, and the wood was thick with fragrant scotch pines, with hazel and with beech, providing a habitat for everything from deer to dormice, from stoats to shrews. One could walk the distance here from Burley, but people seldom did. There were easier paths to follow, and in Robbie's experience people liked their ease.

At the crest of the hill, he made the left turn onto what had long been Hastings land. This comprised thirty-five acres of paddock and wood, with the rooftop of Burley Hill House just visible to the northeast and the peak of Castle Hill Lane beyond it. In one of the paddocks his own two horses happily grazed, delighted not to be carrying his weight round the New Forest on this hot summer day.

Robbie parked near the tumbledown barn and its attendant shed, trying not to see them so he would not have to think about how much work he needed to put into them. He climbed out of the Land Rover and slammed the door. The noise brought his dog loping from round the side of the house where he'd no doubt been sleeping in the shade, his tail wagging and his tongue hanging, and all of himself looking out of character. The Weimaraner was normally elegant in appearance. But he hated the heat and he'd rolled in the compost heap as if this would help him to escape it. He now wore a fragrantly decomposing mantle. He paused to shake himself off.

'Think that's amusing, do you, Frank?' Robbie asked the dog. 'You're a real sight. You know that, eh? I shouldn't let you near the house.'

But no woman lived there to admonish him or to usher Frank from the house herself. So when he went inside and the dog tagged along, Robbie allowed it and was grateful for the company. He fetched the Weimaraner a fresh bowl of water. Frank slopped it happily onto the kitchen floor.

Robbie left him to it and went for the stairs. He was sweaty and he smelled of horse from transporting the pony, but instead of heading for a shower – he could hardly be bothered with that at this time of day, as he'd only get sweaty and smelly again – he went into Jemima's room.

He told himself to be calm. He couldn't think if he got himself into a state and he needed to think. In his experience, there was an explanation for everything, and there was going to be an explanation for the rest of what Meredith Powell had told him.

'Her clothes are there, Rob. But not in the bedroom. He's

boxed them all up and he's put them in the attic. Gina found them because, she said, there was something a little strange – that's how she put it – when he was talking about Jemima's car.'

'So she did what? Took you up to see them? Up to the attic?'

'She just told me about them at first,' Meredith said. 'I asked to look. I reckoned they could've been there a while – from before Gordon and Jemima took the place – so they could've been someone else's. But they weren't. The boxes weren't old, and there was something I recognised. Well, it was mine, actually, and she'd borrowed it and I'd never got it back. So you see . . . ?'

He did and he didn't. Had he not heard from his sister at least weekly since her departure, he would have headed to Sway at once, determined to have a face-to-face with Gordon Jossie. But he *had* heard from her and what she'd repeated at the end of each phone call had been the reassurance, 'Not to worry, Rob. It'll all come right.'

He'd said at first, '*What'll* all come right?' and she'd side-stepped the question. Her avoidance had forced him more than once to ask: 'Did Gordon do something to you, my girl?' to which she'd replied, 'Of course not, Rob.'

Robbie knew he'd now have assumed the worst had Jemima not stayed in touch: Gordon had killed her and buried her on the property somewhere. Or out in the Forest and deep within a wood so that if her body were ever found, it would be in fifty years when it was too late to matter. Somehow, an unspoken prophecy – a belief or a fear – would have been fulfilled by her disappearance because the truth of the matter was: he did not like Gordon Jossie. He'd said to her often enough, 'There's something *about* him, Jemima,' to which she'd laughed and replied, 'You mean he's not like you.'

He'd been forced finally to agree with her. It was easy to like and embrace people just like oneself. It was another matter with people who were different.

In her bedroom now, he phoned her again. Again, no reply. Just the voice and he left a message once he was asked to do so. He kept it cheerful to match her own tone. 'Hey, birthday girl, ring me, eh? Not like you not to get back in touch and I'm having a bit of a worry, I am. Merry Contrary came to see me. She had a cake for you, luv. Got itself all melted in the bloody heat but it's the thought, eh? Ring me, luv. I want to tell you about the foals.'

He found he wanted to go on a bit, but he was talking into a void. He didn't want to leave his sister a message. He wanted his sister herself.

He walked to her bedroom window, its sill yet another depository for what Jemima Clutterduck could not bear to part with, which was nearly everything she'd ever possessed. In this spot, it was plastic ponies, crammed one upon the next and covered with dust. Beyond them he could see the real thing: his horses in the paddock with the sunlight glowing off their well-groomed coats.

The fact that Jemima had not returned for the foaling season was what should have told him, he thought. It had long been her favourite time of year. Like him, she was *of* the New Forest. He'd sent her to college in Winchester as he himself had been sent, but she'd come home when her coursework was completed, rejecting computer technology for baking instead. 'I belong here,' she'd told him. As indeed she did.

Perhaps she'd gone to London not for time to think but just for time. Perhaps she'd wanted to break off with Gordon Jossie but hadn't known how else to bring it about. Perhaps she reckoned if she was gone long enough, Gordon would find someone else and she herself could then return. But none of that was in character, was it?

Not to worry, she'd say. Not to worry, Rob.

What a monstrous joke.

4

David Emery considered himself one of Stoke Newington's very few Cemetery Experts, which he always thought of in upper case letters, David being an Upper Case sort of bloke. He'd made an understanding of Abney Park Cemetery his Life's Work (another upper case situation for him), and it had taken him ages of wandering and getting lost and refusing to be cowed by the general creepiness of the area before he was willing to call himself its Master. He'd been locked in more times than he could begin to count, but he'd never let the cemetery's nightly closure impinge upon his plans while he was there. If he arrived at any of the gates and found them chained against his wishes, he didn't bother to ring the Hackney police for rescue as the sign on the gate recommended he do. For him, it was no huge matter just to hoist himself up the railings and over the top, landing either in Stoke Newington High Street or, preferably, in the back garden of one of the terrace houses that lined the cemetery's northeast boundary.

Making himself a Master of the Park allowed him to use its paths and crannies in any number of ways but particularly in ways amorous. He did this several times a month. He was good with the ladies – they often told him he had soulful eyes, whatever that meant – and since One Thing generally led to Another with women in David's life, a suggestion that they take a stroll in the park was rarely refused, especially since *park* was such a . . . well, such an innocuous word compared to *cemetery*, wasn't it.

His intention was always a shag. Indeed, *taking a walk*, *having a stroll* or *going for a bit of a wander* were all euphemisms for shagging, and the ladies knew that although they pretended not to. They would always say things like, 'Oooh, Dave, that place gives me the jumps, it does,' or words to that effect, but they were perfectly willing to accompany him there once he put an arm round them – going for a bit of breast with his fingers if he could – and told them they'd be safe with him.

So in they'd go, directly through the main gates, which was his preferred route as the path was broad and less intimidating there than it was if they entered by means of Stoke Newington Church Road. There you were beneath the trees and in the clutches of the gravestones before you'd gone twenty yards. On the main path you had at least the illusion of safety till you veered right or left onto one of the narrower routes that disappeared into the towering plane trees.

On this particular day, Dave had coaxed Josette Hendricks to come along with him. At fifteen Josette was a little younger than Dave was accustomed to, not to mention the fact that she was something of a giggler, which he *hadn't* known until he got her onto the first of the narrow paths, but she was a pretty girl with a lovely complexion and those luscious baps of hers were no small matter, in more ways than one. So when he said, 'What d'you say to the park?' and she said, all bright-eyed and moist-lipped, 'Oh *yes*, Dave,' off they went.

He had a little hollow in mind, a place created by a fallen sycamore behind a tomb and between two gravestones. There, Interesting Developments could occur. But he was too much the schemer to head to the hollow straightaway. He started off with a bit of hand-in-hand statue gazing – 'Oooh, dead sad that little angel looks, eh?' – and went on from there to a hand on the back of the neck, a caress – 'Dave, that makes me go all tingly!' – and the kind of kiss that *suggested* but nothing more.

Josette was a little slower than most girls, probably as a result of her upbringing. Unlike other girls of fifteen, she was something of an innocent who'd never even been out on a date – 'Mum and Dad say not yet,' – and therefore she didn't pick up on the signs as well as she might have done. But he was patient and when at last she was pressing against him of her own volition and clearly wanting more of his kisses and at greater length, he suggested they get off the path and 'see if there's somewhere . . . you know what I mean' with a wink.

Who would have bloody thought that the hollow, his own *particular* Site of Seduction, would be flaming occupied? It was an outrage, it was, but there you have it. Dave heard the moaning and groaning as he and Josette approached and there was no mistaking the arms and legs all a'tangle in the undergrowth, especially since there were four of each and none of them had a stitch of clothing on. There was also the naked arse of the bloke pumping madly away, his head turned towards them and a grimace on his face . . . Cor, do we all look like *that?* Dave wondered.

Josette giggled when she saw, and this was a good thing. Anything else would have suggested either fear or prurience and while Dave certainly didn't expect her to be some sort of shrinking Puritan in this day and age, one never knew. He backed away from the hollow, Josette's hand in his, and he gave some thought to where he might take her. There were nooks and hollows aplenty, to be sure, but he wanted a location close to this one, Josette being on the boil.

And then he thought, Of course. They were not far from the chapel at the centre of the cemetery. They couldn't get inside the building, but right next to it – indeed, built *into* it – was a shelter that they could easily use. It offered a roof and walls and that was better than the hollow, come to think of it.

He inclined his head in the direction of the coupling couple and winked at Josette. 'Mmmm, not bad, eh?' he said.

'Dave!' She gave a little gasp of faux horror. How *could* you mention such a thing!

'Well?' he said. 'You saying you don't . . . ?'

'Didn't say that,' was how she replied.

As good as an invitation, that was. It was off to the chapel they went. Hand in hand and in a bit of a hurry. Josette, Dave decided, was definitely a flower ready to be plucked.

They reached the grassy clearing where the chapel stood. 'Just round here, luv,' Dave murmured.

He took her beyond the chapel entrance and around its far corner. And there his plans ground themselves to a sudden halt.

For a teenaged boy with a barrel for a bum was stumbling out of Dave's trysting place. He had such a look on his face that one almost didn't notice he was holding up his obviously unzipped trousers. He dashed across the clearing and then was gone.

All this at first caused David Emery to think the boy had relieved himself inside the trysting place. This cheesed Dave off as he could hardly expect Josette to want to roll round in a spot reeking of piss. But as she was ready and as he was ready and as there *was* the slightest possibility that the boy had not used the shelter as a public convenience, Dave shrugged and urged Josette forward, saying, 'Just in there, luv,' as he followed her.

He was so much thinking of Just One Thing that he nearly jumped out of his skin, he did, when Josette went into the shelter and started screaming.

'No, no, no, Barbara,' Hadiyyah said. 'We can't just go shopping. Not without a plan. That would be far too over*whel*ming. *First* we got to make a list, but before we do that we got to consider what we want. And to do *that* we got to decide on the type of *body* you have. It's how these things are done. One sees it on telly all the time.'

Barbara Havers eyed her companion doubtfully. She wondered whether she should be seeking sartorial advice from a nine-year-old girl. But aside from Hadiyyah, there was only Dorothea Harriman to turn to if she was to take Isabelle Ardery's 'advice' to heart, and Barbara wasn't about to throw herself upon the mercy of Scotland Yard's foremost style icon. With Dorothea at the helm, the ship of shopping was likely to sail straight down the King's Road or – worse – into Knightsbridge, where in a boutique operated by rail thin shop assistants with sculptured hair and similar fingernails, she would be forced to lay out a week's pay on a pair of knickers. At least with Hadiyyah there was a slight chance that what had to be done could be done in M & S.

But Hadiyyah was having none of that. 'Top Shop,' she said. 'We got to go to Top Shop, Barbara. Or Jigsaw. Or *maybe* H & M but just maybe.'

'I don't want to look trendy,' Barbara told her. 'It's got to be professional. Nothing with ruffles. Or spikes sprouting from it. Nothing with chains.'

Hadiyyah rolled her eyes. '*Bar*bara,' she said. 'Really. Do you think *I'd* wear spikes and chains?'

Her father would have had something to say about that, Barbara thought. Taymullah Azhar kept his daughter on what had to be called a very tight rein. Even now in her summer holidays she wasn't allowed to run about with other children her age. Instead, she was studying Urdu and cookery and when she wasn't studying Urdu or cookery, she was being minded by Sheila Silver, an elderly pensioner whose brief period of glory – endlessly recounted – had occurred singing back-up for a Cliff Richard wannabe on the Isle of Wight. Mrs Silver lived in a flat in the Big House, as they called it, an elaborate yellow Edwardian structure in Eton Villas; Barbara lived behind this building on the same property in a hobbit-size bungalow. Hadiyyah and her father were neighbours, domiciled in the ground floor flat of Big House with an area in front of it that served as its terrace. This was where Barbara and Hadiyyah were conferring, each with a Ribena in front of her, both of them bent over a wrinkled section of the *Daily Mail* which Hadiyyah had apparently been saving for an occasion precisely like this one.

She'd fetched the newspaper from her bedroom once Barbara had explained her wardrobe quest. 'I have *just* the thing,' she'd announced happily and, her long plaits flying, she'd disappeared into the flat and returned with the article in question. She laid this open on the wicker table to reveal a story about clothing and body types. Spread across two pages were models who supposedly demonstrated all possibilities of build, excluding anorexia and obesity, of course, as the *Daily Mail* did not wish to encourage extremes.

Hadiyyah had informed Barbara that they had to begin with body type and they couldn't *exactly* work out Barbara's body type if she didn't change into something . . . well, something that would allow them to see what they were working with? She dismissed Barbara back to her bungalow to change her clothes – 'It's awfully hot for corduroy and wool jumpers anyway,' she noted helpfully – and she bent over the paper to scrutinise the models. Barbara did her bidding and returned, although Hadiyyah sighed when she saw the drawstring trousers and T-shirt.

'*What?*' Barbara said.

'Oh, well. Never mind,' Hadiyyah told her airily. 'We'll do our best.'

Their best consisted of Barbara standing on a chair – feeling like a perfect fool – while Hadiyyah crossed the grass 'to get a bit of distance so I c'n compare you to the ladies in the pictures'. This she did by holding up the newspaper and crinkling her nose as she switched her gaze from it to Barbara to it to Barbara before announcing, 'Pear, I think. Short-waisted as well. C'n you lift your trousers? . . . Barbara, you have lovely ankles! Whyever don't you show them? Girls should *always* emphasise their best features, you know.'

'And I'd do that by . . . ?'

Hadiyyah considered this. 'High heels. You have to wear high heels. Do you have high heels, Barbara?'

'Oh yeah,' Barbara said. 'I find them just the thing for my line of work, crime scenes being otherwise rather grim.'

'You're making fun. You *can't* make fun if we're to do this properly.' Hadiyyah bounced across the lawn back to her, trailing the *Daily Mail* article from her fingers. She spread this out on the wicker table once again and perused it for a moment after which she announced, 'A-line skirt. The staple of all wardrobes. Your jacket has to be a length that doesn't draw attention to your hips and as your face is round-ish—'

'Still working to lose the puppy fat,' Barbara said.

'—the neckline of your blouse should be soft, not angular. Blouse necklines, you see, should *mirror* the face. Well, the chin, really. I mean the whole line from the ears to the chin, which includes the jaw.'

'Ah. Got it.'

'We want the skirt mid-knee and the shoes to have straps. *That's* because of your lovely ankles.'

'Straps?'

'Hmm. It says so right here. *And* we must accessorise as well. The mistake so many women make is failure to accessorise appropriately or – what's worse – failure to accessorise at all.'

'Bloody hell. We don't want that,' Barbara said fervently. 'What's it mean, exactly?'

Hadiyyah folded up the newspaper neatly, running her fingers lovingly along each crease. 'Oh, scarves and hats and belts and lapel pins and necklaces and bracelets and earrings and handbags. Gloves as well, but that would be only in winter.'

'God,' Barbara said. 'Won't I be a bit overdone with all that?'

'You don't use it all at *once*.' Hadiyyah sounded like patience itself. 'Honestly, Barbara, it's not really that difficult. Well, maybe it's a *bit* difficult, but I'll help you with it. It'll be such fun.'

Barbara doubted this, but off they went. They phoned her father first at the university, where they managed to catch him between a lecture and a meeting with a post-graduate student. Early in her relationship with Taymullah Azhar and his daughter, Barbara had learned that one did not make off with Hadiyyah without bringing her father fully into the picture. She hated having to admit why she wanted to take Hadiyyah with her on a shopping excursion, so she made do with, 'Got to buy some bits and bobs for work and I thought Hadiyyah might like to come along. Give her something of an outing and all that. Thought we'd stop for an ice cream somewhere when we're finished.'

'Has she completed her studies for the day?' Azhar asked.

'Her studies?' Barbara gave Hadiyyah the eye. The little girl nodded vigorously although Barbara had her doubts about the cookery end of things. Hadiyyah had not been enthusiastic about standing in someone's kitchen in the summer heat. 'Thumb's up on that,' she told Azhar.

'Very well,' Azhar said. 'But not in Camden High Street, Barbara.'

'Last place on earth, I guarantee,' Barbara told him.

The nearest Top Shop turned out to be in Oxford Street, a fact that delighted Hadiyyah and horrified Barbara. The shopping Mecca of London, it was always an undulating mass of humanity on any day save Christmas, and in high summer with schools on holiday and the capital city packed with visitors from around the globe, it was an undulating mass of humanity squared. Cubed. To the tenth. Whatever. Once they arrived, it took them forty minutes to find a car park with space for Barbara's Mini and another thirty to work their way to Top Shop, elbowing through the crowds on the pavement like salmon going home. When they finally arrived at the shop, Barbara glanced inside and wanted to run away at once. It was crammed with adolescent girls, their mothers, their aunts, their grans, their neighbours . . . They were shoulder to shoulder, they were in queues at the tills, they were jostling from racks to counters to displays, they were shouting into mobiles over the pounding music, they were trying on jewellery: earrings to ears, necklaces to necks, bracelets on wrists. It was Barbara's worst nightmare come to life.

'Isn't it wonderful?' Hadiyyah enthused. 'I always want Dad to bring me here, but he says Oxford Street's mad. He says nothing would drag him to Oxford Street. He says wild *horses* couldn't bring him here. He says Oxford Street's London's version of . . . I can't remember, but it's not good.'

Dante's Inferno, no doubt, Barbara thought. Some circle of hell into which women like herself – loathing fashion trends, indifferent about apparel in general, and looking dreadful no matter what she wore – were thrust for their fashion sins.

'But I *love* it,' Hadiyyah said. 'I knew I would. Oh, I just knew it.'

She zipped inside. There was nothing for Barbara to do but follow.

They spent a gruelling ninety minutes in Top Shop, where lack of air conditioning – this was London, after all, where people still believed that there were only 'four or five hot days each year' – and what seemed like a thousand teenagers in search of bargains made Barbara feel as if she'd definitely paid for *every* earthly sin she'd ever committed, far beyond those that she'd committed against the name of haute couture. They went from there to Jigsaw, and from Jigsaw to H & M, where they repeated the Top Shop experience with the addition of small children howling for their mothers, ice cream, lollies, pet dogs, sausage rolls, pizza, fish and chips, and whatever else came into their feverish minds. At Hadiyyah's insistence – 'Barbara, just *look* at the name of the shop, please!' – they followed these experiences with a period of time in Accessorize, and finally they found themselves in M & S, although not without Hadiyyah's sigh of disapproval. She said, 'This is where Mrs Silver buys her *knickers*, Barbara,' as if that information would stop Barbara cold and dead in her tracks. 'Do you want to look like Mrs Silver?'

'At this point, I'll settle for looking like Dame Edna.' Barbara ducked inside. Hadiyyah trailed her. 'Thank God for small mercies,' Barbara noted over her shoulder. 'Not only knickers but air conditioning as well.'

All they'd managed to accomplish so far was a necklace from Accessorize that Barbara thought she wouldn't feel too daft wearing and a purchase of makeup from Boots. The makeup consisted of whatever Hadiyyah told her to buy although Barbara sincerely doubted she'd ever wear it. She'd only given in to the idea of makeup at all because the little girl had been utterly heroic in facing Barbara's constant refusals to purchase anything Hadiyyah had fished out of the racks of clothing they'd seen so far. Thus it seemed only fair to give in on something, and makeup appeared to be the ticket. So she'd loaded her basket with foundation, blusher, eye shadow, eye liner, mascara, several frightening shades of lipstick, four different kinds of brushes and a container of loose powder that was supposed to 'fix it all in place', Hadiyyah told her. Apparently, the purchases Hadiyyah directed Barbara to make were heavily dependent upon her observation of her mother's daily morning rituals, which themselves seemed to be heavily dependent upon 'pots of this and that . . . She always looks brilliant, Barbara, wait till you see her'. Seeing Hadiyyah's mother was something that had not happened in the fourteen months of Barbara's acquaintance with the little girl and her father, and the euphemism *she's gone to Canada on holiday* was beginning to take on a significance difficult for Barbara to continue to ignore.

Barbara groused about the excessive expense, saying, 'Can't I make do with blusher by itself?' To this, Hadiyyah scoffed most heartily. '*Really*, Barbara,' she said, and she left it at that.

Once in M & S, Hadiyyah wouldn't hear of Barbara's trailing off towards racks of anything the child deemed 'suitable for Mrs Silver . . . *you* know.' She had in mind that staple of all wardrobes – the aforementioned A-line skirt – and declared herself content with the fact that at least as it was high summer, the autumn clothing had just been brought in. Thus, she explained, what was on offer hadn't yet been picked over by countless 'working mums who wear this sort of thing, Barbara. They'll be on holiday with their kids just now, so we don't have to worry about having only the pickings left.'

'Thank God for that,' Barbara said. She was drifting towards twin sets in plum and olive green. Hadiyyah took her arm firmly and steered her elsewhere. She declared herself content when they found 'separates, Barbara, which we can put together to make suits. Oh and look, they've blouses with pussy bows. These're rather sweet, aren't they?' She lifted one for Barbara's inspection.

Barbara couldn't imagine herself in a blouse at all, let alone one with a voluminous bow at the neck. She said, 'Don't think that's suitable for my jawline, do you? What about this?' and she pulled a jumper off a neatly folded pile.

'*No* jumpers,' Hadiyyah told her. She replaced the blouse on the rack with, 'Oh, all right. I s'pose the bow's a bit much.'

Barbara praised the Almighty for that declaration. She began to browse through the rack of skirts. Hadiyyah did likewise, and they ultimately came up with five upon which they could agree although they'd had to compromise each step of the way, with Hadiyyah firmly returning to the rack anything she considered Mrs Silverish and Barbara shuddering at anything that might draw attention to itself.

Off they went to the changing rooms, then, where Hadiyyah insisted upon acting the part of Barbara's dresser, which exposed her to Barbara's undergarments, which she declared, 'Shocking, Barbara. You *got* to get those string-back kind.' Barbara wasn't willing to wander even for a moment in the land of knickers, so she directed Hadiyyah to dwell on the skirts they'd chosen. To these the little girl flicked her hand in dismissal of anything 'unsuitable, Barbara', declaring this one to be rucked round the hips, that one to be tight across the bum, another to be a bit nasty looking and a fourth something that even someone's gran wouldn't wear.

Barbara was considering what punishment she might be able to inflict upon Isabelle Ardery for the suggestion that she get herself into this glamorous position in the first place when deep within her shoulder bag, her mobile phone rang, bleating out the musical equivalent of the first four lines of 'Peggy Sue' that she'd gleefully downloaded from the Internet.

'Buddy Holly,' Hadiyyah said.

'I remain gratified to have taught you something.' Barbara fished out the mobile and looked at the number of the caller. She was either saved by the literal bell or her movements were being tracked. She flipped it open. 'Guv,' she said.

'Where are you, Sergeant?' Isabelle Ardery asked.

'Shopping,' Barbara told her, 'for clothes. As recommended.'

'Tell me you're not in a charity shop and I'll be a happy woman,' Ardery said.

'Be a happy woman, then.'

'Do I want to know where?'

'Probably not.'

'And you've managed what?'

'A necklace so far.' And lest the superintendent protest the oddity of this purchase, 'and makeup as well. Lots of makeup. I'll look like . . .' She racked her brain, seeking a suitable image. 'I'll look like Elle MacPherson when next we meet. And at the moment I'm standing in a changing room having my knickers disapproved of by a nine-year-old.'

'Your companion is nine years old?' Ardery said 'Sergeant—'

'Believe me, she has definite thoughts on what I ought to be wearing, guv, which is why we've only managed a necklace so far. I expect we're about to compromise on a skirt, though. We've been at it for hours and I think I've worn her down.'

'Well, effect the compromise and get in gear. Something's come up.'

'Something?'

'We've got a dead body in a cemetery, Sergeant, and it's one that's not supposed to be there.'

Isabelle Ardery didn't want to think of her boys, but her first sight of Abney Park Cemetery made it nearly impossible to think of anything else. They were of an age when having adventures trumped everything save Christmas morning, and the cemetery was decidedly a place for adventures. Wildly overgrown, with gloomy Victorian funerary statues draped in ivy, with fallen trees providing imaginative spots for forts and caches, with tumbling tombstones and crumbling monuments . . . It was like something out of a fantasy novel, complete with the occasional gnarled tree that had been carved at shoulder height to display huge cameos in the shape of moons, stars, and leering faces. All this, and it was just off the high street, behind a wrought iron railing, accessible to anyone through various gates.

DS Nkata had parked their car at the main entrance where already an ambulance was waiting. This entrance was at the junction of Northwold Road and Stoke Newington High Street: an area of tarmac in front of two cream-coloured buildings whose stucco was flaking off in sheets. These sat on either side of enormous wrought iron gates, which, Isabelle learned, were normally open throughout the day but now were closed and guarded by a constable from the local station. He came forward to meet their car.

Isabelle got out into the summer heat. It came off the tarmac in waves. It did nothing to soothe her pounding head, a pain in her skull that was immediately exacerbated by the *thunka-thunka-thunka* of a television news helicopter that was circling above them like a raptor.

A crowd had gathered on the pavement, held back by crime scene tape that was looped tightly from a street lamp to the cemetery fence on either side of the entrance. Among them, Isabelle saw a few members of the press, recognisable by their notebooks, by their recorders and by the fact that they were being addressed by a bloke who had to be the duty press officer from the Stoke Newington station. He'd glanced over his shoulder as Isabelle and Nkata climbed out of the car. He nodded curtly, as did the local constable. They weren't happy. The Met's intrusion into their patch was not appreciated.

Blame politics, Isabelle wanted to tell them. Blame SO5 and the continual failure of Missing Persons not only to *find* a missing person but also to strike from their list persons who were no longer missing. Blame yet another tedious press exposé of this fact and a consequent power struggle between the civilians running SO5 and the frustrated officers demanding a police head to the division, as if that would solve its problems. Above all, blame Assistant Commissioner Sir David Hillier and the manner in which he'd decided to fill the vacant position that Isabelle was now auditioning for. Hillier hadn't said as much, but Isabelle was no fool: this was her test run and everyone knew it.

She'd commandeered DS Nkata to drive her up to the crime scene. Like the constables at the scene, he wasn't happy either. Clearly, he didn't expect a detective sergeant to be required to act the part of chauffeur, but he was professional enough to keep his feelings unspoken. She'd had little choice in the matter. It was either select a driver from among the team or attempt to find Abney Park Cemetery herself, using the *A to Z*. If she was assigned permanently to her new position, Isabelle knew it was likely going to take her years to become familiar with the convoluted mass of streets and villages that had, over the centuries, been subsumed into the monstrous expansion of London.

'Pathologist?' she said to the constable once she had introduced herself and Nkata and had signed the sheet recording those entering the site. 'Photographer? SOCO?'

'Inside. They're waiting to bag her. As ordered.' The constable was polite, just. The radio on his shoulder squawked, and he reached up to turn down the volume. Isabelle looked from him to the gawkers on the pavement and from them to the buildings across the street. These comprised the ubiquitous commercial establishments of every high street in the country: from a Pizza Hut to a newsagent. All of them had living accommodation above them and above one of them – a Polish delicatessen – an entire modern apartment block had been built. Countless interviews would need to be conducted in these places. The Stoke Newington cops, Isabelle decided, should be thanking God the Met was taking the case.

She asked about the tree carvings once they were inside the cemetery and being led into its labyrinthine embrace. Their guide was a volunteer at the burial ground, a pensioner of some eighty years who explained there were no groundsmen or keepers but instead committees of people like himself, unpaid members of the community devoted to reclaiming Abney Park from the encroachment of nature. Of course, it wasn't *ever* going to be what it once had been, the gentleman explained, but that wasn't the point. No one wanted that. Rather, it was meant to be a nature reserve. One'll see birds and foxes and squirrels and the like, he said. One'll note the wildflowers and plants. We aim just to keep the paths passable and make sure the place's safe for people wanting to spend some time with nature. One wants that sort of thing in a city, don't you agree? An escape, if you know what I mean. As to the carvings on the trees, there's a boy doing 'em. We all know him but can't bloody catch him at it. If we do, one of us'll let him have it, he vowed.

Isabelle doubted this. He was as frail as the wild snapdragons that grew along the path they followed.

He took them down trails that grew increasingly narrow as they coursed their way into the heart of the cemetery. Where paths were wide, they were stony, pebbled so variously that they looked like representatives of every possible geological period. Where they were narrow, the paths were thick with decomposing leaves and the ground was spongy and aromatic, sending up the rich scent of compost. At last the tower of a chapel appeared and then the chapel itself, a sad ruin of brick and iron and corrugated steel, its interior thick with weeds and made inaccessible by iron bars.

Over there, the pensioner told them needlessly. He indicated a gathering of white-suited crime scene officers across a parched lawn. Isabelle thanked the man and said to Nkata, 'Track down whoever discovered the body. I'll want a word.'

Nkata gave a look towards the chapel. Isabelle knew he wanted to see the crime scene. She waited for him to protest or argue. He did neither. He said, 'Right,' and she left him to it. She liked him for his response.

She herself approached a small, secondary building abutting one side of the chapel, near to which a body bag waited next to a collapsed ambulance trolley. The body was going to have to be carried out upon it, as the uneven paths in the cemetery would make rolling the trolley impossible till they got near the exit.

Scenes of crime officers were engaged in everything from taping and measuring to marking off footprints, for what little good this would do as there appeared to be dozens. Only a narrow access route consisting of end-to-end boards made the immediate site of the body available, and Isabelle donned latex gloves as she picked her way along it.

The forensic pathologist came out of the secondary building. She was a middle-aged woman with the teeth, skin and disturbing cough of a chain smoker. Isabelle introduced herself and said, 'What is this place?' with a nod at the building.

'No idea,' the pathologist said. She did not give her name, nor did Isabelle want it. 'No door from it into the chapel, so it can't have been a vestry. Gardener's shed, perhaps?' The woman shrugged. It didn't really matter, did it?

Of course, it didn't. What mattered was the corpse, and this turned out to be a young woman. She was half-seated and half-sprawled inside the little annexe, in a position suggesting she'd stumbled backwards upon being attacked and subsequently slid down the wall. The wall itself was mottled by the weather, and above the body a graffito of an eye inside a triangle proclaimed, 'God Goes Wireless'. The floor was stone and littered with rubbish. Death had come to mingle with crisp bags, sandwich wrappers, chocolate bar wrappers and empty Coke cans. There was a pornographic magazine as well, a much more recent bit of rubbish than the rest of the debris as it was fresh and uncrumpled. It was also open at a gleaming crotch shot of a pouting, red-lipsticked woman in patent leather boots, a top hat and nothing else.

Ignominious location in which to meet your end, Isabelle thought. She squatted to have a look at the victim. Her stomach rolled at the scent coming off the body: a smell of meat rotting in the heat, thick as yellow fog. Newly hatched maggots writhed in the body's nostrils and mouth, and her mouth, face and neck – where they could be seen – had turned greenish red.

The young woman's head lolled on her chest, and on the chest itself a vast amount of blood had coagulated. Flies were doing more business there, and the sound of their buzzing was like high tension wires in the close space. When Isabelle carefully moved the young woman's head to expose her neck, more flies rose in a cloud from an ugly wound. It was jagged and torn, suggesting a weapon wielded by a clumsy killer.

'Carotid artery,' the pathologist said. She made a gesture towards the body's bagged hands. 'Looks like she tried to stop the bleeding, but it couldn't have done much good. She would have bled out fast.'

'Weapon?'

'Nothing left at the scene. Till we get her on the table and have a close look, it could be anything sharp. Not a knife, though. The wound's far too messy for a knife.'

'How long d'you reckon she's been dead?'

'Difficult to say because of the heat. Lividity's fixed and rigor's gone. Perhaps twenty-four hours?'

'Do we know who she is?'

'There's nothing on her. No handbag here, either. Nothing to suggest who she is. But the eyes . . . They're going to give you some help.'

'The eyes? Why? What's wrong with them?'

'Have a look for yourself,' the pathologist said. 'They're clouded over as you'd expect, but you can still see something of the irises. Very interesting, you ask me. Don't see eyes like that very often.'

From Alan Dresser's accounts, later confirmed by the take-away's employees, McDonald's was unusually crowded that day. It may be that other parents of young children were also using the break in the weather to get out of the house for the morning, but whatever the case, most of them seem to have converged on McDonald's at the same time. Dresser had a querulous toddler in tow, and he was, he admits, anxious to appease him, to feed him, and to be on his way in order to put him down for a nap. He established the boy at one of the three remaining, available tables – second in from the doorway – and he went to place their order. Although hindsight demands one castigate Dresser for leaving his son unattended for so much as thirty seconds, at least ten mothers were present in McDonald's at that moment and, in their company, at least twenty-two small children. In such a public setting in the middle of the day, how was he to assume that inconceivable danger was approaching? Indeed, if one thinks of danger at all in such a location, one thinks of paedophiles lurking nearby and seeing an opportunity, not of three boys under the age of twelve. No one present looked the least bit dangerous. Indeed, Dresser was himself the only adult male there.

CCTV tape shows three boys later identified as Michael Spargo, Ian Barker and Reggie Arnold approaching McDonald's at twelve-fifty-one. They had been inside the Barriers for more than two hours. They were doubtless hungry, and although they could have assuaged their hunger with the bags of crisps they'd taken from Mr Gupta's snack kiosk, it seems to have been their intention to take food from a McDonald's customer and to make a run for it afterwards. Both Michael's account and Ian's account agree on this point. In every interview, Reggie Arnold refuses to talk about McDonald's altogether. This is likely due to the fact that, no matter whose idea it was to take John Dresser from the premises, it is

Reggie Arnold who has the toddler by the hand as the boys walk towards the Barriers' exit.

In looking upon John Dresser, Ian, Michael and Reggie would have been gazing at the very antithesis of their own past selves. At the moment of his abduction, the child was dressed in a new, azure snow suit, with yellow ducks marching across the front of it. His blond hair was freshly washed and had yet to be cut, so it fell round his face in the sort of cherubic curls one associates with Renaissance putti. He had bright white trainers on his feet and he was carrying his favourite toy: a small brown and black dog with floppy ears and a pink tongue partially torn from its mouth, a stuffed animal later found along the route the boys took once they removed John from McDonald's.

This removal was apparently accomplished without difficulty. It was a matter of moments, and the CCTV film that documents John's abduction makes for chilling viewing. In it, one clearly watches the three boys enter the McDonald's (which, at the time, did not have closed circuit filming of its own). Less than one minute later, out they come. Reggie Arnold emerges first, holding John Dresser by the hand. Five seconds later, Ian Barker and Michael Spargo follow. Michael is eating something from a conical container. These appear to be McDonald's French fries.

One of the questions relentlessly asked after the fact was how could Alan Dresser have failed to notice that his son was being taken? Two explanations exist. One of them is the noise and the crowded conditions of the take-away, which covered any sound John Dresser might have made when approached by the boys who took him. The other is a mobile phone call that Dresser received from his office as he reached the till to place his order. The wretched timing of this call kept him with his back turned from his son longer than he might otherwise have had it turned, and as many people do, Dresser lowered his head and maintained that position as he listened and responded to the caller, likely to avoid distractions that would have made it more difficult for him to concentrate in the raucous atmosphere. By the time he had concluded this phone call, paid for his food and returned with it to the table, John was not only gone but likely had been gone for nearly five minutes, more than enough time to get him out of the Barriers altogether.

Dresser did not at first think that John had been taken. Indeed, with the take-away so crowded, that was the last thing on his mind. Instead, he thought the boy – restless as he'd been in Stanley Wallingford's DIY shop – had climbed down from his seat and wandered off, perhaps attracted by something inside McDonald's, perhaps attracted by something just outside the take-away but still well within the arcade. These were vital minutes, but Dresser did not see them that way. Not unreasonably, he looked round the take-away first before he began asking the adults therein if they had seen John.

One wonders how it is possible. It is midday. It is a public place. It contains other people, both children and adults. Yet three young boys are still able to walk up to a toddler, take him by the hand and make off with him without anyone apparently noticing. How could this happen? Why did it happen?

The how of it is, I believe, contained within the age of the perpetrators of this crime. The fact that they were children themselves made them virtually invisible because what they did was beyond the imagination of the people present in the McDonald's. People simply did not expect malevolence to arrive in the package in which it was presented that day. People tend to have predetermined mental pictures of child abductors, and those pictures do not include schoolboys.

Once it became clear that John was not in the McDonald's and had not been noticed, Dresser widened his search. It was only after he had checked the four nearest shops that he tracked down the arcade's security force and an announcement was made over the public address system, alerting the patrons of the Barriers to be on the lookout for a small boy in a bright blue snow suit. An hour passed during which Dresser continued to look for his son, accompanied by the shopping arcade's manager and the head of the security team. None of them considered looking at the CCTV tapes because none of them at that point wished to think the unthinkable.

5

Barbara Havers had to use her ID to convince the constable she was a cop. He'd barked at her, 'Hey! Cemetery's *closed*, madam,' as she'd approached the main entrance, having finally found a place for her decrepit Mini just behind a skip, where a building was being renovated in Stoke Newington Church Street.

Barbara chalked it up to the outfit. She and Hadiyyah had managed the purchase of that staple of all women's wardrobes – the A-line skirt – but that was it. After returning Hadiyyah to Mrs Silver, Barbara had donned the skirt in a hurry, had seen it was several inches too long, had decided to wear it anyway, but had done nothing else about her appearance other than to loop the necklace from Accessorize round her neck.

She said, 'The Met,' to the constable, who gaped at her before he managed to gather his wits enough to say, 'Inside,' and to offer her the sign-in sheet on a clipboard.

How bloody helpful, Barbara thought. She replaced her ID in her shoulder bag, fished out a packet of fags and lit up. She was about to make a polite request for a wee bit more information as to the pre*cise* location of the crime scene when a slow-moving procession emerged from beneath the plane trees just beyond the cemetery fence. This comprised an ambulance crew, a pathologist with professional bag in hand, and a uniformed constable. The ambulance crew had a body bag on a trolley, which they'd been carrying like a stretcher. They paused to lower its legs. They then continued towards the gates.

Barbara met them just inside. She said, 'Superintendent Ardery?' and the pathologist nodded vaguely in a northernly direction. 'Uniforms along the way,' was the limit of the guidance she gave although she added, 'You'll see them. Fingertip search,' to indicate there would be enough of them to give Barbara further directions should she need them.

She didn't as things turned out, although she was quite surprised she managed to find the crime scene at all, considering the maze that constituted the cemetery. But within minutes, the spire of a chapel came into view and soon enough she saw Isabelle Ardery with a police photographer. They were bent over the screen of his digital camera. As Barbara approached them, she heard her name called. Winston Nkata was emerging from a secondary path near a lichenous stone bench, flipping closed a leather notebook in which, Barbara knew, beautifully legible observations would be written in his maddeningly elegant cursive.

She said, 'So what is it?'

He filled her in. As he was doing so, Isabelle Ardery's voice cut in with a '*Ser*geant Havers,' which was spoken in a tone that indicated neither welcome nor pleasure, despite her orders that Barbara was to come post haste to the cemetery. Nkata and Barbara turned to see the superintendent approaching. Ardery stalked, no walking or strolling here. Her face was stony. 'Are you trying to be amusing?' she asked.

Barbara knew her expression was a blank. She said, 'Eh?' She glanced at Nkata. He looked equally mystified.

'Is *this* your idea of professional?' Ardery asked.

'Oh.' Barbara gave a look to what she could see of her kit. Red high top trainers, navy blue skirt dangling a good five inches below her knees, T-shirt printed with 'Talk to the Fist Cos the Face Ain't Listening,' and necklace of chain, beads and a filigree pendant. She saw how Ardery might take her get-up: a bit of I'll-show-you. She said, 'Sorry, guv. It's as far as I got.' Next to her, she saw Nkata lift his hand to his mouth. She knew the lout was trying to hide a smile. 'Really,' she said, 'God's truth. You said to get out here so I came on the run. I didn't have time—'

'That's enough.' Ardery gave her a once over, her eyes narrowed. She said, 'Remove the necklace. Believe me, it's not an improvement.'

Barbara did so. Nkata turned away. His shoulders quivered. He coughed. Ardery barked at him, 'What have you got?'

He pivoted back to her. 'Kids who found the body're gone now. Locals took them to the station for a complete statement, but I managed a word before they left. It's a boy and girl.' He recited the rest of what he'd learned: two adolescents had seen a boy come out of the murder site; their description was so far limited to 'he had a huge bum and his trousers were falling down' but the male adolescent claimed he probably could help with an e-fit. That was all they were able to contribute because they'd evidently been heading towards the annexe for sex and 'likely wouldn't've noticed the crucifixion if it had been going on in front of them'.

'We'll want whatever statement they give to the locals,' Ardery said. She filled Barbara in on the details of the crime and called the photographer over to run through the digital pictures once again. As Nkata and Barbara looked them over, Ardery said, 'Arterial wound. Whoever did it was going to be, literally, covered in blood.'

'Unless she was taken by surprise from the back,' Barbara pointed out. 'Her head grabbed, pulled back, the weapon driven in from behind. You'd have blood on the arm and the hands, then, but little enough on the body. Right?'

'Possibly,' Ardery said. 'But one couldn't be taken by surprise where the body was, Sergeant.'

Barbara could see the secondary building from where they were standing. She said, 'Taken by surprise then dragged in there?'

'No sign of dragging.'

'Do we know who she is?' Barbara looked up from the pictures.

'No ID. We've got a perimeter search going on, but if that doesn't turn up the weapon or something telling us who she is, we'll do a grid of the entire place and take it in sections. I want you in charge of that. Coordinate with the locals. I want you in charge of a house-to-house as well. Concentrate first on the terraces bordering the cemetery. Handle that and we'll reconvene at the Met.'

Barbara nodded as Nkata said, 'Want me to wait for the e-fit, guv?'

'Do that as well,' Ardery said to Barbara. 'Make sure their statement gets sent over to Victoria Street. And I want you to see if you can squeeze anything else out of them.'

Nkata said, 'I can—'

'You'll continue to drive me,' Ardery told him. She looked towards the perimeter of the clearing in which the chapel sat. Constables were conducting the search there. They'd move outward in circles till they found – or didn't find – the weapon, the victim's bag, or anything else that might constitute evidence. It was a nightmare location that could produce too much or nothing at all.

Nkata was silent. Barbara saw a muscle move in his jaw. He finally said, 'Due respect, guv, but don't you want a constable driving you? Or a special, even?'

Ardery said, 'If I wanted a constable or a special, I'd have got one. Do you have a problem with the assignment, Sergeant?'

'Seems like I could best be used—'

'As I want to use you,' Ardery cut in. 'Are we clear on that?'

He was silent for a moment. Then he said, 'Guv,' politely, in affirmation.

Bella McHaggis was utterly drenched in sweat, but in a good way. She'd just completed her hot yoga class – although *any* yoga class would have turned into hot yoga in the current weather – and she was feeling both virtuous and peaceful. She had Mr McHaggis to thank for this. Had the poor bloke not died on the toilet seat, member in hand and Page Three girl spread out buxomly on the floor in front of him, she'd have likely still been in the shape she was in on that morning she found him gone to his eternal reward. But seeing poor McHaggis like that had been a call to arms. Whereas before his death, Bella hadn't been able to climb a flight of stairs without losing her breath, now she could do that and more. She was particularly proud of her limber body. Why, she could bend from the waist and put her palms on the floor. She could lift her leg to the height of the fireplace mantel. Not at all bad for a bird of sixty-five.

She was on Putney High Street heading for home. She was still wearing her yoga kit, and she had her mat rolled beneath her arm. She was thinking about worms, specifically the composting worms that lived in a rather complicated set up in her back garden. They were amazing little creatures – bless them, they ate virtually anything one handed over – but they needed some care. They didn't like extremes: too much hot or too much cold and off they'd go to the big compost heap in the sky. So she was considering how much heat constituted too much when she passed the local tobacconist where an *Evening Standard* placard stood out front, advertising the day's last edition of that paper.

Bella was used to seeing some dramatic event reduced to three or four scrawled words suitable for bringing people into the shop to purchase a paper. Usually, she walked on by on her way to her home in Oxford Road because as far as she was concerned there were far too many newspapers in London – both broadsheets and tabloids – and, recycling aside, they were eating up every woodland on earth so she was damned if she would contribute to them. But this particular placard slowed her steps: *Woman Dead in Abney Park*.

Bella hadn't a clue where Abney Park was, but she stood there on the pavement with pedestrians passing her by and she wondered if it was at all possible . . . She didn't want to think it was. She *hated* the idea that it might be. But since it *could* be, she went within and purchased a copy of the paper, telling herself that at least she could shred it and feed it to the worms if it turned out that there was nothing to the story.

She didn't read it at once. Indeed, since she didn't like to appear the kind of person who could be seduced into buying a tabloid because of an advertising ploy, she also purchased some breath mints and a packet of Wrigley's spearmint from the shop. She rejected the offer of a plastic bag for these items – one had to draw the line somewhere and Bella refused to participate in the further littering and destruction of the planet through means of the plastic carrier bags one saw blowing along the high street every day – and went on her way.

Oxford Road wasn't far from the tobacconist, a narrow thoroughfare perpendicular both to Putney Bridge Road and to the river. It was less than a quarter of an hour's walk from the yoga studio, so in no time at all she was through her front gate and dodging the eight plastic rubbish bins she used for recycling in her small front garden.

Inside the house, she went into the kitchen where she brewed one of her two daily cups of green tea. She hated the stuff – it tasted like what she imagined horse piss would taste like – but she'd read enough about its value, so she regularly plugged her nose and tossed the brew down her throat. It wasn't until she'd drunk the ghastly cuppa that she spread the paper on the work top and took a look at its unfolded front page.

The photograph was not illuminating. It showed a park entrance guarded by a cop. There was a secondary picture cutting into this one, an aerial shot depicting a clearing in the midst of what looked like a forested area and in the centre of this clearing a church of some kind with white-suited crime scene people crawling round it.

Bella consumed the accompanying story, seeking the relevant bits: young woman, murdered, apparently stabbed, nicely dressed, no identification . . .

She made the jump to page three where she saw an e-fit with the words *person of interest being sought* beneath it. E-fits, she thought, never looked like the person they turned out to be depicting, and this particular one looked so universal that virtually any adolescent boy on the street could have been picked up by the police and questioned as a result of it: dark hair falling over his eyes, chubby face, wearing a hoodie – at least the hood was down and not up – in spite of the heat . . . Totally useless as far as a description went. She'd just seen a dozen such boys on Putney High Street.

The article indicated that this particular individual had been seen leaving the crime scene in Abney Park Cemetery and, reading this, Bella dug out an old *A to Z* from the bookshelves in the dining room. She located this place in Stoke Newington, and the very fact of Stoke Newington, miles upon miles from Putney, gave her pause. She was in the midst of this pause when she heard the front door being unlocked and steps coming down the corridor in her direction.

She said, 'Frazer, luv?' and didn't wait for his reply. She made it her business to know the comings and goings of her lodgers, and it was the hour at which Frazer Chaplin returned from his day job to freshen up and change his clothes for his evening employment. She greatly admired this about the young man: the fact that he had two jobs. Industrious people were the sort of people she liked letting rooms to. 'Got a moment?'

Frazer came to the doorway as she looked up from the *A to Z*. He raised an eyebrow – black like his hair, which was thick and curly and spoke of Spain at the time of the Moors although the boy himself was Irish – and he said, 'Blazing today, eh? Every kid in Bayswater was at the ice and bowl, Mrs McH.'

'No doubt,' Bella said. 'Have a look in here, luv.'

She took him to the kitchen and showed him the paper. He scanned the article then looked at her. 'And?' He sounded perplexed.

'What do you mean "And"? Young woman, dressed nicely, dead . . .'

He twigged then, and his expression altered. 'Oh no. I don' think so,' he said although he did sound slightly hesitant when he went on with, 'Really, it can't be, Mrs McH.'

'Why not?'

'Because why would she be up in Stoke Newington? And why in a cemetery, for God's good love?' He looked at the photographs once again. He looked at the e-fit as well. He shook his head slowly. 'No. No. Truly. More likely she's just gone somewhere for a break, to get away from the heat. To the sea or something, don't you think? Who could blame her, like?'

'She would have said. She wouldn't have wanted anyone to worry. I expect you know that.'

Frazer raised his head from his study of the newspaper photos, alarm in his eyes, a fact that Bella noted with gratification: there were few things in life she loathed more than a slow learner, and she gave Frazer high marks for his ability to infer. He said, 'I've *not* broken the rule again. I might not be the brightest coin in the collection plate, but I'm not—'

'I know, luv,' Bella said quickly. God knew he was a good boy at heart. Easily led, perhaps. Rather too much taken when it came to a bit of skirt. But still good in all the important ways. 'I know, I know. But sometimes young women can be barracudas as you've seen for yourself.'

'Not this time. And not this young woman.'

'But you were friendly with her, yes?'

'Like I'm friendly with Paolo. Like I'm friendly with you.'

'Given,' Bella said, although she couldn't help feeling a wee bit warmed by his declaration of friendship towards herself. 'But being friendly gives one access to people, to what's going on inside them. So don't you think she seemed different lately? Didn't she seem to have something on her mind?'

Frazer rubbed his hand along his jaw as he considered the question. Bella could hear the *scritch* of his whiskers against his palm. He'd have to shave before he went off to work. 'I've not much talent for reading people,' he finally said. 'Not like you.' He was quiet again. Bella liked this about him as well. He didn't rush forward with foolish opinions based on nothing, like so many young people. He was thoughtful and unafraid to take his time. He said, 'Could be – if it *is* her and I'm not saying it is because it hardly makes sense, really – she went up there to think. Needing a quiet place, it being a cemetery.'

'To *think*?' Bella said. 'All the way to Stoke Newington in order to think? She can think anywhere. She can think in the garden. She can think in her bedroom. She can think if she takes a walk by the river.'

'All right. Then what?' Frazer asked. 'Saying it's her. Why would she go?'

'She's been secretive lately. Not her usual self. If it's her, she went up there for no good reason.'

'Such as?'

'Such as meeting someone. Such as meeting someone who killed her.'

'That's dead mad, that is.'

'It may be, but I'm phoning anyway.'

'Who?'

'The cops, luv. They're asking for information and we have it, you and I.'

'What? That there's a lodger hasn't come home in two nights? I expect there's situations like that all over town.'

'May well be. But this particular lodger has a brown eye and a green one, and I doubt you're going to find that description common to anyone else who's gone missing.'

'But if it's her and if she's dead . . .' Frazer said nothing more and Bella looked up from the paper. There was certainly *something* in his tone, and Bella's suspicions were roused. But her concerns were assuaged when he went on with, 'She's such a grand girl, Mrs McH. She's always been open and friendly, hasn't she. She's never acted like someone with secrets. So *if* it's her, the question isn't so much why was she there but who on God's green earth would want to kill her?'

'Some madman, luv,' Bella replied. 'You and I know London's crawling with them.'

*   *   *

Below him, he could hear the usual noise: acoustic guitars and electric guitars, both played badly. The acoustic guitars were bearable as the hesitant chords at least were not amplified. As for the electric guitars, it seemed to him that the worse the player the louder the amplification employed. It was as if whoever the student was, he or she enjoyed being bad. Or perhaps the instructor enjoyed *allowing* the student to be bad and at maximum volume, as if there were a lesson being taught that had nothing to do with music. He couldn't sort out why this might be the case, but he'd long ago given up trying to understand the people among whom he lived.

If you declared, you would understand. If you showed yourself as who you could be. Nine orders but we – we – are the highest. Distort God's plan and you fall like the others. Do you wish to—

A shriek from a chord gone very wrong. It dispelled the voices. There was blessing in that. He needed to be out of this place as he usually was for the hours that the shop beneath him was open for business. But he hadn't been able to leave for two days. It had taken that long to remove the blood.

He had a bed-sit and he'd used its wash basin. It was tiny, though, and tucked into the corner of the room. It was also within sight of the window, so he'd had to be careful because although it was unlikely that someone would see him through the wispy curtains, there was always a chance that a breeze could blow them away from the aperture at the moment when he was wringing cherry-stained water from the shirt or the jacket or even the trousers. Still, he wanted a breeze even as he knew a breeze would be dangerous to him. He'd opened the window in the first place because it was so hot in the bed-sit that he hadn't been able to breathe properly and *useless to us now unless you show yourself* had battered against his eardrums and the thought of air had him stumbling to the window and shoving it open. He'd done it at night, he *had* done it at night which meant he was able to make distinctions and *we are not intended to battle each other. We are meant to battle the sons of Darkness. Do you not see—*

He shoved the earpieces into his ears and turned up the volume. Intermittently, he'd been playing the *Ode to Joy* because he knew it was capable of taking up so much space in his brain that he could have no thoughts that were not those sounds and he could hear no voices that were not the chorus. That was what he needed to see him through, until he could return to the street.

Because of the heat, his clothes had dried quickly, which was a blessing. This had allowed him to soak them a second and third time. Ultimately, the water had altered from bright crimson to cherry to the pale pink of spring blossoms, and while the shirt would not be white again without bleaching or professional laundering, the worst of the staining was gone. And on the trousers and jacket, it couldn't be seen at all. What remained was the ironing, and he had an iron because how he appeared was important to him. He didn't like people to be put off. He wanted them near, he wanted them listening and he wanted them to know him as he really was. But that couldn't happen if he was dishevelled, with filthy clothes suggesting poverty and sleeping rough. Neither of those was accurate. He'd *chosen* his life. He wanted people to know that.

. . . *other choices. Here is one before you. The need is great. Need leads to action and action to honour.*

He'd sought it. Honour, only honour. She'd needed him. He'd heard the call.

It had all turned out wrong. She'd looked at him and he'd seen the recognition in her eyes and he knew it meant surprise because she *would* be surprised but it also meant welcome. He'd walked forward and he'd known what had to be done and there were *no* voices in the moment, no chorus of sound, and he'd heard nothing, not even the music from the earphones he wore.

And he had failed. Blood everywhere, on her and on him and her hands at her throat.

He'd run. He'd hidden at first, rubbing himself with fallen leaves to take the blood away. He removed his shirt and balled it up. He turned his jacket inside out. The trousers were bad but they were black and the black obscured the crimson of her that had spilled down the front of him. He'd had to get home, which meant the bus, which meant more than one bus and he hadn't known when to get off to make the switch so it had taken hours and he'd been seen, gawked at, whispered about, and it could not matter because—

. . . another sign and you should have read it. There are signs around you but you choose to guard when you are meant to fight . . .

—it was his job to get home and to clean himself so that he could do what he had been intended to do.

No one, he told himself, would put it together. In the buses of London there were so many types of people and no one paid attention to anything and even if they had paid attention and had seen and had even remarked upon or remembered what they'd seen, it didn't matter. Nothing mattered. He'd failed and he had to live through that.

6

Isabelle Ardery wasn't pleased that AC Hillier put in an appearance at the morning meeting of her team on the following day. It smacked of checking up on her, which she didn't like, although his claim was that he'd merely wanted to say *well done* in reference to the news conference she'd held the previous afternoon. She wanted to tell him that she wasn't a fool: she understood *exactly* why he'd turned up to stand importantly at the back of the incident room and she also understood that the head of an investigation – that would be me, sir – was meant to listen to whatever the duty press officer advised regarding information to be imparted to the media so she hardly needed to be congratulated on having done her job. But she took the compliment with a formal *thank you, sir*, and she eagerly anticipated his immediate departure. He'd said Do keep me apprised, won't you, Acting Superintendent? and again the message was received as intended. *Acting Superintendent*. She didn't need reminding that this was her audition – for want of a better word – but it appeared to be the man's intention to do that reminding at every possible opportunity. She'd said that the news conference and its call for information from witnesses to anything suspicious was already bearing fruit and asked if he wanted a compendium of each day's phone calls, sir. He eyed her in a way that told her he was evaluating what lay behind her question before he declined the offer, but she kept her face bland. He apparently decided she was being sincere. He'd said, We'll meet later, shall we? and that was that. Off he went, leaving her to the unfriendly gaze of DI John Stewart, which she happily ignored.

The house-to-house in Stoke Newington was in progress,

the slow process of the cemetery search was continuing, phone calls were being fielded and dealt with, diagrams and maps had been drawn. They were bound to get something from the news conference, from the resulting stories on the television news and in the daily papers, and from the e-fit that had been provided by the two adolescents who'd discovered the body. Thus things were clicking along as they were meant to click. Isabelle was satisfied with her performance so far.

She had her doubts about the post mortem, however. She'd never been one for dissection. The sight of blood didn't make her feel anything akin to fainting, but the sight of an open body cavity and the mechanics of removing and weighing what had so recently been living organs did tend to turn her stomach to liquid. For this reason, she determined to take no one with her to observe the proceedings that afternoon. She also skipped lunch in favour of emptying one of the three airline bottles of vodka she'd tucked into her bag for this precise purpose.

She found the mortuary without any trouble and within it, she found the Home Office pathologist awaiting her arrival. He introduced himself as Dr Willeford – 'but do call me Blake . . . let's keep things friendly, shall we?' – and he asked her if she wanted a chair or a stool 'in the event that the coming exploration proves rather more than you feel able to cope with'. He said all of this nicely enough, but there was something about his smile that she didn't trust. She had little doubt that her reaction was going to be reported: Hillier's long tentacles reaching out even here. She vowed to keep upright, told Willeford she didn't anticipate any difficulty as she'd never had difficulty with p.m.s before – an outright lie but how was he to know? – and when he chuckled, then happily said, 'Right, then, here we go,' she stepped right up to the stainless steel trolley and fixed her gaze on the body that lay there, chest up and waiting for the Y-incision, with her fatal wound making a bloody lightning bolt down the right side of her neck.

Willeford recited the salient superficial details first, speaking into the microphone that hung above the trolley. He did so in a chatty fashion, as if with the intention of entertaining whoever would do the transcription. 'Kathy darling,' he said into the microphone, 'we have a female before us this time. She's in good physical condition, no tattoos and no scars. She measures five feet four inches tall – sort out the metrics, my love, as I can't be bothered – and she weighs seven point eight five stone. Do the metrics there as well, will you, Kath? And by the way, how's your mum doing, darling? Are you ready, Superintendent Ardery? Oh, Kath, that's not for you, my dear. We've a new one here. She's called Isabelle Ardery' – with a wink at Isabelle – 'and she's not even asked for a chair on the chance that just-in-case becomes the case. Anyway . . .' He moved to examine the wound at the neck. 'We've got the carotid artery pierced. *Very* nasty. You'll be glad you weren't here, not that you ever are, my love. We've also got a tear in the wound, quite jagged, measuring . . . it's seven inches.' He moved from the victim's neck along the side of her body where he picked up one of her hands and then the other, excusing himself to Isabelle as he passed her and letting Kathy know that the superintendent was still on her feet and her colour was good but they would see, wouldn't they, once he cut the body open? He said, 'No defensive wounds on the hands, Kath. No broken fingernails, no scratches either. Blood on them both but I expect this would have come from her attempt to stop the bleeding once the weapon was withdrawn.' He chatted on for a few more minutes, documenting everything the eye could see. He put her age between twenty and thirty and then he prepared himself for the next step of the process.

Isabelle was ready. Clearly, he expected her to faint. Just as clearly, she intended not to. She found she could have done with another shot of vodka when, after the incision and the exposure of the rib cage, he took out the shears to cut through the victim's chest – it was the sound of metal cutting through bone that she found most repellent – but after that the rest was, if not easy, then at least more bearable.

After Willeford had done his bit, he said, 'Darling Kath, as always, it's been a pleasure. Could you type that up and get it over to Superintendent Ardery, darling? And by the way, she's still upright so I daresay she's a keeper. Remember DI Shatter – *what* an appropriate name, eh? – falling headfirst into the body cavity up in Berwick-on-Tweed that time? Lord, what an uproar. Ah, "but what do we live for but to give" . . . whatever it is that we give to our neighbours and "to laugh at them in our turn." I can*not* ever remember that quote. Adieu, dear Kath, till next time.'

At that point, an assistant swept forward to do the cleanup and Willeford stripped off his scrubs, tossed them in a bin in the corner, and invited Isabelle to '"step into my parlour said the spider," et cetera. I've a bit more for you in here.'

A bit more turned out to be the information that two hairs had been caught up in the victim's hands, and he had little doubt that SOCO would soon inform her that fibres aplenty had been taken from her clothing. 'Got rather close to her killer, if you know what I mean,' Willeford said with a wink.

Isabelle wondered if this counted as sexual harassment, as she asked blandly, 'Intercourse? Rape? A struggle?'

Nothing, he said. Absolutely no evidence. She was, if he might put it this way, a willing participant in whatever went on between herself and the owner of the fibres. Likely that was why she'd been found where she'd been found, as there was no evidence she'd been dragged anywhere against her will: no bruises, no skin under the fingernails, that sort of thing, he said.

Did he have an opinion on what position she was in when she was attacked? Isabelle asked the pathologist. What about time of death? How long had she likely lived after the assault upon her? From what direction did the injury occur? Was the killer left or right handed?

Willeford fished in the pocket of his windcheater at this point – he'd left it behind a door and he fetched it over to where they were sitting – and brought out a nutrition bar. Had to keep his blood sugar up, he confessed. His metabolism was the curse of his life.

Isabelle could see this was the case. Out of his scrubs, he was thin as a garden hoe. At a height of at least six feet six inches, he likely needed to keep eating all day, which had to be difficult in his line of work.

He told her that the presence of the maggots put time of death at twenty-four to thirty-six hours before the body was found although considering the heat, the closer call would be twenty-four. She'd have been upright when she was attacked, and her assailant was right handed. Toxicology would show if drugs or alcohol was involved, but that would take some time, as would the DNA from the hair, as there were 'follicles attached and isn't *that* lovely?'

Isabelle asked if he reckoned the killer had been in front of or behind the young woman.

Definitely standing in front of her, the pathologist said.

Which meant, Isabelle concluded, that she may have known her killer.

Isabelle also went alone on her next call that day. In advance she studied the route, and she was relieved to see that the direction she needed to follow to Eaton Terrace was not a complicated matter. The important bit was not to bollocks things up in the vicinity of Victoria Station. If she kept her wits about her and did not become unnerved by the traffic, she knew she should be able to work her way through the skein of streets without ending up either at the river or – in the other direction – at Buckingham Palace.

As it happened, she did make one wrong turn when she got to Eaton Terrace, choosing left over right, but she saw the error of her ways when she began reading the house numbers on the stately front doors. After turning round, things were simple although she sat in her car for a full two minutes when she arrived at her destination, considering what approach she wished to use.

She finally decided that the truth was best which, she

admitted, was generally the case. Still, in order to speak it, she found that she wanted something to assist, and that something was tucked into the bottom of her bag. She was glad she'd thought to bring more than one airline bottle along for her workday.

She drained the vodka into her mouth. She rested the last of it on her tongue for a good long while till it heated up. She swallowed and then fished for a piece of Juicy Fruit. She chewed this on her walk to the front steps of the house and on the marble draughtsboard that marked what went for the porch, she removed the gum, ran some gloss over her lips, and touched the lapels of her jacket to smooth them. Then she rang the bell.

She knew he had a man – what an odd term, she thought – and it was this individual who answered the door: youngish, owlish and dressed in tennis gear, which seemed an odd enough get-up for a servant, personal assistant, butler, or whatever an earl-in-hiding would have. For that was how Isabelle thought of DI Thomas Lynley, as an earl-in-hiding, because it was frankly inconceivable to her why someone in his social position would choose to spend his life as a cop unless it *was* an incognito sort of thing in which he hid himself away from the rest of his kind. And his kind were the sort of people whose pictures one saw on the cover of tabloids when they got themselves into trouble, or inside the pages of *Hello!*, *OK*, *Tatler* and the like, hoisting champagne flutes at the photographer. They went to nightclubs and stayed till dawn, they skied in the Alps – French, Italian or Swiss, what did it matter? – and they travelled to places like Portofino or Santorini or other multi-syllabic Mediterranean, Ionian or Aegean locations ending in vowels. But they didn't work at ordinary jobs and if they did because they needed the money, they certainly didn't choose to be coppers.

'Afternoon,' the tennis-clad man said. He was Charlie Denton. Isabelle had done her homework.

She showed her ID and introduced herself. 'Mr Denton, I'm trying to locate the inspector. Is he at home by any chance?'

If he was surprised that she knew his identity, Charlie Denton was too careful to let it show. He said, 'As it happens . . .' and he admitted her into the house. He indicated a doorway to her right, which led into a reception room done up in a pleasant shade of green. He said, 'I expect he's in the library.' He gestured to a simple arrangement of furniture round a fire-place and said he could fetch her a drink if she'd like one. She thought about accepting the offer and tossing back a vodka martini straight up, but she declined as she reckoned he was referring to something more in line with the fact that she was still on duty.

While he went to find his . . . Isabelle wondered what the term was: his master? his employer? . . . she took in the room. The building was a townhouse and it likely had been in Lynley's family for quite some time, as no one had got inside to destroy the features that had gone into its making in the nineteenth century. Thus it still possessed its plaster ceiling decorations along with its mouldings above, below and around. Isabelle reckoned there were architectural terms for it all, but she didn't know any of them although she was perfectly capable of admiring them.

She didn't sit but rather walked to the window overlooking the street. A table sat beneath its sill and this held several framed photographs, among them a wedding picture of Lynley and his wife. Isabelle picked this up and studied it: it was casual and spontaneous, the bride and groom laughing and glowing amid a crowd of well-wishers.

She'd been very attractive, Isabelle saw. Not beautiful, porcelain, classical, doll-like or whatever else one wished to call a woman on her wedding day. She was no English rose, either. She'd been dark-haired and dark-eyed, with an oval face and an appealing smile. She'd been fashionably slender as well. But weren't they always? Isabelle thought.

'Superintendent Ardery?'

She turned, the picture still in her hands. She'd expected grey-faced grief – perhaps a smoking jacket, a pipe in hand

and slippers on his feet or something equally and ludicrously Edwardian – but Thomas Lynley was quite tanned, his hair was lightened to blond by exposure to the sun, and he wore blue jeans and a polo shirt with three buttons and a collar.

She'd forgotten his eyes were brown. They were watching her without speculation. He'd sounded surprised when he'd said her name, but whatever else he might be feeling, he didn't reveal it.

She said, 'Acting Superintendent only. I've not been given the position permanently. I'm auditioning for it, for want of a better word. Much like you did.'

'Ah.' He entered the room. He was one of those men who always managed to move with an air of assurance, looking as if they'd fit in anywhere. She reckoned it had to do with his breeding. 'There would be something of a difference,' he said as he joined her at the table. 'I wasn't auditioning, just helping out. I didn't much want the position.'

'I've heard that, but I've found it difficult to believe.'

'Why? Climbing the greasy pole never interested me.'

'Climbing the greasy pole interests everyone, Inspector.'

'Not if they don't want the responsibility and certainly not if they've a marked preference for woodwork.'

'Woodwork? What woodwork?'

He smiled faintly. 'The kind one can fade into.'

He looked at her hands, and she realised she was still holding his wedding picture. She set it back on the table and said, 'Your wife was lovely, Thomas. I'm sorry about her death.'

'Thank you,' he said. And then with a perfect frankness that startled Isabelle, so appealing was it, 'We were completely wrong for each other which ultimately made us right for each other. I quite adored her.'

'How lucky to love so much,' she said.

'Yes.' Like Charlie Denton, he offered her a drink, and again she demurred. Also like Charlie Denton, he gestured towards a seating area, but this one not before the fireplace. Rather, he chose two chairs on either side of a chessboard where a game was in progress. He glanced at this, frowned, and after a moment made a move with his white knight that captured one of the two black bishops. 'Charlie only *appears* to be showing mercy,' Lynley noted. 'That means he's got something up his sleeve. What can I do for you, Superintendent? I'd like to think this is a social call, but I'm fairly sure it's not.'

'There's been a murder in Abney Park. Stoke Newington. It's a cemetery, actually.'

'The young woman. Yes. I heard the report on the radio news. You're investigating? What's wrong with having a local team?'

'Hillier pulled strings. There's also another cock-up with SO5. I think it's more of the former and less of the latter, though. He wants to see how I compare with you. And with John Stewart if it comes to it.'

'I see you've pegged Hillier already.'

'Not a difficult task.'

'He wears a lot on his sleeve, doesn't he?' Lynley smiled again. Isabelle noted, however, that the smile was more form than feeling. He was well-guarded as she supposed any one would be in the same situation. She had no real cause to call upon him. He knew it and was waiting for the reason for her visit.

She said, 'I'd like you to join the investigation, Thomas.'

'I'm on leave,' he replied.

'I realise that. But I'm hoping to persuade you to take a leave from your leave. At least for a few weeks.'

'You're working with the team I worked with, aren't you?'

'I am. Stewart, Hale, Nkata . . .'

'Barbara Havers as well?'

'Oh yes. The redoubtable Sergeant Havers is among us. Aside from her deplorable fashion sense, I've a feeling she's a very good cop.'

'She is.' He steepled his fingers. His gaze went to the chessboard and he seemed to be calculating Charlie Denton's next move although Isabelle knew it was more likely that he was calculating hers. He said, 'So, clearly, you don't need my presence. Not as an investigating officer.'

'Can any murder team have *enough* investigating officers?'

That smile again. 'Facile response,' he told her. 'Good for the politics of the Met. Bad for . . .' He hesitated.

'A relationship with you?' She stirred in her chair and leaned towards him. 'All right. I want you on the team because I want to be able to say your name without a reverential hush falling over the incident room and this is the likeliest route to get me there. Also because I want to get on some sort of normal footing with everyone at the Met, and *that's* because I very much want this job.'

'You're forthright enough when your back's against the wall.'

'And I always will be. With you and with everyone else. *Before* my back's against the wall.'

'That'll play good and bad for you. Good for the team you're directing, bad for your relationship with Hillier. He prefers kid gloves to the iron fist. Or have you already discovered that?'

'It seems to me the crucial association at the Yard is between myself and the team and not between myself and David Hillier. And as for the team, they want you back. They want you as their superintendent – well, all except John Stewart but you're not to take that personally—'

'Nor would I.' He smiled, genuinely this time.

'Yes. Good. All right. They want you back and the only thing that will satisfy them is to know you don't want to be what *they* want you to be and you're quite happy with someone else in the position.'

'With you in the position.'

'I think you and I can work together, Thomas. I think we can work very well together if it comes down to it.'

He seemed to study her, and she wondered what he was reading on her face. A moment passed and she let it hang there and extend, thinking how completely quiet it was in the house and wondering if it had been so when his wife was living. They'd had no children, she recalled. They had been married less than a year at her death.

'How are your boys?' he asked her abruptly.

It was a disarming question and likely intended to be so. She wondered how on earth he knew that she had two sons.

He said as if she had spoken, 'You were on your mobile one day when we met in Kent. Your former husband . . . you were having a discussion with him . . . you mentioned the boys.'

'They're near Maidstone, with him as it happens.'

'That can't be a happy arrangement for you.'

'It's neither happy nor unhappy. There was simply no point moving them to London if I've no idea whether this job is going to be permanent.' She realised after she'd spoken that the words had come out more stiffly than she'd intended. She tried to ameliorate the effect by adding, 'I miss them, naturally. But their summer holidays are probably better spent with their father in the countryside than with me here in London. They can run a bit wild there.'

'And if you're appointed permanently to this job?'

He had a way of watching one when he asked a question. He could probably sort out truth from lie quickly enough, but in this particular case there was simply no way he would be able to suss out the reason for the lie she was about to tell him. 'Then, of course, they would join me in London. But I don't like to make premature moves. That's never seemed wise and in this case it would be completely foolhardy.'

'Like counting your chickens.'

'Exactly,' she said. 'So that's another reason, Inspector—'

'We'd got to Thomas.'

'Thomas,' she said. 'All right. I'm laying out the truth for you. I want you to be involved in this case because I want to improve my chances for a permanent assignment here. With you working with me, it will set minds at rest and put an end to speculation at the same time as it will demonstrate a form of cooperation that will act as . . .' She looked for the appropriate term.

He supplied it. 'As an endorsement of you.'

'Yes. If we work together well, it will do that. As I said, I'll never lie to you.'

'And my part would be played out at your side? Is that how you see it?'

'For the present, yes. It may alter. We'd take it as it comes.'

He was quiet, but she could tell he was considering her request: setting it against his life as he was currently living it, evaluating how things would alter and whether that alteration would make a difference to whatever he was coping with now.

He finally said, 'I must think about it.'

'How long?'

'Have you a mobile?'

'Of course.'

'Give me the number, then. I'll let you know by the end of the day.'

The real question for him was what it meant, not whether he would do it. He'd tried to leave police work behind him, but police work had found him and was likely to continue to find him, whether he willed it or not.

Once Isabelle Ardery left him, Lynley went to the window and watched her stride back to her car. She was quite tall – six feet at least because he was six feet two inches and they'd been virtually eye-to-eye – and everything about her shouted *professional*, from her tailored clothing to her polished pumps to her smooth amber-coloured hair falling just below her ears and tucked behind them. She'd had on gold button-shaped earrings and a necklace with a similarly shaped pendant of gold, but that had been the extent of her jewellery. She wore a watch but no rings, and her hands were well-cared for, with manicured nails cut to her fingertips and skin that looked soft. She was definitely a mixture of masculine and feminine as she would have to be. To succeed in their world, she would be regularly forced to be one of the boys while remaining, at heart, one of the girls. It wouldn't be easy.

He watched her open her bag at her car. She dropped her keys, scooped them up, and unlocked the vehicle. She paused to search through her shoulder bag for something, but apparently she couldn't find it because she tossed her bag inside the car and in a moment she'd started it and had driven off.

He stood looking at the street for a moment once she'd gone. He hadn't done this in quite some time as it was in the street that Helen had died, and he'd not been able to bring himself to look lest his imagination take him back to that moment. But looking now, he saw that the street was merely a street like so many others in Belgravia. Stately white buildings, wrought iron railings that gleamed in the sunlight, window boxes that spilled forth ivy and star jasmine in a sweet perfume.

He turned from the sight. He made for the stairway and climbed, but he did not return to the library where he'd been reading the *Financial Times*. Instead, he went to the bedroom next to the room he'd shared with his wife, and he opened its door for the first time since the previous February. And for the first time since the previous February, he also went inside.

It was not quite finished. A cot required assembling, as they'd only got it as far as unloading from its box. Six rolls of wallpaper tilted against the wainscoting, which had been painted once but definitely needed another coat. A new ceiling light remained in its box, and a changing table stood beneath one of the windows, but it was still bare of appropriate padding. The quilted padding was itself rolled up in a Peter Jones carrier bag, among other carrier bags that contained pillows, nappies, a breast pump, bottles . . . It was astonishing how much gear was required for a creature likely weighing upon birth seven pounds or less.

The room was airless and quite hot, and Lynley moved to the windows and shoved them open. There was little breeze to mitigate the temperature, and he wondered they hadn't thought of that when they'd chosen this room for their son's nursery.

Of course, it had been late autumn then, and on into winter, so summer heat would have been the last thing on their minds. Instead, they'd been consumed with the *fact* of the pregnancy alone, and not actually with what the pregnancy was going to produce. He supposed many couples approached it that way. Get through the tough bits leading up to and through childbirth and then shift into parenting mode. One couldn't be a parent or think like a parent without someone to parent, he concluded.

'M' lord.'

Lynley swung around. Charlie Denton was in the doorway. He knew Lynley disliked the use of his title, but they'd never settled on what Denton was supposed to say or do to get his attention aside from using the title in some form, mumbled if necessary or said in the midst of a cough.

'Yes? What is it, Charlie? Are you off, then?'

He shook his head. 'I've been already.'

'And?'

'One never knows about these things. I thought the manner of dress would do it, but there were no words of approbation from the director.'

'Were there not? Damn.'

'Hmm. I did hear someone murmur, "He has the look," but that was it. The rest is waiting.'

'As always,' Lynley said. 'How long will it take?'

'For a callback? Not long. Commercials, you know. They're picky but they're not that picky.'

He sounded resigned. It was, Lynley thought, the way of the acting world. Making one's way there was a microcosm of life itself. Desire and compromise. Putting oneself in a position of chance and feeling the slap of rejection more often than the embrace of success. But there was no success without taking the chance, without risk and consequence, without a willingness to leap.

He said, 'In the meantime, Charlie, while you're waiting to be cast as Hamlet . . .'

'Sir?' Denton said.

'We need to pack up this room. If you'll make us a jug of Pimm's and bring it up here, we should be able to accomplish it by the end of the day.'

7

Meredith finally tracked Gordon Jossie to Fritham. She'd assumed he'd still be working on the building in Boldre Gardens where Gina Dickens had met him, but when she got there it was obvious that he was long gone to another job. The thatch had been dressed and Gordon's signature piece was in place on the ridge: an elegant peacock whose tail protected the vulnerable corner of the ridge and trailed in sculpted straw several feet down the roof.

Meredith muttered a disappointed expletive – low so that Cammie couldn't hear it – and she said to her daughter, 'Let's wander over to the duck pond, shall we, 'cause there's supposed to be a pretty green bridge over it that we can walk on.'

The duck pond and the bridge ate up an hour, but it turned out to be well spent as things happened. They stopped at the refreshment kiosk afterwards and while purchasing a Cornetto for Cammie and a bottle of water for herself, Meredith learned where she could find Gordon Jossie without having to ring him and thus allow him time to ready himself to see her.

He was working on the pub near Eyeworth Pond. She gathered this from the girl at the till who apparently possessed the information because she'd had her eye on Gordon's apprentice for the entire time the two men had worked at Boldre Gardens. She'd managed to make inroads into this person's affections, apparently and despite – or perhaps because of – having legs so bowed she was shaped like a turkey wishbone. That's where Meredith could find the thatchers, she said, near Eyeworth Pond. She narrowed her eyes and asked which one of the men Meredith was looking for. Meredith wanted to tell her to save her anxiety for something worthwhile. A man in any condition, of any age and in any form was the last thing she wished to add to her life. But she said she was trying to find Gordon Jossie at which point the girl helpfully indicated the exact location of Eyeworth Pond: just east of Fritham. And the pub was nearer to Fritham than it was to the pond anyway, she added.

The idea of another pond and more ducks made it easy to get Cammie from the lawns and flowers of Boldre Gardens into the car, never her favourite place to be because she positively loathed the restrictions of her car seat and the vehicle's lack of air conditioning, and she had long been very happy to make her displeasure known. As luck would have it, though, Fritham was some quarter of an hour only from the gardens, just on the other side of the A31. Meredith drove there with all the windows rolled down and instead of her affirmation tape, she popped in a cassette, which was a favourite of Cammie's. Cammie was partial – of all things – to tenors, and she could actually warble *Nessun Dorma* with astonishing operatic flair.

It was easy enough to find the pub in question. Called the Royal Oak, it was a mishmash of styles that reflected different periods when extensions had been built upon it. So the place blended cob, half-timber, and brick, and its roof was part thatch and another part slate tiles. Gordon had removed the old thatch right down to the rafters. When Meredith arrived he was in the midst of climbing down from the scaffolding where, beneath the pub's eponymous oak, his apprentice was organising bundles of reeds.

Cammie was happy to play upon a swing at the far side of the pub's beer garden, so Meredith knew she'd be well occupied while her mum had a chat with the master thatcher.

Gordon didn't look surprised to see her. Meredith reckoned Gina Dickens had likely reported her visit, and who could blame her? She wondered if, after making her report, Gina had also grilled Gordon on the matter of a car that was not his and on the matter of clothing stored in his attic. She thought the younger woman might have done. She'd seemed unnerved enough when Meredith had brought her more fully into the picture of the place Jemima Hastings had occupied in Gordon Jossie's life.

Meredith wasted no time with preambles once she saw Cammie climb safely onto the swing. She strode up to Gordon Jossie and she said, 'What I'd like to know is how she was supposed to get up to London without her car, Gordon,' and she waited to hear how he'd answer the question and what his face would look like as he did so.

Gordon glanced at his apprentice. He said, 'Let's have a break, Cliff,' and added nothing more till the younger man had nodded and disappeared into the pub. Then he removed the baseball cap he'd been wearing and he wiped down his face and his balding pate with a handkerchief that he took from his jeans. He had his sunglasses on and he didn't remove them which, Meredith knew, was going to make it more difficult to read him. She'd always thought he wore dark glasses because he didn't want people to see his shifty eyes, but Jemima had said, 'Oh, that's nonsense,' and apparently thought there was nothing odd about a man in dark glasses rain or shine, sometimes even indoors as well. But *that* had been the problem from the first: Meredith had thought there were scores of things about Gordon Jossie that just weren't right while Jemima had wanted to see none of them. He was, after all, an m-a-n, one of a subspecies among whom Jemima had been careening for years, like someone controlled by the Pinball Wizard.

Now Gordon removed those dark glasses, but he kept them off only long enough to wipe them down with his handkerchief, whereupon he replaced them, shoved the handkerchief back into his pocket and said calmly, 'What d'you have against me, Meredith?'

'The fact that you separated Jemima from her friends.'

He nodded slowly, as if taking this in. He finally said, 'From you, you mean.'

'From everyone, Gordon. You don't deny it, do you?'

'No point to denying what's dead wrong, eh? Stupid as well, if you don't mind me saying. You stopped coming round, didn't you, so if any separating was being done, you're the one who did it. D'you want to talk about why?'

'What I want to talk about is why her car's in your barn. I want to know why you told that . . . that . . . that *blonde* at your house that the car belongs to you. I also want to know why her clothes're packed up and nothing even vaguely Jemima is on display anywhere.'

'Why am I supposed to tell you all that?'

'Because if you don't or if you do and I'm not satisfied with *what* you tell me . . .' She let the threat hang there. He wasn't a fool. He knew what the rest of the sentence would be.

Still he said, 'What?' He was wearing a long-sleeved T-shirt and from its breast pocket he took a packet of cigarettes. He shook one out and lit it with a plastic lighter. And then he waited for her reply. He turned his head briefly to look beyond her where, across the street from the pub, a red-brick farmhouse stood at the edge of the heath. The heath itself rolled into the distance, purple with heather. A wood lay beyond it. The tree tops seemed to shimmer in the summer heat.

'Oh, just answer me,' Meredith said. '*Where* is she and why'd she not take her car?'

His head turned towards her once again. 'What was she to do with a car up in London? She didn't take it because she didn't need it.'

'Then how did she get there?'

'No idea.'

'That's absurd. You can't expect me to believe—'

'Train, bus, helicopter, hang-glider, roller skates,' he cut in. 'I don't know, Meredith. One day she said she was going and the next day she went. She was gone when I got home from work. I expect she took a taxi into Sway and the train from there. So what?'

'You did something to her.' Meredith hadn't intended to accuse him, not like this and not so quickly. But the thought of that car and the lies about it and Gina Dickens taking up residence while Jemima's belongings languished in boxes up in the attic . . . '*Didn't* you?' she demanded. 'Rob's tried to phone her and she's not answering and she's not returning his messages and—'

'Interested there, are you? Well, he's always been available and, all things considered, I suppose it's a wise move.'

She wanted to strike him. Not so much for the remark, which was totally ridiculous, but for the fact that that's what he would think: that like Jemima she was always looking for a man, that she was somehow incomplete and unfulfilled and otherwise so . . . so . . . so *desperate* without one that she'd have her female antennae up just in case a free bloke floated by in her vicinity. Which – as it applied to Rob Hastings – was completely absurd as he was fifteen years her senior and she'd known him since she was eight years old.

'So where did this Gina person come from?' she demanded. 'How long have you known her? You met her prior to Jemima leaving, didn't you, Gordon. She's at the root of all this.'

He shook his head, eloquently communicating both disbelief and disgust. He drew in deeply on his cigarette, in a breath that looked angry to Meredith.

She said, 'You met this Gina person—'

'Her name is Gina. Gina Dickens, full stop. Don't call her "this Gina person". I don't like it.'

'I'm supposed to care about what you don't like? You met this *person* and you decided you'd rather have her than Jemima, didn't you?'

'That's bloody rubbish. I'm getting back to work.'

Meredith raised her voice. 'You drove her off. She might be in London now but there was never a reason to go there except for you. She had her own business. She'd hired Lexie Streener. She was making a go of the Cupcake Queen, but you didn't like that, did you? You made it rough for her. And somehow you used that or her interest in it or the hours she was gone or *something* to make her feel she had to leave. And then you brought in Gina . . .' It all seemed so reasonable to Meredith, so much the way men behave.

He said again, 'I'm getting back to work,' and he walked to the ladder that gave him access to the scaffolding that stretched the length of the building. Before he climbed, though, he turned to her. He said, 'For the record, Meredith, Gina didn't live here – in the New Forest – till June. She came down from Winchester and—'

'That's where *you're* from! You went to school in Winchester. You met her then.' She knew she sounded shrill, but she couldn't help it. For some reason that she couldn't identify, she'd begun to feel desperate to know what was going on and had been going on for the months that she and Jemima had been estranged.

Gordon waved her off. 'Believe what you want. But what I want is to know why you've hated me from the first.'

'This isn't about me.'

'It's *all* about you, and so's the reason you hated me on sight. Think about that before you come round again. And leave Gina alone while you're at it.'

'Jemima's the reason—'

'Jemima,' he said evenly, 'has easily found someone else by now. You know that like I know that. And I expect it drives you mad, as well.'

Gordon Jossie's pickup wasn't visible when Robbie Hastings pulled beyond the tall hedges and onto the driveway of the man's holding. But that didn't deter him. If Gordon wasn't there, there was still a chance that his new woman might be, and Robbie wanted to see her as much as he wanted to have a conversation with Gordon. He also wanted to have a look round. And he wanted to see Jemima's car with his own eyes although Meredith could not have mistaken it for someone else's. It was a Figaro, and one didn't see a vehicle like that on the road every day.

He had no idea what all of this would or would not prove. But two more phone calls to Jemima's mobile had produced no response and he was beginning to panic. Jemima was flighty, but she wasn't one to ignore her own brother.

Robbie walked over to the paddock where he saw that two ponies were grazing. It was an odd time of year for the animals to be brought in off the forest, and he wondered what was wrong with them. They appeared perfectly fit.

He looked over his shoulder at the cottage. All of its windows were open, as if in hope of a breeze, but there seemed to be no one about. This was all to the good. Meredith had said that Jemima's car was in the barn, so he made for this. He'd got the door wide open when he heard a woman's pleasant voice call out, 'Hullo there. C'n I help you with something?'

The voice came from a second paddock, this one on the barn's east side, across a narrow, rutted farm lane that led off towards the heath. Robbie saw a young woman brushing fragments of weeds from the knees of her blue jeans. She looked like a designer from one of those telly programmes had dressed her: white shirt starched and with the collar turned up, cowboy neckerchief bibbing against her throat, straw hat shading her face from the sun. She wore dark glasses, but he could tell she was pretty. Prettier than Jemima by several yards, tall and possessing curves in places other girls her age usually didn't want to have them. She said, 'Are you looking for someone?'

'My sister,' he said.

She said, 'Oh.' No surprise, he thought. Well, she wouldn't be surprised at this point, would she? Meredith had been there ahead of him and what woman wouldn't ask questions of her man if another woman's name came up unexpectedly as Jemima's name no doubt had done?

He said, 'I've been told her motor's in the barn.'

'Evidently,' she said. 'So is mine. Hang on.'

She ducked through the wire fencing. It was barbed, but she was wearing gloves to hold the barbs away. She was also carrying a map of some sort, ordnance survey by the look of it. 'I'm finished here anyway,' she told him. 'The car's just inside.'

So it was. Not covered by a tarpaulin as it had been before, according to Meredith, but standing there big as life: battleship grey with a cream coloured roof. It was an ancient thing, and it was pulled far into the barn. Another car sat behind it, a late model Mini Cooper, apparently the other woman's.

She introduced herself although he knew she'd be Gina Dickens, Jemima's replacement. She said frankly that she'd been rather put-out, learning that the car wasn't Gordon's but his former partner's. She'd had a few words with him about it, she said. About Jemima's clothing boxed up in the attic as well.

She said, 'He told me she's been gone for months, that he's not heard a single word from her in all that time, that she likely isn't coming back again, that they'd . . . well, he didn't say they'd had a row, just that they'd parted. He said it was something coming on for ages and it had been her idea, and as he was hoping to move on with his life, he'd boxed up everything, but not thrown it away. He reckons she'll want her things eventually and ask to have them sent when she gets . . . settled, I suppose.' She removed her sunglasses and looked at him frankly. 'I'm babbling,' she said. 'Sorry. I'm nervous about all this. I mean about how it looks and everything. Her car here, her things boxed up.'

'You believed Gordon?' Robbie ran his hand along Jemima's car. It was dust free and it shone with a glossy patina. She'd always taken good care of it. So Meredith was right in this: why'd she not taken it with her? True, it would be difficult to have a car in London. But Jemima wouldn't have considered that. When an impulse came upon her, she'd never stopped to consider the details.

Gina said in a somewhat altered voice, 'Well, I actually had no reason not to, Mr Hastings. To believe him, that is. Do you think otherwise?'

'Robbie,' he said. 'You can call me Robbie.'

'I'm Gina.'

'Yes. I know.' He looked at her. 'Where's Gordon, then?'

'Working near Fritham.' She rubbed her arms as if a chill had come over her. She said, 'Would you like to come inside?'

He didn't particularly want to, but he followed her, hoping he might learn something that could settle his concern. They went in through the laundry area and from there to the kitchen. She set her map on the table and he saw that it was indeed an ordnance survey map. She'd marked the property on it, and she'd attached to it a second sheet of paper with a pencilled drawing. This too was of the property, but enlarged. Gina apparently saw him looking it over because she said, 'We're . . .' and she sounded hesitant as if leery of parting with the information. 'Well, we're thinking of making some changes round here.'

That certainly said a great deal about Jemima's absence from the scene. Robbie looked at Gina Dickens. She'd removed her hat. Her hair was pure gold. It was shaped to her head like a close fitting cap, in a style that brought to mind the Roaring Twenties. She removed her gloves and tossed them on the table. 'Amazing weather,' she said. 'Would you like water? Cider? A Coke?' And when he shook his head, she came to the table to stand beside him. She cleared her throat. He could tell she felt uncomfortable. Here she was with the brother of her lover's former lover. It was *bloody* awkward. He felt it as well. She said, 'I was thinking how lovely it would be to have a proper garden, but I wasn't quite sure where. I was trying to determine where the property actually ends, and I thought the map would help, but it doesn't, actually. So I'd decided that *perhaps* in the second paddock . . . as we're not . . . as *he's* not using it. I thought it would make a lovely garden, a place where I could bring my girls.'

'You've children?'

'Oh no. I work with adolescent girls. The sort who might get themselves into trouble if they don't have someone to take an interest. Girls at risk? I hoped to have a place besides an office somewhere . . .' Her voice drifted. She used her teeth to pull on the inside of her lip.

He wanted to dislike her, but he couldn't. It wasn't her fault Gordon Jossie had chosen to move on once Jemima had left him. *If* indeed that was what had happened. Robbie looked at the map and then at Gina's drawing. She'd created a grid from the paddock, he saw, and she'd numbered the squares within it. She said as if in explanation, 'I was trying to get an idea of the exact size. So I'd know what we . . . what I was working with. I'm not sure the paddock itself will do for what I have in mind, so if it doesn't, then perhaps part of the heath . . . ? That's why I'm trying to sort out where the property ends, in case I have to have the garden . . . *we* have to have the garden somewhere else.'

'You do,' Robbie said.

'What?'

'You can't have it in the paddock.'

She seemed surprised. 'Whyever not?'

'Gordon and Jemima' – Robbie wouldn't allow his sister not to be part of the conversation. – 'have common rights here, and the paddocks are meant for the ponies, if they're out of condition.'

Her face fell. She said, 'I had no idea.'

'That he has common rights?'

'I don't even know what the expression means, to tell you the truth.'

Rob explained briefly: how some of the land within the Perambulation had certain rights attached to it – the right of pasture, the right of mast, the right of estovers or marl or turbary – and this particular property had the right of common pasture. It meant that Gordon and Jemima had been allowed ponies which could graze freely upon the New Forest but the proviso was that land near the house had to be kept free for the ponies should they need to be removed from the forest for any reason. 'Gordon didn't tell you this?' he said. 'Odd that he'd be thinking of putting a garden in the paddock when he knows he can't.'

She fingered the edge of the map. 'I haven't actually *told* him about the garden. He knows I'd like to bring my girls out here. So they can see the horses, walk in the forest or in the enclosures, picnic by one pond or another. But I hadn't really gone further than that. I thought I'd make a plan of it first. You know, sketch it out?'

Robbie nodded. 'It's not a bad idea. Are these city girls, then? From Winchester or Southampton or the like?'

'No, no. They'd be from Brockenhurst. I mean they'd go to school in Brockenhurst – the college or the comprehensive? – but they could be from anywhere in the New Forest, I expect.'

'Hmmm. Except they'd be from properties just like this, some of them,' he noted. 'So it wouldn't be that much of a diversion for them, would it?'

She frowned. 'I hadn't thought of that.' She walked to the kitchen window. It overlooked the driveway into the property and the west paddock beyond the driveway. She said with a sigh, 'All this land . . . It seemed such a shame not to put it to good use.'

'Depends on how you define "good use",' Robbie said. As he spoke he looked round the kitchen. It was bare of those items that had belonged to Jemima: her set of cookbooks, her colourful wall hangings, and on a shelf above the table, her model horses – some of that collection which she'd kept at her family home, his own home – were gone. In their place were propped a dozen antique postcards of the sort that predated greeting cards: one for Easter, one for Valentine's Day, two for Christmas, etc. They were not Jemima's.

Seeing these, it came to Robbie that Meredith Powell was correct in her surmise. Gordon Jossie had wiped Robbie's sister completely from his life. That wasn't unreasonable. But having her car and her clothing was. Jossie needed talking to. There was no doubt of that.

8

Gordon lay in bed the next morning with the sweats upon him, and their source had nothing to do with the summer heat as it was early – shortly after six – and the day was not yet baking. He'd suffered through another nightmare, but nightmares were nothing new to him.

Still, he always woke with a start: a gasp for air, a weight on his chest like a test for witchery, and then the sweats. These regularly drenched him, the pyjamas he wore in winter and the bed sheets. And when he was drenched, he began to shiver, which woke Gina up as it had once awakened Jemima.

Their reactions were completely different, though. Jemima always wanted answers to the *whys*. Why do you have nightmares? Why are you not talking to someone about them? Why haven't you seen a doctor about the sweats? There could be something wrong, she told him. A sleep disorder, a lung disorder, a weakness of the heart . . . God only knew. But whatever the reason, he needed to take action because this kind of thing could *kill* him.

Which was how Jemima always thought: people dying. It was her greatest fear and no one needed to explain to him the reason for this. His own fears were different but no less real to him than hers were to her, and that was what life was like. People had fears. They learned to cope. He'd learned to cope with his and he didn't like to talk about them.

Gina didn't require talking about them. With Gina, when he woke with the sweats in the morning after a night she'd spent with him – which was most nights, actually, and there was really no point to her keeping her place in Lyndhurst longer, was there? – she rose from the bed and went to the bathroom for a flannel, which she dampened and then returned to use it upon his body. She brought a bowl of cold water with her, and when the flannel grew too hot from his skin, she dipped it in the water and then used it against him again. He wore nothing in summer when he went to bed, so there were no clammy pyjamas to remove. She smoothed the flannel against his limbs and his face and his chest and when he became aroused by this, she smiled and she mounted him or she did other things equally pleasurable and when she did this, every nightmare he'd had sleeping *or* waking was forgotten and very nearly every thought he harboured was gone from his mind.

Except one. Jemima.

Gina asked nothing of him. She merely wanted to love and be with him. Jemima, on the other hand, had asked the world. She had ultimately asked the impossible. And when he'd explained why he could not give her what she asked for, that had ended everything.

Before Jemima, he'd kept clear of women. But when he'd met her, he'd seen the light-hearted girl that she presented to the world, the fun-loving spirit with a childlike gap between her front teeth. He'd thought, I need someone like this in my life, but he'd been wrong. It hadn't yet been time and it probably never would be, but here he was now with another woman, as unlike Jemima as was humanly possible.

He couldn't say he loved Gina. He knew he ought to love her: she was certainly worthy of any man's love. When they'd first gone into the hotel in Sway for a drink on the afternoon he'd seen her up in the woods, more than one bloke had looked her over and looked at him and he knew what each of them was thinking because one thought such things about Gina Dickens, one couldn't help it and still be a human male. Gina didn't seem to mind. She looked at him frankly in a way that said It's yours if you want it, when you're ready. And when he'd decided that by God he *was* ready because he couldn't live as he'd been living with Jemima gone, he'd accepted her offer and now here she was and he didn't regret his decision in the least even though he'd learned that he couldn't afford to love her or anyone else.

She bathed him now. And all the rest. And if he took her forcefully instead of allowing himself to be taken by her, that was fine with Gina. She gave a breathless laugh as he moved her roughly onto her back and her legs spread and then went round him. He found her mouth and it opened to him like the rest of her and he wondered how he'd got lucky just this once and what he would have to pay for his good fortune.

Afterwards, they both were soaking. They separated and laughed at the sucking sound that came from damp skin disengaging from other damp skin. They showered together and she washed his hair and when he became aroused again, she said, 'Good Lord, Gordon,' with a breathless laugh and she dealt with it – with him – again. He said, 'Enough,' but she said, 'Not enough,' and she proved it to him. His knees went weak.

He said, 'Where'd you learn this, woman?' and she said, 'Did Jemima not like sex?'

He said, 'Not like this,' and by that he meant wanton. For Jemima it had been reassurance. *Love me, don't leave me.* But she had done the leaving.

It was nearly eight when they went down to the kitchen for breakfast. Gina talked to him about her desire for a garden. He didn't want a garden with all the unnecessary disruption it would bring to his life, not to mention the laying of walks, the arranging of borders, the digging, the planting, the building of sheds or greenhouses or conservatories or whatever. He didn't want any of it. He hadn't told her as much because he liked the look of her as she went on about what a garden would mean to her, to them and to 'her girls' as she called them. But then she also brought up Rob Hastings and what he had told her about the land.

Gordon confirmed this, but that was all he intended to say about Rob. The agister had tracked him down to the Royal

Oak pub much as Meredith Powell had done, and just as when Meredith had shown her face, Gordon had told Cliff to take a break so that whatever Rob Hastings had to say could be said out of earshot. To make sure this was the case, they'd walked up the lane to Eyeworth Pond, which wasn't so much a pond as it was a damming of a long-ago stream upon which ducks now floated placidly and on whose banks willows crowded one upon the other and draped leafy branches into the water. There was a small two-tiered car park nearby and a path beyond it led into the wood, where the ground was thick with decades of beech and chestnut leaves.

They walked to the edge of the pond. Gordon lit a cigarette and waited. Whatever Rob Hastings had to say, it would be about Jemima, and he had nothing to tell him about Jemima beyond that which Rob obviously already knew.

'She left because of her,' Rob said, 'didn't she? The one at your house. That's how it was, eh?'

'I see you've been talking to Meredith.' Gordon felt weary with the fuss.

'But Jemima wouldn't want me to know about that,' Rob Hastings said, following the line of conversation that he'd established. 'She wouldn't want me to know about Gina, owing to the shame of it all.'

Despite himself and his reluctance to discuss Jemima, Gordon found this an interesting theory, wrong as it was. He said, 'How'd you reckon, then, Rob?'

'Like this. She must have seen the two of you. You'd've been in Ringwood, maybe, or even Winchester or Southampton if she'd gone for supplies for the Cupcake Queen. She'd've seen something that told her what was going on between the two of you, and she'd've left you because of it. But she couldn't bring herself to tell me because of her pride and the shame of it all.'

'What shame?'

'Being cheated on. She'd be 'shamed of that, knowing I'd warned her from the first something wasn't right about you.'

Gordon flicked ash from his cigarette onto the ground and twisted the toe of his boot upon it. 'Never much liked me, then. You hid it well.'

'I would do, after she took up with you anyways, wouldn't I. I wanted her to be happy and if you were the person making her happy, who was I to make it clear I smelled something bad?'

'What would that something be?'

'You tell me.'

Gordon shook his head, signalling not negation but the fact that it was hopeless to attempt to explain himself since Robbie Hastings would be unlikely to believe whatever he said. He sought to elucidate this with, 'When a bloke like you – like any bloke, really – doesn't like someone, anything looks like a reason for it, Rob. You know what I mean?'

'Truth is, I don't.'

'Well, I can't help you. Jemima left me, full stop. If anyone had someone else on the side, I'd reckon it'd be Jemima 'cause it wasn't me.'

'Who'd you have before her, then, Gor?'

'No one,' Gordon said. 'Ever, actually.'

'Come on, man. You're . . . what?' Rob appeared to think it over. 'Thirty-one years old and you'll have me think you'd not had a woman before you had my sister?'

'That's exactly what I'd have you think because it's the truth.'

'That you were a virgin. That you come to her a blank slate where no other ladies' names've been written, eh?'

'That's it, Rob.'

Robbie, Gordon could tell, didn't believe a word of it. 'You queer, then, Gor?' he asked. 'You a defrocked Catholic priest or something?'

Gordon glanced at him. 'You sure you want to go this way, Rob?'

'What's that supposed to mean?'

'Oh, I think you know.'

Rob's face flamed.

'See, she speculated about you now and again,' Gordon said. 'Well, she would do, wouldn't she? All things considered, it's a bit unusual. Bloke your age. Forty-something, eh?'

'Don't make this about me.'

'Nor about me,' Gordon said. Any conversation along these lines would, he knew, proceed in circles, so he ended it there. What he had to tell Robbie Hastings was what Robbie Hastings had doubtless already heard from Meredith Powell, even from Jemima herself. But he found out quickly enough that that was not going to satisfy Jemima's brother.

'She left because she didn't want to be with me any longer,' Gordon said. 'That's it and that's an end to the matter. She was in a hurry because that's what she always was and you damn well know that. She made up her mind in an instant and then she acted. If she was hungry, she ate. If she was thirsty, she drank. If she decided she wanted a different sort of bloke, no one was going to talk her out of it. That's it.'

'In a nutshell, Gor?'

'That's how it is.'

'Happens I don't believe you,' Rob said.

'Happens I can't do anything about it.'

But when Robbie left him back at the Royal Oak, to which they'd returned in a silence broken only by the sound of their footfalls on the stony verge and the crying of skylarks on the heath, Gordon found he wanted to *make* him believe because anything else meant exactly what happened the next morning while he and Gina were saying their goodbyes for the day outside on the driveway by Gordon's pickup.

An Austin pulled up directly behind the old Toyota. Out stepped a bloke in bottle-thick spectacles with clip-on sunglasses covering them. He had on a tie but he'd loosened it to hang from his neck. He took off the clip-on sunglasses, as if this would allow him to see Gordon and Gina better. He nodded knowingly and said, 'Ah.'

Gordon heard Gina say his name in a questioning murmur,

and he said to her, 'Wait here.' He'd got the door of the pickup open, but he pushed it shut and walked over to the Austin.

'Morning, Gordon,' the bloke said. 'It's going to be hot again, isn't it?'

'It is that,' Gordon replied. He said nothing more because he reckoned things about the visitor would be made clear for him soon enough.

And so they were. The man said affably, 'We need to have a chat, you and me.'

Meredith Powell had phoned in ill to her place of employment, going so far as to plug her nose in order to simulate a summer cold. She didn't like doing this and she certainly didn't like the example it set for Cammie, who watched her with wide-eyed curiosity from the kitchen table. But there'd seemed to be no alternative.

Meredith had paid a call at the police station the prior afternoon and had got exactly nowhere. The conversation had gone a route that had ended with her feeling a perfect fool. What did she have to report that equated to grave suspicions and doubts? Her friend Jemima's car in a barn on the property where she'd lived with her partner for some two years, Jemima's clothes boxed up in the attic, Jemima with a new mobile phone to prevent Gordon Jossie from tracking her down, and the Cupcake Queen deserted in Ringwood. *None of this is like Jemima, don't you see?* had hardly impressed the plod she'd spoken to at the Brockenhurst station. She'd been seen by a sergeant whose name she didn't recall and didn't *want* to recall, and at the end of her tale he'd enquired rather pointedly that couldn't it be, madam, that these people were merely going about their daily lives without reporting their movements to her because this was none of her business? Of course, she'd prompted this remark herself by admitting to the sergeant that Robbie Hastings had spoken to his sister regularly since her removal to London. But still, there had been *no* reason for the sergeant to look upon her as if she'd been something unsavoury that he'd found on the sole of his shoe. She *wasn't* a busybody. She was a concerned citizen. And wasn't a concerned citizen – a taxpayer, mind you – supposed to let the police know when something was off? Nothing sounds *off* to me, the sergeant had said. One woman leaves and this bloke Jossie finds another. How's that measure up to fishy, eh? Way of the world, you ask me. And to her declaration of *for God's sake,* he'd told her to take her troubles to the main station in Lyndhurst if she didn't like what she was getting from him.

Well, she wasn't about to put herself through *that*, Meredith decided. She'd phone the main station but that was *all*. Then she would take matters into her own hands. She knew that something was going on and she had a fairly good idea where to begin digging to find it.

To do this, she needed Lexie Streener. So she made her phone call to the graphic design firm where she herself was employed, talked about a rotten summer cold that she didn't want to pass on to the other employees, and after offering a few artificial sneezes so that Cammie would not suffer damage from this brief exposure to her mother's prevarication, she set out to fetch Lexie Streener.

Lexie hadn't needed the slightest persuading to take a day off from the hair salon, where her future as the Nicky Clarke of Ringwood wasn't exactly arriving on the wings of Mercury. It was no big deal for her to ring the Jean Michel hair salon, groan her way through an excuse of sicking up all night long after a bad beef burger, and then ring off with a 'lemme get meself sorted' to Meredith.

Getting sorted consisted of decking herself in platform shoes, lace tights, a very short skirt – she definitely wouldn't want to be bending over, Meredith thought – and a blouse whose empire waist suggested Jane Austen films or maternity wear. This last bit was a nice touch, indicating that Lexie had somehow worked out Meredith's intentions.

These were devious but not illegal. Lexie was to play the role of a girl in need of serious mentoring, one whose elder sister – that would be Meredith – had heard of a programme being run by a very nice young woman recently down from Winchester. *I can't do a bloody thing with her and I'm that worried she'll go off the rails if we don't take steps* was the general line Meredith planned to take. And she planned to take that line first at Brockenhurst College where girls just Lexie's age took themselves after leaving the comprehensive in the hope of learning something there that would lead to future employment rather than to the dole.

The college was just beyond the Snake Catcher pub, on the Lyndhurst Road. Lexie's role called for her to smoke and sulk and generally act uncooperative, at risk of everything from pregnancy to STDs to rampant heroin addiction. Although Meredith would never have mentioned it to the girl, the fact that her short-sleeved blouse revealed several cutting scars on her arms lent credence to the story they were concocting.

She managed to find a shady spot to leave the car, and together she and Lexie made their way across the baking tarmac to the administrative offices. There they spoke to a harried secretary who was trying to meet the needs of a group of foreign students with limited English. She said to Meredith, 'You want *what*?' And then, 'You need to speak with Monica Patterson-Hughes in Nursing,' which suggested that she didn't quite understand what Meredith was driving at with regard to her 'younger sister's situation'. But Monica Patterson-Hughes being better than no one, she and Lexie went in search of such a person. They found her demonstrating nappy-changing to a group of adolescent girls who had the distinctly attentive look of future nannies. They were quite intent upon a worn-looking Cabbage Patch doll that was being used for the demonstration. Evidently, anatomically correct artificial infants were beyond the limited funding of the organisation.

'We use *actual* infants in part two of the course,' Monica

Patterson-Hughes informed Meredith upon stepping aside to let the future nannies loose on the Cabbage Patch doll. '*And* we're encouraging the use of cloth nappies again. It's all about bringing up baby green.' She looked at Lexie. 'Are you wanting to enrol, my dear? It's quite a popular course. We have girls placed all over Hampshire once they finish up. You'd have to rethink your appearance – the hair's just a *bit* over the top – but with guidance as to dressing and grooming, you could go far. If you've an interest, of course.'

Lexie looked surly, without prompting. Meredith took Monica Patterson-Hughes aside. It wasn't *that*, she explained. It was something quite different. Lexie here has gone a bit wild and I'm the responsible adult in her life and I've been told that there's a programme for girls just like Lexie, girls who need to be taken in hand by someone who sets an example for them, takes an interest, acts like an older sister. Which I of course am, but sometimes a *real* older sister isn't the thing a younger sister wants to listen to, especially a younger sister like Lexie who's already been in a bit of trouble – 'wild boys and binge drinking and such,' Meredith murmured – and who doesn't want to listen to someone she frankly considers a 'bloody preaching cow'.

'I'd heard of a programme?' she repeated hopefully. 'A young lady down from . . . I believe it was Winchester? . . . who's taking on troubled girls?'

Monica Patterson-Hughes frowned. Then she shook her head. There was no such programme associated with the college. Nor did she know of one in the process of being set up. Girls at risk . . . Well, generally they were dealt with at a younger age, weren't they? Mightn't this programme be something more likely to come from the New Forest District Council?

Lexie, apparently getting quite into her role, cooperatively snarled that she wasn't having 'nought to do wiv no fooking council', and she brought out her cigarettes as if she meant to light up there in the classroom. Monica Patterson-Hughes looked suitably appalled. She said, 'My dear, you can't . . .' to which Lexie informed her she'd damn well do what she bloody liked. Meredith thought this might be smearing things on a *bit* thick, and she got her 'younger sister' out of the classroom post haste.

Lexie crowed once they were outside. She said, 'Tha' was great fun, that,' and 'Where're we off to next?' and 'I'll talk 'bout me boyfriend at the next place. What d'you think?'

Meredith wanted to tell her that a wee bit less drama would serve them better but Lexie had few enough diversions in her life and if this little jaunt of theirs had the potential of supplying her with some excitement, that was fine by her. So at the New Forest District Council offices – which they found in Lyndhurst in a U of buildings called Appletree Court – they put on a performance of such conviction that they were immediately ushered into the presence of a social worker called Dominic Cheeters, who brought them coffee and lemony ginger biscuits and seemed so eager to help that Meredith felt a nagging sense of guilt that they were lying to the man.

But here, too, they learned there was no programme being established for girls at risk, and definitely no programme being established by one Gina Dickens from Winchester. Dominic, helpful to the core of his being, even went to the trouble of phoning round various of his 'personal sources', as he called them. But the result was the same. Nothing. So then he went farther afield, phoning the local education offices in Southampton to see if they could be of help. By this time, Meredith reckoned she knew that they could not help and such was the case.

The enterprise with Lexie Streener ate up most of her day, as things turned out. But Meredith considered it time well spent. She now had proof positive, she decided, that Gina Dickens was a flaming liar about her life in the New Forest. And Meredith knew from personal experience that where a person told one lie, dozens of others existed.

*   *   *

When he was alone again, Gordon whistled urgently for Tess. The Golden Retriever came running. She'd been out on the property since early morning, ultimately taking herself to her favourite shady spot, beneath a climbing hydrangea on the north side of the cottage. There she had herself a lair of beaten earth kept moist even on the hottest summer days.

He fetched her brush, and Tess gave him that loopy smile and wagged her tail. She leapt up onto the short-legged table he used for this purpose, and he drew his stool near and began with her ears. She needed a proper brushing daily anyway, and now was a good time to do it.

He wanted a smoke, but he didn't have any fags upon him, so he applied himself forcefully and rapidly to the brushing of the dog. He felt tight from head to toe, and he wanted to get loose and be easy. He didn't know how to manage that, so he brushed the dog and he brushed the dog.

They'd walked away from the car, towards and ultimately into the barn. Gina would have wondered why, but that couldn't be allowed to matter because Gina was untouched, like a lily growing out of an excrement heap, and he meant to keep her that way. So he left her standing in the driveway looking puzzled or frightened or concerned or anxious or *whatever* it was that a woman might feel when the man she's opened her heart to seems to be under the thumb of someone who could hurt him or hurt them both.

He brushed the dog and he brushed the dog. He heard Tess whine. He was being too rough. He eased on the pressure. He brushed the dog.

So they'd gone into the barn and before they got there, Gordon had tried to make it look as if the call from this stranger had to do with the land. He'd gestured here and there, and that had amused. The other chuckled.

'Understand your lady love's gone missing,' he'd said, once they were within the cooler confines of the barn. 'But looks to me' – with a wink and coarse gesture that Gordon was meant to take as sexual and did – 'like you've no worries on that score. She's a nice bit of skirt, that one, nicer than the other. Good, firm thighs, I expect. Strong as well. Other one was littler, wasn't she.'

'What d'you want?' he'd asked. 'Because I've work to do and so does Gina and you're blocking the driveway.'

'That does make it a bit rough, doesn't it? Me blocking the driveway. Where'd the other one go?'

'What other one?'

'You know what I mean, lad. The grapevine tells me someone's got their knickers in a twist over you. Where's the other one? Make the leap here with me, Gordon. I know you can.'

He'd had no choice but to tell him: Jemima, leaving the New Forest without her car for God knows what reason, leaving most of her belongings as well because if he didn't tell it would come out anyway and there'd be hell to pay.

'Just took herself off, you say?' he'd asked.

'That's what happened.'

'Why? You not doing the job on her proper, Gordon? Fine, strapping man like you, man with all the right parts in all the right places?'

'I don't know why.'

The other examined him. He took off his glasses and polished them on a special cloth he removed from his pocket. 'Don't give me that,' he said and his tone of voice was no longer the spuriously jovial one he'd used before but rather icy the way a blade is icy if someone presses it against hot skin. 'Don't you be playing me for a fool. I don't like hearing your name come up in general conversation. Makes me feel dead uneasy, it does. So you still want to say she just left you and you don't know why? I'll not have that.'

Gordon's worry had been that Gina would come into the barn, that she would want to know or to help, to intercede or to protect, for that was her nature.

'She said she couldn't cope,' Gordon said. 'All right? She said she couldn't cope.'

'With what?' And then he'd smiled slowly. No humour in it, but there wouldn't have been. 'Cope with what, my love?' he'd repeated.

'You bloody well know,' said between his teeth.

'Ah . . . Now don't get cheeky with me, lad. Cheekiness? It doesn't become you.'

9

Ultimately, the Stoke Newington house-to-house turned up nothing, nor did the perimeter search of the environs of the chapel and gridding off the whole blooming cemetery and conducting a search that way. They had enough manpower to carry it all off – both from the local station and from officers on loan from other areas – but the end result was no witness, no weapon, no handbag, no shoulder bag, no purse and no identification. Just an admirable rubbish clean-up of the cemetery. On the other hand, they'd had phone calls aplenty, and a description shuffled to SO5 had actually produced a possible lead. In this, they were assisted by the fact that the body in question had unusual eyes: one green and one brown. Once they plugged that into the computer, the field of missing persons narrowed down to one.

She'd been reported as having disappeared from her lodgings in Putney, and it was to Putney that Barbara Havers was sent two days after the discovery of the body; specifically she was sent to Oxford Road, which was equidistant from Putney High Street and Wandsworth Park. There she parked illegally in a residents-only space, propped a police ID in plain sight, and rang the bell on a terrace house whose front garden appeared to be the street's recycling centre, if the bins and plastic containers were anything to go by. She was admitted to the house by an older woman with a military haircut and a bit of military moustache. She wore exercise clothing and pristine white trainers done up with pink and purple laces. She said that she was Bella McHaggis and it was bloody well time a cop'd shown up and was *this* sort of incompetence what her taxes paid for and the bloody government can't do a thing right, can they, because just look at the condition of the streets, not to mention the Underground, *and* she'd phoned the cops two days ago, and . . .

Blah, blah, blah, Barbara thought. While Bella McHaggis gave vent to her feelings, she herself had a look round the place: uncarpeted wood floor, hall stand with umbrellas and coats, and on the wall a framed document announcing itself as House Rules for Occupants, with a sign saying *Landlady on Premises* posted beneath it. 'With lodgers, one can't bang on about the rules enough,' Bella McHaggis asserted. 'I've got them everywhere. The rules, that is. It helps, I find, if people know what's what.'

She led Barbara into a dining room, through a large kitchen, and into a sitting room at the back of the house. There Bella McHaggis announced that her lodger – who was called Jemima Hastings – had gone missing and if the body that had been found in Abney Park had one brown eye and one green eye . . . Here, Bella stopped. She seemed to try to read Barbara's face.

Barbara said, 'Have you got a picture of the young lady?'

Yes, yes indeed, Bella said.

'Come this way.' She led Barbara out of a door on the far side of the sitting room, which took them to a narrow corridor that ran in the direction of the front door of the house. To one side of this corridor, the reverse side of a staircase rose and facing them beneath it was a door otherwise hidden from anyone entering the building. On this door was a poster. The lighting was dim but Barbara could see that the poster featured a black-and-white photograph of a young woman, light hair blowing across her face. She was sharing the picture with three-quarters of a lion's head, somewhat out of focus behind her. The lion was male, marble, slightly streaked from weather, and asleep. The poster itself was an advertisement for the Cadbury Photographic Portrait of the Year. Evidently, it was some sort of contest, and its winners comprised an ongoing show at the National Portrait Gallery in Trafalgar Square.

'So *is* it Jemima?' Bella McHaggis said. 'It's not like her to be gone without telling any of us. When I saw the story in the

Evening Standard, I reckoned if the girl had eyes like those – two different colours . . .' Her words tapered off as Barbara turned to her.

'I'd like to see her room,' Barbara said.

Bella McHaggis made a small sound, something between a sigh and a cry. Barbara saw that she was a decent soul. She said, 'I'm not actually sure, Mrs McHaggis.'

'It's just that they become rather like family,' Bella said. 'Most of my lodgers . . .'

'You've others, then? I'll want to speak with them.'

'They're not here at present. At work, you know. There're just two of them, beyond Jemima, that is. Young men, they are. Very nice young men.'

'Any possibility she could have been involved with either of them?'

Bella shook her head. 'Against the rules. I find it's not a good thing if my gentlemen and ladies begin keeping company while living under the same roof. I had no rule about it at first, once Mr McHaggis died and I started with lodgers. But I found . . .' She looked at poster on the door. 'I found things became unnecessarily complicated if the lodgers . . . Shall we say if they fraternised? Unspoken tensions, the possibility of break-ups, jealousy, tears? Rows over the breakfast table? So I made the rule.'

'And how do you know if the lodgers abide by it?'

'Believe me,' Bella said, 'I know.'

Barbara wondered if this meant an examination of the bed sheets. 'But Jemima was acquainted with the male lodgers, I assume?'

''Course. She knew Paolo best, I expect. He brought her here. That's Paolo di Fazio. Born in Italy but you wouldn't know it. No accent at all. And no . . . well, no odd Italian habits, if you know what I mean.'

Barbara didn't, but she nodded helpfully. She wondered what odd Italian habits might be. Putting tomato sauce on the Weetabix?

'—room nearest to hers,' Bella was saying. 'She worked in a shop somewhere round Covent Garden and Paolo has a stall in Jubilee Market Hall. I had a vacant room; I wanted a lodger; I hoped for another female; he knew she was looking for permanent lodgings.'

'And your other lodger?'

'Frazer Chaplin. He's got the basement flat.' She nodded at the door on which the poster hung.

'So that's his? The poster?'

'No. That's just the way to his flat. She brought the poster to me, Jemima did. I suppose she wasn't altogether happy that I hung it here, where it's out of sight. But, well, there you have it. There wasn't really another suitable space.'

Barbara wondered about that. It seemed to her that there was space aplenty, even with the plethora of signs depicting the household rules. She gave the poster a final quick glance before asking once again to see Jemima Hastings' room. She *looked* like the young woman whose autopsy pictures Barbara had seen Isabelle Ardery put up only that morning in the incident room. But it was, as always, incredible to see the difference between someone in life and someone in death.

She followed Bella to the next floor, where Jemima had a bedroom at the front of the house. Paolo's room was just along the corridor at the back, Bella said, while her own room was yet another floor above.

She opened the door to Jemima's room. It had not been locked, and there was no key stuck in the keyhole on the inside. But that was not to say there wouldn't be a key somewhere in the room, Barbara saw, although it would be a challenge worthy of Hercules in the Augean Stables to find it.

'She was something of a hoarder,' Bella said, which was like declaring that Noah was something of a rowing boat builder.

Barbara had never seen such clutter. The room was a nice size for a lodging, and it contained masses of belongings. Clothes strewn on the unmade bed and across the floor and drooping from drawers in the chest; magazines and tabloids and maps and brochures and handouts from people in the street; decks of playing cards mingling with business cards and postcards; stacks of photographs bound with rubber bands . . .

'How long did she live here?' Barbara asked. It was inconceivable to her that one person could amass so much clobber in anything less than five solid years.

'Nearly seven months,' Bella said. 'I did speak to her about this. She said she'd get round to it, but I think . . .'

Barbara looked at the woman. Bella was pulling thoughtfully at her lower lip. 'What?' Barbara asked.

'I think it gave her some sort of comfort. At the end of the day I daresay she couldn't let any of it go.'

'Yeah. Well.' Barbara gave a sigh. 'All of it's got to be gone through.' She dug out her mobile and flipped it open. 'I'm going to have to ring for backup,' she told Bella.

Lynley used the car as an excuse because that was the easiest thing to tell both himself and Charlie Denton, not that he generally told Denton where he was going but he knew the young man had not yet stopped worrying about his state of mind. So he popped into the kitchen where Denton was applying his considerable culinary skills to making a marinade for a piece of fish and he said, 'I'm off for a bit, Charlie. Over to Chelsea for an hour or so,' and he didn't miss the look of delight that briefly touched the other's features. Chelsea could mean a hundred different destinations, but Denton would reckon there was only a single one that was taking Lynley out of Belgravia. Lynley added, 'Thought I'd show off the motor,' and Denton said, 'Mind how you go, then. You don't want anything marring that paint job.'

Lynley promised he'd do whatever was necessary to prevent such a tragedy, and he walked to the mews where he kept the car that he'd finally bought to replace his Bentley, which had been reduced to a tangle of metallic rubble five months earlier at the hands of Barbara Havers. He unlocked the garage and there it was and the truth of the matter was that he *did* feel the slightest thrill of ownership, looking on the copper beauty of the thing. Four wheels and it was only transport, but there was transport and there was Transport and this was definitely Transport.

Owning the Healey Elliott gave him something to think about when he was driving, besides thinking of the subjects he didn't want to think about. That had been one of the reasons he'd purchased it. One had to consider issues like where to park it and which route to choose from Point A to Point B in order to keep it safe from run-ins with cyclists, taxis, buses and pedestrians pulling wheeled suitcases without a mind for where they were going. Then there was the critical issue of keeping it clean, of keeping it well within sight when parking in a less than salubrious area, of keeping its oil pristine and its spark plugs practically sterilised and its wheels balanced and its tyres filled to the appropriate degree. It was, thus, a vintage English car like all vintage English cars. It required constant vigilance and just as much maintenance. In short, it was exactly what he required at this juncture in his life.

The distance from Belgravia to Chelsea was so minimal that he could have walked it, no matter the heat and the crowds of shoppers along the King's Road. Less than ten minutes from the moment he closed the front door of his house, he was crawling along Cheyne Row in the hope of finding a spot to park near to the corner of Lordship Place. As luck would have it, a spot was vacated by a van making a delivery to the King's Head and Eight Bells as he approached the pub. He was at last walking towards the tall brick house on the corner of Lordship Place and Cheyne Row when he heard his name called out by a woman's voice. '*Tommy*! Hullo!'

This came from the direction of the pub where, he saw, his friends were just rounding the corner from Cheyne Walk and the Embankment beyond it. Likely they'd been for a walk along the river, he decided, for Simon St James was carrying their dog – a long-haired dachshund who hated the heat as much as she hated walkies – and his wife Deborah was at his side, her hand through his arm and a pair of sandals dangling from her fingers.

'Isn't the pavement hot on your feet?' he called back.

'Absolutely horrible,' she admitted. 'I wanted Simon to carry me but given the choice between Peach and myself, the wretch chose Peach.'

'Divorce is the only answer,' Lynley said. They came up to him then, and Peach – recognising him as she would do – squirmed to be put down so that she could jump up and demand to be held again. She barked, wagged her tail and jumped a few more times as Lynley shook St James's hand and accepted Deborah's fierce hug. He said, 'Hullo, Deb,' against her hair.

She said, 'Oh Tommy,' in reply. And then stepping back and scooping up the dachshund who continued to writhe, bark and demand to be noticed, 'You're looking very well. It's so *good* to see you. Simon, doesn't Tommy look well?'

'Almost as well as the car.' St James had gone to have a look at the Healey Elliott. He gave an admiring whistle. 'Have you brought it by to gloat?' he said to Lynley. 'My God, it's a beauty. Nineteen forty-eight, isn't it?'

St James had long been a lover of vintage cars and himself drove an old MG, modified to cope with his braced left leg. It was a TD classic, circa 1955, but the age of the Healey Elliott along with its shape made it rare and a virtual eyeful. St James shook his head – dark hair overlong as always and doubtless Deborah was banging on daily about his need for a haircut – and gave a long sigh. 'Where'd you find it?'

'Exeter,' Lynley said. 'I saw it advertised. Poor bloke spent years of his life restoring it but his wife considered it a rival—'

'And who can blame her?' Deborah said pointedly.

—and wouldn't let go of the matter till he'd sold it.'

'Complete madness,' St James murmured.

'Yes. Well. There I was with cash in hand and a Healey Elliott in front of me.'

'You know, we've been to Ranelagh Gardens having a chat about some new adoption possibilities,' St James said to Lynley. 'That's where we were coming from just now. But truth to tell? Babies be damned. I'd like to adopt this motor instead.'

Lynley laughed.

'Simon!' Deborah protested.

'Men will be men, my love,' St James told her. And then to Lynley, 'How long've you been back, Tommy? Come inside. We were just talking about a Pimm's in the garden. Will you join us?'

'Why else live in summer?' Lynley replied. He followed them into the house, where Deborah placed the dog on the floor and Peach headed towards the kitchen in the eternal dachshund search for food. 'Two weeks,' he said to St James.

'Two weeks?' Deborah said. 'And you've not phoned? Tommy, does anyone know you're back?'

'Denton's not killed the fatted calf for the neighbourhood, if that's what you're asking,' Lynley said dryly. 'But that's at my request. He'd have hired sky writers if I'd allowed it.'

'He must be glad you're home. *We're* glad you're home. You're *meant* to be home.' Deborah clasped his hand briefly and then called out to her father. She threw her sandals at the base of a coat rack, said over her shoulder, 'I'll ask Dad to do us that Pimm's, shall I?' and went in the same direction as the dog, down to the basement kitchen at the back of the house.

Lynley watched her go, realising he'd lost touch with what it was like to be around a woman he knew well. Deborah St James was nothing like Helen, but she matched her in energy and liveliness. That understanding brought with it sudden pain. It came to him, it went. Briefly, it took his breath.

'Let's go outside, shall we?' St James said.

Lynley saw how well his old friend read him. 'Thank you.'

They found a place beneath the ornamental cherry tree, where worn wicker furniture sat round a table. There Deborah joined them. She carried a tray on which she'd placed a jug of Pimm's, a bucket of ice, and glasses displaying the requisite spears of cucumber. Peach followed her and in her wake came the St Jameses' great grey cat Alaska, who immediately took up slinking along the herbaceous border in pursuit of imagined rodents.

Around them were the sounds of Chelsea in summer: distant cars roaring along the Embankment, the twittering of sparrows in the trees, people calling out from the garden next door. On the air the scent of a barbecue rose, and the sun continued to bake the ground.

'I've had an unexpected visitor,' Lynley said. 'Acting Superintendent Isabelle Ardery.' He told them the substance of his visit from Ardery: her request and his indecision.

'What will you do?' St James asked. 'You know, Tommy, it might be time.'

Lynley looked beyond his friends to the flowers in the herbaceous border at the base of the old brick wall defining the edge of the garden. Someone – probably Deborah – had been giving them a great deal of care by recycling the washing-up water. They looked better this year than they had in the past, bursting with life and colour. He said, 'I managed to cope with the nursery at Howenstow and her country clothing. Some of the nursery here as well. But I've not been able to face her things in London. I thought I might be ready when I arrived two weeks ago, but it seems I'm not.' He took a drink of his Pimm's and gazed at the garden wall on which clematis climbed in a mass of lavender blooms. 'It's all still there: in the wardrobe and the chest of drawers. In the bathroom as well: cosmetics, her scent bottles. The hairbrush still has strands of her hair . . . It was so dark, you know, with bits of auburn.'

'Yes,' St James said.

Lynley heard it in Simon's voice: the terrible grief that St James would not express, believing as he did that, by rights, Lynley's own grief was so much greater. And this despite the fact that St James, too, had loved Helen dearly and had once intended to marry her. He said, 'My God, Simon,' but St James interrupted. 'You're going to have to give it time,' he said.

'Do,' Deborah said, and she looked between them. And in this, Lynley saw that she too knew. And he thought of the ways one mindless act of violence had touched upon so many people and three of them sat there in the summer garden, each of them reluctant to say her name.

The door from the basement kitchen opened, and they turned to anticipate whoever was about to come out. This turned out to be Deborah's father, who had long run the household and just as long been an aide to St James. Lynley thought at first he meant to join them but instead Joseph Cotter said, 'More company, luv,' to his daughter. 'Was wondering . . . ?' He inclined his head a fraction towards Lynley.

Lynley said, 'Don't please turn someone away on my account, Joseph.'

'Fair enough,' Cotter said, and to Deborah, ''Cept I thought his lordship might not want—'

'Why? Who is it?' Deborah asked.

'Detective Sergeant Havers,' he said. 'Not sure what she wants, luv, but she's asking for you.'

The last person Barbara expected to see in the back garden of the St James home was her erstwhile partner. But there he was and it took her only a second to process it: the amazing motor out in the street had to be his. It made perfect sense. He suited the car and the car suited him.

Lynley looked much better than when she'd last seen him two months earlier in Cornwall. Then, he'd been the walking wounded. Now, he looked more like the walking contemplative. She said to him. 'Sir. Are you back as in back or are you just back?'

Lynley smiled. 'At the moment, I'm merely back.'

'Oh.' She was disappointed and she knew her face showed it. 'Well,' she said. 'One step at a time. You finished the Cornwall walk?'

'I did,' he said. 'Without further incident.'

Deborah offered Barbara a Pimm's, which Barbara would have loved to toss back. Either that or pour it over her head because she was boiling inside her clothing and cursing DI Ardery once again for directing her to alter her manner of dress. This was just the sort of weather that called for linen draw-string trousers and a very loose T-shirt, not for a skirt, tights, and a blouse courtesy of another shopping event with Hadiyyah, this one more quickly accomplished because Hadiyyah was persistent and Barbara was, if not amenable to Hadiyyah's persistence, then at least detrited by Hadiyyah's persistence. The small favour for which Barbara thanked God was that her young friend had chosen a blouse *without* a pussy-cat bow.

She said to Deborah, 'Ta, but I'm on duty. This is a police call, actually.'

'Is it?' Deborah looked at her husband and then at Barbara, 'Are you wanting Simon, then?'

'You, actually.' There was a fourth chair near the table, and Barbara took it. She was acutely aware of Lynley's eyes on her, and she knew what he was thinking because she knew him. She said to him, 'Under orders, more or less. Well, more like under *serious* advice. You can believe I wouldn't've otherwise.'

He said, 'Ah. I did wonder. Whose orders, more or less?'

'The newest contestant for Webberly's old job. She didn't much like the way I looked. Unprofessional, she told me. She advised me to do some serious shopping.'

'I see.'

'Woman from Maidstone, she is. Isabelle Ardery. She was that—'

'The DI from arson.'

'You remember. Well done. Anyway, it was her idea that I ought to look . . . whatever. This is how I look.'

'I see. Pardon me for asking, Barbara, but are you wearing . . . ?' He was far too polite to go further, and Barbara knew it.

'Makeup?' she asked. 'Is it running down my face? What

with the heat and the fact that I've not the first clue how to put the bloody stuff on . . .'

'You look lovely, Barbara.' Deborah was merely being supportive, Barbara knew, because she herself wore nothing at all on her freckled skin. And her hair, unlike Barbara's own, comprised masses of red curls that suited her even in their habitual disarray.

'Cheers,' Barbara said. 'But I look like a clown and there's more to come. I won't go into it, though.' She heaved her shoulder bag onto her lap and blew a breath upward to cool her face. She was carrying rolled beneath her arm a second poster from the Cadbury Photographic Portrait of the Year exhibition. This one had been tacked to the back of the bedroom door belonging to Jemima Hastings, which Barbara had seen once she'd shut that door to get a better look at the room. The ambient light had afforded her the opportunity to study both the portrait and the information written beneath it. That information had brought Barbara to Chelsea. She said, 'I've got something here that I'd like you to take a look at,' and she unrolled the poster for Deborah's inspection.

Deborah smiled when she saw what it was. 'Have you been to the Portrait Gallery for the show, then?' She went on to speak to Lynley, telling him what he'd missed in his time away from London: a photographic competition in which her entry had been selected as one of the six pictures used for marketing the resulting exhibition. 'It's still on at the gallery,' Deborah said. 'I didn't *win*. The competition was deadly. But it was brilliant to be among the final sixty chosen to be hung, and then she –' with a nod at the picture – 'was selected to be on posters and postcards sold in the gift shop. I was quite over the moon about that, wasn't I, Simon?'

'Deborah's had some phone calls,' St James told them. 'From people wanting to see her work.'

Deborah laughed. 'He's being far too kind. It was *one* phone call from a bloke asking me if I'm interested in doing photo shoots of food for a cookbook his wife is writing.'

'Sounds good to me,' Barbara noted. 'But then anything involving food, you know . . .'

'Well done, Deborah.' Lynley leaned forward and looked at the poster. 'Who's the model?'

'She's called Jemima Hastings,' Barbara told him, and to Deborah, 'How did you meet her?'

Deborah said, 'Sidney – Simon's sister . . . I was looking for a model for the portrait contest and I'd thought at first that Sidney would be perfect, with all the modelling she does. I did *try* with her but the result was too professional looking . . . something about the way Sidney deals with facing a camera? With showing off clothing instead of being a subject? Anyway, I wasn't happy with it and I was casting about afterwards, still looking for someone, when Sidney showed up with Jemima in tow.' Deborah frowned, obviously putting any number of things together at once. She said in a cautious voice, 'What's this about, Barbara?'

'The model's been murdered, I'm afraid. This poster was in her lodgings.'

'Murdered?' Deborah said. Lynley and St James both stirred in their chairs. '*Mur*dered, Barbara? When? Where?'

Barbara told her. The other three exchanged looks, and Barbara said, 'What? Do you know something?'

'Abney Park.' Deborah was the one to reply. 'That's where I took the picture in the first place. That's where this is.' She indicated the great, white, weather-streaked lion whose head filled the frame to the left of the model. 'This is one of the memorials in the cemetery. Jemima had never been there before we took the picture. She told us as much.'

'Us?'

'Sidney went as well. She wanted to watch.'

'Got it. Well, she went back,' Barbara said. 'Jemima did.' She sketched a few more details, just enough to put them all in the picture. She said to Simon, 'Where is she these days? We're going to need to speak to her.'

'Sidney? She's living in Bethnal Green, near Columbia Road.'

'The flower market,' Deborah added helpfully.

'With her latest partner,' Simon said, dryly. 'Mother – not to mention Sid – is hoping this will also be her final partner, but frankly, it's not looking that way.'

'Well, she does rather like them dark and dangerous,' Deborah noted to her husband.

'Having been affected in adolescence by a plethora of romance novels. Yes. I know.'

'I'll need her address,' Barbara told him.

'I hope you don't think Sid—'

'You know the drill. Every avenue and all that.' She rolled the poster back up and looked among them. Certainly there was *something* going on. She said, 'Beyond meeting her with Sidney and then taking the picture, did you see her again?'

'She came to the opening at the Portrait Gallery. All the subjects – the models? – were invited to do that.'

'Anything happen there?'

Deborah looked at her husband as if seeking information. He shook his head and shrugged. She said, 'No. Not that I . . . Well, I think she had a *bit* too much champagne, but she had a man with her who saw she got home. That's really all—'

'A man? Do you know his name?'

'I've forgotten, actually. I didn't think I'd need to . . . Simon, do you remember?'

'Just that he was dark. And I remember that mostly . . .' He hesitated, clearly reluctant to complete the thought.

Barbara did it for him. 'Because of Sidney? You said she likes them dark, didn't you?'

Bella McHaggis had never before been placed into the position of having to identify a body. She'd *seen* dead bodies, of course. She'd even, in the case of the departed Mr McHaggis, doctored the setting in which death had occurred so as to protect the poor man's reputation prior to phoning 999. But she'd never been ushered into a viewing room where a victim of violent death lay, covered by a sheet. Now that she had, she was more than ready to engage in whatever sort of activity would scour from her mind the mental image.

Jemima Hastings – not a single doubt that it was Jemima – had been stretched out on a trolley with her neck wrapped up in thick swathes of gauze like a winter scarf, as if she needed protection from the chilly room. From that, Bella had concluded the girl had had her throat cut and she'd asked if this was the case, but the answer had come in the form of a question, 'Do you recognise . . . ?' Yes, yes, Bella had said abruptly. Of course it's Jemima. She'd *known* the minute that woman officer had come to her house and had peered at that poster. The police-woman – Bella couldn't remember her name at the moment – hadn't been able to keep her expression blank, and Bella had known that the girl in the cemetery was indeed the lodger gone missing from her house.

So to wipe it all away, Bella became industrious. She could have gone to a session of hot yoga, but she reckoned industry was the better ticket. It would get her mind away from the mental picture of poor dead Jemima on that cold steel trolley at the same time as it would prepare Jemima's room for another lodger now the cops had carted away all her belongings. And Bella wanted another lodger, soon, although she had to admit that she hadn't had very much luck with the female variety. Still, she wanted a woman. She liked the sense of balance another woman gave to the household though women were far more complicated than men and even as she wondered if perhaps another male would keep things simpler and prevent the males already in place from *preening* so. Preening and strutting, that's what they did. They did it unconsciously, like roosters, like peacocks, like virtually every male from every species on earth. The calculated dance of notice-me was some-thing Bella generally found rather amusing, but she realised that she had to consider whether it might be easier on everyone concerned if she removed from their household the necessity for it.

Upon her return from viewing Jemima's body, she'd put up her *Room to Let* sign in the dining room window, and she'd made her phone call to *Loot* to run the advertisement. Then she'd gone up to Jemima's room and she'd begun a thorough clean. With the boxes and boxes and *boxes* of her belongings already removed from the house, this was a job that didn't take long. Hoovering, dusting, changing sheets, an application of furniture polish, a beautifully washed window – Bella prided herself particularly on the state of her windows – scented drawer liners removed from the chest and new ones placed there, curtains taken down for cleaning, every piece of furniture moved away from the wall to give the hoover access. No one, Bella thought, cleaned a room the way she did.

She moved on to the bathroom. Generally, she left their bathrooms to her lodgers, but if she was going to have a new lodger soon, it stood to reason that Jemima's drawers and shelves were going to have to be emptied of anything left behind by the police. They'd not removed every item from the bathroom since not everything within had belonged to Jemima, so Bella concentrated on straightening the room as she cleaned it, which was why she found – not in Jemima's drawer but in the top drawer marked for the *other* lodger – a curious item that certainly did not belong there.

It was the result of a pregnancy test. Bella knew *that* the second she clapped her eyes upon it. What she didn't know was whether the result was positive or negative, being of an age at which she would, of course, never have used such a test herself. Her own children – long gone to Detroit and to Buenos Aires – had announced their conception in the old-fashioned manner of wracking her body with morning sickness almost from the instant of sperm-meets-egg, which itself had been achieved in the old-fashioned manner, thank you very much, Mr McHaggis. So Bella, retrieving the incriminating plastic tab from the drawer, wasn't sure about what the indicator meant. Blue line. Was that negative? Positive? She would have to find out. She would also have to find out what it was doing in the drawer of her other lodger because surely *he* hadn't brought it home from a celebratory dinner – or, what was more likely, a confrontational cup of coffee – with the mother-to-be. If a woman he'd been bonking had fallen pregnant and had presented him with the evidence, why would he keep it? A souvenir? Certainly, the coming infant was going to be souvenir enough. No, it stood to reason that the pregnancy test was Jemima's. And if it hadn't been in Jemima's belongings or with Jemima's rubbish, there was a reason. There seemed several possibilities for this, but the one that Bella didn't want to consider was the one telling her that once again, two of her lodgers had pulled the wool over her eyes about what was going on between them.

Bloody hell damn, Bella thought. She had rules. They were *everywhere*. They were signed and sealed and delivered in the contract she made each lodger read and fix his or her name to the bottom of. Were young people so randy that they couldn't stop themselves from jumping in and out of each other's knickers at the first opportunity despite her *very clear rules* about fraternising with other members of the household? It appeared they were. It appeared they could not. Someone, she decided, was going to be talked to.

Bella was going through the mental preparation for such a conversation when the bell went on the front door down below. She gathered up her cleaning supplies, removed her Marigolds, and huffed down the stairs. The bell rang again, and she shouted, 'Coming,' and she opened it to see a girl on her porch, rucksack at her feet, hopeful expression on her face. She didn't look English to Bella and when she spoke, her voice gave her away as someone from what had once probably been Czechoslovakia but was now any one of a number of countries with many syllables, even more consonants, and few vowels because Bella could not keep track of them and no longer tried.

'You have room?' the girl said hopefully, gesturing in the direction of the dining room window where the *Room to Let* sign was displayed. 'I see your notice there . . . ?'

Bella was about to tell her yes, she had a room to let, and how are you at obeying rules, missy? But her attention shifted to a movement on the pavement as someone dodged behind what shrubbery managed to grow in her front garden among the plethora of recycling bins. It was a woman moving out of sight, a woman in a tailored wool suit, despite the heat, with a brightly patterned scarf – her sodding trademark, that was, Bella thought – folded into a band and holding back masses of dyed orange hair.

'You!' Bella shouted at her. 'I'm ringing the cops, I am! You've been bloody told to stay away from this house and this is the limit!'

Whether the activity was going to eat up time or not – and Barbara Havers knew which alternative was actually the case – there was no way she was going to face the sister of Simon St James in her current get-up and with her face attempting to divest itself of its smear of makeup through the means of excessive perspiration. So instead of heading from Chelsea directly to Bethnal Green, she drove home to Chalk Farm first. She scrubbed her face, breathed a sigh of relief, and decided to compromise with the wee-est bit of blusher. She then went for a change of apparel – hallelujah to drawstring trousers and T-shirts – and having thus resumed her normal state of *déshabille*, she was ready to face Sidney St James.

Her conversation with Sidney was not effected immediately, however. Upon leaving her tiny bungalow, Barbara heard Hadiyyah, crying from above, 'Hullo, oh hullo, Barbara!' as if she hadn't seen her in an aeon or so. The little girl went on enthusiastically with, 'Mrs Silver is teaching me how to polish silver today,' and Barbara followed the sound to see Hadiyyah hanging out of a window on the second floor of the big house. 'We're using baking powder, Barbara,' she announced and then she turned as someone within the flat said something to which the little girl corrected herself with, 'Oh! Baking *soda*, Barbara.

'Course Mrs Silver doesn't ackshully *have* any silver so we're using her cutlery, but it makes the cutlery *shine* so. Isn't that brilliant? Barbara, why've you not got on your new skirt?'

'End of the day, kiddo,' Barbara said. 'It's mufti time.'

'And are you—' Hadiyyah's attention was caught by something beyond Barbara's line of vision because she interrupted herself with, 'Dad! Dad! Hullo! Hullo! Sh'll I come home now?' She sounded even more enthusiastic about this prospect than she had about seeing Barbara, which gave Barbara an idea of how much the little girl was actually enjoying learning yet another of Mrs Silver's 'housewifely skills', as she called them. So far this summer they'd done starching, ironing, dusting, hoovering, removing scale from toilet bowls and learning the myriad uses of white vinegar, all of which Hadiyyah had obediently mastered and then dutifully reported to Barbara and demonstrated either for her or for her father. But the bloom had faded from the rose of acquiring domestic skills – how could it be otherwise? Barbara thought – and while Hadiyyah was far too polite to complain to the elderly woman, who could blame her for embracing the thought of escape with a joy that daily increased?

Barbara heard Taymullah Azhar's response, muted from the direction of the street. Hadiyyah's hand fluttered in farewell to Barbara, she disappeared within the flat, and Barbara herself continued down the path that followed the side of the house, emerging from beneath an arbour fragrant with star jasmine to see Hadiyyah's father coming through the front gate, several carrier bags dangling from one hand and his worn leather briefcase in the other.

'Polishing silver,' Barbara said to him by way of greeting. 'I'd no idea baking soda worked a trick on tarnish. You?'

Azhar chuckled. 'There appears to be no end to the domestic knowledge of that good woman. Had I had it mind that Hadiyyah should spend her life in housekeeping, I could not have found her a better instructor. She's quite mastered scones, by the way. Have I mentioned that?' He gestured with the hand that held the carrier bags. 'Will you join us for dinner, Barbara? It's chicken *jalfrezi* with *pilau* rice. And as I recall' – with a smile that showed the sort of white teeth that made Barbara swear she *would* see the dentist in the near future – 'those are among your favourites.'

Barbara told her neighbour she was sorely tempted, but duty called. 'Just on my way out,' she said. Both of them turned as the front door of the old house opened and Hadiyyah clattered down the steps. She was followed closely by Mrs Silver, tall and angular, ensconced in an apron. Sheila Silver, Barbara had learned from Hadiyyah, possessed an entire wardrobe of aprons. They were not only seasonal. They were celebratory as well. She had Christmas aprons, Easter aprons, Halloween aprons, New Year's aprons, birthday aprons and aprons commemorating everything from Guy Fawkes' Night to the ill-fated marriage of Charles and Diana. Each of these was complemented by a matching turban. Barbara reckoned the turbans had been fashioned from tea towels by their wearer, and she had little doubt that when the list of housewifely duties had been mastered by Hadiyyah, turban making would be among them.

As Hadiyyah flung herself in the direction of her father, Barbara waved a farewell. Her last sight of them was of Hadiyyah – arms round Azhar's slender waist – and Mrs Silver in gangly pursuit of her, as if the girl's escape had been pre-emptive and more information about baking soda needed to be imparted.

In her car, Barbara gave a thought to the time of day and concluded that only a bout of creative rat running through London's myriad neighbourhoods would get her to Bethnal Green before nightfall. She skirted as much of the City as she could, ultimately coming on Bethnal Green from Old Street. This was an area that had altered much over the years, as young professionals unable to afford the prices of central London's housing moved in an ever widening circle to embrace parts of town long considered undesirable. Bethnal Green was hence a combination of the old and the new, where sari shops mingled with computer sales centres, and ethnic enterprises like Henna Weddings stood next door to estate agents flogging properties to growing families.

Sidney lived in Quilter Street, a terrace of plain-fronted houses constructed of London brick. A mere two-storeys tall, they comprised the south side of a triangle at the centre of which was a common area called Jesus Green. Unlike so many small parks in town, this one was neither locked nor barred. It was fenced in wrought iron, which was typical of London's squares, but the fence was only waist high and its gate stood open to admit anyone who wanted access to its wide lawn and to the pools of shade offered by the leafy trees that towered over it. Children were playing noisily on the green near to where Barbara parked her old Mini. In one corner a family was having a picnic, and in another a guitarist was entertaining a young adoring female. It was a very good place to escape the heat.

Sidney answered the door to Barbara's knock, and Barbara tried not to feel what she indeed was in the presence of St James's younger sister: a frightening contrast. Sidney was quite tall, she was slender, and she was naturally in possession of the sort of cheekbones that women happily went under the knife to acquire. She had the same coal-coloured hair as her brother and the same blue-today-and-grey-tomorrow eyes. She was wearing capris, which emphasised legs that went from here to China, and a cropped tank-top that showed off her arms, disgustingly tanned like the rest of her. Large hoop earrings dangled from her ears, and she was removing them as she said, 'Barbara. I expect the traffic was a nightmare, wasn't it?' and admitted her into the house.

This was small. All the windows were open, but that was doing little to mitigate the heat inside. Sidney appeared to be one of those loathsome women who did not perspire, but Barbara was not among their number, and she could feel the sweat popping out on her face the moment the front door closed behind her. Sidney said sympathetically, 'Terrible, isn't it? We complain and complain about the rain, and then we get this. There should be some middle ground, but there never is. I'm just this way, if you don't mind.'

Just this way turned out to be a staircase. This rose towards the back of the little house, where a door stood open to a small garden from which the sound of vicious pounding was emanating. Sidney went to the door, saying over her shoulder to Barbara, 'That's just Matt.' And into the garden, 'Matt, darling, come and meet Barbara Havers.'

Barbara looked past her to see a man – burly, shirtless and sweating – who was standing with sledgehammer in hand, apparently in the process of beating a sheet of plywood into submission. There seemed to be no reason for this unless, Barbara thought, he was going for a rather inefficient means of creating mulch for the single, sun-parched herbaceous border. At Sidney's call, he didn't stop what he was doing. Rather, he glanced over his shoulder and nodded curtly. He was wearing dark glasses, and his ears were pierced. His head was shaved to the skull and like the rest of him it shone with sweat.

'Gorgeous, isn't he?' Sidney murmured.

It wouldn't have been Barbara's word of choice. 'What's he doing, exactly?' she said.

'Letting it out.'

'What?'

'Hmmm?' Sidney gazed at the man appreciatively. He didn't appear particularly handsome, but he had a body completely defined by muscle: an eye-catching chest, narrow waist, serious lats and a bum that would have got him pinched just about anywhere on the planet. 'Oh. Aggression. He's letting it out. He hates it when he's not working.'

'Unemployed, is he?'

'Good heavens, no. He does . . . oh, something or other for the government. Come up, Barbara. D'you mind if we talk in the bathroom? I was giving myself a facial. Is it all right if I get on with it?'

Barbara said it was fine by her. She'd never seen a facial being given and now that she was on her relentless course of self-improvement, who knew what tips she might pick up from a woman who'd been a professional model since she was seventeen? As she followed Sidney up the stairs, she said, 'Like what?'

'Matt?' Sidney clarified. 'It's all top secret, according to him. I expect he's a spy or something. He won't say. But he goes off for days or weeks and when he comes home, he fetches the plywood and beats the dickens out of it. He's between jobs at the moment.' She glanced back in the direction of the pounding, concluding with a casual 'Matthew Jones, man of mystery.'

'Jones,' Barbara noted. 'Interesting name.'

'It's probably his whatever . . . his cover, eh? Makes it all rather exciting, don't you think?'

What Barbara thought was that sharing lodgings and a bed with someone who pounded upon wood with a sledge-hammer, possessed shady employment, and had a name that might or might not be his own was akin to playing Russian roulette with a rusty Colt 45, but she kept that to herself. Everyone's boat floated on different water and if the bloke below rang Sidney's chimes – not to mix *too* many metaphors, Barbara thought – then who was she to point out that men of mystery were frequently men of mystery for reasons having nothing at all to do with James Bond. Sidney had three brothers who were doubtless doing their share of pointing that out to her.

She followed Sidney into the bathroom where an impressive line-up of jars and bottles awaited them. Sidney began with the removal of her makeup, chattily explaining the process – 'I like to tone, first, before I exfoliate. How often d'you exfoliate, Barbara?' – as she went along.

Barbara murmured appropriate responses although toning sounded like something one did in a gym and exfoliating surely had to do with gardening, didn't it? When Sidney at last had smoothed on a mask – 'My T-zone is just bloody *murder*,' she confessed – Barbara brought up the reason for her journey to Bethnal Green. She said, 'Deborah tells me you introduced Jemima Hastings to her.'

Sidney acknowledged this. Then she said, 'It was her eyes. I'd posed for Deborah – for the Portrait Gallery competition, you know? – but when the pictures weren't what she wanted, I thought of Jemima. Because of her eyes.'

Barbara asked how she'd come to be acquainted with the young woman, and Sidney said, 'Cigars. Matt likes Havanas – God, they smell awful – and I'd gone there to get him one. I remembered her later because of her eyes, and I reckoned she'd make an interesting face for Deborah's portrait. So I went back and asked her and then took her along to meet Deborah.'

'Went back where?'

'Oh. Sorry. To Covent Garden. There's a tobacconist in one of the courtyards? Round the corner from Jubilee Market Hall? It's got cigars, pipe tobacco, snuff, pipes, cigarette holders . . . all the bits one associates with smoking. Matt and I stopped there one afternoon, which is how I knew where it was and what he bought. Now whenever he's due back from one of his man-of-mystery jaunts, I pop in and get him a welcome home cigar.'

Bleagh, Barbara thought. She was a smoker herself – always intending to give it up although never quite intending *enough* – but she drew the line at anything whose scent reminded her of burning dog poo.

Sidney was saying, 'Anyway, Deborah quite liked the look of her when I introduced them, so she asked her to pose. Why? Are you looking for her?'

'She's dead,' Barbara said. 'She was murdered in Abney Park Cemetery.'

Sidney's eyes darkened. Exactly as her brother's did when he was struck by something, Barbara thought. Sidney said, 'Oh Lord. She's the woman in the paper, isn't she? I've seen the *Daily Mail* . . .' And when Barbara confirmed this, Sidney

went on. She was the sort of woman who chatted compul-
sively – utterly unlike Simon whose reserve was sometimes
completely unnerving – and she sketched in every relevant
and irrelevant detail pertaining to Jemima Hastings and
Deborah St James's photograph of her.

Sidney couldn't make out why Deborah had chosen Abney
Park Cemetery, as it wasn't exactly easy to get to, but you
know Deborah. When she set her mind to something, there
was no suggesting an alternative. She'd apparently scouted
locations for weeks in advance of the photo-shoot and she'd
read about the cemetery – 'something to do with conservation?'
Sidney wondered aloud – and had done an initial recce there,
where she'd found the sleeping lion monument and decided
it was just the thing she wanted for background in the photo.
Sidney had accompanied Deborah and Jemima – 'I admit it.
I was a *bit* put out that my photo hadn't suited, you know?'
– and she'd watched the subsequent photo-shoot, wondering
why she had failed as a subject for the portrait where Jemima
was possibly going to succeed. 'As a professional, you know,
one needs to know. If I'm losing my edge, I must get on top
of my game?'

Right, Barbara agreed. She asked had Sidney seen anything
that day in the cemetery, had she noticed anything. Did she
remember anything? Something unusual? Had anyone watched
the photo-shoot, for example?

Well, yes of course, there were *always* people . . . And lots
of men if it came down to it. Only Sidney couldn't remember
any of them because it had been ages ago and she'd certainly
not thought that she'd *have* to remember and God it was
dreadful that Deborah's picture might have been the means . . .
I mean, wasn't it possible that someone had tracked down
Jemima by using that picture, had found Jemima, had followed
her to that cemetery . . . except what was she *doing* there, did
they know? . . . or perhaps someone had kidnapped her and
taken her there? And *how* had she died?

'Who?' It was Matt Jones speaking. Somehow he'd come

silently up the stairs – Barbara wondered when he'd ceased pounding on the plywood and how long he'd been listening – and he was a looming, sweating presence in the bathroom doorway, which he filled up in a fashion that Barbara would have called menacing had she not also wanted to call it curious. Close to him now, she had a sense of both danger and anger emanating from him. He was sort of a Mr Rochester type, had Mr Rochester been in possession of heavy weaponry in the attic and not a mad wife.

Sidney said, 'That girl from the cigar shop, darling. Jemima . . . What was her surname, Barbara?'

'Hastings,' Barbara said. 'She was called Jemima Hastings.'

'What about her?' Matt Jones asked. He crossed his arms beneath a set of pectorals that were tanned, hairless, impressive, and decorated with a tattoo that said *Mum* surrounded by a wreath of thorns. He possessed three scars on his chest as well, Barbara saw, a puckering of the flesh that had the suspicious look of healed bullet holes. Who *was* this bloke?

'She's dead,' Sidney told her lover. 'Darling, Jemima Hastings was murdered.'

He was silent. Then he grunted once. He moved away from the doorway and rubbed the back of his neck. 'What about dinner?' he asked.

The West Town Road Arcade's CCTV tapes from that day are grainy, making absolute identification of the boys who took John Dresser impossible, should such identification rely on the tapes alone. Indeed, had it not been for Michael Spargo's over-large mustard anorak, there is a chance that John's abductors might have gone unapprehended. But enough people had seen the three boys and enough people were willing to come forward and identify them that the tapes consequently act as confirmation of their identities.

The films show John Dresser walking away quite willingly with the boys, as if he knows them. As they near the arcade exit, Ian Barker takes John's other hand and he and Reggie swing the child between them, perhaps in the promise of more play to come. While they walk, Michael catches them up with a childlike skip and hop, and he seems to offer the toddler some of the French fries he's been eating. This offer of food to a child who was waiting hungrily for his lunch appears to have been what kept John Dresser happy to go with them, at least at first.

It's interesting to note that when the boys leave the Barriers, they do not do so by the exit that would take them to the Gallows, i.e. by the exit most familiar to them. Instead, they choose one of the lesser used exits, as if they already have planned to do something with the toddler and wish to remain as unseen as possible when they make off with him.

In his third interview with the police, Ian Barker claims that their intention was just to 'have a bit of fun' with John Dresser, while Michael Spargo says that he didn't know 'what them other two wanted with that baby', a term ('the baby') that Michael uses throughout his conversations with the police in reference to John Dresser. For his part, Reggie Arnold will not come close to discussing John Dresser until his fourth interview. Instead, he attempts to obfuscate, making repeated references to Ian Barker and his own confusion about 'what he wanted that kitten for', attempting to direct the course of the conversation onto his siblings, or assuring his mother – who was present for all interviews – that he 'didn't nick nothing, never ever, Mum'.

Michael Spargo claims that he wanted to return the toddler to the shopping arcade once they had him outside the Barriers. 'I told them we could drop him back inside, just leave the baby by the door or something, but they were the ones didn't want to. I said we'd get into trouble for nicking him, wouldn't we, [note the objectifying use of *nicking*, as if John Dresser were something they'd pinched from a shop] but they called me a wanker and asked me did I want to grass them up, then.'

Whether this actually happened remains open to doubt as neither of the other two boys refers to Michael having second thoughts. And later nearly every witness – who came to be known collectively as the Twenty-Five – confirms that their sightings of the boys involved all three of them and John Dresser, and all three of them seemed to be actively involved with the little boy.

Considering his past, it seems reasonable to conclude that Ian Barker was the one to suggest they see what would happen if they swung John Dresser as they had been doing but dropped him instead of landing him safely on his feet. This they did, releasing him at the apex of the swing and projecting him ahead of them at some speed, with the apparent and expected effect of John's beginning to cry when he hit the pavement. This fall caused the first of the bruises to John's bottom and, possibly, the first of the ultimately extensive damage done to his clothing.

With a clearly distressed toddler on their hands, the boys made their first attempt to settle him down by offering him the jam roll that Michael Spargo had taken from his home that morning. That John accepted it is clear not only from the extensive report of Dr Miles Neff of the Home Office, but also from witness evidence, for it was at this point that the boys had their first encounter with someone who not only saw them with John Dresser but who also stopped to question them about him.

Trial transcripts show that when seventy-year-old Witness A (all witness names will be withheld from this document for their own protection) saw the boys, John was upset enough to concern her:

'I asked them what was wrong with that baby,' she says, 'and one of them – I think it was the fat one [a reference to Reggie Arnold] – told me he'd fallen and banged his bum. Well, children do fall, don't they? I didn't think . . . I did offer to help. I offered them my handkerchief for his face 'cause he was crying so. But then the taller boy [referring to Ian Barker] said it was his baby brother and they were taking him home. I asked them how far they had to go and they said not far. Just over in Tideburn, they said. Well, as the baby began eating a jam roll they offered him, I couldn't see there would be further trouble.'

She goes on to say that she asked the boys why they weren't at school, and they told her school was finished for the day. This apparently mollified Witness A, who told them to 'get the baby home then' because 'he's obviously wanting his mum'.

She doubtless was additionally mollified by the boys' inspired use of Tideburn as their putative habitation. Tideburn was then and is now safely middle class to upper middle class. Had they said the Gallows – with all that implied – her concerns might have been triggered.

Much has been made of the fact that the boys could have turned John Dresser over to Witness A at that moment, saying they'd found him wandering outside the Barriers. Indeed, much has been said of the fact that the boys had repeated moments when they could have handed John Dresser to an adult and gone on their way. That they didn't suggests that somewhere along the line at least one of them was working on a larger plan. Either that or a larger plan had been earlier discussed among the three of them. But if this latter is the case, it is also something that not one of the boys has ever been willing to reveal.

The police were phoned once the CCTV tapes had been viewed by the Barriers' head of security. By the time they arrived to look at the tapes themselves and to mount a search, however, John

Dresser was approximately one mile away. In the company of Ian Barker, Michael Spargo and Reggie Arnold, he had crossed two heavily trafficked roadways and he was both tired and hungry. He had fallen several more times, apparently, and had cut his cheek on a raised piece of the pavement.

It was becoming trying to be in his company, but still the boys did not release John Dresser to anyone. According to Michael Spargo's fourth interview, it was Ian Barker who first kicked the toddler when he fell and it was Reggie Arnold who hauled the little boy back on his feet and began to drag him. John Dresser was apparently quite hysterical at this point, but this appears to have caused passers-by to believe more firmly in the tale told by the boys that they were attempting to take 'my little brother' home. Whose little brother John Dresser supposedly was was a detail that became a shifting target, dependent solely upon the speakers, (Witnesses B, C, and D) and while Michael Spargo denies in every interview that he ever claimed John Dresser as a sibling, this assertion is contradicted by Witness E, a postal worker who encountered the boys midway to the Dawkins building site.

Witness E's testimony has him asking the boys what's wrong with the toddler, why's he crying so, and what's happened to his face?

'He said – this was the one in the yellow anorak, mind – that it was his brother and that Mum was doing the business with her boyfriend at the house and they were meant to keep the little 'un busy till she was finished. They said they'd walked a bit too far and could I drive them home in my van?'

This was, if anything, an inspired request. Surely the boys knew that Witness E would not be able to accommodate them. He was on his route, and even if that had not been the case, there was probably inadequate room within his vehicle. But the *fact* that this request had been made gave legitimacy to their story. Witness E reports that he 'told them to take the tyke directly home, then, 'cause he was blubbing like nothing I ever seen and I got three of my own', and the boys agreed to do this.

It appears possible that their intentions towards John Dresser, while inchoate when they first snatched him, began to develop with the consecutive string of successful lies they were able to tell about him, as if the easy belief of the witnesses whetted the boys' appetite for abuse. Suffice it to say that they continued on their way, managing to walk the toddler more than two miles despite his protests and his cries of 'Mummy' and 'Da' which were heard, and ignored, by more than one person.

Michael Spargo claims that during this period he asked again and again what they were going to do with John Dresser. 'I told them we couldn't take him home with us. I told them. I did,' the transcript of his fifth interview has him declaring. He also declares that it was at this point that he brought up the idea of leaving John at a police station. 'I said we could leave him on the steps or something. We could leave him inside the door. I said his mum and dad're going to be worried. They're going to think something's happened to him.'

Ian Barker, Michael says, declared that something *had* happened to the toddler. 'He said "Stupid git, something did happen." And he asked Reg did he think the baby'd make a splat when he hit the water.'

Was Ian considering the canal at that point? Possibly. But the fact of the matter was that the boys were nowhere near the Midlands Trans-Country Canal and they were not going to be able to get an exhausted John Dresser there unless they carried him, which they apparently did not wish to do. But had Ian Barker been harbouring a desire to inflict some sort of injury upon John Dresser in the environs of the canal, he had now been thwarted and John himself was the reason why.

John Dresser's company becoming progressively more difficult, the boys made the decision to 'lose the baby in a supermarket somewheres' according to Michael Spargo, because the entire affair had become 'dead boring, innit'. There was no supermarket in the immediate vicinity, however, and the boys set out to find one. It was on their way that Ian, as Michael and Reggie report in separate interviews with the police, pointed out that in a shop they might be seen and even documented on CCTV. He indicated he knew of a much safer location. He led them to the Dawkins building site.

The site itself was a grand idea ruined by loss of funding. Originally intended as three stylishly modern office blocks within 'a lovely, park-like setting of trees, gardens, paths and copious outdoor seating', it had been intended to infuse money into the surrounding community in order to bolster a faltering economy. But poor management on the part of the contractor resulted in the project being called to a halt before the first tower was completed.

On the day that Ian Barker ushered his companions to the site, it had languished untouched for nineteen months. It was fenced by chain link, but it was not inaccessible. Although signage on the fence warned that the site was 'under surveillance 24 hours a day' and that 'trespassers and vandals will be prosecuted to the fullest extent of the law', regular incursions into the property made by children and adolescents indicated otherwise.

It was a tempting area both for playing and for clandestine rendezvous. There were dozens of places to hide; heaps of earth offered launching pads for mountain bikers; discarded boards, tubes and pipes could stand in for weapons in games of war; small chunks of concrete substituted nicely for hand grenades and bombs. While it was a dubious location in which 'to lose the baby' if the boys intended someone to come across him and take him to the nearest police station, it was a perfect spot in which the rest of the day's horrors could play out.

10

When Thomas Lynley pulled up to the kiosk at New Scotland Yard the next morning, he began the process of steeling himself. The constable in charge stepped forward, not recognising the car. When he saw Lynley inside it, he hesitated before bending to the lowered window and saying huskily, 'Inspector. Sir. It's very good to have you back.'

Lynley wanted to say that he wasn't back. But instead he nodded. He understood then what he should have understood before: that people were going to react to his appearance at the Yard and that he was going to have to react to their reacting. So he readied himself for his next encounter. He parked and went up to a set of offices in Victoria Block as familiar to him as his own home.

Dorothea Harriman saw him first. It had been five months since he'd encountered the departmental secretary, but neither time nor circumstances were ever likely to alter her. She was, as always, kitted out to perfection, today in a red pencil skirt and breezy blouse, a wide belt cinching in a waist that would have made a Victorian gentleman swoon. She was standing at a filing cabinet with her back to him, and when she turned and saw him, her eyes filled and she set a file on her desk and clasped both her hands at her throat.

She said, 'Oh, Detective Inspector Lynley. Oh my God, how wonderful. It couldn't *possibly* be better to see you.'

Lynley didn't think he could live through more than one greeting such as this, so he said as if he'd never been gone, 'Dee. You look well today. Are they . . . ?' and he indicated with a nod towards the superintendent's office.

She told him that they were gathered in the incident room

and did he want a coffee? Tea? A croissant? Toast? They'd recently started offering muffins in the canteen and it was no trouble—

He was fine, he told her. He'd had breakfast. She wasn't to bother. He managed a smile and set off for the incident room, but he could feel her eyes on him and he knew he was going to have to get used to it: people assessing him, considering what they should say or not say, unsure how soon or even whether to mention her name. It was, he knew, the way of all people as they navigated the waters of someone else's grief.

In the incident room, it was much the same. When he opened the door and walked in, the stunned silence that fell upon the group told him that Acting Superintendent Ardery hadn't mentioned he'd be joining them. She was standing to one side of a set of china boards on which photos were posted and officers' actions were listed. She saw him and said casually, 'Ah. Thomas. Good morning,' and then to the others, 'I've asked Inspector Lynley to come back on board and I hope his return is going to be a permanent one. Meanwhile, he's kindly agreed to help me learn the ropes round here. I trust no one has a problem with that?' The way she spoke sent the message clearly: Lynley was going to be her subordinate and if anyone *did* have a problem with that, the relevant anyone could request reassignment.

Lynley's gaze took them in, his longtime colleagues, his longtime friends. They welcomed him in their various ways: Winston Nkata with blazing warmth on his dark features, Philip Hale with a wink and a smile, John Stewart with the guarded expectancy of one who knows there's more here than meets the eye, and Barbara Havers with confusion. Her face showed the question that he knew she wanted to ask him: Why didn't you tell me yesterday? He didn't know how he could explain. Of everyone at the Yard, she was closest to him and thus she was the last person to whom he could comfortably speak. She wouldn't understand this, and he didn't yet possess the words to tell her.

Isabelle Ardery continued the meeting that they had been

having. Lynley took out his reading glasses and worked his way closer to the china board upon which the victim's photographs were displayed, in life and in death, including grisly autopsy photos. An e-fit of a person of interest was situated near the pictures of the murder site, and next to this was a close-up of what appeared to be some sort of carved stone. This was an enlargement: the stone was reddish and square and it had the look of an amulet.

'. . . in the victim's pocket,' Ardery was saying in apparent reference to this photograph. 'It looks like something from a man's ring, considering the size and the shape of it, and you can see it's been carved although the carving itself is quite worn. It's with forensics just now. As to the weapon, SO7 are telling us the wound suggests something capable of piercing to a depth of eight or nine inches. That's all they know. There was rust left in the wound as well.'

'Plenty of that on the site,' Winston Nkata pointed out. 'Old chapel, locked off with iron bars . . . Has to be a mountain of clobber round that place could be used for a weapon.'

'Which takes us to the possibility that this was a crime of opportunity,' Ardery said.

'No handbag with her,' Philip Hale said. 'No identification on her. And she'd've had to have something to get up to Stoke Newington. Money, travel card, something. Could've started with bag snatching.'

'Indeed. So we need to put our hands on that bag of hers, if she had one,' Ardery said. 'In the meantime, we've got two very good leads from the porn magazine left near the body.'

Called *Girlicious*, it was the type of magazine that was delivered to the point of sale encased in opaque black plastic, due to the sensitive – and here Ardery rolled her eyes – nature of its contents. This plastic served the purpose of preventing innocent children from pawing through it to have a look at the various pudenda on display. It also served the less obvious purpose of preventing the fingerprints of anyone other than the purchaser to be placed upon it. Now, they had a very good set of dabs to use in the investigation, but better than that, they had a shop receipt tucked within the pages, as if used as a marker. If this shop receipt was the point of purchase of the magazine – and it likely was – then there was a very good chance they were on the trail of whatever sod had bought it.

'He might or might not be our killer. He might or might not be this person—' She indicated the e-fit. 'But the magazine was fresh. It hadn't been there long. And we want to talk to whoever took it into that chapel's annex. So . . .'

She began the assignments. They knew the drill: T.I.E first. The known associates of Jemima Hastings had to be interviewed: at Covent Garden where she was employed, at her lodgings in Putney, at any other place she frequented, at the Portrait Gallery where she had been present for the opening of the exhibition in which her picture hung. All of them would need alibis which would have to be checked out. Her belongings had to be gone through as well, and there were boxes upon boxes of them from her lodgings. An ever-widening search of the area near the cemetery had to be made to attempt to locate her bag, the weapon, or *anything* related to her journey across London to Stoke Newington.

Ardery finished making the assignments. She concluded these with the fact that Detective Sergeant Havers would track down a woman called Yolanda the Psychic.

'Yolanda the *what*?' was Havers' response.

Ardery ignored her. They'd had a phone call from Bella McHaggis, she said, Jemima Hastings' landlady in Putney. A Yolanda the Psychic needed to be looked into. It seemed she'd been stalking Jemima – 'Bella's word, not mine' – so they needed to find her and give her a grilling. 'I trust you have no difficulty with that, Sergeant?'

Havers shrugged. She glanced at Lynley. He knew what her expectation was. So, apparently, did Isabelle Ardery because she announced to everyone, 'Inspector Lynley will work with me for the time being. DS Nkata, you'll be partnered with Barbara.'

*   *   *

Isabelle Ardery handed Lynley the keys to her car. She told him where it was, said she'd meet him down below after she popped into the Ladies, and then she popped into the Ladies. She peed and downed her vodka simultaneously, but the vodka went down a bit too fast for her liking, and she was glad she'd brought the other bottle. So as she flushed the toilet she downed the second one. She tucked both bottles back into her bag. She made sure they kept their distance from each other, each one nicely wrapped in a tissue, for it wouldn't do to go clinking and clanking about like a half-slewed tart with more where that came from. Especially, she thought, since there *wasn't* more where that came from unless she stopped off at a convenient off-licence, which she was highly unlikely to do in the company of Thomas Lynley.

She'd said, 'You and I will take on Covent Garden,' and neither he nor anyone else had questioned her in the matter. She intended to remain close to *any* operation if she got the superintendent's position, and, as far as everyone was concerned, Lynley was there to help her learn the ropes. Having him take her out and about would serve to reinforce the point that she had his support. For her part, she wanted to get to know the man. Whether he realised it, he was the competition in more ways than one, and she meant to disarm him in more ways than one.

She paused at the line of basins to wash, and she used the time also to smooth her hair and tuck it neatly behind her ears, to fish her sunglasses out of her bag and to put on fresh lipstick. She chewed two breath mints and placed a Listerine strip on her tongue for good measure. She went down to the car park where she found Lynley standing alongside her Toyota.

Ever the gentleman he opened the passenger door for her. She told him sharply not to do that again – 'We're not going on a date, Inspector,' – and they set off. He was a very good driver, she noted. From Victoria Street to the vicinity of Covent Garden, Lynley didn't look at anything other than the roadway, the pavements or the Toyota's mirrors, and he didn't bother to make conversation. That was fine with her. Driving with her former husband had always been torture for Isabelle, as Bob was prone to believing he could multi-task and the tasks he engaged in behind the wheel were disciplining the boys, arguing with her, driving and frequently having mobile phone conversations. They'd jumped more red lights, sped through more occupied zebra crossings and made right turns into more oncoming traffic than Isabelle cared to remember. Part of the pleasure of divorce had been the novel security of driving herself.

Covent Garden was no great distance from New Scotland Yard, but their route forced them to cope with the congestion in Parliament Square, which was always worse in the summer months. On this particular day, there was a heavy police presence in the vicinity, since a mass of protestors had gathered near St Margaret's Church and constables wearing bright yellow windcheaters were attempting to herd them in the direction of Victoria Tower Garden.

Things weren't much better in Whitehall, where traffic was stalled near Downing Street. But this turned out to be not because of another protest but rather due to a plethora of gawkers swarming the iron gates in anticipation of God only knew what. Thus, it was more than half an hour between the time Lynley turned the car from Broadway into Victoria Street and the time he managed to park in Long Acre with a police identification propped in the windscreen.

Covent Garden had long since morphed from the picturesque flower market of Eliza Doolittle fame to the commercial nightmare of globalisation run amok that it now was: largely devoted to anything that tourists might be willing to purchase and largely avoided by anyone of sense who lived in the locality. Day workers from the area doubtless used its pubs, restaurants and free-standing food stalls, but its myriad doorways were otherwise undarkened by London's citizenry, unless it was to make a purchase of that which could not easily be purchased elsewhere.

Such was the case with the tobacconist's, where, according to Barbara Havers' report, Sidney St James had first come upon Jemima Hastings. They found this establishment at the south end of the Courtyard Shops, and they wended their way to it through what seemed to be buskers of every shape and form: from individuals artfully posing as statues in Long Acre to magicians, unicycle-riding jugglers, one-man bands and one energetic air guitarist. These all vied for donations in virtually every space that was not otherwise occupied by a kiosk, a table, chairs and people milling about eating ice lollies, jacket potatoes and falafel. It was just the sort of place the boys would have adored, Isabelle thought. It was just the sort of place that made her want to run screaming for the nearest point of solitude, which was likely the church at the far southwest end of the square that Covent Garden comprised.

Things were marginally improved in the Courtyard Shops, most of which were moderately high end so the ubiquitous bands of teenagers and tourists in trainers elsewhere were absent here. The quality of busking was elevated as well. In a lower level courtyard that housed a restaurant with open air seating, a middle-aged violinist played to the orchestral accompaniment of a boom box.

A sign reading *Segar and Snuff Parlour* hung above the tobacconist's multi-paned front window, and near its door stood the traditional wooden figure of the Highlander in full kilted regalia, a flask of snuff in his hands. Printed chalk boards leaned against the door and beneath the window, and they advertised exclusive tobaccos and the shop's daily speciality, which today was the Larranaga Petit Corona.

Five people could not have fitted comfortably within the cigar shop, so tiny was it. Its air fragrant with the perfume of unsmoked tobacco, it comprised a single, old oak display case of pipe-and cigar-smoking paraphernalia, locked glass-fronted oak cabinets of cigars and a small back room devoted to dozens of glass canisters filled with tobacco and labelled with various scents and flavours. The paraphernalia display case also served as the shop's main counter, with an electronic scale, a till and another smaller locked cabinet of cigars standing atop it. Behind this counter, the shop assistant was completing a sale to a woman making a purchase of cigarillos. He called out, 'Be with you shortly, my dears,' in the sort of sing-song voice one might have expected from a fop of an earlier century. As it was, the voice was completely at odds with the age and appearance of the shop assistant. He looked no older than twenty-one and although he was dressed neatly in lightweight summer clothing, he had gauges in his ears and he'd apparently worn them long enough to have stretched his lobes to a skin-crawling size. During the ensuing conversation he had with Isabelle and Lynley, he continually poked his little finger through the holes. Isabelle found the behaviour so repellent that it made her feel rather faint.

'Now. Yes, yes, yes?' he sang out happily once his customer went on her way with her cigarillos. 'How may I help? Cigars? Cigarillos? Tobacco? Snuff? What will it be?'

'Conversation,' Isabelle told him. 'Police,' she added and showed her ID. Lynley did likewise.

'I'm all agog,' the young man said. He gave his name as J-a-y-s-o-n Druther. His father, he revealed, was the owner of the shop. As had been his grandfather and his grandfather's father before him. 'What we don't know about tobacco isn't worth knowing.' He himself was just beginning in the business, having insisted upon taking a degree in marketing before he 'joined the ranks of those who labour'. He wished to expand, but his father disagreed. 'Heaven forbid that we should invest in something not an absolute certainty,' he added with a dramatic shudder. 'Now . . .' He spread his hands – they were white and smooth, Isabelle noted, very likely the objects of weekly manicures – and he indicated he was ready for whatever they asked of him. Lynley stood slightly behind her, which allowed her to do the honours. She liked this.

'Jemima Hastings,' she began. 'I expect you know her, don't you?'

'Rather.' J-a-y-s-o-n extended the word into *raw* and *thur*, and he gave emphasis to the second syllable. He said he wouldn't mind having a word with dear Jemima, as she was the reason he was having to work 'all sorts of mad hours just now. Where *is* the wretched minx, by the way?'

The wretched minx was dead, Isabelle told him.

His jaw dropped open. His jaw snapped shut. 'Good *God*,' he said. 'Not a road accident? She wasn't hit by a car? Heavens, there's not been another terrorist attack, has there?'

'She's been murdered, Mr Druther,' Lynley said quietly. Jayson clocked his highbrow accent and fingered an earlobe in response.

'In Abney Park Cemetery,' Isabelle added. 'The papers have indicated a murder there. Do you read the papers, Mr Druther?'

'God no,' he said. 'No tabloids, no broadsheets and *definitely* no television or radio news. I vastly prefer to live in my own cloud cuckoo land. Anything else sends me into such depression that I can't get out of bed in the morning and the *only* thing that cheers me up is Mum's ginger biscuits. But if I eat them, I'm prone to weight gain, my clothes cease to fit, I must purchase anew, and . . . Surely, you get the idea, yes? Abney Park Cemetery? Where's Abney Park Cemetery?'

'North London.'

'North London?' He made it sound like Pluto. 'My *God*. What was she doing *there*? Was she mugged? Kidnapped? She wasn't . . . She wasn't *interfered* with, was she?'

Isabelle thought that having her jugular vein ripped open was fairly well interfered with, although she knew that wasn't what Jayson meant. She said, 'We'll leave it at *murdered* for the present. How well did you know Jemima?'

Not particularly well, as things developed. It seemed that Jayson had spoken to Jemima by phone but had actually only seen her twice since they shared no work hours and, truth to tell, nothing else either. He knew her more from these than from her actual person, he said. *These* turned out to be a small stack of postcards. Jayson drew them from a cubbyhole near the till, perhaps eight of them in all. They comprised the image that Deborah St James had taken of Jemima Hastings, undoubtedly sold like other images from the collection at the National Portrait Gallery's gift shop. Someone had printed *Have You Seen This Woman* in black marker pen on the front of each card. On the reverse side was a telephone number with *Please Phone* scrawled above it.

Paolo had brought them in for Jemima, Jayson revealed. He knew that much because on the days that he worked and Jemima did not, Paolo di Fazio stopped at the shop anyway if he'd found more cards. This particular set Paolo had delivered several days ago, although Jemima hadn't been there to receive them. Jayson reckoned she had been destroying them as they'd been delivered, since more than once he'd found their shredded remains in the rubbish on the days when he himself worked.

'I think it was some sort of ritual for her.'

Paolo di Fazio. He was one of the lodgers. Isabelle recalled the name from Barbara Havers' report of her conversation with Jemima Hastings' landlady. She said, 'Does Mr di Fazio work nearby?'

'He does. He's the mask man.'

'The masked man?' Isabelle asked. 'What on earth—'

'No, no. Not *masked*. Mask. He creates masks. He's got a stall over in the market hall. He's very good. He's done one of me, actually. They're a bit of a souvenir of . . . well, *more* than a souvenir, really. I think he has a bit of a *thing* for Jemima, if you ask me. I mean, why else would he be scurrying in and out of the shop with postcards he's collected for her?'

'Anyone else come looking for her? On her days off when you were here, that is?' Isabelle asked.

He shook his head. 'Nary a soul,' he told them. 'Only Paolo.'

'What about people she associated with, here at the market?'

'Oh, I wouldn't know them, dear heart, if there are any. There may be, of course, but as I've said, we worked on different days, so . . . ?' He shrugged. 'Paolo could tell you. If he will, that is.'

'Why wouldn't he? Is there something about Paolo we ought to know before we speak to him?'

'Gracious, no. I didn't mean to imply . . . Well, I did get the impression he watched her rather *closely*, if you know what I mean. He did *ask* about her, much like you. Did anyone stop in to the shop looking for her, asking about her, meeting her, waiting for her, that sort of thing . . .'

'How did she come to be working here?' Lynley asked the question, turning from an examination of the Cuban cigars in the large display case.

'Job Centre,' Jayson said. 'And I can't tell you which one because they're all computerised now, aren't they, so she could have come to us from Blackpool, for all I know. We advertised the job with the centre and in she came. Dad interviewed her and hired her on the spot.'

'We'll want to speak to him.'

'With Dad? Why? Heavens, you're not thinking . . .' Jayson laughed, then *whoopsed* and covered his mouth. He arranged his features into a suitably lugubrious expression. 'Sorry. I was just picturing Dad as a murderer. I expect that's why you want to speak with him, isn't it? To get his alibi? Isn't that what you do?'

'We do indeed. We'll need yours as well.'

'My alibi?' A hand pressed to his chest. 'I have no idea where Ashley Park is. And anyway, if Jemima was there and it was during shop hours that she was done in, then I would have been here.'

'It's Abney Park,' Isabelle informed him. 'North London. Stoke Newington, to be precise, Mr Druther.'

'Wher*ev*er. I would have been here. From half past nine until half past six. Until eight if we're talking about a Wednesday. *Are* we? Because as I told you in the beginning, I don't read the papers and I've no idea—'

'Start,' Isabelle instructed.

'What?'

'The papers. Start reading the papers, Mr Druther. You'll be amazed what you can find inside them. Now tell us again where Paolo di Fazio might be found.'

He wondered if they were seraphim. There was something about them that marked them as different. They were not mortal. He could see that. The real question, then, was what type were they? Cherubim, Thrones, Dominions, Principalities? Good, bad, warrior, guardian? Archangels, even, like Raphael, Michael or Gabriel? Archangels that scholars and theologians as yet knew nothing of? Angels of the highest order, perhaps, come to make war with forces so evil that only a sword held in the hand of a creature of light could possibly defeat it?

He didn't know. He couldn't tell.

He'd assumed guardian about himself, but he'd been wrong. He saw that he was meant to be Michael's warrior, but *when* he saw it, it was far too late.

But watching over has power . . .

Watching over is nothing. Watching over is watching evil, and evil destroys.

Destruction destroys. Destruction begets more destruction. Learning is meant. Guarding means learning.

Guarding means fear.

Fear means hate. Fear means anger. Guarding means love.

Guarding means hiding.

Hiding means standing watch which means guarding which means love. I am meant to guard.

You are meant to kill. Warriors defeat. You are called upon to war. I call upon you. Legions upon legions call upon you.

I guarded. I guard.

You killed.

He wanted to strike his mind where the voices were. They were louder today than they'd ever been, louder than shouting, louder than music. He could *see* the voices as well as hear them, and they filled his vision so that he finally made out the wings. They were hidden angels but their wings betrayed them, and they watched him and bore witness from above. They lined up one right next to the other with their mouths opening and their mouths closing and celestial singing should have come from those mouths but what came instead was wind. There was a howling upon it and after the wind came the voices that he knew but would not listen to so he gave himself to the warriors and the guardians and their determination to win him to causes so unlike himself.

He squeezed his eyes shut but still he saw them and still he heard them and still he kept on and on and on till the perspiration wetted his cheeks till he realised it was not perspiration but tears, and then the sound of *bravo* coming from somewhere but not from the angels this time, for they were gone and then so was he. He was stumbling, climbing, making his way to the churchyard and then to the quiet that was not quiet at all for there *was* no quiet, not for him.

Lynley wasn't bothered by the part he was playing in the investigation: something between chauffeur and dogsbody to Isabelle Ardery. The role allowed him to ease his way back into police work, and if he was going to return to police work, it definitely had to be a gradual movement.

'Bit of a wanker,' was Ardery's assessment of Jayson Druther once they left the tobacco shop.

Lynley couldn't disagree. He indicated the route they needed to take to get to Jubilee Market Hall, across the cobbles from the main area of Covent Garden.

Inside the hall, the noise was ear-popping, coming from hawkers, from boom boxes set within the stalls, from shouted conversations and from buyers attempting to broker deals with sellers of everything from souvenir T-shirts to works of art. They found the mask maker's stall after elbowing their way up and down three aisles. He had a good position near a far doorway, making him either the first or the last stall one came to but in any case a stall one would unquestionably see, for it sat at an angle with nothing on either side of it. It was large as well, larger than most, and this was due to the fact that the mask making itself appeared to go on within it. A stool for the artist's subject sat beneath a tall light, and next to it a table held bags of plaster and several other containers. Unfortunately, what the stall did not hold at the present moment was the artist himself although the heavy plastic sheeting that formed its rear wall bore photographs of the masks he produced along with their subjects posed next to them.

A sign on a makeshift counter indicated the time when the artist would return. Ardery glanced at this and then at her watch, after which she said to Lynley, 'Let's have some refreshment.'

They sought said refreshment back the way they'd come, down below the tobacconist in the courtyard. The violinist who'd played there earlier was gone, and it was just as well, because Ardery apparently wanted conversation along with her refreshment. This turned out to be a glass of wine, at which Lynley lifted an eyebrow.

She saw this. 'I've no objection to a glass of wine on duty, Inspector Lynley. We deserve one after J-a-y-s-o-n. Please join me. I hate to feel like a lush.'

'I think I won't,' he said. 'I hit it rather hard after Helen died.'

'Ah. Yes. I expect you did.'

Lynley ordered mineral water to which Ardery lifted her own eyebrow. She said to him, 'Not even a soft drink? Are you always this virtuous, Thomas?'

'Only when I want to impress.'

'And do you?'

'Want to impress you? Don't we all? If you're to be the guv then it serves the rest of us to begin jockeying for positions of prominence, doesn't it?'

'I have serious doubts that you've spent much time jockeying for any position.'

'Unlike yourself? You're climbing quickly.'

'That's what I do.' She looked round the courtyard in which they sat. It wasn't as crowded as the area above them since here there was only the restaurant cum wine bar at the base of a wide stairway. But every table was taken. They'd been lucky to find a spot to sit. 'God, what a mass of humanity,' she said. 'Why d'you reckon people come to places like these?'

'Associations,' he said. She turned back to him. He fingered a crockery bowl holding cubes of sugar, rotating it in his fingers as he went on. 'History, art, literature. The opportunity to imagine. Perhaps a revisiting of a place from childhood. All sorts of reasons.'

'But not to buy T-shirts saying "Mind the gap?"'

'An unfortunate by-product of rampant capitalism.'

She smiled at this. 'You can be mildly amusing.'

'So I've been told, generally with the stress on *mildly.*'

Their drinks arrived. He noticed that she took hers up with some alacrity. She apparently noticed him noticing. 'I'm trying to drown the memory of Jayson. It was the appalling earlobes.'

'An interesting stylistic choice,' he admitted. 'One wonders what the next fad will be now that bodily mutilation is in vogue.'

'Branding, I daresay. What did you make of him?'

'Aside from his earlobes? I'd say his alibi will be simple enough to confirm. The copies of receipts from the till will have the time of day printed on them—'

'Someone could have stood in for him in the shop, Thomas.'

'—and likely there's going to be a regular customer or two, not to mention another shopkeeper hereabouts, who'll be able to confirm he was here. I don't see him as likely to tear open someone's jugular, do you?'

'Admittedly, no. Paolo di Fazio?'

'Or whoever might be at the other end of the postcards. That was a mobile number on it.'

Isabelle reached for her handbag and brought the postcards out. Jayson had given them over with a 'happy to be rid of them, darling,' at her request. She said to Lynley, 'They make things interesting,' and then observing him, 'which brings us to Sergeant Havers.'

'Speaking of interesting,' he noted wryly.

'Have you been happy working with her?'

'I have been, very.'

'Despite her . . .' Ardery seemed to search for a word.

He supplied her with several. 'Recalcitrance? Obstinate refusal to toe the line? Lack of finesse? Intriguing personal habits?'

Ardery brought her wine to her lips, and she examined him over the glass rim as she drank. 'You're rather oddly paired. One wouldn't expect it. I think you know what I mean. I do know she's had professional difficulties. I've read her personnel file.'

'Just hers?'

'Of course not. I've read everyone's. Yours as well. I mean to get this job, Thomas. I mean to have a team that works like a well-oiled machine. If Sergeant Havers turns out to be a loose screw in the works, I'm going to get rid of her.'

'Is that why you're advising change?'

She frowned. 'Change?'

'Barbara's clothing. The makeup. I expect to see her with her teeth repaired and sporting a designer hairdo next.'

'It doesn't hurt a woman to look her best. I'd advise a man on my team to do something about his appearance if he came in looking like Barbara Havers. As it happens, she's the only one who comes to work looking like she's slept rough the night before. Hasn't anyone ever spoken to her before? Didn't Superintendent Webberly? Didn't you?'

'She is who she is,' Lynley said. 'Good mind and big heart.'

'You like her.'

'I can't work with people I don't like, guv.'

'In private conversation, it's Isabelle,' she said.

His eyes met hers. He saw hers were brown, as his were, but not uniformly so. They were richly speckled with hazel and he reckoned that if she wore different colours from what she had on at present – a cream-coloured blouse beneath a well-tailored russet jacket – they might even appear green. He shifted his gaze and took in their surroundings. He said, 'This is hardly private, is it?'

'I think you know what I mean.' She glanced at her watch. She still had half a glass of wine left and before she stood, she tossed the rest of it down. 'Let's find Paolo di Fazio,' she told him. 'He should be back at his stall by now.'

He was. They found him in the midst of attempting to persuade a middle-aged couple to have masks made as souvenirs of their silver wedding anniversary trip to London. He'd brought forth his artistic instruments and laid them on the counter, and he'd set up a collection of sample masks as well. These were mounted on rods that themselves were fixed onto small plinths of finished wood. Fashioned from plaster of Paris, the masks were startlingly lifelike, similar to the death masks that had once been created from the corpses of people of significance.

'The perfect way for you to remember this visit to London,' di Fazio told the couple. 'So much more meaningful than a coffee mug with a Royal's face on it, eh?'

They couple hesitated. They said to each other, 'Should we . . . ?' and di Fazio waited for their decision. His expression was polite, and it didn't alter when they said they would have to think about it.

When they moved off, di Fazio gave his attention to Lynley and Ardery. 'Another fine-looking couple,' he said. 'Each of you has a face *made* for sculpture. Your children are, I expect, as handsome as you.'

Lynley heard Ardery snort with amusement. She showed her warrant card and said, 'Superintendent Isabelle Ardery. New Scotland Yard. This is DI Lynley.'

Unlike Jayson Druther, di Fazio knew at once why they were there. He took off the wire-framed spectacles he wore, began to polish them on the front of his shirt, and said, 'Jemima?'

'You know about what's happened to her, then.'

He returned the glasses to his face and ran a hand over longish dark hair. He was a good-looking man, Lynley saw, short and compact but with shoulders and chest suggesting that he worked with weights. Di Fazio said abruptly, 'Of course I know what's happened to Jemima. All of us know.'

'All? Jayson Druther had no idea what's happened to her.'

'He wouldn't,' di Fazio said. 'He's an idiot.'

'Did Jemima feel that way about him?'

'Jemima was good to people. She would never have said.'

'How did you learn of her death?' Lynley asked.

'Bella told me.' He added what Barbara's report had indicated: that he was one of the lodgers at the home of Bella McHaggis in Putney. In fact, he was the reason, he said, that Jemima had established a lodging place with Mrs McHaggis. He'd told her about a vacant room there not long after he'd met her.

'When was this?' Lynley asked.

'A week or two after she got to London. Some time last November.'

'And how did you meet her?' Isabelle asked.

'At the shop.' He went on to say that he rolled his own, and he bought both his tobacco and his papers from the cigar shop. 'Usually from that idiot, Jayson,' he added. '*Che pazzo.* But one day Jemima was there instead.'

'Italian, are you, Mr di Fazio?' Lynley asked.

Di Fazio took a rollie from the pocket of his shirt – he wore a crisp white shirt and a very clean pair of jeans – and he put it behind his ear. He said, 'With a name like di Fazio, that's an excellent deduction.'

'I think the inspector meant a native of Italy,' Isabelle said. 'Your English is perfect.'

'I've lived here since I was ten.'

'You were born . . . ?'

'In Palermo. Why? What does this have to do with Jemima? I came here legally, if that's what you're interested in, not that it matters much these days with the EU mess and people wandering between borders whenever they feel like it.'

Ardery, Lynley saw, indicated a change of direction with a slight lifting of her fingers from the countertop. She said, 'We understand you were collecting National Portrait Gallery postcards for Jemima. Had she asked you to do that, or was it your idea?'

'Why would it have been my idea?'

'Perhaps you can tell us.'

'It wasn't. I saw one of the cards in Leicester Square. I recognised it from the Portrait Gallery show – there's a banner out front and Jemima's picture's on it, if you haven't seen it – and I picked it up.'

'Where was the postcard?'

'I don't remember . . . near the half price ticket booth? Maybe near the Odeon? It was stuck up with Blu Tac and it had the message on it, so I took it down and gave it to her.'

'Did you phone the number on the back of the card?'

He shook his head. 'I didn't know who the hell it was or what he wanted.'

'"He,"' Lynley noted. 'So you knew it was a man who'd been distributing the cards.'

It was one of those *gotcha* moments, and di Fazio – clearly no fool – understood this. He took a few seconds before he answered. 'She told me her partner was likely doing it. Her *former* partner. A bloke from Hampshire. She knew from the phone number on the back of the card. She said she'd left him, but he hadn't taken it well and now, obviously, he was trying to find her. She didn't want to be found. She wanted to get the cards down before someone who knew where she was saw one and phoned him. So she collected them and I collected them. As many as we could find and whenever we had the chance.'

'Were you involved with her?' Lynley asked.

'She was my friend.'

'Beyond friendship. Were you involved with her or merely hoping to be involved with her?'

Again, di Fazio didn't reply at once. He was obviously no fool, so he knew that any way he answered could make him look bad. Yes, no, maybe, or whatever, there was always the sexual element between men and women to consider and what the sexual element could lead to by way of motive for murder.

'Mr di Fazio?' Ardery said. 'Is there something about the question you don't understand?'

He said abruptly, 'We were lovers for a time.'

'Ah,' Ardery said.

He looked irritated. 'This was before she came to live at Bella's. She had a wretched room up above Keira News, in Charing Cross Road. She was paying too much for it.'

'But that's where you and she . . . ?' Ardery let him complete the thought on his own. 'How long had you known her when you became lovers?'

He bristled. 'I don't know what that has to do with anything.'

Ardery said nothing in answer to this and neither did Lynley. Di Fazio finally spat out, 'A week. A few days. I don't know.'

'You don't know?' Ardery asked. 'Mr di Fazio, I have a feeling that—'

'I went in for tobacco. She was friendly, flirty, you know how it is. I asked her if she wanted to go for a drink after work. We went to that place on Long Acre . . . the pub . . . I don't know what it's called. It was packed, so we had a drink on the pavement with everyone else and then we left. We went to her room.'

'So you became lovers the day you met,' Ardery clarified.

'It happens.'

'And then you began to live together in Putney,' Lynley noted. 'With Bella McHaggis. At her home.'

'No.'

'No?'

'No.' Di Fazio took up his cigarette. He said if they were

going to talk further – and it was costing him in bloody customers, by the way – then they were going to have to do it outside where he at least could have a fag while they spoke.

Ardery told him it was absolutely fine to move outside, and he gathered up his tools and shoved them under the counter along with the sample masks on their wooden plinths. Lynley noted the tools – sharp and well-suited for activities other than sculpting – and knew Ardery had done likewise. They exchanged a glance and followed di Fazio out into the open air.

There he lit his roll-up and told Lynley and Ardery the rest. He'd thought they'd continue as lovers, he said, but he hadn't counted on Jemima's desire to follow the rules.

'No sex,' was how he put it. 'Bella doesn't allow it.'

'Opposed to the whole idea of sex, is she?' Lynley asked.

Sex among the lodgers, di Fazio told them. He'd tried to convince Jemima that they could continue as before with no one the wiser because Bella slept like the dead on the floor above them and Frazer Chaplin – this was the third lodger – had the basement room two floors below, so he wouldn't know what was going on either. The two of them – Jemima and di Fazio – occupied the only two bedrooms on the first floor of the house. There was no bloody way that Bella would find out.

'Jemima wouldn't have it,' di Fazio said. 'When she came to see the room, Bella told her straightaway that she'd tossed out the last lodger for getting involved with Frazer. Caught her coming out of Frazer's room early one morning and that was that. Jemima didn't want that to happen to her – decent lodgings are not easy to find – so she said no more sex. At first it was no sex at Bella's and then it was no sex altogether. It had got to be too much trouble, she said.'

'Too much trouble?' Ardery asked. 'Where were you having it?'

'Not in public,' he replied. 'And not in Abney Park Cemetery, if that's where you're heading. At my studio.' He shared space with three other artists, he said, in a railway arch near Clapham Junction. At first they went there – he and Jemima – but after a few weeks, she'd had enough. 'She said she didn't like the deception,' he said.

'And did you believe her?'

'I hardly had a choice. She said it was over. She made it over.'

'Rather like she'd done with the postcard bloke? According to what she told you?'

'Rather like,' he said.

Which gave them both a motive for murder, Lynley thought.

II

Yolanda the Psychic had an establishment in a market area just off Queensway in Bayswater. Barbara Havers and Winston Nkata found it without too much trouble once they unearthed the market itself, which they accessed by means of an unmarked entry between a tiny newsagent and one of the ubiquitous cheap luggage shops that seemed to pop up in every corner of London. The market was the sort of place one would walk right past without noticing: a low-ceilinged, ethnic-oriented, locals-only warren of passages in which Russian cafés vied with Asian bakeries, and shops selling hookahs sat next to kiosks blaring African music.

A question asked in the Russian café produced the information that there was within the environs of the market a location called Psychic Mews. There, Barbara and Nkata were told, Yolanda the Psychic operated and, considering the hour of the day, she was likely to be present.

A little more wandering brought them to Psychic Mews. This turned out to be what seemed like – but probably wasn't – an authentic old mews complete with cobbled street and buildings having the appearance of former stables, like all mewses in London. Unlike other mewses, however, it was under the protection of a roof as was the rest of the market. This afforded Psychic Mews an appropriate atmosphere of gloom, mystery and even danger. One expected, Barbara thought, Jack the Ripper to leap down from a rooftop at any moment.

Yolanda's business was one of three psychic sanctuaries in the place. Its single window – curtained for the privacy of clients within – bore a sill of accoutrements appropriate to her line of employment: a porcelain hand with its palm outward and all the lines upon it identified, a similar porcelain head with various parts of the skull indicated, an astrological chart, a deck of tarot cards. Only the crystal ball was missing.

'You believe this muck?' Barbara asked Nkata. 'Read your horoscope in the paper or anything?'

Winston examined his palm and compared it to the porcelain one in the window. ''Cording to this, I should've died last week,' he noted, and he shouldered open the door to the place. He had to duck to get inside, and Barbara followed him into an anteroom in which incense burned and sitar music played. Against a wall, the form of the elephant god was rendered in plaster and across from it, a crucifix hung above what seemed to be a kachina doll while an enormous Buddha on the floor appeared to serve the purpose of a doorstop. Yolanda looked to be someone who covered all the spiritual bases, Barbara concluded.

'Anyone here?' she called.

In reply a woman emerged from behind a beaded curtain. She wasn't dressed as Barbara expected. One somehow thought a psychic would be decked out in gypsy gear: all scarves, colourful skirts and heaps of gold necklaces with matching hoop earrings of massive size. But instead, the woman wore a business suit that Isabelle Ardery would have heartily approved of as it was tailored to fit her somewhat stout body and even to Barbara's unschooled eyes it seemed to announce itself with the words *French designer.* Her one bow to stereotype was her scarf, but even this she'd only folded into a band to hold back her hair. And instead of black, the hair was orange, a rather disturbing shade that suggested an unfortunate encounter with a bottle of peroxide.

'Are you Yolanda?' Barbara asked.

In reply, she put her hands to her ears. She clamped her eyes shut. 'Yes, yes, all right!' She had an odd, low voice. She sounded like a man. 'I bloody well *hear* you, don't I!'

'Sorry,' Barbara said although she hadn't spoken loudly at all. Psychics, she thought, must be sensitive to sound. 'I didn't mean—'

'I'll tell her! But you must stop roaring. I'm not deaf, you know.'

'I didn't think I was that loud.' Barbara dug out her ID. 'Scotland Yard,' she said.

Yolanda opened her eyes. She didn't cast even a glance in the direction of Barbara's warrant card. Rather she said, 'Quite a shouter, he is.'

'Who?'

'He says he's your dad. He says you're meant to—'

'He's dead,' Barbara told her.

'Of course he is. I could hardly hear him otherwise. I hear dead people.'

'Like in "I see dead people?"'

'Don't be clever. All right! All right! Don' be so loud! Your dad—'

'He wasn't a shouter. Not ever.'

'He is now, luv. He says you're meant to call on your mum. She's missing you.'

Barbara doubted that. Last time she'd seen her mother, the woman had believed she was looking at their long time neighbour Mrs Gustafson, and her resultant panic – in her final years at home she'd grown to fear Mrs Gustafson as if the old lady had somehow morphed into Lucifer – had not been assuaged by anything Barbara had attempted: from showing her identification to appealing to any of the other residents among whom Mrs Havers lived in a private care home in Greenford. Barbara had not yet been back. It had seemed, at the time, the course of wisdom.

'What shall I tell him?' Yolanda asked. And then with her hands over her ears once again, '*What*? Oh, of course I believe you!' And then to Barbara, 'James, yes? But he wasn't called that, was he?'

'Jimmy.' Barbara shifted uncomfortably on her feet. She looked at Winston who himself seemed to be anticipating an unwelcome message from someone in the great beyond. 'Tell him I'll go. Tomorrow. Whatever.'

'You mustn't lie to the spirit world.'

'Next week then.'

Yolanda closed her eyes. 'She says next week, James.' And then to Barbara, 'You can't manage sooner? He's quite insistent.'

'Tell him I'm on a case. He'll understand.'

Apparently he did, for once Yolanda communicated this matter into the spirit world, she breathed a sigh of relief and gave her attention to Winston. He had a magnificent aura, she told him. Well-developed, unusual, brilliant and evolved. Fan-tas-tic.

Nkata said politely, 'Ta,' and then, 'C'n we have a word, Miss—'

'Just Yolanda,' she said.

'No other name?' Barbara asked her. This would be for the record and all that. Because as this was a police matter . . . Yolanda would surely get the point, eh?

'Police? I'm legal,' Yolanda said. 'Licensed. Whatever you need.'

'I expect you are. We're not here to check your business details. So your full name is . . . ?'

It turned out – no surprise – that Yolanda was a pseudonym: Sharon Price not having quite the same cachet when it came to the psychic trade.

'Would that be Miss or Missus Price?' Nkata asked, having his notebook out and his mechanical pencil poised. It would be missus, she confirmed. Mister was a driver of one of London's black cabs and the children of mister and missus were both grown and flown.

'You're here because of *her*, aren't you?' Yolanda said shrewdly.

'You knew Jemima Hastings, then, yeah?' Nkata said.

Yolanda missed the tense of the verb. She said, 'Oh I know Jemima, yes. But I didn't mean Jemima. I meant *her*, that cow over Putney. She actually rang you, didn't she? She's got a nerve.'

They were all still standing in the anteroom, and Barbara

asked was there a place they could sit for a proper conversation? To this Yolanda waved them through the beaded curtain, where she had a set-up that walked a tightrope between analyst's office with a fainting sofa along one wall and a séance locale with a round table in the middle and a throne-like chair at 12 o'clock, obviously meant for the medium. Yolanda went for this and indicated Havers and Nkata were meant to sit at three and seven o'clock respectively. This had to do with Nkata's aura, evidently and with Barbara's lack of one.

'I'm a bit anxious about *you*,' Yolanda said to her.

'You and everyone else.' Barbara cast a glance at Nkata. He gave her a look of deep and utterly spurious concern over her apparent lack of aura. 'I'll see to you later,' she muttered under her breath, to which he stifled a smile.

'Oh I can see you're unbelievers,' Yolanda said in her strange, man's voice. She reached beneath the table then, whereupon Barbara half expected it to levitate. But instead the psychic brought forth the ostensible reason for her ruined vocal cords: a packet of Dunhills. She lit up and shoved the cigarettes towards Barbara, with the full knowledge, it seemed, that Barbara was a fellow in this matter. 'You're dying to,' she said. 'Go ahead,' and 'Sorry, luv,' to Winston. 'But not to worry. Passive smoking isn't how you're meant to go. More than that, however, and you'll have to pay me five quid.'

'Reckon I'd like to be surprised,' he responded.

'Suit yourself, dearie.' She inhaled with great pleasure and settled back into her throne for a proper natter. She said, 'I don't want her living in Putney. Well, not so much in Putney itself as with *her* and by *her* I s'pose I mean in her house.'

'You didn't want Jemima living in Mrs McHaggis's house?' Barbara said.

'Right.' Yolanda flicked ash onto the floor. This was covered by a Persian carpet, but she didn't seem concerned. She said, 'Houses of death need to be decontaminated. Sage burning in every room and believe you me it doesn't do just to wave it about as one runs through the place. *And* I'm not talking of the sage you get in the market, mind you. One doesn't buy a packet in Sainsbury's from the dried herb shelf and put a teaspoonful in an ashtray and light it and there you have it. Not by a bloody long chalk. One gets the real thing, bound up properly and meant to be burnt. One lights it and appropriate prayers are said. Spirits needing to be released are then released and the place is cleansed of death and only then is it wholesome enough for someone to resume a life within it.'

Winston, Barbara saw, was noting all this down as if with the intention of stopping off somewhere for the appropriate decontaminants. She said, 'Sorry, Mrs Price, but—'

'Yolanda, for God's sake.'

'Right. Yolanda. Are you referring to what's happened to Jemima Hastings?'

Yolanda looked confused. 'I'm referring,' she said, 'to the fact that she lives in a House of Death. Mc*Hag*gis – was ever a woman more appropriately named, I asked you – is a widow. Her husband died in the house.'

'Suspicious circumstances?'

Yolanda *hmmphed*. 'You'll have to ask McHaggis that. *I* can see contagion oozing out of the windows every time I go past. I've *told* Jemima she's meant to clear out of there. And all right, I admit it, I might have been rather insistent about it.'

'Which would be why the cops were phoned?' Barbara asked. 'Who phoned them? I ask because what we know is that you were warned off stalking Jemima at one point. Is our information—'

'That's an *interpretation*, isn't it?' Yolanda said. 'I've expressed my concern. It's grown, so I've expressed it again. P'rhaps I've been a bit . . . Oh, p'rhaps I took things to extremes, p'rhaps I did a bit of *lurking* outside the place, but what am I meant to do? Just let her *languish*? Every time I see her, it's shrunken more, and am I meant to stand by and let that happen? Say nothing about it?'

'"It's shrunken more."' Barbara repeated. '"It" being . . . ?'

'Her aura,' Nkata supplied helpfully, obviously on top of the situation.

'Yes,' Yolanda confirmed. 'When I first met Jemima, she glowed. Well, not like you, luv' – this to Nkata – 'but still more noticeably than most people.'

'How'd you meet her, then?' Barbara asked. Enough of auras, she decided, as Winston was beginning to look decidedly smug about his.

'At the ice rink. Well, not at the ice rink per se, naturally. More like *from* the ice rink. Abbott introduced us. We have coffee together sometimes in the café, Abbott and I. And I run into him in the shop as well. *He's* got something of a pleasant aura himself—'

'Right,' Barbara murmured.

'—and as he gets such grief from his wives – well, this would be his former wives, wouldn't it – I like to tell him not to worry so about that. A man can only do what a man can do, eh? And if he doesn't make enough to pay them all support, then he isn't to drive himself into the grave over it. He does what he can. He teaches, doesn't he? He walks dogs in the park. He tutors children in reading. What more can those three tarts expect from him?'

'What more indeed,' Barbara said.

'Who'd this bloke be?' Winston asked.

Abbott Langer, Yolanda told them. He was an instructor at the Queen's Ice and Bowl, which was just up the street from this market in which they sat.

It turned out that Jemima Hastings had been taking ice skating lessons from Abbott Langer and Yolanda had encountered the two of them having a post-lesson cup of coffee in the Russian café inside this very market. Abbott had introduced them. Yolanda admired Jemima's aura—

'Bet you did,' Barbara muttered.

—and she asked Jemima a few questions which stimulated conversation which in turn prompted Yolanda to hand over her business card. And that was that.

'She's come to see me three or four times,' Yolanda said.

'About what?'

Yolanda managed to draw in on her cigarette and look aghast simultaneously. 'I don't speak about my clients,' she said. 'This is confidential, what goes on in here.'

'We need a general idea . . . ?'

'Oh don't you just.' She blew out a thin stream of smoke. '*Generally* she's like all the rest. She wants to talk about a bloke. Well, don't they all? It's *always* about a bloke, eh? Will he? Won't he? Will they? Won't they? Should she? Shouldn't she? *My* concern, however, is that house she lives in but has she ever wanted to hear about that? Has she ever wanted to hear about where she *ought* to be living?'

'Where would that be?' Barbara asked.

'Not there, let me tell you. I see danger there. I've even offered her a place with my mister and me at a bargain rate. We've got two spare rooms *and* they've both been purified but she hasn't wanted to leave McHaggis. I admit I *might* have been a bit persistent about the matter. I *might* have stopped in to speak to her about it now and then. But that was only because she needs to get *out* of that place and what am I meant to do about that? Say nothing? Let the chips fall? Wait until whatever is going to happen happens?'

It came to Barbara that Yolanda had not caught on that Jemima was dead, which was rather curious since she was supposedly a psychic and here were the rozzers asking questions about one of her clients. On the one hand, Jemima's name had not been released to the media since they'd not yet tracked down her family. On the other hand, if Yolanda was in conversation with Barbara's own father, wouldn't Jemima's spirit be doing some serious shouting from the netherworld as well?

Barbara shot Nkata a look upon the consideration of her father. Had the louse actually tracked down Yolanda and phoned her in advance with pertinent details of Barbara's life? She wouldn't have put it past him. He *would* have his joke.

She said, 'Yolanda, before we go on, I think I need to clarify something: Jemima Hastings is dead. She was murdered four days ago in Abney Park Cemetery in Stoke Newington.'

Silence. And then, as if her bum were on fire, Yolanda shot up from her throne. It toppled backwards. She cast her cigarette to the carpet and ground it out – at least Barbara hoped she ground it out as she didn't fancy a fire – and she flung out her arms. She cried out as if in extremis, saying, 'I knew! I knew! Oh forgive me, Immortals!' And then she fell straight across the table, arms still extended. One hand reached towards Nkata and the other towards Barbara. When they didn't twig what she wanted, she slapped her palms against the table top and then turned her hands towards them. They were meant to clasp hers.

'She's here among us!' Yolanda cried. 'Oh tell me, beloved one. Who? *Who*?' She began to moan.

'Jesus on white bread.' Barbara looked at Winston, aghast. Were they meant to ring for help? Nine, nine, nine or whatever? Should they dash her with water? Was there sage anywhere handy?

'Dark as the night,' Yolanda whispered, her voice hoarser than before. 'He is dark as the night.'

Well, he would be, Barbara thought, if for no other reason than they *always* were.

'Attended by his partner the sun, he comes upon her. *Together* they do it. He was *not* alone. I see him. I *see* him. Oh my beloved!' And then she screamed. And then she fainted. Or she seemed to faint.

'Bloody hell.' Nkata whispered the words. He looked to Barbara for direction.

She wanted to tell him that *he* was the one with the brilliant aura, so he should damn well be able to sort out what to do. But instead, she got to her feet and he did likewise and together they righted Yolanda's throne, seated her, and got her head down between her knees.

When she came too, which happened with an alacrity

suggesting she'd not actually fainted in the first place, she moaned about McHaggis, the house, Jemima, Jemima's questions about him and does he love me, Yolanda, is he the one, Yolanda, should I give in and do what he asks, Yolanda. But aside from 'dark as the night that covers me', which to Barbara sounded suspiciously like a line from a verse, Yolanda was able to relay nothing else. She did say that Abbott Langer was likely to know more because Jemima had been quite regular about her skating lessons and he'd been impressed with her devotion to the ice.

'It's that house,' Yolanda said in summation. 'I tried to warn her about that house.'

Finding Abbott Langer was a simple matter. The Queen's Ice and Bowl was just up the street, as the psychic herself had said. As its name suggested, it combined the pleasures of ten-pin bowling and ice skating. It also offered a video arcade, a food bar and a noise level guaranteed to coax migraines from individuals previously immune to them. The noise came from all directions and comprised an utter cacophony of sounds: rock 'n' roll from the bowling area; shrieks, bleeps, bangs, buzzers and bells from the video arcade; dance music from the skating rink; shouts and screams from the skaters on the ice. Because of the time of year, the place was aswarm with children and their parents and with teenagers in need of a location in which to hang round, send text messages and otherwise look cool. Also, due to the ice, it was quite pleasant in the building itself, and this brought in more people off the street, if only to lower their body temperature.

Perhaps four dozen people were on the ice, most of them clinging to the handrails at the side. The music – what could be heard of it above the din – seemed designed to encourage smooth strokes of the feet, but it wasn't working very well. No one, Barbara noted, save the skating instructors, was keeping time. And there were three of these, obvious by the yellow waistcoats they were wearing, obvious by the fact that they were the only ones who seemed able to skate backwards, which looked to Barbara like an admirable feat.

She and Winston stood against the rail, watching the action for a moment. Several children among the skaters appeared to be taking lessons in an area in the middle of the ice reserved for them. They were being coached by a largish man with a helmet of hair that made him look like an Elvis impersonator. He was far bigger than one associated with ice skaters, well over six feet tall and built like a refrigerator: not at all fat, but solid. He was difficult not to notice, not only because of the hair but also because he was – despite his bulk – remarkably light on his feet. He turned out to be Abbott Langer, and he joined them briefly at the side of the rink when one of the other instructors went out to fetch him.

He had to complete the lesson he was giving, he said. They could wait for him here – 'Watch that little girl in pink . . . She's heading for the gold . . .' – or they could wait for him in the food bar.

They chose the food bar. Since it was past teatime and she'd not even had lunch, Barbara selected a ham salad sandwich, salt and vinegar crisps, a flapjack and a KitKat bar for herself, as well as a Coke to chase everything down. Winston – how could she possibly be surprised at this? – chose an orange juice.

She scowled at him. 'Anyone *ever* comment on your revolting personal habits?' she asked him.

He shook his head. 'Only on my aura,' he replied. 'That your dinner, is it, Barb?'

'Are you out of your mind? I've not yet had my lunch.'

Abbott Langer joined them as Barbara was finishing up her meal. He'd put protective covers on the blades of his ice skates. He had another lesson in half an hour, he said. What could he do for them?

Barbara said, 'We've come from Yolanda.'

'She's completely legitimate,' he said at once. 'Is this a reference? D'you mean to use her? Like on the telly?'

'Ah . . . no,' Barbara said.

'She sent us to have a word with you 'bout Jemima Hastings,' Winston said. 'She's dead, Mr Langer.'

'*Dead*? What happened? When did she die?'

'Few days ago. In Abney—'

His eyes widened. 'She's the woman in the cemetery? I saw it in the papers but there's been no name.'

'Won't be till we find her family,' Nkata said.

'Well, I can't help you with that. I don't know who they are.' He looked away from them, in the direction of the ice rink where a pile-up had occurred at the far end. Instructors were hurrying over to assist. 'God, but that's bad, isn't it?' He looked back to them. 'Murdered in a cemetery.'

'It is,' Barbara said.

'C'n you tell me how?'

Sorry. They could not. Regulations, police work, the rules of investigation. They'd come to the ice rink to gather information about Jemima. How long had he known her? How well did he know her? How did they meet?

Abbott thought about this. 'Valentine's Day. I remember because she brought in balloons for Frazer.' He watched Nkata writing in his notebook and added, 'He's the bloke who hands out the rental skates. Over by the lockers. Frazer Chaplin. I thought at first she was a delivery girl. You know? Making a delivery of Valentine balloons from Frazer's girlfriend? But turned out that she was the *new* girlfriend – or at least she was trying to be – and she'd dropped in to surprise him. We got introduced and we chatted a bit. She was quite keen on having lessons, so we made arrangements to meet. We had to work around her schedule, but that wasn't difficult. Well, I was happy to accommodate, wasn't I? I've got three ex-wives with four children among them, so I don't turn away paying customers.'

'You would have, otherwise?' Barbara asked.

'Turned her away? No, no. Well, I mean I *might* have done if my own circumstances had been different – what with the wives and the kids – but as she showed up regularly and right on time and as she always paid, I couldn't really quibble if her mind seemed on other things when she was here, could I?'

'What sorts of things? Do you know?'

He looked like a man about to say that he hated to speak ill of the dead, but then he eschewed that comment for, 'I expect it had to do with Frazer. I think the lessons were really an excuse to be near him, and that's why she couldn't keep her mind on what she was doing. See, Frazer's got something that attracts the ladies and when they're attracted, he doesn't exactly fight them off, if you know what I mean.'

'We don't, as it happens,' Barbara said. A lie, naturally, but they needed as many details as they could amass at this point.

'He makes the odd arrangement?' Abbott said delicately. 'Now and then? Don't misunderstand, it's always on the up and up as far as the ladies' *ages* go: no underage girls or anything. They turn in their skates and have a word with him, they slip him a card or a note or something, and . . . well, you know. He goes off for a bit with one or the other. Sometimes he phones in late to his night employment – he's a bartender at some posh hotel – and he takes a few hours with one of them. He's not a bad bloke, mind you. It's just how he is.'

'And Jemima had an idea this was going on?'

'A suspicion. Women aren't stupid, are they. But the trouble for Jemima was that Frazer's here for the earliest shift and she could only come in the evening or on her own days off work. So that leaves him free to be more or less available to ladies who want to flirt or to ladies who want more.'

'What was your own relationship with Jemima?' Barbara asked, for she realised that Yolanda's mutterings, as much as she wanted to discount them, could well apply to this man with his helmet of black hair, 'dark as the night'.

'Mine?' he asked, fingertips to his chest. 'Oh, I never get

involved with my skating students. That would be unethical. And anyway, I've three ex-wives and—'

'Four kids, yes,' Barbara said. 'But I expect a poke on the side wouldn't go amiss. If one was on offer and there were no strings.'

The ice skater flushed. 'I won't say I didn't notice she was attractive. She *was*,' he said. 'Unconventional, you know, with those eyes of hers. Bit on the small side, not much meat on her. But she had a real friendliness about her, not like the typical Londoner. I suspect a bloke could have taken that wrong if he wanted to.'

'You didn't, however?'

'As three times were *not* the charm for me, I wasn't about to go for a fourth. I've not had luck in marriage. Celibacy, I find, keeps me safe from involvement.'

'But groundwork laid, you could have had her, I expect,' Barbara pointed out. 'After all, a poke isn't marriage these days.'

'Groundwork or not, I wouldn't have tried it. A poke may not lead to marriage these days, but I had the feeling that wasn't the case for Jemima.'

'Are you saying she was after this Frazer for marriage?'

'I'm saying she wanted marriage full stop. I got the impression it could have been Frazer, but it could have been anyone else as well.'

The time of day was such that Frazer Chaplin was no longer at the Queen's Ice and Bowl, but this was not a problem. The name was an unusual one, and Barbara reckoned there couldn't be two Frazer Chaplins running round town. This had to be the same bloke who lived in Bella McHaggis's house, Barbara informed Nkata. They needed a word with him.

On their way across town, she put Winston in the picture with regard to Bella McHaggis's rules about fraternisation among her lodgers. If Jemima Hastings and Frazer Chaplin *had* been involved, their landlady either had not known it or had turned a blind eye for reasons of her own, which Barbara seriously doubted.

In Putney, they found Bella McHaggis just entering her property with a shopping trolley half filled with newspapers. As Nkata parked the car, Mrs McHaggis began unloading this trolley into one of the large plastic bins in her front garden. She was doing her bit for the environment, she informed them when they came through the gate. Bloody neighbours wouldn't recycle a damn thing if she didn't make an issue of it.

Barbara made an appropriate murmur of sympathy and then asked was Frazer Chaplin at home. 'This is DS Nkata,' she added by way of introduction.

'What d'you lot want with Frazer?' Bella said. 'It's Paolo you ought to be talking to. What I found I found in *his* cupboard, not Frazer's.'

'Beg your pardon?' Barbara asked. 'Look, could we go inside, Mrs McHaggis?'

'When I'm finished here,' Bella said. '*Some* things are important to *some* people, Miss.'

Barbara had an inclination to tell the woman that murder was definitely one of those things, but instead she rolled her eyes at Nkata as Bella McHaggis went back to unloading her trolley. When she'd accomplished this, she told them to follow her inside, and they'd not made it farther than the entry – with its lists of rules and its signs about the landlady's presence on the property – when Bella gave them an earful about her evidence and demanded to know why they hadn't dispatched someone at once to collect it:

'I rang that number, I did. The one in the *Daily Mail* asking for information. Well, I've got information, don't I, and you'd think they'd come and ask one or two of their questions about it. *And* you'd think they'd come on the run.'

She led them into the dining room, where the number of newspapers she had spread on the table suggested she was closely following the progress of the investigation. She said they were meant to sit there while she fetched what they wanted, and when Barbara pointed out that what they wanted was a word with Frazer Chaplin, she said, 'Oh, don't be such a ninny. He's a man but he isn't a *fool*, Sergeant. And have you done anything about that psychic? I rang the police about *her* as well. Hanging about outside my property again. There she was, large as life.'

'We've had a word with Yolanda,' Barbara said.

'Thank God for small mercies.' Bella seemed about to relent on the matter of Frazer Chaplin but then her face altered as she made the mental leap from what Barbara had just said to what Barbara and Winston Nkata wanted: a word with Frazer. She said, 'Why, that mad bloody cow. She's said something about Frazer, hasn't she? She's told you something that's brought you rushing over here and you mean to arrest him. Well, I'm not having that. Not with Paolo and his five engagements and his bringing Jemima here as a lodger and that argument of theirs. Just a friend, he tells me and she agrees and then look what happens.'

'Let me clarify that Yolanda said nothing about Frazer Chaplin,' Barbara said. 'We're coming at him from another angle. So if you'd fetch him? Because if he isn't here—'

'What other angle? There *is* no other angle. Oh, you wait right there and I'll prove it to you.'

She marched out of the dining room. They heard her go up the stairs. When she was gone, Winston looked at Barbara. 'Felt like I ought to salute or summick.'

'She's quite a character,' Barbara admitted. Then, 'Can you hear water running? Could Frazer be having a shower? His room's below us. The basement flat. She doesn't seem to want us to see him, does she?'

'Protecting him? Thinks she fancies him?'

'It fits with what Abbott Langer said about Frazer and the ladies, eh?'

Bella returned, a white envelope in her hand. With the triumphant air of a woman who'd out-Sherlocked the best of them, she told them to have a look at *that*. *That* turned out to be a thin spatulate finger of plastic with a slip of paper emerging from one end of it and a ridged area at the other. In the middle were two small windows, one round and one square. The centre of these was each coloured with a thin blue line, one horizontal and one vertical. Barbara had never seen one before – she'd hardly needed to – but she knew what she was looking at and so, apparently, did Winston.

'A pregnancy test,' Bella announced. 'And it *wasn't* among Jemima's belongings, was it? It was in Paolo's clobber. *Paolo's*. Well, I dare say Paolo's not testing himself, is he?'

'Likely not,' Barbara agreed. 'But how do you reckon this's Jemima's? I assume that's what you're thinking, eh?'

'It's obvious. They shared the bathroom and the toilet's in the bathroom. She either gave this to him' – with a jerk of her head towards the slip of paper – 'or, what's more likely, he saw it in the rubbish and fished it out, and that explains their quarrel. Oh, *he* said it was due to a misunderstanding about Jemima's hanging her smalls in the bath and *she* said it had to do with that male/female nonsense about leaving the toilet seat up, but let me tell you I had a feeling about them from the first. They were butter wouldn't melt and all the rest of it, *friends* from the workplace in Covent Garden. I happened to have a vacant room and *he* happened to know of someone who was looking and could he bring her, Mrs McHaggis? She seems a nice enough sort of girl, he says. And there I was, ready to believe the two of them while all the time they're sneaking round on the floor below me, going at it like monkeys behind my back. Well, let me tell you right now, if she wasn't dead, she'd be gone. Out. Finished. On her ear. On the pavement.'

Right where Yolanda wanted her, Barbara concluded. All well and good, but Yolanda would hardly have sneaked into the house and planted a pregnancy test in the bathroom on the slightest chance that Bella McHaggis would find it, jump to conclusions, and evict the one lodger that Yolanda wanted to get her mitts on. Or would she?

Barbara said, 'We'll take this into consideration.'

'You damn well will,' Bella said. 'It's motive loud and clear and make no mistake. Large as life. Right before your eyes.' She leaned across the table, her palm flat on the front of the *Daily Express*. 'He's been engaged five times, mind you. *Five* times and what does that say about him? Well, *I'll* tell *you* what it says. It says desperate. And desperate means a man who'll stop at nothing.'

'And you're talking about . . . ?'

'Paolo di Fazio. Who else?'

Anyone else, Barbara reckoned, and she could see Winston was thinking the same. She said Right yes, they would have a word with Paolo di Fazio.

'I should certainly hope you will. He's got himself a lock-up somewhere, a place where he does his sculpting. You ask me, he dragged that poor girl into that place and did his worst and dumped her body . . .'

Yes, yes, whatever. All of this would be checked out, Barbara assured her, nodding towards Winston to indicate that he'd been scrupulously taking notes. They'd be having a word with all of the lodgers, and that did include Paolo di Fazio. Now as to Frazer Chaplin—

'*Why* do you want to make this about Frazer?' Bella demanded.

Precisely because you don't, Barbara thought. She said, 'It's a matter of putting a full stop to every possibility. It's what we do.' It was part and parcel of the job. T.I.E. Trace, interview and eliminate.

As Barbara was speaking, the door leading down to the basement flat opened and shut and a man's pleasant voice called, 'I'm off then, Mrs McH.'

Winston got to his feet. He went out into the corridor that led towards the back of the house and said, 'Mr Chaplin? DS Winston Nkata. We'd like a word please.'

A moment. And then: 'Sh'll I ring Duke's and let them know? I'm expected at work in thirty minutes?'

'Won't take long, this,' Nkata told him.

Frazer followed Winston into the room, which gave Barbara her first close look at the man. *Dark as the night.* Yet another, she thought. Not that she intended to give credence to Yolanda's ravings. But still . . . He was a stone and he couldn't be left unturned.

He looked around thirty years old. His olive skin was pockmarked but that didn't detract, and while his shadowy stubble could have covered the scars if he'd grown them into a beard, he was wise not to have done so: he looked piratical and a little dangerous which, Barbara knew, some women found attractive.

He locked eyes with her, then gave her a nod. He was carrying a pair of shoes, and he sat at the table and put these shoes on, lacing them up and saying no thanks to Bella McHaggis's offer of tea. It was an offer that, pointedly, she did not make to the other two. Her attention to the man – she called him *luv* – in addition to what Abbott Langer had told them about his effect on women made Barbara want to suspect him on the spot. Which wasn't exactly good police work, but she had an automatic aversion to men like this bloke because he had one of those unmistakable I-know-what-you-want-and-I've-got-it-here-in-my-trousers expressions on his face. No matter the difference in their ages, if he was giving it to Bella on the side, no wonder she was besotted.

And she was. That much was clear, far beyond the *luv* and the *darling*. Bella looked upon Frazer with a fond expression that Barbara *might* have considered maternal had she not been a cop who'd seen just about every permutation of human entanglement in her years on the force.

'Mrs McH has told me about Jemima,' Frazer said, 'that she's the one from the cemetery. You'll be wanting to know what I know and I'm glad to tell you. I expect Paolo will feel likewise, as will everyone who knew her. She's a lovely girl.'

'Was,' Barbara said. 'As she's dead.'

'Sorry. Was.' He looked something between bland and

solemn, and Barbara wondered if he felt anything at all for the fact that his fellow lodger had been murdered. Somehow, she doubted it.

'We understand she had a bit of thing for you,' Barbara said. Winston did his part with the notebook and pencil, but he was watching Frazer's every move. 'Balloons at Valentine's Day and all the et ceteras?'

'What would those et ceteras be? Because as I see it, sure there's no crime in an innocent delivery of six balloons.'

Bella McHaggis's eyes narrowed at this mention of balloons. Her glance went from the police to her lodger. He said, 'Not to worry, Mrs McH. I said I'd not be making the same mistake twice, and you've got my word on it that I didn't.'

'What mistake would that be?' Barbara asked.

He moved to get more comfortable in his seat. He had a wide-legged posture when sitting, Barbara noted, one of those blokes who liked to show off the family jewels. 'I had a bit of a fling at one time with a lass who lived here,' he said. 'It was wrong, and I know it, and I did my penance. Mrs McH didn't toss me out on my ear as she otherwise might have done, for which I'm grateful. So I wasn't likely to go the wayward son route again.'

Considering what they'd heard from Abbott Langer – if he'd been speaking the truth – Barbara had her doubts about Frazer's sincerity in this matter. She said to him, 'I understand you work at more than one job, Mr Chaplin. Could you tell me where else you're employed besides the ice rink?'

'Why?' Bella McHaggis was the one to ask the question. 'What's that got to do with—'

'It's just procedure,' Barbara told her.

'What *sort* of procedure?' Bella demanded.

'It's nothing, Mrs McH,' Frazer said. 'They're just doing their jobs.' Frazer said that he worked late afternoons and evenings in Duke's Hotel in St James's. He was the bartender there and had been for the last three years.

'Industrious,' Barbara noted. 'Two jobs.'

'I'm saving,' he said. 'It's not a crime, I believe.'

'Saving for what?'

'How's *that* important?' Bella demanded. 'See here—'

'Everything's important till we know it's not,' Barbara told her. 'Mr Chaplin?'

'Emigration,' he said.

'To . . . ?'

'Auckland.'

'Why?'

'I've hopes to open a small hotel. A lovely little boutique hotel, as it happens.'

'Anyone helping you save?'

He frowned. 'What d'you mean?'

'Young lady, p'rhaps, contributing to your hotel fund, making plans, thinking she'll be included?'

'You're speaking of Jemima, I expect.'

'Why would you jump to that conclusion?'

'Because otherwise you'd not have the slightest interest.' He smiled and added, 'Unless you'd like to contribute yourself.'

'No thanks.'

'Alas. You join the score of other ladies who allow me to build my savings on my own. And that would include Jemima.' He slapped his thighs in a gesture of finality and rose from his chair. 'As you said this would take only a moment and as I've another job to go to . . .'

'You run along, luv,' Bella McHaggis told him. She added meaningfully, '*If* there's anything more to be dealt with here, I'll see to it.'

'Thanks, Mrs McH,' Frazer said, and he squeezed her shoulder.

Bella looked gratified at the moment of contact. Barbara reckoned that was part of the Frazer Effect. She said to both of them, 'Do stay in town. I have a feeling we're going to want to talk to you again.'

*   *   *

When they returned to Victoria Street, the afternoon debriefing had already begun. Barbara found herself looking for Lynley as she entered the room and then found herself irritated for doing so. She'd scarcely given her former partner a thought during the day, and she wanted it that way. Nonetheless, she clocked him on the far side of the room.

Lynley nodded at her and a smile lifted just the corners of his mouth. He looked at her over the top of his reading glasses and then back down at a sheaf of papers he was holding.

Isabelle Ardery was standing at the china board, listening to John Stewart's report. Stewart and the constables working with him had been given the unenviable task of dealing with the masses of material they'd taken from Jemima Hastings' lodgings. At the moment, the DI was talking about Rome. Ardery looked impatient, as if waiting for a salient point to emerge.

That didn't seem close to happening. Stewart was saying, 'The common denominator is the invasion. She's got plans from both the British Museum and the Museum of London and the rooms circled relate to the Romans: the invasion, the occupation, the fortresses, all the clobber they left behind. And she bought a mass of postcards from both museums and a book called *Roman Britain* as well.'

'But you said she'd also got a plan of the National Gallery and the Portrait Gallery,' Philip Hale pointed out. He'd been taking notes, and he referred to these. '*And* the Geffrye, the Tate Modern and the Wallace Collection. Looks to me like she was having a recce of London, John. Sightseeing.' Again, from his notes: 'Sir John Soane's house, Charles Dickens' house, Thomas Carlyle's house, Westminster Abbey, the Tower of London . . . She had brochures for all of them, right?'

'True, but if we want to find a connection—'

'The connection is that she was a tourist, John,' Isabelle Ardery said. She went on to tell them that SO7 had sent over a report, and there was good news on that front: the fibres on her clothing had been identified. They constituted a blend of cotton and rayon and they were yellow in colour.

They matched nothing that the girl herself was wearing, so there was a very good chance that they had yet another connection to her killer.

'Yellow?' Barbara said. 'Abbott Langer. Bloke at the ice rink. He wears a yellow waistcoat. All of the instructors do.' She told them about the ice skating lessons Jemima had been taking. 'Could be the fibres were left from a lesson.'

'We'll want that waistcoat, then,' Ardery said. 'His or someone else's. Get someone to fetch one for fabric testing.' She went on with, 'We've also had a curious description phoned in as a result of all the publicity. It seems that a rather filthy man came out of Abney Park Cemetery in the window of time of Jemima Hastings' murder. He was seen by an elderly woman waiting for the bus at an entrance to the cemetery on Stoke Newington Church Street. She recalled him because, she said – and I spoke to her myself, by the way – he looked as if he'd been rolling in leaves, he had quite long hair, and he was either Japanese, Chinese, Vietnamese, or – as she put it – 'one of those Oriental types'. He was wearing black trousers, carrying some sort of case although she couldn't tell me what kind – she thought it might be a briefcase – and he had the rest of his clothing bundled up beneath his arm except for his jacket which he was wearing inside out. We've got someone with her trying to come up with an e-fit, and if we're lucky we'll get some hits on that once we release it. Sergeants Havers and Nkata . . . ?'

Nkata nodded at Barbara, letting her do the honours. Decent bloke, she thought, and she wondered how Winston had come to be so prescient and simultaneously so completely without ego.

She made their report: Yolanda the Psychic, a recap of Abbott Langer and ice skating lessons and the reason for the ice skating lessons, the balloons, the pregnancy test – 'turns out it was negative,' she said – Frazer Chaplin, and Paolo di Fazio. To this she added the argument overheard between Paolo di Fazio and the victim, Paolo's ostensible lock-up where he did his sculpting, Frazer's way with the ladies, Bella McHaggis's possible non-maternal interest in Frazer, Frazer's second job at Duke's Hotel and his plans to emigrate.

'Background checks on all of them,' Isabelle said at the conclusion of Barbara's remarks.

Barbara said, 'We'll get onto to that straightaway,' but Ardery said, 'No. I want you two – you and Sergeant Nkata – down in Hampshire. Philip, you and your people take the background checks.'

'Hampshire?' Barbara said. 'What's Hampshire—'

Ardery put them in the picture, giving them a summary of what they'd missed during the earlier part of the debriefing. She and DI Lynley, she said, had come up with these and 'You'll need to take one along with you to Hampshire'. She handed over a postcard, which Barbara saw was a smaller version of the National Portrait Gallery poster of Jemima Hastings. On the front of it Have You Seen This Woman? was printed in black marker along with an arrow indicating that the card was meant to be flipped over. On the reverse was a phone number, a mobile number by the look of it.

The number, Ardery told her, belonged to a bloke in Hampshire called Gordon Jossie. She and Sergeant Nkata were to go there and see what Mr Jossie had to say for himself. 'Pack a bag because I expect this might take more than one day,' she told them.

There were the usual hoots at this: remarks of 'Oohh, holiday time, you two,' and 'Mind you get separate rooms, Winnie,' to which Ardery said sharply, 'That'll do, you lot,' as Dorothea Harriman came into the room. She had a slip of paper in her hand, a telephone message by the look of it. She handed this to Ardery. The superintendent read it. She looked up, satisfaction playing across her face.

'We've got a name to attach to the first e-fit,' she announced, gesturing to the china board on which hung the e-fit generated from the two adolescents who'd stumbled on the body in the cemetery. 'One of the volunteers at the cemetery thinks it's a boy called Marlon Kay. Inspector Lynley and I will see about him. The rest of you . . . You've got your assignments. Any questions? No? All right, then.'

They would begin again in the morning, she told them. There were several looks of surprise exchanged: an evening off? *What* was she thinking?

No one questioned it, however, there being far too few gift horses in the midst of an investigation. The team began their preparations to depart as Ardery said, 'Thomas?' to Lynley, and 'a word in my office?'

Lynley nodded. Ardery left the incident room. He didn't follow at once, however. Instead, he went to the china board to have a look at the photographs assembled there, and Barbara took the opportunity to approach him. He'd put his reading glasses on again, and he was observing the aerial photographs and comparing them to the drawn diagram of the crime scene.

She said to his back, 'Didn't have a chance earlier . . .' and he turned round from the china board.

'Barbara,' he said, his form of greeting.

She gazed at him intently because she wanted to read him and what she wanted to read was the why and the how and what it all meant. She said, 'Glad to have you back, sir. I didn't say before.'

'Thank you.' He didn't add that it was good to be there, as someone else might have done. It wouldn't be good to be there, she reckoned. It would all be part of just soldiering on.

She said, 'I just wondered . . . How'd she manage it?'

What she wanted to know was what it really meant that he'd come back to the Met: what it meant about him, what it meant about her, what it meant about Isabelle Ardery, and what it meant about who had power and influence and who had nothing of the kind.

He said, 'The obvious. She wants the job.'

'And you're here to help her get it?'

'It just seemed like time. She came to see me at home.'

'Right. Well.' Barbara heaved her shoulder bag into position.

She wanted something more from him, but she couldn't bring herself to ask the question. 'Bit different, is all,' was what she came up with. 'I'm off, then. Like I said, it's good that you're—'

'Barbara.' His voice was grave. It was also bloody kind. He knew what she was thinking and feeling and he *always* had done, which she truly, really hated about the bloke. 'It doesn't matter,' he said.

'What?'

'This. It doesn't matter, actually.'

They had one of those duelling eyeball moments. He was good at reading, at anticipating, at understanding . . . at all those sodding interpersonal skills that made one person a good cop and another person the metaphorical bull knocking about among Mummy's antique Wedgwood.

'All right,' she said, 'yeah. Thanks.'

Another moment of locked eyes till someone said, 'Tommy, will you have a look . . . ?' and he turned from her. Philip Hale was approaching and that was just as well. Barbara took the opportunity to make herself scarce. But as she drove home, she wondered if he'd been speaking the truth about things not mattering. For the fact was that she didn't like it that her partner was working with Isabelle Ardery, although she didn't want to think about why this was the case.

12

The next morning it was largely because of what Barbara *didn't* want to think about that she went about packing a bag for her trip by making sure that not a single item she placed in it would have met with Isabelle Ardery's approval. This was a job that took little time and less thought, and she was just finishing when a knock on her door told her that Winston Nkata had arrived. He'd wisely suggested they take his car, as hers was notoriously unreliable and, besides, fitting his rangy frame into an ancient Mini would have created an excruciating ride for him.

She said, "S open,' and she lit up a fag because she knew she was going to need to toke up on the nicotine since Nkata was, she *also* knew, not about to let her foul the interior of his perfectly maintained Vauxhall with cigarette smoke, not to mention – horrors! – a microscopic bit of ash.

'Barbara Havers, you *know* you're meant to stop smoking,' Hadiyyah announced.

Barbara swung round from the daybed where she'd placed her holdall. She saw not only her little neighbour but Hadiyyah's father, both of them framed in the doorway of her cottage: Hadiyyah with her brown arms crossed and one foot stuck out, as if she was about to begin tapping it like an aggrieved schoolteacher faced with a recalcitrant pupil. Azhar stood behind her, three plastic food boxes stacked in his hands. He used them to gesture with as he smiled and said, 'From last night, Barbara. We decided the chicken *jalfrezi* was one of my better attempts and as Hadiyyah herself made the *chapatis* . . . Perhaps for your own dinner tonight?'

'Brilliant,' Barbara said, 'definitely better than the jar of

Bolognese with cheddar on toast, which was what I'd had planned.'

'*Bar*bara . . .' Hadiyyah's voice was saintly, even in nutritional remonstration.

'Except . . .' Barbara asked would it keep in the fridge as she was actually heading off for a day or so. Before she could explain matters further, Hadiyyah cried out in horror and dashed across the room, where she scooted behind the television set and picked up what Barbara had mindlessly hurled there. 'What've you done with your nice A-line skirt?' she demanded, shaking it out. 'Barbara, why're you not *wearing* it? Why's it behind the telly? Oh look! It's got *slut's wool* all over it now.'

Barbara winced. She tried to play for time by taking the plastic containers from Azhar and stowing them into her fridge without allowing him to see its interior condition, which looked rather like an experiment in creating a new life form. She drew in on her cigarette and kept it clamped between her lips as she managed this manoeuvre, inadvertently spilling ash onto her T-shirt, which asked the world *How many frogs does one girl have to kiss?* She brushed it off, making a smear, swore quietly, and faced the fact that she was going to have to answer at least one of Hadiyyah's questions.

'Got to have it altered,' she told the little girl. 'Bit overlong, which is what we decided when I tried it on, remember? You said it needed to be middle of the knee, and it's definitely not that. Dangling round my legs in a bloody unattractive fashion, it is.'

'But why's it behind the *telly*?' Hadiyyah asked, not illogically. ''Cause if you mean to have it altered—'

'Oh. That.' Barbara did one or two mental gymnastics and came up with, 'I'll forget to do it if I put it in the wardrobe. But there, behind the telly? Turn the telly on and what do I see? That skirt reminding me it needs making shorter.'

Hadiyyah didn't look convinced, and she carried on, 'What about the makeup? You're not wearing your makeup today either, are you, Barbara? I c'n *help* you with it, you know. I used to watch Mummy all the time. She wears makeup. Mummy wears all sorts of makeup, doesn't she, Dad? Barbara, d'you know that Mummy—'

'That will do, *khushi*,' Azhar told his daughter.

'But I was only going to say—'

'Barbara is busy as you can see. And you and I have an Urdu lesson to go to, do we not?' He said to Barbara, 'As I have only one lecture at the university today, we were going to invite you to come with us after Hadiyyah's lesson. A canal trip to Regent's Park for an ice cream. But it seems . . .' He gestured at Barbara's holdall, still unzipped upon her bed.

'Hampshire,' she said, and glimpsing Winston Nkata approaching from beyond the cottage door, which still stood open, 'and here's my date.'

Nkata had to duck to enter the cottage and when he was inside, he seemed to fill the place. Like her, he was wearing something more comfortable than his usual get-up. Unlike her, he still managed to look professional. But then, his sartorial mentor was Thomas Lynley, and Barbara couldn't imagine Lynley ever looking anything but well put together. Nkata was in casual trousers and a pale green shirt. The trousers had creases that would have made a military man weep with joy, and he'd somehow managed to drive across London without getting a single wrinkle in his shirt. *How*, Barbara wondered, was that even possible?

Seeing him, Hadiyyah's eyes grew round and her face solemn. Nkata nodded a hello to her father and said to the little girl, 'I expect you're Hadiyyah, eh?'

'What happened to your face?' she asked him. 'You've got a scar.'

'*Khushi!*' Azhar sounded appalled. His face spoke of a rapid assessment being made of Barbara's visitor. 'Well brought up young ladies do not—'

'Knife fight,' Nkata told her in a friendly fashion. And he said to Azhar, 'It's okay, mon. Get asked all the time. Hard not to notice, innit, girl?' He squatted to give her a better look. 'One of us had a knife, see, and th' other had a razor. Now, thing is this: razor, she's fast and she does damage. But the knife? She's gonna win in the end.'

'Important piece of knowledge, that,' Barbara said. 'Very useful in gang warfare, Hadiyyah.'

'You're in a *gang*?' Hadiyyah asked as Nkata resumed his full height. She looked up at him, her expression awed.

'Was,' he said. 'Tha's where this came from.' And to Barbara, 'Ready? Want me to wait in the car?'

Barbara wondered why he asked the question and what he thought his immediate absence was meant to accomplish: a fond farewell between herself and her neighbour? What a ludicrous idea. She considered the reasons Winston might be thinking that and she took note of Azhar's expression, which spoke of a level of discomfort that she couldn't remember having ever seen in him.

She sifted through various possibilities suggested by three plastic containers of left-over dinner, Hadiyyah's Urdu lesson, a canal trip and Winston Nkata's appearance at her cottage, and she came up with something too stupid to consider in the light of day. She quickly rejected it, then went on to realise she'd referred to Winston as her date and that, in combination with her packing a bag, must have made Azhar – as proper as a Regency gentleman – think she was heading off for a few days in the country with her tall, nice-looking, well-built, athletic and likely delicious-in-all-the-right-ways lover. The very thought made her want to guffaw. Herself, Winston Nkata, candlelit dinners, wine, roses, romance and a few nights of bouncy-bounce in a hotel heavily hung with wisteria . . . She snorted and covered the snort with a cough.

She made a quick introduction between the two men, casually adding 'DS Nkata. We've got a case in Hampshire,' once she'd said Winston's full name. She turned to the daybed before Azhar responded, hearing Hadiyyah say, 'You're a police*man* as well? Like Barbara, you mean?'

'Just like,' Nkata said.

Barbara heaved her holdall to her shoulder as Hadiyyah said to her father, 'C'n *he* come on the canal boat as well, Dad?'

To which Azhar replied, 'Barbara herself said they're going to Hampshire, *khushi*.'

They left the cottage, all of them together. They set off towards the front of the house and Barbara heard Hadiyyah say, 'I forgot. About Hampshire, I mean. But if they weren't? What if they weren't, Dad? Could he come as well?'

Barbara couldn't hear Azhar's reply.

Lynley drove them once again in Isabelle's car. Once again, the arrangement seemed fine with him. He didn't attempt to hold the door open for her another time – he hadn't done so since she'd corrected him about this – and again he gave the driving his complete attention. She'd lost the plot on where in London they were just after Clerkenwell, so when her mobile phone rang as they were coursing by a nameless park, she took the call.

'Sandra wants to know do you want a visit.' It was Bob, speaking without preamble as usual. Isabelle cursed herself for not having examined the number of the incoming call although, knowing Bob, he likely would be ringing her from a phone she couldn't identify anyway. He liked to do that. Stealth was his main weapon.

She said, with a glance at Lynley, who wasn't paying attention to her, 'What d'you have in mind?'

'Sunday lunch. You could come out to Kent. The boys will be happy to—'

'With them, d'you mean? Alone? In a restaurant or something?'

'Obviously not,' he said. 'I was going to say that the boys will be happy to have you join us. Sandra'll do a joint of beef. Ginny and Kate actually have a birthday party to go to on Sunday so—'

'So it would be the five of us, then?'

'Well, yes. I can hardly ask Sandra to leave her own house, can I, Isabelle?'

'A hotel would be better. A restaurant. A pub. The boys could—'

'Not going to happen. Sunday lunch with us is the best offer I'll make.'

She said nothing. She watched what went for London scenery as they passed it: rubbish on the pavements; bleak storefronts with grimy plastic signs naming each establishment; women dressed in black bed sheets with slits for their eyes; sad-looking displays of fruit and veg outside greengrocers; William Hill betting shops . . . Where the hell *were* they?

'Isabelle? Are you there?' Bob asked. 'Is the connection—'

Yes, she thought. That's exactly it. The connection's broken. She closed her phone. When it rang again a moment later, she let her voicemail pick it up. Sunday lunch, she thought. She could picture it: Bob presiding over the joint of beef, Sandra simpering somewhere nearby – although truth to tell, Sandra didn't simper and she was a more than decent sort, for which Isabelle was grateful, all things considered – the twins scrubbed and shiny and perhaps just a little perplexed at this modern definition of *family* with Mummy, Dad and step-mum gathered round the dining table as if it happened every day of the week. Roast beef, Yorkshire pud and sprouts being handed round and everyone waiting for everyone else to be served and grace to be said by whoever said it because Isabelle didn't know and didn't want to know. She damn well *did* know that there was no way in bloody hell she was going to put herself through Sunday lunch at her former husband's house because he didn't mean well, he was out to punish her or to blackmail her further and she couldn't face that or face her boys.

You don't want to threaten me. You don't want this to go to court, Isabelle.

She said abruptly to Lynley, 'Where in God's name are we,

Thomas? How long did it take you to be able to find your way round this bloody place?'

A glance only. He was too well bred to mention the phone call.

He said, 'You'll sort it out faster than you think. Just avoid the underground.'

'I'm a *member* of the hoi polloi, Thomas.'

'I didn't mean it that way,' he said easily. 'I meant that the underground – the map of the underground, actually – bears no relation to the actual layout of the city. It's printed as it is to make it understandable. It shows things north, south, east, or west of each other when that might not necessarily be the case. So take the bus instead. Walk. Drive. It's not as impossible as it seems. You'll sort it out quickly enough.'

She doubted that. It wasn't that one area looked exactly like the next. On the contrary, one area was generally quite distinct from the next. The difficulty was in sussing out how they related to each other: why a landscape of dignified Georgian buildings should suddenly morph into an area of tenements. It simply made no sense.

When they came upon Stoke Newington, she was unprepared. There it was before her, recognisable by a flower shop that she remembered from her earlier journey, housed in a building with *Walker Bros Fount Pen Specialists* painted onto the bricks between its first and second floors. This would be Stoke Newington Church Street, so the cemetery was just up ahead. She congratulated herself on recalling that much. She said, 'The main entrance is on the High Street, to the left on the corner.'

That was where Lynley parked, and they went into the information office just outside the gates. There they explained their purpose to a wizened female volunteer, and Isabelle brought out the e-fit that had prompted the phone call to New Scotland Yard. This individual had not made the call – 'That would most likely have been Mr Fluendy,' she said, '*I'm* Mrs Littlejohn' – but she recognised the e-fit herself.

'I expect that's the boy does the carving, that is,' she said. 'I hope you lot are here to arrest him cos we been ringing the local coppers 'bout that carving since my granny was a girl, let me tell you. You come 'ere, you two. I'll show you what I'm talking about.'

She shooed them out of the information office, hung a sign on the door indicating for the nonexistent hordes of visitors that she'd return momentarily, and toddled into the cemetery. They followed. She took them to one of the trees that Isabelle had seen on her first visit to the place. Its trunk was carved with an elaborate design of quarter moon and stars with clouds obscuring part of the latter. The carving went down to the trunk of the tree, entirely baring it of bark. It was not the sort of thing one could have done quickly or easily. The carving measured at least four feet high and took up perhaps two feet of the tree's circumference. Defacing the tree aside, it was actually quite good.

'He's done this everywhere,' the woman declared. 'We been trying to catch him at it, but he lives over Listria Park, he does, and that backs onto the cemetery. I 'spect he just comes over the wall, so we never know he's here. Easy as pie when you're young, eh?'

Listria Park was not, as Isabelle had first supposed, an actual park. It was instead a street comprising a curve of buildings that had once been individual homes but now were flats with windows overlooking Abney Park Cemetery and gardens over the wall from it, as Mrs Littlejohn had described. It took some doing to find the building in which Marlon Kay lived, but once they'd done so, they discovered themselves in luck as the boy was at home. So was his father, and it was apparently this individual whose disembodied voice replied when they rang the buzzer next to the name D.W. Kay.

He barked out, 'Yeah? Wha' you want?'

Isabelle nodded at Lynley, who did the honours. 'Metropolitan police. We're looking for—'

Even through the crackling connection from the street to the flat, they could hear the commotion Lynley's words provoked: a crash of furniture, a pounding of feet, a 'Wha' the *bloody* hell . . . Where you think you're . . . Wha'd you *do*?' And then the buzzer went to open the door, and they pushed their way inside.

They headed for the stairs just as a heavyset boy came storming down. He ploughed his way towards them, wild-eyed and sweating, making for the door to the street. It was an easy matter for Lynley to stop him. One arm did that much. The other secured him.

'Lemme go!' the boy shrieked. 'He'll murder me, he will!' while above a man roared, 'Get your bum back up 'ere, rotten little lout.'

Little was hardly an accurate adjective. While the boy wasn't obese, he was still a sterling example of modern youth's proclivity for victuals deep fried, fast and loaded with various kinds of fats and sugars.

'Marlon Kay?' Isabelle said to the struggling youth being detained by Lynley's grip upon him.

'Let me go!' he screamed. 'He'll beat me bloody. You don' unnerstan!'

D.W. Kay came hurtling down the stairs at that point, cricket bat in his hands. He was swinging this wildly as he shouted, 'Wha'd you fooking *do*? You fooking better tell me 'fore these coppers do or I'll smack your head from here to Wales and make no mistake!'

Isabelle put herself squarely in his path. She said sharply, 'That will do, Mr Kay. Put that cricket bat down before I have you in the nick for assault.'

Perhaps it was her tone. It stopped the man in his tracks. He stood before her, breathing like a defeated race horse – with breath, however, that smelled like teeth decaying straight up to his brain. He blinked at her.

She said, 'I assume you *are* Mr Kay. And this is Marlon? We want a word with him.'

Marlon whimpered. He shrank back from his father. He said, 'He'll bash me, he will.'

'He'll do nothing of the sort,' Isabelle told the boy. 'Mr Kay, lead us up to your flat. I've no intention of having a discussion in the corridor.'

D.W. looked her up and down – she could tell he was the sort of man who had what pop psychologists would refer to as 'woman issues' – and then he looked at Lynley. His expression said that as far as *he* was concerned, Lynley wore lace panties if he let a woman give orders in his presence. Isabelle wanted to smack *him* into Wales. What century did he think they were living in? she wondered.

She said, 'Do I have to tell you again?' He snarled but co-operated. Back up the stairs he went, and the rest of them followed, Marlon cowering in Lynley's grip. A middle-aged woman in cycling gear was standing at the top of the first flight of stairs. She made a moue that combined dislike, distaste and disgust and said, 'About time, you ask me,' to Mr Kay. He shoved her out of the way and she said, 'Did you see that? Did you *see* that?' to Lynley, ignoring Isabelle altogether. Her cry of, 'Are you finally going to do something about him?' was the last they heard from her as they shut the door behind them.

Inside the flat, the windows were open, but as there was no cross ventilation, their gaping apertures did nothing to mitigate the temperature. The place itself was, remarkably, not a pig sty as Isabelle had been expecting. There was a suspicious white layer upon nearly everything, but this turned out to be plaster dust, as they discovered that D.W. Kay was a plasterer by trade, and he'd been setting out to work when they'd rung the buzzer.

Isabelle told him they needed a word with his son, and she asked Marlon how old he was. Marlon said sixteen, and he winced, as if anticipating that his age was cause for corporal punishment. Isabelle sighed. What his age *was* cause for was the presence of an adult who was not police, preferably a parent, which meant that they were going to have to question the boy either in the presence of his glowering and explosive father or with a social worker.

She looked at Lynley. Appropriately, his expression said it was her call as she was his superior. She said to the boy's father, 'We're going to have to question Marlon about the cemetery. I take it you know that there's been a murder there, Mr Kay?'

The man's face inflamed. His eyes bulged. He was, Isabelle thought, a massive stroke waiting to happen. She went on. 'We can question him here or at the local nick. If we do it here, you'll be required not only to keep quiet but also to keep your hands off this boy from now until eternity. If you do not, you'll be arrested at once. One phone call from him, from a neighbour, from anyone, and in you go. A week, a month, a year, ten years. I can't tell you what the judge will throw at you, but I can tell that what I just witnessed below is something that I will testify to. And I expect your neighbours will be happy to do likewise. Am I being clear or do you require further elucidation on this topic?'

He nodded. He shook his head. Isabelle assumed he was answering both questions and said, 'Very well. Sit down and keep quiet.'

He skulked to a grey sofa, which was part of a sad-looking three-piece suite of a sort Isabelle hadn't seen in years, complete with a tasselled fringe. He sat. Round him, plaster dust rose in a cloud. Lynley deposited Marlon in one of the two chairs and himself went to the window where he remained standing, resting against the sill.

Everything in the room faced a huge flat-screen television, which was featuring a cooking programme at the moment although the sound was muted. A remote lay beneath it, and Isabelle picked this up and switched the set off, which, for some reason, caused Marlon to whimper once again as if a lifeline had been cut. His father curled a lip at him. Isabelle shot him a look. The man rearranged his features. She nodded sharply and went to sit in the other armchair, dusty like everything else.

She told Marlon the bare facts: he'd been seen emerging

from the shelter next to the ruined chapel inside the cemetery. Within that shelter, a young woman's body had been found. A magazine with one person's fingerprints upon it had been dropped in the vicinity of that body. An e-fit had been generated by the persons who'd seen him coming out of that shelter, and should an identity parade be needed, there was little doubt that he'd be picked from it although because of his age, they'd likely use photographs and not require him to stand in a line. Did he want to talk about any of this?

The boy began to blub. His father rolled his eyes but said nothing.

'Marlon?' Isabelle prompted.

He snivelled and said, 'It's only cos I hate school. They bully me. It's cos my bum's like . . . It's big, innit, an' they make fun and it's allas been tha' way an' I *hate* it. So I won't go. I got to leave here, though, don't I, so I go there.'

'Into the cemetery rather than to school?'

'Tha's it, innit.'

'It's summer holidays,' Lynley pointed out.

'I'm talkin bout school time, innit,' Marlon said. '*Now* I go th' cemetery cos tha's what I do. Nuffink else round here and I don't got friends, do I.'

'So you go to the cemetery and you carve on the trees?' Isabelle said.

Marlon shifted round on his barrel of a bum. 'Di'n't *say*—'

'Have you wood carving tools?' Lynley said.

'I di'n't do nuffink to that tart! She was dead when I got there, wa'n't she.'

'So you did go into the shelter by the chapel?' Isabelle said to the boy. 'You admit you're the person our witnesses saw coming out of the shelter four days ago?'

The boy didn't confirm, but he didn't deny. Isabelle said, 'What were you doing there?'

'I do the trees,' he said. 'An' there's no harm in it. Makes 'em pretty is all.'

'I don't mean what were you doing in the cemetery,' Isabelle told him. 'I mean in the shelter. Why'd you go into the shelter?'

The boy swallowed. This was, it seemed, the crux of the matter. He looked at his father. His father looked away.

Marlon whispered, 'Magazine. It was . . . See, I bought it an' wanted to have a glance and . . .' He gazed at her desperately, casting a glance at Lynley as well. 'It was only tha' when I saw them pitchers in the magazine . . . them women . . . You know.'

'Marlon, are you trying to tell me you went into the shelter to masturbate over pictures of naked women?' Isabelle asked baldly.

He began to weep in earnest. His father said, 'Fooking *twat*,' and Isabelle shot him a look. Lynley said, 'That'll do, Mr Kay.'

Marlon hid his face in his hands, pinching his cheeks with his fingers, saying, 'I jus' wanted . . . So I went inside there to – you *know* – but there she was an' I got scared an' I run off. I could see she was dead, couldn't I. There was bugs an' things an' her eyes were open an' the flies were crawling . . . I *know* I shoulda done summat but I couldn't cos I . . . cos I . . . Cops would've asked what I was doing like you're askin now and I'd have to say like I'm sayin now and he *already* hates me and he would find out. I won't go to school. I won't go. I *won't*. But she was dead when I got there. She was dead. She was.'

He was likely speaking the truth, Isabelle reckoned, as she couldn't imagine the boy having the bottle to commit an act of violence. He seemed the least aggressive child she'd ever encountered. But even a boy such as Marlon could snap, and one way or another he needed to be eliminated as a suspect.

She said, 'All right, Marlon. I tend to think you might be telling the truth.'

'I am!'

'I'm going to ask you further questions, though, and you're going to need to be calmer. Can you manage that?'

His father blew a breath of air from his mouth. *Not bloody likely* would have been his words.

Marlon cast a fearful look at his father and then nodded, his eyes welling with more tears. But he wiped his cheeks – he somehow made this a heroic gesture – and he sat up straight.

Isabelle went through the questions. Did he touch the body? No, he did not. Did he remove *anything* from the site? No, he did not. How near did he get to the body? He didn't know. Three feet? Four? He took a step or two inside the shelter but that was all cos he saw her an' . . . Fine fine, Isabelle said, hoping to avoid another descent into hysteria. What happened then? He dropped the magazine and ran. He didn't mean to drop it. He didn't even *know* he'd dropped it. But when he saw he didn't have it with him, he was too scared to go back cos 'I never seen a dead person. Not like that.' He went on to say that she was all bloody down the front of her. Did he see a weapon? Isabelle asked him. He didn't even see where she was cut up, he told her. As far as he could tell, it looked to him like she was sliced up everywhere cos there was so much blood. Wouldn't a person have to be sliced up everywhere to have so much blood on 'em?

Isabelle redirected him, from inside the shelter to outside the shelter. True, it was at least a day after the killing itself when Marlon had come upon the body as things turned out, but whomever he'd seen in the vicinity – whatever he'd seen in the vicinity – could be important to the investigation.

But he'd seen nothing. And when it came to Jemima Hastings' handbag or anything else she might have possessed, the boy swore he'd not taken a thing. If she had a bag with her, he knew nothing of it. It might've been right there next to her, he avowed, and he wouldn't've even known it was there cos all he saw was *her*, he said. An' all that blood.

'But you didn't report this,' Isabelle said. 'The only report we had was from the young couple who saw *you*, Marlon. Why didn't you report it?'

'Them carvings,' he said. 'An' the magazine.'

'Ah.' Defacing public property, buying pornographic magazines, masturbating – or at least intending to do so – in public: these had been his considerations, as had no doubt been the displeasure of his father, and the fact that his father seemed to express that displeasure by means of a cricket bat. 'I see. Well, we're going to need a few things from you. Will you cooperate with us?'

He nodded vigorously. Cooperation? No problem.

They would need a sample of his DNA, which a swab from his mouth would happily provide. They would also require his shoes, his fingerprints, which would be easy enough to obtain. And his carving tools were going to have to be handed over for inspection by forensics. 'I expect,' Isabelle said, 'you've got any number of sharp objects among them? Yes? Well, we need to test them all, Marlon.'

The welling of eyes, the whimper, the father's impatient and bull-like breath.

'It's all to prove you're telling the truth,' she assured the boy. 'Are you, Marlon? Are you telling the truth?'

'Swear,' he said. 'Swear, swear, swear.'

Isabelle wanted to tell him that one swearing was enough, but she reckoned she'd be wasting her time.

As they walked back to the car, the superintendent asked Lynley what he was thinking. She said to him, 'Don't feel you have to keep silent in that sort of situation, you know.'

He glanced at her. Considering the heat of the day and their encounter with the Kays, she was managing to look remarkably collected: unruffled, professional, even cool in the blasting sun. Wisely, if unusually, she wore not a summer suit but a sleeveless dress, and Lynley realised it served more than one purpose in that it likely made her more comfortable at the same time as it made her less intimidating when she questioned people. People like Marlon, he thought, an adolescent boy whose trust she needed to garner.

He said, 'I didn't think you needed my—'

'Help?' She cut in sharply. 'That's not what I was implying, Thomas.'

Lynley looked at her again. 'Actually, I was going to say my participation,' he told her.

'Ah. Sorry.'

'You're prickly about it, then.'

'Not at all.' She fished in her bag and brought out a pair of dark glasses. Then she sighed and said, 'Well, that's not true. I *am* prickly. But one has to be, in our line of work. It's not easy for a woman.'

'Which part isn't easy? Navigating the corridors of power in Victoria Street, dubious though they may be?'

'Oh, it's easy for you to have the odd chuckle at my expense,' she noted. 'But I don't expect any man comes up against the kinds of things a woman has to cope with. Especially a man . . .' She seemed unwilling to finish her thought.

He did it for her. 'A man like me?'

'Well, really, Thomas. You can hardly argue that a life of privilege – the family pile in Cornwall, Eton, Oxford . . . remember I *do* know a bit about you – has made it difficult for you to succeed in your line of work. And why do you do it, anyway? Certainly you don't *need* to be a policeman. Doesn't your sort of man generally do something less—' She seemed to be searching for the right term and she settled on, 'less elbow-rubbing with the great unwashed?'

'Such as?'

'I don't know. Sit on boards of hospitals and universities? Breed thoroughbred horses? Manage property – his own, naturally – and collect rent from farmers wearing flat caps and Wellingtons?'

'Those would be the ones who come to the kitchen door and keep their eyes cast downward? The ones who hastily remove those flat caps in my presence? Pulling on their forelocks and all the rest?'

'What in God's name is a forelock?' she asked. 'I've always wondered. I mean, it's clear that it's hair and it's in the front but how much of it constitutes a "fore" of it and why on earth would someone pull it?'

'It's all part of the bowing and scraping,' he said solemnly. 'Part of the general peasant-and-master routine that comprises life for my sort of man.'

She looked at him. 'Damn you, your eyes are *actually* twinkling.'

He said, 'Sorry,' and he smiled.

She said, 'It's bloody hot, isn't it. Look, I need something cool to drink, Thomas. And we could use the time to talk. There's got to be a pub nearby.'

He reckoned there was, but he also wanted to have a look at the spot where the body had been found. They'd arrived back at her car at the front of the cemetery, and he made his request: would she take him to the chapel where Jemima Hastings' body had been found? Even as he spoke the words, he recognised another step being taken. Five months since his wife's murder on the front steps of their house: in February even a hint that he might be willing to look upon a place where someone had died had been unthinkable.

As he reckoned she might, the superintendent asked why he wanted to see it. She sounded suspicious, as if he was checking up on her work. She pointed out that the site had been checked, had been cleared, had been reopened to the public, and he told her that it was curiosity and nothing more. He'd seen the pictures; he wanted to see the place.

She acquiesced. He followed her inside the cemetery and along paths that twisted into the trees. It was cooler here with foliage sheltering them from the sun and no concrete pavements sending the heat upward in unavoidable waves. He noticed that she was what once would have been called 'a fine figure of a woman' as she strode ahead of him, and she walked as she seemed to do everything else: with total confidence.

At the chapel, she directed him round the side. There the shelter stood and beyond it the baked grass of a clearing gave onto more of the graveyard, a stone bench sitting on the edge of this. Another stone bench was across from the first, with three overgrown tombs and one crumbling mausoleum behind it.

'Fingertip, perimeter and a grid, producing a diligent search,' Ardery told him. 'Nothing except what you'd expect in this kind of place.'

'Which would be . . . ?'

'Soft drink cans and other assorted rubbish, pencils, pens, plans of the park, crisp bags, chocolate wrappers, old Oyster cards – yes, they're being checked into – and enough used condoms to give one hope that sexually transmitted diseases might one day be a thing of the past.' And then, 'Oh. Sorry. That wasn't appropriate.'

He'd been standing in the doorway to the shelter, and he turned to see that a dark flush was climbing up her neck.

She said, 'The condom thing. Other way round, it could be construed as sexual harassment. I apologise for the comment.'

'Ah,' he said. 'Well, no offence taken. But I'll be on guard in the future, so take care, guv.'

'Isabelle,' she said. 'You *can* call me Isabelle.'

'I'm on duty,' he said. 'What d'you make of the graffito?' He indicated the wall of the shelter where GOD GOES WIRELESS and the eye in the triangle were rendered in black.

'Old,' she said. 'Placed here long before her death. And smacking of the Masons. You?'

'We're of the same mind on that.'

'Good,' she said. He saw that the flush on her skin was receding. She said, 'If you've seen enough, then, I'd like that drink. There're cafés on Stoke Newington Church Street, and I expect we can find a pub as well.'

They left the cemetery by a different route, this one taking them past the monument which Lynley recognised as the background that Deborah St James had used for her photograph of Jemima Hastings. It sat at the junction of two paths: a marble life-size male lion on a plinth. He paused and read the monument's inscription that they 'would all meet again on some happy Easter morning.' Were that only the truth, he thought.

The superintendent was watching him, but she said nothing other than, 'It's this way, Thomas,' and led him to the street.

They found both a café and a pub in very short order. Ardery chose the pub. Once inside, she disappeared into the Ladies, telling him to order her a cider and saying, 'For God's sake, it's *mild*, Thomas,' when he apparently looked surprised at her choice, as they would be on duty for hours. She told him that she wasn't about to police her team regarding their choice of liquid refreshment. If someone wanted a lager in the middle of the day, she didn't care. It's the work that matters, she informed him, and the quality of that work. Then off she went to the Ladies. For his part, he ordered her cider – 'And make it a pint, please' she'd said – and got a bottle of mineral water for himself. He took these to a table tucked away in a corner, then he changed his mind and chose another one, more suitable, he thought, for two colleagues at work.

She proved herself a typical woman, at least in matters pertaining to her disappearance into the Ladies. She was gone at least five minutes and when she returned, she'd rearranged her hair. It was behind her ears now, revealing earrings. They were navy, edged in gold, he saw. The navy matched the colour of her dress. He wondered about the little vanities of women. Helen had never merely *dressed* in the morning: she had put together entire ensembles.

For God's sake, Helen, aren't you only going out to buy petrol?

Darling Tommy, I might actually be seen*!*

He blinked, poured water into his glass. There was lime with it, and he squeezed the wedge hard.

Ardery said, 'Thank you.'

He said, 'They had only one brand.'

'I didn't mean the cider. I meant thank you for not standing up. I expect you usually do.'

'Ah. That. Well, the manners *are* beaten into one from birth, but I reckoned you'd rather I eschewed them at work.'

'Have you ever had a female superior officer before?' And when he shook his head, 'You're coping rather well.'

'It's what I do.'

'You cope?'

'Yes.' When he said it, though, he saw how it could lead to a discussion he didn't want to have. So he said, 'And what about you, Superintendent Ardery?'

'You won't call me Isabelle, will you?'

'I won't.'

'Whyever not? This is private, Thomas. We're colleagues, you and I.'

'On duty.'

'Will that be your answer for everything?'

He thought about this, how convenient it was. 'Yes. I expect it will.'

'And should I be offended?'

'Not at all. Guv.'

He looked at her and she held the look. The moment became a man-woman thing. That was always the risk when the sexes mixed. With Barbara Havers it had always been something so far out of the question as to be nearly laughable. With Isabelle Ardery, this was not the case. He looked away.

She said lightly, 'I believed him. You? I realise he could have been going back to the scene of the crime, checking on the body to see if she'd been found yet, but I don't think it's likely. He doesn't seem clever enough to have thought it all through.'

'You mean taking the magazine with him so it would appear he had a reason to duck into the shelter?'

'That's what I mean.'

Lynley agreed with her. Marlon Kay was an unlikely killer. The superintendent had gone the way of wisdom in dealing with the situation, though. Before they'd left the boy and his surly father, she made the arrangements for his fingerprints to be taken and his mouth to be swabbed, and she'd had a look through his clothing. There was nothing yellow among it. As for the trainers he'd worn that day in the cemetery, they were devoid of visible signs of blood but would be sent to forensics anyway. In all of this Marlon had been completely cooperative. He seemed anxious to please them at the same time as he was eager to show he had nothing to do with the death of Jemima Hastings.

'So we're left with the sighting of the Oriental man, and let's hope that something comes of it,' Ardery said.

'Or that something comes of this bloke in Hampshire,' Lynley noted.

'There's that as well. How d'you expect Sergeant Havers will cope with that part of the investigation. Thomas?'

'In her usual fashion,' he replied.

13

'Bloody incredible. I've never seen anything like it.' This was Barbara Havers' reaction to the New Forest and the herds of ponies running wild upon it. There were hundreds of them – thousands perhaps – and they grazed freely wherever they had a mind to graze. On the vast swatches of the grassland, they munched upon greenery with their foals nearby. Beneath primeval oaks and beeches and wandering among both rowan and birch, they fed upon the scrub growth and left in their wake a woodland floor dappled with sunlight, spongy with decomposing leaves, and devoid of weeds, bushes and brambles.

It was nearly impossible not to be enchanted by a place where ponies lapped water in splashes and ponds and thatched cottages of white-washed cob looked like buildings scrubbed on a daily basis. Grand vistas of hillsides displayed a patchwork in which the green of the bracken had begun to brown and the yellow of gorse was giving way to the increasing purple of heather.

'Almost makes me want to pack in London,' Barbara declared. She had the big *A to Z* road atlas open upon her lap, having acted as navigator for Winston Nkata during their drive. They'd stopped once for lunch and another time for coffee and now they were wending their way from the A31 over to Lyndhurst where they would make their presence known to the local coppers whose patch they were invading.

'Nice, yeah,' was Nkata's assessment of the New Forest. 'Expect it'd be a bit quiet for me, though. Not to mention . . .' He glanced at her. 'There's the raisin in the rice pud aspect of things.'

'Oh. Right. Well,' Barbara said, and she reckoned he was correct on that score. The county wasn't a place where they'd be finding a minority population and certainly not a population with Nkata's background of Brixton via West Africa and the Caribbean, with a bit of a sidetrack into gang warfare on the housing estate. 'Good place for a holiday, though. Mind how you go through town. We've got a one-way system coming up.'

They negotiated this with little trouble and found the Lyndhurst police station just beyond town in the Romsey Road. An undistinguished brick building in the tedious architectural style that fairly shouted 1960s, it squatted on the top of a small knoll, with a crown of concertina wire and a necklace of CCTV cameras marking it as an area of out-of-bounds to anyone not wishing his every movement to be monitored. A few trees and a flower garden in front of the building attempted to soften the overall dismal air of the place, but there was no disguising its institutional nature.

They showed their identification to the special constable apparently in charge of reception, a young bloke who emerged from an internal room once they rang a buzzer placed on the counter for this purpose. He looked interested but not overwhelmed by the idea that New Scotland Yard had come calling. They told him they needed to speak to his chief super and he made much of going from their ID pictures to their faces as if suspecting them of ill intentions. He said, 'Hang on, then,' and disappeared with their IDs into the bowels of the station. It was nearly ten minutes before he reappeared, handed back their warrant cards, and told them to follow him.

Chief Super, he said, was a bloke called Zachary Whiting. He'd been in a meeting but he'd cut it short.

'We won't keep him long,' Barbara said. 'Just a courtesy call, this, if you know what I mean. Bring him into the picture so there's no misunderstanding later.'

Lyndhurst was the operational command headquarters for all the police stations in the New Forest. It was under the authority of a chief superintendent who himself reported to the constabulary in Winchester. One cop didn't wander onto another cop's patch without making nice and all the et ceteras, and that was what Barbara and Winston were there to do. If anything currently going on in the area happened to apply to their investigation, all the better. Barbara didn't expect this to be the case, but one never knew where a professional obligation like this one could lead.

Chief Superintendent Zachary Whiting stood waiting for them at his desk. Behind spectacles, his eyes watched them with some speculation, but this was hardly a surprising response to a call from New Scotland Yard. When the Met arrived, it often meant trouble of the internal investigation sort.

Winston gave Barbara the nod, so she did the honours, making the introductions and then sketching out the details of the death in London. She named Jemima Hastings as the victim. She concluded with the reason for their incursion into his patch.

'There was a mobile number on a postcard related to the victim,' Barbara told Whiting. 'We've traced that number to a Gordon Jossie here in Hampshire. So . . .' She didn't add the rest. The chief inspector would know the drill.

Whiting said, 'Gordon Jossie?' and he sounded thoughtful.

'You know him?' Nkata asked.

Whiting went to his desk and leafed through some paperwork. Barbara and Winston exchanged glances.

'Has he been in trouble round here?' Barbara asked.

Whiting didn't reply directly at first. He repeated the surname, and then he said, 'No, not in trouble,' putting a hesitation before the final word as if Gordon Jossie had been in something else.

'But you know the bloke?' Nkata said again.

'It's just the name.' The chief superintendent apparently found what he was searching for in his stack of paperwork, and this turned out to be a phone message. 'We've had a phone call about him. Crank call, if you ask me, but evidently she was insistent, so the message got passed along.'

'Is that normal procedure?' Barbara asked. Why would a chief superintendent want to be informed about phone calls, crank or otherwise?

He said that it wasn't normal procedure at all, but in this case the young lady wasn't taking no for an answer. She wanted something done about a bloke called Gordon Jossie. She'd been asked did she want to make a formal complaint against the man, but she was having none of that. 'Said she finds him a suspicious character,' Whiting said.

'Bit odd that you'd be informed, sir,' Barbara noted.

'I wouldn't have been in the normal course of things. But then a *second* young lady phoned, saying much the same thing, and that's when I learned about it. Seems odd to you, no doubt, but this isn't London. It's a small, close-knit place and I find it wise to know what's going on in it.'

'Anticipating this bloke Jossie might be up to something?' Nkata asked.

'Nothing suggests that. But this' – Whiting indicated the phone message – 'puts him onto the radar.'

He went on to tell the Scotland Yard officers they were welcome to go about their business on his patch, and when they gave him Jossie's address, he told them how to find the man's property near the village of Sway. If they needed his help or the help of one of his officers . . . There was something about the way he made the offer. Barbara had the feeling he was doing more than just making nice with them.

Sway was located off the regularly travelled routes in the New Forest, the apex of a triangle created by itself, Lymington, and New Milton. They drove there on lanes that became progressively narrower, and they ended up in a stretch of road called Paul's Lane, where houses had names but no numbers and tall hedges blocked most of them from view.

There were a number of cottages strung along the lane, but only two substantial properties. Jossie's turned out to be one of them.

They parked on the verge next to a tall hawthorn hedge.

They walked up the lumpy driveway, and they found him within a paddock to the west of a neat cob cottage. He was inspecting the rear hooves of two restless ponies. Under the baking sun, he wore a dark glasses as well as a baseball cap, and he was protected further by long sleeves, gloves, trousers and boots.

This was not the case for the young woman watching him from outside the paddock. She was calling out, 'D'you think they're ready for release yet?' and she was wearing a striped sundress that left her arms and legs bare. Despite the heat, she looked fresh and cool, and her head was covered by a straw hat banded by material that matched the dress. Hadiyyah, Barbara thought, would have approved.

'Dead silly to be afraid of ponies,' Gordon Jossie replied.

'I'm *trying* to make friends with them. Honestly.' She turned her head and caught sight of Barbara and Winston, her gaze taking them both in but then going back to linger on Winston. She was very attractive, Barbara thought. Even with her own limited experience, she could tell that young woman wore her makeup like a pro. Again, Hadiyyah would have approved. 'Hullo,' the woman said to them. 'Are you lost?'

At this, Gordon Jossie looked up. He watched their progress up the driveway and over to the fence. This was barbed wire strung between wooden posts, and his companion had been standing with her hands clasped on top of one of the latter.

Jossie had the wiry sort of body that reminded Barbara of a footballer. When he took off his cap and wiped his brow with his arm, she saw his hair was thinning, but its ginger colour suited him well.

Barbara and Winston fished out their IDs. Winston did the honours this time. When he'd finished the introductions, he said to the man in the paddock, 'You're Gordon Jossie?'

Jossie nodded. He walked towards the fence. His pace was slow, and nothing much showed upon his face. His eyes, of course, they could not read. The glass in his lenses was virtually black.

The young woman identified herself as Gina Dickens. 'Scotland Yard?' she said, with a smile. 'Like Inspector Lestrade?' And then to tease Jossie, 'Gordon, have you been naughty?'

There was a wooden gate nearby, but Jossie didn't come through it. Rather, he went to a hosepipe that was looped round a newish-looking fencepost and attached to a free-standing water tap outside the paddock. He removed the hosepipe and unspooled it in the direction of a stone trough. Absolutely pristine, this was, Barbara saw. It was either new like the fencepost or the man was more than a bit compulsive about keeping things tidy. The latter didn't seem likely since part of the paddock was overgrown and in disrepair, as if he'd given up in the midst of repairing the area. He began adding water to the trough. Over his shoulder, he said, 'What's the trouble, then?'

Interesting question, Barbara thought. Directly to trouble. But then who could blame him? A personal visit from the Met wasn't one's common or garden experience.

She said, 'Could we have a word, Mr Jossie?'

'Seems like we're having it.'

'Gordon, I think they might mean . . .' Gina hesitated, as if unwilling to push him. Then she said to Winston, 'We've a table and chairs beneath the tree in the garden,' and indicated the front of the cottage. 'Shall we meet you there?'

'Works for me,' Nkata said and went on with, 'Hot today, innit?' giving Gina Dickens the benefit of his high wattage smile.

'I'll fetch something cool for us to drink,' she said, and she went off towards the cottage, but not before she cast a puzzled glance in Jossie's direction.

Barbara and Nkata waited for Jossie, the better to make sure he took a direct route from the paddock to the front garden with no sidetracking. When he'd finished topping off the trough for the ponies, he returned the hosepipe to the post and came through the wooden paddock gate, removing his gloves.

'It's this way,' he said to them, as if they couldn't find the front garden without his help. He led them to it, a patch of parched lawn at this time of year, but containing flowerbeds that were thriving. He saw Barbara looking at these and said, 'Gina uses the dishwater. We do the washing up with special detergent,' as if to explain why the flowers weren't dead in the middle of hosepipe bans and a very dry summer.

'Nice,' Barbara noted. 'I kill most everything and it doesn't take special washing up soap for me to do it.' She got down to business as they sat at the table. This looked to be part of a little outdoor dining area, featuring candles, a floral table-cloth, and complementary cushions on the chairs. Someone, it seemed, had a flair for decorating. Barbara pulled the postcard photo of Jemima Hastings from her bag. She laid it on the table in front of Gordon Jossie. She said, 'C'n you tell us anything about this woman, Mr Jossie?'

'Why?'

'Because your mobile number' – she flipped the card over – 'is on the back here. And what with "Have you seen this woman?" on the front, it seems like you probably know her.' Barbara turned the postcard face up again, sliding it within inches of Jossie's hand. He did not touch it.

Gina came round the side of the cottage, carrying a tray on which sat a pink concoction in a squat glass jug. Sprigs of mint and a few pieces of ice floated in it. She placed the tray on the table and her gaze took in the postcard. She looked from it to Jossie. She said, 'Gordon? Is something . . . ?'

Abruptly Jossie said, 'This is Jemima,' and indicated the picture on the card by flicking his fingers towards it.

Gina sat slowly. She looked perplexed. 'On the card?'

Jossie didn't reply. Barbara didn't want to hasten to any conclusions about his reticence. She reckoned, among other things, his lack of response might well be due to embarrass-ment. Clearly this woman Gina Dickens was something to Jossie, and she'd likely be wondering why he was being faced with a postcard featuring another woman whom he clearly knew.

Barbara waited for Jossie's answer to Gina's question.
She and Nkata exchanged a look. They were of one mind
in the matter and that mind was of the *let him swing for a
moment* variety.

Gina said, 'May I?' and when Barbara nodded, she picked
up the postcard. She made no comment about the photo itself,
but her gaze took in the query at the bottom of the card and,
when she flipped it over, the phone number printed across
the back. She said nothing. Instead, she placed the card gently
on the table and poured each of them a glass of whatever it
was she'd concocted.

The heat seemed to grow more oppressive in the silence.
Gina herself was the one to break it. She said, 'I'd no idea . . .'
Her fingers touched her throat. Barbara could see her pulse
beating there. It put her in mind of the manner in which
Jemima Hastings had died. 'How long have you been looking
for her, Gordon?' Gina asked.

Jossie fixed his eyes on the postcard. He finally said, 'This
is months old, this is. I got a stack of them . . . I dunno . . .
round April, it was. I didn't know you then.'

'Want to explain?' Barbara asked him. Nkata opened his
neat leather notebook.

Gina said, 'Is something going on?'

Barbara wasn't about to give any more information than
was necessary at this point, so she said nothing. Nor did
Winston, except to murmur, 'So . . . Mr Jossie?'

Gordon Jossie made a restless movement in his chair. The
story he told was brief but direct. Jemima Hastings was his
former lover; she'd left him after more than two years together;
he'd wanted to find her. He'd seen an advertisement for the
photographic portrait show in the *Mail on Sunday* by purest
chance and this – with a nod at the postcard – was the photo
that had been used in the advert for that show. So he'd gone
to London. No one at the gallery would tell him where the
model was, and he hadn't a clue how to contact the photographer. So he bought up the postcards – forty, fifty, or sixty

because he couldn't recall but they'd had to fetch more from their storage room – and he'd stuck them in phone boxes, in shop windows, in any spot where he thought they'd get noticed. He'd worked in widening rings round the gallery itself till he ran out of cards. And then he waited.

'Any luck?' Barbara asked him.

'I never heard from anyone about her.' He said again to Gina, 'This was before I'd met you. It's nothing to do with you and me. Far as I knew, far as I *know*, wasn't anyone who ever saw them, saw her, and put two-and-two together. Waste of time and money, it was. But I felt like I had to try.'

'To find her, you mean,' Gina said in a quiet voice.

He said to her, 'It was the *time* we'd put in together. Over two years. I just wanted to know. It doesn't mean anything.' Jossie turned to Barbara, 'Where'd you get this, anyway? What's going on?'

She answered his question with one of her own. 'Care to tell us why Jemima left you?'

'I've no bloody idea. One day she decided it was over, and off she went. She made the announcement and the next day she was gone.'

'Just like that?'

'I reckoned she'd been planning it for weeks. I phoned her at first once she'd gone. I wanted to know what the hell was going on. Who wouldn't, after two years together when someone says it's over and just disappears and you've not seen it coming? But she never took the calls and she never returned them and then the mobile number got changed altogether or she got a new mobile or *whatever* because the phone calls stopped going through. I asked her brother about it—'

'Her brother?' Nkata looked up from his notebook and when Gordon Jossie identified the brother as Robbie Hastings, Nkata jotted this down.

'But he said he didn't know anything about what she was up to. I didn't believe him – he never liked me and I expect he was dead chuffed when Jemima ended things – but I couldn't get a single detail out of him. I finally gave up. And then—' with a look at Gina Dickens that had to be called grateful – 'I met Gina last month.'

'When did you last see Jemima Hastings, then?' Barbara asked.

'The morning of the day she left me.'

'Which was?'

'Day after Guy Fawkes. Last year.' He took a swig of his drink and then wiped his mouth on his arm. He said, 'Now are you going to tell me what this is all about?'

'I'm going to ask you if you've made any journeys out of Hampshire in the last week or so.'

'Why?'

'Will you answer the question, please?'

Jossie's face suffused with colour. 'I don't think I will. What the hell is going on? Where'd you get that postcard? I didn't break any laws. You see postcards in phone boxes all over London and they're a damn sight more suggestive than that one.'

'This was among Jemima's belongings in her lodgings,' Barbara told him. 'I'm sorry to tell you that she's dead. She was murdered in London about six days ago. So again, I'll ask you if you've made any journeys out of Hampshire.'

Barbara had heard the expression *pale to the lips* but she'd never seen it occur so rapidly. She reckoned it had to do with Gordon Jossie's natural colouring: His face gained colour quickly, and it seemed to lose it in much the same manner.

'Oh my God,' Gina Dickens murmured. She reached for his hand.

Her movement made him flinch away. 'What d'you mean murdered?' he asked Barbara.

'Is there more than one meaning to *murdered*?' she inquired. 'Have you been out of Hampshire, Mr Jossie?'

'Where did she die?' he asked as a response and when Barbara didn't answer he said to Nkata, 'Where did this happen? How? Who?'

'She was murdered in a place called Abney Park Cemetery,' Barbara told him. 'So again, Mr Jossie, I'll have to ask you—'

'Here,' he said numbly. 'I've not left. I've been here. I was here.'

'Here at home?'

'No. 'Course not. I've been working. I was . . .' He seemed dazed. Either that, Barbara reckoned, or he was trying to do a mental two-step to come up with an alibi that he hadn't expected to have to give. He explained that he was a thatcher and that he'd been working on a job, which was what he did every day except weekends and some Friday afternoons. When asked if someone could confirm that fact, he said yes, of course, for God's sake, he had an apprentice. He gave the name, Cliff Coward, and the phone number as well. Then he said, 'How?' and licked his lips. 'How did she . . . die?'

'She was stabbed, Mr Jossie,' Barbara said. 'She bled out before anyone found her.'

Gina did clasp Jossie's hand at that point, but she didn't say anything. What, really, *could* she say, given her position?

Barbara considered this last: her position, its security, or its lack thereof. She said, 'And you, Ms Dickens? Have you been out of Hampshire?'

'No, of course not.'

'And six days ago?'

'I'm not sure. Six days? I've only been to Lymington. The shopping . . . in Lymington.'

'Who can confirm that?'

She was silent. It was the moment when someone was supposed to say, 'You aren't bloody well suggesting that I had something to do with this?' but neither of them did. Instead they glanced at each other and then Gina said, 'I don't expect anyone can confirm it except Gordon. But why should someone be able to confirm it?'

'Keep the receipts from your shopping, did you?'

'I don't know. I don't think so. I mean, one doesn't, ordinarily.

I can look, but I certainly didn't think . . .' She looked frightened. 'I'll try to find them,' she said. 'But if I can't . . .'

'Don't be stupid.' Jossie directed this remark not to Gina but to Barbara and Winston. 'What's she supposed to have done? Obliterated the competition? There isn't any. We were finished, Jemima and me.'

'Right,' Barbara said. She gave a nod to Winston and he made much of flipping his notebook closed. 'Well, you are now, aren't you, you and Jemima? Finished is definitely the word for it.'

He went into the barn. He thought to brush Tess – as he usually did at such moments – but the dog wouldn't come despite his whistling and his calls. He stood stupidly at her brushing table, fruitlessly and with a very dry mouth shouting, 'Tess! Tess! Get in here, dog!' with absolutely no result because, of course, animals were intuitive and Tess damn well knew something wasn't right.

Gina did come, however. She said quietly, 'Gordon, why didn't you tell them the truth?' She sounded fearful and he cursed himself for that fear in her voice.

She *would* ask, of course. It was, after all, the question of the hour. He wanted to thank her for having said nothing to the Scotland Yard cops because he knew what it must look like that he'd lied to them.

She said, 'You *did* go to Holland, didn't you? You *were* there, weren't you? That new source for reeds? That site where they're growing them? Because the reeds from Turkey are becoming rubbish? That's where you were, isn't it? Why didn't you tell them?'

He didn't want to look at her. He heard it all in her voice, so he bloody well didn't want to see it in her face. But he had to look her in the eye for the simple reason that she was Gina, and not just anyone.

So he looked, but he saw not fear but rather concern. It

was for him and he knew it and knowing it made him weak and desperate. He said, 'Yes.'

'You went to Holland?'

'Yes.'

'Then why didn't you just tell them? Why did you say . . . ? You weren't at work, Gordon.'

'Cliff'll say I was.'

'He'll lie for you?'

'If I ask him, yes. He doesn't like coppers.'

'But why would you ask him? Why not just tell them the truth? Gordon, has something . . . Is something . . . ?'

He wanted her to approach him as she'd done before, early in the morning, in bed and then in the shower because although it was sex and only sex, it *meant* more than sex, and that was what he needed. How odd that he'd understand in that moment what Jemima had wanted from him and from the act. A lifting up and a carrying off and an end to that which could never be ended because it was imprisoned within and no simple conjoining of bodies could free it.

He set down the brush. Obviously, the dog was not going to obey, even for a brushing, and he felt like a fool for waiting for her. He said, 'Geen,' and Gina said in return, 'Tell me the truth.'

He said, 'If I told them I was in Holland, they'd take it further.'

'What do you mean?'

'They'd want me to prove it.'

'Can't you? Why would you not be able to prove it? Did you not *go* to Holland, Gordon?'

'Of course, I went. But I threw away the ticket.'

'But there're records. All sorts of records. And there's the hotel. And whoever you saw . . . the farmer . . . whoever . . . Who grows the reeds? He'll be able to say . . . You can phone the police and just tell them the truth and that'll be the end of it.'

'It's easier like this.'

'How on earth can it be easier to ask Cliff to lie? Because if he lies and if they find out that he lies . . . ?'

Now she did look frightened, but frightened was something that he could deal with. Frightened was something he understood. He approached her the way he approached the ponies in the paddock, one hand out and the other visible: no surprises here, Gina, nothing to fear.

He said, 'Can you trust me on this? *Do* you trust me?'

'Of course I trust you. Why shouldn't I trust you? But I don't understand . . .'

He touched her bare shoulder. 'You're here with me. You've been with me, what? A month? Longer? Are you thinking I would've hurt Jemima? Gone up to London? Found her and stabbed her to death? Is that how I seem to you? That sort of bloke? He goes to London, murders a woman for no reason since she's already long gone out of his life, then comes home and makes love to this woman, this woman right here, the centre of his whole flaming world? Why? *Why?*'

'Let me look at your eyes.' She reached up and took off his dark glasses, which he hadn't removed coming into the barn. She set them on the brushing table and then she put her hand on his cheek. He met her gaze. She looked at him and he didn't flinch and finally her expression softened. She kissed his cheek and then his closed eyelids. Then she kissed his mouth. Then her own mouth opened, and her hands went down to his arse and she pulled him close.

After a moment, breathless, she said, 'Take me right here,' and he did so.

They found Robbie Hastings between Vinney Ridge and Anderwood, which were two stopping-off spots on the Lyndhurst Road between Burley and the A35. They had reached him on his mobile, from a number that Gordon Jossie had given them. 'He'll doubtless tell you the worst about me,' Jossie said abruptly.

It was no easy matter to locate Jemima Hastings' brother since so many roads in the New Forest had convenient names but no signs. They finally discovered exactly where he was by chance, having stopped at a cottage where the road they were taking made a dogleg, only to discover it was called Anderwood Cottage. By heading farther along the route, they were led to believe by the cottage owner, they would locate Rob Hastings on a track leading to Dames Slough Enclosure. He was an agister, they were told, and he'd been called to do 'the usual bit of sad business'.

This business turned out to be the shooting of one of the New Forest ponies that had been hit by a car on the A35. The poor animal had apparently managed to stagger across acres of heath before collapsing. When Barbara and Nkata found the agister, he'd put the horse to death with one merciful shot from a .32 pistol, and he'd brought the animal's body to the edge of the lane. He was talking on his mobile, and sitting attentively next to him was a majestic looking Weimaraner, so well-trained as to ignore not only the interlopers but also the dead pony lying a short distance from the Land Rover in which Robbie Hastings had apparently come to this lonely spot.

Nkata pulled off the lane as far as he was able. Hastings nodded as they approached him. They'd told him only that they wanted to speak with him at once, and he looked grave. It was hardly likely that he had many calls from the Metropolitan police in this part of the world.

He said, 'Stay, Frank,' to the dog and came towards them. 'You might want to keep back from the pony. It's not a happy sight.' He said he was waiting for the New Forest Hounds and then added, 'Ah. Here he is,' in reference to an open-bed lorry that rumbled towards them. It was pulling a low trailer with shallow sides, and into this the dead animal was going to be loaded. It would be used for meat to feed the dogs, Robbie Hastings informed them as the lorry got into position. At least some good would come of the reckless stupidity of drivers who thought the Perambulation was their personal playground, he added.

Barbara and Nkata had already decided there was no way that they were going to inform Robbie Hastings of his sister's death on the side of a country road. But they had also reckoned that their very presence was likely to set the man on edge, and it did so. Once the pony was loaded and the lorry from New Forest Hounds had negotiated a difficult turn to get back to the main road, Hastings swung round to them and said, 'What's happened? It's bad. You wouldn't be here otherwise.'

Barbara said, 'Is there somewhere we could have a conversation with you, Mr Hastings?'

Hastings touched the top of his dog's smooth head. 'Might tell me here,' he said. 'There's no place nearby for private talk 'less you want to go into Burley, and you don't want that, not at this time of year.'

'Do you live nearby?'

'Beyond Burley.' He took off the baseball cap he was wearing, revealing a head of close-cropped hair. This was greying and would have been thick otherwise, and he used a kerchief he had round his neck to scrub over his face. His face was singularly unattractive with large buckteeth and virtually no chin. His eyes, however, were deeply human and they filled with tears as he looked at them. He said, 'So she's dead, eh?' and when Barbara's expression told him this was so, he gave a terrible cry and turned from them.

Barbara exchanged a look with Nkata. Neither of them moved at first. Then Nkata was the one to put his hand on Hastings' shoulder and the one to say, 'We're that sorry, mon. 'S bad when someone goes like this.'

He himself was upset. Barbara knew this from the way Nkata's accent altered, becoming less South London and more Caribbean, with the *th*'s morphing into *d*'s. He said, 'I'm drivin' you home. Sergeant here, she follow in my car. You tell me how to go, we get you there. No way you need to be out here now. You good to tell me how to get t'your place?'

'I can drive,' Hastings said.

'No way you're doing that, mon.' Nkata jerked his head at Barbara and she hastened to open the Land Rover's passenger door. On its seat were a shotgun and the pistol the man had used to shoot the pony. She moved these beneath the seat and together she and Nkata got Hastings inside. His dog followed: one graceful leap and Frank was leaning against his master in the silent way all dogs have of comforting.

They made a sad little procession out of the area, proceeding not back the way they had come but rather farther along the lane through a woodland of oaks and chestnuts. These afforded a canopy that arced over the lane in a verdant tunnel of leaves. Back out on the Lyndhurst Road, though, there was broad lawn on one side giving way to tangled heath on the other. Herds of ponies grazed freely here, and where they wished to cross the road, they simply did so.

Once in Burley, it became quickly clear why Hastings had said they would not want to have private conversation there. Tourists were massing everywhere, and they seemed to be taking their cues from the ponies and the cows wandering through the village at will: they walked where their fancy took them, bright sunlight falling upon their shoulders.

Hastings lived through and beyond the village. He had a holding at the top of a strip of road called Honey Lane – actually marked with a sign, Barbara noted – and when they finally pulled onto the property, she saw it was similar to a farm, with several outbuildings and paddocks, one of which held two horses.

The door they used led directly into the kitchen of the house, where Barbara went to an electric kettle upended on a draining board. She filled it, set it to work, and sorted out mugs and bags of PG Tips. Sometimes a shot of the bloody national beverage was the only way in which fellow-feeling could be expressed.

Nkata sat Hastings at an old Formica-topped table, where the agister took off his hat and blew his nose on his kerchief, which he then balled up and shoved to one side. He said, 'Sorry,' and his eyes filled. 'I should have known when she didn't answer my calls on her birthday. And not ringing back at once the day afterwards. She always rang back. Within the hour, generally. When she didn't, it was easier to think she was just busy. Caught up in things. You know.'

'Are you married, Mr Hastings?' Barbara brought mugs to the table, along with a battered tin canister of sugar that she'd found on a shelf with matching old canisters of flour and coffee as well. It was an old-fashioned kitchen with old-fashioned contents: from the appliances to the objects on the shelves and in the cupboards. As such, it looked like a room that had been lovingly preserved, rather than one that had been artfully restored to wear the guise of an earlier period.

'Not very likely, that,' was how he answered the question. It seemed to be a resigned and bleak reference to his unfortunate looks. That was sad, Barbara thought, a self-prophecy fulfilled.

'Ah,' she said. 'Well, we're going to want to speak to everyone in Hampshire who knew Jemima. We hope you'll be able to help us with that.'

'Why?' he asked.

'Because of how she died, Mr Hastings.'

At this point Hastings seemed to realise something he hadn't yet considered despite the fact that he was being spoken to by representatives of the Metropolitan police. He said, 'Her death . . . Jemima's death . . .'

'I'm very sorry to tell you that she was murdered six days ago.' Barbara added the rest: not the means of death but the place in which it had occurred. And even then she kept it general, by mentioning the cemetery but not its location and not the location of the body within it. She finished with, 'So everyone who knew her will have to be interviewed.'

'Jossie.' Hastings sounded numb. 'She left him. He didn't like that. She said he couldn't come to terms with it. He rang her and rang her and he wouldn't stop ringing her.' That said, he raised his fists to his eyes, and he wept like a child.

The electric kettle clicked off, and Barbara went to fetch it. She poured water into the mugs, and she found milk in the fridge. A shot or two of whisky would have been better for the poor man, but she wasn't up to rustling through his cupboards so the tea was going to have to do, despite the heat of the day. At least the interior of the cottage was cool and kept that way by its construction of thick cob walls, which were rough and white-washed outside and painted pale yellow within the kitchen.

It was the presence of the Weimaraner that seemed to soothe Robbie Hastings at last. The dog had placed his head on Hastings' thigh, and the low long whine that issued from the animal roused the master. Robbie Hastings wiped his eyes and blew his nose again. He said, 'Aye, Frank,' and he cupped his hand over the dog's smooth head. He lowered his own head and pressed his lips to the animal. He didn't look at either Barbara or Nkata when he raised his head again. Instead he stared at the mug of tea.

Perhaps knowing what their questions were going to be, he began to talk, slowly at first, then with more reassurance. Next to him, Nkata took out his notebook.

At Longslade Bottom, Hastings began, there was a wide expanse of lawn where people went regularly to exercise their dogs off lead. He took his own dog there one day several years back and Jemima went along. That's where she'd met Gordon Jossie. This would have been more than two years ago.

'Somewhat new to the area, he was,' Hastings said. 'Broken away from a master thatcher round Itchen Abbas – a bloke called Heath – and come down the New Forest to start his own business. Never had much to say, but Jemima fancied him at once. Well, she would do, wouldn't she, 'cause she was tweenem at that point.'

Barbara frowned, wondering at the expression. She reckoned it was some strange Hampshirean term. '"Tweenem?"'

'"Tween men,' he clarified. 'Jemima always liked to have a partner. From the time she was . . . I don't know . . . twelve or thirteen? She wanted boyfriends. I always reckoned it was our dad's dying like he did, Mum's well. Killed in a car crash, both of them at once. Made her think she had to have someone that was truly and permanently hers, I think.'

'More 'n yourself,' Nkata clarified.

'I reckon it seemed to Jemima that she needed someone more special. I was her brother, see. Didn't mean anything if her brother loved her since he was meant to love her.' Hastings pulled the mug towards him. A bit of tea sloshed onto the table. He smeared this with the palm of his hand.

'Was she promiscuous?' Barbara asked, adding when the agister looked at her sharply, 'Sorry, but I have to ask. And it doesn't *matter*, Mr Hastings. Only as it might relate to her death.'

He shook his head. 'To her, it was all about being in love with some bloke. Given, she partnered up with one or two eventually, if you know what I mean, but only if she thought they were in love. "Madly in love" was what she always called it. "We're madly in love with each other, Rob." Typical young girl, you ask me. Well, nearly.'

'Nearly?' Barbara and Nkata spoke simultaneously.

Hastings looked thoughtful, as if examining his sister in a new light. He said slowly, 'She did cling a bit, I s'pose. And could be that made it hard for her to hold onto a boy. Same with men. She wanted a bit too much from them, I think, and that would . . . well, it would eventually end things. I wasn't much good at it, but I'd try to explain things to her: how blokes don't like someone holding onto them so. But I reckon she felt alone in the world 'cause of our parents, though she wasn't alone, not ever, not the way you'd think. But *feeling* that way, she had to stop the aloneness. She wanted to—' He frowned and seemed to consider how to put his next remarks. 'It was a bit like she wanted to climb into their skin, get that close to them, *be* them in a manner of speaking.'

'A stranglehold?' Barbara said.

'She didn't intend it, never. But, aye, I s'pose that's what happened. And when a bloke wanted his bit of space, Jemima couldn't cope. She clung all the tighter. I expect they felt like they had no air, so they sloughed her off. She'd cry a bit, then she'd blame them for not being what she really wanted, and she'd go on to another.'

'But this didn't happen with Gordon Jossie?'

'The strangling part?' He shook his head. 'With him, she got as close as she wanted. He seemed to like it.'

'How did you feel about him?' Barbara asked. 'And about her being involved with him?'

'I *wanted* to like him 'cause he made her happy, 's well as one person *can* make another happy, you know. But there was something about him didn't ever strike me right. His feet kept shifting round and he always wore them dark glasses. He wasn't much like blokes round here. I wanted her to find someone, settle down, make a family for herself as that's what she wanted, and I didn't see it as something could happen with him. Mind, I didn't tell her so. Wouldn't have made a difference if I had.'

'Why not?' Nkata asked. He had not, Barbara noted, touched his tea. But then Winston had never been much of a tea man. Lager was more his thing, but not a lot of it. Winston was nearly as abstemious as a monk: little drinking, no smoking, his body a temple.

'Oh, when she was "madly in love", the deal was sealed. There'd have been no point. Anyway I reckoned it was nothing to worry over 'cause Jemima'd likely run through him like she'd done the others. A few months and things would be over and she'd be searching for a man again. That didn't happen, though. Soon enough she was spending whole nights with him in his lodgings. Then they found that property over Paul's Lane, and they snapped it up and set up house and that was that. Well, I wasn't 'bout to say anything *then*. I just hoped for the best. It looked like that's what happened for a time. Jemima seemed quite happy. Starting her business with them cupcakes and all, over Ringwood. And he was building his thatching business. They seemed good with each other.'

'Cupcake business?' Nkata asked the question. 'What'd that be?'

'The Cupcake Queen. Sounds daft, eh? But thing is, she was that good in the kitchen, quite a hand with baking, Jemima. She had a score of customers buying cupcakes off her, fancy decorated and the like, special occasions, holidays, birthdays, anniversaries, gatherings. Worked herself up to being able to open a business of it in Ringwood – that would be the Cupcake Queen – and it was doing good but then it all came to naught 'cause she left Jossie and she left the area.'

As Nkata noted this, Barbara said, 'Gordon Jossie tells us he has no idea why Jemima left him.'

Hastings snorted. 'He told *me* he reckoned she had someone on the side and left him for that one.'

'What did she tell you?'

'That she was going off to think.'

'That's all?'

'That's the limit. That's what she said. She needed time to think.' Hastings rubbed his hands on his face. 'Thing is, I didn't see that as bad, you know? That she wanted to go off? I reckoned that finally she didn't want to rush things with some bloke, that she wanted to get herself sorted before she settled it permanently with someone. I thought it was a good idea.'

'But she didn't indicate anything more than that?'

'Nothing more than she was going off to think. She stayed in touch with me regular. Got herself a new mobile and let me know she'd done it 'cause Gordon kept ringing her but I didn't consider what that could mean, see. Just that he wanted her back. Well, so did I.'

'Did you?'

'I bloody well did. She's all I had in the way of family. I wanted her home.'

'Here, you mean?' Barbara asked.

'Just *home*. However she wanted that to mean. Long as it was Hampshire.'

Barbara nodded and asked for a list of Jemima's friends and acquaintances in the area, as best he could give it them. She also told him they would need – regretfully – to know his own whereabouts on the day his sister died. Last, they asked him what he knew of Jemima's activities in London and he said that he knew little enough except that she had 'someone up there, some new bloke that she was "madly in love with". As usual.'

'Did she give you his name?'

'Wouldn't even whisper it. It was all brand new, she said, this relationship, and she didn't want to throw a spanner in it. All she'd say was that she was over the moon. That and "this is the one". Well, she'd said that before, hadn't she? She always said it. So I didn't take much notice.'

'That's all you know? Nothing at all about him?'

Hastings appeared to consider this. Next to him, Frank gave a gusty sigh. He'd lowered himself to the floor but when Hastings moved restlessly in his chair, the dog was up at once, attending to him. Hastings smiled at the animal and pulled gently on one of his ears. He said, 'She'd started taking ice skating lessons. God knows why, but that was Jemima. There's a rink named after the Queen or some other Royal maybe the Prince of Wales, and . . .' He shook his head. 'I expect it was her skating instructor. That'd be just like Jemima. Someone skating her round the rink with his arm round her waist? She'd fall for that. She'd think it meant something when all it meant was that he was keeping her on her feet.'

'Like that, was she?' Nkata asked. 'Taking things wrong?'

'Always taking things to mean love when they meant nothing of the sort,' Hastings said.

Once the police had left, Robbie Hastings went upstairs. He wanted to remove the smell of dead pony with a shower. He also wanted a place to weep.

He realised how little the police had told him: death in a

cemetery somewhere in London and that was all. He also
realised how little he had asked them. Not how she had died,
not where she had died within the cemetery, and not even
when, exactly. Not who had found her. Not what did they
know so far. And recognising this, he felt deep shame. He wept
for that as much as he wept for the incalculable loss of his
little sister. It came to him that as long as he'd had Jemima,
no matter where she was, he hadn't ever been completely alone.
But now his life seemed finished. He couldn't imagine how
he would cope.

But that was the absolute end of what he would allow
himself. There were things to be done. He got out of the
shower, put on fresh clothes, and went out to the Land Rover.
Frank hopped in beside him and together he and the dog
travelled west, towards Ringwood. It was slow country driving,
which gave him time to think. What he thought of was Jemima
and what she had told him in their many conversations after
she'd gone to London. What he tried to recall was anything
that might have indicated she was on a path to her death.

It could have been a random killing, but he didn't think it
was. Not only could he not begin to face the possibility that
his sister had merely been the victim of someone who had
seen her and decided that she was perfect for one of those
sick thrill killings so commonplace these days, but also there
was the matter of where she had been. The Jemima he knew
didn't go into cemeteries. The last thing she wanted was to be
reminded of death. She never read obituaries, she didn't go
to films if she knew a leading character was going to die, she
avoided books with unhappy endings, and she turned newspapers facedown if death was on the front page as it so often
was. So if she'd entered a cemetery on her own, she had a
reason for doing so. And a reflection upon Jemima's life led
him to the one reason he didn't really want to consider.

A rendezvous. The latest bloke she'd been mad about was
likely married. That wouldn't have mattered to Jemima.
Married or single, partnered or partnerless . . . These were

fine distinctions she wouldn't have made. Where love, as she considered it, was concerned, she would have seen the greater good as making a connection with a man. She would have defined as love whatever it was between them. She would have *called* it love, and she would have expected it would run the course of love as she saw it: two people fulfilling each other as soul mates – another daft term of hers – and then having miraculously found each other, walking hand in hand into happily ever after. When that did not happen, she would cling and demand. And then what? he asked himself. Then what, Jemima?

He wanted to blame Gordon Jossie for what had happened to his sister. He knew that Jossie had been looking for her: Jemima had told him as much although not *how* she knew this, so at the time he'd thought it could well be just another one of her fancies. But if Gordon Jossie *had* been looking and if he had found her, he could have gone up to London . . .

Why was the problem. Jossie had another lover now. So had Jemima if she was to be believed. So what was the point? Dog in the manger? It had been known to happen. A bloke is rejected, finds another woman, but still cannot rid his mind of the first one. He decides the only way to scour his brain of the memories associated with her is to eliminate her so he can move on with her replacement. Jemima had been, upon Jossie's own admission and despite his age, his first lover. And that first rejection is always the worst, isn't it?

Those eyes of his behind those dark glasses, Robbie thought. Those shifting feet. The fact that he had so little to say. Hard worker, Jossie, but what did that mean? Strong focus on one thing – building his business – could just as easily turn into strong focus on something else.

Robbie thought all this as he made his way to Ringwood. He would face off with Jossie, he decided, but now wasn't the time. He wanted to see him without Jemima's replacement at his side.

Ringwood was tricky to negotiate. Robbie came at it from Hightown Hill. This forced him to drive past the abandoned

Cupcake Queen, which he couldn't bear to look at. He parked the Land Rover not far from the parish church of St Peter and Paul, overlooking the market square from a hillock where it rose among ancient graves. From the car park, Robbie could hear the constant rumble and even smell the exhaust of the lorries chugging along the Ringwood Bypass. From the market square he could see the bright flowers in the church's grave-yard and the hand-washed fronts of the Georgian buildings along the High Street. It was in the High Street that Gerber & Hudson Graphic Design had its small suite of offices, above a shop called Food for Thought. He told Frank to stay in the doorway there, and he went up the stairs.

Robbie found Meredith Powell at her computer, in the process of creating a poster for a children's dance studio there in the town. It wasn't, he knew, the job that she wanted. But unlike Jemima, Meredith had long been a realist, and as a single parent forced to live with her own parents in order to save money, she would know that her dream of designing fabrics was not something immediately attainable.

When she saw Robbie, Meredith rose. She wore a caftan of bright summer hues: boldly lime shot through with violet. Even he could see the colours were all wrong on her. She was gawky and out of place, like him. The thought made him feel a sudden, awkward tenderness for her.

He said, 'A word, Merry?' and Meredith seemed to read something on his face. She went to an interior office, where she popped her head in the doorway to speak briefly to someone. Then she came across to him. He led her down the stairs and, once out on the High Street again, reckoned that the church or the churchyard was the best place to tell her.

She greeted Frank with a 'Hello, doggie-Frank,' and the Weimaraner wagged his tail and followed them along the street. She peered at Robbie and said, 'You look . . . Has something happened, Rob? Have you heard from her?' and he said that he had. For indeed he had, after a fashion. If not *from* her, then *of* her. The result was the same.

They went up the steps and into the graveyard but it was too hot there, he reckoned, with the sun beating down and not a breeze stirring. So he found Frank a shady spot under a bench on the porch and took Meredith inside the church and by then she was saying, 'What is it? It's bad. I can see that. What's happened?'

She didn't weep when he told her. Instead, she went to one of the battered pews. She didn't take a red leather cushion off its holder in order to kneel, though. Rather, she sat. She folded her hands in her lap and when he joined her in the pew, she looked at him.

She murmured, 'I'm most horribly sorry, Rob. This must be so awful for you. I know what she means to you. I know she was . . . She's everything.'

He shook his head because he couldn't reply. The church was cool inside, but he was still hot. He marvelled when, next to him, Meredith shivered.

'*Why* did she leave?' Meredith's voice was anguished. He could tell, however, that she asked the question as a form of one of those universal *why*s: why do terrible things happen at all? Why do people make incomprehensible decisions? Why does evil exist? 'God, Rob. Why did she leave? She loved the New Forest. She wasn't a city girl. She could barely cope with college in Winchester.'

'She said—'

'I *know* what she said. You told me what she said. So did he.' She was silent for a moment, thinking. Then she said, 'And this is down to him, isn't it? This is down to Gordon. Oh, maybe not the killing itself, but part of it. Some small part. Something we can't see or understand just yet. Somehow. Some part of it.'

And then she did begin to cry, which was when she took one of the kneelers from its holder and dropped to her knees upon it. He thought she intended to pray, but she talked instead: to him but with her face towards the altar and its reredos of carved angels holding up their quatrefoil shields. These depicted the instruments of the passion. Interesting, he thought help-lessly, they had nothing to do with instruments of defence.

Meredith told him about looking into Gordon's new partner, Gina Dickens, about looking into the claims she had made about what she was doing in this part of Hampshire. There was no programme for girls at risk that anyone knew of, Meredith told him and she sounded bitter as she gave him the news, no programme at the college in Brockenhurst, no programme through the district council, not one anywhere at all. 'She's lying,' Meredith concluded. 'She met Gordon somewhere a long time ago, believe me, and she wanted him and he wanted her. It wasn't enough that they just *do* it in a hotel or something—' She said this last with the bitterness of a woman who'd done exactly that – 'with no one the wiser. She wanted more. She wanted it all. But she couldn't get it with Jemima around, could she, so she got him to drive Jemima off. Rob, she isn't who she pretends to be.'

Robbie didn't know how to respond to this, so far fetched seemed the notion. Truth was, he wondered about Meredith's real purpose in looking into Gina Dickens and into what Gina Dickens claimed to be doing in Hampshire. Meredith had something of a history of disapproving of people whom she herself could not understand, and more than once over the years of their friendship Jemima had found herself at odds with Meredith because of this, because of Meredith's inability to see why Jemima could simply not *be* without a man as Meredith herself was fully and perfectly capable of being. Meredith was not a serial manhunter; ergo, in her mind, neither should Jemima be.

But there was more to it than that in this particular matter, and Robbie reckoned he knew what it was: if Gina had wanted Gordon and had wanted him to remove Jemima from his life in order to have him, then Gordon had done for Gina what Meredith's long ago London lover had not done for her, despite what had been a greater need in the form of her pregnancy. Gordon had driven Jemima off, opening the door to Gina's complete entry into his life, no secret lover but rather overt life partner. This would rankle with Meredith. She wasn't made of stone.

'Police have been to talk to Gordon,' Robbie told her. 'I expect they talked to her as well. To Gina. They asked me where I was when Jemima . . . when it happened and—'

Meredith whirled to him. 'They didn't!'

''Course. They have to. So they also asked him. Her too, probably. And if they didn't, they will. They'll come to talk to you as well.'

'Me? Why?'

'Because you were her friend. I was meant to give them names of anyone who might tell them something, anything. That's what they're here for.'

'What? To accuse us? You? Me?'

'No. No. Just to make sure they know everything there is to know about her. Which means . . .' He hesitated.

She cocked her head. Her hair touched her shoulder. He saw in places where her skin was bare that it was also freckled as her face was freckled. He recalled her and his sister in a state about the spots on their young adolescent faces, trying this and that product and using makeup and just being growing girls together. The acuteness of the memory struck him.

He said, 'Ah, Merry,' and could go no further. He didn't want to weep in front of her. It felt weak and useless. He was suddenly, stupidly, selfishly aware of how bloody ugly he was, of how weeping would make him seem all the uglier to Jemima's friend and where that had never mattered before, it mattered now, because he wanted comfort. And he thought how there *was* no comfort and never had been and never would be for ugly men such as he.

She said, 'I should have stayed in contact with her, this last year, Rob. If I had done, she might've not gone off.'

'You mustn't think that,' he said. 'It's not your doing. You were her friend and the two of you were just going through a bad patch. That happens, sometimes.'

'It was more than a bad patch. I wanted her to listen, Rob, to hear, just for once. But there were things she never would change her mind about and Gordon was one of them. Because they were sexual by that time and whenever she was sexual with a bloke—'

He gripped her arm to stop her. He felt a cry building in him, but he wouldn't let it escape. He couldn't look at her, so he looked at the stained glass windows round the altar and he thought how they had to be Victorian because the church had been rebuilt, hadn't it, and there was Jesus saying 'It is I, be not afraid,' and there was St Peter, and there the Good Shepherd, and there oh there was Jesus with the children and he was suffering the little children to come unto him and that was the problem, wasn't it, that the little children with all their troubles had not been suffered? Wasn't that the real problem when everything else was stripped away?

Meredith was silent. His hand was still on her arm and he became aware of how hard he was gripping her and how he must be hurting her, actually. He felt her fingers move against his where they were like claws on her bare skin and it came to him that she wasn't trying to loosen his grip but rather she was caressing his fingers and then his hand, making small slow circles to tell him that she understood his grief although the truth of the matter was that she could not understand, nor could anyone else, what it was like to be robbed of everyone, and to have no hope of filling the void.

14

'**C**ourse he was here,' had been Cliff Coward's confirmation of Gordon Jossie's alibi. 'Where else's he s'posed to be, eh?' A short cocky little bloke wearing crusty blue jeans and a sweat-stained headband, he'd been leaning against the bar at his regular watering hole in the village of Winstead, a pint in front of him and an empty crisp bag balled up next to his fist. He played with this as they spoke. He gave few details: they were working on a pub roof near Frith and he expected he'd know well enough if Gordon Jossie hadn't been there six days ago as it was only the two of them and *someone* was up on that scaffold grabbing the bundles of reeds as he'd hoisted them up. ''Spect that was Gordon,' he'd said with a grin. 'Why? What's he s'posed to've done? Mug some old lady in Ringwood market square?'

'It's more a question of murder,' Barbara told him.

Cliff's face altered, but his story did not. Gordon Jossie had been with him, he said, and Gordon Jossie was no murderer. 'I think I'd bloody well know,' he noted. 'Been working for him over a year. Who's he s'posed to have done?'

'Jemima Hastings.'

'*Jemima*? Not a chance.'

They went from Winstead up to Itchen Abbas, bypassing Winchester on the motorway. On a small property between Itchen Abbas and the hamlet of Abbotstone, they found the master thatcher at whose side Gordon Jossie had worked years earlier to learn the trade. He was called Ringo Heath – 'Don't ask,' Heath said sourly. 'It might have been John, Paul, or George and don't I bloody well know it' – and when they arrived, he was seated on a battered bench, on the shady side of a brick house. He seemed to be whittling, as in one hand he had a wicked-looking knife with a sharp blade curving into a hook, and he was applying this to a thin switch, splitting it first and then sharpening both of its ends into arrow-tip points. At his feet lay a pile of switches yet to be seen to. In a wooden box next to him on the bench, he was placing those that had already been whittled. To Barbara, they looked like toothpicks for a giant, each of them perhaps a yard or more long. They also looked like potential weapons. As did the knife itself, which she learned was called a spar hook. And the toothpicks were the spars, which were used to make staples.

Heath held one up, extended between his two palms. He bent it nearly double and then released it. It sprang back to its original straight line. 'Pliable,' he told them although they hadn't asked. 'Hazel wood. You c'n use willow at a pinch, but hazel's best.' It would be twisted into a staple, he told them, and the staple would be used to hold the reed in place once it was in position on the rooftop. 'Gets buried in the reeds and eventually rots away, but that's no matter. Reeds're all compressed by then and that's what you want: compression. Best rooftop money can buy, thatch is. It's not all about chocolate-box houses and front gardens done up with pansies, is it?'

'I expect not,' Barbara said cooperatively. 'What d'you think, Winnie?'

'Looks good to me, roof like that,' Nkata said. 'Bit of a problem with fire, I'd 'spect.'

'Bah, nonsense,' Heath said. 'Old wives' tale.'

Barbara doubted it. But they weren't there to talk about the flammable nature of reeds on rooftops. She stated their purpose: Gordon Jossie and his apprenticeship with Ringo Heath. They'd phoned Heath in advance to track him down. He'd said, 'Scotland Yard? What're you lot doing out here?' but he'd been cooperative.

What could he tell them about Gordon Jossie? Barbara began. Did he remember him?

'Oh. Aye. No reason to forget Gordon.' Heath continued

his work as he gave his history with Jossie: he'd come to work as an apprentice a bit older than usual. He'd been twenty-one. Usually an apprentice was sixteen 'which's better for training as they don't know a thing about a thing, do they, and they're still at the point when they even might *believe* they don't know a thing about a thing, eh? But twenty-one's a bit old 'cause you don't want some bloke set in his ways. I was a bit reluctant to take him on.'

But take him on he did, and things turned out well. Hard worker, Jossie was. A bloke who talked very little and listened a lot and 'didn't go round wearing those sodding earphones with music blasting away like kids do now. Half the time you can't even get their attention, eh? You're up on the scaffold shouting at 'em and they're down below listening to whoever and bobbing their heads to the *beat*.' He said this last word scornfully, a man who obviously did not share his namesake's passion for music.

Jossie, on the other hand, hadn't been like the typical apprentice. *And* he'd been willing to do anything he'd been assigned to do, without claiming something was 'beneath him or rubbish like that'. Once he was given actual thatching jobs to do – which, by the way, did not happen for the first nine months of his apprenticeship – he wasn't ever above asking a question. And it would be a *good* question and never once did it have to do with '"How much money c'n I expect to make, Ringo?" like he was thinking he'd be going out to buy some Maserati on what a thatcher makes. It's a good living, I tell him, but it's not *that* good so if you're 'specting to impress the ladies with golden cufflinks or whatever, you're barking up a tree with no leaves, if you know what I mean. What I tell him is that there's always need for a thatcher 'cause we're talking 'bout listed buildings, eh? And they're all round the south and up into Gloucestershire and beyond and they got to *stay* thatched. There's no replacing 'em with tiles or anything else. So if you're good – and he meant to be good, let me tell you – you work all year and you've gen'rally got more bookings than you c'n handle.'

Gordon Jossie had apparently been a model apprentice:
With no complaint he'd started out doing nothing more than
fetching, carrying, hoisting, cleaning up, burning rubbish
and according to Heath he 'did it all *right*, mind you. No
cutting corners. I could tell he was going to be good when
I got him on the scaffold. This is detail work, this is. Oh it
looks like slapping reeds onto the rafters and that's that,
doesn't it, but it's step-by-step and a decent roof – a big
one, say – takes months to put on 'cause it's not like laying
tiles or pounding shingles, is it? It's working with a natural
product, it is, so there's no two reeds the same diameter and
the length of them's not exact. This is something takes
patience and skill and it takes years to get it down so you
can do a roof properly.'

Gordon Jossie worked for him as an apprentice for nearly
four years, and by that time he'd gone far beyond the apprentice stage and was more like a partner. In fact, Ringo Heath
had wanted to bring him on as a bonafide partner, but Gordon
wanted to have his own business. So he'd left with Heath's
blessing, and had begun the way they all began: subcontracted
to someone with a larger concern till he was able to break out
on his own.

'Ever since, I end up with one after 'nother lazy sods to
work as apprentices,' Heath concluded, 'and believe me, I'd
take an older bloke like Gordon Jossie in the blink of an eye,
if one came round.'

He'd filled the wooden box with completed spars as they
were speaking, and he heaved it up and took it over to an
open-back lorry, where he slung it alongside various crates
that sat among a collection of curious implements, which Heath
was happy to identify for them without being asked to do so.
He was building up a real head of steam on his topic. They
had shearing hooks for carving into the thatch –

'Takes about a millimetre off, it does, sharp as anything,
and you got to use it with care lest you slice into your hand.'

– leggetts which were used to dress the thatch and which,

to Barbara, looked like nothing more than an aluminium grill with a handle, something one might use on the cooker to fry up bacon; the Dutchman, which was used in *place* of the leggett to dress the thatch when the roof was curved . . .

Barbara nodded sagely and Nkata jotted everything in his notebook, as if expecting he'd be tested on it later. She was having trouble keeping it all straight and determining how she would bring the thatcher away from his lengthy exposition on the process of thatching a roof and back to the subject of Gordon Jossie, when Heath mentioned 'and ever'one of them's different', which made her pay closer attention to what he was saying.

'. . . bits an' bobs that the blacksmith provides, like the crooks an' the pins.' The crooks were curved at one end – hence the name, as they resembled a shepherd's crook in miniature – and these were hooked round the reeds and driven into the rafters to hold them in place. The pins, which resembled long spikes with an eye at one end and a sharp point at the other, held the reeds in place while the thatcher was working. These came from the blacksmith, and the interesting bit was that every blacksmith made them according to however he wanted to make them, especially as far as the point was concerned.

'Forged on four sides, forged on two sides, cut to give it a slash-tip, spun on a grinding wheel . . . Whatever the blacksmith fancies. I like the Dutch ones best. I like a *proper* forging, I do.' His said this last as if one could not expect such a thing as proper forging to go on in England any longer.

But Barbara was taken by the very idea of blacksmithing and how it might relate to making a weapon. The thatching tools *themselves* were weaponlike, if it came to that, no matter Heath's referring to them dismissively as the bits and bobs of his job. Barbara picked one up – she chose a pin – and found its tip was nice and sharp and suitable for murder. She handed it to Nkata and saw by his expression that they were of the same mind on the matter.

She said, 'Why was he twenty-one years old when he came to you, Mr Heath? Do you know?'

Heath took a moment, apparently to adjust to the abrupt change in topic as he'd been nattering on about why the Dutch took more pride in their work than the English and this seemed to have to do with the EU and the mass migration of Albanians and other Eastern Europeans into the UK. He blinked and said, 'Eh? Who?'

'Twenty-one was old for an apprentice, you said. What had Gordon Jossie been doing before he came to you?'

College, Ringo Heath told them. He'd been a student in some college in Winchester, studying one trade or another although Heath couldn't recall which it was. He'd brought two letters with him, though. Recommendations these were, from someone or other who'd taught him. It wasn't the typical way an apprentice presented himself for potential employment, so he'd been quite impressed with that. Did they want to see the letters? He thought he still had them.

When Barbara told him that they did indeed want to see them, Heath turned towards his house and bellowed, 'Kitten! You're needed.' To this a most unkittenlike woman emerged. She carried a rolling pin under her arm and she looked the type who'd be happy to use it: big, brawling, and muscular.

Kitten said, 'Really, pet, why've you got to yell? I'm only just inside, in the kitchen,' in a surprisingly genteel voice, completely at odds with her appearance. She sounded liked an upstairs someone from a costume drama, but she looked like someone who'd be washing the pots and pans in a decidedly downstairs scullery.

Heath simpered at her, saying, 'Darling girl. Don't know the strength of my own voice, do I. Sorry. Have we still got them letters that Gordon Jossie handed over when he first wanted a job? You know which ones I mean, don't you? The ones from his college? You remember them?' And to Barbara and Winston, 'She keeps the books and such, does my Kitten. And the girl's got a mind for facts and figures that'd make you dizzy. I keep telling her to go on telly. One of those quiz programmes or summat. I say we could be millionaires if she got herself on a quiz show.'

'Oh, you do go on, Ringo,' Kitten said. 'I made that chicken and leek pie you love, by the by.'

'Precious girl.'

'Silly boy.'

'I'll see you when I see you.'

'Oh, you do talk, Ring.'

'Uh . . . About those letters?' Barbara cut in. She glanced at Winston who was watching the exchange between man and wife like a bloke at an amorous ping-pong match.

Kitten said that she would fetch them as she reckoned they were in Ringo's business files. She wouldn't be a moment, she said, because she liked to stay organised since 'leave things to Ringo, we'd be living under mounds of paperwork, let me tell you'.

'True enough,' Ringo said, 'darling girl.'

'Handsome—'

'*Thank* you, Mrs Heath,' Barbara said pointedly.

Kitten made kissy noises at her husband who made a gesture that seemed to indicate he'd love to swat her on the bum, at which she giggled and disappeared inside the house. Within two minutes, she was back, and she carried a manila folder from which she extricated the aforementioned letters for their inspection.

These were, Barbara saw, recommendations attesting to Gordon Jossie's character, his work ethic, his pleasant demeanour, his willingness to take instruction and all the et ceteras. They were written on the letterhead of Winchester Technical College II, and one of them came from a Jonas Bligh while the other had been written by a Keating Crawford. They'd both indicated knowledge of Gordon Jossie from within the classroom and from outside the classroom. Fine young man, they declared, trustworthy and good-hearted and well deserving of an opportunity to learn a trade like thatching. One would not go wrong in hiring him. He was bound to succeed.

Barbara asked could she keep the letters. She'd return them to the Heaths, of course, but for the time being, if they didn't mind . . .

They didn't mind. At this point, however, Ringo Heath asked what Scotland Yard wanted with Gordon Jossie anyway. 'What's he s'posed to've done?'

'We're investigating a murder up in London,' Barbara told them. 'A girl called Jemima Hastings. D'you know her?'

They didn't. But what they did know and were willing to assert was that Gordon Jossie was definitely no killer. Kitten, however, added an intriguing detail to the Jossie resumé as they were about to leave.

He couldn't read right, she told them, which always made her wonder at the fact that he somehow completed courses in college. While obviously there were classes one took that might not *require* reading, she had always found it a bit odd that he'd managed such *success* at the Winchester college. She said to her husband, 'You know, darling boy, that *does* suggest something not quite right about Gordon, doesn't it? I mean, if he could actually manage to get through his coursework and still hide the fact that he couldn't read, it does rather imply an ability to hide other things, wouldn't you say?'

'What d'you mean he couldn't read?' Ringo demanded. 'That's rubbish, that is. Bah.'

'No, precious. It's the truth. I saw it. He absolutely could not read.'

'D'you mean he had trouble with reading?' Nkata asked. 'Or he couldn't read.'

He couldn't read, she said. In fact, while he knew the alphabet, he had to print it out in order to know it for certain. It was the most peculiar thing she'd ever seen. Because of this, she'd wondered more than once about how he'd got through school. 'Reckoned he'd been performing for the instructors in ways not entirely academic,' she concluded, 'if you know what I mean.'

★   ★   ★

Throughout the rest of the day, Meredith Powell felt a dull fire burning within her. It was accompanied by a pounding in her head, one that wasn't connected to pain but rather to the words *she's dead.* The simple fact of Jemima's death was bad: it put Meredith into a state of disbelief and sorrow, and the sorrow was more profound than she would ever have expected to feel for someone who was not a member of her immediate family. Beyond the fact of her death, though, was the additional fact that Jemima had been taken away before Meredith had been able to put things right between them, and this gnawed at her conscience and her heart. She could no longer remember what it even was that had so damaged their long friendship. Had it been a slow chipping away of their affection for each other, or had it been one deadly blow? She couldn't recall, which told her how unimportant it must have been.

'I'm not like you, Meredith,' Jemima had said so many times. 'Why can't you just accept that?'

Because having a man's not going to make you stop being afraid had been the answer. But it had been a reply that Jemima had pooh-poohed as an indication of Meredith's jealousy. Except she hadn't been jealous, not really. She'd merely been concerned. She'd watched Jemima flit from boy to boy to man to man for years in a restless search for something not a single one of them would ever be able to give her. And *that* had been what she'd wished her friend to understand and what she'd tried again and again to get across to her until finally she'd thrown up her hands – or Jemima had done, because she couldn't remember now – and that had been that as far as friendship went between them.

She phoned Gordon Jossie's house before leaving work at the end of the day. Gina Dickens answered, and this was good, as it was Gina Dickens whom Meredith wished to see. She said, 'I need to talk to you. Will you meet me? I'm in Ringwood just now but I can meet you anywhere, wherever you like. Just not at . . . not at Gordon's please.' She didn't want to see the house again. She didn't think she could face it just now, not with another woman there, happily going about a life with Gordon Jossie while Jemima lay dead, cold and murdered up in London.

Gina said, 'The police have been here. They said that Jemima—'

Meredith squeezed her eyes shut, and the telephone felt cold and slick in her hand. She said, 'I need to speak with you.'

'Why?'

'I'll meet you. You name the place.'

'Why? You're making me nervous, Meredith.'

'I don't mean to. Please. I'll meet you anywhere. Just not at Gordon's.'

There was a pause. Then Gina named Hinchelsea Wood. Meredith didn't want to risk a wood, with all its solitude and everything that solitude suggested about danger, no matter what Gina Dickens said about being nervous of *her* and all that this was supposed to imply about Gina Dickens' apparent innocence. Meredith suggested a heath instead. What about Longslade Heath? There was a car park and they could—

'Not a heath,' Gina said at once.

'Why not?'

'Snakes.'

'What snakes?'

'Adders. There're adders on the heath. You must know that. I read that somewhere, and I don't want to—'

'Hatchet Pond, then,' Meredith cut in. 'It's outside of Beaulieu.' They agreed on this.

There were other people at Hatchet Pond when Meredith arrived. There were ponies and foals as well. The people strolled along the edge of the water, they walked their dogs, they sat in cars reading, they fished, they chatted to each other on benches. The ponies lapped water and grazed.

The pond itself stretched out a good distance, with a finger of land on the far side that reached into the water and was topped with beech and chestnut trees and a single, graceful willow. It was a good trysting place for young people at night, tucked off the road so that parked cars could not be seen, but still conveniently located at the intersection of several routes: with Beaulieu immediately to its east, East Boldre to the south and Brockenhurst to the west. All sorts of trouble between hot-blooded adolescents could be got into here. Meredith knew that from Jemima.

She waited some twenty minutes for Gina to arrive. She herself had barrelled the distance from Ringwood, driven by determination. It was one thing to be deeply suspicious about Gordon Jossie, Gina Dickens and the fact that most of Jemima's belongings were packed neatly away in Gordon's house. It was another thing to learn that Jemima had been murdered. All the way from Ringwood, Meredith had engaged in a mental conversation with Gina about these and other matters. When Gina finally arrived in her little red convertible with her enormous film star dark glasses covering half her face and a scarf keeping her hair in place, as if she was Audrey flipping Hepburn or something, Meredith was quite ready for her.

Gina got out of the car. She cast a look at one of the ponies nearby, as Meredith crossed the car park to her. Meredith said, 'Let's walk,' and when Gina hesitated, saying, 'I'm a bit leery of the horses,' Meredith countered with, 'Oh for God's sake. They won't hurt you. They're just *ponies*. Don't be stupid.' She took Gina's arm.

Gina pulled away. 'I can walk on my own,' she said stiffly. 'But not near the horses.'

'Fine.' Meredith headed along a path that skirted the water. She cooperatively chose a direction away from the ponies, towards a lone fisherman who was casting his line not far from a heron, motionless, as it waited to scoop up an unsuspecting eel.

'What's this about?' Gina demanded.

'What do you *think* this is about? Gordon has her car. He has her clothes. Now she's dead in London.'

Gina stopped walking, and Meredith turned to her. Gina said. 'If you're suggesting or even *trying* to get me to believe that Gordon—'

'Wouldn't she have sent for her clothes? *Eventually*?'

'She wouldn't need her country clothing in London,' Gina said. 'What was she going to do with it there? The same goes for her car. She didn't need a car. Where would she keep it? Why would she drive it?'

Meredith tore at the skin round her fingernails. There was truth here somewhere. She meant to have it. She said, 'I know all about you, Gina. There's no programme anywhere round here for young girls at risk. Not at the college in Brockenhurst, and not at the comprehensive. Social services haven't even heard of a programme and social services haven't even heard of *you*. I know because I checked, all right? So why don't you tell me what you're doing here, *really*. Why don't you tell me the truth about you and Gordon? About when you really met and how you met and what that meant to him and Jemima.'

Gina lips parted then pursed. She said, 'Honestly. You've been checking on me? What's wrong with you, Meredith? Why are you so—'

'Don't you dare turn this on me. That's clever of you, but I'm not about to be dragged in that direction.'

'Oh, don't be ridiculous. No one's dragging you anywhere.' She pushed past Meredith on the narrow path along the water. 'If we're going to walk, let's bloody well walk.'

Gina stalked off. After a moment, she began to speak over her shoulder, saying sharply, 'Just think, if you're capable of it. I told you I was *establishing* a programme. I didn't tell you it existed. And the first step in establishing a programme is assessing need, for heaven's sake. *That's* what I'm doing. That's what I *was* doing when I met Gordon. And yes, all right, I admit I haven't been as diligent as I could have been about it, I haven't been as . . . as dedicated as I was when I first came to the New Forest. And yes, all right, the reason for that is that I got involved with Gordon. And I've rather liked being

Gordon's partner and having Gordon provide for me. But as far as I know, none of that is a *crime*, Meredith. So what I want to know – if you don't mind – is why you dislike Gordon so much? Why can't you stand the thought of me, or anyone else I dare say, being with him? Because this really isn't about me, is it? This is about Gordon.'

'How did you meet him? How did you *really* meet him?'

'I told you! I've told you the absolute truth from the first. I met him last month, in Boldre Gardens. I saw him later that day and we went for a drink. He *asked* me for a drink and he looked harmless enough and it was a public place and . . . Oh, why am I bothering with all this? Why don't you just come out with it? Why don't you tell me what you suspect me of? Murdering Jemima? Encouraging the man I love to murder her? Or is it loving him at all that bothers you and why would that be?'

'This isn't about loving anyone.'

'Oh, isn't it? Then perhaps you're accusing me of sending Gordon off to murder Jemima for some reason. Perhaps you see me standing on the front step and waving a handkerchief as he drives off to do *whatever* he was supposed to do. But *why* would I do that? She was gone from his life.'

'Perhaps she got in touch with him. Perhaps she wanted to come back. Perhaps they met somewhere and she said she wanted him and you couldn't have that because then you'd have to—'

'So *I* killed her? Not Gordon at all, but me this time? Do you know how ridiculous you sound? And do you want to be meeting out here in the wilds of Hatchet Pond with a killer?' She put her hands on her hips as if thinking about the answer to her question. She smiled and said bitterly, 'Ah. Yes. I see why you didn't want Hinchelsea Wood. How foolish of me. I might have killed you there. I've no idea how I would have done it, but that's what you think. That I'm a killer. Or that Gordon is. Or that we both are: somehow in cahoots to eliminate Jemima for reasons that are so *bloody* obscure . . .'

She turned away. There was a weather-beaten bench nearby and she made for this and dropped upon it. She whipped off her scarf and shook back her hair. She removed her dark glasses, folded them up and held them tightly in her hand.

Meredith stood before her, arms crossed against her chest. She was suddenly and acutely aware of how *different* they were: Gina tanned and voluptuous and obviously appealing to any man and herself a miserable, freckled beanpole of a thing, alone and likely to stay that way. Only that *wasn't* the issue here.

Yet as if Gina had read her mind, she said in a tone no longer bitter at all but instead resigned, 'I'm wondering if this is just what you do to any woman who has a nice relationship with a man. I know you didn't approve of Gordon and Jemima: he said you didn't want him to be with her. But I couldn't sort out why, what it was to you if she and Gordon were partners. Was it because you yourself have no one? Because, perhaps, you keep trying and failing while all round you women and men get attached with no trouble at all? I mean, I know what happened to you. Gordon told me. Jemima told him. Because, of course, he was trying to sort out why you disliked him so much and she said it had to do with London, with when you lived there and got involved with the married man, the one you didn't know was married, and there you were pregnant . . .'

Meredith felt her throat close. She wanted to stop the flow of words but she couldn't: the catalogue of her personal failures. She felt weak and dizzy as Gina kept talking . . . about betrayal and then desertion and then *bloody little fool, don't claim you didn't know I was married because you are simply not that stupid and I never lied, I never once lied, and why the hell weren't you taking precautions unless it was that you wanted to trap me is that what it was did you want to trap me well I won't be trapped not by the likes of you or by anyone if it comes down to it and yes, yes, you can damn well sort out exactly what that means my dear.*

'Oh, I'm sorry. I'm *sorry*. Here. Please sit.' Gina rose and urged Meredith onto the bench next to her. She said nothing more for several minutes as across the surface of the placid water dragonflies flitted, their fragile wings flashing purple and green in the light.

'Listen,' Gina said quietly, 'can you and I possibly be friends? Or if not friends, perhaps nodding acquaintances? Or maybe nodding acquaintances at first and then *afterwards* friends?'

'I don't know,' Meredith said dully, and she wondered how widely her shame was known. She reckoned it was known everywhere. It was, she thought, as much as she deserved. For stupid is as stupid does, and she'd been unforgivably stupid.

By the time John Dresser's body was found two days after his disappearance, he was national news. What was known to the public at that point was what was seen in the CCTV films from the Barriers, in which a toddler seems to walk off happily hand in hand with three little boys. The still photos released by the police thus offered images that could be interpreted in one of two ways: as children having found the toddler wandering and setting out to take him to an adult who ultimately did him harm or as children intent upon the abduction and possible terrorising of another child. These images played across the front page of every national and local newspaper, and on the television.

With Michael Spargo wearing that unmistakable, overlarge mustard anorak, his identity was quickly established by his own mother. Sue Spargo took her son straight to the police station. That he'd been beaten beforehand was evident by the heavy bruising on his face, although there is no record of anyone's having questioned Sue Spargo about this beating.

Following the rules of law, Michael Spargo was interrogated in the presence of a social worker and his mother. The detective in charge of this questioning was a twenty-nine-year veteran of the police force, DI Ryan Farrier, a man with three children and two grandchildren of his own. Farrier had been working criminal investigations for nineteen years of his twenty-nine year career, but he had never come across a killing that affected him as did the murder of John Dresser. Indeed, so deeply was he harrowed by what he saw and heard during the investigation that he has since retired from the police and has remained under the care of a psychiatrist. It's worth noting, as well, that the police department made both psychological and psychiatric services available to all the individuals who worked upon the crime once John Dresser's body was found.

As might be expected, Michael Spargo denied everything at first, claiming that he was in school that day and maintaining that claim until presented not only with the CCTV film but also with evidence from his teacher as to his truancy. 'All right, I was with Reg and Ian,' is all that he says on tape at this point. When asked for their surnames, he tells the police, 'It was their idea, wasn't it. I didn't never want to nick that kid.'

This enrages Sue Spargo, whose eruption into verbal abuse and whose attempts at physical abuse are immediately halted by the other adults in the room. Her screams of 'You tell them the bloody truth or I'll fucking kill you, I will,' are the last words she will speak to Michael during the course of the investigation and up until the moments she shares with him following his sentencing. This abandonment of her son at a crucial moment in his life is characteristic of her parenting style and perhaps speaks more loudly than anything else as to the source of Michael's psychological disturbance.

Arrests of Reggie Arnold and Ian Barker quickly followed Michael Spargo's mentioning of their names, and what was known at the time of their arrests was only that John Dresser had been seen with them and had disappeared. When they were brought to the police station (each boy was taken to a different station, and they did not see each other until their trial began), Reggie was accompanied by his mother Laura and later joined by his father Rudy, and Ian was alone although his grandmother arrived prior to his being interviewed. The whereabouts of Ian's mother Tricia at the time of his arrest are never made clear in the documentation, and she did not attend his trial.

At first no one suspected that John Dresser was dead. Transcripts and tapes of early questioning by the police indicate that their initial belief was that the boys took John in an act of mischief, grew tired of his company, and left him somewhere to fend for himself. Although each of the boys was already known to the police, they were none of them known for anything more than truancy, acts of petty vandalism and minor thefts. (One does wonder how Ian Barker, with a history of small animal torture, managed to go unnoticed for so long, however.) It was only when repeated witnesses began to step forward in the first thirty-six hours following John's disappearance – communicating the level of the toddler's distress – that the police seem to have developed a sense that something more ominous than a prank had occurred.

A search for the little boy had already begun, and as the area surrounding the Barriers was picked through by police and by concerned citizens in an organised and ever-widening circumference, it was not overlong before the Dawkins building site came under scrutiny.

Constable Martin Neild, twenty-four years old at the time and a brand new father, was the individual who found the body of John Dresser, alerted to the possibility of its proximity by the sight of John's blue snow suit crumpled and bloodied on the ground near a disused Portaloo. Inside this loo, Neild found the baby's body, stuffed callously into the chemical toilet. Neild reports that he 'wanted to think it was a doll or something', but he knew otherwise.

15

'What's the decision about Sunday lunch, Isabelle? I've mentioned it to the boys, by the way. They're quite keen.'

Isabelle Ardery pressed her fingers to her forehead. She'd taken two paracetamol but they'd done nothing to ease her headache. Nor had they done much for her stomach. She knew she should have eaten something before gulping them down, but the thought of food on top of an already roiling gut was more than she could manage.

She said, 'Let me speak to them, Bob. Are they there?'

He said, 'You don't sound quite yourself. Are you unwell, Isabelle?' Which wasn't what he meant, of course. *Unwell* was a euphemism, and only barely. *Unwell* stood in place of everything else he didn't intend to ask but fully intended to communicate.

She said, 'I was up late last night. I'm on a case. You might have read about it. A woman's been murdered in a north London cemetery.'

He clearly wasn't interested in that part of her life. He said, 'Hitting it rather hard then, are you?'

'There are usually late nights when it comes to a murder investigation,' she replied, deliberately choosing to misunderstand him. 'You know that, Bob. So may I speak to the boys? Where are they? Certainly they're not out somewhere at this hour of the morning.'

'Still asleep,' he said. 'I don't like to wake them.'

'Surely they can go back to sleep if I just say hello.'

'You know how they are. And they need their rest.'

'They need their mother.'

'They have a mother, as things are. Sandra's quite—'

'Sandra has two children of her own.'

'You aren't suggesting she treats them differently, I hope. Because, frankly, I won't have that. Because, *also* frankly, she treats them a damn sight better than their natural mother does since she's fully conscious and in possession of all her faculties when she's around them. Do you really want to have this conversation, Isabelle? Now, are you coming for lunch on Sunday or are you not?'

'I'll send the boys a note,' she said quietly, beating down her incipient rage. 'May I assume, Bob, that you and Sandra aren't forbidding my sending a note to them?'

'We're not *forbidding* anything,' he said.

'Oh please. Let's not pretend.' She rang off without a goodbye. She knew she'd pay for that later – *Did you actually hang up on me, Isabelle? Surely we must have been disconnected somehow, yes?* – but at the moment, she could do nothing else. To remain on the line meant being exposed to an extended display of his ostensible paternal concern, and she wasn't up to it. She wasn't, in fact, up to much that morning, and she was going to have to do something about that before heading into work.

Four cups of black coffee – all right, it was Irish coffee, but she could be forgiven for that as she'd used only a *dash* of spirits – one slice of toast and a shower later, she was feeling fit. She was actually in the middle of the morning briefing before she felt the urge once more. But then, it was easy to fight it off because she could hardly duck into the Ladies, and that was just how it was. What she could do instead was keep her mind on her work and vow to have a different kind of evening and night at the end of this day.

Sergeants Havers and Nkata had reported in first thing from the New Forest. They were staying in a hotel in Sway – Forest Heath Hotel, it was called, Havers said – and this bit of information was met with guffaws and remarks of the 'Hope Winnie's managed to get his own room' ilk, which Isabelle cut off with a sharp 'That'll do,' while they assessed the information the two sergeants had unearthed so far. Havers appeared to be building up a head of steam over the fact that Gordon Jossie was a master thatcher and that thatching tools were not only deadly but made by hand. For his part, Nkata seemed to be more interested in the fact of another woman being present in Gordon Jossie's life. Havers also mentioned Gordon Jossie's letters of reference from a Winchester college and then brought up a thatcher called Ringo Heath. She concluded by listing the names of individuals still needing to be spoken to.

'C'n we get you lot on to background checks?' Havers then asked. 'Hastings, Jossie, Heath, Dickens . . .' They'd spoken to the local rozzers, by the way, but there wasn't a lot of joy from that quarter. New Scotland Yard were welcome to nose round the locals' patch, according to the CS in Lyndhurst, but as the murder was in London, it wasn't the locals' problem.

Ardery assured the sergeant that they'd get on things at this end, since she herself wished to know everything there was to know about anyone even remotely concerned with Jemima Hastings. 'I want to know every detail there is, down to whether their bowels move regularly,' she told the team. She instructed Philip Hale to carry on with the names from Hampshire and she ticked off the additional London names in case he'd forgotten them: Yolanda the Psychic, aka Sharon Price, Jayson Druther, Abbott Langer, Paolo di Fazio, Frazer Chaplin, Bella McHaggis. 'Alibis for everyone, with confirmation, and try for two sources. John, I'll want you handling that part. Coordinate with SO7 as well. Light a fire over there. We need some good information.'

Stewart gave no indication that he'd heard her, so Isabelle said, 'Did you get that, John?' to which he smiled sardonically and pointed an index finger to his temple.

'All in there . . . guv,' he noted, and, 'Anything else?' as if he suspected that she was the one in need of a good prodding.

She narrowed her eyes. She was about to respond when Thomas Lynley did so. He was standing at the back of the room, politely keeping himself out of the way although she couldn't decide if this was a benefit to her or merely a reminder to everyone else of the immense contrast between their styles. He said, 'Perhaps Matt Jones? Sidney St James's partner? It's likely nothing, but if he'd been to the cigar shop as Barbara indicated . . .'

'Matt Jones as well,' Isabelle said. 'Philip, someone on your team?'

'Will do,' Hale said.

She told them all to get on with it, then, and said, 'Thomas? If you'll come with me?'

They would seek out Paolo di Fazio's studio, she told him. Between their interview with the sculptor and Barbara Havers' report of her conversation with Bella McHaggis about Paolo and the pregnancy test, there existed an ocean that wanted swimming.

Lynley nodded, amenable to anything, it seemed. She said she would meet him at her car. Five minutes for her to use the Ladies, she told him. He said certainly in that well-bred fashion of his and she felt him watching her as she walked off. She stopped in her office to grab her handbag, and she took it with her to the toilet. No one could possibly fault her for that, she thought.

As before, he was waiting patiently at her car, but this time on the passenger's side. She raised an eyebrow, to which he said, 'I expect you need the practice, guv. London traffic and all that?'

She tried to read him for underlying meanings, but he was very good at a poker face. 'Very well,' she told him. 'And it's Isabelle, Thomas.'

'Due respect, guv.'

She sighed impatiently. 'Oh for God's sake, Thomas. What did you call your last superintendent behind the scenes?'

'*Sir*, mostly. Other times it would have been *guv*.'

'Fine. Wonderful. Well, I'm ordering you to call me Isabelle when we're alone together. Have you an aversion to that?'

He seemed to consider this: the aversion bit. He examined the door handle on which he'd already placed his hand. When he looked up, his brown eyes were candidly on her face and the sudden openness of his expression was disconcerting. 'I think "guv" gives a distance you might prefer,' he said. 'All things considered.'

'What things?' she said.

'All things.'

The frank look they exchanged made her wonder about him. She said, 'You play your cards quite close, don't you, Thomas.'

He said, 'I have no cards at all.'

She snorted at this and got into the car.

Paolo di Fazio's studio was near Clapham Junction. This was south of the river, he told her, not terribly far from Putney. Their best course was to drive along the Embankment. Did she want him to give her directions?

'I think I can just about manage the route to the river,' she told him.

Paolo di Fazio himself had indicated where to find him. Upon being contacted he'd declared that he had given them *all* the information there was to give about himself and Jemima Hastings, but if they wanted to spend their time going over old ground, then so be it. He'd be where he was most mornings: at the studio.

The studio turned out to be tucked into one of the many railway arches created by the viaducts leading out of Clapham Junction. Most of these had long ago been put to use, being converted from tunnels into wine cellars, clothing outlets, car repair shops and – in one case – even a delicatessen selling imported olives, meats and cheeses. Paolo di Fazio's studio was between a picture framer and a bicycle shop, and they arrived to find its front doors open and its overhead lights brightly illuminating the space. This space was whitewashed and set up in two sections. One section appeared to be given over to the early work that went on when an artist took a sculpture from clay on its way to bronze, so there were masses of wax, latex, fibre glass and bags of plaster everywhere, along with the grit and the grime one might associate with working with such substances. The other section accommodated work stations for four artists, whose pieces were currently shrouded in plastic and likely in varying stages of completion. Finished bronze sculptures had places in a row along the centre of the studio, and they ranged in style from the realistic to the fantastical.

When they came upon it, Paolo di Fazio's style turned out to be figurative, but of a nature that favoured bulbous elbows, long limbs, and disproportionately small heads. Lynley murmured, 'Shades of Giacometti,' and he paused in front of it, and Isabelle glanced at him sharply to gauge his expression. She had no idea what he was talking about, and she absolutely hated a show-off. But she saw he was taking out his spectacles to give the sculpture a closer look, and he seemed unaware that he'd even spoken. She realised yet again that he was impossible to read, and she additionally wondered if she could work with someone who'd so mastered the art of keeping his thoughts to himself.

Paolo di Fazio wasn't in the studio. Nor was anyone else. But he entered as they were having a look at his work area, which was identifiable by more of the masks, similar to those he made in Jubilee Market Hall, that stood on dusty wooden pedestals upon shelves at the rear. Specifically, they were having a look at his tools and at his tools' potential to do harm.

Di Fazio said, 'Please touch nothing,' as he came in their direction. He was carrying a takeaway coffee and a bag from which he brought out two bananas and an apple. These he placed carefully on one of the shelves as if arranging them for a still life. He was dressed as he'd been dressed when they'd earlier seen him: blue jeans, a T-shirt and dress shoes, which as before, seemed an odd get-up for someone at work with clay, particularly the dress shoes as he somehow managed to keep them perfectly clean. They would have passed muster at a military inspection. He said, 'I'm at work here, as you can see.' He gestured with his coffee in the direction of a shrouded piece.

Isabelle said, 'And may we look at your work?'

He apparently needed to think about this for a moment before he shrugged and removed its swaddling of plastic and cloth. It was another elongated, knobby-limbed piece, apparently male and apparently in agony if the expression was anything to go by. A mouth gaped open, limbs stretched out, the neck curved back and the shoulders arched. At its feet lay a grill of some sort, and to Isabelle it looked for all the world as if the figure were in anguish over a broken barbecue. She reckoned it all meant something deep and she readied herself to hear Lynley make an insufferably illuminating remark about it. But he said nothing, and di Fazio himself didn't shed any light on matters for Isabelle when he identified the figure only as St Lawrence. He went on to tell them that he was doing a series of Christian martyrs for a Sicilian monastery, by which Isabelle took it that St Lawrence's gruesome means of death had actually been by barbecue. This made her wonder what belief, if any, she'd be willing to die for, and *this* in turn made her wonder how or if the deaths of martyrs tied in with Jemima Hastings' own end.

'I've done Sebastian, Lucy and Cecilia for them,' di Fazio was saying. 'This is the fourth of a series of ten. They'll be placed in the niches in the monastery chapel.'

'You're well known in Italy, then,' Lynley said.

'No. My uncle is well-known in the monastery.'

'Your uncle's a monk?'

Di Fazio gave a sardonic laugh. 'My uncle is a criminal. He thinks he can buy his way into heaven if he makes enough donations to them. Money, food, wine, my art. It is all the same to him. And as he pays me for the work, I don't question the . . .' He looked thoughtful, as if seeking the proper word. '. . . the effectiveness of his actions.'

At the street end of the studio, a figure appeared in the

double doorway, silhouetted by the light outside. It was a
woman, who called out, 'Ciao, baby,' and strode over to one
of the other work areas. She was short and rather plump
with an enormous shelf-like bosom and coils of espresso
coloured hair. She whipped the protective covering off her
piece of sculpture and set to work without another look in
their direction. Nonetheless, her presence seemed to make
di Fazio uneasy, for he suggested that they continue their
conversation elsewhere.

'Dominique didn't know Jemima,' he told them, with a nod
at the woman. 'She'd have nothing to add.'

But she knew di Fazio, Isabelle reckoned, and she might
come in useful down the line. She said, 'We'll keep our voices
down, if that's what worries you, Mr di Fazio.'

'She will want to concentrate on her work.'

'I daresay we won't prevent her from doing so.'

Behind his gold-framed spectacles, the sculptor's eyes
narrowed. It was just a fractional movement, but Isabelle did
not miss it. She said, 'This actually won't take long. It's about
your argument with Jemima. And about an at-home
pregnancy test.'

Di Fazio gave no reaction to the remark. He looked briefly
from Isabelle to Lynley as if evaluating the nature of their
relationship. Then he said, 'I had no argument with Jemima
that I remember.'

'You were overheard. It would have taken place in your lodgings in Putney and chances are it might have had to do with
that pregnancy test which was found among your belongings.'

'You have no warrant—'

'As it happens, we aren't the ones who found it.'

'Then it's not evidence, is it. I know how these things work.
There's a procedure that must be followed. And this *was* not
followed so this pregnancy test or whatever it is cannot be
evidence against me.'

'I applaud your knowledge of the law.'

'I've read enough of injustice in this country, madam. I've

read how the British police work. People who have been unjustly accused and unjustly convicted. The Birmingham gentlemen. The Guildford group.'

'You may have done.' Lynley was the one to speak, and Isabelle noted that he didn't bother to lower his voice to prevent Dominique from hearing. 'So you'll also know that in building a case against a suspect in a murder investigation, some things go down as background information and some as evidence. The fact that you had an argument with a woman who turned up dead may be neither here nor there, but if it *is* neither here nor there, it seems the wiser course to clear things up about it.'

'Which is another way of saying,' Isabelle noted, 'that you have some explaining to do. You indicated that you and Jemima ultimately stopped having sexual relations when she took up lodgings with Mrs McHaggis.'

'That was the truth.' Di Fazio cast a look in Dominique's direction. Isabelle wondered if the other artist had taken Jemima's place.

'Had she become pregnant during the time when you and she were still lovers?'

'She had not.' Another look in Dominique's direction. 'Can we not have this conversation elsewhere?' he asked. 'Dominique and I . . . We hope to marry this winter. She doesn't need to hear—'

'Do you indeed? And this would be your sixth engagement, wouldn't it?'

His face grew stormy, but he mastered this. He said, 'Dominique doesn't need to hear facts about Jemima. Jemima was done with.'

'That's an interesting choice of words,' Lynley noted.

'I didn't hurt Jemima. I didn't touch Jemima. I wasn't there.'

'Then you won't mind telling us everything you've so far failed to tell us about her,' Isabelle said. 'You also won't mind providing us with an alibi for the time of Jemima's death.'

'Not here. Please.'

'All right. Then at the local nick.'

Di Fazio's face went completely rigid. 'Unless you place me under arrest, I do *not* have to take a step out of this studio in your company, and this I know. Believe me, I know. I've read about my rights.'

'That being the case,' Isabelle said, 'you'll also know that the sooner you clear up this matter of you, Jemima, the pregnancy test, the argument and your alibi, the better off you'll be.'

Di Fazio cast another look in Dominique's direction. She seemed intent upon her work, Isabelle thought, but who could really tell. They appeared to be at the point of impasse when Lynley made the move that resolved the situation: He went to Dominique's area to examine her work, saying, 'May I have a look? I've always thought that the lost wax process . . .' and on he went till Dominique was fully engaged.

'So?' Isabelle said to di Fazio.

He turned his back on Lynley and Dominique, the better to prevent his intended bride's reading of his lips, Isabelle reckoned. He said, 'It was before Dominique. It was Jemima's test, in the rubbish in the toilet. She'd told me there was no one else in her life. She'd said she wanted a break from men altogether. But when I saw the test, I knew that she'd lied. There was someone new. So I spoke with her. And it was hot, this conversation, yes. Because she would not be with me but I *knew* that she would be with him.'

'Who?'

'Who else? Frazer. She wouldn't risk with me. But with him? If she lost her place in the lodging as a result of Frazer, it didn't matter.'

'She *told* you it was Frazer Chaplin?'

He looked impatient. 'She didn't need to tell me. This is Frazer's way. Have you seen him? Have you spoken to him? There's no woman that he wouldn't try to take because that's who he is. Who else would it be?'

'He wasn't the only man in her life.'

'She went to the ice rink. For lessons, she said, but I knew better. And sometimes she went to Duke's Hotel as well. She wanted to see what Frazer was up to. And he was up to finding ladies.'

Isabelle said, 'Perhaps. But there are other men whose lives touched hers. At her own place of employment, at the ice rink—'

'What? You suppose she was . . . what? With Abbott Langer? With Jayson Druther? She went to work, she went to the ice rink, she went to Duke's Hotel, she went home. Trust me. She did nothing else.'

'If that's the case,' Isabelle said, 'you do see how this gives you a motive for murdering her, don't you?'

Colour rushed into his face, and he grabbed up one of his tools and used it to gesture with. 'Me? It's *Frazer* who would want her dead. Frazer Chaplin. He would want to shake her away from him. Because she wouldn't give him the freedom he required to do what Frazer does.'

'Which is?'

'He fucks the ladies. All the ladies. And the ladies like it. And he makes them want it. And *when* they want it, they seek him out. So this is what she was doing.'

'You seem to know quite a lot about him.'

'I've *seen* him. I've watched them. Frazer and women.'

'Some might say he's merely had better luck with women, Mr di Fazio. What do you make of that?'

'I know what you're trying to say. Don't think I'm foolish. I'm telling you how it is with him. So I ask you this: if Frazer Chaplin wasn't the man she'd taken as her lover, then who was it?'

It was an interesting question, Isabelle thought. But far more interesting at the moment was the fact that di Fazio had seemed to know what Jemima Hastings' every movement had been.

Two of them hovered. Their form was different. One rose from an ashtray on a table, a cloud of grey that became a cloud of light from which he had to turn his head even as he heard the booming cry of *The eighth choir stands before God.*

He tried to block the words.

They are the messengers between man and man's Deity.

The cries were loud, louder than they had ever been and even as he filled his ears with music, another cry came from another direction, saying *Battlers of those who themselves were born of the bearer of light. Distort God's plan and be thrown into the jaws of damnation.*

Although he tried not to seek the source of this second shrieking, he found it anyway because a chair swept into the air before him and it began to take shape and it began to approach him. He shrank away.

What he knew was that they came in disguises. They were travellers, they were healers of the sick, they were inhabitants of the pool of Probatica at whose shores the infirm lay waiting the movement of the water. They were the builders, the slave masters of demons.

He who healed was also present. He spoke from within the cloud of grey and he became flame and the flame burned emerald. He called not for righteous anger but for a flood of music to issue forth in praise.

But the other fought him. He who was destruction itself, known by Sodom, called Hero of God. But he was Mercy as well, and he claimed to sit at the left hand of God, unlike the other. Incarnation, conception, birth, dreams. These were his offerings. *Come with me.* But a price would be paid.

I am Raphael and it is you who are called.

I am Gabriel and it is you who are chosen.

Then there was a chorus of them, a veritable flood of voices, and they were everywhere, and he worked against being taken by them. He worked and he worked till the sweat poured from him and still they came on. They descended till there was one mighty being above all, and he approached. He would not be denied. He would overcome. And to this there was no other answer that might be given so he had to escape he had to run he had to find a place of safety.

He himself gave the cry against the multitude that he now

knew was indeed the Eighth Choir. There was a stairway that emerged from the light and he made for this, for wherever it headed. To the light, to God, to some other Deity, it didn't matter. He began to climb. He began to run.

'Yukio!' came the cry from behind him.

'So I have the impression the engagement is all in Paolo di Fazio's head,' Lynley said. 'Dominique did a bit of eye-rolling when I offered her my congratulations.'

'Now that's interesting,' Isabelle Ardery said. 'Well, I did think six times engaged was rather pushing the envelope in the human relationship area. I mean, I've heard of six times married – well, perhaps only with American film stars in the days when they actually *did* get married – but it's rather odd that with all the engagements, he's never made it to the altar. It does make one wonder about him. How much is real and how much is imagined.'

'He may have done.'

'What?' Ardery turned to him. They'd stopped at the delicatessen, which occupied one of the railway arches. She was making a purchase of olives and meats. She'd already bought a bottle of wine at the wine cellar.

Lynley reckoned these would likely stand in place of her dinner. He knew the signs, having worked so many years with Barbara Havers and having thus become accustomed to the single policewoman's eating habits. He considered extending an invitation to the superintendent: dinner at his home in Eaton Terrace? He rejected the idea as he couldn't imagine as yet sharing his dining table with anyone.

'He may have made it to the altar,' he said. 'Married. Philip Hale will be able to tell us. Or perhaps John Stewart. We're developing a rather long list for the background checks. John can help out there if you've a mind to move him.'

'Oh, I'm sure he'd adore that assignment.' The superintendent took her bag of goods, said thanks to the shop girl, and headed for her car. The day was heating up. Surrounded by and composed of bricks, concrete and macadam, possessing all the possible charms that overfull wheelie bins and rubbish on the street could provide, the area immediately round the railway arches was like a wrestler's armpit: steaming and malodorous.

They got into the car before Isabelle Ardery responded. She wound down the window, cursed that she did not have air conditioning, pardoned herself for cursing, and then said, 'What d'you make of him, then?'

'Isn't there a song about it?' Lynley said. 'Looking for love in all the wrong places?' He wound down his window as well. They headed off. His mobile rang. He looked at the number and felt an unaccustomed moment of dread. Assistant Commissioner Hillier was phoning, or at least his office was.

Where was the inspector and could he come to the AC's office? Hillier's secretary wanted to know. And welcome back to New Scotland Yard, Detective Inspector. This is an unofficial meeting, by the way. No need to mention it to anyone.

Code for don't mention this meeting to Isabelle Ardery and why, accordingly, didn't you let the assistant commissioner know you would be returning to work? Lynley didn't much like the inference that could be drawn from it all. He said that he was out at the moment but he would come in to see the assistant commissioner as soon as he could. He included the words *assistant commissioner* with a slow deliberation. He felt Ardery glance in his direction.

He said to her as he ended the call, 'Hillier. Wanting a word.'

She drove on, her gaze on the road. She said, 'Thank you, Thomas. Are you always so decent?'

'Virtually never.'

She smiled. 'I meant John Stewart, by the way.'

'Pardon?'

'When I asked what you make of him.'

'Ah. Right. Well. He and Barbara have nearly come to blows over the years, if that's any help.'

'Women in general, then? Or women coppers?'

'That's something I've never been quite able to work out. He was married once. It ended badly.'

'Ha. I expect we know who wanted to end it.' Isabelle said nothing more till they'd crossed over the river again. And then, 'I'm going to want a warrant, Thomas.'

'Hmm. Yes. I expect that's the only course. And he knows his rights rather too well, doesn't he. Hillier would call it an unfortunate sign of the times.'

It came to Lynley as he spoke that he'd followed Ardery's line of thought with ease. They'd gone smoothly from John Stewart to Paolo di Fazio without the need for clarification and without the further need for Ardery to explain why a search warrant was required: they were going to want to gather up the artist's sculpting tools. Indeed, they were going to need the tools of every one of the artists with whom Paolo di Fazio shared space. Forensic examinations would have to be done on everything.

'Paolo,' Lynley noted, 'isn't going to be popular with his mates.'

'Not to mention what this will do to his "engagement" to Dominique. Did she alibi him, by the way?'

'She didn't. Except to say she reckoned he was at Covent Garden. If it's afternoon you're talking about, that's where he usually is, she said, and someone there will have seen him. She also knew why I was asking. And contrary to what di Fazio said, she did know Jemima, at least by sight. She called her "Paolo's ex".'

'No jealousy? No concern?'

'Not that I could see. She seemed to know, or at least to believe, that it was finished between them. Between Jemima and Paolo, I mean.'

They rode the rest of the way in silence and they were in the underground car park at New Scotland Yard when Isabelle Ardery spoke again, gathering up her purchases from the railway arches. She said, 'What d'you make of Paolo's declaration that Frazer Chaplin was involved with Jemima?'

'Anything's possible at this point.'

'Yes. But it also supports what Sergeant Havers said about the bloke.' She slammed the door and locked it, adding, 'And that, frankly, comes as something of a relief. I have my concerns about Barbara Havers and her reaction to men.'

'Do you?' Lynley walked at her side. He was unused to a woman so tall. Barbara Havers didn't reach to his collarbone and while Helen had been above average height, she had not been nearly as tall as Isabelle Ardery. He and the acting superintendent were shoulder to shoulder. He said, 'Barbara has very good instincts about people. You can generally rely on her input.'

'Ah. What about you, then?'

'My input is, I hope—'

'I meant your instincts, Thomas. How are they?' She looked at him. It was an even gaze.

He wasn't sure what to make of her question. 'When the wind is southerly, I generally know my hawks from my handsaws,' he settled on saying.

Back in the incident room, bits of information were filtering in: Jayson Druther had indeed been present in the cigar shop when Jemima Hastings was killed in Stoke Newington, and he'd provided the names of three customers to confirm this. He'd gone on to alibi his father, if there was interest in that. 'Betting shop,' John Stewart reported, 'over in the Edgware Road.' Abbott Langer had finished up his afternoon lessons at the ice rink, walked dogs in Hyde Park and then returned to the ice rink for his evening clients. *But* the dog walking bit gave him a good size window to get up to Stoke Newington because there was no dog owner to swear the family canine had been walked. Obviously, a dog walker was employed when no one was at home.

As to background information, progess had been made there as well. Although Yolanda the Psychic had been warned off stalking Jemima Hastings, Jemima Hastings hadn't been the one to report her. That reporting had been done by Bella McHaggis.

'McHaggis's husband died at home, but there's nothing

suspicious associated with it,' Philip Hale reported. 'His heart gave out while he was on the toilet. Yolanda's daughter is dead. Starved herself slimming. Same age as Jemima.'

'Interesting,' Ardery said. 'Anything else?'

Frazer Chaplin, born in Dublin, one of seven children, no record and no complaints. Shows up on time to the job, he reported.

'He has two jobs,' Isabelle told him.

Shows up on time to both of his jobs. He seems a bit too interested in money, but then, who isn't? There's something of a joke at Duke's Hotel: him looking for a rich American-Brazilian-Canadian-Russian-Japanese-Chinese-*anything* to support him. Male or female. He doesn't care. He's a bloke with plans, according to the hotel manager, but no one faults him and he's well-liked. 'One of those "That's our lad Frazer" types,' Hale said.

'Anything on Paolo di Fazio?' Isabelle asked.

It turned out that Paolo had an interesting background: born in Palermo from which his family fled the Mafia. His sister had been married to a minor Mafioso there only to be beaten to death by him. The husband himself had been found hanged in his cell while awaiting trial and no one thought it was a suicide.

As to the rest? Isabelle Ardery asked.

There was very little. Jayson Druther had an ASBO, apparently having to do with a relationship that went sour. But this was with a man, not a woman, for whatever good that piece of news could do them. Abbott Langer, on the other hand, was a bit of a puzzle. It was true that he was an Olympic ice skater turned coach and dog walker. It was completely bogus that he had ever been married with children. He was fairly close to Yolanda the Psychic, apparently, but this didn't seem to be a sinister connection as it was looking more and more as if Yolanda the Psychic did as much trolling for surrogate children – adult or otherwise – as she did reading palms or getting in touch with the spirit world.

'We'll want more on this marriage business,' Ardery noted. 'He's a real person of interest, then.'

Lynley slipped out of the meeting as the superintendent was giving further instructions about confirming alibis and the time of death, which was set between two o'clock and five o'clock. This should make it easy, she was saying. Most of these people have jobs. Someone saw something not quite right somewhere. Let's find out who and what it is.

Lynley crossed over to Tower Block, and he made his way to the assistant commissioner's office. Hillier's secretary – in an uncharacteristic move – rose from her chair and came to greet him, her hand extended. Usually the soul of discretion when it came to things Hillier, Judi MacIntosh murmured, 'Brilliant to see you, Inspector,' and added, 'Don't be fooled. He's quite pleased about this.'

This was apparently Lynley's return and *he*, naturally, was Sir David Hillier. The assistant commissioner, however, did not want to talk about Lynley's return other than to say, 'You're looking fit. Good,' when Lynley entered his office. Then he set down to business. The business was, as Lynley suspected it might be, the permanent assignment of someone to the detective superintendent's position, which was nearly nine months vacant.

Hillier broached the topic in his usual fashion, at an oblique angle. He said, 'How're you finding the job?' which, of course, Lynley might have taken any way he wished and which, of course, Hillier would use to steer the conversation any way he desired.

'Different and the same at once,' Lynley replied. 'Everything's a bit shaded with odd colours, sir.'

'She's got a good mind, I dare say. She wouldn't have climbed as fast as she's climbed without that, would she.'

'Actually . . .' Lynley had been talking about returning to work with the world as he'd known it utterly transformed in an instant, on the street, at the hands of a child with a gun. He thought about making this point, but he instead he said,

'She's clever and quick,' which seemed to him a good response, making a reply but saying little enough.

'How are the team responding to her?'

'They're professionals.'

'John Stewart?'

'No matter who takes the job, there'll be a period of adjustment, won't there? John has his quirks, but he's a good man.'

'I'm being pressed to name a permanent replacement for Malcolm Webberly,' Hillier said. 'I tend to think Ardery's a very good choice.'

Lynley nodded, but that was the extent of his response. He had an uneasy feeling where this was heading.

'Naming her will bring a lot of publicity.'

'Not necessarily a bad thing,' Lynley said. 'The opposite, in fact. Promoting a female officer, indeed an officer from outside the Met . . . I can't see how that could be interpreted as anything other than a positive move, fairly guaranteed to give the Met good press.' Which, he didn't add, they rather badly needed. In recent years they'd faced charges of everything from institutionalised racism to gross incompetence and all points in between. A story in which there were no skeletons lurking in anyone's closet would be a welcome one, no doubt about it.

'If it *is* a positive move,' Hillier noted. 'Which brings me to the point.'

'Ah.'

Hillier shot him a look at that *ah*. He apparently decided to let it go. He said, 'She's good on paper, and she's good from every verbal report about her. But you and I know there's more than verbiage involved in being able to do this job well.'

'Yes. But weaknesses always come out eventually,' Lynley said. 'Sooner or later.'

'They do. But the point is, I'm being asked to make this sooner, if you understand what I mean. And if I'm going to make it sooner, then I'm also going to make it right.'

'Understandable,' Lynley acknowledged.

'It seems she's asked you to work with her.'

Lynley didn't inquire how Hillier knew this. Hillier generally knew everything that was going on. He hadn't got to his
present position without developing an impressive system of
snouts. 'I'm not sure I'd call it "working with her",' he said
carefully. 'She's asked me to come on board and show her the
ropes, to allow her to move more quickly into the job. She has
her work cut out: not only new to London but new to the Met
and having a murder case landing in her lap. If I can help her
make a quick transition, I'm happy to.'

'So you're getting to know her. Better than the rest, I dare
say. That brings me to the point. I can't put this delicately,
so I'm not going to try: if you come across anything that gives
you pause about her, I want to know what it is. And I do
mean anything.'

'Actually, sir, I don't think I'm the one to—'

'You're exactly the one. You've been in the job, you don't
want the job, you're working with her, and you've a very good
eye for people. You and I have disagreed over the years—'

Which was putting it mildly, Lynley thought.

'—but I'd never deny that you've rarely been wrong about
someone. You've a vested interest – we *all* have a vested
interest – in this job going to someone good, to the best
person out there, and you're going to know if she's that
officer in very short order. What I'm asking you to do is to
tell me. And, frankly, I'm going to need details because the
last thing we need is a charge of sexism if she doesn't get
the job.'

'So what is it exactly that you want me to do, sir?' If he
was going to be asked to spy upon Isabelle Ardery, then the
assistant commissioner, Lynley decided, was going to have to
come out and say it. 'Written reports? A regular briefing?
Meetings like this?'

'I think you know.'

'As it happens, I—' His mobile rang. He looked at it.

'Let it go,' Hillier said.

'It's Ardery,' Lynley replied. Still, he waited for the assistant commissioner's sharp nod, telling him to take it.

'We've got an ID on the second e-fit,' Ardery told him. 'He's a violinist, Thomas. His brother identified him.'

16

Barbara Havers did the telephone work and Winston Nkata did the route planning. Without much difficulty, she was able to track down Jonas Bligh and Keating Crawford, the two instructors at Winchester Technical College II – no one was shedding any light on whether there was actually a Winchester Technical College I – and both of these individuals agreed to speak to the Scotland Yard detectives. Both of them also asked what the coming visit from Scotland Yard was about. When she said it was about a bloke called Gordon Jossie for whom a letter of reference had been written, the response of 'Who?' was identical.

Barbara repeated Jossie's name. This would have been eleven years ago, she told them.

Again they were virtual echoes in reply: eleven years? One could hardly be expected to remember a student from such a long time ago, Sergeant. But each went on to assure her he would be waiting for the detectives to show up.

Meantime, Nkata was studying the map to get them up to Winchester, into Winchester, and in the general environs of the college. He was growing less and less happy about being in Hampshire, and Barbara couldn't blame him. He was the only black person she herself had seen since they'd entered the New Forest, and from the reaction of everyone they'd come into contact with at the hotel in Sway, he appeared to be the first black man they'd ever encountered other than on the telly.

She'd said to him *sotto voce* at dinner on the previous evening, 'First, it's that people think we're a couple, Winnie,' to excuse the obvious curiosity of their server.

He said, 'Yeah?' and she could sense him bristling. 'So wha' if we are? Something wrong with mixed couples? Something *wrong* with that?'

''Course not,' Barbara said at once. 'Bloody hell, Winnie. I should be so lucky. And *that's* why they're staring. Him and *her*? they're thinking. How'd she score *that* bloke? *Defi*nitely not on her looks, by God. Have a look at the two of us: you and me having dinner in a hotel. The candlelight, the flowers on the table, the music playing—'

'It's a CD, Barb.'

'Bear with me, okay? People jump to conclusions based on what they see. You can believe me. I get it all the time when I'm with DI Lynley.'

He seemed to think about this. The hotel dining room *was* moderately special, even if the music did indeed come from a CD playing old Neil Diamond hits and the flowers on the table were plastic. It remained the only establishment in Sway where one could have anything remotely resembling a romantic evening. Still, he said, 'Second?' to which she said, 'Huh?'

'You said *first*. What's second?'

She said, 'Oh. Second, it's just that you're tall and you've got that scar on your face. Makes you look a type. And then there's the way you dress contrasted with the way I dress. They also might be thinking you're "someone" and I'm your secretary or assistant or whatever. Probably a footballer. That would be you, not me. Or maybe a film star. I reckon they're trying to decide where they saw you last: *Big Brother*, some game show, maybe on *Morse* when you were still in nappies.'

He gazed at her, looking mildly amused. He said, 'You do this with Inspector Lynley, Barb?'

'Do what?'

'Worry so much. 'Bout him, I mean. Like you're doing with me.'

She could feel herself colouring. 'Was I? I mean, am I? Sorry. Just that—'

'Nice of you,' he told her. 'But I been stared at worse'n here, believe me.'

'Oh,' she said. 'Well.'

'*And*,' he added, 'you don't dress half bad, Barb.'

To which she guffawed. 'Right. And Jesus didn't die on the cross. But it's no matter. Superintendent Ardery is seeing about that. Soon, believe me, I'll be the Met's answer to . . .' She pulled at her lip. 'See, that's the problem. I don't even know the latest fashion icon. That's how far out of the loop I am. Well, whatever. It can't be helped. But life was easier when emulating the dress sense of the Queen was good enough, let me tell you.' Not that she herself had ever emulated the Queen's dress sense, Barbara thought. Although she *did* wonder if sensible shoes, gloves and a handbag looped over her arm would satisfy Superintendent Ardery.

Winchester being a city and not a village, Winston Nkata was not marked for special observation there. Nor was he much noted on the campus of Winchester Technical College II, which they found easily as a result of his advanced planning. Jonas Bligh and Keating Crawford proved to be more challenging, however. Expecting to find them in a department somehow related to thatching, Barbara had neglected to ask their whereabouts. It turned out that Bligh was involved with computers in some arcane fashion while Crawford dealt with telecommunications.

Bligh was 'having his surgery hours', they were told, and they found his office tucked beneath a stairway up and down which, during their initial conversation with him, herds of students pounded incessantly. Barbara couldn't imagine anyone actually accomplishing anything in this environment, but when they introduced themselves to Bligh, the wax earplugs he removed explained how he managed to cope with the place. He suggested they go for a coffee, have a walk, whatever. Barbara counter-suggested that they track down Crawford, a plan that she hoped would save them some time.

That was managed by way of mobile phone, and they met the telecommunications instructor in the car park where a caravan selling ice cream and juice was attracting a crowd.

Crawford was one of them. Well-covered was a sympathetic way to describe him. He certainly didn't need the Cornetto he was attacking. He finished it and immediately purchased another, calling over his shoulder, 'You lot want one?' to the detectives and his colleague.

Fully capable of seeing her future when her feet were held to the flames, Barbara demurred. Winston did likewise. So did Bligh, who muttered, 'Dead before he's fifty, just you wait,' although he said pleasantly, 'Don't blame you,' to Crawford in reference to the second Cornetto. 'Damned hot summer, eh?'

They went through the usual prefatory conversational motions that were peculiar to the English: a brief discussion of the weather. They strolled to a patch of browning lawn that was shaded by a sturdy sycamore. There were no benches or chairs here, but it was a relief to get out of the sun.

Barbara handed each of the men the letter of reference he'd written for Gordon Jossie. Bligh put on a pair of spectacles; Crawford dropped a dollop of vanilla ice cream on the sheet. He wiped it off on his trouser leg, said, 'Sorry, occupational hazard,' and began to read. In a moment, he frowned and said, 'What the hell . . . ?' and Bligh simultaneously shook his head. They spoke nearly in unison.

'This is bogus,' Bligh said as Crawford declared, 'I didn't write this.'

Barbara and Winston exchanged a glance. 'Are you sure?' she asked the instructors. 'Could you have forgotten? I mean, you must be asked to write a lot of letters at the end of students' coursework, right?'

'Naturally,' Bligh agreed. His voice was dry. 'But I'm generally asked to write letters in my own field, Sergeant. This is college letterhead, I'll give you that, but the letter itself deals with Gordon Jossie's accomplishments in Accounts and Finance, which I don't teach. And that's not my signature.'

'You?' Barbara said to Crawford. 'I take it . . . ?'

He nodded. 'Large appliance repair,' he said, indicating the contents of the letter by extending it to her. 'Not my bailiwick. Not even close.'

'What about the signature?'

'Same thing, I'm afraid. Someone likely nicked letterhead from an office – or even designed it on their computer, I suppose, if they had an example in front of them – and then wrote their own recommendations. It happens sometimes, although you'd think this bloke would have checked first to see who taught what. Looks to me like he gave a quick glance at a list of the staff and chose our names at random.'

'Exactly,' Bligh said.

Barbara looked at Winston. 'It explains how someone who can't read or write managed to "complete" coursework at the college, eh?'

Winston nodded. 'But not how someone who can't read or write wrote these letters, cos he didn't.'

'That looks like the case.'

Which meant, of course, that someone else had written them for Gordon Jossie, someone who knew him from years gone by, someone they likely hadn't spoken to yet.

Robbie Hastings knew that if he was going to get to the bottom of what had happened to his sister and why, and if he was going to be able to go on living, no matter how bleakly, he had to begin looking squarely at a few basic truths. Meredith had been attempting to tell him at least one of those truths in the church in Ringwood. He'd stopped her abruptly because he was a bloody coward. But he knew he couldn't go on that way. So he finally picked up the phone.

She said, 'How are you?' when she heard his voice. 'I mean how are you doing, Rob? How are you coping? I can't sleep or eat. Can you? I just want to do—'

'Merry.' He cleared his throat. Part of him was shouting *better not to know better never to know* and part of him was trying to ignore those cries. 'In the church when you and I were talking about her . . . What did you mean?'

'When?'

'You said *whenever*. That was the word you used.'

'I did? Rob, I don't know—'

'With a bloke, you said. Whenever she was with a bloke.' God, he thought, don't make me say more.

'Oh.' Meredith's voice was small. 'Jemima and sex, you mean.'

He whispered it. 'Aye.'

'Oh, Rob. I s'pose I shouldn't actually have said that.'

'But you did, didn't you. So you need to tell me. If you know something that's to do with her death.'

'It's nothing,' she said quickly. 'I'm sure of it. It's not that.'

He said nothing, reckoning that if he was silent, she would be forced to continue, which she did.

She said, 'She was younger, then. It was years ago anyway. And she would have changed, Rob. People change.'

He wanted so much to believe her. Such a simple matter to say, 'Oh. Right. Well, thanks,' and ring off. In the background he could hear murmurs of conversation. He'd phoned Meredith at work, and he could have used this alone as an excuse to end their conversation at that point. So could she, for that matter. But he didn't take that turn. He couldn't do so now and live with the knowledge that he'd run again, just as he'd turned a blind eye to what he knew at heart she was likely to tell him if he insisted upon it.

'Seems it's time for me to know it all, Merry. It's no betrayal on your part. Mind, there's nothing you can say would make a difference now.'

When she spoke at last, it sounded to him as if she were talking inside a tube, as the sound was hollow although it could well have been that his heart was hollow. She said finally, 'Eleven, then, Rob.'

'Eleven what?' he asked. Lovers? he wondered. Had Jemima had so many already? And by what age? And had she actually kept count?

'Years,' Meredith said. 'That's how old.' And when he said nothing, she rushed on with, 'Oh, Rob. You don't want to know. Really. And she wasn't *bad*. She just . . . See, she equated things. 'Course, I didn't know that at the time: why she did it, I mean. I just knew she might end up pregnant but she said no because she took precautions. She even knew that word: precautions. I don't know what she used or where she got it because she wouldn't say. Just that it wasn't up to me to tell her right from wrong and if I was her friend, I would know that, wouldn't I. And then it became a matter of me not having boyfriends, see. "You're only jealous, Merry." But that wasn't it, Rob. She was my *friend*. I only wanted to keep her safe. And people talked about her so. Specially at school.'

Robbie wasn't sure he could speak. He was standing in the kitchen and he felt blindly behind him for a chair onto which he could lower himself with infinite slowness. 'Boys at school?' he said. 'Boys at school were having sex with Jemima when she was eleven? Who? How many?' Because he would find them, he thought. He would find them and he would sort them even now, so many years after the fact.

Meredith said, 'I don't know how many. I mean, she always had boyfriends but I don't expect . . . Surely not all of them, Rob.'

But he knew she was lying to protect his feelings or perhaps because she believed she'd betrayed Jemima enough, even as he was the one who'd betrayed her by not seeing what was in front of him all along.

'Tell me the rest,' he said. 'There's more, isn't there?'

Her voice altered as she replied and he could tell she was crying. 'No, no. There's really no more.'

'God damn it, Merry—'

'Really.'

'*Tell* me.'

'Rob, please don't ask.'

'What *else?*' And then his own voice broke when he said, 'Please,' and perhaps that was what made her continue.

'If there was a boy she was doing it with and another boy wanted her . . . She didn't understand. She didn't know how to be faithful. She didn't mean anything and she wasn't a tart. She just didn't understand how it looked to other people. I mean what they thought or might do or might ask of her. I *tried* to tell her but there was this boy and that boy and this man and that man and she just couldn't see that it really had nothing to do with love, what they wanted, and when I tried to tell her, she reckoned I was being—'

'Yes,' he said. 'All right. Yes.'

She was quiet again although he could hear the rustle of something against the phone. Tissue likely. She'd wept the entire time she'd spoken. She said, 'We used to quarrel. Remember? We used to talk for hours in her bedroom. Remember?'

'Aye. Aye. I remember that.'

'So you see, I tried. I should have told someone, but I didn't know who.'

'You didn't think to tell me?'

'I did. But then sometimes I thought . . . All the men and perhaps even you . . .'

'Oh God, Merry.'

'I'm sorry. So sorry.'

'Why did you . . . ? Did she say . . . ?'

'Never. Nothing. Not that.'

'But still you thought . . .' He felt a laugh bubbling in him, one of simple despair at so outrageous an idea, so far from the truth of who he was and how he lived his life.

At least, he thought, with Gordon Jossie had come an alteration in his sister. Somehow she'd found what she was looking for because surely she'd been faithful to him. She had to have been. He said, 'She stuck with Jossie, though. She was true to him. I mean, he wanted to marry her and he wouldn't have done if he had the slightest suspicion or indication that—'

'*Did* he?'

Something about the way she asked the question stopped

him. She spoke not in a challenge to his statement but with outright surprise.

'Did he what?'

'Want to marry her.'

'He did. She left because she wanted time to think about it and I expect he worried it was over between them because he phoned her and phoned her and she got herself a new mobile. So you see, she'd finally got to the point...' What point? he wondered. He was fairly babbling, and he knew it because he reckoned there was something more to come.

There was. Meredith said, 'But, Rob, before our ... what do I call it? Our break-up? Our row? The end of our friendship? Before that, she told me Gordon didn't want to marry at all. It wasn't her, she said. He didn't want to marry full stop. He was afraid of marriage, she said. He was afraid of getting too close to anyone.'

'Blokes always say that, Merry. At the beginning.'

'No. Listen. She told me it was all she could do to talk him into living together, and before that it was all she could do to talk him into letting her spend the night with him, and before that it was all she could do to coax him into having sex. So to think he was mad to marry her ... What would have changed him?'

'Living with her. Getting used to that. Seeing that there was no big fear to being with someone. Learning that—'

'What? Learning what? Truth is, Rob, if there was something to learn, something to discover, wouldn't it likely be that he discovered that Jemima—'

'*No.*' He said it not because he believed it but because he wanted to believe it: that his sister had been to Gordon Jossie what she hadn't been to her own brother. An open book. Wasn't that what couples were meant to be to each other? he asked himself. But he had no answer. How bloody could he since being one half of a couple was for him the stuff of fantasy?

Meredith said, 'I wish you hadn't asked. I wish I hadn't said. What does it matter really, now? I mean, at the end of the day she only wanted someone to love her, I think. I didn't see that at the time, when we were girls. And when I finally did see it, when we were older, our paths were so different that when I tried to talk to her about it, it seemed like I had a problem, not Jemima.'

'It got her killed,' he said. 'That's what happened, isn't it?'

'Surely not. Because if she'd changed as you said she'd changed, if she was faithful to Gordon . . . And she'd been with him longer than anyone else, hadn't she? More than two years? Three?'

'She left in a rush. He kept ringing her.'

'You see? That means he wanted her back, which he wouldn't have if she'd been unfaithful. I think she'd grown out of all that, Rob. Really, I do.'

But Robbie could tell by the eagerness of Meredith's tone that whatever she said from this moment onwards would be said to assuage his feelings. He felt turned every which way, and he was dizzy. Among all the new information he had gathered, there had to be an essential truth about his sister. There had to be a way to explain both her life and her death. And he had to find that truth, for he knew that its discovery would be the only way he could forgive himself for failing Jemima when she had needed him most.

Barbara Havers and Winston Nkata returned to the Operational Command Unit where they handed over the forged letters from Winchester Technical College II to the Chief Superintendent. Whiting read them. He was the sort of reader who formed the words with his lips as he went along. He took his time.

Barbara said, 'We've spoken to these two blokes, sir. They didn't write the letters. They don't know Gordon Jossie.'

He looked up. 'That,' he said, 'is problematical.'

In a nutshell, Barbara thought, although he didn't seem wildly interested in the matter. She said, 'Last time we were here, you said two women had phoned up about him.'

'Did I.' Whiting seemed to be musing on the matter. 'There *were* two calls, I believe. Two women suggesting that Jossie needed looking into.'

'And?' Barbara asked.

'And?' Whiting said.

Barbara exchanged a glance with Winston. He did the honours. 'We got these letters now, see. We got a dead girl up in London connected with this bloke. He went up there on a search for her some time back, which he doesn't deny, and he stuck up cards with her picture on them, asking for phone calls should anyone see her. And you got two phone calls yourself drawing your 'tention to him.'

'Those calls didn't mention a card in London,' Whiting said. 'Nor did they mention your dead girl.'

'Point is the calls themselves and how things're stacking up 'gainst Jossie.'

'Yes,' Whiting said. 'That can make things look iffy. I do see that.'

Barbara decided indirection was clearly *not* the path to take with the chief superintendent. She said, 'Sir, what do you know about Gordon Jossie that you're not telling us?'

Whiting handed the letters back to her. 'Not a bloody thing,' he said.

'Did you check him out based on those phone calls?'

'Sergeant . . . Is it Havers? And Nkata?' Whiting waited for their nods although Barbara could have sworn he knew their names very well despite the fact that he mispronounced both of them. 'I'm not very likely to use manpower to investigate someone based on a phone call from a woman who might well be upset because a gentleman stood her up for a date.'

'You said two women,' Nkata pointed out.

'One woman, two women. The point is that they had no complaint, only suspicions and their suspicions amounted to being suspicious, if you understand.'

'Meaning what?' Barbara asked.

'Meaning that they had nothing to be suspicious about. He

wasn't peeping in windows. He wasn't hanging about primary schools. He wasn't snatching handbags from old ladies. He wasn't moving questionable bits of this or that into his house or out of it. He wasn't inviting women on the street to step into his vehicle for a bit of you-know-what. As far as they could tell us – these phone callers who, by the way, wouldn't leave their names – he was just a suspicious type. Those letters of yours' – he indicated the forgeries from the college – 'don't add anything to the mix. Seems to me the important bit is not that he forged them—'

'He didn't,' Barbara said. 'He can't read or write.'

'All right. Someone else forged them. A mate of his. A girl-friend. Who knows. Have you ever considered that he wouldn't have got himself hired as an apprentice at his age had he not had something to show he was a worthwhile risk? I dare say that's all these letters show.'

'True enough,' Barbara said. 'But the fact remains—'

'The fact remains that the important bit is whether he did his job well once he got it. And that's what he did, yes? He served a fine apprenticeship up in Itchen Abbas. Then he began his own business. He's built that business up and, as far as I know, he has kept his nose clean.'

'Sir—'

'I think that's the end of the story, don't you?'

As it happened, she didn't, but Barbara said nothing. Nor did Nkata. And as she was careful not to look at Winston, so was he careful not to look at her. For there was something that the chief superintendent wasn't dealing with: they'd said nothing at all to him about Gordon Jossie's serving an apprenticeship to Ringo Heath or to anyone else, and the fact that Whiting knew about one suggested once again that there was more to Gordon Jossie and his life in the New Forest than met the eye. To Barbara there was no question about it: Chief Superintendent Zachary Whiting was fully apprised as to what the *more* was.

*   *   *

Meredith decided further action was called for after the phone
call from Rob Hastings and because of the phone call. She
could tell the poor man was equal parts crushed to the core
and ridden by guilt and since part of this was due to her mouth
running on about matters best left unsaid, she took a step to
rectify things. She had seen just enough cop shows on the telly
to know what to do when she made the decision to go to
Lyndhurst. She was fairly confident that Gina Dickens wouldn't
be in the lodging that she claimed was hers above the Mad
Hatter Tea Rooms since Gina had seemed fairly intent upon
establishing her life with Gordon Jossie. Meredith reckoned
that, in the pursuit of this end, she likely hadn't darkened her
own doorway in days. Should she actually be in, Meredith had
her excuse ready: came to say sorry for being such a pest. I'm
just upset. That part was the truth, at least, although being
upset was only the half of it.

She'd begged the rest of the day off work. Splitting headache,
the heat and that time of the month. She'd work at home if
they didn't mind, where she could put a cold compress on her
head. She nearly had most of the graphic done anyway. An
hour more was all it would take to get it finished.

That was fine with the boss and off she went, and when
she got to Lyndhurst she parked by the New Forest Museum
and walked the short distance up to the tea rooms on the High
Street. Midsummer and Lyndhurst was thick with tourists.
The town sat squarely in the centre of the Perambulation and
was generally the first stop for visitors wishing to familiarise
themselves with this part of Hampshire.

Gina's lodgings above the Mad Hatter Tea Rooms were
accessed by a doorway that was separate from the tea rooms
themselves, from which at this time of day the scent of baked
goods rolled out onto the street. There were two lodging rooms
only and since from one hip hop music was blasting, Meredith
chose the other. It was here she applied the knowledge she'd
gained from watching police programmes on the telly. She
used a credit card to ease the catch back. It took five tries

and she was drenched in sweat – both from nerves and from the ambient temperature in the building – before she got inside. But when she managed it, she knew she'd made the right decision. For a mobile phone on the nightstand was ringing and as far as she was concerned, the ringing was fairly screaming *clue*.

She made a dash for it. She picked it up. She said, 'Yes?' with as much authority as she could muster and as breathlessly as she could manage, in order to disguise her voice. As she did this, she looked round the room. It was furnished simply: a bed, a chest of drawers, a bedside table, a desk, a wardrobe. There was a basin with a mirror above it, but no *en suite* bath. As the window was closed, it was deadly hot.

There was silence on the other end of the phone. She thought she'd missed the call and she cursed to herself. Then a man's voice said, 'Babe, Scotland Yard's been. How the *hell* much longer?' and she went cold from head to toe, as if a blast of refrigerated air shot through the room.

She said, 'Who is this? Tell me who this is!'

Silence in reply. Then, 'Shit,' in a low mutter. And then nothing.

She said, 'Hello? Hello? Who is this?' but she knew that whoever it was, he had already disconnected himself from the call. She punched the *send* button to return the call, although she reckoned that the man on the other end would hardly answer. But she didn't need him to do so. She needed only to see the number from which the call had come. What she got, though, was *Private Number* printed on the small screen. Damn, she thought. Whoever he was, he was calling from a withheld number. When the call went through, it rang and rang as she'd expected. No voice mail, no message. And a call from someone in cahoots with Gina Dickens.

Meredith felt a surge of triumph at this knowledge. It proved that she'd been right from the first. She'd *known* that Gina Dickens was dirty. All that remained was to find out the real purpose of her presence in the New Forest because no matter what Gina had declared about her programme to help girls at risk, Meredith didn't buy it. As far as she was concerned, the only girl at risk had been Jemima.

Through the walls of the room, the hip-hop music continued to thump. From below, the noise from the tea rooms rose. From without, the street noise reverberated through the windows: lorries passing through the High Street and grinding through their gears when they hit the gentle slope, cars heading for Southampton or Beaulieu, tour coaches the size of small cottages ferrying their passengers south to Brockenhurst or even as far as the port town of Lymington and an excursion over to the Isle of Wight. Meredith remembered how Gina had spoken of the cacophony in the street beneath her window. In this, at least, she had not been lying. But in other matters . . . Well, that was what Meredith was here to discover.

She had to be quick. She was going from cold to hot again, and she knew she couldn't risk opening a window and drawing attention to the room in this way. But the temperature made the air close and herself claustrophobic.

She attacked the bedside table first. The clock radio upon it was tuned to Radio Five, which didn't seem to indicate anything, and within the single drawer of the table there was nothing but a box of tissues and an old, opened package of Blu Tac with a small chunk of it missing. On the shelf of the table was a stack of magazines, too ancient to have belonged to Gina Dickens, Meredith reckoned.

In the wardrobe there were clothes, but not the quantity that one would associate with permanency. They were of good quality, though, in keeping with what Meredith had already seen Gina wearing. She had expensive taste. Nothing was trendy rubbish. But the clothes gave no other clue about their owner. They *did* make Meredith wonder how Gina expected to maintain her wardrobe on what Gordon Jossie made as a thatcher, but that was it.

She had similar luck with the chest of drawers, where the one piece of information she gleaned was that Gina definitely did not buy her knickers at discount prices. They seemed to be silk or satin, at least six different colours and prints and each pair of knickers possessed a bra to match. Meredith allowed herself a moment of knicker envy before she looked through the rest of the drawers. She saw neatly folded T-shirts, jerseys and a few scarves. That was it.

The desk offered even less information. It displayed some tourist brochures in a wooden holder atop it and some exceedingly cheap stationery in its centre drawer along with two postcards featuring the Mad Hatter Tea Rooms. There was a single pen in a shallow depression within this drawer, but that was all. Meredith pushed it shut, sat on the desk chair, and thought about what she had seen.

Virtually nothing of use. Gina had nice clothes, she liked nice knickers and she had a mobile phone. Why she didn't have that phone *with* her was an interesting point: had she forgotten it? Did she not want Gordon Jossie to know that she had it? Was she worried that possession of it would indicate something she didn't wish him to know? Was she avoiding a caller to whom she didn't wish to speak? Was she therefore on the run? The only way to get an answer to any of those questions was to ask her directly, which Meredith could hardly do without revealing she'd broken into her room, so she was out of luck.

She gazed round the place. For want of anything else to do, she looked under the bed but was not surprised when she found nothing but a suitcase, which itself contained nothing. She even examined it for a false bottom – at this point feeling fairly ridiculous – but she came up empty handed at that. She heaved herself to her feet, once again noting the closeness of the room. She thought about splashing some water on her face, and reckoned it wouldn't hurt to use the basin to revive herself, but the water was tepid and would have needed running for several minutes to become cool enough to do any good.

She patted her face on the hand towel provided, rehung it neatly on its rack, and then gave a closer look to the sink.

It hung from the wall and was fairly modern in appearance. It was feminine as well, with flowers and vines painted onto the porcelain. Meredith ran her hand along it and then, thinking that as she'd noted it so also might have Gina, she ran her hand beneath it as well. Her fingers came to something that didn't feel right. She squatted to have a better look.

There, beneath the basin, something had been lodged with Blu Tac. It appeared to be a small, taped and folded package made of paper. She eased it off the underside of the basin and carried it to the desk. Carefully, she removed both the tape and the Blu Tac for future use.

Unfolded, the paper turned out to be a piece of the room's cheap stationery. It had been fashioned into something akin to a pouch and what that pouch held appeared to be a small medallion. Meredith would have vastly preferred a message, cryptic or otherwise. She would have liked to see 'I asked Gordon Jossie to murder Jemima Hastings so that he would be free for me' although she would not have said no to, 'I believe Gordon Jossie is a killer although I myself had nothing to do with it.' Instead what she had was a roundish object, looking as if it had been made as part of a metallurgy class. Clearly, it was supposed to be a perfect circle, but it hadn't quite made it. The metal in question looked like dirty gold, but it could have been anything that headed remotely in the direction of gold as Meredith reckoned there weren't a lot of classes on offer that allowed students to experiment with something so expensive.

The thought of classes took her inexorably to Winchester where Gina Dickens had come from. There seemed to be possible fruit to be borne from a fuller exploration of this. Meredith didn't *know* whether this object actually belonged to Gina, nor had she the slightest idea why Gina or anyone else would have placed it beneath the basin, but the opened packet of Blu Tac in the bedside table suggested it was hers. And as long as Gina's ownership was a possibility, Meredith was not at a dead end in her investigation.

The question now was whether to take the little medallion with her or try to remember what it looked like so that she could describe it later. She considered drawing it, and she even went to the desk, sat, and brought out a sheet of the cheap stationery to try her hand at sketching. The problem was that the workmanship wasn't particularly clear and while there seemed to be embossing on the thing, she couldn't make any of it out very well. So it seemed to her that there was nothing for it but to engage in one small act of burglary. It was in a good cause, after all.

When Gordon Jossie arrived back at his holding, he found Gina in the last place he would have expected to see her: in the west paddock. She was at the far side of it, and he might have missed her altogether had not one of the ponies whinnied, which directed his attention over to them. He saw the blonde of Gina's hair against the dark green backdrop of the wood in the distance. At first he thought she was merely walking on the far side of the paddock and beyond the fence, perhaps returning from a ramble in the trees. But when he climbed out of the pickup with Tess at his heels, he ventured over to the fence and found that Gina was actually within the paddock itself.

This sent his hackles soaring. From the first, Gina had made a considerable topic out of her fear of the New Forest ponies. So to find her inside the paddock with them aroused the sleeping cobra of distrust within him.

She hadn't noticed his arrival. She was pacing along the line of the barbed wire fencing, and she seemed intent upon ignoring the ponies as well as watching for their droppings or taking care with her footwork since she had her eyes on the ground.

He called to her. She started, one hand clutching at the collar of her shirt. In the other hand she appeared to be carrying a map.

She was wearing, he saw, her knee-high Wellingtons. This told him that whatever else she was doing, once again she was worried about adders. Briefly he thought about explaining to her that adders wouldn't likely be in the paddock, that the paddock was not the heath. But this wasn't a moment for explanations on his part. There was a question to be answered about what she was doing in the paddock in the first place and about the map she was holding. She smiled and waved and folded it. She said with a laugh, 'You gave me quite a fright.'

'What're you doing?' He couldn't help it: his voice was sharp. He made a concerted effort to soften it but he didn't quite manage to make his tone normal. 'I thought ponies scared you.'

She cast a look at the animals. They were meandering across the paddock in the direction of the water trough. Gordon went over to the fence with Tess. The water was low, and he went for the hosepipe and unspooled it to the paddock. He entered, telling the dog to stay where she was – which she didn't much like, pacing back and forth to show her displeasure – and he began topping up the trough.

As he did this, Gina picked her way in his direction, but she didn't do it by crossing directly over to him as another person might. Rather she went by way of the fence, keeping within inches of it as she moved along. She didn't answer him till she'd reached the eastern part of the paddock in this diligent fashion.

'You've found me out,' she said. 'Pooh. I did so want to make it a surprise.' She cast a wary eye on the ponies. As she got closer to him, so also did she get closer to them.

'What surprise?' he asked. 'And is that a map? What're you doing with a map? How c'n a map be part of a surprise?'

She laughed. '*Please*. One thing at a time.'

'Why're you inside the paddock, Gina?'

She observed him for a moment before she answered. Then she said with care, 'Is something wrong? Should I not be in here?'

'You said the New Forest ponies . . . You said that horses in general—'

'I know what I said about horses. But that doesn't mean I wouldn't try to get over it.'

'What are you talking about?'

Gina reached his side before she replied again. She ran her hand through her sparkly hair. Despite his agitation, he liked to see her do this. He liked the way it fell back into place so perfectly no matter how she – or he – dishevelled it. 'Getting over an irrational fear,' she told him. 'It's called desensitisation. Haven't you ever heard of people who get over their fears by being exposed to them?'

'Bollocks. People don't get over their fears.'

She'd been smiling but her smile faltered at his tone. She said, 'What nonsense, Gordon. Of *course* they do, if they want to. They expose themselves to their fear in increments till they're no longer afraid. Like getting over a fear of heights by slowly exposing oneself to progressively higher and higher places. Or getting over a fear of flying by getting used to the aeroplane jetway first and then going to the doorway of the plane and then just inside with the doors open and then to the seats. Haven't you heard of that?'

'What's that have to do with being in the paddock? And carrying a map with you. What the hell are you doing with a map?'

She frowned outright then. She shifted her weight in that womanly way, one hip jutted out. She said, 'Gordon, are you accusing me of something?'

'Answer the question.'

She looked as startled as she'd looked when he first called out her name. Only this time, he knew, it was because of how sharply he spoke to her.

She said quietly, 'I just explained. I'm trying to get used to them by being in the paddock with them. Not close to them, but not on the other side of the fence either. I was going to stay there until they didn't make me so nervous. Then I was going to take a step or two closer to them. That's all.'

'The map,' he said. 'I want to know about the map.'

'Good grief. I took it from my *car*, Gordon. It's something to wave at them, to frighten them off if they got too close.'

He said nothing in reply to this. She looked at him so closely that he turned his head to keep her from reading his expression. He felt his blood pulsing in his temples and he knew his face must look red and revealing.

She said with what sounded like great care, 'Are you aware that you're acting like you suspect me of something?'

Again, he made no reply. He wanted out of the paddock. He wanted her out of the paddock as well. He went to the gate and she followed him, saying, 'What's wrong, Gordon? Has something happened? Something else?'

'What d'you mean?' he demanded, swinging to her. 'What's supposed to have happened?'

'Well, heavens, I don't know. But first that strange man came to speak with you. Then those detectives from Scotland Yard to tell you that Jemima—'

'This isn't about Jemima!' he cried.

She gaped at him, then closed her mouth. She said, 'All right. It's not about Jemima. But you're clearly upset and I can't think it's just that I went into the paddock to get used to the horses. Because that doesn't make sense.'

He forced out the words because he had to say something. 'They've talked to Ringo. He phoned me about it.'

'*Ringo?*' Clearly, she was nonplussed.

'He gave them letters, and the letters are false. He didn't know that, but they'll suss it out. Then they'll be back here at the double. Cliff lied like I asked him to, but he'll break if they press him. They'll force the issue and he won't hold out.'

'Does any of that matter?'

'Of *course* it matters!' He jerked the gate open. He'd forgotten about the dog. Tess raced inside and greeted Gina ecstatically. Seeing this, Gordon told himself that it had to mean something if Tess liked Gina. Tess read people well and if she read Gina as decent and good, what else mattered?

Gina knelt to rub the dog's head. Tess wagged her tail and bumped closer to her for more. Gina looked up at him and said, 'But you went to Holland. That's all it was. If it comes to it, you can tell the police you lied because you don't have the paperwork. And what does it matter anyway if you don't have the itinerary or the ticket or whatever? You went to Holland, and you can prove it *somehow*. Hotel records. Internet searches. The person you talked to about the reeds. Really, how difficult can it be?' And when he didn't answer, 'Gordon, you *were* in Holland, weren't you?'

'Why d'you want to know?' He spoke explosively. It was the very last thing he intended but he *wouldn't* be pressed.

She'd risen from the dog as she spoke, and she took a step away from him now. Her gaze drifted beyond him and he swung round to see who was there, but it was only her car she was looking at and it came to him that she was thinking about leaving. She seemed somehow to master this desire because once again she spoke calmly enough although he could see from the way her mouth formed the words that she was on the alert and prepared to run away. He wondered how they'd got to this point, but he knew at heart that this would always be the end point he reached with a woman. It might as well have been written in stone.

She said, 'Darling, what's going on? Who's Ringo? What letters are you talking about? Have those police come to see you again today? Or, at heart, is this just about me? Because if it is, I had *no* idea . . . I didn't intend harm. It only seemed to me that if we're to be together – I mean permanently – then I need to get used to the New Forest animals. Don't I? The horses are part of your life. They're part of the holding. I can't avoid them forever.'

It was, if not an olive branch, then at least a fork in the road that he could take if he wanted to take it. He thought about the choices that lay ahead before he finally said, 'If you wanted to get used to them, I would have helped you.'

'I know that. But then it wouldn't have been a surprise.

And that's what I wanted it to be.' Some small tension seemed to release within her before she went on. 'I'm sorry if I've somehow overstepped the mark. I didn't think it would actually hurt anything. Look. Will you watch?' She took the map and unfolded it. She said, 'Will you let me show you, Gordon?'

She waited for his nod. When he gave it, she turned from him. She approached the trough slowly, the map held at her side. The ponies were drinking but they raised their heads warily. They were wild, after all, and meant to remain so.

Next to him, Tess whined for attention, and he grasped her collar. Near the trough, Gina raised the map. She waved it at the ponies, and cried, 'Shoo, horse!' Tess gave a sharp bark as the ponies wheeled round and trotted to the far side of the paddock.

Gina turned back to him. She said nothing. Nor did he. It was another point of choice for him, but there were so many now, so many choices and so many paths and every day there seemed to be more. One wrong move was all it would take, and he knew that better than anything.

She came back to him. When she was outside the paddock once again, he released his hold on the dog and Tess bounded to Gina. A moment for another caress and the retriever was off in the direction of the barn, loping for the shade and her water dish.

Gina stood before him. As was his habit, he was wearing his dark glasses still, and she reached up and removed them, saying, 'Let me see your eyes.'

'The light,' he said, although this wasn't quite the truth, and 'I don't like to be without them,' which was.

She said, 'Gordon, can you be easy? Will you let me help you let everything go?'

He felt tight from head to foot, held in a vice of his own creation. 'I can't.'

'You can,' she said. 'Let me, my darling.'

And the miracle of Gina was that how he had been with her moments before did not matter to her. She was *now* incarnate. The past was the past.

She slid one hand up his chest and her arm round his neck. She drew him near her while her other hand slid down and down in order to make him hard.

'Let me help you let everything go,' she repeated, this time close and against his mouth. 'Let me, darling.'

He groaned helplessly and then he chose. He closed the remaining space between them.

17

'He's called Yukio Matsumoto,' Isabelle Ardery told Lynley when he walked into her office. 'His brother saw the e-fit and phoned in.' She fingered through some paperwork on her desk.

Lynley said, 'Hiro Matsumoto?'

She looked up. 'That's the brother. D'you know him?'

'I know of him. He's a cellist.'

'In a London orchestra?'

'No. He's a soloist.'

'Well-known?'

'If you follow classical music.'

'Which you do, I take it?' She sounded marginally piqued, as if he'd been intent upon demonstrating knowledge that she considered both arcane and offensive. She also seemed on edge. Lynley wondered if this had to do with whatever she might be thinking about his meeting with Hillier. He wanted to tell her to have no fear on that score. While he and Hillier had reached a point of personal rapprochement after Helen's death, he had a feeling it wouldn't last and soon enough they'd be back on their previous footing, which was at each other's throats.

He said, 'I've heard him play. If, indeed, that's the Hiro Matsumoto who phoned you.'

'I can't think there're two blokes with that name, and anyway he wouldn't come to the Yard. He said he'd speak to us at his solicitor's office. Some backing and forthing over that and we compromised with the bar at the Milestone Hotel. Not far from the Albert Hall. Do you know it?'

'It can't be difficult to find,' he said. 'But why not at his solicitor's office?'

'I don't like the image of cap-in-hand.' She looked at her watch. 'Ten minutes,' she said. 'I'll meet you at the car.' She tossed him her keys.

It was actually fifteen minutes later when she joined him. In the closer confines of the car, she smelled of mint. 'Right,' she said as they headed up the ramp. 'Tell me, Thomas.'

He glanced at her. 'What?'

'Don't be coy. Did Hillier order you to watch me and give him reports?'

Lynley smiled to himself. 'Not in so many words.'

'But it *was* about me, wasn't it, this meeting with Sir David.'

At the street he braked and looked in her direction. 'You know, in some situations that conclusion would smack of narcissism. The appropriate response would be "The world is not all about you, guv."'

'Isabelle,' she said.

'Guv,' he repeated.

'Oh *bother*, Thomas. I don't intend to let that go. The Isabelle bit. As to the other, are you going to tell me or shall I just assume? I want loyalists working for me, by the way. You'll have to choose sides.'

'And if I don't wish to?'

'Out on your handsome ear. You'll be back on traffic duty in the blink of an eye.'

'I was never on traffic duty in the first place, guv.'

'Isabelle. And you know damn well what I mean, behind those impeccable manners of yours.'

He pulled out into Broadway and considered his route. He settled on making for Birdcage Walk and weaving over to Kensington from there.

The Milestone Hotel was one of the many boutique establishments that had been springing up round town in the last few years. Fashioned from one of the distinguished redbrick mansions that faced Kensington Gardens and the palace, it was oaken, quiet and discreet, an oasis from the bustle of High Street Kensington, not far from the hotel's front door. It was also air-conditioned, a real blessing.

The hotel's staff wore expensive uniforms and spoke in the hushed voices of people at a religious service. The moment that Lynley and Isabelle Ardery walked into the place, they were approached by a pleasant concierge who asked if he could be of assistance.

They wanted the bar, Ardery told him. She was brisk and official. Where is it? she asked.

The man's moment of hesitation was something Lynley recognised as an indication of a disapproval that he wouldn't voice. For all he knew, she was a hotel inspector or someone getting ready to write about the Milestone in one of the myriad guides to London. It would serve everyone's interests if he cooperated as blandly as possible with only a minuscule display of his judgment of her manners. He said, 'Of course, madam,' and he took them personally to the bar, which turned out to be an intimate setting for a colloquy.

Before he left them, Isabelle asked him to fetch the bartender and when that individual arrived, she ordered a vodka and tonic. To Lynley's carefully expressionless face, she said, 'Are you going to tell me about Sir David or not,' which surprised him as he thought she'd likely remark about the drink.

'There's little to report. He's interested in filling the position soon. It's been too long without someone permanently in Webberly's place. You've a good shot at it as—'

'As long as I keep my nose clean, wear tights to the office, don't ruffle anyone's feathers, and walk the straight and narrow,' she said. 'Which I suppose includes not having a vodka and tonic during working hours, whatever the temperature of the day.'

'I was going to say "as far as I can tell",' he told her. He'd ordered a mineral water for himself.

She narrowed her eyes at him and frowned at the bottle of

San Pellegrino when it arrived. 'You disapprove of me, don't you?' she said. 'Will you tell Sir David?'

'That I disapprove? I don't, actually.'

'Not even of the fact that I have the occasional drink on duty? I'm *not* a lush, Thomas.'

'Guv, you've no need to explain yourself to me. And as to the rest, I'm not eager to become Hillier's snout. He knows that.'

'But your opinion counts with him.'

'I can't think why. It never did before.'

The sound of quiet conversation came in their direction, and in a moment two people entered the room. Lynley recognised the cellist at once. His companion was an attractive Asian woman in a smartly tailored suit and stiletto heels that clicked like whip cracks against the floor.

She glanced at Lynley but spoke to Ardery. 'Superintendent?' she said. At Ardery's nod, she introduced herself as Zaynab Bourne. 'And this is Mr Matsumoto,' she told them.

Hiro Matsumoto bent fractionally from the waist although he also extended his hand. He gave a firm handshake and murmured a conventional greeting. He had, Lynley thought, a pleasant face. Behind his wire-rimmed spectacles, his eyes appeared kind. For an international celebrity in the world of classical music, he seemed inordinately humble as well, asking politely for a cup of tea. Green tea if they had it, he said. If not, black tea would do. He spoke without an apparent accent. Lynley recalled that he'd been born in Kyoto, but he'd studied and played abroad for many years.

He was appearing now at the Albert Hall, he said. He was in London for only a fortnight, also teaching a master class at the music college. It was purest chance that he'd seen the e-fit – which he called the artist's rendition – of his brother in the newspaper and also on the television news.

'Please believe me,' Hiro Matsumoto said quietly, 'when I assure you that Yukio did not kill this woman the papers are speaking of. He could not have done so.'

'Why?' Ardery said. 'He was in the vicinity – we've a witness to that – and he seems to have been running from the scene.'

Matsumoto looked pained. 'There will be an explanation. Whatever else he might be, whatever else he does, my brother Yukio is not a killer.'

Zaynab Bourne said as if to explain, 'Mr Matsumoto's younger brother suffers from paranoid schizophrenia, Superintendent. Unfortunately, he won't take medication. But he's never been in trouble with the police since he first came to London – if you check your records you'll find this is true – and he leads a quiet life in general. My client' – with a brief, proprietary touch on Hiro Matsumoto's arm – 'is identifying him so that you can concentrate your efforts elsewhere, where they belong.'

'That may be the case, the schizophrenia bit,' Ardery said, 'but as he was seen running from the area of a murder and as some of his clothing appeared to have been removed and was balled up—'

'It's been hot weather,' the solicitor cut in.

'—he's going to have to be questioned. So if you know where he is, Mr Matsumoto, you do need to tell us.'

The cellist hesitated. He removed a handkerchief from his pocket and used it on his glasses. Unshielded by them, his face looked quite young. He was in his late forties, Lynley knew, but he could have passed for a man fifteen years younger.

He said, 'First, I must explain to you.'

Ardery looked as if the last thing she wanted was an explanation for anything, but Lynley himself was curious. As secondary officer to Ardery, it wasn't his place but still he said, 'Yes?'

His brother was a gifted musician, Hiro Matsumoto said. They were a musical family, and the three of them – there was also a sister who was a flautist in Philadelphia – had all been given instruments as children. They were expected to learn, to practise long and hard, to play well, and to excel. Towards this end they were educated in music at great cost to their parents and at personal sacrifice of them all.

'Obviously,' he said, 'there is not a normal childhood when one has this sort of . . . focus.' He chose the last word carefully. 'In the end, I went to Juilliard, Miyoshi studied in Paris and Yukio came to London. He was fine at first. There was no indication that anything was wrong. It was only later that the illness appeared. And because of this, because it happened in the midst of his studies, our father believed he was malingering. Out of his depth, perhaps, and unable to admit it or to cope with it. This was not the case, of course. He was seriously ill. But in our culture and in our family—' Matsumoto had continued polishing his glasses as he spoke, but now he paused, put them on, and adjusted them carefully on his nose. 'Our father is not a bad man. But his beliefs are firm, and he could not be convinced that Yukio needed more than merely a good talking to. He came here from Kyoto. He made his wishes known to Yukio. He gave him instructions, and he expected them to be followed. Since his instructions had always been obeyed, he thought he'd done enough. And at first it seemed so. Yukio drove himself hard, but the illness . . . This is not something you can wish away or work away. He had a collapse, he left the college and he simply disappeared. For ten years he was lost to us. When we located him, we wanted to help him, but he would not be forced. His fears are too great. He distrusts the medicines. He has a terror of hospitals. He manages to survive on his music, and my sister and I do what we can to watch over him when we come to London.'

'And do you now know where he is? Exactly where he is?'

Matsumoto looked to his solicitor. Zaynab Bourne took up the thread of the conversation. 'I hope Mr Matsumoto has made it clear that his brother is ill. He wants an assurance that nothing will be done that might frighten him. He understands that Yukio will need to be questioned, but he insists that your approach be cautious and that any interview be conducted in my presence and in the presence of a mental health professional. He also insists upon your acknowledgement and assurance that, as his brother is someone diagnosed with untreated paranoid schizophrenia, his words – whatever they might be once you speak to him – can hardly be used against him.'

Lynley glanced at Ardery. She had her hands clasped round her vodka and tonic, and her fingers tapped against the cool sides of the glass. She'd drunk most of it during their conversation, and now she drained the rest. She said, 'I acknowledge that we'll take care. You'll be there. A specialist will be there. The Pope, the Home Secretary and the Prime Minister will be there if you want it. You'll have as many witnesses as you like if that's your pleasure, but if he admits to murder, he's going to be charged.'

'He's seriously ill,' the solicitor said.

'And we have a legal system that will make that determination.'

There was a little silence as the cellist and his solicitor thought this over. Ardery leaned back in her chair. Lynley waited for her to remind them that they were at the moment sheltering someone who could be a material witness to a crime or, worse, the actual killer. But she didn't play that card and she looked as if she knew she didn't need to.

Instead she said, 'There's a simple reality you must face, Mr Matsumoto. If you don't give your brother up to us, someone else will eventually.'

Another silence before Hiro Matsumoto spoke. He looked so pained that Lynley felt a powerful surge of compassion for him, a surge so strong that he wondered if he was actually meant to do police work at this juncture in his life. The whole point was to manoeuvre people into a corner. Ardery was perfectly willing to do this, he could see, but he thought he himself might not have the stomach for it any longer.

Matsumoto said quietly, 'He is in Covent Garden. He plays his violin there, as a busker, for money.' He dropped his head, as if the admission were somehow a humiliation, as perhaps it was.

Ardery rose. She said, 'Thank you. I have no intention of frightening him.' And to his solicitor she went on with, 'When we have him in custody, I'll ring you and tell you where he is. We won't speak to him until you're there. Contact whatever mental health expert you need and bring her along.'

'I will want to see him,' Hiro Matsumoto said.

'Of course. We'll arrange that as well.' She gave him a nod and indicated to Lynley that they needed to be off.

Lynley said to the cellist, 'You've done the right thing, Mr Matsumoto. I know it wasn't easy.' He found he wanted to go on, forging a fellowship with the man because his own brother had in the past been deeply troubled. But Peter Lynley's difficulties with both alcohol and drugs were insignificant compared to this, so he said nothing else.

Isabelle made the phone call once they were on the pavement in front of the hotel, heading back to her car. They had their man, she told DI Hale brusquely. Get over to Covent Garden at once and take a team with you. Five blokes should do it. Fan out when you get there, look for a middle-aged Japanese man sawing away on a violin. Box him in. Do not approach him. He's barking mad and just as dangerous. Phone me with his exact location. I'm on my way.

She snapped her phone off and turned to Lynley. 'Let's pick up the miserable shite.'

He looked surprised or taken aback or *something* that she couldn't quite make out. She said, 'This bloke is very likely a killer, Thomas.'

'Right, guv.' He spoke politely.

She said, '*What?* I'll give them their bloody psycho-whatever-they-want-kind-of-expert and I'll not say a word to him till Ms Stiletto Heels is sitting in his lap, if necessary. But I'm not about to risk his getting away from us when we've finally got him.'

'You'll get no objection from me.'

But she knew he objected to something and she pressed him. 'I dare say you have a better approach?'

'Not at all.'

'God *damn* it, Thomas, if we're to work together, you're going to be frank with me even if I have to twist your arm.'

They were at the car and he hesitated before unlocking his door. At least, she thought, she'd apparently cured him of opening her door for her. He said, 'You're certain about that?'

'Well, of course I'm certain. Why else would I say it? I want to know what you think and I want to know it *when* you think it.'

'Have you a drinking problem, then?' he asked her.

It wasn't what she'd been expecting, but she knew she should have been prepared. The fact that she hadn't been caused her to explode. 'I had a bloody vodka and tonic. Do I look like I'm staggering drunk to you?'

'And before the vodka and tonic?' he asked. 'Guv, I'm not a fool. I expect you've got it in your bag. Likely it's vodka because most people think that has no odour. You've got breath mints as well, or chewing gum or whatever else you use to hide the smell.'

She said in automatic response, gone icy to her fingertips, 'You're out of order, Inspector Lynley. You are so bloody *far* out of order that I ought to send you packing to walk a patch in south London.'

'I can understand that.'

She wanted to strike him. It came to her that it didn't matter to him and that likely it had *never* mattered to him: what threats were used against him to control him as a cop. He was unlike the rest because he didn't need the job, so if they took it from him or threatened to take it from him or acted in a way that met with his aristocratic displeasure, he could walk away. And this was more than maddening, she realised. It made him a loose cannon, with loyalties to no one.

'Get in the car,' she told him. 'We're going to Covent Garden. Now.'

They drove in absolute silence, along the south side of Kensington Gardens and then Hyde Park. And she wanted a drink. The vodka and tonic had been a typical hotel bar vodka and tonic: a meagre finger-and-a-half of vodka in the glass with the tonic provided alongside in a bottle so she could make the drink as strong or as weak as she wished. Because of Lynley's presence, she'd used the entire tonic, and now she regretted it. She bloody, *sodding* regretted it. She also went over her movements feverishly, in her mind. She'd been perfectly careful. He was making a guess and waiting to see what she would do about it.

She said to him, 'I'm going to forget we had that exchange on the pavement, Thomas.'

He said, 'Guv,' in a tone that telegraphed *as you wish*.

She wanted to go further. She wanted to know what, if anything, he would say to Hillier. But to make any additional mention of the topic could give it a credence she couldn't afford.

They were attempting to negotiate Piccadilly Circus when her mobile rang. She barked, 'Ardery,' into it, and Philip Hale spoke. They'd found the Japanese bloke with the violin, he told her. 'Down a set of stairs in a courtyard just beyond—'

'The cigar shop,' Isabelle said, for she recalled that she and Lynley had seen the damn busker themselves. He'd been playing to the accompaniment of a boom box. With long salt and pepper hair, he'd been wearing a dinner jacket and standing in the lower courtyard in front of a wine bar. Why the hell hadn't she remembered the man?

That was the bloke, Philip Hale said when she'd described him.

'Have you uniforms with you?'

No. Everyone was in plain clothes. Two blokes were sitting at tables in the courtyard and the rest were—

Hale broke off. Then he said, 'Damn. Guv, he's packing up. He's shut off the boom box and he's putting the violin . . . You want us to nab him?'

'No. *No*. Do not approach him. Follow him, but keep everyone away. And keep well back. Do not let him see he's being tailed, all right?'

'Right.'

'Good man, Philip. We'll be there presently.' She said to Lynley, 'He's on the move. *Get* us there, for God's sake.'

She could feel her nerves jangling to the tips of her toes. He, on the other hand, was perfectly calm. But once they made it through Piccadilly Circus, a tailback of taxis seemed to stretch into infinity.

She cursed. She said, 'Bloody *hell*, Thomas. Get us *out* of here.'

He gave no reply. But he made the virtue of being a long-time Londoner apparent when he began to take side streets, coolly, as if in possession of the Knowledge. He finally parked as Isabelle's mobile rang again.

Philip Hale's voice said, 'There's a church at the southwest end of the square.'

'Has he gone inside?'

He hadn't, Hale said. In front of the church was a garden and he had begun to play there, in the middle of the central path. There were benches lining this and people were listening and, 'Guv, there's quite a crowd gathered.'

Isabelle said, 'We'll be there.' And to Lynley, 'A church?'

'That would be St Paul's Covent Garden.' As they came into the vicinity of the old flower market, he took her arm briefly and pointed her towards it. She saw the building over the heads of the crowd: a classical structure of brick with quoins of pale stone. She headed towards it, but the route wasn't easy. There were buskers everywhere and hundreds of people enjoying them: magicians, balloon sellers, tap dancers, even a group of grey-haired women playing marimbas.

Isabelle was thinking it was the perfect spot for something dreadful to happen – anything from a terrorist attack to a runaway vehicle – when a sudden commotion to one side of the church caught her attention just as her mobile rang. A shout went up, and she snapped, 'What's going on?' into the phone. For it was clear to her that something was happening and it wasn't what she wanted to happen and even as she

e arrival of ambulances, the rush of feet, exigent
g barked as trolleys wheeled the injured into exam-
. Lynley saw and heard all of this and was swept
e moment he'd walked in and learned that his wife
shot on the front steps of their house, that help did
ve for twenty minutes and that in that time Helen had
ithout oxygen as her heart pumped blood uselessly into
ity of her chest. It was all so real that he gasped, stopped
tly, and did not come round till he heard Isabelle Ardery
's name.

er tone cleared his head. She was saying to him,
uniforms down here, round the clock, wherever he is,
wherever they move him. Christ, what a cock-up. I bloody well
told him not to approach.'

He noticed that she was wringing her hands and he thought
inanely how he'd never seen someone do that although he'd
read the expression often enough in books, as an indication
of someone's anxiety. Doubtless, she'd be feeling anxiety in
spades. The Metropolitan police in pursuit of someone who
ends up in hospital? No matter that they were identifying
themselves as they pursued him. It wouldn't play that way
in the newspapers, and she'd know that. She would also know
that the ultimate head to roll, if it came down to it, was going
to be hers.

e doors opened. Philip Hale came in, his expression
ght. Sweat made rivulets from his temples and beaded
orehead. He'd removed his jacket. His shirt clung to

moved. She had him by the arm and then against
d she was inches from his face before he had even
ocation in the room. She hissed, 'Do you *ever* bloody
d you not to approach the man.'

idn't—'

him, Philip, you're taking the blame. I'll see to

thought this, she saw him: Yukio Matsumoto tearing through the
crowd, his violin in one hand and sheer unmitigated panic on
his face.

On the mobile Philip Hale said, 'He clocked us, guv. Don't
know how. We've got—'

'I see him,' she said. 'Get in pursuit. If we lose him here,
we've lost him for good.' And to Lynley, 'Damn. *Damn,*' as
the violinist broke into a crowd. Cries of protest were followed
almost at once by shouts of 'Police! Stop! Stop that man!' and
afterwards a form of madness ensued. For part of the dark
history of the Metropolitan police in pursuit of *anyone* was a
history that included the shooting to death of an unarmed and
innocent civilian in an underground train, and no one wanted
to be in the line of fire. No matter that these plainclothes cops
were not armed, the crowd wouldn't know that. People began
running in all directions as mothers grabbed children, husbands
grabbed wives, and those individuals with a score to settle
against the police did what they could to get in the way.

'Where's he gone?' Isabelle demanded of Lynley.

He said, 'There!' and indicated roughly the north. She
followed his gesture and saw the bobbing head of the man
and then the black of his dinner jacket, and she set off after
him, shouting into her phone, 'Philip, he's going north on . . .
What it is?' to Lynley.

'James Street,' Lynley said. 'In the direction of Long Acre.'

'James Street,' she repeated. 'In the direction . . . where?' to
Lynley. And then, 'Bloody hell. You talk to him.' She thrust
her mobile at Lynley and began to run, forcing her way through
the crowd with shouts of 'Police! Police! Get out of the way!'

Matsumoto had made it to the top of the street, charging
down the middle of it with no regard for whom or what he
ran into. Fallen children, one upended kiosk and trampled
shopping bags lay in his wake, but to her cries of 'Stop him!'
no one did a thing.

In pursuit, she and Lynley had the advantage over Philip
Hale and his men. But Matsumoto was fast. He was driven

by fear and by whatever demons were inside his head. In front of her, she saw him dash directly into Long Acre, where the blast of a horn told her he'd nearly missed being hit by a car. She redoubled her speed in time to see him go roaring up another street. He ran as if his life depended upon escape, his violin clutched to his chest, its bow long discarded. Isabelle cried, 'Where does that go?' to Lynley. 'Where's he heading?'

'Shaftesbury Avenue,' Lynley told her and into the phone, 'Philip, can you head him off by another route? He's about to cross Shelton Street. He's paying no attention to where he's running or what's around him. If he makes it as far as Shaftesbury . . . Yes. Yes. Right.' And to Isabelle, 'There'll be uniforms somewhere nearby. He's got the Met on it.'

'Christ, we don't want uniforms, Thomas.'

'We don't have a choice.'

They raced after him. Matsumoto knocked pedestrians right and left. He stumbled against a placard for the *Evening Standard*. She thought they had him because the vendor jumped forward and managed to grab his arm, yelling, 'Just you bloody wait.' But he shoved the irate man into the window of a shop front with tremendous force. The glass cracked, then exploded and showered the pavement in shards.

He made it into Shaftesbury Avenue. He veered to the right. In vain, Isabelle hoped for a uniformed constable or anything else because as she and Lynley rounded the corner, she could see the danger and she understood in a flash what was likely to happen if they didn't stop him at once.

Which they could not do. They could *not* do.

'What is this place?' she called to Lynley. He'd gained upon her and was surging ahead, but she was close after him.

'High Holborn, Endell, New Oxford . . .' His breathing was heavy. 'We can't let him cross.'

She saw that well enough. Cars, taxis, lorries, and buses were all debouching into this one spot and from every direction.

But cross he intended and cross he attempted, without a

glance to the right or the left, as ⸺ and not upon a congested st⸺

The taxi that hit him had ⸺ the northeast and like every o⸺ vast confluence of streets that h⸺ and in every direction, it came fast⸺ off the pavement, intent upon crossin⸺ into him, sending his body in a horrify⸺

'Jesus God!' Isabelle heard Lynley cry⸺ shouting into her mobile, 'Philip! Philip! He's ⸺ ambulance at once. Top of Shaftesbury Avenue, ⸺ High Street,' as everywhere round them the screech ⸺ and the blaring of horns filled the air, as the taxi driver ⸺ out of his vehicle and – hands to his head – ran towards ⸺ crumpled body of Yukio Matsumoto, as a bus driver join⸺ him and then three others till the violinist was hidden from ⸺ view, as Lynley shouted, 'Police! Keep back! Don't move him!'

And as she herself realised she'd made the wrong decision – the very worst decision – to have a team go after the man.

When he'd agreed to be part of Isabelle Ardery's murder squad for this investigation, the last spot Lynley would have considered as one of the locations in which he might have ⸺ in an appearance was St Thomas' Hospital, ⸺ Emergency, the very rooms and corridors i⸺ to make the decision to let go of Helen⸺ that was where the ambulance took⸺ when Lynley walked through the do⸺ of the casualty ward, it was as ⸺ between this moment and the ⸺ to his wife. The smells were ⸺ The sights were as they ⸺ chairs linked together ⸺ about AIDS, other sexua⸺ importance of frequent hand⸺

362

universal: th⸺
orders bein⸺
ining area⸺
back to ⸺
had bee⸺
not ⸺

⸺der ⸺
⸺wall ⸺
⸺ned her ⸺
⸺listen? I to⸺
'Guv, I d⸺
If we los⸺
it personally.'
'But, guv⸺

'Under review, in the dock, in the box. What*ever* it takes to get your attention because when I say you are not to approach a suspect, I do not sodding mean anything else so you tell me – you God damn bloody tell me, Philip – which part of that you didn't understand because we've got a man who's been hit by a car and likely to die and if you think *anyone*'s about to let this go and pretend it didn't happen, then you'd better have another God damn think and you'd better do it now.'

The DI glanced Lynley's way. There could not be, Lynley knew, a better cop and more decent person than Philip Hale. Given an order, he'd follow it to the letter, which was what he'd done and all of them knew it.

Hale said, 'Something spooked him, guv. One moment he was playing the violin and the next he was on the run. I don't know why. I swear to God—'

'You swear to God, do you?' She shook his arm. Lynley could see the tension in her fingers, and her grasp had to be a raw one because the tips of her fingers were red and the skin beneath her nails had gone crimson. 'Oh that's *very* pretty, Philip. Step onto the pitch. Take responsibility. I've no time for men who snivel like—'

'Guv.' Lynley intervened quietly. 'That'll do.'

Ardery's eyes widened. He saw that she'd eaten the lipstick from her mouth and what replaced it for colour on her face were two circles of red fury high on her cheeks. Before she could reply, he said to her urgently, 'We need to get to his brother and let him know what's happened.'

She began to speak and he added, 'We don't want him to hear this from a news report. We don't want anyone significant learning it that way.' By which he meant Hillier and she *had* to know that, even as she was driven by demons he well recognised but had never actually understood.

She released Hale's arm. 'Get back to the Yard,' she said and then to Lynley, 'That's twice now. You're warned.'

'Understood,' he said.

'And it makes no bloody difference, does it?' Then she

swung on Philip Hale once again. 'Are you an idiot, Philip? Did you not hear me? Get back to the Yard!'

Philip Hale looked from Ardery to Lynley and back to Ardery. He said, 'Guv' with a nod and he left them. Lynley saw him shake his head as he went.

Ardery said to Lynley, 'Get on to the brother, then,' and she began to pace. As Lynley made the necessary calls, he watched her and he wondered at what point she'd make another trip to the Ladies because there was little doubt in his mind that she desperately needed a drink.

However, during the forty minutes they waited for Hiro Matsumoto's solicitor to find the cellist and to bring him to St Thomas' Hospital, the acting superintendent remained in the waiting area and Lynley developed a reluctant respect for the manner in which she mastered herself. She made the appropriate phone calls to the Yard, putting the press office into the picture and passing along information to AC Hillier's office as well. Hillier, Lynley reckoned, would ultimately give Isabelle Ardery an earful. There was nothing the assistant commissioner hated more than bad press. Half of London could shoot the other half in the street and Hillier would not be as bothered as he would be by a tabloid screaming *More Brutality from the Met.*

When they finally arrived, Hiro Matsumoto was far calmer than his solicitor, who breathed fire and threatened lawsuits, neither of which was unexpected. She was interrupted only when they were joined by the physician who'd initially seen to the violinist's injuries. He was a gnomelike man with overlarge and oddly translucent ears and a nametag reading Hogg. He spoke directly to Hiro Matsumoto, obviously recognising him as the party likely to be most intimately connected to the injured man. He ignored the others.

A broken shoulder and a broken hip constituted the initial information, which sounded hopeful considering how bad things could have been. But then Mr Hogg added fractured skull and acute subdural haematoma to the mix, as well as the fact that the size of the injury was going to cause a dangerous increase in intracranial pressure, which in turn would result in damage to delicate brain tissue if something was not done immediately. That something was decompression, effected only by surgery and Yukio Matsumoto was being prepared for the operating theatre as they spoke.

'This is a murder suspect,' Isabelle Ardery informed the doctor. 'We're going to want to speak with him before *anything* is done to him incommunicado.'

'He's not in any condition—' the doctor began, to be interrupted by both the brother and the brother's solicitor.

One said, 'My brother did not kill that woman,' as the other said, 'You're not speaking to anyone but me, madam, and let's make certain that's *very* clear. And if you so much as approach Yukio Matsumoto without my knowledge—'

'Don't you threaten me,' Isabelle Ardery cut in.

'What I'll do – what I *intend* to do – is to find out exactly what led to this unbelievable development and when I find out, you'll be under a legal scrutiny the likes of which you have never seen. I hope I'm being completely clear.'

The doctor snapped, 'My interest is in the injured and not on whatever quarrel you two are having. He's going into surgery and there's an end to the matter.'

'Please,' Hiro Matsumoto said quietly. His eyes were liquid. 'My brother. He'll live?'

The doctor's expression softened. 'It's a traumatic injury, Mr Matsumoto. We'll do our very best.'

When he departed, Isabelle Ardery spoke, saying to Lynley, 'We need to collect his clothing for forensics.'

'I'll have something to say about that,' Zaynab Bourne snapped.

'He's a principal suspect in a murder investigation,' Ardery snapped back. 'We'll have the appropriate paperwork and we'll take the clothing and *if* you have a problem with that, you can take it up via the proper channels.' To Lynley, 'I'll want someone posted here as well, someone capable of staying on top of every development. The moment he's able to speak, we want an officer in the room with him.' She turned to Hiro Matsumoto and asked if he could tell them where his brother had his digs.

His solicitor was winding up to protest, but Matsumoto said, 'No, please, Mrs Bourne. I believe it is in Yukio's best interests to clear this matter up.'

'Hiro, you *can't* . . .' Mrs Bourne drew him away from Lynley and Ardery. She spoke urgently into his ear and he listened gravely. But the end result was no different. He shook his head. A few more words passed between them and Zaynab Bourne made for the outer doorway, flipping open her mobile phone as she went. Lynley had little doubt the solicitor had resources upon whom she was calling to light a fire under the Met.

Hiro Matsumoto returned to the police. He said, 'Come. I'll take you there.'

Isabelle fielded a phone call from AC Hillier as they crossed the river, heading up Victoria Embankment to avoid Parliament Square. Previously, she'd spoken only to the AC's secretary, grateful for the opportunity to rehearse the passing along of information that was likely to send Hillier into orbit. He said, 'Tell me,' by means of greeting. Isabelle, cognisant of Hiro Matsumoto's presence in the back seat of the car, gave him as little information as possible. She concluded her recitation with, 'He's in the operating theatre and his brother is with us. We're heading to his digs.'

'Have we got our man?'

'It's very possible.'

'Considering the situation, I don't need *possible*. I need probable. I need yes.'

'We should know quite soon.'

'God knows, we had better. Get to my office when you're done out there. We need a meeting with Deacon.'

She didn't know who the hell Deacon was, but she wasn't about to ask Hillier to identify him. She said she'd be there as soon as she could and when she ended the call, she asked Lynley the question.

He said, 'Head of the Press Bureau. Hillier's lining up the cavalry.'

'How do I prepare?'

He shook his head. 'I've never known.'

'Philip cocked this up, Thomas.'

'Do you think so.'

The fact that he said those words as a statement was, she decided, a declaration of his own opinion, not to mention of his judgement. And, perhaps, a declaration of his loyalties as well.

They said nothing more, merely riding in a tense silence to Charing Cross Road where Hiro Matsumoto directed them to its intersection with Denmark Street. There a red brick structure of eight floors housed living accommodation that was called Shaldon Mansions, which appeared to be flats that filled a building whose ground floor comprised a line of shops. These carried on a theme of music that extended down Denmark Street – which itself appeared to comprise nothing but outlets for guitars, drums and various types of horns – and combined this theme with newsagents, luggage shops, cafés and bookstores. The entrance to the flats consisted of an opening tucked between Keira News and Mucci Bags, and as they walked towards it, Isabelle sensed Lynley's steps slowing, so she turned to find he was gazing intently at the building. She said, 'What?' and he said, 'Paolo di Fazio.'

'What about him?'

'This is where Jemima Hastings took him.' He gave a nod to the entrance to the flats. 'That first night they met. He said she took him to a flat above Keira News.'

Isabelle smiled. 'Well done, Thomas. So we know how Yukio came to meet her.'

Hiro Matsumoto said, 'Knowing they might have met does not mean—'

'Of *course* it doesn't,' Isabelle said grimly. Anything to keep him moving. Anything to get him to take them to the flat, as there appeared to be no concierge to direct them.

Unfortunately, the cellist had no key. But as things turned out, a few bells rung, followed by a few knocks upon doors and a few questions here and there led them into Keira News. There Isabelle's identification produced a master key to every flat in Shaldon Mansions, held by the shop's owner who did double duty as a recipient of packages and emergency contact should a crisis arise within the building.

They definitely had a crisis on their hands, as Isabelle explained to the man. He handed over the key and they were about to set out when Lynley paused to ask him about Jemima Hastings. Did he know her? Did he remember her? Unusual eyes, one green and one brown?

The eyes did it. She had indeed lived in Shaldon Mansions, in a bedsit, quite similar to the one into which they were seeking entrance.

This confirmed another connection between Yukio Matsumoto and Jemima Hastings, and the fact gratified Isabelle hugely. It was one thing to connect them by means of Covent Garden. It was quite another to connect them through their living accommodation. Things were looking up.

Yukio's bedsit was on the fifth floor of the building, a point at which the spaciousness of the floors below gave way to crow-stepped gables and a mansard roof. As much accommodation as possible had been crammed into the space, and these rooms opened off a narrow corridor where the air was so close it had likely gone unrefreshed since the first Gulf War.

Inside Yukio Matsumoto's bedsit, the atmosphere was oppressively hot, and the place was quite disturbingly fitted out with floor to ceiling figures that had been drawn on the walls with marker pens. They loomed everywhere, dozens of them. A scrutiny indicated they depicted angels.

'What in God's name . . .' Isabelle murmured as next to her Lynley fished out his reading glasses to give the scrawled thought this, she saw him: Yukio Matsumoto tearing through the crowd, his violin in one hand and sheer unmitigated panic on his face.

On the mobile Philip Hale said, 'He clocked us, guv. Don't know how. We've got—'

'I see him,' she said. 'Get in pursuit. If we lose him here, we've lost him for good.' And to Lynley, 'Damn. *Damn*,' as the violinist broke into a crowd. Cries of protest were followed almost at once by shouts of 'Police! Stop! Stop that man!' and afterwards a form of madness ensued. For part of the dark history of the Metropolitan police in pursuit of *anyone* was a history that included the shooting to death of an unarmed and innocent civilian in an underground train, and no one wanted to be in the line of fire. No matter that these plainclothes cops were not armed, the crowd wouldn't know that. People began running in all directions as mothers grabbed children, husbands grabbed wives, and those individuals with a score to settle against the police did what they could to get in the way.

'Where's he gone?' Isabelle demanded of Lynley.

He said, 'There!' and indicated roughly the north. She followed his gesture and saw the bobbing head of the man and then the black of his dinner jacket, and she set off after him, shouting into her phone, 'Philip, he's going north on . . . What it is?' to Lynley.

'James Street,' Lynley said. 'In the direction of Long Acre.'

'James Street,' she repeated. 'In the direction . . . where?' to Lynley. And then, 'Bloody hell. You talk to him.' She thrust her mobile at Lynley and began to run, forcing her way through the crowd with shouts of 'Police! Police! Get out of the way!'

Matsumoto had made it to the top of the street, charging down the middle of it with no regard for whom or what he ran into. Fallen children, one upended kiosk and trampled shopping bags lay in his wake, but to her cries of 'Stop him!' no one did a thing.

In pursuit, she and Lynley had the advantage over Philip Hale and his men. But Matsumoto was fast. He was driven by fear and by whatever demons were inside his head. In front of her, she saw him dash directly into Long Acre, where the blast of a horn told her he'd nearly missed being hit by a car. She redoubled her speed in time to see him go roaring up another street. He ran as if his life depended upon escape, his violin clutched to his chest, its bow long discarded. Isabelle cried, 'Where does that go?' to Lynley. 'Where's he heading?'

'Shaftesbury Avenue,' Lynley told her and into the phone, 'Philip, can you head him off by another route? He's about to cross Shelton Street. He's paying no attention to where he's running or what's around him. If he makes it as far as Shaftesbury . . . Yes. Yes. Right.' And to Isabelle, 'There'll be uniforms somewhere nearby. He's got the Met on it.'

'Christ, we don't want uniforms, Thomas.'

'We don't have a choice.'

They raced after him. Matsumoto knocked pedestrians right and left. He stumbled against a placard for the *Evening Standard*. She thought they had him because the vendor jumped forward and managed to grab his arm, yelling, 'Just you bloody wait.' But he shoved the irate man into the window of a shop front with tremendous force. The glass cracked, then exploded and showered the pavement in shards.

He made it into Shaftesbury Avenue. He veered to the right. In vain, Isabelle hoped for a uniformed constable or anything else because as she and Lynley rounded the corner, she could see the danger and she understood in a flash what was likely to happen if they didn't stop him at once.

Which they could not do. They could *not* do.

'What is this place?' she called to Lynley. He'd gained upon her and was surging ahead, but she was close after him.

'High Holborn, Endell, New Oxford . . .' His breathing was heavy. 'We can't let him cross.'

She saw that well enough. Cars, taxis, lorries, and buses were all debouching into this one spot and from every direction.

But cross he intended and cross he attempted, without a

universal: the arrival of ambulances, the rush of feet, exigent orders being barked as trolleys wheeled the injured into examining areas. Lynley saw and heard all of this and was swept back to the moment he'd walked in and learned that his wife had been shot on the front steps of their house, that help did not arrive for twenty minutes and that in that time Helen had gone without oxygen as her heart pumped blood uselessly into the cavity of her chest. It was all so real that he gasped, stopped abruptly, and did not come round till he heard Isabelle Ardery say his name.

Her tone cleared his head. She was saying to him, '. . . uniforms down here, round the clock, wherever he is, wherever they move him. Christ, what a cock-up. I bloody well *told* him not to approach.'

He noticed that she was wringing her hands and he thought inanely how he'd never seen someone do that although he'd read the expression often enough in books, as an indication of someone's anxiety. Doubtless, she'd be feeling anxiety in spades. The Metropolitan police in pursuit of someone who ends up in hospital? No matter that they were identifying themselves as they pursued him. It wouldn't play that way in the newspapers, and she'd know that. She would also know that the ultimate head to roll, if it came down to it, was going to be hers.

The doors opened. Philip Hale came in, his expression distraught. Sweat made rivulets from his temples and beaded on his forehead. He'd removed his jacket. His shirt clung to his body.

Ardery moved. She had him by the arm and then against the wall and she was inches from his face before he had even noted her location in the room. She hissed, 'Do you *ever* bloody listen? I told you not to approach the man.'

'Guv, I didn't—'

'If we lose him, Philip, you're taking the blame. I'll see to it personally.'

'But, guv—'

glance to the right or the left, as if he were running in a park and not upon a congested street.

The taxi that hit him had no chance to stop. It came from the northeast and like every other means of transport in the vast confluence of streets that hurled vehicles by the dozens and in every direction, it came fast. Matsumoto flung himself off the pavement, intent upon crossing, and the taxi slammed into him, sending his body in a horrifying arc of flight.

'Jesus God!' Isabelle heard Lynley cry. And then he was shouting into her mobile, 'Philip! Philip! He's been hit. Get an ambulance at once. Top of Shaftesbury Avenue, near St Giles High Street,' as everywhere round them the screech of brakes and the blaring of horns filled the air, as the taxi driver burst out of his vehicle and – hands to his head – ran towards the crumpled body of Yukio Matsumoto, as a bus driver joined him and then three others till the violinist was hidden from view, as Lynley shouted, 'Police! Keep back! Don't move him!'

And as she herself realised she'd made the wrong decision – the very worst decision – to have a team go after the man.

When he'd agreed to be part of Isabelle Ardery's murder squad for this investigation, the last spot Lynley would have considered as one of the locations in which he might have to put in an appearance was St Thomas' Hospital, Accident and Emergency, the very rooms and corridors in which he'd had to make the decision to let go of Helen and their child. But that was where the ambulance took Yukio Matsumoto, and when Lynley walked through the doors into the hushed urgency of the casualty ward, it was as if no time at all had passed between this moment and the aftermath of what had happened to his wife. The smells were the same: antiseptics and cleansers. The sights were as they had been before: the institutional blue chairs linked together and lining the walls, the notice boards about AIDS, other sexually transmitted diseases, and the importance of frequent hand washing. The sounds remained figures a closer examination. Behind her, she heard Hiro Matsumoto sigh tremulously. She glanced his way. He looked infinitely sad.

'What is it?' she asked.

The cellist's gaze went from one drawing to the next to the next. 'He thinks they speak to him. The celestial host.'

'The what?'

'All the different kinds of angels,' Lynley put in.

'There's more than one kind?'

'There are nine different kinds.'

And he could no doubt list them, Isabelle thought grimly. Well, she didn't want to know – nor did she need to know – the categories of celestial whatever-they-were. What she needed to know was what, if anything, they had to do with Jemima Hastings' death. She reckoned nothing. But Hiro said, 'They battle for him. In his head, of course, but he hears them and he sometimes thinks he sees them. What he sees are people but angels have come in human guise in the past. And of course they are always depicted in a human form in art and in books and because of this, he thinks he's one with them. He believes they're waiting for him to declare his intention. It's the very heart of his illness. Yet it proves, doesn't it, that he harmed no one?'

Isabelle took in the drawings as Lynley moved along them slowly. There were angels descending into pools of water where humans lay crumpled with arms extended in supplication; there were angels driving demons before them to work on a temple in the distance; there were angels with trumpets, angels holding books, angels with weapons and one enormous wing-spread creature leading an army while nearby another cast destruction upon a Biblical-looking town. And one entire section appeared to be given to a struggle between two types of angels: one armed with weapons and one with wings spread to cover cowering humans below.

'He believes he must choose,' Hiro Matsumoto said.

'Choose what?' Isabelle asked. Lynley, she saw, had moved

to a narrow single bed, where a bedside table held a lamp, a book and a filmy looking glass of water. The book he picked up and opened. A card fell out and he bent to take it up from the floor as Hiro Matsumoto answered.

'Between guardian angel and warrior angel,' he said. 'To protect or to . . .' He hesitated, so Isabelle finished the thought.

'To punish,' she said. 'Well, it seems he made his choice, doesn't it?'

'Please, he did not—'

'Guv.' Lynley was looking at the card. She crossed the room to him. It was, she saw, yet another of the National Portrait Gallery postcards featuring the photograph of Jemima Hastings. It also bore *Have You Seen This Woman?* upon it but over the image of the sleeping lion had been scrawled an angel like those in the room. It had its wings spread out to create a shield but no weapons were in its hands. 'It looks as if he was leaning towards guarding, not punishing,' Lynley said.

Isabelle was about to tell him it didn't look like anything of the sort when Yukio's brother cried out. She swung round. She saw that he'd approached the room's basin and he was staring at something lying on its edge. She said sharply, 'Keep away from it!' and she strode across the room to see what he'd stumbled upon.

Whatever it was, it was crusted with blood. Indeed it was crusted with so *much* blood that other than its shape, it was indefinable.

'Ah,' Isabelle said. 'Yes indeed. Don't touch that thing, Mr Matsumoto.'

The time of day limited his options for parking in Chelsea. Lynley had to make do with a hike over from Carlyle Square. He crossed the King's Road and walked towards the river via Old Church Street. As he did so, he considered the various ways in which he might avoid AC Hillier over the next few days and the other various ways in which he might colour what he'd been experiencing at Isabelle Ardery's side should he be forced into conversation with the assistant commissioner.

He wanted to give Ardery leeway. New to the job of super-intendent, she would be anxious to prove her worth. But he also wanted the appropriate arrest made when the time came to make an arrest, and he was unconvinced Yukio Matsumoto was guilty of the crime of murder. Guilty of something, there could be little doubt. But murder . . . Lynley couldn't see it.

'That's because of the brother,' Isabelle had told him brusquely upon their return to the Yard. 'You admire him so you want to believe whatever he says. I don't.'

There was an unnatural hush in the incident room for their final meeting of the day. The other officers knew what had earlier happened to Yukio Matsumoto in the street, so this would have been one source of their reticence. The other, however, would have been Isabelle Ardery's confrontation with Philip Hale at St Thomas' Hospital. It was a clear case of telegraph, telephone, tell-a-cop. Even if Philip had said nothing to the others, they would have known something was up simply from his demeanour.

By the end of the afternoon, there had been no additional information from the hospital about Yukio Matsumoto's condition, so they were operating from a no-news-is-good-news perspective. SOCO had been dispatched to the violinist's digs and the bloody object found on his wash basin had been sent to forensics for complete analysis. Everything was clicking along and checking out: Marlon Kay's woodcarving tools were clean; all the sculpting tools from the studio near Clapham Junction were clean as well. Frazer Chaplin's whereabouts had been confirmed for the day of the murder by his colleagues at the ice rink, by his colleagues at Duke's Hotel and by Bella McHaggis. Her whereabouts had been confirmed by a yoga studio and her neighbours. There was still some question about where and if Abbott Langer had actually done the dog walking he'd claimed to be doing, and Paolo di Fazio's presence in Jubilee Market Hall *could* have applied to any day or to no day because no one really paid that much attention. But he'd likely been there, and *likely* was good enough for Detective Superintendent Ardery. She had high hopes that charges could be brought against Yukio Matsumoto as soon as the rest of the forensic reports were in.

Lynley had his doubts about this, but he said nothing. When the meeting concluded, he approached the china boards and spent a few minutes studying what was on them. He examined one of the photographs in particular, and when he left Victoria Street, he took a copy of this with him. It was, at least in part, his reason for coming to Chelsea instead of heading directly home.

St James wasn't in, as things turned out. But Deborah was, and she ushered Lynley into the dining room. There she'd laid out afternoon tea, but not for consumption. She was trying to decide whether she wanted to pursue food photography, she told him. First approached with the idea of doing so, she'd thought it was 'rather an insult to achieving the ex*ceed*ingly high art of my dreams', she said. 'But as the ex*ceed*ingly high art of my dreams isn't exactly bringing in vast sums of money and as I hate the thought of poor Simon supporting his arty wife into her dotage, I thought that photographing food might be the very thing until I'm discovered as the next Annie Leibovitz.'

Success in this arena, she told him, was all about lighting, props, colours and shapes. Additionally, there were considerations having to do with over-crowding the pictures, with suggesting that the viewer was actually *part* of the scene and with focusing on the food without overlooking the importance of mood.

'I'm just thrashing about,' she admitted. 'I'd say you and I can consume all this when I'm done, but I wouldn't recommend it as I made the scones myself.'

She'd created quite a scene, Lynley saw, something straight out of the Ritz with everything from a silver tray of sandwiches to a bowl piled high with clotted cream. There was even an ice bucket with a bottle of champagne tucked away in one corner and as Deborah chatted about everything from the angle of the photograph to the manner in which one created what looked like beads of water on the strawberries, Lynley recognised in her conversation the effort to bring normality back into their relationship.

He said, 'I'm quite all right, Deb. It's difficult, as you might expect, but I'm finding my way.'

Deborah averted her gaze. A rose in a bud vase needed adjusting, and she made this adjustment before she replied quietly. 'We miss her terribly. Particularly Simon. He doesn't like to say. I think he believes he'll make it worse. Worse for me, *and* for him. He won't, of course. How could he possibly? But it's all mixed up.'

Lynley said, 'We've always been something of a tangle, the four of us, haven't we?'

She looked up then although she didn't reply.

He said, 'It'll sort itself out.' He wanted to tell her that love was an odd thing, that it bridged divides, it faded and it re-discovered itself. But he knew she understood this already because she was living it, as was he. So instead he said, 'Simon's not here? I've something I wanted to show him.'

'He's on his way home. He's been in a meeting at Gray's Inn. What've you got for him?'

'A picture,' he said, and even as he said it he realised that there could exist additional pictures that might come to his aid. He went on to ask, 'Deb, have you any photos of your opening at the Portrait Gallery?'

'D'you mean my own photos? I didn't take my camera.'

No, he meant publicity photos. Had there been anyone at the National Portrait Gallery that night, taking pictures of the opening of the Cadbury show? Perhaps for use in a brochure, perhaps for a magazine or a newspaper.

'Ah,' she said. 'You're talking about pictures of celebrities and celebrities-to-be? The beautiful people holding champagne flutes and showing off their spray tans and dental work? I can't say we had an enormous number of those turn up, Tommy. But there *were* some photos being taken. Come with me.'

She took him to Simon's study, at the front of the house. There, from an old canterbury next to Simon's desk, she unearthed a copy of *Hello!*. She made a face and said, 'It was a rather slow day for glamorous events in town.'

Hello!, he saw, had done its usual business with those who might be considered the Beautiful People. These individuals had posed obligingly. It was a gratifying two-page spread of pictures.

There had been quite a crowd at the photographic exhibit. Lynley recognised a few movers and shakers of London society in addition to those longing to become such. Among the pictures, there were candid shots as well, and within these, he found Deborah and Simon in conversation with Jemima Hastings and a saturnine man who looked like trouble. He expected to learn that the bloke was one of the men connected in some way to the dead girl, and he was surprised to learn he was looking upon Matt Jones, the new partner of Sidney St James, Simon's younger sister.

'Sidney's mad about him,' Deborah said. 'Simon, on the other hand, thinks she's merely mad. He's rather a mystery – this is Matt, not Simon, of course. He disappears for weeks at a time and says he's off working for the government. Sidney thinks he's a spy. Simon thinks he's a hit man.'

'What do you think?'

'I can never get ten words out of him, Tommy. To be honest, he makes me a bit nervous.'

Lynley found a picture of Sidney, then: tall, lithe, striking a pose with champagne in hand and her head thrown back. It was supposed to be candid – indeed, she was in conversation with a swarthy bloke tossing his drink down his throat – but it was not for nothing that Sidney was a professional model. Despite the crowd round them, she knew when a camera was on her.

There were other pictures, posed and spontaneous. They needed closer scrutiny. Indeed, the magazine itself would likely have a score of photos on file that hadn't even been printed in these pages and Lynley realised they might be valuable and that they might want tracking down. He asked Deborah if he could keep the magazine. She said of course, but did he think that Jemima's killer had been there?

He said anything was possible. So everything had to be explored.

St James arrived then. The front door opened, and they heard his uneven footsteps in the entry. Deborah went to the door of his study, saying, 'Tommy's here, Simon. He's wanting you.'

St James joined them. There was an awkward moment in which Lynley's old friend assessed his state – with Lynley wondering when the time would arrive that awkward moments with friends would be a thing of the past – and then St James said, 'Tommy. I'm in need of a whisky. You?'

Lynley wasn't, but he obliged with, 'I wouldn't say no.'

'Lagavulin, then?'

'Am I that special an occasion?'

St James smiled. He went to the drinks trolley beneath the window and poured two glasses as well as a sherry for Deborah. He handed them round and then said to Lynley, 'Have you brought me something?'

'You know me too well.' Lynley handed over the copy of the picture he'd brought from the incident room. As he did so, he told St James something of what had happened that day: Yukio Matsumoto, the chase through the streets, the accident in Shaftesbury Avenue. Then he told of the implement they'd found in the violinist's room, ending with Ardery's conclusion that they had their man.

'Hardly unreasonable, all things considered,' St James said. 'But you're reluctant to agree?'

'I find motive a difficulty.'

'Obsessive love? God knows that happens enough.'

'If obsession's involved, it seems more likely he's obsessed with angels. He's got them all over the walls in his room.'

'Has he indeed? That's curious.' St James gave his attention to the picture.

Deborah joined him. She said, 'What is this, Tommy?'

'It was found in Jemima's pocket. SO7's saying it's carnelian, but that's as far as we've got. I was hoping you might have some thoughts on it. Or failing that—'

'That I might know someone who'd be able to suss it out? Let me have a closer look.' St James carried the picture to his desk, where he used a magnifying glass upon it. He said, 'It's well worn, isn't it? The size suggests a stone from a man's ring or perhaps a woman's pendant. Or a brooch, I suppose.'

'Jewellery, in any case,' Lynley agreed. 'What d'you make of the carving?'

St James bent over the photo. He said, after a moment, 'Well, it's pagan. That much is obvious, isn't it?'

'That's what I thought. It doesn't appear Celtic.'

'No, no. Definitely not Celtic.'

'How d'you know?' Deborah asked.

St James handed over the magnifying glass to her. 'Cupid,' he said. 'One of the carved figures. He's kneeling in front of the other. And she's . . . Minerva, Tommy?'

'Or Venus.'

'But the armour?'

'Something belonging to Mars?'

Deborah looked up. 'That makes this . . . how old, then, Simon? A thousand years?'

'Bit more, I dare say. Third or fourth century, likely.'

'But how did she get it?' She asked Lynley this.

'That's the question, isn't it?'

'Could this be why she was killed?' Deborah asked. 'For a carved bit of stone? It must be valuable.'

'It does have value,' Lynley said. 'But if her killer wanted it, he'd hardly have left it on her body.'

'Unless he didn't know she was carrying it,' Deborah said.

'Or was interrupted before he could make the search,' St James added.

'As to that...' Lynley told them more about the murder weapon, or at least what they were assuming was the murder weapon. It was, he said, saturated in blood.

'What is it?' St James asked.

'We're not entirely sure,' Lynley told him. 'All we have to go on at the moment is the shape.'

'Which is...?'

'Deadly sharp at one end, perhaps nine inches long, a curved handle. Very like an oddly shaped spike.'

'Used for what?'

'I've no idea.'

With the presence of police cars, forensic vehicles, an ambulance and dozens of officers of the law in the vicinity of the Dawkins building site, it was only a matter of minutes before the press arrived and the community as a whole became aware that a body had been found. While local police efforts to control the flow of information were admirable, the nature of the crime was difficult to conceal. Thus the superficial condition of John Dresser's body and exactly where the body had been found were details both widely reported and widely known within four hours. Also widely known and reported was the arrest of three boys (their names withheld for obvious reasons) who were 'helping the police with their enquiries,' which of course had long been a euphemism for 'suspects in the case'.

Michael Spargo's mustard anorak had made him identifiable not only to those individuals in the Barriers who recognised it and him on the CCTV film, having seen him that day, and not only to the witnesses who came forward with descriptions of him, but also to his neighbourhood. In short order, community outrage led a threatening mob to the front door of the Spargo home. Within thirty-six hours, this resulted in the entire family's being removed from the Gallows and established in another part of town (and after the trial to another part of the country) under an assumed name. When the police came for Reggie Arnold and Ian Barker, it was with much the same consequences, and their families were moved to other locations as well. Of them all, only Tricia Barker has ever spoken to the press in the intervening years, having resolutely refused to change her name. There is some speculation that her cooperation has to do with garnering publicity for a hoped-for appearance on reality television.

It could well be said that the hours of interviews with the

three boys in the subsequent days reveal much about their psychopathology and the dysfunction of their families. Of the three, it would appear on the surface that Reggie Arnold came from the strongest home situation because in his every interview both Rudy and Laura Arnold were present, along with the interviewing detective and a social worker. But of the three boys Reggie, it must be remembered, displayed the most overt symptoms of inner turmoil according to his teachers, and the tantrums, hysteria and self-destructive activities that characterised his classroom experience became more pronounced as the days of interviews wore on and as it became more evident to him that whatever manipulations he'd used in the past to get himself out of trouble were not going to work in the situation in which he found himself.

On the tape his voice wheedles at first. Then it whines. His father instructs him to sit up straight and 'be a man not a mouse' and his mother weeps about what Reggie is 'doing to us all'. Their focus remains consistently upon themselves: how the exigency of Reggie's situation is affecting them. They seem oblivious not only to the nature of the crime about which he's being questioned and what the nature of this crime indicates about the state of his mind, but also to the jeopardy he faces. At one point Laura tells him that she 'can't sit here all day while you whinge, Reg', because she has Reggie's 'brother and sister to think of, don't you understand that? Who d'you think's taking care them while I'm here with you? While your dad's here with you?' Even more troubling, neither of the parents seems to notice when the questions directed at Reggie begin to home in on the Dawkins building site, on the body of John Dresser and on what the evidence found at the site suggests happened to John Dresser there. Reggie's behaviour escalates – even repeated breaks and interventions by the social worker do not settle him – and although it's clear that he was very likely involved in something horrendous, his parents don't take note of that, as they continue to attempt to mould his behaviour to something that they themselves will approve of. In this we see the very essence of the narcissistic parent, and in Reggie we see the extreme to which a child's reaction to such parenting can take him.

Ian Barker faces a situation not unlike Reggie's, although he remains stoic throughout. It is only through his later drawings during sessions with a child psychiatrist that the extent of his participation in the crime will be revealed. While interviewed, he maintains his story that he knows 'nothing about no baby' even when shown the CCTV film and read the statements of the witnesses who saw him in the company of the other boys and John Dresser. During all this, his grandmother weeps. One can hear her on the tape, as her ululations rise periodically and the social worker's murmurs of 'Please, Mrs Barker' fail to calm her. Her only remarks are 'I've a duty here', but there is no indication that she sees communication with her grandson as part of that duty. While she understandably must have felt a tremendous sense of guilt for having abandoned Ian to his mother's inadequate and often abusive care, she does not appear to connect this abandonment and the emotional and psychological abuse that followed to what happened to John Dresser. For his part, Ian never asks for his mother. It's as if he knows in advance that he will stand alone throughout the investigation, supported mainly by a social worker who was unknown to him before the crime.

As for Michael Spargo, we have already seen that Sue Spargo's abandonment of him occurred almost at once, during his first encounter with the police. This was also consistent with the rest of his life: his father's departure from the home would have had a profound effect on all of the Spargo boys; his mother's drinking and her other inadequacies would only have exacerbated Michael's sense of desertion. Sue Spargo had already been incapable of putting a stop to the hand-me-down abuse that was going on among her nine sons. Michael likely had no expectation that his mother would be able to stop anything else that was going to happen to him.

Once they were arrested, Michael, Reggie and Ian were interviewed repeatedly, up to seven times in a single day. As can be imagined, considering the enormity and the horror of the crime committed, each of them pointed the finger at the others. There were certain events that none of the boys would discuss at all, particularly those having to do with the hairbrush they had stolen from Items-for-a-Pound, but suffice it to say that both Michael Spargo and Reggie

Arnold were aware of the iniquitous nature of what they had done. Their initial protestations of innocence notwithstanding, the multitudinous references to 'stuff what was done to that baby' along with their growing distress when certain topics were brought up (and, in the case of Reggie Arnold, the repeated hysterical begging of his parents not to hate him) tell us that they were fully cognisant of every line of propriety and humanity that was crossed during their time with John Dresser. To the end, on the other hand, Ian Barker remained unmoved, stoic, as if his life circumstances had bled from him not only conscience but also every feeling of empathy he might otherwise have had towards another human being.

'Do you understand what forensic evidence is, lad?' were the words that cracked open the door to confession, for a confession was what the police wanted from the boys, just as a confession is what police want from all criminals. Upon their arrests, the boys' school uniforms, their shoes and their outer wear had all been gathered for examination, and the trace evidence from these articles would later not only place them at the Dawkins building site but also put them in the company of John Dresser in the final terrible moments of his life. Shoes belonging to all three boys were spattered with the toddler's blood; fibres from their clothing were caught up not only in John's snowsuit but also in his hair and on his body; their fingerprints were on the back of the hairbrush, on copper tubing from the building site, on the door of the Portaloo, on the seat of the commode inside, and on John Dresser's little white trainers. The case against them was open and shut, but in the earliest interviews the police, of course, would not have known that as the evidence had not yet been analysed.

As the police ultimately saw it and as the social workers agreed, a confession from the boys would serve a number of purposes: it would trigger the recently passed Contempt of Court Act, putting an end not only to the growing, hysterical press speculation about the case but also to any possibility of details prejudicial to the trial being leaked to the public; it would allow the police to focus their attention on building whatever sort of case against the boys that they intended to present to the Crown Prosecutors; it would give psychologists the necessary material for an evaluation of the boys. The police did not as a whole consider the value of a confession as it pertained to the boys' own healing. That there was 'something deeply wrong in all of the families' (the words of Detective Superintendent Mark Bernstein in an interview two years after the trial) was obvious to everyone, but the police did not see it as their duty to mitigate the psychological and emotional damage done to Michael Spargo, Ian Barker and Reggie Arnold within their own homes. One can certainly not fault them for this, despite the fact that the frenzied nature of the ultimate crime speaks of deep psychopathology in all of them. For the brief of the police was to bring someone to justice for the murder of John Dresser and to give, through this, some small measure of relief to his suffering parents.

As might be suspected, the boys begin by accusing each other, once they are informed that John Dresser's body has been located and that, in the vicinity of the Portaloo, everything from footprints to faecal matter has been found and is going to be analysed by criminologists and, doubtless, connected to his abductors. 'Was Ian's idea to nick the kid,' comes from Reggie Arnold, who addresses this cry not to the police interviewer but rather to his mother, to whom he says, 'Mum, I never. I never took that kid.' Michael Spargo accuses Reggie, and Ian Barker says nothing until he's told of Reggie's accusation at which point he says, 'I wanted that kitten, is all.' All of them begin with protestations that they did not 'hurt no baby' and Michael is the first to admit that they 'might've took him outside the Barriers for a walk or something but that was cause we didn't know where he belonged'.

All of the boys are urged throughout to tell the truth. 'The truth is better than lying, son,' Michael Spargo is told repeatedly by his interviewer. 'You've got to say. Please, luv, you've got to say,' is what Ian Barker hears from the grandmother. Reggie is counselled by his parents to 'spit it out, now, like something bad from your tummy that you've got to get rid of.' But the full truth is clearly a form of abomination that the boys are afraid to touch upon, and their reactions to the aforementioned injunctions illustrate the various degrees to which they raise their defences against having to speak it.

18

He drove onto the property once again while Gordon was watering the ponies. Ten minutes more and Gordon would have been off for the day, working on the roof of the Royal Oak pub. As it was, he was trapped. He stood inside the paddock with a hosepipe in his hand and Gina watching him from the fence. She'd not wanted to enter the paddock this time. The ponies seemed skittish this morning, she'd said. She'd lost her nerve for the moment.

Over the sound of the water burbling into the trough, Gordon didn't notice the car's engine as the vehicle rumbled onto the driveway. Gina, however, was near the edge of it, and she tentatively called his name at the same moment as the car door slamming caught his attention.

He saw the sunglasses. They caught the morning light like the wings of misplaced bats. Then he was coming towards the fence, and the movement of his lips told Gordon that whatever was to happen next, the other man was determined to enjoy it.

The man said to Gina with a tone perfectly gauged to convey an utter lack of fellow feeling, 'Gorgeous day, my dear, wouldn't you say? Bit hot again but who's complaining? We get little enough good weather in this country, eh?'

Gina glanced at Gordon, a quick look shot through with questions that she wouldn't ask. She said, 'I could do with a few more cool breezes, to be honest.'

'Could you, now? Can't get our Gordon to wave the fan over you when you're both hot and sweaty?' He smiled, a baring of teeth that was as disingenuous as everything else about him.

'What d'you want?' Gordon flung the hosepipe to one side. The water continued to burble from it. The ponies, surprised by his sudden movement, trotted away across the paddock. Gordon thought that Gina might enter the enclosure at that point, with the ponies safely away, but she did not do so. She remained by the fence, her hands fixed atop one of the newer posts. Not for the first time, he cursed that upright piece of wood and all of its brothers. He should have let the whole damn thing rot to hell, he thought.

'That's not very friendly,' was the reply to his question. 'What I want is a bit of conversation. We can have it here or we can go for a drive.'

'I've work to do.'

'Won't take long.' He made a minute adjustment to his trousers: a hitch, a shift and the bollocks put into a more comfortable position. It was the sort of movement that had a hundred different interpretations, depending upon circum- stances and the bloke making it. Gordon looked away. The other said, 'What's it to be, my dear?'

'I've a job to do.'

'That I do know. So . . . a drive?' And to Gina, 'I won't take him far. He'll be back before you know how to miss him.'

Gina cast a look from Gordon to the other man and back to Gordon. He could see she was frightened, and he felt a surge of futile rage. This was, of course, what the other man wanted him to feel. He needed to get the bastard off the property.

He strode to the spigot and cranked the water off. He said, 'Let's go,' and then quietly to Gina as he passed her, 'It's all right. I'll be back.'

'But why must you—'

'I'll be back.'

He got into the car. Behind him, he heard a chuckle and, 'That's our lovely boy,' and in a moment they were reversing down the driveway and into the lane. On the lane and heading in the direction of Sway, 'You're a sweet little piece of filth, aren't you? She wouldn't be looking at you like you're God's gift to her wet hole, would she, if she knew the truth of the matter?'

Gordon said nothing although he felt a churning in his stomach. At the end of the lane, they jigged to the left and began to work over to Sway. At first he thought their destination was the village itself, but they passed the hotel, rumbled over the railway tracks and headed northwest past a line of suburban cottages. They were coursing in the direction of the cemetery, with its neat rows of graves sheltered on all four sides by stands of alders, beeches and birch. This, Gordon realised, was likely where Jemima would be buried. The ancient churchyards nearby were full, and he doubted there was a family plot somewhere, for she'd never mentioned one to him and he knew her parents had been cremated. She'd never spoken of death at all aside from telling him about her parents, and he'd been grateful for this although he had not considered that until this moment.

They went past the cemetery as well. Gordon was about to ask where the hell they were going when a left turn into a rutted track took them into a bumpy car park. And then he knew. This was Set Thorns Enclosure, an area of woodland like many others across the Perambulation, fenced off from the free roaming New Forest animals while the timber within it grew to a size that made it impossible for it to be harmed.

Walking paths wound through this vast acreage of woods, but only one other car stood nearby and no one was in it. Thus they had the woodland virtually to themselves, just as the other man would want it.

'Come along, darling,' Gordon was told. 'Let's have a bit of a stroll, eh?'

Gordon knew there was little point playing for time. Things would be as they would be. There were certain situations over which he had at least nominal control. But this was not one of them.

He got out into the morning air. The scent was fresh and

pure. There was a gate up ahead of the car, and he went to this, opened it, went inside the enclosure where he waited for instruction. It was soon in coming. Paths went in three directions from this point: deep into the enclosure or following the woodland's boundaries. It didn't matter to him which path was chosen as the outcome was likely to be the same.

An examination of the ground was sufficient to indicate which way they should go. Paw prints and footprints looking rather fresh led into the heart of the trees, so they would take an alternate route, this one skirting southeast along the enclosure's boundary before dipping downward into a swale and then rising again beneath chestnuts and through thick copses of holly. In open spots, the Perambulation's foresters had stacked wood cut from the trees or felled by storms. Here the bracken was thick and lush, encouraged into growth by filtered sunlight, but now beginning to brown at the edges. By the end of the summer and into autumn it would form a covering of brown lace wherever the sun hit the floor of the wood most strongly.

They trudged along, Gordon waiting for whatever was to come. They saw no one although they could hear a dog barking in the distance. Other than that, the only sound came from the birds: harsh corvine calls from avian predators and the occasional short burst of song from chaffinches hidden deep within the trees. It was a place rich in wildlife, where squirrels fed on the thick windfall from the chestnut trees and a flash of auburn in the undergrowth was a sure indication of foxes.

There were shadows everywhere as well, and the air was fragrant. Walking and waiting, he could almost forget, Gordon thought, that he was being trailed by someone intent upon doing him harm.

'This is far enough,' the other said. He came up behind Gordon and dropped a hand on his shoulder. 'Now let me tell you a tale.'

They were inches from each other. Gordon could feel the

hot, eager breath on the back of his neck. They'd come to a widening of the path at this point, more like a small clearing, and up ahead there seemed to be an intersection of some sort with a gate beyond it. In the distance the woodland ceased, and he could see a lawn spreading out. Ponies grazed there placidly and safely, at some great distance from any road.

'Now, darling, you'll need to turn round and face me. There. Just like that. Nicely done.'

Face to face, Gordon could see much more than he wanted to see – large pores, blackheads, a patch of whiskers missed in that morning's shave – and he could smell the sweat of anticipation. He wondered what it felt like to have such supremacy over another, but he knew not to ask that of the man. Things would go worse for him if he played this badly and he'd learned long ago just to get *through* things so that he could go on.

'So we've been found out, my darling.'

'What d'you mean?'

'Oh, I think you know. You've had a visit from the coppers. They're on your tail. What d'you make of that?'

'The cops know nothing that you don't tell them,' Gordon said.

'Think that, do you? Hmmm. Yesssss. But they're onto Winchester Technical. Where d'you think they'll go now they know that's fiction? Someone somewhere should have sorted *that* one.'

'Well, no one did. And I can't see that it matters. I didn't need the bloody letters in the first place.'

'That's what you think?' He took a step closer. They were chest to chest now and Gordon wanted to step away, so invaded did he feel. But he knew how that step would be interpreted. The other wanted fear to overwhelm him.

'I learned the trade. I've worked the trade. I've got a business. What more do you want?'

'Me?' His voice was all innocence and surprise. 'What do *I* want? My dear boy, this isn't about me.'

Gordon made no reply. He swallowed a sour flavour in his mouth. He heard a dog yelp excitedly somewhere. He heard its master call out in response.

The other man raised his hand and Gordon felt its heat cradling the back of his neck. And then the fingers tightened just behind his ears, thumb and forefinger slowly increasing their pressure until the grip was agony to him. He refused to react, to blink, to groan. He swallowed again. He tasted bile.

'But we both know who wants something, don't we? And we both know what that something is. You know what *I* think should be done, don't you?'

Gordon gave no answer. The pressure increased.

'Don't you? Answer me now. You know what I think should be done, don't you?'

'I suspect it,' Gordon said.

'A few little words from me. That's all it takes. Five or six words. That can't be what you want, eh?' He gave a little shake to Gordon's head, a movement wearing the guise of fondness, except for the pain of the pressure behind his ears. Gordon's throat ached; his head felt light.

'You're obliged,' he said.

For a moment, nothing. And then the other whispered, 'I. Am. What?'

'Obliged. You know it. This game of yours—'

'I'll bloody well show you a game . . .' And the smile, that baring of teeth like an animal except to think of the other man as an animal was to dishonour animals.

'Down,' he said through his teeth. 'Down you go. That's right. On your knees.' He forced the issue with the pressure of his hand. There was nothing for it but to obey.

Gordon was inches only from the other's groin, and he saw the hairy fingers go deftly for the trousers' zip. They lowered it smoothly, as if it had been oiled in anticipation of this moment and the purpose behind it. The hand slid inside.

The dog ended things. An Irish setter bounded onto the path, coming from the intersection of trails up ahead. It trotted along and gave a bark. Someone called out, 'Jackson! Come boy. Come.'

Gordon found himself jerked to his feet. The setter reached him and snuffled round his feet.

'Jackson! Jackson! Where are you? Come!'

'He's here,' Gordon shouted. 'He's over here.'

The other smiled, no teeth this time, but an expression that said things had been merely postponed, not cancelled. He whispered, 'One word from me and you know who shows up. One word from me and *poof* . . . everything's gone. You'll keep that in mind, won't you?'

'You rot in hell,' Gordon said.

'Ah, but not without you, my dear. That's the real beauty of your position.'

Meredith Powell found the office she was looking for without much trouble. It was in Christchurch Road near the fire station, and she walked there from Gerber & Hudson Graphic Design on her morning break.

She didn't know what to expect from a private investigator. She'd seen depictions of private eyes on the telly, and the emphasis always seemed to be on their quirkiness. She didn't want quirky, however. She wanted efficient. She had little enough money to spend on this venture although she knew it had to be spent.

That phone call to Gina's mobile had convinced her, as had the fact that the mobile wasn't in Gina's possession in the first place. While Meredith knew that Gina could merely have forgotten to take it with her prior to setting off on that particular day, it looked as if she was, more or less, a permanent fixture on Gordon's holding and, that being the case, why would she not have returned for her mobile phone once she realised it was missing? It seemed to Meredith that there was only one possible answer: she hadn't returned for it because she hadn't wanted it with her, ringing, vibrating, messaging, texting or anything else-ing while Gordon Jossie was about. All of this made Gina a suspicious character once again. All of this made Meredith turn to Daugherty Enquiries, Inc.

The Daugherty in question turned out to be an elderly woman, much to Meredith's surprise. No rumpled trench coat was involved in her attire and no dusty office plant or pockmarked steel desk sat in her office. Rather she wore a green summer suit and sensible shoes, and her office furniture was polished to a glow. There was no plant at all, dusty or otherwise. Just prints on the walls, these of the New Forest wildlife.

She had pictures on her desk, comforting shots of children and grandchildren. She had a laptop computer open on her desk as well and a neat stack of papers next to it, but she closed the lid of the laptop and gave her full attention to Meredith in the few minutes that they spoke.

Meredith called her Mrs Daugherty. She said it was Ms but that Michele would do. She pronounced it Me-shell, with the accent on *me*. She said, 'Unusual name for someone my age, but my parents were forward thinkers.'

Meredith was unsure what this meant. She stumbled once with the placement of emphasis on the woman's name, but she got the hang of it after a single correction, which seemed to please Michele Daugherty because she beamed and winked.

Meredith wasted no time in telling the investigator what she wanted: any information to be uncovered about one Gina Dickens. Anything at all, she said. She didn't know what the investigator would be able to find but she was looking for as much as possible.

'The competition?' The investigator's tone suggested this wasn't the first time a woman had come seeking information about another woman.

'You might say that,' Meredith said. 'But this is for a friend.'

'It always is.'

They spent a few moments on the fee and Meredith brought out her chequebook because on the telly there was always a retainer given. But Michele Daugherty waved this away: Meredith would pay once services were rendered.

That was that. It hadn't taken long. Meredith walked back to Gerber & Hudson feeling as if she'd taken an appropriate step.

She began to doubt this almost at once, however. Gina Dickens was waiting for her. She was perched on a chair in the square of space that went for reception, feet flat on the floor and shoulder bag in her lap. When Meredith entered, she rose and approached.

'I didn't know where else to turn.' She spoke in an anxious whisper. 'You're the only person I actually *know* in the New Forest. They said you were gone for a bit but that I could wait.'

Meredith wondered if somehow Gina had made a few unwelcome discoveries: that she'd been in her digs above the Mad Hatter Tea Rooms, that she'd answered the ringing mobile phone there, that she'd removed what had been hidden beneath the basin, that she'd only just now hired a private eye to look into the whats and wherefores of Gina's entire existence. She felt an immediate surge of guilt, but then she quelled it. Despite the look on Gina's face, which seemed to blend importuning and fear, this was not the moment to let one's conscience get the better of one. Besides, what was done was done. Jemima was dead and there were too many questions that needed to be answered.

Meredith looked across the room to the little alcove in which she did her work. This was meant to convey that she did not have a moment to spare, but Gina apparently wasn't going to read anything into Meredith's actions that she didn't want to read just now. She said, 'I found . . . Meredith, what I found . . . I don't know what to make of it but I *think* I know and I don't *want* to know and I need to talk to someone . . .' and the mention of finding something hooked Meredith at once.

'What is it?'

Gina winced, as if Meredith had spoken too loudly. She glanced round the office and said, 'C'n we talk outside?'

'I'm just off my break. I've got to—'

'Please. Five minutes. Less, even. I . . . I phoned Robbie Hastings to find out where you were. He didn't want to tell me. I don't know what he thought. But I told him you and I had spoken and that I needed another woman and as I've no friends yet . . . Oh it's *stupid* ever to tie oneself to a man. I knew it and I did it anyway with Gordon because he seemed so different from other men I've known . .' Her eyes filled but no tears spilled over. Instead, the moisture made them luminous. Meredith wondered, ridiculously, how she managed that. How did any woman manage to look attractive so close to tears? She herself got all red in the face.

Meredith gestured towards the doorway. They stepped into the corridor. It seemed that Gina meant to go down the stairs and out into the High Street, but Meredith said to her, 'It'll have to be here.' She added, 'Sorry,' when Gina turned back and looked a little taken aback by the abruptness of Meredith's declaration.

'Yes. Of course.' Gina smiled tremulously. 'Thank you. I'm grateful. You see, I just didn't . . .' She began to fumble with the straw bag she was carrying. She brought out a simple envelope. She lowered her voice. 'The police from London have been to see us. From Scotland Yard. They came about Jemima and they asked Gordon – they asked us both – where we were the day she was killed.'

Meredith felt a piercing of pleasure. Scotland Yard! A triumphant *Yes!* shot through her brain.

'And?' she asked.

Gina looked round as if to see who might be listening. 'Gordon had been there,' she said.

Meredith grabbed her arm. '*What?* In London? The day she was murdered?'

'The police came because there was a postcard they found. It had her picture on it. Meredith, he'd put them up them all round London. At least round the area where he thought she was. He admitted this when the police showed it to him.'

'A *postcard*? With her picture? What in God's name . . . ?'

Gina stumbled through an explanation that Meredith scarcely followed: the National Portrait Gallery, a photograph, a competition of some sort, an advertisement, whatever. Gordon had seen it, had gone to London months earlier, had bought God only knew how many postcards and had put them up like wanted posters. 'They had his mobile number on the back,' Gina said.

Meredith felt ice run down her arms. 'Someone phoned him because of the postcard,' she whispered. 'He found her, didn't he?'

'I don't know,' Gina said. 'He *said* he didn't. He told me he was in Holland.'

'When?'

'The day. That day. You know what day. When Jemima . . . *You* know. But that's not what he said to the police, Meredith. He told *them* he was working. I asked him why did he tell them that and he said Cliff would give him an alibi.'

'Why didn't he just tell them that he was in Holland?'

'That's what I asked him. He said he couldn't prove it. He said he'd thrown everything away. *I* said they could phone the hotel he stayed in and they could phone the farmer he'd talked to but . . . Meredith, that wasn't the point, really.'

'What do you mean? Why wasn't it the point?'

'Because . . .' Her tongue came out and licked her lips, pink with a lipstick that matched one of the colours in the sundress she was wearing. 'I already knew, you see.'

'What?' Meredith felt her head was spinning. '*Had* he been to London? On the day she died? Then why didn't you tell?'

'Because he didn't know – he *doesn't* know – that I'd found out. He's been avoiding certain topics for ages, and whenever I've got close to whatever he doesn't want to talk about, he just changes the subject. Twice, even, he's gone a bit wild, and last time he did that, he frightened me. And now I'm thinking, what *if* he's the one? What if he . . . ? I can't stand to think he might be but I'm afraid, and I don't know what to do.' She shoved the envelope into Meredith's hands. She said, 'Look.'

Meredith slid her finger beneath the flap, which didn't seal the envelope but merely folded inward to contain the contents. There were just three items: two rail tickets to and from London and a hotel receipt for one night's stay. The hotel bill had been paid by credit card and Meredith reckoned the date of stay was the same as Jemima's death.

Gina said, 'I'd found these already. I was taking out the rubbish – this was the day after his return – and they were tucked into the bottom. I wouldn't have seen them at all had I not dropped an earring into the wastepaper basket. I reached in to find it and I saw the colour of the ticket and I knew what it was, of course. And when I saw it, I reckoned he'd gone up there because of Jemima. I thought at first that it wasn't over between them like he'd told me or *if* it was, they had unfinished business of some sort. And I wanted to talk to him about it at once, but I didn't. I was . . . You know how it is when you're afraid to hear the truth?'

'What truth? God, did you *know* he'd done something to her?'

'No, no! I didn't know she was dead! I mean I thought it wasn't *over* between them. I thought he still loved her and if I confronted him, that's what he'd have to say. Then it would be over between *us* and she'd return and I hated the thought of her returning.'

Meredith narrowed her eyes. She could see the trick, if trick it was: For perhaps Jemima and Gordon *had* mended their fences. Perhaps Jemima *had* intended to return. And if that was the case, what was to prevent Gina herself from making the trip to London, doing away with Jemima, and keeping the ticket and the hotel receipt to pin the crime on Gordon? What a nice bit of vengeance from a woman scorned.

Yet something wasn't right in all this. But the various possibilities made Meredith's head pound.

Gina said, 'I've been afraid. Something's very wrong, Meredith.'

Meredith handed the envelope back to her. 'Well, you've got to turn this over to the police.'

'But then they'll come to see him again. He'll know I was the one to turn him in and if he *did* hurt Jemima—'

'Jemima's dead. She's not hurt. She's murdered. And whoever killed her needs to be found.'

'Yes. Of *course*. But if it's Gordon . . . It *can't* be Gordon. I refuse to think . . . There has to be an explanation somewhere.'

'Well, you'll have to ask him, won't you?'

'No! I'm not safe if he . . . Meredith, don't you see? Please. If you don't help me, I can't do it on my own.'

'You must.'

'Won't you . . . ?'

'No. You've got the story. You know the lies. There'd be only one outcome if I went to the police.'

Gina was silent. Her lips quivered. When her shoulders dropped, Meredith saw that Gina had worked things out for herself. Should Meredith take the rail tickets and the hotel receipt to the local police or to the Scotland Yard cops, she would only be repeating what someone else had told her. That someone else was exactly the person the police would seek next, and Gordon Jossie would likely be right there when the detectives arrived to put questions to Gina.

Gina's tears fell then, but she brushed them away. She said, 'Will you come with me? I'll go to the police, but I can't face it alone. It's such a betrayal and it might mean nothing and if it means nothing, don't you see what I'm doing?'

'It doesn't mean nothing,' Meredith said. 'We both know that.'

Gina dropped her gaze. 'Yes. All right. But what if I get to the station and lose my courage when it comes to going inside and talking? What will I do when they come for Gordon? Because they *will* come, won't they? They'll see he lied and they'll come and he'll know. Oh God. Oh God. How did I *do* this to myself?'

The door to Gerber & Hudson opened, and out popped

Randall Hudson's head. He didn't look pleased and he made the reason clear when he said, 'Are you coming back to work today, Meredith?'

Meredith felt heat in her cheeks. She'd never been scolded at her work before. She said in a low voice to Gina Dickens, 'All right. I'll go with you. Be here at half past five.' And then to Hudson, 'Sorry, sorry, Mr Hudson. Just a small emergency. It's taken care of now.'

Not quite true. But it would be settled in a very few hours.

Barbara Havers had made the phone call to Lynley earlier, out of Winston Nkata's presence. It wasn't so much because she hadn't wanted Winston to know she was phoning her erstwhile partner. It was more a matter of timing. She'd wanted to get in touch with the inspector prior to his arrival at the Yard that day. This had necessitated an early morning call, which she'd made from her room in the Sway hotel.

She'd reached Lynley at the breakfast table. He'd brought her up to speed on the goings on in London, and he'd sounded guarded on the topic of Isabelle Ardery's performance as superintendent, which made Barbara wonder what it was that he wasn't telling her. She recognised in his reticence that peculiar form of Lynley loyalty that she herself had long been the recipient of, and she felt a pang that she didn't want to name.

To her question of, 'If she thinks she's got her man, why hasn't she recalled us to London?' he said, 'Things have moved quickly. I expect you'll hear from her today.'

'What do you reckon about what's going on?'

In the background she heard the clink of cutlery against china. She could picture Lynley in the dining room of his town-house, *The Times* and the *Guardian* nearby on the table and a silver pot of coffee within reach. He was the sort of bloke who'd pour that coffee without spilling a drop, and when he stirred it within his cup, he'd manage to do so without making a sound. How did people *do* that? she wondered. 'She's not jumping to a wild conclusion,' he settled on saying. 'Matsumoto had what looked like the weapon in his room. It's gone to forensics. He also had one of the postcards tucked into a book. His brother doesn't believe he harmed her, but I don't think anyone else will go along with him on that.'

Barbara noted that he'd avoided her question. 'And you, sir?' she persisted.

She heard him sigh. 'Barbara, I just don't know. Simon has the photo of that stone from her pocket, by the way. It's curious. I want to know what it means.'

'Someone killing her to get it?'

'Again, I don't know. But there are more questions than answers just now. That makes me uneasy.' Barbara waited for more. Finally, he said, 'I can understand the desire to sew the case up quickly. But if it's mismanaged or botched altogether because of someone rushing to judgement, that's not going to look good.'

'For her, you mean. For Ardery.' And then she had to add because of what it meant to her and to her own future with the Yard: 'You care about that, sir?'

'She seems a decent sort.'

Barbara wondered what that meant, but she didn't ask. It wasn't her business, she told herself, even as it felt like her business in every way.

She brought up the reason for her call: Chief Superintendent Zachary Whiting, the forged letters from Winchester Technical College II, and Whiting's knowledge of Gordon Jossie's apprenticeship in Itchen Abbas with Ringo Heath. She said, 'We didn't mention any apprenticeship, let alone where it was, so why would he know about it? Does he keep his fingers on the pulse of every individual in the whole bloody New Forest? Seems to me there's something going on with Whiting and this Jossie bloke, sir, because Whiting definitely knows more than he's willing to tell us.'

'What are you considering?'

'Something illegal: Whiting taking payoffs for whatever

Jossie's doing when he's not off thatching old buildings. He's working on people's houses, Jossie is. He sees what's inside them, and some of them will have valuables. This isn't exactly a poverty-stricken part of the country, sir.'

'Burglaries orchestrated by Jossie and discovered by Whiting? Pocketing ill-gotten gains instead of making an arrest?'

'Or could be they're into something together.'

'Something that Jemima Hastings discovered?'

'That's definitely a possibility. So I'm wondering, could you do some checking on him? Bit of snooping. Background and such. Who is this bloke Zachary Whiting? Where'd he do his police training? Where'd he come from before he ended up here?'

'I'll see what I can sort out,' Lynley said.

While all roads weren't exactly leading to Gordon Jossie, Barbara thought, they were certainly circling round the bloke. It was time to see what the rest of the team in London had come up with when checking on him – not to mention when checking on every other name she'd handed over – so after breakfast when she and Winston were making their preparations for the day, she took out her mobile to make the call.

It rang before she had a chance. The caller was Isabelle Ardery. Her remarks were brief, of the pack-up-and-come-home variety. They had a solid suspect, they had what was undoubtedly the murder weapon, they had his shoes and his clothing which were going to test positive for Jemima's blood, they had an established connection between them.

'And he's a nutter,' Ardery concluded. 'Schizophrenic who won't take meds.'

'He can't be tried, then,' Barbara said.

'Trying him's hardly the point, Sergeant,' Ardery told her. 'Getting him permanently off the street is.'

'Understood. But there's more than one curious person

down this way, guv,' Barbara told her. 'I mean, just considering Jossie, f'r instance, you might want us to stay and nose round till we—'

'What I want is your return to London.'

'C'n I ask . . . where we are with the background checks?'

'So far there's nothing questionable on anyone,' Ardery told her. 'Especially not down there. Your holiday's over. Get back to London. Today.'

'Right.' Barbara ended the call and made a face at the phone. She knew an order when she heard an order. She wasn't convinced, however, that the order made sense.

'So?' Winston said to her.

'That's definitely the question of the hour.'

19

Although Bella McHaggis liked to think that her lodgers would scrupulously do their own recycling, she'd learned over time that they were far more likely to toss items into the rubbish. So, every week, she made rounds inside her house. She found newspapers piled here and there, old magazines under beds, Coke cans crushed inside wastepaper baskets and all sorts of otherwise valuable articles in nearly every location.

It was for this reason that she emerged from her house with a laundry basket whose contents she intended to deposit among the many receptacles she had placed in her front garden for this purpose. On the step, however, basket in arms, Bella halted abruptly. For after their previous encounter, the last person she expected to see just inside her front gate was Yolanda the Psychic. She was in the midst of waving in the air what looked like a large green cigar. A plume of smoke rose from it, and as she waved it, Yolanda chanted sonorously in her husky masculine tone.

This was the bloody limit, Bella thought. She dropped her basket and yelped, '*You*! What the bloody hell will it take? Get off my property this instant.'

Yolanda's eyes had been shut, but they flew open. She appeared to shake off some trance she was in. *That* was likely another one of her completely spurious performances, Bella thought. The woman was an utter charlatan.

Bella kicked the laundry basket to one side and strode over to the psychic, who was holding her ground. 'Did you hear me?' she demanded. 'Leave the property this instant or I'll have you arrested. And stop waving that . . . that *thing* in my face.'

Closer to it now, Bella saw that *thing* was a collection of pale leaves, rolled tightly and bound up with thin twine. Its smoke was, frankly, not bad smelling, more like incense than tobacco. But that was hardly the point.

'Black as the night,' was Yolanda's reply. Her eyes looked odd, and Bella wondered if the woman was high on drugs. 'Black as the night and the sun, the sun.' Yolanda waved her stick of smoking whatever-it-was directly in Bella's face. 'Ooze from the windows. Ooze from the doors. Purity is needed or the evil within—'

'Oh for God's sake,' Bella snapped. 'Don't pretend you're here for *anything* other than causing trouble.'

Yolanda continued to wave the smoking object like a priestess in the performance of an arcane rite. Bella grabbed her arm and attempted to hold it in place. She was surprised to find the psychic was quite strong, and for a moment they stood there like two ageing female wrestlers, each trying to throw the other to the mat. Bella finally won, for which she was thankful as it did her good to see that her hours of yoga and athletic training were doing *something* besides lengthening her life on this miserable planet. She mastered Yolanda's arm, lowered it, and knocked the green cigar from her hand. She stamped upon it till it was extinguished while Yolanda moaned, mumbled and murmured about God, purity, evil, black, the night and the sun.

'Oh, *stop* your nonsense.' Yolanda's arm still in her grasp, Bella began to march her towards the gate.

Yolanda, however, had other things on her mind. She put on the metaphorical brakes. Legs as stiff as a two-year-old's in the midst of a tantrum, she planted herself firmly and would not be budged.

'This is a place of evil,' she hissed. To Bella, the woman's expression looked wild. 'If you won't purify, then you must leave. What happened to her will happen again. *All* of you are in danger.'

Bella rolled her eyes.

'Listen to me!' Yolanda cried. 'He died within, and when that happens in a place of abode—'

'Oh *rubbish*. Stop pretending you're here to do anything other than spy and cause trouble. Which you've done from the first and don't deny it. What do you want now? *Who* do you want now? Looking to talk someone else out of living here? Well, there's no one else yet. Are you satisfied? Now, get the hell . . . Be gone before I phone the police.'

It seemed that the idea of police finally got through. Yolanda immediately stopped resisting and allowed herself to be propelled towards the gate. But still she nattered on about death and the need for a ritual of purification. Bella was able to determine from Yolanda's rambling that all of this was due to the untimely passing of Mr McHaggis, and truth to tell, the fact that Yolanda seemed to know about McHaggis's death inside the house did give Bella pause. But she shook off the pause – because, obviously, Jemima could have told her about McHaggis's death since Bella herself had mentioned it more than once – and with no further conversation between them, she directed Yolanda from the property to the pavement.

There, Yolanda said, 'Heed my warning.'

To which Bella said, 'You bloody heed mine. Next time you show your face round here, you'll be explaining your presence to the coppers. Understand? Now *scarper*.'

Yolanda started to speak. Bella made a threatening movement towards her. That apparently did it, because she hustled down the pavement in the direction of the river. Bella waited till she disappeared round the corner into Putney Bridge Road. Then she went back to what she'd intended to do. She grabbed the laundry basket and approached the serried rank of rubbish bins with their neat labels upon them.

It was in the Oxfam bin that she found it. Later she would think what a miracle it was that she'd opened that particular bin at all, for she emptied the Oxfam bin least often, as items for Oxfam were tossed away infrequently by herself, by residents of her house, and by people who lived nearby. As it was, she had nothing to deposit in the Oxfam bin on this day. She merely removed its lid to take note of when it was likely to need emptying. The newspaper bin was itself nearly full and the plastics bin was likewise; the glass bins were fine – separating green from brown from clear kept them from filling too quickly – and since she was looking at the bins in general, she'd gone on to the Oxfam bin as a matter of course.

The handbag was buried beneath a jumble of clothing. Bella had removed this, with a curse about people's enduring laziness as evidenced by the fact that they couldn't be bothered to fold what they wished to have carted off to the charity, and she was about to fold it all herself, item by item, when she saw the handbag and recognised it.

It was Jemima's. There was no doubt about it, and even if there had been doubt, Bella scooped it up and opened it and there inside were Jemima's purse, her driving licence, her address book and her mobile phone. There were other bits and bobs as well, but these didn't matter as much as the fact that Jemima had died in Stoke Newington where she'd no doubt had her handbag with her, and here it was now in Putney, as large as the life she no longer possessed.

There was no question in Bella's mind what she had to do about this sudden discovery. She was headed for the front door with the handbag in her grasp when the front gate opened behind her and she turned, expecting to see Yolanda's stubborn return. But it was Paolo di Fazio coming through, and when his eyes lit on the handbag that Bella was carrying, she saw from his expression that, like her, he knew exactly what it was.

By returning to St Thomas' Hospital and remaining there for most of the previous night to await word on Yukio Matsumoto's condition, Isabelle had managed to put off the meeting with AC Hillier. Since he'd instructed her to deliver herself to his office upon her return to the Yard, she'd decided merely not to return to the Yard until long after the assistant commissioner had vacated Tower Block for the night. This would give her time to sort through what had happened in order to be able to speak clearly about it.

That plan had worked. It had also allowed her to be first in line to know what was going on with the violinist's condition. This was simple enough: he remained in a coma throughout the night. He was not out of danger, but the coma was artificial: induced to allow the brain time to recover. Had she been given suzerainty in this situation, Yukio Matsumoto would have been brought round and then thoroughly questioned once he'd emerged from the operating theatre. As it was, the most she was able to manage was a police guard in the vicinity of intensive care to make certain the man didn't suddenly regain consciousness on his own, realise the depth of the trouble he was in, and do a runner. It was, she knew, a laughable possibility. He was in no condition to go anywhere. But appropriate procedure had to be followed, and she was going to follow appropriate procedure.

She believed she had done so from the first. Yukio Matsumoto was a suspect; his own brother had identified him from an e-fit in the newspaper. It was not down to her that the man had panicked and had tried to outrun the police. Besides that, as things turned out, he was in possession of what had to be the murder weapon and when his clothing and his shoes had undergone analysis along with the weapon, there were going to be blood splatters somewhere upon them – no matter how minute and no matter how he'd tried to clean them – and those blood spatters would belong to Jemima Hastings.

The only problem was that this information could not be passed onto the press. It could not come out until a trial. And that was a problem indeed because the moment the word got out that a member of London's foreign citizenry had been hit by a vehicle while running from the coppers – which hadn't taken long – the press had gathered like the wolf pack they were, on the scent of a story that smacked of police incompetence. They were baying to bring down the responsible party, and the job of the Met was to position itself to handle things when the wolves closed in for the kill.

Which, naturally, was one of two reasons that Hillier had wanted to see her: to determine what the Met's position was going to be. The other reason, she knew, was to assess if or how badly she'd cocked things up. Should he decide blame lay with her, she was finished, the opportunity for promotion gone.

The broadsheets that morning had taken a wait-and-see attitude, reporting the bare facts. The tabloids, on the other hand, were doing their usual. Isabelle had watched BBC1 as she'd made her preparations for the day, and the morning talking heads did their typical bit with both kinds of newspaper, holding them up for the delectation of their viewers and commenting upon the stories featured. Thus in advance of heading to the Yard, she knew that gallons of newsprint were being devoted to the *Copper Chase Disaster*. This gave her time to prepare. Whatever she reported to Hillier had to be good, and she damn well knew it. For once the papers connected the victim with his famous brother, which would hardly take long, considering Zaynab Bourne's threats of the previous day, the story would have even stronger legs. Undoubtedly then it would run for days. Things could have been worse, but Isabelle couldn't quite see how.

She had an Irish coffee prior to leaving for work. She told herself that the caffeine would counteract the effects of the whisky, and besides, after being up for most of the night, she had earned it. She drank it down quickly. She also tucked four airline bottles of vodka into her bag. She assured herself that she likely wouldn't need them, and anyway they were not enough to do anything but help her think clearly if she felt muddled during the day.

She stopped in at the incident room at work. She told Philip Hale to relieve the officer at St Thomas' Hospital and to remain there. His startled expression replied that as a DI, he should not be asked to do something that a uniformed constable could easily do as it was a waste of manpower. She waited for him actually to make a comment, but he sucked in a breath and said nothing but 'Guv,' in polite response. No matter because John Stewart talked for him, saying laconically, 'Due respect, guv . . .' which, Isabelle knew, he felt nothing of anyway. She snapped, 'What is it?' and he pointed out that using a detective inspector as some sort of single-headed Cerberus at the hospital when he could otherwise be handling what he'd earlier been told to handle – all of the background checks which were, by the way, mounting up – was hardly a wise use of Philip's expertise. She told him she didn't need his advice. 'Get on to forensics and stay glued to them. Why's the analysis of those hairs found on the body taking so long? And where the hell is DI Lynley?'

He'd been called up to Hillier's office, she was informed. Stewart did the informing, and he looked as if nothing could have pleased him more than to be the person sharing that bit of news with her.

She might otherwise have avoided her meeting with Hillier, but because Lynley had been there, doubtless making his own report on the goings-on of the previous day, she had no choice but to take herself to the assistant commissioner's office. She refused to fortify herself before heading there. Lynley's impertinent question about her drinking still plagued her.

She met him in the corridor near Hillier's office. He said, 'You look like you've had no sleep.'

She told him she'd returned to the hospital and remained there long into the night. 'How are things?' she asked in conclusion, with a nod towards the AC's office.

'As expected. It could have gone better with Matsumoto yesterday. He wants to know why it didn't.'

'Does he see that as your position, Thomas?'

'What?'

'Making those sorts of determinations. Making reports to him about my performance. Official snout. Whatever.'

Lynley gazed at her in a fashion she found disconcerting. It wasn't sexual. She could have dealt with that. It was, instead, intolerably kind. He said quietly, 'I'm on your side, Isabelle.'

'Are you?'

'I am. He's thrown you headfirst into the investigation because he's being pressured from above to fill Malcolm Webberly's position and he wants to know how you do the job. But what's going on with him is only partly about you. The rest is politics. Politics involve the commissioner, the Home Office and the press. As you're feeling the heat, so is he.'

'I wasn't wrong: the situation yesterday wasn't mismanaged.'

'I didn't tell him it was. The man panicked. No one knows why.'

'That's what you told him?'

'That's what I told him.'

'If Philip Hale hadn't—'

'Don't throw Philip into the midst of feeding sharks. That sort of thing will return to haunt you. The position to take is no one's to blame. That's the position that will serve you best in the long run.'

She thought about this. She said, 'Is he alone?'

'When I went in, he was. But he's phoned for Stephenson Deacon to come to his office. There's got to be a briefing and the Directorate of Public Affairs wants it as soon as possible. That will mean today.'

Isabelle acknowledged a fleeting wish that she'd tossed back at least one of the bottles of vodka. There was no telling how long the coming meeting would take. But then she assured herself that she was up to the challenge. This wasn't about her, as Lynley had said. She was merely present to answer questions.

She said to Lynley, 'Thank you, Thomas,' and it was only when she was approaching the desk of Hillier's secretary that she realised Lynley had earlier used her Christian name. She turned back to say something to him, but he was already gone.

Judi MacIntosh made a brief call into the sanctum sanc-
torum of the assistant commissioner. She said, 'Superintendent
Ardery—' but got no further. She listened for a moment and
said, 'Indeed, sir.' She told Isabelle that she was to wait. It
would be a few minutes. Did the superintendent want a cup
of coffee?

Isabelle declined. She knew she was supposed to sit, so that
was what she did, but didn't find it easy. As she was waiting,
her mobile rang. Her ex-husband, she saw. She wouldn't talk
to him now.

A middle-aged man came into the area, a litre bottle of
soda water tucked into his arm. Judi MacIntosh said to him,
'Do go in, Mr Deacon,' so Isabelle knew she was looking at
the head of the Press Bureau, sent by the Directorate of Public
Affairs to get to grips with the situation. Oddly, Stephenson
Deacon had a football stomach although the rest of him was
thin as a towel in a third rate hotel. This inadvertently gave
the impression of a pregnant woman blindly determined to
watch her weight.

Deacon disappeared into Hillier's office, and Isabelle spent
an agonising quarter of an hour waiting to see what would
happen next. What happened was Judi MacIntosh's being
informed to send Isabelle within, although how Judi
MacIntosh received this information was a mystery to Isabelle
as nothing had seemed to intrude upon what the woman was
doing – which was beavering away at some typing on her
computer – when she looked up and announced, 'Do go
inside, Superintendent Ardery.'

Isabelle did so. She was introduced to Stephenson Deacon
and she was asked to join him and Hillier at the conference
table to one side of the AC's office. There she was subjected to
a thorough grilling by both men on the topic of what had
happened, when, where, why, who did what to whom, what sort
of chase, how many witnesses, what had been the alternatives
to giving chase, did the suspect speak English, did the police
show their identification, was anyone in uniform, etc, etc.

Isabelle explained to them that the suspect in question had bolted out of the absolute blue. They'd been watching him when something apparently spooked him.

Any idea what? Hillier wanted to know. Any idea how?

None at all. She'd sent men there with strict instructions not to approach, not to have uniforms with them, not to cause a scene—

Fat lot of good *that* did, Stephenson Deacon put in.

But somehow he was frightened anyway. It seems that he might have taken the police for invading angels.

Angels? What the—

He's a bit of an odd egg, sir, as things turned out. Had we known about that, had we known he was likely to misinterpret anyone's approaching him, had we even thought he would take the sight of someone coming near to mean he was in danger—

Invading angels? *Invading angels?* What the bloody hell do angels have to do with what happened?

Isabelle explained the condition of Yukio Matsumoto's digs. She described the drawings on the walls. She gave them Hiro Matsumoto's interpretation of the depiction of the angels his brother had drawn, and she concluded with the connection that existed between the violinist and Jemima Hastings as well as what they'd found in the room itself.

At the end, there was silence, for which Isabelle was grateful. She had her hands clasped tightly in her lap because she'd realised they'd begun shaking. When her hands trembled it was always a signal that thinking was shortly going to become difficult for her. It was a result of not eating breakfast, she decided, a simple matter of blood sugar and caffeine.

Finally, Stephenson Deacon spoke. The solicitor for Hiro Matsumoto, he informed her with a glance at what appeared to be a phone message, would be holding a press conference in just three hours. The cellist would be with her, but he wouldn't speak. Zaynab Bourne was going to lay blame for what had occurred in Shaftesbury Avenue directly at the feet of the Met.

Isabelle started to speak, but Deacon held up a hand to stop her.

They themselves would prepare for a counter press conference – he referred to it as a pre-emptive strike – and they would hold it in exactly ninety minutes.

At this, Isabelle felt a sudden dryness develop in her throat. She said, 'I expect you want me there?'

Deacon said they did not. 'We expect no such thing,' was how he put it. He would give out the relevant information that he'd just gathered from the superintendent. If she was wanted further, he said, he would let her know.

She was thus dismissed. As she left the room, she saw the two men lean towards each other in the sort of huddle that indicated an evaluation being made. It was an unnerving sight.

'What are you doing here?' Bella McHaggis demanded. She didn't like surprises in general, and this one in particular disturbed her. Paolo di Fazio was supposed to be at work. He was not supposed to be coming through her garden gate at this time of day. The juxtaposition of Paolo's being there in Putney with her having just discovered Jemima's handbag caused a frisson of warning to run through Bella's body.

Paolo didn't answer her question. His eyes were fixed – they were absolutely *paralysed*, Bella thought – upon the handbag. He said, 'That's Jemima's.'

'Interesting that you know,' was her reply. 'I myself had to look inside.' And then she repeated her question. 'What are you doing here?'

His reply of 'I live here,' did not amuse. He then said, as if she hadn't already told him, 'Have you looked inside?'

'I just told you I looked inside.'

'And?'

'And what?'

'Is there . . . Was there anything?'

'What sort of question is that?' she asked him. 'And why aren't you at work where you're supposed to be?'

'Where did you find it? What are you going to do with it?'

This was the limit. She began to say, 'I have no intention—' when he cut in with, 'Who else knows about it? Have you phoned the police? Why are you holding it that way?'

'What way? How am I supposed to be holding it?'

He fished in his pocket and brought out a handkerchief. 'Here. You must give it to me.'

That sent the alarm bells absolutely *clanging*. All at once Bella's mind was filled with details, and rising to the top of them was that pregnancy test. That fact floated there with others equally damning: all of Paolo di Fazio's engagements to be married, that argument Bella had heard between him and Jemima, Paolo's being the one to bring Jemima to her house in the first place . . . And there were probably more if she could gather her wits and not be put off her mental stride by the expression on his face. She'd never seen Paolo look so intense.

She said, 'You put it there, didn't you? With everything for Oxfam. You play the innocent now with all these questions, but you can't fool me, Paolo.'

'I?' he said. 'You must be mad. Why would I put Jemima's bag in the Oxfam bin?'

'We both know the answer to that. It's the perfect place to hide the handbag. Right here on the property.' She could, indeed, see how the plan would have worked. No one would look for the bag so far from the place where Jemima had been killed, and if someone found it by chance, as she herself had done, then it could easily be explained away: Jemima herself had discarded it, never bloody mind the fact that it held her essential belongings! But if no one found it prior to its being carted off to Oxfam, all the better. When the bin was emptied, it would doubtless be months after her death. The contents would be taken away and perhaps the bag would be opened wherever things were gone through for distribution to the shops.

By that time no one would know where it had come from or, perhaps, even remember the death in Stoke Newington. No one would think the bag had anything to do with murder. Oh, it was all so clever of him, wasn't it?

'You think I hurt Jemima?' Paolo asked. 'You think I killed her?' He ran his hand over his head in a movement she knew she was meant to take for agitation. '*Pazza!* Why would I hurt Jemima?'

She narrowed her eyes. He sounded so convincing, didn't he? And wouldn't he just, him with his five or fifteen or fifty engagements to women who always threw him over and why, why, *why*? Just what was wrong with Mr di Fazio? What did he do to them? What did he want from them? Or better yet, what did they come to know about him?

He took a step closer, saying, 'Mrs McHaggis, at least let's—'

'Don't!' She backed away. 'You stay right there! Don't come an inch closer or I'll scream my head off. I know your sort.'

'My "sort"? What sort is that?'

'Don't you play the innocent with me.'

He sighed. 'Then we have a problem.'

'How? Why? Oh don't you try to be clever.'

'I need to get into the house,' he said. 'This I cannot do if you won't let me approach you and pass you by.' He returned his handkerchief to his pocket. He'd been holding it all along – and she knew he'd meant to wipe fingerprints from the bag because one thing he *wasn't* was a bloody fool and neither was she – but obviously he could see that she knew what he intended and he'd given it up. 'I have left in my room a postal order that I wish to send to Sicily. I must fetch this, Mrs McHaggis.'

'I don't believe you. You could have sent it straight away, directly you bought it.'

'Yes. I could have. But I wished to write a card as well. Would you like to see it? Mrs McHaggis, you're being silly.'

'Don't use that ruse on me, young man.'

'Please think things through because what you've concluded

makes no sense. If Jemima's killer lives in this house, as you seem to think, there are far, *far* better places to have put her bag than in the front garden. Don't you agree?'

Bella said nothing. He was trying to confuse her. That was what killers always did when they were backed into a corner.

He said, 'To be honest, I'd thought Frazer was likely responsible for what's happened, but this bag tells me—'

'Don't you dare blame Frazer!' Because *that* was what they did as well. They tried to blame others, they tried divert suspicion. Oh, he was bloody clever, indeed.

'—that it makes no sense to think he's guilty, either. For why would Frazer kill her, bring her bag here and put it in the rubbish in front of the house where he lives?'

'It's not rubbish,' she said inanely. 'It's for recycling. I won't have you call the recycling rubbish. It's because people think that that they won't recycle in the first place. And if people would simply begin recycling, we might save the planet. Don't you understand?'

He raised his eyes skyward. It came to Bella that he looked, for a moment, exactly like one of those pictures of martyred saints. This was due to the fact that he was darkish skinned because he was Italian and most of the martyred saints were Italian. Weren't they? If it came to it, was he really Italian? Perhaps he was merely pretending to be. Lord, what was happening to her brain? Was this what abject terror did to people? Except, she realised, she perhaps wasn't as terrified as she'd earlier been or as she was supposed to be.

'Mrs McHaggis,' Paolo said quietly, 'please consider that someone else might have put Jemima's bag in that bin.'

'Ridiculous. Why would anyone else – ?'

'And *if* someone else put the bag there, who might that person be? Is there someone who might want to make one of us look guilty?

'There's only one person looking guilty, my lad, and that person is you.'

'It isn't. Don't you see? That bag's presence makes you look bad as well, doesn't it? Just as it makes me look bad, at least in your eyes, and it makes Frazer look bad.'

'You're shifting blame! I told you not to. I told you . . .' And suddenly the penny dropped: the vague mutterings about black, night, sun and ooze; the prayers and the smoking green cigar. 'Oh dear Lord,' Bella murmured.

She turned from Paolo and fumbled for the door to get into the house. If he followed her inside at this point, she knew it did not matter.

20

'I think your best course is going to be to get someone from Christies to look at it,' St James said. 'Or, failing that, someone at the B.M. You can check it out from the evidence officer, can't you?'

'I'm not exactly in a position to take that decision,' Lynley said.

'Ah. The new superintendent. How is it going?'

'A bit unevenly, I'm afraid.' Lynley glanced around. He and St James were speaking via phone. References to Isabelle Ardery had to be circumspect. Besides, he felt for the acting superintendent's position. He didn't envy her, having to cope with Stephenson Deacon and the Directorate of Public Affairs so soon into her employment at the Yard. Once the press came howling into the picture in an investigation, the pressure for a result mounted. With someone now in hospital, Ardery was going to feel that pressure from every quarter.

'I see,' St James said. 'Well, if not the stone itself, what about the photo you showed me? It's quite clear and you can see the scale. That might be all that's necessary.'

'For the British Museum, possibly. But certainly not for Christies.'

St James was silent for a moment before he said, 'I wish I could be more help, Tommy. But I'm loath to send you in the wrong direction.'

'Nothing to apologise for,' Lynley told his friend. 'It might mean nothing anyway.'

'But you don't think so.'

'I don't. On the other hand, I may be merely clutching at a straw.'

So it definitely seemed because right, left and centre everything was either utterly confusing matters or checking out as inconsequential. There was no middle ground between the extremes.

The background checks completed so far served as evidence of this: of the principals in London involved in the case, tangentially or otherwise, everyone was turning out to be exactly who he seemed to be and nobody's copy book was blotted. There was still the matter of Abbott Langer's supposed marriages to be sorted, and Matt Jones – paramour of St James's sister – continued to be a question mark as there were more than four hundred Matthew Joneses spread out in the UK so tracking each down and sorting them all out was proving a problem. Other than that, no one had so much as a parking ticket. This made things look grim as far as Yukio Matsumoto was concerned, despite his brother's protestations of the violinist's harmless nature. For with everyone else turning up clean and no one else in London apparently having a motive to murder Jemima Hastings, the killing either had to have been committed in the sort of act of madness one could easily associate with Yukio Matsumoto and his angels or it had to have arisen from something and someone connected to Hampshire.

Of the Hampshire principals, there were two curious points that had been uncovered and only one of them seemed likely to lead anywhere. The first point was that Gina Dickens had so far been untraceable in Hampshire although various forms of her name were still being tried: Regina, Jean, Virginia, etc. The second, and more interesting, piece of information was about Robert Hastings who, as things turned out, had trained to be a blacksmith prior to taking over his father's position as agister. And this might have merely been shoved aside as another useless bit of data had forensics not given a preliminary assessment of the murder weapon. According to microscopic examination, the thing was hand-forged, and the blood upon it had come from Jemima Hastings, as well. When this information was added to Yukio Matsumoto's possession of the spike, to the eyewitness report of an Oriental man stumbling from Abney Park Cemetery, to the e-fit generated by that report and to what was likely to be blood residue on the violinist's clothing and his shoes, it was difficult to disagree with Isabelle Ardery's conclusion that they had their man.

But Lynley liked to have everything accounted for. Thus he returned to the stone that Jemima Hastings had carried in her pocket. It wasn't that he assumed it was valuable and, possibly, the reason for her death. It was just that the stone remained a detail that he wanted to understand.

He was once again studying the photo of the stone when he received a phone call from Barbara Havers. She'd had the word to return to London, she told him, but before she did so she wanted to know if he'd unearthed anything about Chief Superintendent Zachary Whiting. Or, for that matter, about Ringo Heath because it could be that there was a connection between those two that wanted exploring.

What he'd discovered was little enough, Lynley told her. All of Whiting's training as a police officer had followed the usual, legitimate pattern: he'd done his required training weeks at a Centrex centre, he'd taken additional instruction at several area training units, and he'd attended an admirable number of courses in Bramshill. He had twenty-three years of service under his belt, all of them spent in Hampshire. If he was involved in anything untoward, Lynley hadn't sorted what it was. *He can be a bit of a bully on occasion* had been the nastiest comment anyone cared to make about the bloke, although *He's been sometimes too enthusiastic about the job in hand* could, Lynley knew, have several interpretations.

As for Ringo Heath, there was nothing. Especially there was no connection of record between Heath and Chief Superintendent Whiting. As to a connection between Whiting and Gordon Jossie, whatever it was, it was going to have to come out of Jossie's background because it certainly wasn't coming out of Whiting's.

'So it's sod bloody all on a biscuit, eh?' was how Havers

received the information. 'I s'pose her order to come home makes sense.'

'You're on your way, aren't you?' Lynley asked her.

'With Winston at the wheel? What d'*you* think?'

Which meant that Nkata who, unlike Havers, had a history of taking orders seriously, was returning them to London. Had she been given her way in matters, Barbara would have likely dallied until she was satisfied by what she was able to gather about everyone in Hampshire even remotely connected to Jemima Hastings' death.

He concluded his call as Isabelle Ardery returned from her meeting with Hillier and Stephenson Deacon. She looked no more harried than usual, so he concluded the meeting had gone marginally well. Then John Stewart fielded a phone call from SO7 that put a full stop to the case as far as Ardery was concerned. They had the analysis of the two hairs found on the body of Jemima Hastings, he told them.

'Well thank God for that,' Ardery declared. 'What've we got?'

'Oriental,' he told her.

'Hallelujah.'

It would have been a moment for packing everything in then, and Lynley could see that Ardery was inclined to do so. But Dorothea Harriman came into the room in the very next moment and, with her words, burst everything wide open.

One Bella McHaggis was downstairs in reception, Harriman told them, and she wanted to speak to Barbara Havers.

'She was told the detective sergeant is in Hampshire, so she's asked to see whoever's in charge of the case,' Harriman said. 'She's got evidence, she says, and she doesn't mean to hand it over to just anyone.'

Bella was no longer suspicious of Paolo di Fazio. That was finished the moment she'd seen the error in her thinking. She didn't regret setting the coppers after him since she watched enough police dramas on the telly to know that everyone had to be eliminated as suspects in order to find the guilty party and, like it or not, he was a suspect. So was she, she supposed. Anyway, she reckoned he'd get over whatever offence he might be feeling because of her suspicions and if he didn't, he'd find other lodgings but in any case she couldn't be bothered because Jemima's handbag had to be turned over to the officers investigating the case.

As she didn't intend waiting at home for them finally to show their faces *this* time round, she didn't bother with the phone, Instead, she'd dropped Jemima's handbag into the canvas carryall that she used for her grocery shopping, and she'd carted it off to New Scotland Yard because that was where that Sergeant Havers person had come from.

When she learned that Sergeant Havers wasn't in, she'd demanded someone else. The head, the chief, the whoever's-in-charge, she said to the uniform in reception. And she wasn't leaving till she talked to that person. *In* person, by the way. Not on the phone. She parked herself near the eternal flame and there she determined to remain.

And damn, if she didn't have to wait exactly forty-three minutes for a responsible party finally to appear. Even when this happened, she didn't think she was looking at the responsible party at all. A tall, nice-looking man approached her and, when he spoke from beneath his head of beautifully groomed blond hair, he didn't sound like anyone she'd ever heard yapping away on *The Bill*. He was Inspector Lynley, he said in the plummy tone that had always proclaimed Public School in One's Past. Did she have something related to the investigation?

'Are you in charge?' she demanded and when he admitted that he was not, she told him to fetch whoever was and *that*, she said, was how it was going to be. She was in need of police protection from the killer of Jemima Hastings, she said, and she had a feeling he wasn't going to be able to provide that on his own. 'I know who did it,' she told him and she lifted the carryall to her chest, 'and what I've got in here proves it.'

'Ah,' he said politely. 'And what have you got in there?'

'I'm *not* a nutter,' she told him sharply because she could tell what he was thinking about her. 'You fetch who needs to be fetched, my good man.'

He went to make a phone call. He regarded her from across the lobby as he spoke to whoever was at the other end of the line. Whatever he said proved fruitful, though. In another three minutes, a woman came out of the elevator and through the turnstile that kept the general public away from the mysterious workings of New Scotland Yard. This individual strode over to join them. She was, Inspector Lynley told Bella, Detective Superintendent Ardery.

'And are *you* the person in charge?' Bella said.

'I am,' the superintendent replied. Her facial expression added the comment, And this better be worth my time, madam.

Right, Bella thought, it bloody well will be.

The handbag was so hopelessly compromised for purposes of evidence that Isabelle wanted to shake the woman silly. The fact that she did not was, she decided, a testimony to her self-control.

'It's Jemima's,' Bella McHaggis announced as she produced it with a flourish. This flourish included adding fingerprints to what were doubtless dozens more of her own, in the process smearing everyone else's and, in particular, smearing the killer's. 'I found it with the Oxfam goods.'

'A discarded bag or one that she carried daily?' Lynley asked, not unreasonably.

'It's her regular bag. And it wasn't discarded because it's got all her clobber in it.'

'You went through it?' Isabelle gritted her teeth in preparation for the inevitable answer which was, naturally, that the woman had pawed through everything, depositing more fingerprints, creating more compromised evidence.

'Well, of course I went through it,' Bella asserted. 'How else was I to know it's Jemima's?'

'How else indeed,' Isabelle said.

Bella McHaggis gave her a narrow-eyed look that told Isabelle she was being evaluated. The woman seemed to reach a conclusion that no offence was intended by Isabelle's tone, and before she could be stopped from doing so, she opened the handbag, said, 'See here, then,' and dumped its contents onto the seat where she'd been awaiting them.

'Please don't—' Isabelle began as Lynley said, 'This all must go to—' and Bella picked up a mobile phone and waved it at them, declaring, 'This is hers. And this is her purse and her wallet,' and on and on as she pawed through everything. There was nothing for it but to grab her hands in the unlikely hope that something had gone untouched on Bella's first time through the handbag and that it could remain so. 'Yes, yes. Thank you,' Isabelle said. She nodded at Lynley to replace the handbag's contents and to put the bag itself into the carryall. When he'd accomplished this, Isabelle asked the woman to take her through everything that had led to her finding the handbag. This Bella McHaggis was pleased to do. She gave them chapter and verse on recycling and saving the planet, and from this Isabelle concluded that the handbag had come from a bin that was not only situated in front of Bella McHaggis's house but was also accessible to anyone who happened to pass by and see it. This, apparently, was a point that Bella herself wished to make because the conclusion of her recitation contained a fact she declared 'the most important bit of all.'

'And that is?' Isabelle enquired.

'Yolanda.'

It seemed that the psychic had been lurking round Bella's front garden again, and she'd been there this time moments before Bella had made the discovery of Jemima's handbag.

She'd been ostensibly having 'some sort of bloody psychic *experience*,' Bella scoffed, which had been characterised by muttering, moaning, praying, and waving round a stick of burning whatever that was supposed to do something magical or 'rubbish like that'. Bella had given her a few choice words, and the psychic had scurried off. Moments later, checking the Oxfam bin, Bella had uncovered the handbag.

'Why were you checking the bin?' Lynley asked.

'To see how soon it would need emptying, obviously,' was her withering reply. It seemed, not unreasonably, that the other bins collected recycling matter far more quickly than did the Oxfam bin. While they were emptied twice each month, the Oxfam bin was not.

'*She'd* have no way of knowing that,' Bella said.

'We'll want to go through this bin,' Isabelle said. 'You've not done anything with its contents, have you?'

She hadn't done, for which Isabelle praised God. She told the woman that someone would come and fetch the bin from her and in the meantime, she wasn't to open it again or even touch it.

'It's important, isn't it?' Bella looked quite pleased with herself. 'I *knew* it was important, didn't I.'

There was no doubt of that, although how to interpret the handbag's importance was something over which Isabelle found herself at odds with Lynley. As they rode the lift on their return to the incident room, she said to him, 'He had to have known where she lived, Thomas.'

Lynley said, 'Who?' and the way he said it told her he was thinking in another direction entirely.

'Matsumoto. It would have been a simple matter for him to put the handbag in that bin.'

'And keep the murder weapon?' Lynley asked. 'How d'you reckon his thinking went on that one?'

'He's mad as a hatter. He isn't thinking. He *wasn't* thinking. Or if he *was* thinking, he was thinking about doing what the angels told him to do. Get rid of this, hold onto that, run, hide, follow her, whatever.' She glanced at him sharply. He was gazing at the floor of the lift, his brow furrowed and the knuckle of his index finger to his lips in a posture that suggested consideration of her words and of everything else. She said, 'Well?'

He said, 'We've Paolo di Fazio inside that house. We've Frazer Chaplin inside it as well. And then there's the matter of Yolanda.'

'You can't mean to suggest another *woman* killed Jemima Hastings. By driving a spike into her carotid artery? Heavens, Thomas, the entire means of murder isn't the least bit feminine, and I dare say you know it.'

'I agree it's unlikely,' Lynley said. 'But I don't want to discount the fact that Yolanda might be protecting someone who handed the bag over to her and asked her to be rid of it. She needs talking to.'

'Oh, for God's bloody sake . . .' And then she saw his expression. She knew that he was assessing her, and she also knew what he was assessing. She felt a bubble of anger that *any* man should stand in judgement of her in a situation in which he would not likely stand in judgement of another male. She said, 'I want to have a close look at the contents of that bag before we hand it over to forensics. And don't bloody tell me that's irregular, Thomas. We don't have time to wait round for those blokes to tell us every fingerprint is useless. We need a result.'

'You're—'

'We'll wear gloves, all right? And the bag won't leave my sight or yours. Will that do or do you want more guarantees?'

'I was going to say you're in charge. You give the orders,' he replied. 'I was going to say it's your case.'

She doubted that. He was as smooth as icing on a cake. She said, 'Mind you remember that,' as they left the lift together.

The most important belonging of Jemima Hastings inside the bag was the mobile phone, and this Isabelle handed over to John Stewart with orders to deal with it, to listen to voice messages, to trace calls, to read and make note of any and all texts, and to get his hands on the mobile's records. 'We'll want

to use the mobile phone towers as well,' she added. 'The
pinging, or whatever the hell they call it.' The rest of the contents
she and Lynley went through together, most of it seeming to
be perfectly straightforward: a small folding map of London,
a paperback novel showing a predilection for historical
mysteries, a wallet holding thirty-five pounds along with two
credit cards; three biros, a broken pencil, a pair of sunglasses
in a case, a hairbrush, a comb, four lipsticks and a mirror.
There was also a list of products from the cigar shop, along
with an advertisement for Queen's Ice and Bowl – Great Food!
Birthday Parties! Corporate Events! – an offer for member-
ship to a Putney gym and spa and business cards from Yolanda
the Psychic, London Skate Centre, Abbott Langer Professional
Ice Instructor and Sheldon Pockworth Numismatics.

This last gave Isabelle pause as she tried to recall what
numismatics referred to. She came up with stamps. Lynley
said coins.

She told him to check it out. He said, 'Along with Yolanda?
Because I still think—'

'All right. Along with Yolanda. But I swear she has nothing
to do with this, Thomas. A woman did *not* commit this crime.'

Lynley found Yolanda the Psychic's place of business in
Queensway with little trouble although he had to wait outside
the faux mews building where she plied her trade because a
sign on the door declared *In Session! No Entry!*, and from
this he assumed that Yolanda was in the process of doing
whatever it was that psychics did for their clients: tea leaves,
tarot cards, palms, or the like. He fetched himself a takeaway
coffee from a Russian café tucked in the junction of two of
the indoor market's corridors, and he returned to Psychic
Mews with cup in hand. By that time, the sign had been
removed from the door, so he finished the coffee quickly and
let himself in.

'That you, dearest?' Yolanda called from an inner room,

shielded from the reception area by a beaded curtain. 'Bit early, aren't you?'

'No,' Lynley replied to her first question. 'DI Lynley. New Scotland Yard.'

She came through the curtain. He took in her startling orange hair and her tailored suit that he recognised – thanks to his wife – as either vintage Coco Chanel or a Coco Chanel rip-off. She wasn't what he had expected.

She stopped when she saw him. 'It throbs,' she said.

He blinked. 'Pardon?'

'Your aura. It's taken a terrible blow. It wants to regain its strength but something's got in the way.' She held her hand up before he could reply. She cocked her head as if listening to something. 'Hmm. Yes,' she said. 'It's not for nothing, you know. She intends to return. In the meantime your part is to become ready for her. That's a dual message.'

'From the great beyond?' He asked the question lightly but, of course, he thought at once of Helen, no matter the irrationality of applying the idea of return to someone so completely gone.

Yolanda said, 'You'd be wise not to make light of these matters. Those who make light generally regret it. What'd you say your name was?'

'DI Lynley. Is that what happened to Jemima Hastings? Did she make light?'

Yolanda ducked behind a screen for a moment. Lynley heard the scratch of a match. He thought she was lighting incense or a candle – either seemed likely and there was already a cone of incense burning at the crossed legs of a seated Buddha – but she emerged with a cigarette. She said to him, 'It's good that you gave it up. I don't see you dying because of your lungs.'

He absolutely refused to be seduced. He said, 'As to Jemima?'

'She didn't smoke.'

'That didn't much help her in the end, did it?'

Yolanda took a heavy hit from the tobacco. 'I already talked to the cops,' she said. 'That black man. Strongest aura I've seen in years. P'rhaps ever, to tell you the truth. But that woman with him? The one with the teeth? I'd say she has issues impeding her growth, and they aren't only dental. What would you say?'

'May I call you Mrs Price?' Lynley asked. 'I understand that's your real name.'

'You may not. Not on these premises. Here, I'm Yolanda.'

'Very well. Yolanda. You were in Oxford Road earlier today. We must talk about that, about Jemima Hastings as well. Shall we do it here or elsewhere?'

'Elsewhere being . . . ?'

'They'll have an interview room at the Ladbroke Grove station. We can use that if you prefer.'

She chuckled. 'Cops. You best be careful how you act else it'll disappear altogether. There's such a thing as karma, Mr Lynley. That's what you said your name is, didn't you?'

'That's what I said.'

She examined him. 'You don't look like a cop. You don't talk like a cop. You don't belong.'

How true, he thought. But this was hardly a startling deduction for her to have made. He said, 'Where would you like to talk, Yolanda?'

She went through the beaded curtain. He followed her.

There was a table in the centre of the inner room, but she didn't sit there. Instead, she went to an overstuffed armchair that faced a Victorian fainting sofa. She lay upon this latter and closed her eyes, although she still managed to smoke her cigarette unimpeded. He took the chair and said to her, 'Tell me about Oxford Road first. We'll get to Jemima in a moment.'

There was little enough to tell, according to Yolanda the Psychic. She'd been in Oxford Road because of its inherent evil, she declared. She'd failed to save Jemima from it despite her warnings to move house, and with Jemima having fallen victim to its depravity, she was duty bound to try to save the rest of them. Clearly, they weren't about to leave the place, so she was trying to purify it from without: She was burning sage. 'Not that that bloody woman will listen to anything I try to tell her,' she declared. 'Not that she would even begin to appreciate my efforts on her behalf.'

'What sort of evil?' Lynley asked.

Yolanda opened her eyes. 'There aren't different *sorts* of evil,' she replied. 'There's just it. *It*. Evil. So far it's taken two people from that house, and it's after more. Her husband died there, you know.'

'Mrs McHaggis's husband?'

'So you'd think she'd purify the place, but will she? No. She's too much the dim bulb to see the importance. Now Jemima's gone as well, and there'll be another. Just you wait.'

'And you were there solely to perform a . . .' Lynley sought the term that best fitted burning sage in someone's front garden and settled on, 'a rite of some kind?'

'Not of "some kind". Oh I know what your sort think about my sort. You've no belief till life brings you to your knees and then you come running, don't you?'

'Is that what happened to Jemima? Why did she come to see you? Initially, I mean.'

'I don't speak about my clients.'

'I know that's what you told the other officers but we've a problem, you see, as you're not a psychiatrist, a psychologist, a solicitor. There's no privilege to invoke, as far as I can tell.'

'Which means what, exactly?'

'Which means your failure to disclose information can be seen as obstructing a police investigation.'

She was silent, digesting this. She drew in on her cigarette and blew the smoke heavenward, thoughtfully.

Lynley went on. 'So my suggestion is that you tell me whatever seems relevant. Why did she come to see you?'

Yolanda seemed to be tossing round the ramifications of speaking or not speaking. She finally said, 'I told the others already: love. It's why they usually come.'

'Love for whom?'

Again a hesitation before she said, 'The Irishman. The one who works at the ice rink.'

'Frazer Chaplin?'

'She wanted to know what they always want to know.' Yolanda moved restlessly on the sofa. She reached for an ashtray beneath it and stubbed out her cigarette. She said, 'I *told* the others that, more or less. The black man and the woman with the teeth. I don't see how going over it all again with you is going to make a difference.'

Lynley gave passing wry thought to how Barbara Havers would react to being called 'the woman with the teeth'. He said, 'Call it a new perspective: mine. What, exactly, did you tell her?'

She sighed. 'Love's risky.'

Isn't it just, Lynley thought.

'I mean as a topic,' she went on. 'One can't make predictions about it. There're too many variables, always the unexpected bits, especially if one doesn't have the other person there to . . . well, to scrutinise, you see. So one keeps things *vague*, in a manner of speaking. That's what I did.'

'To keep the client coming back, I should guess.'

She glanced his way, as if to evaluate his tone. He kept his face impassive. She said, 'This is a business. I don't deny it. But it's also a service that I provide and, believe me, people need it. 'Sides, all sorts of things come up when I'm engaged with a client. They come to see me for one reason, but they find others. 'S not *me* keeping them coming back, I can tell you that. It's what I know. It's what I tell them that I know.'

'And Jemima?'

'What about her?'

'She had other reasons, beyond her questions about love?'

'She had.'

'And what were those?'

Yolanda sat up. She swung her legs round. They were chunky, without ankles, a single plane from her knees to her feet. She plopped her hands down on either side of her thighs as if for balance, and while she held herself straight, her head was lowered. She shook this.

Lynley thought she meant to refuse: no more information, sir. But instead, she said, 'Something's standing between me and the others. Everything's gone quiet. But I intended no harm. I didn't know.'

Lynley felt strongly disinclined to play along. He said, 'Mrs Price, if you know something, I must insist—'

'Yolanda!' she said, her head rising with a jerk. 'It's Yolanda in here. I'm having enough trouble with the spirit world as it is, and I don't need someone in this room reminding them I've another life out there, d'you understand? Ever since she died – ever since I was *told* that she died – it's gone quiet and dark. I'm going through the motions, I've been doing that for days, and I don't know what I'm failing to see.' Then she rose. The room was dim and gloomy, in keeping with her line of work, and she went to the curtained entry where she switched on an overhead light. The illumination brought the dismal little space into an unforgiving relief: dust on the furniture, slut's wool in the corners, secondhand belongings that were chipped and cracked. Yolanda paced the small area. Lynley waited although his patience was wearing thin.

She finally said, 'They come for advice. I try not to give it directly. That's not how it works. But in her case, I could feel something more and I needed to know what it was in order to work with her. She had information that would have helped me, but she didn't want to part with.'

'Information about whom? About what?'

'Who's to tell? She wouldn't say. But she asked where she should meet someone if hard truths had to be spoken between them and if she feared to speak them.'

'A man?'

'She wouldn't tell me that. I said the obvious, what anyone would say: she must choose a public place for her meeting.'

'Did you mention—'

'I did *not* tell her that cemetery.' She stopped her pacing. She was on the other side of the table and she faced him across it, as if she needed the safety of this distance. She said, '*Why* would I tell her that cemetery?'

'I take it you didn't recommend her local Starbucks either,' Lynley pointed out.

'I said choose a place where peace predominates and where she could feel it. I don't know why she chose that cemetery. I don't know how she even knew about it.' She resumed her pacing. Round the table once, twice, before she said, 'I should have told her something else. I should have seen. Or felt. But I didn't tell her to stay away from that place because I didn't see danger.' She swung round on him. 'Do you know what it means that I didn't see danger, Mr Lynley? Do you understand the position that puts me in? I've never doubted the gift for a moment, but now I do. I don't know truth from lies. I can't *see* them. And if I couldn't protect her from danger, I can't protect anyone.'

She sounded so wretched that Lynley felt a surprising twinge of compassion although he did not for a moment believe in psychic phenomena. The thought of protecting someone, however, made him think of the stone Jemima was carrying. A talisman, a good luck charm? He said, 'Did you try to protect her?'

'Of *course* I did.'

'Did you give her anything to keep her safe prior to this meeting she intended to have?'

But she hadn't. She had sought to protect Jemima Hastings only with words of advice – 'vague mutterings and imaginings,' Lynley thought – and they'd been useless.

At least, however, they now knew what Jemima had been doing in Abney Park Cemetery. On the other hand, they had only Yolanda's word for what she herself had been doing in Oxford Road that day. He asked her about this; he also asked her what she'd been doing at the time of Jemima's death. To the latter she said she'd been doing what she was always doing:

meeting with clients. She had the appointment book to prove it and if he wanted to phone them he was welcome to do so. As to the former, she'd already said: she was attempting to purify the bloody house before someone else met death unexpectedly. 'McHaggis, Frazer, the Italian,' she said.

Did Yolanda know them all? Lynley asked her.

By sight if not by acquaintance. McHaggis and Frazer she'd spoken to. The Italian, not.

And did she have occasion to open any of the recycling bins in the garden? he enquired.

She looked at him as if he were mad. Why the bloody hell would she open the bins? she asked. The bins don't need purifying, but that house does.

He didn't want to go down that road again. He reckoned he'd got all there was to be had from Yolanda the Psychic. Until the spirit world revealed more to her, she seemed like a closed book to him.

21

When Robbie Hastings pulled onto Gordon Jossie's holding, he wasn't sure what he intended to do, for Jossie had lied to him not only about wanting to marry Jemima, but also, as things turned out, about when he'd last seen her. Rob had had this latter piece of information from Meredith Powell, and it was a phone call from her that had sent him to Jossie's property. She'd been to see the police in Lyndhurst; she'd given them proof positive that Gordon had travelled into London on the morning of Jemima's death. He'd even stayed the night in a hotel, she told Rob, and she'd given the police that information as well.

'But, Rob,' she had said and through his mobile he could hear anxiety in her voice, 'I think we've made a mistake.'

'"We"?' Half of *we* turned out to be Gina Dickens, in whose company Meredith had been ushered into the presence of Chief Superintendent Whiting – 'because we said, Rob, that we wouldn't talk to *anyone* but the man at the top' – and there they'd demanded to know the whereabouts of the two detectives who'd come to the New Forest from New Scotland Yard. They had something of grave importance to hand over to those detectives, they told him, and of course he asked what it was. Once he knew what it was, he asked to see it. Once he saw it, he put it into a folder and asked where it had come from. 'Gina didn't want to tell him, Rob. She seemed afraid of him. Afterwards she told me he's been on the property to talk to Gordon and *when* he came to talk to Gordon, she didn't know he was police. He didn't say, and Gordon didn't either. She said she went all cold when we walked into his office and she saw him cos she reckons Gordon must've known who he was all along. So now she's nearly out of her mind with fear because *if* this bloke shows up on the property and *if* he takes that evidence with him, *then* Gordon'll know how he got it because how else could he have got it except from Gina?'

As the information continued to pile up, Robbie had difficulty taking it all in. Train tickets, a hotel receipt, Gina Dickens in possession of both, Gordon Jossie, Chief Superintendent Whiting, New Scotland Yard . . . And then there was the not small matter of Gordon's complete lie about Jemima's departure: that she had someone in London or elsewhere, that he himself had wanted to marry and *she* had left *him* rather than what the truth likely was: that he had driven her off.

Meredith had gone on to say that Chief Superintendent Whiting had kept the rail tickets and the hotel receipt in his possession, but once she and Gina had left him and once Gina had revealed the man's connection – 'whatever it is, Rob' – to Gordon Jossie, Meredith herself had known absolutely that he was *not* going to give the information to New Scotland Yard although she couldn't say why. 'And we didn't know where to find them,' Meredith wailed, 'those detectives, Rob. I've not even talked to them yet anyway, so I don't know who they are, so I wouldn't recognise them if I saw them on the street. Why haven't they come to *talk* to me? I was her friend, her best friend, Rob.'

To Rob, only one detail actually mattered. It wasn't that Chief Superintendent Whiting had potential evidence in his hands and it wasn't the whereabouts of the Scotland Yard detectives or why they hadn't spoken yet to Meredith Powell. What mattered was that Gordon Jossie had been to London.

Rob had taken the call from Meredith just at the end of a meeting of the New Forest's verderers, which they'd held, as usual, in the Queen's House. And although this location was not far from the police station where the chief superintendent operated, Rob didn't even think about going there to question Chief Superintendent Whiting about what he intended to do with the information from Meredith and Gina Dickens. He

had only one destination in mind and he set off for it with a
grinding of the Land Rover's gears and Frank lurching on
the seat next to him.

When he saw from the absence of vehicles that no one was
at home on Jossie's holding, Rob paced intently round the
cottage as if he'd be able to find evidence of the man's guilt
leaping out of the flower beds. He looked into windows and
tested doors and the fact that they were locked in a place
where virtually no one locked their doors seemed to declare
the worst.

He went from the cottage to the barn and swung open the
doors. He strode inside to his sister's car, saw that the key was
in the old Figaro's ignition, and tried to make something of
this, but the only thing he could make of it didn't amount to
sense, anyway: that Jemima had never gone to London but
had been murdered here and buried on the property, which
of course hadn't happened at all. Then he saw that the ring
attached to the ignition key held another, and assuming this
was the key to the cottage, Robbie took it and hurried back
to the door.

What he intended to look for, he didn't know. He only
understood that he had to do something. So he opened drawers
in the kitchen. He opened the fridge. He looked in the oven.
He went from there to the sitting room and took the cushions
off the sofa and the chairs. Finding nothing, he dashed up the
stairs. Clothes cupboards were neat. Pockets were empty.
Nothing languished under the beds. Towels in the bathroom
were damp. A ring in the toilet bowl spoke of cleaning needing
to be done, and although he wanted something to be hidden
inside the cistern, there was nothing.

Then Frank started barking outside. Then another dog
began barking as well. This took Robbie to one of the windows
where he saw two things simultaneously: one was that Gordon
Jossie had come home in the company of his Golden Retriever.
The other was that the ponies in the paddock were *still* in
the damn paddock when Rob would have sworn to God that

they belonged out on the forest, so why the hell were they still here?

The barking increased in frenzy, and Rob dashed down the stairs. Never mind that he was the one trespassing. There were questions to be asked.

Frank sounded insane, as did the other dog. Rob saw as he burst out of the cottage that for some reason Jossie had stupidly opened the door of the Land Rover and had let Frank jump out and he himself was now bent into the vehicle and searching through it as if he didn't bloody well already know who owned it.

The Weimaraner was howling, not at the other dog but at Jossie himself. This fuelled Rob's rage because if Frank howled it was because he'd been harmed and *no* one was meant to lay a hand on his dog and certainly not Jossie who'd laid hands elsewhere and death was the result.

Tess was yelping now because Frank was howling. Two dogs from the property across the lane joined in and the resulting cacophony set the ponies in motion inside the paddock. They began to trot back and forth along the line of the fence, tossing their heads, neighing.

'What the hell're you doing?' Robbie demanded.

Jossie swung round from the Land Rover and asked a variation of the same question and with far more reason, as the door to the cottage stood wide open and it was only too clear what Rob had been up to. Rob shouted at Frank to be quiet, which only set the dog into a complete paroxysm of barking. He ordered the Weimaraner back into the vehicle, but instead Frank approached Jossie as if he intended to go for the thatcher's throat. Jossie said, 'Tess. That'll do,' and his own animal ceased barking at once, and this made Rob think of power and control and how a need for power and control could be at the heart of what had happened to Jemima and then he thought of the railway tickets, of the hotel receipt, of Jossie's trip to London, of his lies, and he strode over to the thatcher and heaved him against the side of the Land Rover.

He said through his teeth, '*London*, you bastard.'

'What the hell . . .' Gordon Jossie cried.

'She didn't leave you because she had someone else,' Robbie said. 'She wanted to marry you, although God knows why.' He pressed Jossie back, had his arm across the thatcher's throat before Jossie could defend himself. With his other hand, he knocked the man's sunglasses to the ground because he damn well intended to see his eyes for once. Jossie's hat went with them, a baseball cap that left a line across his forehead like the mark put on Cain. 'But you didn't want that, did you?' Rob demanded. 'You didn't want *her*. First you used her, then you drove her away, and then you went after her.'

Jossie pushed Rob away. He was breathing hard, and he was, Rob found, far stronger than he looked. He said, 'What're you talking about? Used her for *what*, for the love of God?'

'I can even see how it worked, you bastard.' It seemed so obvious now that Rob wondered he hadn't seen it before. 'You wanted this place, this holding, didn't you? And you reckoned I could help you get it, because it's part of my area, and land with common rights isn't easy to come by. And I'd want to help because of Jemima, eh? It's all fitting now.'

'You're round the bend,' Jossie said. 'Get the hell out of here.' Rob didn't move. Jossie said, 'If you don't get off this property, I'll—'

'What? Call the cops? I don't think so. You were in London, Jossie, and they know it now.'

That stopped him cold. He was dead in whatever tracks he thought he was about to make. He said nothing but Robbie could tell he was thinking like mad.

The upper hand his, Rob decided to play it. 'You were in London the very day she was murdered. They've got your rail tickets. How d'you like that? They've got the receipt from the hotel and I expect your name's on it large as life, eh? So how long d'you expect it'll be before they come after you for a little chat? An hour? More? An afternoon? A day?'

If Jossie had been considering lying at this point, his face betrayed him. As did his body, which went limp, all fight gone because he knew he was done for. He bent, picked up his sunglasses, rubbed them against the front of his T-shirt, which was marked by sweat and stained from work. He returned the glasses to his face, likely to hide his eyes but it didn't matter now because Rob had seen in them everything he wanted to see.

'Yes,' Robbie said. 'End game, Gordon. And don't think you can run because I'll follow you to hell if I have to and I'll bring you back.'

Jossie reached for his cap next, and he slapped it against his jeans although he didn't put it back on. He'd removed his windcheater and left it in a lump on the Land Rover's seat. He grabbed it up in the same lump and said, 'All right, Rob.' His voice was quiet and Rob saw that his lips had gone the colour of putty. 'All right,' he said again.

'Meaning what exactly?'

'You know.'

'You were there.'

'If I was, whatever I say won't make a difference.'

'You've lied about Jemima from the first.'

'I've not—'

'She wasn't running to someone in London. She didn't leave you for that. She *had* no one else, in London or anywhere. There was only you, and you were who she wanted. But you didn't want her: commitment, marriage, whatever. So you drove her away.'

Jossie looked towards the ponies in the paddock. He said, 'That's not how it was.'

'Are you denying you were there, man? Cops check the CCTV films from the railway station – in Sway, in London – and you'll not be on them the day she died? They take your photo to that hotel and no one'll remember you were there for a night?'

'I had no reason to kill Jemima.' Gordon licked his lips. He glanced over his shoulder, back towards the lane, as if seeking someone coming to rescue him from this confrontation. 'Why the hell would I want her dead?'

'She'd met someone new once she got to London. She told me as much. And then it was dog in the manger for you, wasn't it. You didn't want her but, by God, no one else would have her.'

'I'd no idea she had anyone else. I still don't know that. How *was* I to know?'

'Because you tracked her. You found her, and you talked to her. She would have told you.'

'And if that's what happened, why would I care? I had someone else as well. I *have* someone else. I didn't kill her. I swear to God—'

'You don't deny being there. There in London.'

'I wanted to talk to her, Rob. I'd been trying to find her for months. Then I got a phone call . . . Some bloke had seen the cards I'd put up. He left a message saying where Jemima was. Just where she worked, in Covent Garden. I phoned there – a cigar shop – but she wouldn't talk to me. Then she rang me a few days later and said yes, all right, she was willing to meet me. Not where she worked, she said, but at that place.'

At the cemetery, Rob thought. But what Jossie was saying didn't make sense. Jemima had someone new. Jossie had someone new. What had they to talk about?

Rob walked to the paddock, where the ponies had gone back to grazing. He stood at the fence and looked at them: they were too sleek, too well-fed. Gordon was doing them no service by keeping them here. They were meant to forage all year long; they were part of a herd. Rob opened the gate and went into the paddock.

'What are you doing?' Jossie demanded.

'My job.' Behind him, Rob heard the thatcher follow him into the paddock. 'Why're they here?' he asked him. 'They're meant to be on the forest with the others.'

'They were lame.'

Rob went closer to the ponies. He *shushed* them gently as,

behind him, Jossie closed the paddock gate. It didn't take any longer than a moment for Rob to see that the ponies were perfectly fine and he could feel their restless need to be out of there and with the others in the herd.

He said, 'They're not lame now. So why've you not . . .' And then he saw something far more curious than the oddity of healthy ponies locked up in a paddock in July. He saw the way their tails were clipped. Despite the growth of hair since the last autumn drift when the ponies had been marked, the pattern of the clipping on these ponies' tails was still quite readable and what that pattern said was that neither one of the animals belonged in this particular area of the New Forest at all. Indeed, the ponies were branded as well, and the brand identified them as coming from the north part of the Perambulation, near Minstead, from a holding located next to Boldre Gardens.

He said, unnecessarily, 'These ponies aren't yours. What the hell are you up to?'

Jossie said nothing.

Robbie waited. They had a moment of stalemate. It came to Rob that further conversation or argument with the thatcher was going to be pointless. It also came to him that it didn't matter. The cops were onto him now.

He said, 'Right then. Whatever you want. I'll come tomorrow with a trailer to fetch them. They need to go back where they belong. And you need to keep your hands off other people's livestock.'

At first Gordon tried to believe Robbie Hastings had been bluffing because to believe anything else would mean one of two things. Either he himself had blindly misplaced trust yet another mad time in his life or someone had broken into his house, found damning evidence that he had not even known would be damning, and taken it away to bide his time or her time and to present it to the cops when it could do the most damage to him.

Of the two possibilities, he preferred the second one because although it would mean the end was near, at least it would not mean he'd been betrayed by someone he trusted. If, on the other hand, it was the first one, he believed he might not recover from the blow.

Yet he knew it was far more likely that Gina had found the railway tickets and the hotel receipt than it was that Meredith Powell or someone with equal antipathy for him had entered his house, gone through the rubbish, and pocketed those materials without his knowledge. So when Gina returned home, he was waiting for her.

He heard her car first. It was odd because she cut the engine as she came into the driveway, and she coasted to a stop behind his pickup. When she got out, she closed the door so quietly that he couldn't even hear the click of it. Nor could he hear her footsteps on the gravel or the sound of the back door opening.

She didn't call his name as she usually did. Instead, she came up the stairs and into the bedroom and she gave a start when she saw him by the window, the sun behind him and the rest of him, he knew, just a silhouette to her. But she made a quick recovery. She said, 'Here you are,' and she smiled as if nothing was wrong, and for that single moment *how* he wanted to believe that she had not given him up to the police.

He said nothing, as he tried to gather his wits together. She brushed an errant lock of hair from her cheek. She said his name and when he didn't reply, she took a step towards him and said, 'Is something wrong, Gordon?'

Something. Everything. Had there been a moment when he'd thought that things could ever be right? And why had he thought that? A woman's smile, perhaps, the touch of a hand that was soft and smooth against his skin, his hands on the fullness of hips or buttocks, his mouth on the sweetness of breasts . . . Had he been so much of a fool that the mere act having a woman somehow could obliterate all that had gone before?

He wondered what Gina knew at this point. The fact that she was here suggested it was little enough, but the fact that she had possibly – probably – found the rail tickets, found the hotel's receipt, keeping them close to her until she could use them to harm him . . . And *why* had he not thrown them away on the platform in Sway upon his return? That was the real question. Had he only thought to do so, he and this woman would not be standing here in this bedroom, in the insufferable summer heat, facing each other with the sin of betrayal in both of their hearts, not only in hers, because he could not claim she was the only sinner.

He hadn't thrown the tickets away on the station platform and he hadn't rid himself of the receipt because he hadn't considered that something might happen to Jemima, that his possession of those bits of paper might damn him, that Gina might find them and keep them and say nothing about his lie to her of having gone to Holland, allowing him to dig himself in deeper and deeper and still not saying a word about what she knew about where he had really been, which was not in Holland, not on a farm talking to someone about reeds, not out of the country at all but rather in the heart of a London cemetery trying to wrest from Jemima's possession those things she could use to destroy him if she chose.

Gina said, 'Gordon, why're you not answering me? Why're you looking at me like that?'

'Like what?'

'Like you're . . .' She brushed at her hair again although this time none of it was out of place. Her lips curved but her smile faltered. 'Why won't you answer? Why're you staring? Is something wrong?'

'I went to talk to her, Gina,' he said. 'That's all I did.'

She furrowed her brow. 'Who?'

'I needed to talk to her. She agreed to meet me. I didn't tell you only because there was no reason to tell you. It was over between us, but she had something of mine that I wanted back.'

She said, the realisation apparently coming to her, 'You saw *Jemima*? When?'

He said, 'Don't pretend you haven't sussed that out. Rob Hastings was here.'

She said, 'Gordon, I don't see how . . . Rob Hastings?' She gave a small laugh but it held no humour. 'You know, you're actually frightening me. You sound . . . I don't know . . . fierce? Did Rob Hastings say something to you about me? Did he do something? Did you argue with him?'

'He told me about the rail tickets and the hotel receipt.'

'What rail tickets? What hotel receipt?'

'The ones you found. The ones you handed over.'

Her hand rose. She placed the tips of her fingers between her breasts. She said, 'Gordon, honestly. You're . . . What are you talking about? Did Rob Hastings claim that I gave him something? Something of yours?'

'The cops,' he said.

'What about them?'

'You gave the rail tickets and that hotel receipt to the cops. But if you'd asked me about them instead, I would have told you the truth. I didn't before this because I didn't want you to worry. I didn't want you to think there might still be something between us because there wasn't.'

Gina's eyes – wide, blue, more beautiful than the northern sky – observed him as her head slowly tilted to one side. She said, 'What on earth are you talking about? *What* tickets? *What* receipts? What did Rob Hastings claim I did?'

He'd claimed nothing, of course. Gordon had merely concluded. And he'd done that because it seemed to him that, unless someone had surreptitiously gone through his rubbish, no one else could have come across those items save Gina. He said, 'Rob told me the cops in Lyndhurst have what proves I was in London that day. The day she died.'

'But you weren't.' Gina's voice sounded perfectly reasonable. 'You were in Holland. You went about the reeds because those from Turkey are rubbish. You didn't keep the tickets to

Holland so you had to say you were working that day. And Cliff told the police – that man and woman from Scotland Yard – that you were working because you knew they'd think you were lying if you didn't produce those tickets. And that's what happened.'

'No. What happened is I went to London. What happened is that I met Jemima in the place she died. On the day she died.'

'Don't say that!'

'It's the truth. But when I left her, she was alive. She was sitting on a stone bench at the edge of a clearing where there's an old chapel and she was alive. I'd not got from her what I wanted to get, but I didn't hurt her. I came home the next day so you'd think I'd gone to Holland, and I threw those tickets in the rubbish bin. That's where you found them.'

'No,' she said. 'Absolutely not. And if I *had* found them and been confused by them, I would've talked to you. I would've asked you why you lied to me. You know that, Gordon.'

'So how do the cops—'

'Rob Hastings told you they have the tickets?' She didn't wait for an answer. 'Then Rob Hastings is lying. He wants you to be blamed. He wants you to . . . I don't know . . . to do something crazy so the police will think . . . Good heavens, Gordon, *he* could've gone through the rubbish himself, found those tickets and handed them over to the police. Or he could be holding on to them, just waiting for the moment to use them against you. Or if not him, then someone else with equal dislike for you. But why would I do anything with any tickets other than simply talk to you about them? Have I the slightest reason to do something that might cause you trouble? Look at me. Have I?'

'If you thought that I'd hurt Jemima . . .'

'Why on earth would I think that? You were through with each other, you and Jemima. You told me that and I believed you.'

'It was true.'

'Well, then . . . ?'

He said nothing.

She approached him. He could tell she was hesitant, as if he were an anxious animal in need of calming. And she was just as anxious, he could tell. What he couldn't sense was the source of her anxiety: his paranoia? his accusations? her guilt? the desperation each of them felt to be believed by the other? And why was there desperation at all? He knew what he had to lose. But what had she?

She seemed to hear the question, and she said, 'So few people have anything good between them. Don't you see that?'

He didn't reply, but he felt compelled to look at her, right into her eyes, and the fact of this compulsion made him tear his gaze from her and look anywhere else, which was out of the window. He turned to it. He could see the paddocks and the ponies within.

He said slowly, 'You said you were afraid of them. But you went inside. You were *in* there with them. So you weren't afraid, were you? Because if you were, you wouldn't have gone inside for any reason.'

'The horses? Gordon, I tried to explain—'

'You would have just waited for me to release them onto the forest again. You knew I'd do that eventually. I'd *have* to do it. Then it would have been perfectly safe to go in but then you wouldn't have had a reason, would you.'

'Gordon. Gordon.' She was near him now. 'Listen to yourself. That doesn't make sense.'

Like an animal, he could smell her, so close was she. The odour was faint, but it combined the scent she wore, a light sheen of perspiration, and something else. He thought it might be fear. Equally, he thought it might be discovery. His discovery or hers, he didn't know, but it was there and it was real. Feral.

The hair on his arms stirred as if he were in the presence of danger, which he was. He always had been and this fact was so odd to him that he wanted to laugh like a wild man as he realised the simple truth that everything was completely backwards in his life: he could hide but he could not run.

She said, 'What are you accusing me of? *Why* are you accusing me of anything? You're acting like . . .' She hesitated, not as if she was searching for a word, but rather as if she knew quite well what he was acting like and the last thing she wanted was to say it.

'You want me to be arrested, don't you?' Still, it was the ponies he looked at. They seemed to him to hold the answers. 'You want me to be in trouble.'

'*Why* would I want that? Look at me. Please. Turn around. Look at me, Gordon.'

He felt her hand on his shoulder. He flinched. She withdrew it. She said his name. He said, 'She was alive when I left her. She was sitting on that stone bench in the cemetery. And she was alive. I swear it.'

'Of course she was alive,' Gina murmured. 'You had no reason to harm Jemima.'

The ponies outside trotted along the fence, as if knowing it was time to be released.

'No one will believe that, though,' he said, more to himself than to her. 'He – above all – won't believe it now he has those tickets and that receipt.' So he would return, Gordon thought bleakly. Again and again. Over and over until the end of time.

'Then you must just tell the truth.' She touched him again, the back of his head this time, her fingers light on his hair. 'Why on earth didn't you simply tell the truth in the first place?'

That was the question, wasn't it? he thought bitterly. Tell the truth and to hell with the consequences, even when the consequences were going to be death. Or worse than death because at least death would put an end to how he had to live.

She said, so near to him now, 'Why didn't you tell me? You can always talk to me, Gordon. Nothing you tell me could ever change how I feel about you.' And then he felt her cheek pressing against his back and her hands upon him, her knowing hands. They were first at his waist. Then her arms went round him and her soft hands were on his chest. She said, 'Gordon, Gordon,' and then the hands descended, first to his stomach and then, caressing, between his thighs, reaching for him, reaching. 'I would never,' she murmured. 'I would never, ever, *ever*, darling . . .'

He felt the heat, the pressure and the surge of blood. It was such a good place to go, so good that whenever he was there, nothing else intruded upon his thoughts. So happen, happen, let it happen, he thought. For didn't he deserve—

He jerked away from her with a cry and swung round to face her.

She blinked at him. 'Gordon?'

'*No!*'

'Why? Gordon, so few people—'

'Get away from me. I can *see* it now. It's down to you that—'

'Gordon? Gordon!'

'I don't want you here. I want you gone. Go bloody God-damn-you-to-hell away.'

Meredith was heading for her car when her mobile rang. It was Gina. She was sobbing, unable to catch her breath long enough to make herself clear. All Meredith could tell was that something had happened between Gina and Gordon Jossie in the aftermath of the visit she and Gina had made to the Lyndhurst police station. For a moment Meredith thought that Chief Superintendent Whiting had shown up on Gordon's property with the evidence they'd given him, but that didn't seem to be the case or if it was, Gina didn't say so. What she *did* say was that Gordon had somehow discovered that his railway tickets and his hotel receipt were in the hands of the cops and he was in a terrifying rage about it. Gina had fled the property and was now holed up in her bedsit above the Mad Hatter Tea Rooms.

'I'm that scared,' she cried. 'He knows I'm the one. I don't know what he'll do. I tried to pretend . . . He accused me . . . What could I say? I didn't know how to make him believe . . . I'm so afraid. I can't stay here. If I do, he'll come. He knows where . . .' She sobbed anew. 'I should never have . . . He wouldn't have hurt her. But I thought he should explain to the police . . . because if they found it . . .'

Meredith said, 'I'll come over straightaway. If he bangs on the door, you ring nine, nine, nine.'

'Where are you?'

'Ringwood.'

'But that'll take . . . He'll come after me, Meredith. He was so angry.'

'Sit in the tea room then. He won't go after you there. Not in public. Scream your head off if you have to.'

'I shouldn't have—'

'What? You shouldn't have gone to the cops? What else were you supposed to do?'

'But how did he know they have those tickets? How *could* he know? Did you tell someone?'

Meredith hesitated. She didn't want to admit she'd told Robbie Hastings. She picked up her pace to get to her car, and she said, 'That bloke Whiting. Likely, he'd've gone out there with questions straightaway when we gave him that stuff. But this is good, Gina. It's what we wanted to happen. Don't you see that?'

'I *knew* he'd know. That's why I wanted you to be the one to—'

'It's going to be all right.' Meredith ended the call.

She was, at this point, some distance from Lyndhurst but the dual carriageway out of Ringwood was going to help her.

She steamed into Lyndhurst some twenty minutes later. She left her car by the New Forest Museum and hurried back along the car park's narrow entry towards the High Street, where a tailback from the traffic lights for the Romsey Road made crossing between the vehicles easy.

Gina wasn't in the tea rooms. These were closed for the day anyway, but the proprietress was still there doing her evening clean-up so Meredith knew that had Gina wanted to sit and wait and be perfectly safe, she could have done so. Which meant, she concluded, that Gina had calmed down.

She climbed the stairs. It was silent above, with just the noises from the High Street drifting in from the open doorway. As before, it was hotter than Hades in the building, and Meredith felt the sweat trickle down her back, although she knew it was only partly due to the heat. The other part was fear. What if he was here already? In the room? With Gina? Having followed her back to Lyndhurst and ready to do his worst.

Meredith had barely knocked on the door when it was flung open. Gina presented an unexpected sight: her face was puffy and red. She was holding a flannel to the upper part of her arm, and a seam had given way on the sleeve of the shirt she was wearing.

Meredith cried out, 'Oh my God!'

'He was upset. He didn't mean to . . . I didn't say the right things.'

'What did he *do*?'

Gina crossed to the basin where, Meredith saw, she'd put a few pathetic cubes of ice. These she wrapped into the flannel and when she did so, Meredith saw the ugly red mark on her arm. It looked the size of a fist.

She said, 'We're phoning the police. That's assault. The police have to know.'

'I should never have gone to them. He wouldn't have hurt her. That's not who he is. I should have known that.'

'Are you mad? Look at what he just did to you! We must—'

'We've done enough. He's frightened. He admits he was there. Then she died.'

'He *admitted* it? You must tell the police. Those detectives from Scotland Yard. Oh, where the hell are they?'

'Not that he killed her. Never that. He admitted he saw her. They had arranged to meet. He said he had to know for sure it was finished between them before he and I could . . .' She began to cry. She held the flannel back to her arm and she gave a gasp when it touched her.

'We must get you to casualty. That could be a serious injury.'

'It's nothing. It'll bruise, that's all.' She looked down at her arm. Her lips move convulsively. 'I deserved it.'

'That's mad! That's what abused women *always* say.'

'I didn't believe in him. And not to believe him and then to betray him when I could have just asked him and when all he did was go to talk to her to make sure they were done with each other so that he and I . . . ? He hates me now. I betrayed him.'

'Don't *talk* like that. If anyone did any betraying, we both know who it was. Why would you believe him, anyway? He says he went there to make sure it was finished between them, but what else would he say? What else *could* he say now he knows the cops have the evidence they need? He's in trouble, and he's running scared. He's going to cut down anyone in his way.'

'I can't believe it of him. It's that policeman, Meredith. The chief superintendent we saw.'

'You think *he* killed Jemima?'

'I told you earlier: He's been to see Gordon. There's something between them. Something not right.'

'You think it's Jemima?' Meredith asked. 'Jemima's between them? They killed her together?'

'No, no. Oh, I don't *know*. I wouldn't have thought a thing about him, about him coming out to see Gordon at home those times but then when we walked into his office today and I saw who he really is . . . I mean, that he's a cop, that he's someone important. When he came to the cottage, he *never* said he was a cop. And Gordon never said either. But he must know, mustn't he?'

Meredith finally saw how all of it fitted. More, she saw how they'd put themselves into real danger, she and Gina. For if Gordon Jossie and the chief superintendent were engaged in something together, she and Gina had handed over a piece of evidence that Whiting would need to destroy at once. But he wouldn't need to destroy only the tickets and the hotel receipt, would he? He would also need to destroy those people who knew about them.

He would have recognised Gina, obviously. But he didn't know who Meredith was and she didn't think she'd given him her name. So she was safe, for the moment. She and Gina could . . . Or had she? she wondered. Had she said her name? Had she introduced . . . shown identification . . . something? Isn't that what one always did? No, no. She hadn't done so. They'd merely gone to his office. They'd handed over the evidence, they'd spoken to him, and . . . God. *God.* She couldn't remember. Why on earth couldn't she remember? Because she was in a muddle, she thought. There was too much going on. She was getting confused. There was Gina, there was Gina's panic, there was evidence, there was Gordon's rage and there was probably something else as well but she couldn't remember.

She said to Gina, 'We've got to get out of here. I'm taking you home.'

'But—'

'Come on. You can't stay here and neither can I.'

She helped Gina gather her belongings, which were few enough. They threw them into a carrier bag and got underway. Gina would follow Meredith in her own car, and they would go to Cadnam. It seemed the safest possible place. They would have to share not only a room but also a bed and they would have to cook up some story for Meredith's parents, but Meredith had time to work on that on the drive home, and when she pulled into the driveway at her parents' house, she told Gina that a gas leak at the Mad Hatter Tea Rooms had made her lodging unfit for habitation. At such short notice, it was the best she could do.

She said, 'You've just come to work at Gerber and Hudson as the receptionist, all right?'

Gina nodded but she looked fearful, as if Meredith's parents might phone up Gordon Jossie and announce her whereabouts should she get part of the story wrong.

She relaxed a bit as Cammie came charging out of the house, shouting, 'Mummy! Mummy!' The little girl flung herself at Meredith, wrapping her arms tightly round Meredith's legs. 'Gran wants to know where you *been*, Mummy.' And to Gina, 'My name's Cammie. What's yours?'

Gina smiled and Meredith could see her shoulders change, as if tension was draining out of them. She said, 'I'm Gina.'

'I'm five years old,' Cammie told her, demonstrating her age with her fingers as Meredith lifted her to her hip. 'I'll be six years old next, but not for a long time cos I jus' turned five in May. We had a party. D'you have parties on your birthday?'

'I haven't in a long time.'

'That's too bad. Birthday parties are lovely, especially if you have cake.' And then, typically, she was off in another conversational direction. 'Mummy, Gran's cross cos you didn't ring her and say you'd be late. You're meant to *ring* her.'

'I'll apologise.' Meredith kissed her daughter with the loudest smack of her lips that she could manage, the way Cammie liked. She set her on the ground. 'Could you run inside and tell her we have company, Cam?'

Whatever pique Janet Powell might have been feeling thus was dissipated when Meredith ushered Gina into the house. Her parents were nothing if not hospitable, and once Meredith told them the spurious tale of the gas leak at the Mad Hatter Tea Rooms, nothing more needed to be said.

Janet murmured, 'Terrible, terrible, pet,' and patted Gina on the back. 'Well, we can't have you stopping there, can we? You sit right here and let me make you a nice plate of ham salad. Cammie, you take Gina's bag to your mum's room and put out fresh towels in the bathroom. And ask your granddad will he scrub the bath.'

Cammie scampered off to do all this, announcing that she'd even let Gina use her own personal bunny towels and calling out, 'Granddad! We're to clean the bath, you an' me,' as Gina sat at the table.

Meredith helped her mother put together the ham salad. Neither she nor Gina was actually hungry – how could they have been, considering the circumstances? – but they both made an effort as if with the mutually unspoken knowledge that failure to do so would arouse suspicion where further suspicion was unwanted.

Gina went along with the idea of the gas leak with an ease that Meredith found herself admiring greatly, putting aside her worries about Gordon Jossie in a way that Meredith herself could never have managed in the same situation. Indeed, she soon had engaged Janet Powell in a conversation on the topic of Janet herself: her long marriage to Meredith's father, motherhood and grandmotherhood. Meredith could tell her mother was charmed.

Nothing disturbed the evening and by the time darkness fell, Meredith's guard had melted away. They were safe, for now. Tomorrow would be time enough to consider what to do next.

She began to see that she had been wrong about Gina Dickens. Gina was just as much a victim in this as Jemima had been. Each of them had made the same mistake: for some reason that Meredith herself would never be able to under-stand, each of the women had fallen for Gordon Jossie, and Gordon Jossie had deceived them both.

She couldn't comprehend how two intelligent women had failed to see Gordon for what he so obviously was, but then she had to admit that her distrust of men wasn't something that other women would naturally share. Besides, people gener-ally learned from their *own* encounters with the opposite sex. People didn't usually learn from hearing tales about others' relationships gone sour.

This had been the case for Jemima, and it was undoubtedly

the case for Gina. She was learning now, that was true, although it still seemed that she didn't want to believe.

'I still can't think he hurt her,' Gina said in a low voice when they were alone in Meredith's bedroom. And then she added before Meredith could make an acidulous comment about Gordon Jossie, 'Anyway, thank you. You're a real friend, Meredith. And your mum's lovely. So is Cammie. And your dad. You're very lucky.'

Meredith considered this. She said, 'For a long time, it didn't feel that way.' She told Gina then about Cammie's father. She recited the whole wretched tale. She finished by saying, 'When I wouldn't have an abortion, that was that. He said I'd have to prove in court that he was the dad, but at that point I actually didn't care to.'

'He doesn't help you at all? He doesn't support her?'

'If he sent me a cheque, I'd set fire to it. Way I see it, he's the one losing out. I have Cammie, and he'll never know her.'

'What does she think about her dad?'

'She knows that some kids have dads and others don't. We reckoned – Mum and Dad and me – if we didn't make it a tragedy, she wouldn't see it that way.'

'But she must ask.'

'Sometimes. But at the end of the day, she's more interested in seeing the otters at the wildlife park, so we don't have to have much of a conversation about it. In time, I'll tell her some version of the story, but she'll be older then.' Meredith shrugged, and Gina squeezed her hand. They were sitting on the edge of the bed, in the dim light of a single bedside lamp. The house was silent aside from their whispers.

Gina said, 'I expect you know you did the right thing, but it's not been easy for you, has it?'

Meredith shook her head. She found herself grateful for the understanding, for she knew that it looked to others as if it *had* been easy and she never spoke about it in any other way. She lived with her parents, after all, and they loved Cammie. Meredith's mum looked after the little girl while

Meredith went off to work. What could be simpler? Many
things, of course, as it turned out and topping the list was
being single, being free and being in pursuit of the career she'd
set off to London to have in the first place. That was gone
now, but not forgotten.

Meredith blinked quickly as she realised how long it had
been since she'd had a close friend of her own age. She said,
'Ta,' to Gina and then she considered what real friendship
actually meant: confidences shared, no secrets kept. Yet she
had one that she needed to part with.

She said, 'Gina,' and she took a deep breath, 'I've got something of yours.'

Gina looked puzzled. 'Mine? What?'

Meredith fetched her bag from the top of the chest of
drawers. She dumped its contents next to Gina, and she pawed
through them till she had what she was looking for: the tiny
packet she'd found beneath the basin in Gina's lodging. She
held it in the palm of her hand and she extended it to Gina.

'I broke into your bedsit.' She could feel her face flush pure
red. 'I was looking for something that would tell me . . .'
Meredith thought about it. What *had* she been looking for?
She hadn't known then and she didn't know now. She said, 'I
don't know what I was looking for, but this is what I found,
and I took it. I'm sorry. It was a terrible thing to do.'

Gina looked at the little packet of folded paper, but she
didn't take it. Her shapely eyebrows drew together. 'What
is it?'

Meredith hadn't for a moment considered that what she'd
found might not actually belong to Gina. She'd discovered it
in Gina's room; ergo, it was hers. She withdrew her hand and
removed the wrapping from the roughly shaped circle of gold.
Again, she extended her hand to Gina and this time Gina
picked the small piece of gold from Meredith's palm and held
it in her own.

She said, 'D'you think it's real, Meredith?'

'Real what?'

'Real gold.' Gina peered at it closely. She said, 'It's quite old, isn't it. Look how it's worn down. I c'n make out a head. And there're some letters as well.' She looked up. 'I think it's a coin. Or p'rhaps a medal, an award of some kind. Have you a magnifying glass?'

Meredith thought about this. Her mother used a small one to thread the needle of her sewing machine. She went to fetch it and handed it over. Gina used it to try to make out what was depicted on the object she held. She said, 'Some bloke's head, all right. He's wearing one of those circlet crowns.'

'Like a king would wear into battle, over his armour?'

Gina nodded. 'There're words as well, but I can't make them out. Only they don't look English.'

Meredith thought. A coin or medal possibly fashioned from gold, a king, words in a foreign language. She thought also of where they lived: in the New Forest itself, a place long ago established as the hunting grounds for William the Conqueror. He didn't speak English. None of the court spoke English then. French was their language.

'Is it French?' she asked.

Gina said, 'Can't tell. Have a look yourself. It's not easy to read.'

It wasn't. The letters were blurred, likely with time and usage, which suggested the way any coin would become less easy to read, having been carried round, handled and passed from one person to another.

'I expect it's valuable,' Gina said, 'if only because it's gold. 'Course, I'm only assuming it's gold. I s'pose it could be something else.'

'*What* else?' Meredith said.

'I don't know. Brass? Bronze?'

'Why hide a brass coin? Or a bronze one? I expect it's gold, all right.' She raised her head. 'Only if it's not yours—'

'Honestly? I've never seen it in my life.'

'—then how did it get into your room?'

Gina said, sounding delicate about it, 'Truth to tell, Meredith, if you broke into the room so easily . . .'

Meredith finished the thought. 'Someone else could have done the same. *And* left the coin beneath the basin as well.'

'Is that where you found it?' Gina was quiet, mulling this over. 'Well, either whoever had the room before me hid the coin, left in a hurry, and forgot about it,' she finally said, 'or someone put it there while I've had the room.'

'We need to know who that person was,' Meredith said.

'Yes. I think we do.'

22

Lynley took a call from Isabelle Ardery as he emerged from Psychic Mews. Luckily, he'd set his phone on vibrate or he wouldn't have heard it as the noise from a shop playing Turkish music made hearing anything else impossible. He said, 'Hang on, I've got to get out of here,' and he went outside.

'—has to be the quickest work he's managed to do,' Isabelle Ardery was saying as he brought the mobile to his ear once he reached the pavement. At Lynley's question, she repeated what she'd been telling him: that DI John Stewart, in an admirable display of what he was actually capable of when he wasn't being deliberately difficult, had tracked down all of the phone calls made to and from Jemima Hastings' mobile in the days leading up to her death, on the day of her death and in the days after her death as well. 'We've one call from the cigar shop on the day she died,' Ardery said.

'Jayson Druther?'

'And he confirms that. He says it was about an order for Cuban cigars. He couldn't find them. Her brother phoned her as well, as did Frazer Chaplin, and . . . I admit I've saved what's most intriguing for last. There was a call from Gordon Jossie.'

'Was there indeed?'

'There was his number, large as life. Same one as on the postcard he put up round the Portrait Gallery and Covent Garden. Interesting, isn't it?'

'What've we got on the mobile phone towers?' Lynley asked. 'Anything yet?' They'd want to track the location of the callers when the calls to Jemima's mobile had been made, and checking the pinging off the mobile phone towers was the way to do this. It couldn't pinpoint exactly where a caller had been, but it would get them close to the spot.

'John's checking into that. It's going to take time.'

'Calls following her death?'

'There were messages from Yolanda, from Rob Hastings, from Jayson Druther, from Paolo di Fazio.'

'Nothing from Abbott Langer, then, or Frazer Chaplin? Nothing from Jossie?'

'Nothing at all. Not afterwards. Suggests to me that one of those blokes knew there was no point in phoning, doesn't it?'

'What about calls she made on the day she died?'

'Three to Frazer Chaplin – this is in advance of the one she received from him – and one to Abbott Langer. They need talking to again, those two.'

Lynley told her he would get onto that. He was yards away from the ice rink.

He added what Yolanda had said about her last meeting with Jemima. If Jemima had sought advice from the psychic about hard truths needing to be spoken to someone, it seemed to Lynley that those hard truths were meant to be heard by a man. Since, if the psychic was to be believed, Jemima had apparently been in love with the Irishman, one of the possibilities was that he was the recipient of those hard truths, which she needed to tell. Of course, Lynley told the superintendent, he was not blind to the fact that there were other equally strong potential recipients of Jemima Hastings' message: Abbott Langer would be one of them as would Paolo di Fazio, Jayson Druther, Yukio Matsumoto and any other man whose life touched upon Jemima's such as Gordon Jossie as well as Jemima's own brother Rob.

'Go with Chaplin and Langer first,' Ardery said when he'd finished. 'We'll keep digging at this end.' She was silent for a moment before adding, 'Hard truths? That's what she told you? D'you reckon Yolanda's telling her own truths, Thomas?'

Lynley considered what Yolanda had said about him, about his aura, about the return of a woman – gone but never forgotten – into his life. He had to admit that he didn't know how much of what Yolanda said was based on intuition, how much on watching for subtle reactions in her listener as she spoke, and how much on what she really knew from the 'other side'. He reckoned they could discount just about everything she proclaimed that had no basis in cold facts, and he said, 'But when it comes to Jemima, the psychic wasn't making predictions, guv. She was reporting on what Jemima actually told her.'

'Isabelle,' she said. 'Not guv. We'd got to Isabelle, Thomas.'

He was quiet for a moment, considering this. He finally said, 'Isabelle, then. Yolanda was reporting on what Jemima told her.'

'But she also has a vested interest in leading us astray if she herself put that handbag in the bin.'

'True. But someone else could have put it there. And she could be protecting that person. Let me talk to Abbott Langer.'

The mobile phone records were simultaneously good news and bad news for Isabelle. Anything that led them in the direction of the killer had to be a plus. At the same time, however, anything that led them *away* from Yukio Matsumoto as that killer made her own position perilous. It was one thing if a killer attempting to run from the police was hit by a taxi and severely injured. This was bad for her situation, but it wasn't fatal. It was quite another thing if an innocent psychiatric patient off his meds was hit while in the act of fleeing God-only-knew-what cooked up by his feverish brain. That didn't look good in the present climate of people being mistaken for terrorists and taken out by gunfire in hideous error. The long and short of it was that, mobile phone calls or not, they needed something definitive – something absolutely ironclad – to be the nail in Matsumoto's coffin.

She had watched the Met's pre-emptive press conference, which Stephenson Deacon and the Directorate of Public Affairs had put together. She had to admit that the press office was as smooth and cool as sculpted marble, but they would be, having had years of practice in the subtle art of imparting information meant to be explicative when the very last thing they wanted was to give out incriminating details about any officer from or any action taken by the Met. Deacon and Hillier himself had appeared before the cameras. Hillier had made the prepared statement. The accident in Shaftesbury Avenue was deemed unfortunate, undesirable, unavoidable and every other *un-* that could be excavated from someone's thesaurus. *But* the officers were not armed, he intoned, they had *clearly* identified themselves as officers repeatedly, and *if* a suspect runs from the police when the police want to question him, those police are going to give chase for obvious reasons. In a murder investigation, the safety of the public at large trumps other considerations, especially when someone is making an attempt to evade an interaction with the police. Who those police were by name Hillier didn't divulge. That would come later, Isabelle knew, in the unfortunate event of someone needing to be thrown to the wolves.

Isabelle had a good idea who that person would be. There were follow-up questions from journalists at the press conference, but she didn't listen to them. She got back to work and she was still at work when a phone call came in from Sandra Ardery. The call didn't come through her mobile, which was clever of Sandra, Isabelle thought, since she would have recognised the number and refused to answer. Rather, the call came through channels, ending up on Dorothea Harriman's line. Harriman came personally to share the blessed news: Sandra Ardery would be that grateful for 'a quick word with you, guv. She says it's about the boys?' That inflection on the noun indicated Harriman's unfounded assurance that surely Isabelle would jump to talk to anyone who had something to say about 'the boys'.

Isabelle restrained herself from snatching up the phone and barking '*What*?' at Sandra. She had nothing against Bob's wife, who always made an heroic attempt to remain a neutral party in Isabelle's disputes with her former husband. She nodded at Harriman and took the call.

Sandra's voice was breathy as always. She spoke like someone either doing a bad impersonation of Marilyn Monroe or exhaling clouds of cigarette smoke although she didn't indulge in the latter as far as Isabelle knew. 'Bob said he tried to reach you earlier,' Sandra told her. 'He left a message on your mobile? I did tell him to try your office, but . . . You know Bob.'

Ah yes, Isabelle thought. She said, 'I've been caught up in things here, Sandra. We've had an incident with a bloke in the street.'

'Are you involved in *that*? How dreadful. I saw the news conference. It interrupted my programme.'

Her programme was medical, Isabelle knew. Not a daily hospital drama, this, but rather an intense scientific exploration of debilitating conditions and numerous afflictions, fatal and otherwise. Sandra watched it religiously and took copious notes as a means of monitoring her children's health. As a result, she regularly ferried them to their GP in a state of panic, most recently because of a rash on the younger girl's arm, which Sandra had firmly believed was an outbreak of something called Morgellons disease. Sandra's obsession with this programme was the single subject that Isabelle and Bob Ardery could actually share a chuckle over.

'Yes, I'm involved in an investigation related to that incident,' Isabelle told her, 'which is why I wasn't able to—'

'Shouldn't you have been at the press conference? Isn't that how it's done?'

'It's not "done" any particular way. Why? Is Bob monitoring me?'

'Oh no. Oh no.' Which meant that he was. Which meant that he had probably phoned his wife and told her to switch on the telly post haste because his ex had blotted her copy book properly this time and the proof was at that very moment being offered up for public consumption on the airwaves. 'Anyway, that's not why I'm phoning.'

'Why are you phoning? Are the boys all right?'

'Oh yes. Oh yes. Not to worry about that. They're right as rain. A bit noisy, of course, and a bit rambunctious—'

'They're eight-year-olds.'

'Of course. Of course. I don't mean to imply . . . Isabelle, not to *worry*. I love those boys. You know I do. They're just wildly different to the girls.'

'They don't like dolls and tea parties, if that's what you mean. But you didn't expect them to, did you?'

'Not at all. Not at all. They're lovely. We had an outing yesterday, by the way, the girls and the boys and I. I thought they might enjoy the cathedral in Canterbury.'

'Did you?' A cathedral, Isabelle thought weakly. For eight-year-olds. 'I wouldn't think—'

'Well of course, of course, you're right. It didn't go quite as well as I hoped. I'd *thought* the Thomas Becket part would appeal. You know what I mean. Murder on the high altar? This renegade priest? And it did, rather. At first. But holding their attention was a bit of a problem. I think they would have preferred a trip to the seaside, but I do so worry about sun exposure what with the ozone layer and global warming and the alarming increase in basal cell carcinoma. And they don't like sun block, Isabelle, which I can't understand. The girls slather it right on, but one would think I'm trying to torture the boys, the way they react to it. Did you never use it?'

Isabelle drew in a steadying breath. She said, 'Perhaps not as regularly as I might have done. Now—'

'But it's crucial. You must have known—'

'Sandra. Is there something particular you've phoned about? I'm quite tied up here, you see, so if this is just to chat . . . ?'

'You're busy, you're busy. Of *course*, you're busy. It's only this: do come to lunch. The boys want to see you.'

'I don't think—'

'Please. I do plan to take the girls to my mum's, so it will be just you and the boys.'

'And Bob?'

'And Bob, naturally.' She was silent for a moment and then she said impulsively, 'I did try to get him to *see*, Isabelle. I told him it was only fair. I said you need time with them. I told him I would cook the lunch and have it ready for you and then we could all be off to my mum's. We'd leave you with them and it would be just like a restaurant or a hotel only it would be in our house. But . . . I'm afraid he wouldn't consider that. He just *wouldn't*. I'm so sorry, Isabelle. He means well, you know.'

He means nothing of the kind, Isabelle thought.

'Please come, won't you? The boys . . . I do think they're caught in the middle, don't you? They don't understand. Well, how could they?'

'Doubtless Bob has explained it all.' Isabelle didn't bother to try to keep bitterness at bay.

'He hasn't, he hasn't. Not word, not a *word*. Just that Mummy's in London settling into a new job. Just as you agreed.'

'I *didn't* agree. Where the hell did you get the idea that I agreed?'

'It's only that he said—'

'Would *you* have agreed to hand over your children? *Would* you? Is that the sort of mother you think I am?'

'I know you've tried to be a very good mother. I know you've tried. The boys dote on you.'

'Tried? *Tried*?' Isabelle suddenly heard herself and wanted to pound her fist against her skull as she realised she'd begun to sound exactly like Sandra, with her infuriating habit of doubling words and phrases, a nervous tic that always sounded as if she believed the world was partially deaf and in need of her constant reiteration.

'Oh, I'm not saying this right. I'm not *saying*—'

'I must get back to work.'

'But will you come? Will you consider coming? This isn't

about you and it's not about Bob. It's about the boys. It's about the boys.'

'Don't you bloody dare tell me what this is about.' Isabelle slammed the phone down. She cursed and dropped her head into her hands. I will not, I will *not*, she told herself. And then she laughed although even to her own ears she sounded hysterical. It was that bloody doubling of words. She thought she might go mad.

'Uh . . . Guv?'

She looked up although she knew before she did so that the marginal deference in the tone marked the interruption as coming from DI John Stewart. He stood there with an expression on his face that told her he'd overheard at least part of her conversation with Sandra. She snapped, 'What is it?'

'The Oxfam bin.'

It took her a moment before she got her brain round that one: Bella McHaggis and her recycling front garden. She said to Stewart, 'What about it, John?'

'We've got more than a handbag inside it. We've something you're going to want to see.'

The continued heat wave was, Lynley found, making it a big day at the Queen's Ice and Bowl, particularly on the ice itself. This was likely the coolest spot in London, and everyone from toddlers to pensioners appeared to be taking advantage of it. Some of them simply clung to the railing at the rink's edge and pulled themselves along haphazardly. Others more adventurous wobbled round the rink without assistance, with the more expert skaters trying to avoid them. In the very middle of the rink, future Olympians practised jumps and spins with varied degrees of success while, negotiating the crowd for space wherever possible, ice dancing instructors plied their trade with inept partners, making brave attempts to mirror Torvill and Dean.

Lynley had to wait to speak to Abbott Langer who was

giving a lesson in the middle of the ice. He'd been pointed out to Lynley by the skate hire bloke who referred to Langer as 'the git with the hair'. Lynley hadn't been certain what was meant by that until he caught a glimpse of the instructor. Then he saw there was no other description needed. He'd not seen such a hirsute Swiss roll outside of a photograph, ever.

No matter the case, Langer could certainly skate. He launched himself off the ice in an effortless jump as Lynley watched, demonstrating its ease for a young male pupil who looked round ten years old. The child tried it and landed on his bum. Langer glided over and lifted him to his feet. He bent his head to the child's, they spoke for a moment, and Langer demonstrated a second time. He was very good. He was smooth. He was strong. Lynley wondered if he was also a killer.

When the lesson finished, Lynley intercepted the skating instructor as he said goodbye to his pupil and put guards on the blades of his skates. Could he have a word? Lynley enquired politely. He showed his identification.

Langer said, 'I've spoken to the other two. Black bloke and some dumpy woman. I don't see how I could have anything else to say.'

'Loose ends,' Lynley told him. 'This shouldn't take long.' He indicated the café that formed a division between the ice rink and the bowling alley. He said, 'Let's have a coffee, Mr Langer,' and he waited till Langer resigned himself to a conversation.

Lynley bought two coffees and took them to the table where Langer dropped his bulky body. He was turning a salt cellar in his fingers. These were thick and strong looking, and his hands were large like the rest of him.

'Why did you lie to the other officers, Mr Langer?' Lynley asked him without preamble. 'You must have known every-thing you said would be checked.'

Langer made no reply to this. Wise man, Lynley thought. He was waiting for more.

'There are no ex-wives. Nor are there children,' Lynley said. 'Why lie about something so easy to disprove?'

Langer took a moment to tear open two packets of sugar, which he dumped into his coffee. He did not stir it. 'It's nothing to do with what happened to Jemima. *I've* nothing to do with that.'

'Yes, but you would say that, wouldn't you?' Lynley pointed out. 'Anyone would.'

'It's a matter of consistency. That's all.'

'Explain.'

'I tell everyone the same. Three ex-wives, children. It keeps things simple.'

'That's important to you?'

Langer looked away. From where they sat, the ice rink was visible: all the lovely young things flying about – or otherwise – in their colourful tights and skimpy skirts. 'I like to remain uninvolved,' he said. 'Ex-wives and children help, I find.'

'Uninvolved with whom?'

'I'm an instructor. That's all I do with them, whatever their ages. Sometimes a young one or a middle-aged one or *any* of them develop an interest because we're close on the ice. It's stupid, it doesn't mean anything, and I don't take advantage. Ex-wives make that possible.'

'With Jemima Hastings as well?'

'Jemima took lessons from me,' Langer told him. 'That's the extent of it. She used me, rather.'

'For what?'

'I told the others this already. I wasn't lying about that. She wanted to keep her eye on Frazer.'

'She phoned you on the day she died. Along with the truth about ex-wives and children, you didn't mention that to the other detectives.'

Langer took up his coffee. 'I hadn't remembered the call.'

'And do you now?'

He looked reflective. 'Yes, actually. She was looking for Frazer.'

'Was she supposed to be meeting him at the cemetery?'

'I rather think she was checking up on him. She did that often. Anyone Frazer was involved with ended up doing that. Jemima wasn't the first and she wouldn't have been the last. Long as he worked here that went on.'

'A woman checking up on him?'

'A woman, who didn't quite trust him, making sure he was walking the straight and narrow. He rarely did.'

'And for Jemima?'

'It was likely business as usual for Frazer, but I don't know, do I? Anyway, I couldn't help her that day, which she ought to have realised before she rang me.'

'Why?'

'Because of the time. He isn't here at that hour. Had she thought about it, she would have known he wouldn't be here. But he wasn't answering his mobile, she said. She rung him a few times and he wasn't answering and she wanted to know was he still here where, perhaps, he wouldn't be able to hear it with all the noise.' He indicated the clamour round them. 'But really, she had to have known he'd already left for home. Anyway, that's what I told her.'

For home, Lynley thought. 'He didn't go from here directly to Duke's Hotel?'

'He always goes home first. He says he doesn't like to keep his Duke's kit here where it could get dirty, but knowing Frazer, there's another reason.' He made a crude gesture with his hands, an indication of sexual intercourse. 'Likely he's been doing the job on someone en route, between here and Duke's. Or there at home, even. It wouldn't surprise me. That would be his style. Anyway, Jemima said she'd been leaving him messages and she was feeling panicky.'

'She used that term? Panicky?'

'No. But I could hear it in her voice.'

'Was it fear perhaps? Not panic, but fear? She was phoning from a cemetery, after all. People are sometimes frightened in cemeteries.'

Langer shrugged off this idea. He said, 'I don't think that's what it was. 'f you ask me, I think it was dread of having to look squarely at something she's been denying.'

Interesting point, Lynley thought. He said, 'Carry on.'

'Frazer,' he said. 'I expect she wanted very much to think Frazer Chaplin was the one, if you know what I mean, the one in inverted commas. But I expect in her heart she knew he wasn't.'

'What makes you draw the latter conclusion?'

Langer smiled thinly. 'Because it's the conclusion they always reached, Inspector. Every last woman who hooked up with the bloke.'

Thus Lynley greatly anticipated meeting the male paragon he'd been hearing about. He made his way to St James's Place, a nearly hidden cul-de-sac where Duke's Hotel formed a stately L of red-brick, decorative ironwork, oriel window and sumptuous swathes of ivy tumbling from first floor balconies. He left the Healey Elliott under the watchful eye of a uniformed doorman and entered into the reserved hush one usually encounters in places of worship. Could he be helped? he was asked by a passing bellboy.

The bar, he replied.

The bar ran heavily to naval portraits and prints of ruined castles, with a painting of Admiral Nelson in his post-arm days taking a predominant position as one would expect of a sea-oriented décor. The bar comprised three rooms – two of which were separated by a fireplace in which, mercifully, no fire was burning – and it was furnished with upholstered armchairs and round, glass-topped tables at which were gathered mostly business people at this time of day. They appeared to be tossing back gins and tonic, with a few hardier souls getting glassy-eyed over martinis. This was apparently the signature drink of one of the bartenders, an Italian man with a marked accent who asked Lynley if he wanted the speciality which, he was told, was neither shaken *nor* stirred but rather babied along into some sort of miraculous nectar.

Lynley demurred. He said he wouldn't mind a Pellegrino, if they had it. Lime and no ice. And was Frazer Chaplin available for a chat? He produced his identification. The bartender – who bore the unlikely non-Italian name of Heinrich – gave no reaction at all to the presence of a policeman, in possession of a cultured accent or not. Indifferently, he said Frazer Chaplin had not yet arrived. He was expected – with a glance at an impressive watch – in the next quarter hour.

Did Frazer work regular hours? Lynley enquired from the bartender. Or did he, perhaps, just fill in when things were busy in the hotel?

Regular hours, he was told. 'Wouldn't have taken the job otherwise,' Heinrich said.

'Why not?'

'Evening shift is busiest. The tips are better. So are the customers.'

Lynley raised an eyebrow, seeking elucidation, which Heinrich was happy to give him. It seemed Frazer enjoyed the attention of various ladies of varying ages who frequented the bar at Duke's Hotel most evenings. These were international businesswomen mostly, in town for one reason or another, and Frazer was apparently willing to give them additional reasons to hang about.

'Has an eye out for a lady who'll keep him how he wants to be kept,' was how Heinrich put it. He shook his head, but his expression was unmistakably fond. 'Fancies himself a gigolo.'

'Is that working for him?'

Heinrich chuckled. 'Not yet. But that's not kept the lad from trying. He wants to own a boutique hotel, just like this place. But he wants someone else to buy it for him.'

'He's looking for a great deal of money, then.'

'That's Frazer.'

Lynley thought about this and how it related to the truths

Jemima had wished to speak. To a man hoping for money from
a woman, the message that she wouldn't be handing it over
to him would indeed be a very hard truth. As would be the
possible truth that she wanted nothing more to do with him
because she'd discovered he was after her money . . . *if* she had
money in the first place. But again and maddeningly, there
were other truths when it came to Jemima. To Paolo di Fazio
there was a hard truth that might have been told: that she was
going to take up life with Frazer Chaplin despite Paolo's feelings for her. As to everyone from Abbott Langer to Yukio
Matsumoto, doubtless a little delving was going to reveal there
were truths everywhere needing to be spoken.

Lynley did the maths on the time of Frazer Chaplin's daily
arrival in the bar of Duke's Hotel: the Irishman had ninety
minutes between the hour he left the ice rink and when he
began work at this location. Was it time enough to race up to
Stoke Newington, murder Jemima Hastings, and get to his
second job? Lynley didn't see how. Not only had Abbott Langer
suggested that the man went to Putney before heading to
Duke's, but even had that not been the case, the London traffic
would have made it next to impossible. And Lynley couldn't
see the killer getting to that cemetery on public transport.

When Frazer Chaplin arrived at Duke's, Lynley had the
uneasy feeling he'd seen the man before. Exactly where he'd
seen him hovered on the edge of his consciousness, but for
the moment he couldn't insert the face into a location. He
thought about where he'd been in recent days, but nothing
clicked. He let it go for the moment.

He was no judge of male looks, but he could see Chaplin's
appeal to women who liked their men dark and edgy, possessing
an air of danger, a cross between a modern day Heathcliff and
Sweeney Todd. He wore a cream jacket and white shirt with
a red bow tie over his dark trousers, an outfit giving reasonable testimony to why he would want to change his clothes at
home and not carry them round with him or leave them at
the ice rink. Like Abbott Langer, his hair verged on black,

but unlike Langer's it was styled more in keeping with the times. It looked newly washed and he appeared to be freshly shaven. His hands looked manicured as well, and he wore an opal ring on his left ring finger.

He joined Lynley at once, having been given the word by the bartender. Lynley had taken a table quite near to the gleaming mahogany bar, and Frazer dropped into one of the chairs, extended his hand, and said, 'Heinrich tells me you'd like a word? Have you something new to ask me? I've spoken to some other coppers already.'

Lynley introduced himself and said, 'You appear to be the last person to speak to Jemima Hastings, Mr Chaplin.'

He replied in his lilting accent which, Lynley noted, would likely have appealed to the ladies as much as Chaplin's tough masculinity, 'Do I, now,' but he made it a statement and not a question. 'And how would you reckon that, Inspector?'

'From her mobile phone records,' Lynley told him.

'Ah,' he said. 'Well I expect the very last person to speak to Jemima would be the bloke who killed her, unless she was jumped on without preliminaries.'

'She seems to have phoned you a number of times in the hours leading up to her death. She phoned Abbott Langer as well, looking for you, according to him. Abbott seems to feel she was romantically involved with you, and he isn't the only person to make that observation.'

'Would I be wrong to expect the other person is one Paolo di Fazio?' Chaplin asked.

'Where there's smoke, there's generally something in flames, in my experience,' Lynley said. 'What was your phone call about, Mr Chaplin?'

Frazer tapped his fingers on the glass-topped table. A silver bowl of mixed nuts sat upon it, and he reached for a few and held them in the palm of his hand. He said, 'She was a lovely girl. I'll give you that. But while I might have seen her on the outside now and again—'

'On the outside?'

'Away from Mrs McHaggis's lodgings. While I might have seen her now and again – the pub, the high street, having a meal somewhere, at a film, even? – that would be the extent of it. Now, I'll also grant that it could have appeared to others we were involved. Truth to tell, it could have appeared that way to Jemima as well. Her coming to the ice rink like she did, her talking to that gypsy woman who does the fortunes, that sort of thing makes it look like the two of us had it going. But more than being friendly to her? More than being friendly like I would to anyone I shared lodgings with? More than merely having or *trying* to have a friendship? That's the stuff of fantasy, Inspector.'

'Whose?'

'What?'

'Whose fantasy?'

He popped the nuts into his mouth. He sighed. 'Inspector, Jemima leaped to conclusions. Have you never known a woman to do that? One moment you're buying a lager for a girl, and the next she's got you married with kids and living in a rose-covered cottage in the countryside. That's not happened to you?'

'Not in my memory.'

'Lucky you are, then, for it's happened to me.'

'Tell me about the phone call on the day of her death.'

'I swear to the Holy Ghost, man, I don't even remember making it. But if I did, and if, as you say, she'd been phoning me as well, then likely as not I was merely returning her call, fending her off in one way or another. Or at least attempting to. She had it for me. I won't deny that. But there's no way I was encouraging the girl.'

'And the day of her death?'

'What about it?'

'Tell me where you were. What you did. Who saw you.'

'I've been over all this with the other two—'

'But not with me. And sometimes there are details that one officer misses or fails to put in a report. Please humour me.'

'There's nothing to humour you with. I worked at the ice rink, I went home to shower and change, I came here. It's what I do every day, for Jesus' sake. There's someone at every point to confirm this, so you can't be thinking that I somehow scarpered up to Stoke Newington to kill Jemima Hastings. Especially as I had no bloody reason to do it.'

'How do you get from the ice rink to this job, Mr Chaplin?'

'I've a scooter,' he said.

'Have you indeed?'

'I do. And if you're thinking that I'd've had the time to weave through traffic and make it up to Stoke Newington and then back here . . . Well, you best come with me.' Frazer rose, picking up a few more nuts and tossing them into his mouth. He had a brief word with Heinrich and then led the way out of the bar and out of the hotel as well.

At the far end of the cul de sac that was St James's Place, Frazer Chaplin's motor scooter stood. It was a Vespa, the sort of vehicle that zips up and down the streets of every major town in Italy. But unlike those scooters, this one was not only painted a violent and completely unforgettable lime green, it was also covered with bright red advertising transfers for a product called DragonFly Tonics, in effect becoming a mobile billboard not unlike those seen occasionally on black cabs round town.

Chaplin said, 'Would I be mad enough to take myself up to Stoke Newington on that? To leave it parked *anywhere* and then do a dash to kill Jemima? What d'you take me for, man, a fool? Would you be likely to forget you'd seen that thing parked hither or thither? *I* wouldn't, and I doubt anyone else would either. Take a bloody photo of it if you want. Show it round up there. Go to every house and shop in every street there is, and you'll see the truth of it.'

'Which is what?'

'That I bloody well didn't kill Jemima.'

When the police ask Ian Barker on tape, 'Why did you make the baby naked?' he does not reply at first. His grandmother keens in the background, a chair scrapes the floor, and someone taps on the table top. 'You know that baby was naked, don't you? When we found him, he was naked. You know that, don't you, Ian?' are the next questions, and they are followed by, 'You yourself made him naked before you used the hairbrush on him. We know that because your fingerprints are on that hairbrush. Were you angry, Ian? Had Johnny done something to make you angry? Did you want to sort him out with the hairbrush?'

Ian finally says, 'I didn't do nothing to that kid. You ask Reggie. You ask Mikey. Mikey was the one changed his nappy, anyways. He knew how. He got brothers. I don't. And Reg was the one nicked the bananas, eh?'

Michael says in response to the first mention of the hairbrush, 'I never. I never. Ian told me he poohed. Ian said I was meant to change him. But I never,' and when asked about the bananas, he begins to cry. Ultimately he says, 'It got poo on it, didn't it. That baby was in the muck there on the ground . . . He was just laying there . . .' whereupon his weeping turns to wailing.

Reggie Arnold addresses his mother, as before, saying, 'Mum, Mum, there wasn't no hairbrush. I never made that baby naked. I never touched him. Mum, I never touched that baby. Mikey kicked him, Mum. See, he was on the ground and he was on his face 'cause . . . Mum, he must've fell. And Mikey kicked him.'

When told of Reggie's claim, following on the heels of Ian's claims, Michael Spargo finally begins to tell the rest of the story in what is an attempt to defend himself against what he obviously sees as an effort on the part of the other two boys to shift blame to him. He admits to using his foot on John Dresser, but he claims it was only to turn the baby over in order 'to help him breathe right'.

From this point forward, the excruciating details slowly come out: the blows to little John Dresser from the boys' feet, the use of copper tubing upon him like swords or whips, and ultimately the discarded concrete blocks. Parts of the story, however – the exact details of what happened with the banana and the hair-brush, for example – Michael refuses to speak about altogether, and this silence about those two pieces of evidence remains when the other two boys are questioned as well. But the postmortem examination of John Dresser's body in addition to the level of the boys' continued distress when the subject of the hairbrush comes up indicates the sexual component of the crime just as its terrible ferocity substantiates the deep well of anger each boy called upon in the final moments of the toddler's life.

Once a confession was obtained from the boys, the Crown Prosecutors took the highly unusual and equally controversial decision *not* to present the full details of John Dresser's ante-mortem injuries to the court during the subsequent trial. Their reasoning was twofold. First, they had not only the confessions but also the CCTV films, the eyewitness testimonies and copious forensic evidence, all of which they believed established without doubt the guilt of Ian Barker, Michael Spargo and Reggie Arnold. Second, they knew that Donna and Alan Dresser were going to be present for the trial as was their right, and the CPS did not wish to exacerbate the parents' agony and grief by revealing to them the extent of the brutality that had been inflicted upon their child prior to and after his death. Wasn't it enough, they reasoned, to learn one's child – so recently out of infanthood – had been abducted, dragged across town, stripped naked, whipped with copper tubing, stoned with broken concrete and dumped into an abandoned Portaloo? Additionally, they had complete confessions from at least two of the boys (Ian Barker only going so far as admitting finally that he was in the Barriers that day and he saw John Dresser, before holding firm to 'Maybe I did something and maybe I didn't' for the rest of his interviews), and more than that seemed completely unnecessary for a conviction. It must be argued, however, that a third reason could well exist for the CPS's silence on the matter of John Dresser's *internal* injuries: had these injuries become known, questions regarding the psychological state of his killers would have arisen, and these questions might have led the jury ineluctably towards manslaughter instead of murder because they would necessarily have been instructed to consider the 1957 Act of Parliament, which declares that a person 'shall not be convicted of murder if he was suffering from such abnormality of mind . . . as substantially impaired his mental responsibility for his acts' at the time of the crime. *Abnormality of mind* are the key words here, and John's further injuries do much to suggest deep abnormality on the part of all three of his killers. But a verdict of manslaughter would have been unthinkable, considering the climate in which the boys were tried. While the venue for the trial had been changed, the crime had gone from being a national story to an international story. Shakespeare declares that 'blood will have blood', and this situation was an example of that.

Some have argued that when the boys stole the hairbrush from the Items-for-a-Pound shop in the Barriers, they knew full well what they were going to do with it. But to me, this suggests both reasoning and planning far beyond that of which they were capable. I don't deny that perhaps my reluctance to believe in such a degree of premeditation is attached to a personal disinclination for considering the potential for pure iniquity to exist in the minds and hearts of ten- and eleven-year-old boys. Nor will I deny my preference for believing that the use of that hairbrush was the work of impulse. What I certainly will agree with is what the fact of that hairbrush illustrates about the boys: those who abuse and violate have been abused and violated themselves, not once but repeatedly.

When the hairbrush was brought up in interviews, it was a subject that not one of the boys was willing to talk about. On tape, their reactions vary, from Ian's assertion that 'wasn't no hairbrush that I ever saw', to Reggie's attempt at innocence with, 'Mikey might've nicked one from that shop but I don't know that, do I' and 'I never took no hairbrush, Mum. You got to believe I never would've took no hairbrush', to Michael's 'We didn't have no hairbrush, we didn't have no hairbrush, we didn't, didn't,' which rises in what sounds like panic with every denial. When Michael is gently told, 'You know one of you boys took that hairbrush, son,' he agrees that, 'Reggie might've, then, but I didn't see' and 'I don't know what happened to it, do I.'

It is only when the presence of the hairbrush at the Dawkins building site is brought up (along with the fingerprints upon it, in conjunction with the blood and the faecal matter on its handle) that the reactions of the boys escalate to their most emotive. Michael's begins with 'I never . . . I told you and told you I didn't . . . I didn't take no hairbrush . . . there weren't no hairbrush at all' and segues to 'It were Reggie done it to that baby . . . Reggie wanted to . . . Ian took it from him . . . I said to stop and Reggie did it.' Reggie, on the other hand, addresses all his remarks to his mother, saying, 'Mum, I never . . . I wouldn't hurt no baby . . . Maybe I hit him once but I never . . . I took his snowsuit off him but it was all mucked up, that's why . . . He were crying, Mum. I knew not to hurt him if he were crying.' During this, Rudy Arnold is silent, but Laura can be heard throughout, moaning, 'Reggie, Reggie, what've you done to us?' as the social worker quietly asks her to drink some water, perhaps in an attempt to silence her. As for Ian, he finally begins to cry when the extent of John Dresser's injuries are read to him. His grandmother can be heard weeping along with him and her words, 'Sweet Jesus, save him. Save him, Lord,' suggest she's accepted the boy's culpability.

It is at the point of the hairbrush's introduction into the interviews – three days after the toddler's body was found – that the boys confess fully to the crime. It is, perhaps, one of the additional horrors of the murder of John Dresser that when the perpetrators of this ghastly crime confessed, only one of them had a parent present. Rudy Arnold sat by his son through-out. Both Ian Barker and Michael Spargo were accompanied only by social workers.

23

Whoever had killed Jemima Hastings, as things turned out, was someone who'd worn a yellow shirt to do it. Lynley learned the details of this article of clothing upon his return to New Scotland Yard, where the team was meeting in the incident room and a photo of the shirt – now in the possession of forensics – was newly up on one of the china boards.

Barbara Havers and Winston Nkata had arrived from the New Forest, Lynley saw, and he also saw from Barbara's expression that she wasn't happy about being recalled to London, blood-stained yellow shirt or not. She was fighting back a need to speak, which in her case meant fighting back a need to argue with the acting superintendent. Nkata, on the other hand, seemed acquiescent enough, displaying the easiness of disposition that had long been an integral part of his character. He lounged at the back of the room, sipping from a plastic cup. He nodded at Lynley and tilted his head towards Havers. He, too, knew she was itching to walk on the wrong side of whatever line Isabelle Ardery had drawn for her.

'. . . still unconscious,' Ardery was saying. 'But the surgeon indicates he'll be brought round tomorrow. When that happens, he's ours.' And to Lynley, bringing him fully into the picture, 'The shirt was among the clobber in the Oxfam bin. It's got a significant blood stain on the front of it, right side, and on the right sleeve and cuff. It's with forensics but for the moment we're assuming the blood is our victim's. Agreed?' She didn't wait for Lynley's reply. 'Right, then. Let's put a few things together. We've two Oriental hairs in the victim's hand, no defensive wounds on her, a pierced carotid artery and a Japanese man in possession of the murder weapon and with her blood on his clothing. What've you got to add from today, Thomas?'

For the team, Lynley recapped what he'd learned from Yolanda. He added for them, and for Isabelle as well, the details he'd had from Abbott Langer, the bartender Heinrich and Frazer Chaplin. He knew he was about to devastate Isabelle's position, but there was no way round it: he concluded by saying, with a nod at the large photo of the shirt, 'I think we have two individuals interacting with Jemima in Abney Park Cemetery, guv: there was nothing in Matsumoto's wardrobe even vaguely resembling that shirt. He wears black and white – not bright colours – and even if that weren't the case, the clothing he had on that day, a dinner jacket, was itself stained with her blood as you've just said. He can't have been wearing both the dinner jacket and the yellow shirt. So with yet another article of clothing blood-stained and with Jemima going to the cemetery to speak with a man, we've got two blokes there instead of one.'

'That's how I've got it figured,' Barbara Havers put in quickly. 'So, guv, it seems to me that recalling Winnie and me to London—'

'One bloke to kill her and the other to . . . what?' John Stewart asked.

'To watch over her, I suspect,' Lynley said. 'Something at which Matsumoto, seeing himself as her guardian angel, failed miserably.'

'Hang on, Thomas,' Ardery said.

'Hear me out,' Lynley replied. He saw her eyes widen slightly and he knew she wasn't pleased. He was going in a completely different direction, and God knew she had very good reason for the investigation's maintaining its progress towards Matsumoto as the killer. 'A bloke met her there to hear her hard truths,' Lynley said. 'We've got this from the psychic and, her profession aside, I think she's to be believed. If we ignore all Yolanda's additional maundering about Jemima and the house in Oxford Road, she's merely relating to us her own encounters with the woman. So from her we know that a man in Jemima's life needed to hear something and Yolanda suggested a "place of peace" for their meeting. Jemima knew about the cemetery as she'd been photographed there. That was the spot she chose.'

'With Matsumoto just happening to be there?' Ardery demanded.

'He probably followed her.'

'All right. But let's assume this wasn't the only time he followed her. Why would it have been? Why only on this particular day? That makes no sense. So if he was stalking her, he likely was the man who needed to hear the hard truths, those being leave me alone or I'll have you for stalking. But he anticipates this is the way the conversation will go and, like all mad stalkers, he's come with a weapon. Yellow shirt or not, blood-stained dinner jacket or not, how do you explain that weapon in his possession, Thomas?'

'How do *you* explain the blood on two kinds of clothing?' John Stewart put in.

Glances were exchanged among the others present. It was his tone. He was taking sides. Lynley didn't want this. It was not his intention to turn the investigation into a political intrigue. He said, 'He sees her meet someone in the cemetery. They decamp to the chapel annexe for a more private word.'

'*Why?*' Isabelle asked. 'They're already in a private spot. Why does it need to be more private?'

'Because whoever she's there to meet is there to kill her,' Havers put in. 'So *he* makes the request. "Let's go over there. Let's go in that building." Guv, we need to—'

Lynley held up a hand. 'Perhaps they're arguing. One of them gets up, begins to pace. The other follows. They go inside but only the killer emerges. Matsumoto sees this. He waits for Jemima to come out as well. When she doesn't, he goes to investigate.'

'For God's sake wouldn't he notice the other bloke had *blood* on his shirt?'

'He may have done. Perhaps that's why he went to investigate. But I think it's more likely that the other bloke would have taken that shirt off and hidden it. He'd *have* to have done so. He can't leave the cemetery with blood all over him.'

'Matsumoto did.'

'Which is what suggests to me that he *didn't* kill her, not that he did.'

'This is bollocks,' Ardery said.

'Guv, it isn't.' Havers broke in, and her tone declared she was serious this time. She *would* be heard and damn the consequences. 'There's something not right in Hampshire. We need to get back there. Winnie and I—'

'Oh you two lovebirds,' John Stewart put in.

Lynley said automatically, 'That'll do, John,' forgetting his return from acting superintendent to inspector.

'Sod off,' Havers told Stewart, undeterred. 'Guv, there's more to be looked into in the New Forest. This bloke Whiting . . . ? Something's not right about him. There're contradictions all over the place.'

'Such as?' Isabelle asked.

Havers began leafing through her disaster of a notebook. She shot a look at Winston, saying *Get involved* here, mate. Winston stirred and came to her aid. 'Jossie's not what he seems, guv,' he said. 'He and Whiting are connected somehow. We've not got to the root of things but the fact that Whiting knew 'bout Jossie's apprenticeship suggests to us – to Barb an' me – that he was behind Jossie getting it in the first place. An' *that* suggests he forged those letters from the technical college. We can't see who else might've done it.'

'For God's sake, why would he do that?'

'Could be Jossie's got something on him,' Nkata said. 'We don't know what. Yet.'

Havers said, 'But we could find out if you'd let us—'

'You'll stay here in London as you've been ordered.'

'But, guv—'

'No.' And to Lynley, 'It's just as easy to work this the other way round, Thomas. She meets Matsumoto in the cemetery. She goes with Matsumoto into the chapel annexe. They have their words, he uses the weapon on her and he flees. The *other*, wearing a yellow shirt, sees this. He goes into the annexe. He comes to her aid but she has a wound that's beyond aid. He gets her blood on him. He panics. He *knows* how this is going to look once his history with Jemima comes to light. He *knows* the cops look hard at whoever first comes upon the victim and reports it, and he can't afford that. So he runs.'

'And then what?' John Stewart asked. 'He puts that shirt in McHaggis's Oxfam bin? Along with the handbag? And what *about* the handbag? Why take it?'

'Could be Matsumoto took the handbag. Could be he put it in the bin. He'd want to cast blame, to muddy the waters.'

'So,' Stewart said acerbically, 'let me get this straight. This Matsumoto and the other bloke – damn well unbeknownst to each other – *both* put a piece of incriminating evidence in the very same bin? In an entirely different area of London from where the crime was committed? Bloody hell, woman. Jesus God. What exactly d'you think are the odds of that?' He blew out a derisive breath and looked at the others. *Idiot cow*, his expression said.

Isabelle's face was perfect stone. She said to Stewart, 'In my office. Now.'

Stewart hesitated just long enough to signal his scorn. He and Isabelle engaged in a moment of locked gazes before the acting superintendent strode out of the room. Stewart rose in a lazy movement and followed her.

A tight silence ensued. Someone whistled low. Lynley approached the china board for a closer look at the photo of the yellow shirt. There was a movement next to him, and he saw that Havers had come to join him.

She said to him in a low voice, 'You know she's making the wrong decisions.'

'Barbara—'

'You *know*. No one wants to kick his arse into the next time zone as much as I do, but he's right this time.'

She meant John Stewart. Lynley couldn't disagree. Isabelle's desperation to bend the facts to fit what she needed to believe about Matsumoto was truncating the investigation. She was in the worst position possible: her temporary status at the Met, her first investigation and its deterioration into a welter of inconceivable circumstances with a suspect in hospital because he'd done a runner, that suspect the brother of a famed cellist with access to a fiery solicitor, the press taking up the story, Hillier involved, and the abominable Stephenson Deacon on board to attempt to manipulate the media, and evidence pointing in every possible direction. Lynley wasn't sure how things could get worse for Isabelle. Hers was turning out to be a baptism not by fire but rather by conflagration.

He said, 'Barbara, I'm not sure what you'd have me do.'

'Talk to her. She'll listen to you. Webberly would've and you'd've talked to Webberly if he'd been going at things like this. You know you would. And if you were in the same position as she is just now, you'd listen to *us*. We're a team for a reason.' She drove her hands into her ill-cut hair in typical fashion, pulling on it roughly. '*Why* did she call us back from Hampshire?'

'She has limited resources. Every investigation has.'

'Oh bloody *hell*!' Havers stalked off.

Lynley called after her, but she was gone. He was left facing the china board, staring at the yellow shirt. He saw at once what it was telling him and what it should have told Isabelle. He realised he too was in an unenviable position. He considered how best to use the information before him.

Barbara couldn't understand why Lynley wouldn't take a stand. She *could* understand why he might not want to do that in front of the rest of the team since John bloody Stewart hardly needed encouragement to pull a Mr Christian on the acting superintendent's Captain Bligh. But why not have a word with her in private? That was the part that didn't make sense. Lynley wasn't intimidated by anyone – his thousand-and-one run-ins with AC Hillier surely gave testimony to that – so she knew he wasn't unnerved by the prospect of going eyeball-to-eyeball with Isabelle Ardery. That being the case, what was stopping him? She didn't know. What she did know was that for some reason, he wasn't being himself when she needed him to be just that person, the one he'd always been, to her and to everyone.

That he wasn't being the Thomas Lynley she recognised and had worked with for years troubled her more than she wanted to admit. It seemed to mark the degree to which he'd changed and the degree to which things that had once mattered to him no longer mattered. It was as if he was floating out there in some sort of unnamable void, lost to them in ways that were crucial but undefined.

Barbara didn't want to define them now. She just wanted to get home. Because Winston had driven them up from the New Forest, she was forced into a journey on the blasted Northern Line at the worst time of day in the worst possible weather, and she was additionally forced to make this journey crammed into the area in front of the carriage doors, wondering why the hell people would *not* move down the aisle into the bloody carriage itself, as she was jostled into the broad back-side of a woman shrieking into her mobile phone about 'fooking get home an' I mean it this time, Clive, or I swear I'm taking the knife and cutting them off', when she wasn't being pushed into the odoriferous armpit of a T-shirted adolescent listening to something loud and obnoxious through his earphones.

To make matters worse, she had her holdall with her and when she finally reached Chalk Farm station, she had to jerk it out of the carriage and in the process she broke one of its straps. She swore. She kicked it. She scraped her ankle against one of its buckles. She swore again.

She trudged home from the station wondering when the weather would break, bringing a storm that would wash the dust from the leaves and scour the smog-laden air. Her mood grew even fouler as she lugged the holdall behind her, and everything that was infuriating her seemed to have as its source Isabelle Ardery. But considering Isabelle Ardery led her back to considering Thomas Lynley, and Barbara had had enough of that for one day.

I need a shower, Barbara decided. I need a fag. I need a drink. Hell on wheels: I need a life.

By the time she arrived home, she was dripping perspiration and her shoulders ached. She tried to tell herself it was the weight of the holdall, but she knew it was tension, plain and simple. She reached the front door of her bungalow with more relief than she'd felt in ages at being home. She didn't even care that, inside the place, it was hot enough to bake bread. She opened windows and dug her small fan from a cupboard. She lit a cigarette, inhaled deeply, blessed the mere existence of nicotine, fell into one of the plain kitchen chairs and looked round her extremely humble little abode.

She'd dropped her holdall by the door, so she hadn't seen what was on the daybed at first. But now, sitting at the kitchen table, she saw that her A-line skirt – that article best suited to a woman with a figure like hers, according to Hadiyyah – had been tailored. The hem had been taken up, the skirt had been ironed and a complete outfit had been assembled upon the bed: the skirt, a crisp businesslike new blouse, sheer tights, a scarf, even a chunky bracelet. And her shoes had been polished as well. They fairly gleamed. The good fairy had been here.

Barbara rose and approached the bed. She had to admit, it all looked good together, especially the bracelet which she never would have considered purchasing, let alone wearing. She picked it up for a closer inspection. A gift tag was tied to it with a purple ribbon. *Surprise!* had been printed on the card along with *Welcome Home!* and the gift giver's name, as if she had not known who had arranged these items for her: Hadiyyah Khalidah.

Barbara's mood altered at once. Amazing, she thought, how such a little thing, a mere act of thoughtfulness . . . She stubbed out her cigarette and ducked into the tiny bathroom. A quarter of an hour saw her showered, refreshed and dressed. She brushed some blusher on her face in a bow to Hadiyyah's make-over efforts, and she left her bungalow. She went to the lower ground floor flat of the Big House, which faced onto the summer-dry lawn.

The French windows were open, and cooking sounds along with conversation came from within. Hadiyyah was chatting to her father and Barbara could hear from her voice that she was excited.

She knocked and called out, 'Anyone home?' to which Hadiyyah cried, 'Barbara! You're back! Brilliant!'

When Hadiyyah came to the door, she looked altered to Barbara. Taller, somehow, although that didn't make sense as Barbara had hardly been gone long enough for the little girl to have grown. 'Oh, this is so lovely,' Hadiyyah cried. 'Dad! Barbara's here. C'n she stay for dinner?'

'No, no,' Barbara stammered. 'Please, don't, kiddo. I only came to say thank you. I've just got back. I found the skirt. And the rest. And what a bloody nice surprise it was.'

'I hemmed it myself,' Hadiyyah informed her proudly. 'Well, *maybe* Mrs Silver helped a bit 'cause *sometimes* I make my stitches crooked. But were you surprised? I ironed it as well. Did you find the bracelet?' She bounced from foot to foot. 'Did you like it? When I saw it, I asked Dad could we buy it 'cause you know how you got to accessorise, Barbara.'

'From your lips to my memory,' Barbara told her reverently. 'But I couldn't've found anything as perfect as that.'

'It's the colour, isn't it?' Hadiyyah said. 'And part of what makes it so wonderful is the size. See, what I learned is that *size* of the accessory depends upon *size* of the person wearing it. But *that* has to do with one's features and bones and body type, not with one's weight and height, if you know what I mean. So if you look at your wrists – like if you compare them to mine – what you c'n see—'

'*Khushi.*' Azhar came to the door of the kitchen, wiping his hands on a tea towel.

Hadiyyah turned to him. 'Barbara found the surprise!' she announced. 'She likes it, Dad. And what about the blouse, Barbara? Did you like the new blouse? I wished I picked it out, but I didn't. Dad picked it out, didn't you, Dad? I wanted a different one.'

'Don't tell me. You wanted one with a pussy bow.'

'Well . . .' She shifted on her feet, doing a little tap dancing in the doorway. 'Not exactly. But it *did* have ruffles. Not a lot, you see. But there was a sweet little ruffle down the front hiding the buttons and I liked it awfully. I thought it was brilliant. But Dad said you wouldn't ever wear ruffles. *I* said fashion is all about expanding one's horizons, Barbara. But *he* said horizons can be expanded only so far, *and* he said the tailored blouse was better. *I* said the neckline of a blouse is meant to copy the shape your jawline makes and your face is rounded, isn't it, not angular like the tailored blouse is. And *he* said let's try it and you c'n always take it back if you don't like it. And d'you know where we got it?'

'*Khushi, khushi*,' Azhar said warmly. 'Why do you not invite Barbara inside?'

Hadiyyah laughed, hands to her mouth. 'I got so excited!' She stepped back from the door. 'We have fizzy lemonade to drink. D'you want some? We're having a celebration, aren't we, Dad?'

'*Khushi*,' Azhar said to her meaningfully, his eyebrows raised.

Some sort of message passed between them, and Barbara realised that Azhar and his daughter had been in the midst of a private conversation. Her presence was clearly an interruption. She said hastily, 'Anyway, I'm off, you two. I wanted to say thanks straightaway. It was awfully kind. C'n I pay you for the blouse?'

'You may not,' Azhar told her.

'It was a present,' Hadiyyah declared. 'We even bought it in Camden High Street, Barbara. Not in the Stables or anything—'

'God no,' Barbara said. Uneasy personal experience had

taught her how Azhar felt about Hadiyyah wandering round the warren comprising the Stables and Camden Lock Market.

'—but we *did* go into Inverness Street Market, and it was just lovely. I've never been there before.'

Azhar smiled. He cupped the back of his daughter's head and jiggled it lightly in a fond gesture. He said, 'How you chatter tonight.' And to Barbara, 'Will you stay for dinner, Barbara?'

'Oh, *do* stay, Barbara,' Hadiyyah said. 'Dad's making chicken *saag masala*, and there's *dal* and *chapatis* and mushroom *dopiaza*. I gen'rally don't like mushrooms, you know, but I love them how Dad cooks. Oh, an' he's making rice *pilau* with spinach and carrots.'

'That sounds like quite a feast,' Barbara said.

'It is, it is! 'Cause like I said—' She clapped her hands to her mouth. Her eyes fairly danced above them. She said against her palms, 'Oh, I wish and wish I could say more. Only I can't, you see. I promised.'

'Then you mustn't,' Barbara said.

'But you're *such* a friend. Isn't she, Dad? C'n I . . . ?'

'You may not.' Azhar shot Barbara a smile. 'Now, we have stood here chatting long enough. Barbara, we insist that you join us for dinner.'

'There's lots of food,' Hadiyyah announced.

'Put that way,' Barbara told her, 'I can hardly do anything but fall straight into it.'

She followed them inside, and she felt a warmth that had nothing to do with the day's temperature, which had hardly been lessened by the cooking that had gone on within the flat. Indeed, the beastly heat of the waning day was something she hardly noticed at all. Instead, she noticed the manner in which her mood lifted, she no longer was caught up in considering what was happening to Thomas Lynley, and the concerns of the murder inquiry melted away.

* * *

The confrontation with John Stewart left Isabelle rattled, a reaction she hadn't expected. She was long used to dealing with men on the force, but theirs was generally a covert sexism, displayed by the sly innuendo whose interpretation could, conveniently, be attributed to everything from thin skin to complete misinterpretation on the part of the listener. Matters were different with John Stewart. Sly innuendo was not his style. At least Isabelle found that this was the case behind closed doors when Stewart knew very well that any move she made against him would be an instance of her-word-against-his with the higher-ups. And this in a situation in which the last thing she wanted to do was to go to her superior officers with a complaint about sexual harassment or anything else. John Stewart, she realised, was clever as the devil. He knew the ice she was skating on was thin. He was happy to shove her directly into the middle of the pond.

She wondered briefly how a man could be so short-sighted as to set himself in warfare with someone who might be selected as his superior officer. But she gave that consideration only a moment before she saw their stand-off from Stewart's point of view: clearly, he didn't expect her to be selected. And at the end of the day, she couldn't blame him for believing she'd soon be shown the door.

What a cock-up, she thought. How could things possibly get any worse? God, how she wanted a drink.

But she steeled herself not to have one, not even to look inside her handbag where her airline bottles nestled like sleeping infants. She didn't *need* the stuff. She merely wanted it. Want was not need.

A knock on her office door and she swung round from the window, where she'd been standing to gaze at a view she did not even see. She called enter, and Lynley stood there. He held a manila envelope in his hand.

He said, 'I was out of order earlier. I'm terribly sorry.'

She laughed shortly. 'You and everyone else.'

'Still and all—'

'It's no matter, Thomas.'

He said nothing for a moment, observing her. He tapped the envelope against his palm, as if he was thinking how to go on. At last he said, 'John is . . .' but still he hesitated, perhaps looking for the proper word.

She said, 'Yes. It's hard to pin down, isn't it? Just the right term to capture the essence of John Stewart.'

'I suppose. But I shouldn't have disciplined him, Isabelle. It was rather a knee-jerk reaction, I'm afraid.'

She waved him off. 'As I said, it doesn't matter.'

'It's not you,' Lynley said. 'You need to know that. He and Barbara have been at it for years. He has difficulty with women. His divorce . . . I'm afraid it rather turned him. He's not come back from it, and he's not been able to see any fault on his part for what went on.'

'What did go on?'

Lynley entered, shutting the door behind him. 'His wife had an affair.'

'Ask me if I'm surprised about that.'

'She had an affair with another woman.'

'I can hardly blame her. That bloke would make Eve choose the snake over Adam.'

'They're a couple now, and they have custody of John's two girls.' He observed her steadily as he said this. She shifted her gaze away.

'I can't feel sorry for him.'

'Who could blame you? But sometimes these things are good to know, and I doubt his file said it.'

'You're right. It didn't. Are you thinking we have something in common, John Stewart and I?'

'People at odds often do.' And then in a shift, 'Will you come with me, Isabelle? You'll need to bring your car as I won't be coming back this way. There's someone I want you to meet.'

She frowned. 'What's this about?'

'Not much, actually. But as it's the end of the day . . . We can have a meal afterwards, if you'd like. Sometimes talking over a case brings out something not considered before. Arguing about it does the same.'

'Is that what you want to do? Argue?'

'We do have areas of disagreement, don't we? Will you come with me?'

Isabelle looked round the office. She thought, Whyever not? and she nodded curtly. 'Give me a moment to collect my things. I'll meet you downstairs.'

When he'd left her, she used the time to make a quick trip into the Ladies, where she observed herself in the mirror and saw the day playing out on her face, especially between her eyes where a deep line was making the sort of vertical incision that became permanent. She decided to repair her makeup, which gave her a reason to open her handbag. There she caught sight of those nestling infants. She knew it would take only a moment to toss one of them back. Or all of them. But she firmly closed the bag and went to join her colleague.

Lynley didn't tell her where they were going. He merely nodded when she joined him and said he'd keep her within sight. That was the limit of their exchange before he set off in his Healey Elliott and gunned its engine as he headed upward, out of the underground car park and into the street. He manoeuvred over to the river. He was as good as his promise: he kept her within view and didn't allow a change in traffic lights to separate them. She was oddly comforted by this.

Unfamiliar with London as she was, she hadn't a clue where they were going as they headed southwest along the river. It was only when she saw the golden orb atop a distant obelisk to her right that she realised they'd come to the Royal Hospital, which meant they'd reached Chelsea. The broad lawns of Ranelagh Gardens were desiccated from the weather, she saw, although a few brave souls gathered there anyway: a late afternoon game of football was in progress.

Just beyond the gardens, Lynley turned right. He coursed along Oakley Street and then went left and left again. They were in an established Chelsea neighbourhood now, and it was characterised by quite tall red-brick homes, wrought iron railings and leafy trees. He pointed out a parking space to her, and he pulled ahead to wait for her to fit her car into it. When she joined him in his own car, he drove a bit farther. She saw the river up ahead of them again, along with a pub, which was where he parked. He said he'd be a moment and he went inside. He had an arrangement with the publican, he told her when he returned. When there was no parking available in Cheyne Row, which appeared to be the street's usual condition, he left his car alongside the pub and his keys with the barman as security.

He said, 'It's just this way,' and he directed her to one of the houses, this one at the junction of Cheyne Row and Lordship Place. She expected this building, like the others, to be a conversion as she couldn't imagine someone actually owning an entire piece of this pricey London real estate. But then she saw from the doorbell that she was wrong, and when Lynley rang it, a dog began barking almost at once, quieting only when a man's rough voice said, 'Enough! 'ell, you'd think we was gettin invaded,' as he swung the door open. He saw Lynley even as the dog rushed out, a longhaired dachshund who did not attack but rather leapt round their legs, as if wanting to be noticed.

'Watch out for Peach,' the man said to Isabelle. 'She's wanting food. Fact, she's always and *only* wanting food.' And with a nod to Lynley, 'Lord Ash'rton,' in something of a mumble, as if he knew Lynley preferred another way of being addressed but was reluctant to be less formal with him. Then he said with a smile, 'I was doing a tray of G and T. You as well?' as he held open the door.

'Planning to get addled, are they?' Lynley enquired as he gestured for Isabelle to precede him inside.

The man chuckled. 'S'pose miracles can happen,' he replied and he said, 'That pleased, Superintendent,' when Lynley introduced Isabelle.

He was called Joseph Cotter, she discovered, and while he

didn't appear to be a servant – despite his making drinks for someone – he also didn't appear to be the primary resident of the house. That was someone they would apparently 'find above', as Joseph Cotter said. He himself went into a room just to the left at the front of the house. 'G and T, then, m'lord?' he called over his shoulder. 'Superintendent?'

Lynley said he would gladly have one. Isabelle demurred. 'A glass of water would be lovely, though,' she replied.

'Will do,' he said.

The dachshund had been sniffing around their feet as if in the hope they'd brought something edible in on their shoes. Finding nothing, she'd scarpered up the stairs, and Isabelle could hear her paws clicking against the wooden risers as she ascended higher and higher in the house.

They did likewise. She wondered where on earth they were going and what the man Joseph Cotter had meant by *above*. They passed floor after floor of dark wainscoting below pale cream walls on which hung dozens of black-and-white photos, mostly portraits although some interesting landscapes were also scattered among them. On the final level of the house – Isabelle had lost count of the number of flights of stairs they'd climbed – there were two rooms only and no corridor although even more of the photos hung here, and in this spot they hung straight to the ceiling. The effect was like being in a photographic museum.

Lynley called out, 'Deborah? Simon?' to which a woman's voice replied with, 'Tommy? Hullo!' and a man's voice said, 'In here, Tommy. Mind the puddle there, my love,' and her reply, 'Let me see to it, Simon. You'll only make a mess.'

Isabelle preceded Lynley into the room which took most of its illumination from an enormous skylight that comprised the greater part of the ceiling. Beneath this, a redheaded woman knelt on the floor sopping up liquid. Her gaunt-faced companion stood nearby, a few towels in his hands. These he passed to her as she said, 'Two more and I think we've got it. Lord, what a mess.'

She could have been referring to the room itself, which looked like the den of a mad scientist with worktables cluttered with files and documents being blown about by fans that stood in the room's two windows in a futile attempt to mitigate the heat. There were bookshelves crammed with journals and volumes, racks of tubes and beakers and pipettes, three computers, china boards, video machines, television monitors. Isabelle couldn't imagine how anyone was able to function in the place.

Neither, apparently, could Lynley, for he looked round, said, 'Ah,' and exchanged a look with the man whom he introduced as Simon St James. The woman was St James's wife Deborah, and Isabelle recognised the name as that of the photographer who'd taken the portrait of Jemima Hastings. She recognised St James's name as well. He was a longtime expert witness, an evaluator of forensic data who worked equally for the defence or for the prosecution when a case of homicide came to trial. She could tell from their interaction that Lynley knew Simon and Deborah St James rather well, and she wondered why he had wanted her to meet them.

St James said to Lynley, 'Yes, as you see,' in answer to his *ah*. He employed an even tone in which something about the state of the room was communicated between them.

Beyond this work place, a second door opened into what was apparently a darkroom, and it was from this space that liquid pooled out. Fixer, Deborah St James explained as she finished mopping it up. She'd spilled an entire gallon of the stuff. 'One never *spills* when a container is nearly empty, have you noticed?' she asked. Job done, she stood and shook back her hair. She reached in the pocket of the bib overalls she was wearing – these were olive linen, wrinkled, and they suited her in ways that would have seemed ridiculous on another woman – and she brought out an enormous hair slide. She was the kind of woman who could gather up her hair in a single deft movement and make it look fashionably dishevelled. She wasn't at all beautiful, Isabelle thought, but she was natural and that was her appeal.

That she appealed to Lynley was something he didn't hide. He said, 'Deb,' and hugged her, kissing her on the cheek. Briefly, Deborah's fingers touched the back of his neck. 'Tommy,' she said in reply.

St James watched this, his face perfectly unreadable. Then he removed his gaze from his wife and Lynley to Isabelle and said lightly, 'How're you getting on with the Met, then? You've been thrown in feet first, I dare say.'

'I suppose that's better than head first,' Isabelle replied.

Deborah said, 'Dad's doing us drinks. Did he offer you . . . ? Well, of course he did. Let's not have them up here. There's got to be air in the garden. Unless . . .' She looked from Lynley to Isabelle. 'Is this business, Tommy?'

'It can be done in the garden as easily as here.'

'With me? With Simon?'

'Simon this time,' and to St James, 'if you've a moment. It shouldn't take long.'

'I was finished here anyway.' St James looked round the room and added, 'She had the maddest system of organising things, Tommy. I swear to you, I still can't work it out.'

'She meant to make herself indispensable to you,' Lynley said.

'Well, she was that.'

Isabelle looked between them once again. Some sort of code, she reckoned.

Deborah said, 'It'll come right eventually, don't you think?' but it seemed that she wasn't speaking of the files. Then she smiled at Isabelle and said, 'Let's get out of here.'

The little dog had settled on a tattered blanket in one corner of the room, but she heroically scuttled back down the stairs she'd just come up when she realised their intentions. At the ground floor, Deborah called, 'Dad, we're going into the garden,' and Joseph Cotter replied, 'Be there in a tick, then,' from the study where the sound of glass clinking against metal suggested that drinks were being placed on a tray.

The garden comprised lawn, brick patio, herbaceous borders and an ornamental cherry tree. Deborah St James led Isabelle to a table and chairs beneath this, chatting about the weather. When they'd sat, she changed gears, directing a long look at Isabelle. 'How's he getting on?' she asked frankly. 'We worry about him.'

Isabelle said, 'I'm not the best judge as I've not worked with him before. He seems to be doing perfectly well as far as I can tell. He's very kind, isn't he?'

Deborah didn't reply at first. She gazed at the house as if seeing the men within it. After a moment she said, 'Helen worked with Simon. Tommy's wife.'

'Did she? I'd no idea. She was a forensic specialist?'

'No, no. She was . . . Well, she was rather uniquely Helen. She helped him when he needed her, which usually worked out to be three or four times each week. He misses her terribly, but he won't talk about it.' She removed her gaze from the house back to Isabelle. 'Years ago, they intended to marry – Simon and Helen – but they never did. Well, obviously, they didn't,' she added with a smile, 'and Helen eventually married Tommy. Bit of a difficult situation, isn't it, making the change from lovers to friends.'

Isabelle didn't ask why Lynley's wife and Deborah's husband had not married. She wanted to do so, but the arrival of the two men supervened, and on their heels came Joseph Cotter with the tray of drinks and the household dog who bounded across the lawn with a yellow ball in her mouth that she proceeded to chew upon, plopping herself at Deborah's feet.

More conversation about the weather followed, but soon enough, Lynley brought up the ostensible reason for this visit to Chelsea: he handed to Simon the manila envelope he'd been carrying in Isabelle's office. Simon opened it and drew out its contents. Isabelle saw it was the photograph of the yellow shirt from the Oxfam bin.

'What d'you make of it?' Lynley asked his friend.

St James studied it for a minute in silence before he said,

'I should think it's arterial blood. The pattern on the front of the shirt? It's a spray.'

'Suggesting?'

'Suggesting this was worn by the killer, and he stood quite close to the victim when he struck the fatal blow. Look at the spray on the collar of the shirt.'

'What d'you reckon that means?'

St James thought about this, his expression distant. He responded with, 'Oddly enough, I'd say in the midst of an embrace. Anything else and the heaviest spray would surely be on the sleeve, not on the collar and the front of the shirt. Let me show you. Deborah?'

He rose from his chair, no easy business for him because he was disabled. Isabelle hadn't noticed this earlier. He wore a leg brace, which made his movements awkward.

His wife rose as well and stood as directed by her husband. He put his left arm round her waist and drew her to him. He bent as if to kiss her and as he did so, he lifted his right hand and brought it down on her neck. The demonstration completed, he touched his wife lightly on the hair and said to Lynley with an indication of the photo, 'You can see the heaviest part of the spray is high on the right breast of the shirt. He's taller than she was, but not by much.'

'Not a defensive wound on her, Simon.'

'Suggesting she knew him well.'

'She was there with him willingly?'

'I dare say.'

Isabelle said nothing. She saw the purpose of this call upon the St Jameses, and she didn't know whether to be grateful that Lynley hadn't made these points – which she reckoned he'd already deduced from the photo – during the team's meeting at the Met or angry that he had decided to do it this way, in the presence of his friends. She was hardly likely to argue with him here, and he must have known that. It was yet another nail in the coffin of Matsumoto as killer. She had to regroup and she had to do it in haste.

She stirred in her seat. She nodded sagely and made noises about being grateful for their time and, unfortunately, having to be on her way: there were various things to see to, an early morning, the expectation of a witness to be interviewed, undoubtedly a meeting with Hillier . . . They would understand, of course.

Deborah was the one to see her to the door. Isabelle thought to ask her if, on the day of the photo, she remembered anything, anyone, any circumstance remotely unusual?

Deborah said the expected. It had been more than six months ago. She could remember virtually nothing about it other than Sidney – 'Simon's sister' – St James being present. 'Oh, and there would be Matt as well,' Deborah added. 'He was there.'

'Matt?'

'Matt Jones. Sidney's partner. He brought her to the cemetery and watched for a few minutes. But he didn't stay. Sorry. I should have mentioned it earlier. I hadn't really considered him till now.'

Isabelle was thinking about this as she began to trace the route back to her car. But she hadn't got far in her speculation when she heard her name called. She turned to see Lynley coming towards her down the pavement. She said when he reached her, 'Matt Jones.'

He said, 'Who?' He had the manila envelope in his possession again. She gestured for it. He handed it over.

'Sidney St James's boyfriend. Her partner. Whatever. He was there that day, in the cemetery according to Deborah. She'd forgotten till now.'

'When?' And then he put it together. 'The day she took the photo?'

'Right. What do we know about him?'

'So far, we know that there're hundreds of Matthew Joneses. Philip was on it but—'

'All right, all right. I take your meaning, Thomas.' She sighed. She'd pulled Hale off and forced him to stand watch at St

Thomas' Hospital. If there was critical information out there about Matt Jones, it was still out there, waiting to be uncovered.

Lynley looked towards the river. He said, 'Are you interested in dinner, Isabelle? I mean, are you hungry? We could have something in the pub. Or, if you prefer, I don't live far from here. But you know that, don't you, as you've been to the house.' He sounded rather awkward with the invitation, which Isabelle – despite her growing concerns about the investigation – found a bit charming. She recognised the immediate dangers of getting to know Thomas Lynley better, however. She didn't particularly want to expose herself to any of them.

He said, 'I'd like to talk to you about the case.'

She said, 'That's all?' and she was very surprised to see him flush. He didn't strike her as a flushing kind of man.

He said, 'Yes. Yes. Of course. What else?' Then he added, 'Well, I suppose there's Hillier as well. The press. John Stewart. The situation. And then there's Hampshire.'

'What about Hampshire?' She asked the question sharply.

He indicated the pub. 'Come to the King's Head,' he said. 'We need to take a break.'

They stayed three hours. Lynley told himself it was all in service of the case in hand. Still, there was more to their elongated sojourn at the King's Head and Eight Bells than sorting out the various aspects of the investigation. There was the matter of getting to know the acting superintendent and seeing her somewhat differently.

She was careful with what she revealed about herself, like most people, and what she *did* reveal was painted in positives: an older brother sheep farming in New Zealand; two parents alive and well near Dover where Dad was a ticket agent for a ferry line and Mum was a housewife who sang in the church choir; education in RC schools although she was not now a member of any religion; former husband a childhood sweetheart whom she married too young, unfortunately, before either of them was really prepared for what it takes to make a marriage work.

'I hate to compromise,' she admitted. 'I want what I want and there you have it.'

He said, 'And what do you want, Isabelle?'

She looked at him frankly before she answered. It was a long look that could have communicated any one of a number of things, he supposed. She said at last with a shrug, 'I expect I want what most women want.'

He waited for more. Nothing more was offered. Round them in the pub the noise of the nighttime drinkers seemed suddenly muted, until he realised what muted them was his heartbeat, which was unaccountably loud in his ears. 'What's that?' he asked her.

She fingered the stem of her glass. They'd had wine, an entire bottle of it, and he'd pay the price the following morning. But they'd stretched the drinking over the hours, and he didn't *feel* the least drunk, he told himself.

He said her name to prompt her to reply, and he repeated his question. She said, 'You're an experienced man, so I think you know very well.'

His heartbeat again, and this time it occluded his throat, which didn't make sense. But it did prevent him from giving a reply.

She said, 'Thank you for dinner. For the St Jameses as well.'

'There's no need—'

She rose from the table then, adjusted her bag over her shoulder, and laid her hand on his as she made ready to depart. She said, 'Oh, but there is. You could have presented what you'd already concluded about that shirt during our meeting. I'm not blind to that, Thomas. You could have made a perfect fool of me and forced my hand with regard to Matsumoto, but you chose not to. You're a very kind and decent man.'

24

An establishment called Sheldon Pockworth Numismatics had sounded to Lynley like a place tucked away in an alley in Whitechapel, a shop whose proprietor was a Mr Venus type, articulating bones instead of dealing in medals and coins. The reality was far different. The shop itself was clean, sleek and brightly lit. Its location was not far from Chelsea's Old Town Hall, in a spotless brick building on the corner of the King's Road and Sydney Street where it shared what was doubtless expensive space with a number of dealers in antique porcelain, silver, jewellery, paintings and fine china.

There was no Sheldon Pockworth, nor had there ever been. There was instead one James Dugué, who looked more like a technocrat than a purveyor of coins and military medals from the Napoleonic Wars. When Lynley entered that morning, he found Dugué leafing through a heavy volume set upon a spotless glass counter. Beneath this gleamed gold and silver coins on a rotating rack. When Dugué looked up, his chic steel-rimmed spectacles caught the light. He wore a crisp pink shirt and a navy tie striped diagonally in green. His trousers were navy as well and, when he moved from beyond the counter to a second display case, Lynley saw that he had on blindingly white trainers and no socks. *Brisk* was a very good word to describe him. So, as things turned out, was *certain*.

Lynley had come to the shop directly from his home rather than going into the Yard. He lived so close that it made more sense, and he'd phoned Isabelle on her mobile to tell her this as a courtesy. They'd spoken briefly, haltingly and politely. The ground had slightly shifted beneath them.

At the end of their dinner on the previous night, he'd walked with her to her car although she'd told him such a show of good breeding was hardly necessary as she was perfectly adept at defending herself in the unlikely event that she should be accosted in the fashionable Chelsea neighbourhood. Then she seemed to realise exactly what she'd said because she'd stopped completely on the pavement, turned to him, impulsively put her hand on his arm, and murmured, 'Oh my God. I am so sorry, Thomas,' which told him she'd connected her remarks to what had happened to Helen, murdered in a neighbourhood not so different from this one and less than a mile away.

He'd said, 'Thank you. But you've no need, really . . .' and he hesitated about saying more, stumbling rather with, 'It's only that . . .' before he stopped again, in a search for words.

They stood in the deep shadows of a leafy beech, the pavement beneath it already beginning to collect its leaves, fallen in the hot dry summer. Once again he was aware of being nearly eye to eye with Isabelle Ardery: a tall woman, slender without being thin, cheekbones prominent – a fact he hadn't noticed before – and eyes large, which he also hadn't noticed. Her lips parted as if to say something.

He held her gaze. A moment passed. A car door slammed nearby. He looked away. He said, 'I do want people to take less care with me.'

She made no reply.

He said, 'They're afraid they'll say something and I'll be reminded. I understand that. I'd probably feel the same. But what I don't understand is how anyone might think I actually *need* reminding or am afraid of being reminded.'

Still, she said nothing.

'What I mean is that she's always there anyway. She's a constant presence. How could she not be? She was doing such a simple thing, bringing in her shopping, and there they were. Two of them. He was twelve years old, the one who shot her. He did it for no reason really. Just because she was there. They've caught him but not the other and he – the boy – won't name him. He won't say a word about what happened.

He hasn't done since they found him. But the truth is, all I want to know was what she might have *said* to them before they . . . Because somehow I think I might feel . . . If I knew . . .' He suddenly found his throat was so tight that he knew he would, to his horror, weep if he did not stop speaking. He shook his head and cleared his throat. He kept his gaze on the street.

Her hand was extraordinarily soft when she touched his. She said, 'Thomas. You've no need. Really. Walk along with me.'

As if she thought he might not do so, she put her hand at his elbow and with her other hand she held onto his arm. She brought him close to her side and it was oddly comforting. He realised that other than his immediate family and Deborah St James, no one had touched him for months, aside from shaking his hand. It was as if people had become frightened of him, as if by touching him they believed the tragedy that had visited his life would somehow visit theirs. He found he felt such *relief* at her touch that he walked with her, and their steps fell into a natural rhythm.

'There,' she said when they reached her car. She faced him. 'I've had a pleasant evening. You're very good company, Thomas.'

'I've my doubts about that,' he said quietly.

'Do you?'

'Yes. And it's Tommy, actually. That's what most people call me.'

'Tommy. Yes. I've noticed.' She smiled and said, 'I'm going to hug you now and you're meant to know that this is in friendship.' She did so. She held him close to her – but only for a moment – and she also brushed her lips against his cheek. 'I think I shall call you Thomas for now, if that's all right,' she said before she left him.

Now in the coin shop Lynley waited while the proprietor put his heavy volume away. Lynley handed him the card they'd found in Jemima Hastings' bag, and he showed Dugué the

Portrait Gallery photo of Jemima. He also showed his police identification.

Surprisingly, after Dugué examined the warrant card he said to Lynley, 'You're the policeman who lost his wife last February, aren't you?'

'I am.'

'I remember these things,' Dugué told him. 'Terrible business, that. How can I help you?' And when Lynley nodded at the Portrait Gallery picture of Jemima, he said, 'Yes. I remember her. She's been into the shop.'

'When?'

Dugué considered the question. He looked out of the shop, which was mostly windows, and studied the corridor beyond it. He said, 'Round Christmas. I can't be more exact than that, but I do remember the decorations. Seeing her backlit by the fairy lights we put up in the corridor. So it would have been round Christmas, give or take two weeks in either direction. Unlike some establishments, we don't keep our decorations up all that long. We all of us loathe them, to be honest. Along with the carols. Bing Crosby may dream of snow. I, for one, dream of strangling Bing Crosby at the end of one week having to listen to him.'

'Did she make a purchase?'

'As I recall, she wanted me to look at a coin. It was an aureus, and she thought it might be worth something.'

'"Aureus."' Lynley considered his schoolboy Latin. 'Gold, then. Was it worth a great deal?'

'Not as much as one would think.'

'Despite its being gold?' It seemed to Lynley that the price of gold alone would make it valuable. 'Did she want to sell it?'

'She just wanted to know what it was worth. And what it *was*, actually, because she'd no idea. She reckoned it was old and she was right about that. It was old. Round one-fifty AD.'

'Roman, then. Did she say how she came to have it?'

Dugué asked to look at the picture of Jemima again, as if this would stimulate his memory. After studying it for a moment he said slowly, 'I believe she said it was among her father's things. She didn't tell me exactly but I reckoned he'd died recently and she'd been going through his belongings the way one does, trying to sort out what to do with this and that.'

'Did you offer to buy it?'

'As I said, aside from the gold itself, it wasn't worth enough. On the open market, I wouldn't have been able to get a lot for it. You see . . . Here, let me show you.'

He went to a desk behind the counter where he opened a drawer that had been fashioned to hold books. He ran his fingers along them and brought out one, saying, 'What she had was an aureus minted during the reign of Antoninus Pius, the bloke who came to be emperor directly after Hadrian. Know about him?'

'One of the Five Good Emperors,' Lynley said.

Dugué looked impressed. 'Not the sort of knowledge I'd think a copper would have.'

'I read history,' Lynley admitted. 'In another life.'

'Then you know his was an unusual reign.'

'Only that it was peaceful.'

'Right. As one of the good guys, he wasn't . . . Well, let's say he wasn't sexy. Or, at least, he's not sexy now, not to collectors. He was intelligent, well-educated, experienced, protective of Christians, clement towards conspirators and happy to stay in Rome and delegate responsibility to his provincial leaders. Loved his wife, loved his family, assisted the poor, practised economy.'

'In a word, boring?'

'Certainly compared to Caligula or Nero, eh?' Dugué smiled. 'There's not been a lot written about him, so I think collectors tend to dismiss him.'

'Which makes his coins of less value on the market?'

'That and the fact that there were two thousand different coins minted during his reign.' Dugué found what he was looking for in the volume, and he swung it to face Lynley.

The page, Lynley saw, displayed both the obverse and the

reverse of the aureus in question. The former depicted the emperor in profile, draped in the fashion of a bust, with CAES and ANTONINVS in relief, parenthesising the emperor's head. The latter showed a woman enthroned. This was Concordia, Dugué explained, a patera in her right hand and cornucopiae beneath her. These images were fairly standard stuff, the coin dealer went on, which was what he'd also told Jemima. He'd explained to her that although the coin itself was rare enough – 'One generally comes across coins of baser metals because they were minted more regularly than the aureus' – its true value would come from the marketplace. That was defined by the demand for the coin among collectors.

'So what are we talking about, exactly?' Lynley asked.

'The value?' Dugué considered this, tapping his fingers against the top of the display case. 'I'd say between five hundred and a thousand quid. *If* someone wanted it and *if* that person were bidding against someone else who wanted it. What you must remember,' Dugué concluded, 'is that a coin needs to be—'

'Sexy,' Lynley said. 'I understand. The bad boys are the sexy ones, aren't they?'

'Sad,' Dugué confimed, 'but true.'

Could he then assume, Lynley asked, that Sheldon Pockworth Numismatics did not have an aureus from the period of Antoninus Pius among its stock?

He could, Dugué said. If the inspector wanted to look at an actual aureus from that time, he would likely find one in the British Museum.

Barbara Havers had been forced to begin her day by shaving her legs, which hadn't done much to elevate her mood. She was fast discovering that there was a domino effect to altering her physical appearance: for example, the wearing of a skirt – A-line or otherwise – dictated either the wearing of tights or going barelegged, and either choice demanded that something be done about the condition of her legs. *This* required the application of razor to skin. *That* required shaving cream or some other kind of lather, which she did not possess so she used a dollop of Fairy Liquid instead to develop some suds activity. But the entire operation led to the excavation of a plaster from her medicine cabinet when she sliced into her ankle and blood gushed forth. She shrieked then cursed. What the flaming hell, she wondered, did how she dress have to do with what she was able to accomplish as a cop, anyway?

There was no question, however, that she would wear the skirt. That had been dictated not only by the acting superintendent's pointed suggestion but more by the fact that Hadiyyah had gone to such an extreme to make it ready for her. Indeed, what was also demanded of the morning was that Barbara stop at the big house upon leaving her bungalow, her purpose to show Hadiyyah how she looked. She had on the new bracelet and the blouse as well, but she'd eschewed the scarf. Too hot, she reasoned. She'd save it for autumn.

Azhar came to the door. Hadiyyah appeared behind him at once, when she heard Barbara's voice. They both exclaimed over the dubious alteration in Barbara's appearance. 'You look lovely!' Hadiyyah cried, hands clasped beneath her chin as if to keep herself from bursting into applause. 'Dad, doesn't Barbara look *lovely*?'

Barbara said, 'Not exactly the word, kiddo, but thanks all the same.'

'Hadiyyah is right,' Azhar said. 'All of it suits you, Barbara.'

'And she's got on *make*up,' Hadiyyah said. 'See how she's got on makeup, Dad? Mummy always says makeup's just to enhance what you got, and Barbara's used it *just* like Mummy. Don't you think so, Dad?'

'Indeed.' Azhar put his arm round Hadiyyah's shoulders. 'You've both done very well, *khushi*,' he told her.

Barbara felt the pleasure of their compliments. She knew they were due to kindness and friendship and nothing more – she was not nor would she ever be a remotely attractive woman – but still, she fancied that their gazes remained fixed on her as she went to the garden gate for the walk to her car.

Once at work, she put up with the hoots and good-natured teasing of her colleagues. She suffered their remarks in silence as she looked round for Lynley and found him missing. As was the acting superintendent, she learned. First thing that had happened that day: Hillier had demanded Isabelle Ardery's presence in his office.

Had Lynley gone with her? She asked the question of Winston Nkata. She tried to make it casual, but he wasn't deceived.

'Got to wait and see, Barb,' was how he put it. 'Anyt'ing else, you make yourself crazy.'

She scowled. She hated the fact that Winston Nkata knew her so well, and she couldn't reckon how he'd managed the accomplishment. Was she that bloody obvious about everything? What else had Nkata worked out?

She asked, abruptly, if anyone had gathered any useful information about Zachary Whiting. Was there anything besides the fact that he was once or twice too enthusiastic about being a cop, whatever that meant when it was home for supper? But there was nothing. Everyone was working on something else. Barbara sighed. It seemed that if anything was to be dug out about anyone in Hampshire, she was going to have to do the digging.

This was down to what SO7 had reported about the hairs found clasped in Jemima Hastings' hand. With Oriental hairs on the body, stacked alongside a murder weapon in the possession of a Japanese violinist, *and* the victim's blood on his clothing, *and* witnesses seeing him in the vicinity wearing that clothing on the day of her death, it wasn't going to appear to be a matter of urgency to go digging deeper into the background of one marginally suspicious cop. And this despite the discovery of a yellow, bloodstained shirt in a recycling bin across the river in Putney. That had to mean something, as did the presence of the victim's handbag in that same bin.

Barbara went for Whiting first. Since someone had reported

him being rather too enthusiastic about policing, surely there were going to be records somewhere that further defined exactly what his enthusiasm had been about. One merely had to follow the trail of Whiting's career to find someone willing to talk frankly about the bloke. Where, for example, had he been before Lyndhurst? He could hardly have spent his entire career climbing the ranks in a single station. That just didn't happen.

The Home Office was going to be the likeliest source of information, but excavating for it was not going to be quick or easy. The hierarchy of the place constituted a labyrinth, and it was peopled by the Under-Secretary, the Deputy Under-Secretaries, the Assistant Under-Secretaries and the Assistant Secretaries. Most of these individuals commanded their own staffs, and these staffs manned all of the different departments that were responsible for policing in the country. Of all the departments, the section that dealt with powers and procedure seemed the best option to Barbara. The question was: whom did she ring, pay a call upon, invite out for a coffee, arm twist, bribe, or beg? That was a real problem because unlike other cops who cultivated connections the way farmers grow their crops, Barbara had never possessed the social skills to rub elbows with people who might later be useful to her. But there had to someone who did have those skills, who'd used them, who could come up with a name . . .

She considered her colleagues. Lynley was the best possibility but he wasn't there. Philip Hale was also likely, but he remained at St Thomas' Hospital under Ardery's orders, ill-conceived though they were. John Stewart was out of the question as he was the last person on the planet from whom Barbara would ask a favour. Winston Nkata's connections were street-oriented as a result of the time he'd spent as chief battle counsel for the Brixton Warriors. This left the constables and the civilian staff, which in turn left the most obvious person of all. Barbara wondered that she hadn't reckoned from the first that Dorothea Harriman could be of assistance in this matter.

She located the departmental secretary in the copy room,

where in lieu of copying she appeared to be applying nail enamel
to her tights for some reason. She was wearing one of her stylish
pencil skirts – Barbara felt she was becoming something of an
expert in the matter of skirts – which was appropriate to her
lanky figure, and she had this hiked to the middle of her thighs
as she used the nail polish against her tights.

'Dee,' Barbara said.

Harriman started. 'Oh my goodness,' she said. 'What a fright,
Detective Sergeant Havers.'

For a moment, Barbara thought she was referring to her
own appearance. Then she realised what Harriman actually
meant, and she said, 'Sorry. Didn't mean to surprise you.
What're you doing with that?'

'This?' Harriman held up the bottle of nail enamel. 'Ladder,'
she said. And when Barbara looked at her blankly, 'On my
tights? It stops ladders from going further. Didn't you know?'

Barbara said hastily, 'Oh yeah. Ladders. Sorry. Don't know
what I was thinking. Got a moment, then?'

'Well, of course.'

'C'n we . . . ?'

Since she was going her own way in matters, Barbara knew
the wisdom of keeping this situation strictly *entre nous*. She
tilted her head towards the corridor and Harriman followed
her. They went along it and into the stairwell.

Barbara explained what she wanted: a snout at the Home
Office, someone willing to do a little snoop-and-talk about
one Chief Superintendent Zachary Whiting of the Hampshire
Constabulary. She reckoned this potential snout had to be
employed within the powers and procedures section of the
Home Office because that was where information about criminal
records, regional crime squads, detective work and complaints
was housed. She had a feeling that within one of those areas
there was going to be some tiny detail – possibly something that
might seem otherwise insignificant to a person not actually
looking for it – that would put her on to what Whiting was up
to out in Hampshire. Surely, she said, Dorothea Harriman knew

someone who might be able to direct them to another someone who in turn could find a third someone . . . ?

Harriman pursed her well-defined lips. She fingered her scrupulously highlighted and fashionably cut hair. She tapped her blusher-enhanced cheek. Had they been in other circumstances Barbara acknowledged that she might have asked the young woman for lessons in applying her make-up as she was definitely a practitioner of Hadiyyah's mum's philosophy of enhancement only. As it was, Barbara could only note and admire as Harriman considered the question.

She gazed at the soft drinks machine on the landing. Two floors below a door opened, a voice spoke loudly about being served 'a plate of mash tasting like gravel in drying cement', and footsteps came clomping up the stairs. Barbara grabbed Harriman by the arm and pulled her back into the corridor and, from there, into the copying room again.

This, evidently, gave Harriman time to consider all the various possibilities she no doubt had either in her Rolodex or in her personal directory because when they'd sequestered themselves on the far side of the copier, she said in a stage whisper, 'There *was* a bloke whose sister's flatmate . . .'

'Yeah?' Barbara said.

'I dated him briefly. We met at a drinks party. You know how it is.'

Barbara hadn't a clue how it was but she nodded helpfully. 'C'n you ring him? See him? Whatever?'

Harriman tapped a fingernail against her teeth. 'It's a *bit* tricky. He was rather keen and I wasn't, if you know what I mean. But . . .' She brightened. 'Let me see what I can do, Detective Sergeant Havers.'

'C'n you do it now?'

'This is important, isn't it?'

'Dee,' Barbara said fervently, 'I can't even stress how important it is.'

*   *   *

There had been no further avoiding a meeting with the assistant commissioner. Judi MacIntosh had phoned Isabelle early enough in the morning – and on her mobile at that – to make Sir David Hillier's wishes perfectly clear. The acting detective superintendent was meant to come to Sir David's office the moment she got to Victoria Street.

To make certain that Isabelle understood, the request was repeated when she reached her office. It came this time in the person of Dorothea Harriman, teetering into Isabelle's domain in what had to be five inch high heels bound to condemn her feet to podiatric surgery in later years.

'He does say you're meant to go now,' Dorothea explained apologetically. 'Would you like me to fetch you a coffee to take with, Acting Detective Superintendent Ardery? I don't ordinarily,' she added as if to clarify her duties, 'but as it's early and as you might want to fortify yourself . . . ? Since the assistant commissioner can be a bit overwhelming . . . ?'

What she wanted to fortify herself with wasn't coffee, but Isabelle didn't intend to go that route. Instead, she declined the offer, stowed her belongings in her desk, and made her way to Hillier's office in Tower Block where Judi MacIntosh greeted her, sent her directly into the assistant commissioner, and told her that the head of the press office would be joining them.

This wasn't good news. It meant further machinations were in the works. Further machinations meant Isabelle's position was even more tenuous than it had been on the previous day.

Hillier was just finishing a phone call. This consisted of, 'I'm asking you to hold back on it for a few hours more till I get things sorted out . . . This isn't deal-making . . . There are points to clarify and I'm about to do so . . . Of course, you'll be the first to know . . . If you think this is the sort of call I actually *like* to make . . . Yes, yes. All right.' With that he rang off. He gestured to one of the two chairs in front of his desk. Isabelle sat and he did likewise, which went a small distance towards reassuring her.

He said, 'It's time for you to tell me precisely what you knew in advance, and I suggest you take care with your answer.'

Isabelle drew her eyebrows together. She saw that on the assistant commissioner's desk a tabloid and a broadsheet lay face down, and she determined the press had picked up on something that she hadn't revealed to Hillier and Deacon or something that she had not previously known and did not know now. She realised she should have had a look at the morning papers prior to coming in to work, if for no other reason than to prepare herself. But she'd not done so, nor had she turned on the morning television news for the presenters' usual report on the front pages of the papers.

She said, 'I'm not sure what you mean, sir,' even though she recognised that this was what he wanted her to say because it put him into a more powerful position, where he liked to be. She waited for what would come next. She was fairly sure it would be the dramatic moment in which he flipped the papers right side up, and so it was. Thus she saw in short order that Zaynab Bourne's afternoon news conference, the legs of which had been intended to be summarily amputated by the Met's pre-emptive meeting with the media, had instead attained such prominence in the news cycle that the Met's conference might never have occurred. Zaynab Bourne had managed this by releasing a piece of information that Isabelle herself had not mentioned to either Hillier or Deacon during their meeting: that Yukio Matsumoto was a long-diagnosed paranoid schizophrenic. The Met's withholding of this information constituted – in the words of the solicitor – 'an obvious and disgraceful attempt at subreption for which they cannot and will not be held blameless.'

Isabelle didn't need to read the rest to know that Mrs Bourne had asserted the investigating officers' prior knowledge of Yukio Matsumoto's condition, revealed to them in a meeting they'd had with the violinist's own brother in advance of setting off after him. So now the police were in the position of not only chasing a man into the afternoon traffic of Shaftesbury Avenue, which certainly *could* have been forgiven as an unfortunate but unavoidable circumstance brought about by an individual's attempting to evade a reasonable conversation with unarmed policemen, but *now* of chasing a terrified psychiatric patient into said traffic, a man who doubtless was in the midst of a psychotic episode that the police had already been told to anticipate by the man's own brother. It did not help matters that the man's own brother was international virtuoso cellist Hiro Matsumoto.

Isabelle considered her approach. Her palms were damp, but the last thing she intended to do was to wipe them casually along her skirt. Should she do so, she knew that Hillier would see that her hands were shaking as well. She schooled herself to relax. What was called for here was a show of strength through a clear indication that she would not be cowed by tabloids, broadsheets, solicitors, news conferences, or Hillier himself. She looked at the assistant commissioner squarely and said, 'The fact that Yukio Matsumoto is mental hardly matters, as I see it, sir.'

Hillier's skin went rosy. Isabelle continued confidently before he could speak.

'His mental state didn't matter when he avoided our questions and it matters even less just now.'

Hillier's skin went rosier still.

Isabelle plunged on. She made her voice certain and she kept it cool. Cool would mean that she had no fear of the assistant commissioner's disagreeing with her assessment of matters. It would mean she believed that her assessment had been and was rock solid. She said, 'The moment Matsumoto's ready for an identity parade, we have a witness who'll place him in the vicinity of the crime. This is the very same witness who created the e-fit recognised by the man's own brother. Matsumoto was, as you know, in possession of the murder weapon and wearing bloodied clothes, but what you might not yet know is that two hairs found in the hand of the victim have been identified as oriental in origin. When DNA tests are completed on them, those hairs are going to belong to him. He was acquainted with the victim, she'd lived in the same building as he, and he's known to have followed her. So frankly, sir, whether he's a mental case or not is incidental. I didn't consider mentioning it when I met with you and Mr Deacon because in light of everything else we knew about the man, the fact that he has a mental condition – which hasn't been attested to by anyone save his own brother and his brother's solicitor, by the way – is a minor point. If anything, it's yet another detail that weighs against him: he wouldn't be the first untreated mental patient to murder someone in the midst of an episode of some sort and, sad to say, he won't be the last.' She stirred in her seat, leaning forward and placing her arms along Hillier's desk in a gesture to show that her assumption was that she was his equal and the two of them – and by extension the Met – were in this together.

'Now,' she said, 'this is what I recommend. Incredulity.'

Hillier didn't reply at once. Isabelle could feel her heart beating – *slamming*, really – against her rib cage. She reckoned it could have been seen in the pulse on her temples had she worn her hair differently and she knew it probably was evident on her neck. But that, too, was somewhat out of Hillier's view and as long as she said nothing more, merely waiting for his reply, obviously communicating to him nothing but confidence in the decisions she'd made . . . She merely needed to keep her eyes on his, which were icy and rather soulless, weren't they, and she hadn't noticed that before this moment.

'Incredulity,' Hillier finally repeated. His telephone rang. He snatched it up, listened for a moment and said, 'Tell him to hang on. I'm nearly finished here.' Then to Isabelle, 'Go on.'

'With?' She made it sound as if she assumed he'd followed her logic, all surprise that he needed her to clarify.

His nostrils moved, not a flare so much as a testing of the air. For prey, no doubt. She held her ground. He said, 'With your point, Superintendent Ardery. Just how do you see this playing out?'

'With our astonishment that someone's mental condition – unfortunate though it may be – would ever trump the safety of the general public. Our officers went to the site unarmed. The man in question panicked for reasons we haven't yet ascertained. In our possession is very hard evidence—'

'Most of which was gathered after the fact of his accident,' Hillier noted.

'Which is beside the point, of course.'

'The point being?'

'That we have our hands on a person of serious interest who can, as the phrase goes, "help us with our enquiries" in a fashion that no one else can. What we're looking for, good people of the press, is – might I remind you – whoever is responsible for the brutal murder of an innocent woman in a public park, and if *this* gentleman can lead us to that party, then that's what we're going to demand he do. The press will fill in the blanks. The last thing they'll ask is the order in which events occurred. Evidence is evidence. They'll want to know what it is, not when we found it. And even if they unearth the fact that we found it after the accident on Shaftesbury Avenue, the point is the murder, the park and our belief that the public might prefer we protect them from madmen wielding weapons rather than tiptoe round someone who might or might not be hearing Beelzebub muttering in his ear.'

Hillier considered this. Isabelle considered Hillier. She wondered idly what he'd received his knighthood for because it was odd that someone in his position would be given an honour that generally went to the higher-ups. That he'd been knighted spoke not so much of a service to the public hero-ically rendered but rather to Hillier's knowing people in high places and, more important, knowing how to use those people in high places. He was, thus, not a man to cross. But that was fine. She didn't intend to cross him.

He said to her, 'You're a wily one, aren't you, Isabelle? I've not missed the fact that you've managed to swing this meeting your way.'

'I wouldn't expect you to miss that fact,' Isabelle said. 'A man like you doesn't rise to the position you have because things get past him. I quite understand that. I quite admire it. You're a political animal, sir. But, make no mistake about it, so am I.'

'Are you.'

'Oh yes.'

A moment passed between them during which they were locked in an assessing look. It had about it the air of the distinctly sexual, and Isabelle allowed herself to imagine going at it with David Hillier, the two of them locked in an entirely different kind of combat on her bed. She reckoned he imagined much the same. When she was as certain of that as she could be, she dropped her gaze.

She said, 'I assume Mr Deacon's waiting outside, sir. Would you like me to stay for that meeting?'

Hillier didn't reply until she raised her eyes. Then he said slowly, 'That won't be necessary.'

She rose. She said, 'Then I'll get back to work. If you want me' – her choice of verb was deliberate – 'Ms MacIntosh has my mobile number. As, perhaps, do you?'

'I do,' he said. 'We'll speak again.'

25

S he went directly to the Ladies. The only problem was that she hadn't thought to bring her bag with her to Hillier's office, so at the moment she was without resources and she was left relying on what was available, which was water from the tap. This was hardly an efficacious substance for what ailed her. But she used it for want of anything else: on her face, her hands, her wrists.

Thus she felt little improved when she left Tower Block and made her way back to her office. She heard her name called by Dorothea Harriman – who for some reason seemed incapable of referring to her in any terms briefer than *Acting Detective Superintendent Ardery* – but this she ignored. She closed her office door and went directly to her desk where she'd left her bag. Upon opening it, she discovered in short order that she had three messages on her mobile phone. She ignored them as well. She thought Yes yes yes as she brought forth one of her airline bottles of vodka. In her rush to have it, she dropped the bottle onto the lino floor. She scrambled on her knees beneath her desk to fetch it, and she downed it as she rose to her feet. It wasn't enough, of course. She emptied her bag on the floor to find the other. She downed this and went for the third one. She *deserved* it. She'd survived an encounter that by all rights she shouldn't have survived at all. She'd avoided the participation of Stephenson Deacon and the Directorate of Public Affairs in that encounter. She'd argued her case, and she'd won, if only for the moment. And because it *was* only for the moment, she bloody well needed a drink, she bloody well deserved one, and if there was anyone between here and hell who didn't understand that—

'Acting Detective Superintendent Ardery?'

Isabelle spun towards the door. She knew, of course, who'd be standing there. What she didn't know was how long she'd been there or what she'd seen. She snapped, 'Don't you *ever* come into this office without knocking!'

Dorothea Harriman looked startled. 'I did knock. Twice.'

'And did you hear me reply?'

'No. But I—'

'Then do *not* enter. Do you understand that? If you ever do that again . . .' Isabelle heard her own voice. To her horror, she sounded like a termagant. She realised she still had the third airline bottle clutched in her hand, and she closed her fingers round it in a concealing fist. She drew a breath.

Harriman said, 'Detective Inspector Hale's rung from St Thomas' Hospital, ma'am.' Her tone was formal and polite. She was, as ever, the consummate professional and her being so at such a moment as this reduced Isabelle to feeling like a scrofulous cow. 'I'm sorry to disturb,' Harriman said, 'but he's phoned twice. I did tell him you were with the assistant commissioner but he said it was urgent and to tell you the moment you returned to your office. He said he'd rung your mobile but couldn't reach you—'

'I'd left it here, in my bag. What's happened?' Isabelle said.

'Yukio Matsumoto's conscious. The detective inspector said you were meant to know the moment you returned.'

When Isabelle arrived, the first person she saw was DI Philip Hale who, she mistakenly presumed, was pacing down the pavement to meet her. As things turned out, however, he was instead on his way back to the Yard, having reached the infuriating conclusion that he'd followed her orders sufficiently by remaining at the hospital until their principal suspect had regained consciousness, whereupon he'd made the call to inform her. He had gone on, he told her, to bring in two uniformed constables to stand guard at Matsumoto's doorway.

Now he was heading to the incident room to get back to the checks he and his constables had been making on—

'Inspector Hale,' Isabelle interrupted him. '*I* tell *you* what you'll be doing. You do not tell me. Are we clear on that?'

Hale frowned. 'What?'

'What do you mean by "what"? You're not a stupid man, are you? You certainly don't look stupid. *Are* you stupid?'

'Look, guv, I was—'

'You were at this hospital, and here at this hospital you shall remain until ordered otherwise. You'll be at the doorway to Matsumoto's room – seated or standing and I don't care which. You'll be holding the patient's hand if necessary. But what you won't be doing is going off on your own and ringing up constables to take your place. Until you're directed otherwise, you're here. Is that clear?'

'Due respect, guv, this isn't the best use of my time.'

'Let me point something out to you, Philip. We're where we are at this precise moment because of your earlier decision to confront Matsumoto when you were told to keep your distance from the man.'

'That's not what happened.'

'And now,' she went on, 'despite being told to remain here at the hospital, you've taken it upon yourself to arrange for your own replacement. Is this not true, Philip?'

He shifted his weight. 'It is, in part.'

'And which part isn't?'

'I didn't confront him at Covent Garden, guv. I didn't say a word to the bloke. I may have got too close to him, I may have . . . whatever. But I didn't—'

'Were you told to approach him? To get close to the man? To breathe the same air in his vicinity? I think not. You were told to find him, report back, and keep him in sight. In other words, you were told to keep your distance, which you did not do. And now here we are, *where* we are, because you took a decision you weren't meant to take. Just as you're doing now. So get back into that hospital, get back to Matsumoto's doorway, and until you hear otherwise from me, remain there. Am I being clear?'

As she'd been speaking, she'd watched the muscle in Hale's jaw jumping. He didn't reply and she barked, 'Inspector! I'm asking you a question.'

To which he finally said, 'As you wish, guv.'

At that she went towards the hospital entrance and he followed as she preferred him to follow: several paces behind her. She wondered at the fact of these detectives under her command all wanting to go their own way in the investigation and what this said about the leadership provided first by the former superintendent, Malcolm Webberly, and by everyone subsequent to him, including Thomas Lynley. Discipline was called for but having to administer that in the midst of everything else going on was particularly maddening. Changes were going to have to be made with this lot. There was no question about that.

As she reached the door with Hale as her shadow, a taxi arrived. Hiro Matsumoto stepped out, a woman in his company. This was, thank God, not his solicitor but a Japanese woman close to his own age. The third Matsumoto sibling, Isabelle concluded, Miyoshi Matsumoto, the Philadelphia flautist.

She was correct. She paused, jerking her thumb at the door for Hale to go ahead into the hospital. She waited till Matsumoto had paid for the taxi, whereupon he introduced her to his sister. She had arrived from America on the previous evening, he said. She had not yet seen Yukio. But they'd had word this morning from Yukio's doctors—

'Yes,' Isabelle said. 'He's conscious. And I must speak with him, Mr Matsumoto.'

'Not without his attorney.' It was Miyoshi Matsumoto who replied, and her tone was nothing like her brother's. Obviously, she'd been in big city America long enough to know that *lawyer up* was rule number one when dealing with the police force. 'Hiro, call Mrs Bourne right now.' And to Isabelle, 'Keep away. I don't want you near Yukio.'

Isabelle wasn't unaware of the irony of being told exactly what she herself had told Philip Hale in the moments leading up to Yukio Matsumoto's flight. She said, 'Ms Matsumoto, I know you're upset—'

'You've got that much right.'

'—and I don't disagree that this is a mess.'

'*That's* what you call it?'

'But what I ask you to see—'

'Get away from me.' Miyoshi Matsumoto pushed past Isabelle and stalked towards the hospital doors. 'Hiro, call that lawyer. Call someone. Keep her *out* of here.'

She went within, leaving Isabelle outside with Hiro Matsumoto. He looked at the ground, his arms crossed on his chest. She said to him, 'Please intercede.'

He seemed to consider her request and Isabelle felt momentarily hopeful until he said, 'This is something I can't do. Miyoshi feels much as I do.'

'Which is?'

He looked up. Behind his gleaming spectacles, his eyes looked bleak. 'Responsible,' he said.

'You didn't do this.'

'Not for what happened,' he said, 'but for what didn't happen.' He nodded at Isabelle and moved towards the hospital doors.

She followed him at first, then walked at his side. They entered the hospital and began to make their way to Yukio Matsumoto's room. Isabelle said, 'No one could have anticipated this. I've been reassured by my officer on the scene that he didn't approach your brother, that instead Yukio saw something or heard something or perhaps *felt* something – we can't even work out which it was – and he simply bolted. As you've said yourself—'

'Superintendent, that's not what I mean.' Matsumoto paused. Round them, people went on their way: visitors bearing flowers and balloons to loved ones, members of the hospital's staff striding purposefully from one corridor to another. Above their heads the public address system asked Dr Marie Lincoln to report to the operating theatre, and next to them pardon was requested by two orderlies whisking a patient somewhere on a trolley. Matsumoto seemed to take all of this in before he went on. 'We did what we could for Yukio for many years, Miyoshi and I, but it was not enough. We had our own careers, and it was easier to let him drift so that we could pursue our music. With Yukio to concern ourselves with, to weigh us down . . .' He shook his head. 'How could we have climbed so far, Miyoshi and I? And now this. How could we have sunk so low? I am most deeply shamed.'

'You've no need to be,' Isabelle told him. 'If he's sick, as you say, and without medication, if he's got a mental condition that caused him to do something, you bear absolutely no responsibility.'

He'd walked on as she was speaking and he'd rung for the lift and then faced her. When the doors opened in near silence, he turned and she followed him inside. He said to her quietly, 'Again, you misunderstand me, Superintendent. My brother did not kill that poor woman. There is an explanation for everything: for the blood on him, for that . . . that thing you found in his lodgings . . .'

'Then for God's sake, let him give me the explanation,' Isabelle said. 'Let him tell me what he *did* do, what he knows, what actually happened. You can be present, right at his bedside. Your sister can be present. I'm not in uniform. He won't know who I am, and you don't need to tell him if you think he'll panic. You can speak to him in Japanese if that would make it easier for him.'

'Yukio speaks perfect English, Superintendent.'

'Then speak to him in English. *Or* Japanese. Or both. I don't care. If, as you say, he's guilty of nothing but being in the cemetery, then he may have seen something that can help us find Jemima Hastings' killer.'

They reached the floor he'd rung for and the doors slid open. In the corridor, Isabelle stopped him a final time. She said his name in such a way that even she could hear the desperation in her voice. And when he looked at her gravely, she went on to say, 'We're in a time crunch here. We can't wait for Zaynab Bourne to show up. If we *do* wait, you and I both know she's not going to let me speak to Yukio. Which means, if as you say he's guilty of nothing more than being in Abney Park Cemetery when Jemima Hastings was attacked and murdered, he himself could well be in danger because the killer will know from every newspaper in town that Yukio is a person of interest because he was there. And *if* he was there, he likely saw something and he's likely to tell us. Which he won't be able to do if your solicitor shows up.' She was more than desperate at this point, she realised. She was verging on babbling and it made no difference to her what she said or whether she believed what she said – which she didn't, actually – because the only thing that mattered just then was bending the cellist's will to hers.

She waited. She prayed. Her mobile phone rang and she ignored it.

Finally, Hiro Matsumoto said, 'Let me speak to Miyoshi,' and he went to do so.

Barbara discovered that Dorothea Harriman had hidden talents. From Harriman's appearance and demeanour, she'd always reckoned that the departmental secretary had no real trouble pulling men, and this was, of course, true. What she hadn't known was the length of time Harriman evidently managed to linger in the memories of her victims and to produce within them a willingness to cooperate with anything she desired.

Within ninety minutes of Barbara's making the request, Dorothea was back with a slip of paper fluttering from her fingers. This was their 'in' at the Home Office, the flatmate of the sister of the bloke who was, apparently, still lost within Dorothea's thrall. The flatmate was a minor cog in the well-oiled machine that was the Home Office, her name was

Stephanie Thompson-Smythe, and – 'This is what's truly excellent,' Dorothea breathed – *she* was dating a bloke who apparently had access to whatever codes, keys, or magical words were necessary to create an open sesame situation with an individual policeman's employment records.

'I had to tell her about the case,' Dorothea confessed. She was, Barbara found, rather full of her success and desirous of waxing eloquent on the topic, which Barbara reckoned she owed her so she listened cooperatively and waited for the slip of paper to be handed over. 'Well, of course, she *knew* about it. She reads the papers. So I told her – well, I had to bend the truth just a *bit*, naturally – that a trail seems to be leading to the Home Office which of course made her think that *perhaps* the guilty party is there somewhere and being protected by one of the higher ups. Rather like Jack the Ripper or something? Anyway, I told her that anything she could help us out with would be brilliant and I swore her name wouldn't come up at all anywhere. *But*, I told her, she would be doing an *heroic* service to help us out even in the smallest way. She seemed to like that.'

'Wicked,' Barbara said. She indicated the slip of paper Dorothea still held.

'*And* she said she'd phone her boyfriend and she did and you're to meet them both at the Suffragette Scroll in' – Dorothea glanced at her wristwatch which, like the rest of her, was slender and golded – 'twenty minutes.' She sounded quite triumphant, her first venture into the underworld of snouts and blackguards a rousing success. She handed over the slip of paper at last, which turned out to be the mobile phone number of the boyfriend of the flatmate. This was, Dorothea told her, just in case something happened and they 'failed to show', in her words.

'You,' Barbara told her, 'are a marvel.'

Dorothea blushed. 'I do think I carried things off rather well.'

'Better than that,' Barbara told her. 'I'll head over there now.

If anyone asks, I'm on a mission of grave importance for the superintendent.'

'What if the superintendent asks?' Dorothea said. 'She's only gone over to St Thomas' Hospital. She'll be back eventually.'

'You'll think of something,' Barbara told her as she grabbed her disreputable shoulder bag. She headed off to meet her potential Home Office snout.

The Suffragette Scroll was no great distance, either from the Home Office or from New Scotland Yard. A monument to that eponymous movement of the early Twentieth Century, it stood at the northwest corner of the green that comprised the intersection of Broadway and Victoria Street. The journey comprised a five-minute walk for Barbara – including her wait for the lift inside Victoria Block – so she had adequate time to fortify herself with nicotine and to lay her plans before two individuals came strolling hand-in-hand towards her, doing their best to look like lovers having a bit of a walk on the green in their break from the daily grind.

One was Stephanie Thompson-Smythe – Steph T-S, as she introduced herself – and the other was Norman Wright, the thinness of whose bridge of nose spoke of serious inbreeding among his forebears. He could have sliced bread with the top of his proboscis.

Norman and Stephanie T-S looked round like agents from MI5. Stephanie said to her man, 'You talk. I'll watch,' and retreated to a bench some distance away. Barbara thought this was a good idea. The fewer people involved, the better it was.

Norman said to her, 'What d'you think of the Scroll?' He gazed upon it intently and spoke from the side of his mouth. From this Barbara took it that they were to play at being admirers of Mrs Pankhurst and her fellows, which was fine by her. She walked round the scroll, gazing up at it, and murmuring to Norman about what she needed and hoped to attain from their acquaintance, brief though it might likely be.

'Whiting's his name,' she concluded. 'Zachary Whiting.

Chapter and verse is what I need. There's got to be something somewhere in his records that looks ordinary but isn't.'

Norman nodded. He pulled at his nose, which gave Barbara a chill as to the damage this might to do the delicate thing, and he considered her words. He said, 'So you'll want the lot, eh? That could be difficult. I send it online and I leave a trail.'

'We're going to have to be antique in our methods,' Barbara told him. 'Careful and antique.'

He looked at her blankly, clearly a child of the electronic age. His eyes narrowed as he thought about this. 'Antique?' he asked.

'A photocopier.'

'Ah,' he said. 'And if there's nothing to copy? Most of this is stored on computer.'

'A printer then. Someone else's printer. Someone else's computer. There are ways, Norman, and you've got to find one. We're talking life and death. A female corpse up in Stoke Newington and something rotten—'

'– in the state of Denmark,' Norman said. 'Yes. I see.'

Barbara wondered what the hell he was talking about, but she twigged it before she made a fool of herself and asked what Denmark had to do with the price of salami. She said, 'Ah. Very good. Too bloody right. Thing to remember is that what *looks* ordinary might not *be* ordinary. This bloke's managed to get as far as chief superintendent in the Hampshire Constabulary, so we're not likely to stumble on smoking guns.'

'Something subtle. Yes. Of course.'

'So?' Barbara asked him.

He would see what he could do, Norman told her. Meantime, did they need a code word? Perhaps a signal? Some way for him to tell her that he had the goods for her without phoning New Scotland Yard? And if he was to make copies of anything, where would the drop be located?

Obviously, Barbara thought, he'd been reading far too much early John Le Carré. She decided she would have to play along. The drop, Barbara told him, *sotto voce*, would be at the cash point machine in front of Barclays in Victoria Street. He would ring her personal mobile phone and say 'Drinks tonight, luv?' and she would know to meet him in that spot. She would stand behind him. He would leave the goods at the cash point machine when he withdrew money or at least pretended to withdraw money. She would then pick it up with her own cash when she used the machine. Not the most sophisticated system, she knew, considering all the CCTV cameras that would be documenting every movement in the vicinity, but it couldn't be helped.

Norman said, 'Right, then,' and waited for her to hand over her mobile number. They parted.

Barbara said to his retreating back, '*Soon*, Norman.'

'Life and death,' was his reply.

God, she thought, the lengths she went to in the cause of finding a killer. She returned to Victoria Block.

Back in the incident room, there was some serious milling about going on. She learned this had to do with a report from SO7 that had just come in: the blood sprayed on the yellow shirt from the Oxfam bin did indeed belong to Jemima Hastings. Well, Barbara thought, they had reckoned as much.

She approached the china board with its array of photos, its scrawled information, its names listed and its timelines drawn. She hadn't had a decent look at it since being recalled from Hampshire, and among other things up there was a decent photo of the yellow shirt. It might tell her something, she thought. She wondered how Whiting looked in yellow.

But it was not the shirt that caught her attention, as things turned out. It was another photograph altogether. She looked upon the picture of the murder weapon, of the ruler placed next to it to indicate its size.

When she saw it, she spun round from the photo to seek out Nkata. From across the room he glanced up at that moment, a phone pressed to his ear, and he obviously clocked her expression because he said a few more words to whoever was on the other end of the line, before ringing off and coming to join her.

She said, 'Winnie . . .' and pointed to the picture. She didn't need to say more. She heard him breathe out in a whistle, so she knew he was thinking what she was thinking. The only question was whether his conclusion was the same.

She said, 'We've got to get back to Hampshire.'

He said, 'Barb—'

'Don't argue.'

'Barb, we been ordered back. We can't head off like we're in charge here.'

'Phone her, then. She's got her mobile.'

'We c'n ring down there. We c'n tell th' cops to—'

'Ring where? Hampshire? With *Whiting* in charge? Winnie, good God, d'you think that makes sense?'

He looked at the photo of the weapon, then at the photo of the yellow shirt. Barbara knew he was thinking of the politics behind what she was proposing, and in his hesitation, she had her answer to the question concerning on what side of the line Winnie would always walk. She couldn't blame him. Her own career was so chequered that a few more black marks hardly mattered. His career was not.

She said, 'All right. *I'll* phone the guv. But then I'm going. It's the only way.'

To Isabelle's relief Hiro Matsumoto did have some influence over his sister. After some conversation in their brother's hospital room, Miyoshi Matsumoto emerged and told Isabelle she could speak to Yukio. But *if* her younger brother became upset either by Isabelle's questions or her presence, the interview would end at once. And *she* – not Isabelle – would be the one to determine how 'upset' might manifest itself.

Isabelle had no choice but to agree to Miyoshi's rules. She fished her mobile out of her bag and switched it off. She wanted to take no chances that anything external to her own questions might disturb the violinist.

Yukio's head was bandaged, and he was hooked up to

various machines and IV drips. But he was conscious and he seemed to be taking some comfort from the presence of his two siblings. Hiro had positioned himself near his brother's shoulder where he'd laid his hand. Miyoshi took a place on the other side of the bed. She fussed maternally with the neck of his hospital gown as well as with the thin blanket that covered him. She eyed Isabelle suspiciously. She said, 'You've the time it will take Mrs Bourne to arrive.'

That, Isabelle saw, had been the compromise the siblings had reached. Hiro had phoned the solicitor in exchange for his sister's agreement to allow Isabelle a few minutes' access to their brother. She said, 'Very well,' and she studied the violinist. He was smaller than he'd seemed in flight. He looked far more vulnerable than she would have expected.

She said to him, 'Mr Matsumoto . . . Yukio, I'm Detective Superintendent Ardery. I need to speak with you, but you're not to worry. What we're saying here – in this room – is not being recorded or documented. Your brother and sister are here to make sure I don't upset you, and you can be assured that upsetting you is the least of my intentions. Do you understand me?'

Yukio nodded although his gaze fluttered over to his brother first. There was, Isabelle saw, only a faint resemblance between them. Although Hiro Matsumoto was the elder, he looked years younger.

'When I went to your lodgings in Charing Cross Road,' Isabelle told Yukio, 'I found a piece of iron, pointed like a spike, on the edge of the basin. It had blood on it and that blood turned out to belong to a woman called Jemima Hastings. Do you know how that spike got there, Yukio?'

Yukio didn't respond at first. Isabelle wondered if he would at all. She'd never before confronted a paranoid schizophrenic, so she had no idea what to expect.

When he finally spoke, he indicated his neck, in the approximate location of the wound to Jemima Hastings. 'I pulled it out,' he said.

'The spike?' Isabelle clarified. 'You pulled the spike from Jemima's neck?'

He said, 'Tore.'

'The spike tore her skin? Made the wound worse? Is that what you're saying?' It certainly matched the condition of her body, Isabelle thought.

'Don't direct him to say what you want him to say,' Miyoshi Matsumoto said sharply. 'If you're going to ask my brother questions, he's going to answer them in his own way.'

Yukio said, 'Life's fountain came forth, like God telling Moses to tap upon stone. From the stone comes water to soothe their thirst. The water is a river and the river turns to blood.'

'Jemima's blood?' Isabelle asked. 'You got it on your clothing when you removed the spike?'

'It was everywhere.' He closed his eyes.

His sister said, 'That's enough,' to Isabelle.

Are you mad? was what Isabelle wanted to reply, hardly the question to ask the sister of a paranoid schizophrenic. She'd heard virtually nothing from the man, and certainly not a single word that could be used in court. Or used even to press charges against him. Or against anyone. She'd be laughed off the force if she even tried. She said, 'Why were you there, in the cemetery, on that day?'

Still with his eyes closed – and God only knew what he was seeing behind his lids – Yukio said, 'It was the choice they gave me. To guard or to fight. I chose to guard but they wanted something else.'

'So you fought? Did you have a fight with Jemima?'

'That's *not* what he's saying,' Miyoshi said. 'He didn't fight with that woman. He tried to save her. Hiro, she's trying to bend his words.'

'I'm trying to learn what happened that day,' Isabelle told her. 'If you can't see that—'

'Then try bending the conversation in another direction,' Miyoshi snapped. And then to her brother, with her hand stroking his forehead, 'Yukio, were you there to protect that woman in the cemetery? Is that why you were there when she was attacked? Did you try to save her? Is that what you're saying?'

Yukio opened his eyes. He looked at his sister but didn't seem to see her. He said, and for the first time his voice was quite clear, 'I watched her.'

'Can you tell me what you saw?' Miyoshi asked him.

It came out haltingly and half of it was obscured by what Isabelle assumed were either biblical references or products of his fevered mind. He spoke of Jemima in the clearing where the cemetery's chapel stood. She sat on a bench, read a book, used her mobile phone. Ultimately she was joined by a man. Sunglasses and a baseball cap constituted the limit of the description that Yukio Matsumoto provided, which could have applied to one quarter of the male population of the country, if not the world. It telegraphed *disguise* so loudly and clearly that Isabelle thought Yukio Matsumoto was either manufacturing it on the spot or they had an image – completely useless – of their killer at last. She wasn't sure which. But then things got dicey.

This man had a conversation with Jemima upon the stone bench where Jemima sat. Yukio had no idea how long the conversation lasted, but when it ended, the man left.

And when he left, Jemima Hastings was, decidedly, still alive.

She used her mobile again. Once, twice, three times? Five hundred times? Yukio didn't know. But then she *took* a call. After that, she walked to the side of the chapel and out of his range of vision.

And then? Isabelle asked.

Nothing. At least not at first, not for some minutes. Then a man appeared from that same side of the ruined chapel. A man in black – God, why were they *always* in black? Isabelle wondered.

– who carried a rucksack and who made for the trees. Away from the chapel, out of sight altogether.

Yukio waited then. But Jemima Hastings did not return to the chapel clearing. So he went to look for her and that was how he discovered what he had not seen before: that there was a tiny building abutting the chapel. In this building Jemima lay wounded, her hands scrabbling round her throat, which was how he saw the spike. He thought she was trying to pull it out, and so he helped her.

And thus, Isabelle thought, the river of blood from her artery which had already spurted out upon the yellow shirt worn by her killer, began to pulse out with every beat of her heart. Nothing Yukio could have done would have saved her. Not with a wound like that, exacerbated when he'd removed the spike.

If, she thought, he was to be believed. And she had a terrible feeling that he was.

One man in sunglasses and a baseball cap. The other in black. They would need to try to get e-fits of both of them, and Isabelle prayed only that this could be managed before Zaynab Bourne got there and threw a spanner in everything.

26

Robbie Hastings had encountered no difficulty when he went to the Lyndhurst police station. His thought had been to insist on quick action, but that wasn't necessary as it turned out. Upon identifying himself, he'd been ushered into the chief superintendent's office, where Zachary Whiting had offered him midmorning coffee and heard him out with not a single interruption. As Rob spoke, Whiting frowned in concern, but the frown turned out to be about Rob's upset rather than about the questions he was asking or the demands for action he was making. At the conclusion of Rob's recitation of concerns, Whiting had said, 'Good God, it's all in hand, Mr Hastings. You should have been informed of this, and I can't think why you weren't.'

Rob wondered *what* was in hand, and this he asked, adding that there were train tickets, there was a hotel receipt. He knew that these had been given to Whiting and what had Whiting done about them? What had he done about Jossie, as a matter of fact? Again, Whiting reassured him. What he meant when he said that things were in hand was that everything he – Whiting – knew, everything he had been told, and everything that had been handed to him was now in the possession of the Scotland Yard detectives who'd come down to Hampshire in connection with the London murder inquiry. That meant the tickets and the hotel receipt as well, Whiting told him. They were likely in London at this point, as he'd sent them up by special messenger. Mr Hastings wasn't to worry about that. If Gordon Jossie had perpetrated this crime against Mr Hastings' sister –

'*If?*' Rob had said.

– then Mr Hastings could expect Scotland Yard to come calling again in very short order.

'I don't understand why the London police and not you lot here—'

Whiting held up his hand. He said it was a complicated matter because more than one police jurisdiction was involved. As to why it was Scotland Yard looking into matters and not the locals from where Mr Hastings' sister had been killed, he couldn't say. That was likely due to some political situation up in London. But what Whiting *could* say was that the reason the Hampshire constabulary was not handling the case had to do with this being a killing that had not occurred in Hampshire in the first place. The Hampshire police *would* cooperate and *were* cooperating fully with London, naturally. That meant handing over whatever they had or were given or what they learned, and once again he wanted to assure Mr Hastings that this had been done and was continuing to be done.

'Jossie admits to being in London,' Rob told Whiting again. 'I spoke to him myself. The bastard *admits* it.'

And that, too, would be transmitted to the London police. There would be someone brought to justice, Mr Hastings. That was likely to happen very soon.

Whiting personally ushered Rob to the reception area at the end of their meeting. He introduced him along the way to the duty press officer, to the sergeant in charge of the custody suite, and to two special constables who liaised with the community.

In Reception, Whiting informed the special on duty that until an arrest had been made in the London murder of Jemima Hastings, whenever her brother needed to see the chief superintendent, he was to be given access. Rob appreciated all of this. It went a great way towards soothing his mind.

He returned to his home and hooked up the horse trailer. With Frank as his companion – head hanging out of the window, tongue and ears flapping – he trundled from Burley along the lanes to Sway and from there to Gordon Jossie's holding.

The narrowness of the roads and the fact of the horse trailer made the going slow, but it was of no account. He didn't expect Gordon Jossie to be on the property at this time of day.

That turned out to be the case. When Rob reversed up the cottage drive and positioned the horse trailer near the paddock that contained the two ponies from the Minstead area, no one came out of the cottage to stop him. The absence of Jossie's Golden Retriever told him, as well, that no one was home. He let Frank out of the Land Rover to have a run, but told the Weimaraner to keep his distance when he brought the ponies from the paddock. As if he understood this perfectly, Frank headed in the direction of the barn, snuffling along the ground as he went.

The ponies weren't as skittish as some within the Perambulation, so it wasn't difficult to get them into the horse trailer. This went some way towards explaining how Jossie had managed them when he brought them here as, unlike Rob, he wasn't an experienced horseman. It did not, however, explain what Jossie was doing with the two ponies in the first place, so far from where they normally grazed and belonging to someone else. He would have seen how their tails were clipped, so even had he mistaken them for his own ponies, a closer look would have told him they were from another area. Keeping them on his holding when they weren't his responsibility and longer than they clearly needed to be there was an expense any other commoner would have avoided. Rob couldn't reckon why Gordon Jossie had taken it on.

When he had them ready for transport, Rob returned to the paddock to close its gate. There he noticed what he might have noticed on earlier visits to the holding had he not been first consumed with concerns about his sister and then later taken up by considerations ranging from Gina Dickens' presence to that of the ponies. Jossie had been putting some work into the paddock. The gate was relatively new, a number of the fence posts were new, and the barbed wire strung between them was new as well. The freshness of all this, however, comprised only one part of the paddock. The rest had yet to be seen to. Indeed, the rest was something of a ruin, with posts atilt and areas overgrown with weeds.

This gave him pause. It wasn't, he knew, unusual for a commoner to make improvements upon his holding. This was generally necessary. It was, however, odd that someone like Jossie – characterised by the nearly compulsive care with which he did everything else – would have left a job such as this one unfinished.

Rob recalled Gina Dickens' desire for a garden, and for a moment he wondered if she and Jossie had taken the unlikely decision to have that garden here. If Gordon intended to build another paddock somewhere else for ponies, it would explain why the thatcher had gone no further with his scheme to improve this one as a holding pen for stock. On the other hand, discontinuing this paddock's use as a holding pen would mean moving the heavy granite trough to another location, a task requiring the sort of equipment Gordon didn't possess.

Rob frowned at this. The trough suddenly seemed to him very much like the presence of the ponies: unnecessary. For hadn't there been a trough here already? Within the paddock? Surely there had.

He looked for it. It didn't take long. He found the old trough in the unrestored section of the paddock, heavily overgrown with brambles, vines and weeds. It stood some distance from the water source, which made the new trough not altogether unreasonable as it could be more easily reached by hosepipe. Still, it was strange that Gordon would go to the expense of a new trough without having uncovered the old one. He had to have suspected it was there.

It was a curiosity. Rob intended to have a word with Gordon Jossie about it.

He returned to his vehicle and murmured to the ponies moving restlessly within the trailer. He called to Frank, the dog came running, and they set off to the northernmost part of the Perambulation.

It took nearly an hour to get there, even keeping to the main roads. Rob was stymied in his progress by a train stopped on the railway tracks in Brockenhurst, blocking the crossing, and then again by a tour coach with a flat tyre that caused a tailback on the south side of Lyndhurst. When he finally got beyond it and into Lyndhurst itself, the restiveness of the animals in the trailer told him that taking them up to Minstead was a bad idea. As a result, he veered onto the Bournemouth Road and made for Bank. Beyond it and along a sheltered lane stood the tiny enclave of Gritnam, a circle of back-to-back gardenless cottages facing outward onto the lawns, the trees and the streams that comprised the expanse of Gritnam Wood. The lane itself went no farther than Gritnam, so there was likely no safer place in the New Forest to release ponies which had too long been kept in Gordon Jossie's paddock.

Rob parked in the middle of the lane that encircled the cottages as the place was so tiny there was no other spot to leave a vehicle. There amid a silence broken only by the call of chaffinches and the trill of wrens, he eased the ponies out into freedom once more. Two children emerged from one of the cottages to watch him at work, but long schooled in the ways of the New Forest, they did not approach. Only when the ponies were making their way towards a stream that gleamed some distance into the trees did either child speak and then it was to say, 'We got kittens here, if you want to see 'em. We got six. Mum says we're meant to give 'em way.'

Rob went over to where the two children stood, barefooted and freckled in the summer heat. A boy and girl. Each of them held a kitten in their arms.

'Why've you got the ponies?' the boy asked. He seemed to be the elder of the two by several years. His sister watched him adoringly. She put Rob in mind of the way Jemima had once watched him. She put Rob in mind of how he'd failed her.

He was about to explain what he was doing with the ponies when his mobile rang. It was on the seat of his Land Rover, but he could hear it clearly. He set off to take the call, heard the news all of the agisters dreaded hearing, and swore when he was given it. For the second time in a week, a New Forest pony had been hit by a motorist. Rob's services were wanted in the manner in which he least wished to give them: the animal was going to have to be killed.

The worry Meredith Powell felt had grown to full blown anxiety by the morning. All of it had to do with Gina. They'd shared the double bed in Meredith's bedroom, and Gina had asked in the darkness if Meredith didn't mind holding her hand till she went to sleep. She'd said, 'I know it's ridiculous to ask but I think it might settle me a bit . . .' and Meredith had told her yes, of course, she didn't even *need* to explain, and she'd covered Gina's hand with her own and Gina's hand had turned and clasped hers and there their hands had lain for hours upon hours on the mattress between them. Gina had fallen asleep quickly – which of course made perfect sense as the poor girl was exhausted by what she'd gone through at Gordon Jossie's cottage – but her sleep was light and fitful and every time Meredith had tried to ease her hand away from Gina's, Gina's fingers tightened, she gave a small whimper, and Meredith's heart had gone out to her again. So in the darkness, she'd thought about what to do about Gina's situation. For Gina had to be protected from Gordon, and Meredith knew that she herself might be the only person willing to protect her.

Asking for police participation in the matter was out of the question. Chief Superintendent Whiting and his relationship with Gordon – whatever it was – put paid to that, and even if that were not the situation, the police weren't about to deploy their resources upon the protection of a single individual based on the strength of her bruises. Truth was that cops wanted a lot more than a few bruises before they did anything. They generally wanted a court order, an injunction filed, charges made and the like, and Meredith had a very good feeling that Gina Dickens was too frightened to apply herself to any of this anyway.

She could be urged to remain at Meredith's house, but that could hardly go on indefinitely. While it was true that no one was more accommodating than Meredith's own parents, it was also true that they were already sheltering Meredith and her daughter and anyway since Meredith had impulsively come up with the gas leak tale to explain Gina's presence, her mum and dad would assume the gas leak would be fixed within twenty-four hours.

That being the case, Gina would be expected to return to her bedsit above the Mad Hatter Tea Rooms. This, of course, was the worst place for her because Gordon Jossie knew where to find her. So an alternative needed to be developed, and by morning Meredith had an idea what that alternative might be.

'Rob Hastings will protect you,' she told Gina over breakfast. 'Once we tell him what Gordon did to you, he'll certainly help. Rob's never liked him. He's got rooms in his house that no one's using and he'll offer one without our even asking.'

Gina hadn't eaten much, merely picking at a bowl of grapefruit segments and taking one bite of a piece of dry toast. She was silent for a moment before she said, 'You must have been a very good friend to Jemima, Meredith.'

That was hardly the case since she hadn't been able to talk Jemima out of taking up with Gordon and look what happened. Meredith was about to say this, but Gina went on.

'I need to go back.'

'To your bedsit? Bad idea. You can't put yourself where he knows where to find you. He'll never think you might be at Rob's. It's the safest place.'

But, surprisingly, Gina had said, 'Not the bedsit. I must go back to Gordon's. I've had the night to sleep on it, and I've thought about what happened. I can see how I was the one to provoke—'

'No, no, no!' Meredith cried. For this was how abused

women always acted. Given time to 'think', what they generally ended up thinking was that *they* were at fault, somehow provoking their men to do what they'd done to hurt them. They ended up telling themselves that if they'd only kept their mouths shut or acted compliant or said something different, fists would *never* have been swung in their direction.

Meredith had tried her best to explain this to Gina, but Gina had been obdurate. She'd said to Meredith in reply, 'I know all that, Meredith. I've got my degree in sociology. But this is different—'

'That's also what they always say!' Meredith had cut in.

'I know. Trust me. I *do* know. But you can't think I'd let him hurt me again. And the truth is . . .' She looked away from Meredith, as if gathering the courage to admit the worst. 'I do honestly love him.'

Meredith was aghast. Her face must have shown it because Gina went on to say, 'I just can't think, at the end of the day, that he hurt Jemima. He's not that kind of man.'

'He went to London! He lied about going! He lied to you, to Scotland Yard as well. Why would he lie if he didn't have a reason to be lying? *And* he lied to you from the very first about going there. He said it was Holland. He said it was to buy reeds. You told me that and you must see what it means.'

Gina let Meredith have her entire say in the matter before she herself drew the conversation to its conclusion. She said, 'He knew I'd be upset if he told me he'd gone to see Jemima. He knew I'd be a bit unreasonable. Which is what I've been, which is certainly what I was last night. Look. You've been good to me. You've been the best friend I have in the New Forest. But I love him and I *must* see if there's a chance he and I can make things work. He's under terrible stress right now because of Jemima. He's reacted badly but I've not reacted well either. I can't throw it all away because he did something that hurt me a bit.'

'He may have hurt you,' Meredith cried, 'but he *killed* Jemima!'

Gina said firmly, 'I don't believe that.'

There was no more talking to her about the matter, Meredith discovered. There was only her intention to return to Gordon Jossie, to 'give things another try' in the fashion of abused women everywhere. This was bad, but what was worse was that Meredith had no choice: she had to let her go.

Still, worry over Gina Dickens dominated most of her morning. She had no creative energy to apply to her work for Gerber & Hudson and when a phone call came into the office for her, she was happy enough to have to use her elevenses in a dash over to the office of Michele Daugherty who'd made that call and said to her, 'Got something for you. Have you time to meet?'

Meredith purchased a takeaway orange juice and drank it on her route to the private investigator's office. She'd nearly forgotten that she'd hired Michele Daugherty, so much having happened since she'd asked her to look into Gina Dickens.

The investigator was on the phone when she arrived. At long last Michele Daugherty called her into her office, where a reassuring stack of papers seemed to indicate she'd been hard at work on the brief that Meredith had given her.

The investigator wasted no time with social preliminaries. 'There is no Gina Dickens,' she said. 'Are you sure you've got the right name? The right spelling?'

At first, Meredith didn't understand what the investigator meant so she said, 'This is someone I *know*, Ms Daugherty. She's not just a name I heard mentioned in a pub or something. She's actually . . . rather . . . well, she's rather a friend.'

Michele Daugherty didn't question why Meredith was having a friend investigated. She merely said, 'Be that as it may. There's no Gina Dickens that I can find. There're Dickenses aplenty but no one called Gina in her age range. Or in any other age range, if it comes down to it.'

She went on to explain that she'd tried every possible spelling and variation of the given name. Considering that Gina was likely a nickname or an abbreviated form of a longer name, she'd gone into her databases with Gina, Jean, Janine, Regina, Virginia, Georgina, Marjorina, Angelina, Jacquelina, Gianna, Eugenia and Evangelina. She said, 'I *could* go on like this indefinitely, but I expect you'd rather not pay for that. At the end of the day when things go in this direction, I tell my clients it's safe to say that there is no person by that name 'less she's managed to slip through the system without having left a mark on it anywhere, which isn't possible. She *is* a Brit, isn't she? No doubt of that? Chance she might be a foreigner? Aussie? New Zealander? Canadian?'

'Of course she's British. I spent last night with her, for heaven's sake.' As if *that* meant anything, Meredith thought as soon as she said it. 'She's been living with a man called Gordon Jossie, but she has a bedsit in Lyndhurst above the Mad Hatter Tea Rooms. Tell me how you searched. Tell me where you looked.'

'Where I always look. Where any investigator, including the police, would look. My dear, people leave records. They leave trails without knowing: birth, education, health, credit history, financial dealings throughout their lives, parking tickets, the ownership of *anything* that might have required financing or provided a guarantee or warranty and thus needed to be registered, magazine subscriptions, newspaper subscriptions, phone bills, water bills, electricity bills. One searches through all this.'

'What exactly are you saying, then?' Meredith was feeling quite numb.

'I'm saying that there is no Gina Dickens, full stop. It's impossible not to leave a trail, no matter who you are or where you live. So if a person *doesn't* leave a trail, it's fairly safe to conclude she isn't who she says she is. And there you have it.'

'So who is she?' Meredith considered the possibilities. '*What* is she?'

'I've no idea. But the facts suggest she's someone very different from whoever it is she's pretending to be.'

Meredith stared at the investigator. She didn't want to understand, but the fact was that she was understanding all too terribly well. She said numbly, 'Gordon Jossie, then. J-o-s-s-i-e.'

'What about Gordon Jossie?'

'Start on him.'

Gordon had to return to his holding for a load of Turkish reeds. These had been held for inspection at the port for a maddening length of time, a circumstance that had considerably slowed his progress on the roof of the Royal Oak Pub. It seemed to Gordon that the terrorist attacks of recent years had resulted in all port authorities believing there were Muslim extremists hidden within every crate on every ship that docked in England. They were especially suspicious of items having their provenance in countries with which they were not personally familiar. That reeds actually *grew* in Turkey was a piece of information most port officials did not possess. So those reeds had to be examined at excruciating length, and if such examination ate up a week or two, there was not much he could do about it. It was yet another reason to try to get the reeds from the Netherlands, Gordon thought. At least Holland was a familiar place in the eyes of the hopeless blokes who were assigned the duty of inspecting that which was shipped into the country.

When he and Cliff Coward returned to his holding for the delivery of the reeds, he saw at once that Rob Hastings had made good on his word. The two ponies were gone from the paddock. He wasn't sure what he was going to do about this, but then perhaps, he thought wearily, there was nothing to be done, things being the way they were at the moment.

This was something that Cliff had wanted to discuss. Seeing Gina's car gone from the vicinity of Gordon's house, Cliff asked about her. Not where she was but how she was, the same 'How's our Gina then,' that he asked nearly every day. Cliff had been quite taken with Gina from the first.

Gordon had told him the truth. 'Gone,' was how he put it.

Cliff repeated the word dumbly, as if the term were slow to sink into his head. When it got to his brain, he said, 'What? She's left you?'

To which Gordon replied, 'That's how it works, Cliff.'

This prompted a lengthy discourse from Cliff on the subject of what kind of shelf life – as he put it – girls like Gina generally had. 'You got six days or less to get her back, man,' Cliff informed. 'You think blokes're going to let a girl like Gina walk round the streets without trying it on? Ring her up, say sorry, get her back. Say sorry even if you didn't do nothing to make her leave. Say anything. Just *do* something.'

'Nothing to be done,' Gordon told him.

'You're off your nut,' Cliff decided.

So when Gina actually showed up while they were loading reeds into the back of Gordon's pickup, Cliff made himself scarce. From the elevated bed of the truck, he saw her red Mini Cooper coming along the lane, said 'Give you twenty minutes to sort this one, Gordon,' and then he was gone, heading in the direction of the barn.

Gordon walked towards the end of the driveway so when Gina drove in, he was in the vicinity of the front garden. At heart, he knew that Cliff was right: she was the kind of woman blokes lined up to have the slightest chance of winning over, and he was a fool if he didn't try to get her back.

She braked when she saw him. The car roof was down, and her hair was windblown from the drive. He wanted to touch it because he knew how it would feel, so soft against his hands.

He approached the car. 'Can we talk?'

She was wearing her sunglasses against the brightness of another fine summer day, but she shoved them to the top of her head. Her eyes, he saw, were red-rimmed. She'd been crying, he realised. He was the one who'd brought this on. It was another burden. Yet another failure to be the man he wanted to be.

'Please. Can we talk?' he repeated.

She looked at him warily. She pressed her lips together, and he could see her bite down on them. Not as if she wanted to keep herself from speaking but as if she feared what might happen if she did speak. He reached for the handle of the door, and she flinched slightly.

He said, 'Oh, Gina.' He took a step back, in order to allow her to decide. When she opened the door, he felt he could breathe again. He said, 'C'n we . . . ? Let's sit over here.'

Over here was the garden she'd made so lovely for them, with the table and chairs, the torches and the candles. *Over here* was where they'd had their suppers in the fine weather of the summer amid the flowers she'd planted and painstakingly watered. He walked to the table and waited for her. He watched her but said nothing. She had to make the decision on her own. He prayed she'd make the one that would give them a future.

She got out of the car. She glanced at his pickup, at the reeds he was loading into it, at the paddock beyond it. He saw her draw her eyebrows together. She said, 'What's happened to the horses?'

He said, 'They're gone.'

She looked at him. Her expression told him she thought he'd done this for her, because she was afraid of the animals. Part of him wanted to tell her the truth: that Rob Hastings had taken them because Gordon hadn't the need – let alone the right – to hang onto them. But the other part of him saw how he could use the moment to win her and he wanted to win her. So he let her believe whatever she wanted to believe about the ponies' removal.

She came to join him in the garden. They were separated from the lane by the hedge. They were also sequestered from Cliff Coward's curious eyes by the cottage that stood between the front garden and the barn. They could speak here and not be heard or seen. This went some distance towards making Gordon easier although it seemed to have the opposite effect on Gina, who looked round, shivered as if with cold, and clasped her arms to her body.

'What've you done to yourself?' he asked her. For he saw deep bruises upon her arms, ugly marks that made him move towards her. 'Gina, what's happened?'

She looked down at her arms, as if she'd forgotten. She said, 'I hit myself.'

'What did you say?'

She said, 'Have you never wanted to hurt yourself because nothing you do ever seems to come out right?'

'What? How did you . . . ?'

'I pounded,' she said. 'When it wasn't enough, I used . . .' She'd not been looking at him, but now she did, and he saw her eyes were full.

'You used something to hurt yourself with? Gina . . .' He took a step towards her. She backed away. He felt struck. He said, 'Why did you do this?'

A tear spilled over. She wiped it away with the back of her hand. 'I'm so terribly ashamed,' she said. 'I did it.'

'What?' For a horrible moment he thought she meant that *she'd* killed Jemima, but she clarified with, 'I took those tickets, that hotel receipt. I found them and I took them and I was the one who gave them to . . . I'm so *sorry.*'

She began to weep in earnest then, and he went to her. He drew her into his arms and she allowed this and when she allowed it and because she allowed it, he felt his heart open to her as it had not opened to anyone, even to Jemima.

He said, 'I shouldn't have lied to you. I shouldn't have said I was going to Holland. I should have told you from the first that I was seeing Jemima, but I thought I couldn't.'

'Why?' She clenched her fist against his chest as if she would hit him, but she didn't do so. 'What did you think? Why don't you trust me?'

'Everything I told you about seeing Jemima was true. I swear to God. I saw her but she was alive when I left her. We didn't part well, but we didn't part in anger.'

'Then what?' Gina waited for his answer, and he struggled to give it, with his body, his soul and his very life hanging on the balance of whatever words he chose. He swallowed and she said, 'What on earth are you so afraid of, Gordon?'

He put his hands on either side of her lovely face. He said, 'You're only my second.' He bent to kiss her, and she allowed this. Her mouth opened to him and she accepted his tongue and her hands went to the back of his neck and held him to her so the kiss went on and on and on. He felt enflamed, and he – not she – was the one to break off. He was breathing so hard that he might have been running. 'Only Jemima and you. No one else,' he said.

'Oh Gordon,' she said.

'Come back to me. What you saw in me . . . that anger . . . the fear . . .'

'Shh,' she murmured. She touched his face with those fingers of hers, and where she touched he felt his skin take fire.

'You make it all disappear,' he said. 'Come back. Gina. I swear.'

'I will.'

27

Lynley took the first of the phone calls on his mobile as he left Sheldon Pockworth Numismatics, heading for his car on his way to the British Museum. It was from Philip Hale. Initially, his message was positive. Yukio Matsumoto, he reported, was conscious, and Isabelle Ardery was interviewing him in the presence of his brother and sister. However, there was something more and as Hale was the last of the detectives ever to raise a protest in the midst of an investigation, when he did so, Lynley knew the situation was serious. Ardery was ordering him to stay at the hospital when he could better be used elsewhere, he told Lynley. He'd tried to explain to her that guarding the suspect was something best left to constables so that he could return to more useful occupation, but she wouldn't hear of it, he said. He was a team player as much as anyone, Tommy, but there came a time when someone had to protest. Obviously, Ardery was a micromanager and she was never going to trust her murder squad to take any initiative. She was—

'Philip,' Lynley cut in, 'hang on. I can't do anything about this. It's just not on.'

'You can *talk* to her,' Hale replied. 'If you're showing her the ropes like she claimed you are, then show her that one. Can you see Webberly . . . or yourself . . . or even John Stewart and God knows John's obsessive enough . . . ? Come on, Tommy.'

'She's got a lot on her plate.'

'You can't tell me she won't listen to you. I've seen how she . . . Oh hell.'

'Seen how she what?'

'She got you to come back to work. We all know that. There's a reason for it, and likely it's personal. So *use* the reason.'

'There's no personal—'

'Tommy. For God's sake. Don't play at being blind when no one else is.'

Lynley didn't reply for a moment. He considered what had passed between himself and Ardery: how things looked and what they were. He finally said he'd see what he could do although he reckoned it would be little enough.

He phoned the acting superintendent, but Ardery's mobile went immediately to her voice message. He asked her to ring him, and he kept onward to his car. She *wasn't* his responsibility, he thought. If she asked his advice, he could certainly give it. But the point was to let her sink or swim without his interference, no matter what anyone else wanted from him. In what other way could she show that she was up to the job?

He made his way over to Bloomsbury. The second call on his mobile came while he was stuck in traffic in the vicinity of Green Park station. This time it was Winston Nkata ringing him. Barb Havers, he said, in 'best Barb fashion' was on her way to defying the superintendent's instructions that she remain in London. She was, he went on, driving down to Hampshire. Winston had not been able to talk her out of it. 'You know Barb' was how Winston put it.

'She'll listen to you, man,' Nkata said. ''Cos she bloody well i'n't listening to me.'

'Christ,' Lynley muttered, 'she's a maddening woman. What's she up to, then?'

'The weapon,' Nkata said. 'She recognised it.'

'What d'you mean? She knows who it belongs to?'

'She knows what it is, guv. So do I. We di'n't see the picture of it till today. Di'n't have a look at the china board before this morning. And *what* it is narrows the field to Hampshire.'

'It's not like you to keep me in suspense, Winston.'

'Called a crook,' Nkata told him. 'We saw 'em by the crate in Hampshire, when we talked to that bloke Ringo Heath.'

'The master thatcher.'

'Tha's the bloke. Crooks's what's used to hold reeds in place when you're putting them on a roof. Not exactly something we'd be used to seeing in London, eh, but in Hampshire? Any place they got thatched roofs and thatchers, you're goin' to see crooks.'

'Jossie,' Lynley said.

'Or Hastings. 'Cos these're made by hand. Crooks, that is.'

'Hastings? Why?' Then Lynley remembered. 'He trained as a blacksmith.'

'And blacksmiths're the ones who make the crooks. Each one makes 'em different, see. They end up—'

'Like fingerprints,' Lynley concluded.

'Tha's about it. Which's why Barb's heading down there. She said she'd ring Ardery first, but you know Barb. So I thought you might . . . you know. Barb'll listen to you. Like I said, she wasn't having anything off me.'

Lynley cursed beneath his breath. He rang off. Traffic began moving, so he continued on his way, determined to track down Havers via mobile as soon as he could. He hadn't managed this when his mobile rang again. This time it was Ardery.

'Where've you got with the coin dealer?' she asked.

He briefed her, telling her he was on his way to the British Museum. She said, 'Excellent. It's a motive, isn't it? And we've found no coin among her things, so someone took it off her at some point. We're getting somewhere at last. Good.' She went on to tell him what Yukio Matsumoto had informed her: there had been two men in the vicinity of the chapel in Abney Park Cemetery, not just one. Indeed, there had been three, if they wanted to include Matsumoto himself. 'We're working with him on an e-fit. His solicitor showed up while I was talking to him and we had something of a set-to – God, that woman's like a pit bull – but she's on board for the next two hours. As long as the Met admits culpability in Yukio's accident.'

Lynley drew in a sharp breath. 'Isabelle, Hillier's never going to go for that.'

'This,' Isabelle said, 'is more important than Hillier.'

It would, Lynley thought, be a very snowy day in hell before David Hillier saw things that way. Before he could tell the acting superintendent as much, however, she had rung off. He sighed. Hale, Havers, Nkata and Ardery. Where to begin? He chose the British Museum.

There at last, he tracked down a woman called Honor Robayo who had the powerful build of an Olympic swimmer and the handshake of a successful politician. She said frankly and with an appealing grin, '*Never* thought I'd be talking to a cop. Read masses of mysteries and detective novels, I do. Who d'you reckon you're more like, then: Rebus or Morse?'

'I have a fatal proclivity for vintage vehicles,' Lynley admitted.

'Morse it is.' Robayo crossed her arms on her chest, high up as if her biceps wouldn't allow her arms to get closer to her body. 'So. What c'n I do for you, then, Inspector Lynley?'

He told her why he'd come: to talk to the curator about a coin from the time of Antoninus Pius. This coin would be an aureus, he said.

'Got one you want to show me?' she asked.

'I was hoping for the opposite,' he replied. And could Ms Robayo tell him what such a coin might be worth? 'I'd heard between five hundred and a thousand pounds,' Lynley said. 'Would you agree?'

'Let's just have a quick look.'

She took him to her office where amid books, magazines and documents on her desk, she also kept her computer. It was a small matter to access a site on which coins were sold and a smaller matter to find on this site an aureus from the time of Antoninus Pius offered for bidding on the open market. The amount being asked was given in dollars: three thousand, six hundred. More than Dugué had thought likely. Not a huge sum, but a sum to kill for? Possibly.

'Do coins like these need a provenance?' Lynley asked.

'Well, they're not like art, are they? No one's going to care who's owned it in the past unless, I suppose, it was some Nazi who took it off a Jewish family. The real questions about it will circle round its authenticity and its material.'

'Meaning?'

She indicated the computer screen on which the aureus for sale was pictured. 'It's either an aureus or it's not an aureus: it's pure gold or not. And that's not something that'd be tough to sort out. As to its age – is it really from the period of Antoninus Pius? – I *suppose* someone could fake one, but any coin expert would be able to spot that. Besides, there's the question of why one would go to all the trouble of faking a coin like this. I mean, we're not talking about faking a "newly discovered" painting by Rembrandt or Van Gogh. You c'n imagine what something like that would be worth if someone could pull the wool successfully. Tens of millions, eh? But a coin? One would have to ask if thirty-six hundred dollars makes it worth the effort.'

'Over time, however?'

'You mean, if someone had faked a lorry load of coins to sell in dribs and drabs? Possibly, I s'pose.'

'May I have a look at one?' Lynley asked, 'Aside from on the computer screen, I mean. D'you have any here in the museum?'

They did indeed, Honor Robayo told him. If he'd follow her? They'd have to toddle over to the collection itself, but it wasn't far and she expected Lynley would find it interesting.

She led him back through time and place in the museum – ancient Iran, Turkey, Mesopotamia – until they got to the Roman collection. Lynley had been here but not in years. He'd forgotten the extent of the treasure.

Mildenhall, Hoxne, Thetford. They were called the hoards because that was how they had each been found: as a hoard hidden through burial during the time of the Romans' occupation of Britain. Things hadn't always gone swimmingly for the Romans as they attempted to subdue the people whom they'd come to rule. Since those people hadn't generally taken well to being vanquished, rebellions occurred. During these intermittent periods of revolt, Roman riches were concealed to keep them safe on the chance that the revolt might be successful. Sometimes the owners of these riches were unable to return for them, so they remained buried for centuries: in sealed jars, in wooden cases lined with straw, in whatever was available at the time.

This had been the case for the Mildenhall, Hoxne and Thetford Hoards, which comprised the main treasures that had been found. Buried for more than one thousand years, each had been unearthed during the twentieth century and they included everything from coins to vessels, from body ornaments to religious plaques.

There were minor treasure hoards in the collection as well, each representing a different area of Britain where the Romans had settled. The most recently discovered was the Hoxne hoard, Lynley saw, which had been uncovered in Suffolk on county council land in 1992. The discoverer – a bloke called Eric Lawes – had miraculously left the treasure exactly where and as it lay and had phoned the authorities at once. Out they came to scoop up more than fifteen thousand gold and silver coins, silver tableware and gold jewellery in the form of neck-laces, bracelets and rings. It was a sensational find. Its value, Lynley reckoned, was incalculable.

'Much to his credit,' Lynley murmured.

'Hmm?' Honor Robayo said.

'The fact that Mr Lawes turned it in. The treasure and this gentleman who found it.'

'Well, of course,' she said. 'But really, less to his credit than you might think.' She and Lynley were standing in front of one of the cases that contained the Hoxne Hoard, where a reconstruction of the chest in which the hoard had been buried was rendered in acrylic. She moved from this across the room to the immense silver platters and trays from the Mildenhall Hoard. She leaned against the case and said, 'Remember, this bloke Eric Lawes was out there looking for metal objects anyway. And *as* that's what he was doing in the first place, he likely would've known the law. 'Course the law's been changed round a bit since this hoard was found, but at the time, a hoard like Hoxne would've become the property of the Crown.'

'Doesn't that indicate he'd have had a motive to hang onto it?' Lynley asked.

She shrugged. 'What's he supposed to do with it? Especially when the law said a museum could purchase it from the Crown – at fair market value, mind you – and whoever found it would get that money as a reward. That's some considerable dosh.'

'Ah,' Lynley said. 'So someone would be motivated to hand it over, not to hang onto it.'

'Right.'

'And now?' He smiled, feeling rather foolish for the last question. He said, 'Forgive me. I probably ought to know the law about this, as a policeman.'

'Bah,' was her reply. 'I doubt you come across many cases of people unearthing treasures in your particular line of work. Anyway, the law's not *much* changed. Finder has fourteen days to report the treasure – if he *knows* it's a treasure – to the local coroner. He actually could be prosecuted if he doesn't ring up the coroner, as a matter of fact. Local coroner—'

'Hang on,' Lynley said. 'What d'you mean: if he *knows* it's a treasure.'

'Well, that's the thing about the 1996 law, you see. It defines what a treasure is. One coin, f'r instance, does not a treasure make, if you know what I mean. Two coins, however, and you're on shaky ground if you don't let the proper authorities know.'

'So that they can do what?' Lynley asked. 'On the off chance that all you've found is two coins and not twenty thousand?'

'So that they can bring out an archaeological team and dig the hell out of your property, I expect,' Honor Robayo said. 'Which, to be frank, most people don't mind because they end up with fair market value for the treasure.'

'*If* a museum wants to buy it.'

'Right.'

'And if no one does? If the Crown claims it?'

'That's another interesting bit about the change in law. The Crown can only put its mitts on treasures from the Duchy of Cornwall and the Duchy of Lancaster. As to the rest of the country . . . ? While it's not exactly a case of finders-keepers/losers-weepers, the finder *will* end up with a reward when the treasure is finally sold and if the treasure is anything like these' – with a nod at the cases of silver and gold and jewellery in Room 49 – 'you can lay good odds on the reward being hefty.'

'So what you're saying,' Lynley said, 'is that the finder of something like this has absolutely no motivation for keeping the news to himself or to herself.'

'None at all. Of course, I s'pose he could hide it under his bed and bring it out at night and run his hands through it gleefully, for all the good that's going to do him. Sort of a Silas Marner kind of thing. But at the end of the day, most people'd prefer the cash, I expect.'

'And if all that's been found is a single coin?'

'Oh, he can keep that. Which bring us to . . . Over here. We've got the aureus you were looking for.'

It was inside one of the smaller cases, one in which various coins were displayed and identified. The aureus in question looked no different from the one he'd seen on the screen of James Dugué's computer at Sheldon Pockworth Numismatics a short time earlier. Lynley gazed at it, willing the coin to tell him something about Jemima Hastings who'd supposedly had it in her possession at some point. If, as Honor Robayo had so colourfully indicated, one coin did not a treasure make, then there was every chance that Jemima had possessed it merely as a memento or a good luck charm that she was considering selling, perhaps to help her with her finances in London once she came to live in town. She would have needed to know what it was worth first. There was nothing unreasonable about that. But part of what she'd told the coin dealer had been a lie: her father hadn't died recently. From Havers' report on the matter, as he recalled, Jemima's father had been dead for years. Did that lie matter? Lynley didn't know. But he *did* need to talk to Havers.

He moved away from the case containing the aureus, thanking Honor Robayo for her time. She seemed to think she'd disappointed him in some way because she apologised and said, 'Well. Anyway. I do wish there was something . . . Have I helped at all?'

Again, he didn't really know. It was certain that he had more information than he'd had earlier in the day. But as to how it reflected a motive for killing Jemima Hastings—

He frowned. The Thetford Treasure caught his attention. They'd not looked so closely at that one because it comprised not coins but rather tableware and jewellery. The former was mostly done in silver. The latter was gold. He went for a look.

It was the jewellery that interested him: rings, buckles, pendants, bracelets and necklaces. The Romans had known how to adorn themselves. They'd done so with precious and semi-precious stones, for the larger pieces along with some of the rings contained garnets, amethysts and emeralds. Among these nestled one stone in particular, reddish in colour. It was, he could see at once, a carnelian. But what caught his eye was not so much the stone's presence among the others but what had been done with it: Venus, Cupid and the armour of Mars were engraved upon it, according to the description given. It was, in short, nearly identical to the stone that had been found on Jemima's body.

Lynley swung round to look at Honor Robayo. She raised an eyebrow as if to say What is it?

He said, 'Not two coins but a coin and a gem stone together. Do we have a treasure? Something that has to be reported to that local coroner you were mentioning a moment ago?'

'Something governed by the law?' She considered this, scratching her head. 'I s'pose that could be argued. But you could equally argue that someone who happens to find two superficially unrelated objects might merely clean them up, set them aside, and not think about them in relation to the law. I mean, how many people out there actually *know* this law? Find a treasure like the Hoxne Hoard and you're highly likely to make a few enquiries as to what you're supposed to do next, right? Find a single coin and a stone – both of which probably needed massive cleaning, mind you – and why would you jump to the phone over that? I mean, it's not like newsreaders are announcing on the telly once a week that their viewers must ring up the coroner on the off chance that they've unearthed a treasure chest while they're planting their tulips. Besides, people think of coroners and death, don't they, not coroners and treasure hoards.'

'Yet according to law, two items constitute treasure, don't they?'

'Well . . . Right. They do. Yes.'

It was little enough, Lynley thought, and Honor Robayo could certainly have sounded more robust in her agreement. But it was something. If not a torch then at least a match, and as he knew, a match was better than nothing when one was wandering in the dark.

Barbara Havers had stopped for both petrol and sustenance when her mobile rang. Otherwise, she would have religiously ignored it. As it was, she'd just pulled into the vast car park of a service station and she was striding towards the Little Chef – first things first, she'd told herself, and first things meant a decent fry-up to see her through the rest of the day – when she heard 'Peggy Sue' emanating from her shoulder bag. She rooted out the mobile to see that DI Lynley was ringing her. She took the call as she marched towards the promise of food and air conditioning.

'Where are you, Sergeant?' Lynley asked without preamble.

His tone told her that someone had sneaked on her, and it could only have been Winston Nkata since no one else knew what she was up to and Winnie was nothing if not scrupulous about obeying orders, no matter how maddening they were. Winnie, in fact, even obeyed non-orders. He *anticipated* orders, damn the man.

She said, 'About to sink my teeth into a major food group that's been dipped into batter and thoroughly fried, and let me tell you I don't much care which food group it is at this point. *Peckish* doesn't begin to describe, if you know what I mean. Where are you?'

'Havers,' Lynley said, 'you didn't answer my question. Please do so.'

She sighed. 'I'm at a Little Chef, sir.'

'Ah. Centre for all that's nutritious. And where might this particular branch of that fine eating establishment be?'

'Well, let me see . . .' She considered how to dress up the information but she knew it was useless to make it sound like anything other than what it was. So she finally said, 'Along the M3.'

'*Where* along the M3, Sergeant?'

Reluctantly she gave him the nearest exit number.

'And does Superintendent Ardery know where you happen to be going?'

She didn't reply. This was, she knew, a rhetorical question. She waited for what was coming next.

'Barbara, is professional suicide really your intention?' Lynley enquired politely.

'I rang her, sir.'

'Did you.'

'It went to her voice mail. I told her I was on to something. What else was I supposed to do?'

'Perhaps what were you meant to be doing? In London?'

'That's hardly the point. Look, sir, did Winnie tell you about the crook? It's a thatching tool and—'

'He did indeed tell me. And your intention in heading off to Hampshire is what, exactly?'

'Well, it's obvious, isn't it? Jossie's got thatching tools. Ringo

Heath's got thatching tools. Rob Hastings likely once *made* thatching tools, which're probably lying round his barn. Then there's the bloke that works with Jossie – Cliff Coward – who could put his mitts on a thatching tool and there's that cop Whiting as well because something's not right with him, in case you're about to tell me I should've rung up the Lyndhurst station and given *him* the news about the crook. I've got a snout at the Home Office, by the way, looking into Whiting.' Which is more than you were able to do, she wanted to say but she did not.

If she thought Lynley would be impressed with the leaps and bounds she was making while he'd been swanning round London doing *whatever* Isabelle Ardery had asked him to do, she was proven wrong almost at once. He said, 'Barbara, I want you to stay where you are.'

She said, '*What*? Sir, listen to me—'

'You can't take matters—'

'. . . into my own hands? Well, I wouldn't have to if the superintendent – the *acting* superintendent – had something other than tunnel vision. She's dead wrong about that Japanese bloke and you know it.'

'And she knows it now as well.' He told her what Ardery had managed to get from her interview with Yukio Matsumoto.

Barbara said, '*Two* men in the cemetery with her? Aside from Matsumoto? Bloody hell, sir. Don't you see that one of them – and possibly both of them – came up from Hampshire?'

'I don't disagree,' Lynley told her. 'But you've only got one part of this puzzle under your pillow, and you know as well as I that if you play that part too soon, you've lost the game.'

Barbara smiled then, in spite of herself. 'Are you aware how many metaphors you just mixed?'

She could hear the smile in his own voice when he said, 'Call it the passion of the moment. It prevents me from thinking cleverly.'

'Why? What's going on?'

She listened then to what he had to say: about Roman

treasure hoards, about the British Museum, about the law, about finders of treasures and what they were owed. When he was finished, she whistled and said, 'Brilliant. Whiting must know this. He has to.'

'Whiting?' Lynley sounded incredulous. 'Barbara—'

'No. Listen. Someone unearths a treasure. Jossie, let's say. In fact, it's got to be Jossie. He doesn't know what to do, so he rings the coppers. Who else to ring if you don't know the law, eh? Word gets up the food chain at the Lyndhurst station to Whiting and Bob's your uncle: out he trots. He lays eyes on the booty; he sees what the future could hold for him if he manages to claim it as his own – cops' pensions being what they are – and then . . .'

'What?' Lynley demanded. 'He scarpers up to London and kills Jemima Hastings? Might I ask why?'

''Cause he's got to kill *anyone* who knows about the treasure and if she went to see this Sheldon Mockworth bloke—'

'Pockworth,' Lynley said. 'Sheldon Pockworth. And he doesn't exist. That's just the name of the shop.'

'Whatever. She goes to see him. She verifies what the coin is. She knows there's more – lots more, *piles* of more – and now she knows it's the real thing. Vast amounts of lolly all waiting to be scooped up. And Whiting bloody knows it as well.' Barbara was building a real head of steam on the topic. They were so close to cracking what was going on. She could feel her entire body tingling with the knowledge.

Lynley said patiently, 'Barbara, are you aware of how much you're ignoring with all this?'

'Like what?'

'Just to begin: why did Jemima Hastings abruptly leave Hampshire in the first place if there was a vast treasure of Roman coins sitting there waiting for her to share in it? Why, after she identified the coin – months and months ago, by the way – did she apparently do nothing more about it? Why, if the man she lived with in Hampshire had dug up an entire Roman treasure, did she never mention the slightest thing about this to anyone, including a psychic whom she apparently visited numerous times to ask about her *love life* instead?'

'There's an explanation, for God's bloody sake.'

'All right. Do you have it?'

'I damn well would if you—'

'What?'

If you would work with me. That was the answer. But Barbara couldn't bring herself to say it because of what the declaration implied.

He knew her well, though. Far too well. He said in that most reasonable tone of his, 'Listen, Barbara. Will you wait for me? Will you stay where you are? I can be there in less than an hour. You were about to have a meal. Have it. Then wait. Will you do that much?'

She thought about this, even though she knew what her answer would be. He was, after all, still her longtime partner. He was, after all, still and always Lynley.

She sighed. 'All right. I'll wait,' she told him. 'Have you had lunch? Sh'll I order you a fry-up?'

'Good God, no,' he replied.

Lynley knew that the last thing Barbara Havers was was a woman given to cooling her heels merely because she'd agreed to hold off momentarily on a course of action she was determined to take. So he was unsurprised when he walked into the Little Chef some ninety minutes later – frustratingly delayed by a burst water main in south London – to discover that she was burning up minutes on her mobile phone. The remains of her meal lay before her. In typical Havers fashion, it was a veritable monument to arterial blockage. To her credit, at least a few of the chips remained uneaten, but the presence of a bottle of malt vinegar told him that the rest of the meal had likely consisted, as she'd promised, of cod deep fried and sealed in copious amounts of batter. She'd followed this up with sticky toffee pudding, it seemed. He looked at all this and then at her. She was incorrigible.

She nodded a hello as he examined the plastic chair opposite her for the remains of a previous diner's meal. Finding it free of grease and food scraps, he sat. She said, 'Now that's interesting,' to whomever was the recipient of her phone call, and when she had at last ended the conversation, she jotted a few lines in her tattered spiral notebook. She said to Lynley, 'Something to eat?'

'I'm thinking of giving it up entirely.'

She grinned. 'My dining habits inspire you that much, do they, sir?'

'Havers,' he replied solemnly, 'believe me: words fail.'

She chuckled and rooted her cigarettes from her shoulder bag. She would know, of course, that smoking was forbidden inside the eatery. He waited to see if she would light up anyway and wait to be thrown out of the place. She did not. Instead, she set the Players to one side and did some further excavation, which produced a roll of Polos. She dislodged one for herself and offered him another. He demurred.

'Bit more on Whiting,' she told him, with a nod at her mobile on the table between them.

'And?'

'Oh, I definitely think we're heading where we need to be heading when it comes to *that* bloke. Just you wait. Heard from Ardery yet? D'we have an e-fit from Matsumoto on either of the blokes he saw in the cemetery?'

'I think that's in hand, but I haven't heard.'

'Well, I c'n tell you if one of them's a ringer for Jossie then the other will be Whiting's identical twin if it's not Whiting himself.'

'And what are you basing this inference upon?'

'That was Ringo Heath I was talking to. You know. The bloke—'

'—under whom Gordon Jossie learned his trade. Yes. I know who he is.'

'Right. Well. Seems our Ringo's had more than one visit from Chief Superintendent Whiting over the years, and the first of them came *before* Gordon Jossie ever signed on as Ringo's apprentice.'

Lynley considered what Havers was saying. To him, she was sounding rather more triumphant than the information seemed to call for. He replied with, 'And this is important because?'

'Because of what he wanted to know when he first came to see him: did Ringo Heath take on apprentices. And, by the way, what was Mr Heath's familial situation?'

'Meaning?'

'Did he have a wife, kids, dogs, cats, mynah birds, the whole cricket match. Two weeks later – p'rhaps three or four, but who knows as it was a long time ago, he says – along comes this bloke Gordon Jossie with, it turns out and we bloody well know *this,* phony letters from Winchester Technical College II in hand. So Ringo, who's already told Whiting he takes on apprentices, remember, hires our Gordon and that should've been that.'

'I take it that that wasn't that?'

'Too bloody right. On the odd occasion, Whiting shows up. Sometimes he runs into Ringo at his local, even. Which, you can bet, isn't Whiting's local. He makes enquiries, casual ones. They're in the nature of how's-the-work-coming-along-my-friend, but Ringo isn't exactly dead between the ears, is he, so he reckons this has to do with more than just a friendly enquiry from one of the local rozzers as he hoists a pint. 'Sides, who likes to have the local rozzers being friendly? That'd make *me* dead nervous and I'm one of them.' She drew in a breath. It seemed to Lynley the first time she'd done so. Clearly, she was heading for the peroration of her remarks because she said, 'Now. Like I told you, I've got a snout in place at the Home Office looking into our Zachary Whiting. Meantime, there's the thatching crook to be dealt with. None of the principals in London're going to have got their mitts on a thatching tool—'

'Hang on,' Lynley said. 'Why not?'

That stopped her in her tracks. She said, 'What d'you mean "why not?" You can't expect these things to be growing in flowerbeds.'

'Havers, this particular tool was old and rusty,' Lynley said. 'What does that suggest to you?'

'That it was old and rusty. Left lying about. Taken from an old roof. Discarded in a barn. What else is it supposed to mean?'

'Sold in a London market by a dealer in tools?'

'No bloody way.'

'Why not? You know as well as I do that there are antique markets in every part of town: from formal markets to casual affairs set up on Sunday afternoons. If we come down to it, there's a market right inside Covent Garden where one of the suspects – you do remember Paolo di Fazio, don't you? – actually has a stall. The crime was committed in London, not Hampshire, and it stands to reason—'

'No bloody way!' Havers' voice was loud. Several diners in the Little Chef glanced in their direction. She saw them do so and said, 'Sorry,' to Lynley, adding in a hiss, 'Sir. *Sir.* You can't be telling me that the use of a thatching tool to kill Jemima Hastings was an absolute and completely incredible coincidence. You can't, you just *can't*, be saying that: that our killer conveniently picked out something to do away with her and that something just happened to be one of the very same somethings that Gordon Jossie uses in his work? *That* horse won't run once round the track, and you bloody well know it.'

'I'm not saying that.'

'Then what? *What?*'

He considered this. 'Perhaps it was used to frame Gordon Jossie. Can we believe that Jemima never told a soul in London about the man she left behind in Hampshire, about the fact that her former lover was a master thatcher? Once Jossie came looking for her, once he began leaving those cards round the streets with his phone number on them, doesn't it stand to reason that she would have told someone – Paolo di Fazio, Jayson Druthers, Frazer Chaplin, Abbott Langer, Yolanda, Bella McHaggis . . . *someone* – who this person was?'

'What would she have told them?' Havers said. 'Okay, my ex-boyfriend, p'rhaps. I'll give you that. But my ex-boyfriend the thatcher? Why would she tell someone he was a thatcher?'

'Why wouldn't she?'

Havers threw herself back in her seat. She'd been leaning forward, intent upon making her every point, but now she observed him. Round them, the noise of the Little Chef rose and fell. When Havers finally spoke again, Lynley was unprepared for the direction she took.

She said, 'It's Ardery, isn't it, sir?'

'What's Ardery? What are you talking about?'

'You know bloody well. You're talking like this because of her, because she thinks this's a London situation.'

'It *is* a London situation. Havers, I hardly need remind you that the crime was committed in London.'

'Right. Excellent. Bloody brilliant of you. You *don't* need to remind me. And I don't think I need to remind you that we aren't living in the age of transport-by-horseback. You seem to think that no one from Hampshire – and for that you c'n read Jossie or Whiting or Hastings or Father Bleeding Christmas – could've got up to London in any number of ways, done the deed, and then gone home.'

'Havers, listen. Don't be—'

'What? Absurd? That's the word you'd use, isn't it. But at the end of the day the real issue here is you're protecting her and we *both* know it although only one of us knows why you're doing it.'

'That's outrageous and untrue,' Lynley replied. 'And, might I add although it's never stopped you before, now you're out of order.'

'Don't you bloody pull rank on me,' Barbara told him. 'From the first, she's wanted to think this is a London case. She had it that way when she decided Matsumoto did it, and she'll have it that way once she gets an e-fit off him, just you wait. Meantime, Hampshire's crawling with nasties that no one's beginning to want to look at—'

'For the love of God, Barbara, she *sent* you to Hampshire.'

'And she ordered me back before I was finished. Webberly would've never done that. You wouldn't have done it. Even that wanker Stewart wouldn't *ever* have done it. She's wrong, wrong, wrong, and—' Havers stopped abruptly. She seemed to have run out of steam. She said, 'I need a fag,' and she grabbed up her belongings. She strode towards the doors of the place. He followed her, weaving between the tables of onlookers who'd become understandably curious about what was going on between them.

Lynley thought he knew. It was a logical leap that Havers was making. It was just the wrong one.

Outside, she was striding towards her car, on the far side of the car park in the direction of the petrol pumps. He was parked nearer to the Little Chef than she, so he got into the Healey Elliott and drove after her. He came up alongside her. She was smoking furiously, muttering to herself. She tossed a glance his way and increased her speed.

He said, 'Havers, get in.'

'I'd rather walk.'

'Don't be stupid. Get in. That's an order.'

'I don't obey orders.'

'You will now, Sergeant.' And then, seeing her face and reading the pain that he knew was at the heart of why she was acting as she was, he said 'Barbara, please get into the car.'

She stared at him. He stared at her. Finally, she tossed away her cigarette and climbed into the car. He said nothing until he'd driven across the car park to the only spot of shade available, provided by an enormous lorry the driver of which was likely inside the Little Chef as they themselves had just been.

Havers groused, 'This car must've cost you a mint. Why's it not got air conditioning, for God's bloody sake?'

'It was built in 1948, Barbara.'

'Stupid excuse.' She didn't look at him, nor did she look straight ahead of them into the shrubbery beyond which the M3 offered a broken view of traffic whizzing towards the south. Instead, she looked out of her side window, offering him the sight of the back of her head.

'You've got to stop cutting your own hair,' he told her.

'Shut up,' she said quietly. 'You sound like her.'

A moment passed. He raised his head and looked at the pristine ceiling of the car. He thought about praying for guidance, but he didn't really need it. He knew what had to be said between them. Yet it constituted the Great Unmentionable that had been governing his life for months. He didn't want to mention it. He just wanted to get on.

He said quietly, 'She was the light, Barbara. That was the most extraordinary thing about her. She had this . . . this ability that was simply at the core of who she was. It wasn't that she made light of *things* – situations, people, you know what I mean – but that she was able to *bring* light with her, to uplift merely by virtue of who she was. I saw her do this time and again: with Simon, with her sisters, with her parents, and then of course with me.'

Havers cleared her throat. Still she did not look at him.

He said, 'Barbara, do you believe – do you honestly believe – that I could walk away from that so easily? That, so desperate to get out of the wilderness because I admit I *am* desperate to get out of it, I would take any route that appeared before me? Do you believe that?'

She didn't reply. But her head lowered. He heard a small sound emanate from her, and he knew what it meant. God, how he knew.

He said, 'Let it go, Barbara. Stop worrying so. Learn to trust me because if you don't, how will I learn to trust myself?'

She began to weep in earnest, then, and Lynley knew what her show of emotion was costing her. He said nothing else for there was, indeed, nothing more to say.

Moments passed before she turned to him, and then it was

to say, 'I don't have a damn tissue.' She began to scramble round her seat, as if looking for something. He fished out his handkerchief and handed it over. She used it, saying, 'Ta. Trust you to have the linen ready.'

'The curse of my upbringing,' he told her. 'It's even ironed.'

'I noticed,' she said. 'I bet you didn't iron it, though.'

'God, no.'

'Figures. You don't even know how.'

'Well, I admit that ironing isn't among my talents. But I expect if I knew where the iron was kept in my house – which, thank God, I don't – I could put it to use. On something simple like a handkerchief, mind you. Anything more complicated would completely defeat me.'

She chuckled wearily. She leaned back in the seat and shook her head. Then she seemed to examine the car itself. The Healey Elliott was a saloon with room for four, and she squirmed round for a look in the back. She noted, 'This's the first time I've been in your new motor.'

'The first of many, I hope, as long as you don't smoke.'

'Wouldn't dare. But I can't promise I won't eat. Nice bit of fish and chips to make the insides smell sweet. You know what I mean. What's this then? Up for some light reading?' She fished something from the back seat and brought it to the front. It was, he saw, the copy of *Hello!* he'd had from Deborah St James. Havers looked from it to him and cocked her head, 'Checking up on the social scene, are you? Not what I'd expect you to do 'less you take this with you when you go for your manicures. You know. Something to read while the nails are being buffed?'

'It's Deborah's,' he said. 'I wanted to have a look at the photos from the Portrait Gallery opening.'

'And?'

'Lots of people holding champagne glasses and looking well turned out. That's about it.'

'Ah. Not my crowd, then?' Havers opened the magazine and began flipping through it. She found the appropriate set of pages, where the photos of the portrait competition's opening show were spread out. 'Right,' she said, 'not a hoisted pint anywhere, more's the pity. 'Cause a decent ale's better than some thimbleful of champagne any day of the—' Her hand tightened on the magazine. She said, 'Holy hell,' and she turned to him.

'What is it?' Lynley asked.

'Frazer Chaplin was there,' Havers said, 'and in the picture—'

'Was he?' Then Lynley remembered how in person Frazer had seemed so familiar to him. That was it, then. He'd obviously seen the Irishman in one of the pictures of the Gallery opening, forgetting about it later. Lynley glanced at the magazine and saw that Havers was indeed indicating a photo of Frazer. He'd been the swarthy man in the picture of Sidney St James. 'More evidence he was involved with Jemima,' Lynley said, 'no matter that he's posing with Sidney.'

'No, no,' Havers said. 'Frazer's not the point. It's her. *Her.*'

'Sidney?'

'Not Sidney. *Her.*' Havers pointed to the rest of the crowd and specifically to another woman, this one young, blonde and very attractive. Some socialite, he reckoned, the wife or daughter of a gallery sponsor, likely. But Havers disabused him of that notion when next she spoke. 'It's Gina Dickens, Inspector,' she said, and she added unnecessarily because at that point he knew quite well who Gina Dickens was, 'She lives in Hampshire, with Gordon Jossie.'

Much has been made not only of the British criminal justice system but also of the trial that followed the boys' confessions. Words such as *barbaric*, *Byzantine*, *archaic* and *inhuman* have been used, and commentators around the globe have taken strong positions on both sides of the matter, some of them passionately arguing that inhumanity, no matter its source, should be met with like inhumanity (invoking Hammurabi) and others of them just as passionately contending that nothing is served by the public pillorying of children and, indeed, further damage is done to them. What remains is this singular fact: governed by a law that makes children responsible for their behaviour at the age of ten in the case of capital crimes, Michael Spargo, Reggie Arnold and Ian Barker had to be tried as adults. Thus, they faced trial by judge and jury.

What is also worthy of note is that, when a serious crime has been committed by children, they are forbidden by law to have any therapeutic access to psychiatrists or psychologists prior to trial. While such professionals *are* tangentially involved in the developing proceedings against children, their examination of the accused is strictly limited to determining two things: whether the child in question was – at the time of the crime – capable of distinguishing between right and wrong and whether such child was responsible for his acts.

Six child psychiatrists and three psychologists examined the boys. Interestingly, they reached identical conclusions: Michael Spargo, Ian Barker and Reggie Arnold were of average to above-average intelligence; they were fully cognisant of the difference between right and wrong; they were well aware of the notion of personal responsibility, despite (or perhaps because of) their attempts to blame each other for John Dresser's torture and death.

In the climate that surrounded the investigation into John Dresser's abduction and murder, what other conclusions could have been drawn? As has already been noted, 'Blood will have blood'. Yet the sheer enormity of what was done to John Dresser begged for a disinterested approach from all parties involved in the investigation, the arrest and the trial. Without that kind of approach in these matters, we are doomed to cling to our ignorance, believing that the torture and murder of children *by* children is somehow normal, when no rational mind would accept this as the case.

We do not need to forgive the crime, nor do we need to excuse it. But we do need to see the *reason* for it so as to prevent its ever occurring again. Yet whatever the true cause was that lay at the root of the three boys' heinous behaviour that day, it was not presented at their trial because it did not need to be presented. The police's function was not to delve into the psychological make-up of the boys once they were arrested. Rather, their function was to make that arrest and to organise the evidence, the witnesses' statements and the boys' confessions for the prosecution. For their part, the prosecution's function was to obtain a conviction. And because any *therapeutic* psychological or psychiatric attention to the boys prior to their trial was forbidden by law, whatever defence could be mounted on their behalf had to rely upon their counsels' attempts to shift blame from one boy onto another or to chip away at what testimony and evidence the CPS presented to the jury.

In the end, of course, none of this mattered. The preponderance of evidence against the three boys made the outcome of their trial ineluctable.

Abused children carry abuse forward through time. This is the unthinkable gift that keeps on giving. Study after study underscores this conclusion, yet that salient piece of information was not part of the trial of Reggie Arnold, Michael Spargo and Ian Barker. It could not have been, based not only on criminal law but also on the thirst (we might call it 'bloodthirst') for some form of justice to be handed down. Someone had to pay for what had happened to little John Dresser. The trial established guilt beyond any doubt. It was up to the judge to determine punishment.

Unlike many more socially advanced countries in which children accused of crimes are remanded into the custody of their parents, foster parents, or some sort of care pending what is usually a hearing held in camera, child criminals in the UK are placed in 'Secure Units' designed to house them prior to facing a court of law. During their trial, the three boys daily came and went from three separate secure units – in three armed vans that had to be protected from surging crowds waiting for them at the Royal Court of Justice – and while court was in session, they sat in the company of their individual social workers inside a dock designed especially for them and built so that they could see over the side in order to watch the proceedings. They were well-behaved throughout, although occasionally restless. Reggie Arnold had been given a colouring book with which to entertain himself during tedious moments; the other boys had pads of paper and pencils. Ian Barker was stoic throughout the first week, but by the end of the second week, he continually looked around the courtroom as if seeking his mother or grandmother. Michael Spargo spoke frequently to his social worker, who often had her arm around him and who allowed him to rest his head on her shoulder. Reggie Arnold cried. Frequently, as testimony was given, members of the jury observed the accused. Sworn to do their duty, they could not have helped wondering what exactly their duty was in the situation they faced.

The verdict of guilty took only four hours. The decision on punishment would take two weeks.

28

The pony lay thrashing on the ground on Mill Lane, which was just outside of Burley.

The injured animal writhed on the ground with both of its back legs broken, desperately attempting to rise and run from the group of people who gathered at the rear end of the car that had hit it. Every few moments it shrieked horribly as it arched its back and flailed its legs.

Robbie Hastings pulled over to the narrow bit of verge. He told Frank to stay, and he got out of the vehicle and into the noise: pony, conversation, cries. As he approached the scene, one of the group broke away and strode to meet him, a man in jeans, Wellingtons and T-shirt. The jeans were worn and stained brown at the knees.

Rob recognised him from his occasional nights at the Queen's Head. Billy Rodin, he was called, and he worked as a full-time gardener at one of the large homes along the road. Rob didn't know which one.

'American.' Billy winced at the noise from the stallion and jerked his thumb at the rest of group. There were four of them: two middle-aged couples. One of the women was crying, and the other had turned her back on the scene and was biting her hand. 'Got confused, is what happened.'

'Wrong side of the road?'

''Bout it, yeah. Car coming towards'm too fast round that curve.' Billy gestured the way Rob himself had come. 'Startled them. They veered right instead of left and then tried to correct, and the stallion was there. Wanted to give 'em a piece of my mind, but lookit 'em, eh?'

'Where's the other vehicle?'

'Just kept going.'

'Number plates?'

'Didn't get 'em. I was over there.' Billy pointed towards one of the many brick walls on the lane, this one some fifty yards away.

'Heard the racket, I did.'

Rob nodded and went to look at the stallion. The pony screamed. One of the two American men came towards him. He wore dark glasses and a golf shirt with a logo, Bermuda shorts and sandals. He said, 'God damn, I'm sorry. C'n I help you get him into the trailer or something?'

Rob said, 'Eh?'

'The trailer. Maybe if we support his rump . . . ?'

Rob realised that the man thought he'd brought the horse trailer to drive the poor creature on the ground in front of them to some veterinary surgery. He shook his head. 'Got to destroy him.'

'We can't . . . ? There's no vet around? Oh, shit. Oh damn. Did that guy tell you what happened? There was this other car and I totally blew it because—'

'He told me.' Rob squatted to take a closer look at the pony, whose eyes were rolling and from whose mouth a slight froth was issuing. He hated the fact that it was one of the stallions. He recognised this one since he and three others had only been moved into Rob's area to service the mares this past year: a strong young bay with a blaze on his forehead. He should have lived more than twenty years.

'Listen, do we have to stay while you . . . ?' the man asked. 'I only want to know because Cath is upset enough and if she has to watch you kill that horse . . . She's a real animal person. This pretty much ruins our vacation anyway – not to mention the front end of the car – and we only got to England three days ago.'

'Go into the village.' Rob told the man how to get there. 'Wait for me at the Queen's Head. You'll see it on the right. I expect there're phone calls you need to make anyway, about the car.'

'Look, how bad a trouble're we in? C'n I make this right somehow?'

'You're not in trouble. There are just formalities—'

The pony neighed wildly. It sounded like a scream.

'Do something, *do* something,' one of the women cried.

The American nodded and said, 'Queen's Head. Okay,' and then to the others, 'Come on. Let's go.'

They made short work of vacating the scene, leaving Billy Rodin on the side of the lane. 'Worst part of the job, eh?' he said. 'Poor dumb brute.'

Rob wasn't sure which of them the phrase suited best: the American, the stallion, or himself. He said, 'Happens too often, especially in summer.'

'Need my help?'

Rob told him he didn't. He would dispatch the poor animal and ring New Forest Hounds to pick up the body. 'You needn't stay,' he told him.

'Right then,' Billy Rodin said, and he headed back to the gardening from which he'd come on the run.

This left Rob to deal with the stallion, and he went to his Land Rover to fetch the pistol. Two ponies in less than a week, he thought. Things were getting worse and worse. His charge was to protect the animals on the forest – especially the ponies – but he didn't see how he could do it if people didn't learn to value them. He didn't blame the poor foolish Americans. Likely they hadn't been driving fast anyway. He told Frank once more to stay as he jerked open the Land Rover's door and reached in the back.

The pistol was gone. He saw this at once, and for an unnerving moment, he thought ridiculously that somehow one of the Americans had got it since they'd driven right by the Land Rover on their way towards Burley. Then he thought of the children at Gritnam while he was unloading the two ponies into the woodland just a short time ago. *That* consideration made his stomach churn and drove him to thrust himself into the Land Rover and begin a frantic search. He always kept the pistol secured behind the driver's seat in a disguised holster fashioned for just this purpose, but it wasn't there. It hadn't fallen to the floor, it wasn't under the seat, nor was it under the passenger's seat. He thought about the last time he'd used it – the day the two Scotland Yard detectives had found him on the side of the road with another injured pony – and he considered briefly that one of them . . . perhaps the black man *because* he was black . . . And then he realised how horrible a thought it was and what it said about him that he even considered it . . . and behind him the stallion continued to thrash and shriek.

He grabbed up the shotgun. God, he didn't want to have to do it this way, but he had no choice. He loaded the thing and approached the poor pony, but all the time his mind was feverishly casting up images of the past few days, of all the people who'd been near enough to the Land Rover . . .

He should have been removing the pistol and the shotgun from the vehicle every evening. He'd been too distracted: Meredith, the Scotland Yard detectives, his own visit to the local police, Gordon Jossie, Gina Dickens . . . *When* had he last removed the pistol and the shotgun as he was meant to do anyway? He couldn't say.

But there was a single certainty and he damn well knew it. He had to find that gun.

Meredith Powell faced her boss, but she couldn't look at him. He was in the right and she was in the wrong and there were no two ways about it. She *had* been off her stride. She *had* been enormously distracted. She *had* been ducking out of the office on the least pretext. She certainly couldn't deny any of this, so what she did was nod. She felt as humiliated as she'd ever felt, even in the worst moments all those years ago in London when she'd had to face the fact that the man to whom she'd given her love had been merely a worthless object of a feminine fantasy long fed by the cinema, by certain novels and by advertising agencies.

'So I want to see a change,' Mr Hudson was saying as a conclusion to his remarks. 'Can you guarantee a change, Meredith?'

Well, of course she could. That was what he expected her to say, so she said it. She added that her dearest and oldest friend had been murdered in London recently and that was causing her to be preoccupied, but she would pull herself together.

'Yes, yes, I'm sorry about that,' Mr Hudson said abruptly, as if he was already in possession of the facts surrounding Jemima's death as indeed he likely was. 'Tragedy, it is. But life continues for the rest of us, and it's not going to continue if we let the walls collapse round our ears, is it.'

No, no, of course. He was right. She *was* sorry she'd not been pulling her weight round Gerber & Hudson, but she would resume doing so the very next day. That is, unless Mr Hudson wanted her to remain into the evening to make up for lost time, which she would do except that she had a five year old at home and—

'That won't be necessary.' Mr Hudson used a letter opener to clean beneath his fingernails, digging round industriously in a way that made Meredith feel rather faint. 'As long as I see the old Meredith back here at her desk tomorrow.'

He would, oh he *would*, Meredith vowed. Thank you, Mr Hudson. I appreciate your confidence in me.

When he dismissed her, she returned to her cubicle. End of the day, so she could go home. But to leave so soon on the heels of Mr Hudson's reprimand would not look good no matter how he'd concluded their interview. She knew that she ought to spend at least one hour longer than usual with her nose to the grindstone of whatever it was that she was supposed to be doing.

Which, of course, she could not remember. Which, of course, had been Randall Hudson's point.

She had a pile of telephone messages on her desk, so she fingered through these in the hope of finding a clue. There were certainly names and there were pointed questions and ultimately she reckoned she *could* start looking a few things up since almost everyone seemed to be concerned about how the designs for this and for that were coming along, according to the messages. But her heart wasn't in it, and her mind would not cooperate at all. She had, she concluded, far more important subjects with which to be concerned than the colour scheme she would recommend for the advertisement of a local bookshop's new reading group.

She put the messages to one side. She used the time to straighten her desk. She made an effort to look industrious as her colleagues called out goodbyes and faded into the late afternoon, but all the time her thoughts were like a flock of birds circling a food source, lighting upon it briefly and taking flight again. Instead of a food source, though, the flock of birds circled Gina Dickens, only to find out that there were far too many places for them to land without a single one offering either a decent foothold or safety from predation.

But how could it actually be otherwise? Meredith asked herself. For in every matter that touched upon Gina, Meredith had been outmanoeuvred from the first.

She forced herself to consider each of her interactions with the other young woman, and she felt every which way the fool. The truth of the matter was that Gina had read her as easily as she herself read Cammie. She had no more sense and even less art than a five year old, and it had likely taken fewer than ten minutes for Gina Dickens to work that out.

She'd done so on the very first day when Meredith had taken that stupid, melting birthday cake to Jemima's cottage. Gina had claimed knowledge of nothing relating to Jemima, and Meredith had believed her, just like that. And hearing a claim that the programme for young girls at risk was merely in its embryonic stage, she'd believed that as well. As she had also believed that Gordon Jossie – and not Gina herself, which, let's face it was far more likely – had gone into London on the very day that Jemima died. As she had also believed that

Gordon Jossie – and not Gina herself – had caused the bruising on Gina's body. As to everything Gina had claimed about a relationship of some sort between Chief Superintendent Whiting and Gordon . . . Gina could have announced they'd both landed as conjoined twins from Mars and Meredith would have believed her.

It seemed that there was only one alternative now. So Meredith rang her mother and told her she'd be just a bit late coming home because she had a stop to make. Fortunately that stop was on the way, so she needn't worry. And give Cammie a kiss and a cuddle please.

Then she went for her car and headed for Lyndhurst. She put on an affirmation tape to accompany her on the A31. She repeated the sonorous declarations of her ability, her value as a human being and the possibility of her becoming an agent of change.

The usual rush hour tailback slowed her progress on the Bournemouth Road as she approached Lyndhurst. The traffic lights in the High Street didn't help matters either, but Meredith found that the repetition of her affirmations kept her centred, so that when she finally reached the police station, her nerves were steady and she was ready to make certain that her demands for action were well-understood.

She expected to be thwarted, frankly. She reckoned that the special constable in reception would recognise her and, with much eye rolling, would tell her she could not see the chief superintendent on the spur of the moment. This wasn't, after all, a drop-in centre. Zachary Whiting had more important concerns than to meet with every hysterical woman who happened to call in.

But that didn't occur. The special constable asked her to be seated, disappeared into the station for less than three minutes, and returned with the request that she follow him because although Chief Superintendent Whiting had intended to leave for the day, once he heard Meredith's name, he remembered it from her earlier visit – so she *had* given her name, she thought – and asked that she be ushered in to his office.

She told him everything. She gave him A to Z and then some on the topic of Gina Dickens. She saved the very best for the end: her own hiring of a private investigator in Ringwood and what that private investigator had turned up about Gina.

Whiting jotted notes throughout. At the end, he clarified that this Gina Dickens was the same woman who had accompanied Meredith to the police station here in Lyndhurst with evidence suggesting that one Gordon Jossie had been in London during the time his former lover had been murdered. This *was* that woman, was it not?

It was, Meredith said. And she realised, Chief Superintendent Whiting, how that looked: that she herself was a nutter of the first water. *But* she'd had her reasons for delving into Gina's background because everything Gina told her had been suspect from the first and wasn't the important bit the fact that now they knew every word the woman spoke was a lie? She'd even lied about himself and Gordon Jossie, Meredith told him. She'd said he – Whiting himself! – had paid more than one mysterious call upon Gordon.

Had she indeed? Whiting frowned. This would be looked into, he assured her. He said he would handle the matter personally. He said that there was obviously more here than could be understood by merely skimming the surface and since he had access to a far better set of investigatory tools than were had by any private investigator, Meredith should let the matter rest with him.

'But will you *do* something about her?' Meredith asked, and she even wrung her hands.

He would indeed, Whiting told her. There was nothing she needed to worry about from this moment forward. He recognised the urgency of the situation, especially as it had to do with a murder.

So she left. She felt, if not lighthearted, then at least moderately relieved. She'd taken a step towards dealing with the problem of Gina Dickens, and that made her feel somewhat less foolish about being seduced – there was no other word for it – by Gina's lies.

There was a car in the drive of her parents' home in Cadnam when Meredith arrived. She didn't recognise it, and the sight of it gave her pause. She briefly considered the possibility she always considered and hated herself for considering when something unexpected happened that might concern Cammie: her daughter's father had decided to visit. This was never the case, but Meredith had not yet managed to school her mind not to go there at the least provocation.

Inside the house, she was startled to see the private investigator from Ringwood sitting at the kitchen table with a cup of tea and a plate of Fig Newtons before her. On her lap was Cammie, and Michele Daugherty was reading to her. Not a children's book, for Cammie was not remotely interested in stories about elephants, boys and girls, puppies, or bunnies. Rather the investigator was reading to Meredith's daughter from an unauthorised biography of Placido Domingo, a book whose purchase Cammie had insisted upon when she'd seen it in a shop in Ringwood and recognised one of her favourite tenors on the cover.

Meredith's mother stood at the cooker, doing fish fingers and chips for Cammie's tea. She said unnecessarily, 'We've a visitor, luv,' and to Cammie, 'That's enough for now. Put Placido back on the shelf, there's a good girl. We'll have more of him after your bath.'

'But Gran . . .'

'Camille.' Meredith used her *mother* tone. Cammie made a face but slid off Michele Daugherty's lap and trudged dramatically in the direction of the sitting room.

Michele Daugherty gave a glance in the direction of the cooker. Meredith decided pleasantries were in order until her mum was supervising Cammie's meal. Indeed, since she didn't know whether her mother had been told exactly what Michele Daugherty did for a living, she decided to wait and see what this unexpected visit was all about rather than to question it.

Janet Powell, unfortunately, was taking her time, probably in order to hear why this stranger had come calling upon her daughter. They'd run out of chat and still she cooked. There was nothing for it but to offer Michele Daugherty a look at the back garden, which Meredith did. Michele accepted with alacrity. Janet Powell shot Meredith a look. *I'll get it out of you anyway* was the message.

There was, thank God, at least a back garden to see. Meredith's parents were both avid about roses and they were in full bloom, and since the Powells insisted upon planting roses with fragrance and not just with colour, the scent was heady: impossible not to notice and to comment upon. Michele Daugherty did both, but then took Meredith by the arm and led her as far from the house as possible.

'I couldn't ring you,' she said.

'How did you know where to find me? I didn't tell you where—'

'My dear, you did hire me because I'm a PI, didn't you? How difficult do you suppose it is to find someone who isn't worried about being found?'

There was that, of course, Meredith realised. She wasn't exactly in hiding. Which brought her immediately to the person who *was* in hiding. Or in something else. She said, 'You've found out . . . ?' and she waited for her thought to be completed by the other woman.

'It's not safe,' she said. 'Nothing appears to be. That's why I couldn't phone you. I don't trust the phone in my office and when it comes to mobiles, they're just about as risky. Listen, my dear. I went on with my research once you left me. I started in on the other name, Gordon Jossie.'

Meredith felt a shiver crawl up her arms like fingertips tapping from the other world. 'You've found out something,' she murmured. 'I knew it.'

'It's not that.' Michele glanced round, as if expecting

someone to leap over the brick wall and come charging across the roses to accost her. 'It's not that at all.'

'More on Gina Dickens, then?'

'Not that either. I had a visit from the cops, my dear. A gentleman called Whiting showed up. He let me know in very clear terms having a great deal to do with my licence to do business that a bloke called Gordon Jossie was off limits to me and to my endeavours. "It's all in hand," is how he put it.'

'Thank God,' Meredith breathed.

Michele Daugherty frowned. 'What's that you say?'

'I stopped to see him on my way home this afternoon. Chief Superintendent Whiting. I told him what you'd discovered about Gina Dickens. And I'd *already* told him about Gordon. I'd been to talk to him about Gordon earlier. Before I came to you, in fact. I'd tried to interest him in what was going on, but—'

'You're not understanding me, my dear,' Michele Daugherty said. 'Chief Superintendent Whiting came to see me this morning. Not an hour after you left me. I'd begun my search but I'd not got far. I'd not even rung the local police. Or *any* police for that matter. Did you ring him and tell him I was investigating? Before you saw him this afternoon?'

Meredith shook her head. She began to feel ill.

Michele lowered her voice. 'Do you see what this means?'

Meredith had an idea but she didn't particularly want to give it voice. She said, 'You'd only begun the process when he showed up? What does that mean, exactly?'

'It means I went into the national data banks. It means that somehow entering Gordon Jossie's name into those national databanks set off bells and whistles somewhere and brought Chief Superintendent Whiting on the run to my doorstep. It means there's far more here than meets the eye. It means I can't help you further.'

Barbara Havers drove directly to Gordon Jossie's holding, arriving there in late afternoon and without being intercepted by a phone call from Isabelle Ardery, for which she thanked her lucky stars. She only hoped that DI Lynley would run interference for her with the acting superintendent when it came to light that Barbara had taken herself to Hampshire. If he did not, her goose was in the oven.

No cars were in the driveway that ran alongside the cottage. Barbara parked and knocked on the cottage's back door for good measure although she reckoned no one was at home, which turned out to be the case. No matter, she thought. Time to have a look round. She took herself over to the barn and tried its vast sliding door. It was conveniently unlocked. She left it ajar to give herself some light.

It was cool within, and musty smelling: a combination of stone, dust and cob. The first thing she saw was an ancient car, two tones of colour on it in the fashion of the 1950s. It was in pristine condition and looked as if someone came out to the barn to dust it every day. Barbara went to have a closer look. A Figaro, she saw. Italian? Inspector Lynley would know, car buff that he was. She herself had never seen a vehicle like it. It wasn't locked so she checked it over, stem to stern, beneath the seats and in the glove box as well. There was nothing of interest.

The Figaro was parked towards the back of the building, to give clear access to the rest of the barn. This space contained any number of unsealed crates, which Barbara reckoned had to do with Gordon Jossie's employment. She went to them next.

There were crooks galore, she found. This was unsurprising since they were a principal element of thatching. It wasn't rocket science to work out how they were used, either. The hooked end did just that: it hooked over one end of a bunched collection of reeds and held them in place. The pointed end got pounded into the rafters beneath. When it came to murder, the use of the crook was equally simple to sort out. The hooked end was the handle and the pointed end did the business on the victim.

What was interesting about the crooks that Jossie had was that they were not all the same. Among the wooden boxes, three contained crooks but in each of the boxes the crooks were slightly different. This difference had to do with the business end of the tool: each pointed tip had been created differently. In one box, the points had been fashioned as a diagonal cut. In another, the points had been created by turning and pounding the iron four times upon taking the crook from the blacksmith's fire. In the third, a smoother point had been achieved by rolling the iron when it was molten. The end was the same in each case, but the means of getting there apparently formed the blacksmith's signature. For a city denizen like Barbara, the fact that these implements were made by hand in this day and age was nothing short of remarkable. Seeing them was like stepping back in time. But then, she reckoned, so was seeing thatched roofs.

She needed to ring Winston. He was likely in the incident room at this time of day, and he could have a close look at the photo of the murder weapon and tell her how the point was shaped. That wouldn't sign, seal and deliver anyone's guilt in the matter of Jemima's death, but at least it would let them know whether Jossie's crooks here in his barn bore any resemblance to the one that was used on his former lover.

She headed towards the barn door to fetch her mobile from her car. Outside, she heard the sound of a vehicle in the drive, the quick slam of a door, and the barking of a dog. It seemed that Gordon Jossie had just arrived home from his workday. He wouldn't be happy to find her prowling round his barn.

She was right in that. Jossie came striding towards her and despite the baseball cap that shaded part of his face, Barbara could see from the ruddiness of the rest of his complexion that he was not pleased.

'What the hell are you doing?'

'Nice supply of crooks you've got in there,' she replied. 'Where d'you get them?'

'What difference does that make?'

'Amazing that they're still made by hand. 'Cos they are, aren't they? I'd reckon at this point someone would be manufacturing them, what with the Industrial Revolution having come along. Can't you get them from China or somewhere? India maybe? Someone's got to be turning them out in masses.'

The Golden Retriever – absolutely worthless as a guard dog – had apparently recognised her from her earlier visit to the holding. Barbara patted her on the head. The dog leapt up and licked her cheek.

'Tess!' Jossie said. 'Down! Get away!'

'S'okay,' Barbara said. 'I generally prefer men, but in a pinch a female dog will do.'

'You didn't answer me,' Jossie said.

'Makes us even. You didn't answer me either. Why're the crooks made by hand?'

'Because the others are crap and I don't work with crap. I take pride in my work.'

'We have that in common, then.'

He wasn't amused. 'What do you want?'

'Who d'you get them off? Someone local?'

'One's local. The others are from Cornwall and Norfolk. You need more than one supplier.'

'Why?'

'The obvious. You need masses of them to do a roof and you can't get caught short in the middle of a job. Are you going to tell me why we're talking about crooks?'

'I'm thinking of a career change.' Barbara went to the Mini and fetched her bag. She dug out her Players and said, 'Mind?' to Jossie. She offered him one but he refused. She lit her own and observed him. All of this gave her time to consider what it actually meant that, when long came to short, he was asking her as much about the crooks as she was asking him. He was either very clever or he was very something else. Innocent of the crime came to mind. But she'd seen enough of the criminal element to know that the criminal element was the criminal element because it had been quite successful at *being* the criminal element. Talking to one of their sort was like dancing in one of those Regency costume dramas on the telly: one had to know the proper steps and in which order one was supposed to make them.

'Where's your lady friend?' Barbara asked him.

'I've no idea.'

'Moved out, has she?'

'I didn't say that. You c'n see for yourself that her car's not here, so—'

'Jemima's is, though. That's hers in the barn, isn't it?'

'She left it here.'

'Why?'

'Haven't a clue. I assume she meant to come back for it when she had a use for it or a place to keep it. She didn't tell me, and I didn't ask.'

'Why not?'

'What the hell does it matter? What do you want? Why are you here?' He looked round as if he could sort out what she'd been up to by glancing from the barn to the west paddock and from there to the east paddock and from there to the cottage.

The dog picked up on his agitation and began to pace, looking from her master to Barbara. After a few moments, she yelped once and headed for the back door to the cottage. Barbara said to Jossie, 'I think your dog wants feeding.'

He said, 'I know how to care for a dog.'

He went to the cottage and disappeared inside. Barbara took the opportunity to fetch the magazine she'd had from Lynley when she'd met him earlier on the motorway. She rolled it up and went to the cottage, where she let herself in.

Jossie was in the kitchen, where the dog was gulping down a bowl of dry food. Jossie stood at the sink looking out of the window. It gave a view of his pickup, Barbara's car and the paddock beyond. Earlier, she remembered, there'd been animals in it.

'Where'd the horses go?' she asked him.

'Ponies,' he said.

'There's a difference?'

'They went back on the forest, I presume. I wasn't here when he fetched them.'

'Who?'

'Rob Hastings. He said he'd come for them. Now they're gone. I reckon it's safe to assume he returned them to the forest as they weren't likely to let themselves out of the paddock, were they.'

'Why were they here?'

He turned to her. 'Prime Minister's question time,' he said, 'is over.'

For the first time he sounded a shade menacing, and Barbara saw a glimpse of the real man beneath the exterior that he kept so controlled. She drew in on her cigarette and wondered about her personal safety. She concluded he was unlikely to dispatch her right there in his kitchen, so she approached him, flicked cigarette ash into the sink, and said, 'Sit down, Mr Jossie. I have something to show you.'

His face hardened. He looked as if he'd refuse at first, but then he went to the table and dropped into a chair. He'd not removed his cap or his sunglasses, but he did so now. 'What,' he said. Not even a question. He sounded tired to the bone.

Barbara unrolled the magazine. She found the pages of social photos. She sat down opposite him and turned the magazine so that he could see it. She said nothing.

He glanced at the pictures and then at her. 'What?' he said again. 'Posh folk drinking champagne. Am I supposed to care about this?'

'Have a closer look, Mr Jossie. This is the opening of the photo show at the National Portrait Gallery. I think you know which show I'm talking about.'

He looked again. She saw that he was giving his attention to the picture of Jemima posing with Deborah St James, but that was not the picture of interest. She indicated the one in which Gina Dickens appeared.

'We both know who this is, don't we, Mr Jossie?' Barbara said to him.

He said nothing. She saw him swallow, but that was his only reaction. He didn't look up and he didn't move. She looked at his temple but saw no wild pulsing. There was nothing at all. Not what she expected, she thought. Time for a bit of a push.

She said, 'Personally, I believe in coincidence. Or synchronicity. Or whatever. These things happen and there's no doubt about that, eh? But let's just say that it wasn't coincidence that Gina Dickens was at the Portrait Gallery for the opening of this show. That would mean she had a reason to be there. What d'you expect that reason was?'

He didn't reply, but Barbara knew his mind must be racing.

'P'rhaps she's wild for photography,' Barbara said. 'I s'pose that's possible. I rather like it myself. P'rhaps she happened to be wandering by and thought she could score a glass of the bubbly and a cheese stick or something. I could see that, as well. But there's another p'rhaps and I reckon you and I know what it is, Mr Jossie.'

'No.' He sounded a little hoarse. This was good, Barbara thought.

'Yes,' she said. 'P'rhaps she had a reason for being there. P'rhaps she knew Jemima Hastings.'

'No.'

'She didn't? Or you can't believe she did?'

He said nothing.

Barbara took out her card, wrote her mobile number on the back, and slid it across the table towards him. 'I want to talk to Gina,' she said. 'I want you to ring me when she gets home.'

29

Isabelle had remained at St Thomas' Hospital for most of the afternoon, excavating for information in the twisted passageways that comprised the mind of Yukio Matsumoto when she wasn't sparring with his solicitor and making promises that she was not remotely authorised to make. The result was that, by the end of the day, she had a disjointed scenario of what had happened in Abney Park Cemetery along with two e-fits. She also had twelve voice messages on her mobile.

Hillier's office had rung three times, which wasn't good. Stephenson Deacon's office had rung twice, which was just as bad. She skipped those five messages plus two from Dorothea Harriman and one from her ex-husband. That left her with messages from John Stewart, Thomas Lynley and Barbara Havers. She listened to Lynley's. He'd phoned twice: once about the British Museum, once about Barbara Havers. Although she took note of the fact that the sound of the inspector's well-bred baritone was vaguely comforting, Isabelle paid scant attention to the messages. For unrelated to the fact of his messages was the additional fact that her insides felt as if they wanted to become her outsides, and while she knew very well that there was one quick way to settle both her stomach and her nerves, she did not intend to employ it.

She drove back to Victoria Street. On the way she phoned Dorothea Harriman and told her to have the team in the incident room for her return. Harriman tried to bring up the subject of AC Hillier – as Isabelle reckoned she might – but Isabelle cut her off with, 'Yes, yes, I know. I've heard from him as well. But first things first.' She rang off before Harriman told her the obvious: that in Hillier's head *first things first* meant attending to Sir David's desires. Well, that couldn't matter at the moment. She had to meet with her team, and that took priority.

They were assembled when she arrived. She said, 'Right,' as she walked into the room, 'we've got e-fits on two individuals who were in the cemetery and seen by Yukio Matsumoto. Dorothea's running them through the copier so you'll each have one shortly.' She went over what Matsumoto had told her about that day in Abney Park Cemetery: Jemima's actions, the two men he'd seen and where he had seen them, and Yukio's attempt to help Jemima upon finding her wounded in the chapel annexe. 'Obviously, he made the wound worse when he removed the weapon,' she said. 'She would have died anyway, but removing the weapon hastened things. It also got him drenched in her blood.'

'What about his hair in her hand?' It was Philip Hale who asked the question.

'He doesn't remember her reaching up to him, but she may have done.'

'And he may be lying,' John Stewart noted.

'Having talked to him—'

'Sod talking to him.' Stewart threw a balled piece of paper onto his desk. 'Why didn't he phone the police? Go for help?'

'He's a paranoid schizophrenic, John,' Isabelle said. 'I don't think we can expect rational behaviour from him.'

'But we *can* expect usable e-fits?'

Isabelle clocked the restless movement among those gathered in the room. Stewart's tone was, as usual, bordering on snide. He was going to have to be sorted out eventually.

Harriman entered the room, the stack of duplicated e-fits in hand. She murmured to Isabelle that AC Hillier's office had phoned again, apparently with the knowledge that Acting Superintendent Ardery was now in the building. Should she . . . ?

She was in a meeting, Isabelle told her. Tell the assistant commissioner she would get to him in good time.

Dorothea looked as if *that way lies madness* was the response on the tip of her tongue, but she scurried off as well as she could scurry on her ridiculous high heels.

Isabelle handed out the e-fits. She'd already anticipated the reactions she was going to get once the officers looked at what Yukio Matsumoto had come up with, so she began talking to head them off. She said, 'We've got two men. One of them our victim met in the vicinity of the chapel, in the clearing, on a stone bench where she apparently had been waiting for him. They spoke at some length. He then left her and when he left her, she was alive and unharmed. Matsumoto says that Jemima took a phone call from someone at the conclusion of her conversation with this bloke. Shortly after that she disappeared round the side of the chapel, out of Yukio's view. It was only when Man Number Two appeared, coming from the same direction that Jemima had herself taken, that Yukio went to see where she was. That was when he saw the annexe to the chapel and discovered her body within it. Where are we with the mobile phone towers, John? If we can triangulate where that phone call came from just before she was attacked—'

'Jesus. These e-fits—'

'Hang on,' Isabelle cut in. John Stewart was the one who had spoken – no surprise there that he went his own way rather than answer her question – but she could tell from the expression on Winston Nkata's face that he wished to speak as well. Philip Hale moved restlessly and Lynley had gone to stand by the china boards for a look at something or, perhaps, to hide his own expression, which she had no doubt was deeply concerned. As well it might be. She was concerned herself. The e-fits were nearly useless, but that was not a subject she intended to countenance. She said, 'This second man is dark. Dark is consistent with three of our suspects: Frazer Chaplin, Abbott Langer and Paolo di Fazio.'

'All with alibis,' Stewart managed to put in. He counted them off with his fingers. 'Chaplin at home, confirmed by McHaggis; di Fazio inside Jubilee Market at his regular stall confirmed by four other stall holders and no doubt seen by three hundred people; Langer walking dogs in the park, confirmed by his customers.'

'None of whom saw him, John,' Isabelle snapped. 'So we'll break the goddamn alibis. One of these blokes put a spike through a young woman's neck, and we're going to get him. Is that clear?'

''Bout that spike,' Winston Nkata said.

'Hang on, Winston.' Isabelle continued her previous line of thought. 'Let's not forget what we already know about the victim's mobile phone calls either. She's rung Chaplin three times and Langer once on the day of her death. She's taken one call from Gordon Jossie, another from Chaplin, and another from Jayson Druther – our cigar shop bloke – on the same day and within our window of time when she was killed. *After* her death, her mobile took messages from her brother, Jayson Druther again, Paolo di Fazio and Yolanda, our psychic. But *not* Abbott Langer and *not* Frazer Chaplin, both of whom fit the description of the man seen leaving the area of the murder. Now, I want the neighbourhoods canvassed again. I want those e-fits shown at every house. Meantime, I want the CCTV films we've got from the area looked over once again for a Vespa motorbike, lime green, with transfers advertising DragonFly Tonics on it. And I want that to be part of the house-to-house as well. Philip, coordinate the house-to-house with Stoke Newington station. Winston, I want you on the CCTV films. John, you'll—'

'Bloody *hell*, this is stupid,' John Stewart said. 'The sodding e-fits are worthless. Just look at them. Are you trying to pretend there's a single defining characteristic? The dark bloke looks like a villain in a television drama and the one in the cap and glasses could be a bloody woman, for all we know. D'you actually *believe* this slant-eye's tale that—'

'That'll do, Inspector.'

'No, it won't. We'd have an arrest if you hadn't run this bugger into traffic and then hung about waiting to find out he wasn't the killer in the first place. You've bloody well mishandled this case from the first. You've—'

'Give it a rest, John.' Of all people, it was Philip Hale speaking. Winston Nkata joined him, saying, 'Hang on, man.'

'*You* lot might start thinking about what's going on,' was Stewart's reply. 'You've been tiptoeing round every mad thing this woman's said, like we owe the bloody slag allegiance.'

'Jesus, man . . .' This came from Hale.

'You pig!' was the cry from one of the female constables.

'And you wouldn't know a killer if he stuck his in you and tickled you with it,' was Stewart's reply to her.

At this, chaos erupted. Aside from Isabelle, there were five young women in the room, three constables and two typists. The nearest constable came out of her chair as if propelled, and one typist threw her coffee cup at Stewart. He shot up and went for her. Philip Hale held him back. He swung at Hale. Nkata grabbed him. Stewart turned on him.

'You fucking nig—'

Nkata slapped his face. The blow was hard, fast and loud like a crack. Stewart's head flew back.

'When I say hang on, I mean it,' Nkata told him. 'Sit down, shut your gob, act like you know something, and be glad I didn't punch your lights out and break your goddamn nose.'

'Well done, Winnie,' someone called out.

'That'll do, all of you,' Isabelle said. She could see that Lynley was watching her from his place by the china board. He hadn't moved. She was grateful for this. The last thing she wanted was his intervention. It was bad enough that Hale and Nkata had had to sort out Stewart when it was her job to do the sorting. She said to Stewart, 'In my office. Wait there.' She said nothing more until he'd slammed his way out of the room. Then, 'What else do we have, then?'

Jemima Hastings had possessed a gold coin – currently

missing from her belongings – and a carnelian that were Roman in origin.

Barbara Havers had recognised the murder weapon and—

'Where is Sergeant Havers?' Isabelle asked, realising for the first time that the dowdy woman wasn't among the officers in the room. 'Why isn't she here?'

There was silence before Winston Nkata said, 'Gone to Ham'shire, guv.'

Isabelle felt her face go rigid. She said, 'Hampshire,' simply because she could not think of another response in the circumstances.

Nkata said, 'Murder weapon's a crook. Barb an' I, we saw 'em in Ham'shire. It's a thatcher's tool. We got two thatchers on our radar down there, and Barb thought—'

'Thank you,' Isabelle said.

''Nother thing is crooks're made by blacksmiths,' Nkata continued. 'Rob Hastings's a blacksmith and since—'

'I said thank you, Winston.'

The room was silent. Phones were ringing in another area, and the sudden sound of them served as an unwelcome reminder of how out of control their afternoon briefing had become. Into this silence, Thomas Lynley spoke, and it became immediately apparent that he was defending Barbara Havers.

'She's unearthed another connection among Ringo Heath, Zachary Whiting and Gordon Jossie, guv,' he said.

'And how do you come to know this?'

'I spoke to her on her way to Hampshire.'

'She rang you?'

'I rang her. I managed to catch her when she'd stopped on the motorway. But the important thing is—'

'You're not in charge here, Inspector Lynley.'

'I understand.'

'By which I take it that you also understand how out of order you were to encourage Sergeant Havers to do anything other than to get her bum back to London. Yes?'

Lynley hesitated. Isabelle locked eyes with him. The same

silence came over the room again. God, she thought. First Stewart, now Lynley. Havers gallivanting to Hampshire. Nkata coming to blows with another officer.

Lynley said carefully, 'I see that. But there's another connection Barbara's come up with, and I think you'll agree it's worth looking at.'

'And this connection is?'

Lynley told her about a magazine and its photos of the opening of the Cadbury Photographic Portrait of the Year show. He told her about Frazer Chaplin in those pictures and, there in the background, Gina Dickens. He concluded with, 'It seemed best to let her go to Hampshire. If nothing else, she can get us photos of Jossie, Ringo Heath and Whiting to show round Stoke Newington. And to show to Matsumoto. But, knowing Barbara, she's likely to come up with more than that.'

'Is she indeed,' Isabelle said. 'Thank you, Inspector. I'll chat with her later.' She looked at the rest of them and read on their faces the varying degrees of discomfort. She said to them, 'The lot of you have your activities for tomorrow. We'll speak again in the afternoon.'

She left them. She heard her name called as she strode to her office. She recognised Lynley's voice but she waved him off. 'I need to deal with DI Stewart,' she told him, 'and then with Hillier. And that, believe me, is all I can cope with today.' She turned quickly before he could reply. She'd not made it to her office door when Dorothea Harriman told her that the assistant commissioner had personally just phoned – the emphasis she placed on *personally* expressing the urgency of the communication – and he was giving the superintendent a choice: she could either come to his office at once or he could come to hers.

'I took the liberty . . .' Dorothea said meaningfully. 'Because with all due respect, Detective Superintendent Ardery, you don't want the assistant commissioner coming—'

'Tell him I'm on my way.'

John Stewart, she decided, would have to wait. Briefly, she wondered how her day could possibly become worse, but she reckoned she was about to find out.

The key was to hold things together for another hour or so. Isabelle told herself she was capable of that. She didn't need to fortify herself for a final sixty minutes at the Yard. She might have wanted to but she didn't need to. Want and need were completely different.

At AC Hillier's office, Judi MacIntosh told her to go straight in. The assistant commissioner was expecting her, she said, and did she want tea or a coffee? Isabelle accepted tea with milk and sugar. She reckoned that being able to drink it without her hands shaking would make a statement about the control she was maintaining over the situation.

Hillier was sitting behind his desk. He nodded towards his conference table, and he told her they would wait for Stephenson Deacon's arrival. He joined her there when Isabelle sat. He had several telephone messages in his hand, slips of paper that he laid out on the table in front of him and made a show of studying. The office door opened after two minutes' tense silence, and Judi MacIntosh came in with Isabelle's tea: cup and saucer, milk jug and sugar, stainless steel spoon. These would be trickier to handle than a plastic or Styrofoam cup. This teacup would rattle on its saucer when she lifted it, sounding a betrayal. Very clever, Isabelle thought.

'Please enjoy your tea,' Hillier told her. She reckoned his tone was similar to that which Socrates heard prior to the hemlock.

She took milk but decided against the sugar. Sugar would have required her dexterous use of the spoon and she didn't think she could manage that. As it was, when she stirred the milk into the tea, the sound of steel hitting china seemed earsplitting. She didn't dare raise the cup to her lips. She set the spoon in the saucer and waited.

It was less than five minutes before Stephenson Deacon joined them although it seemed much longer. He nodded at her and sank into a chair, placing a manila folder in front of him. His hair was thin and the colour of mouse fur and he ran his hands through it as he said, 'Well,' after which he levelled a gaze at her and added, 'We do have something of a problem, Superintendent Ardery.'

The problem had two parts and the head of the press bureau shed light upon them without further prefatory remarks. The first part constituted unauthorised deal-making. The second part constituted the result of that unauthorised deal-making. Both were equally damaging to the Met.

Damaging to the Met had nothing to do with real damage, Isabelle quickly discovered. It did not mean the police had lost any power over the criminal element. Rather, damage to the Met meant damage to the *image* of the Met and whenever the Met's image was sullied, the sullying generally came from the press.

In this case, what the press were reporting appeared to have come verbatim from Zaynab Bourne. She had embraced the deal offered by Detective Superintendent Isabelle Ardery at St Thomas' Hospital: unfettered access to Yukio Matsumoto in exchange for the Met's admission of culpability for the Japanese man's flight and his subsequent injuries. The final edition of the *Evening Standard* was leading with the story, but unfortunately the *Standard* was leading with only half of it and that was the culpability half. *Met Admits Wrongdoing* was how the paper was phrasing it, and they were doing their phrasing in a three-inch banner below which were printed photos of the accident scene, photos of the solicitor at the press conference where she'd made this announcement, and a publicity shot of Hiro Matsumoto and his cello, as if he and not his brother were the victim of the accident in question.

Now that Scotland Yard had admitted its part in causing the terrible injuries from which Yukio Matsumoto was hero-ically trying to recover, Mrs Bourne had said, she would be exploring the monetary compensation owed to him. They could all thank God that no armed officers had been involved in chasing the poor man, by the way. Had the police been wielding guns, she had little doubt that Mr Matsumoto would now be awaiting burial.

Isabelle reckoned that the real reason she was sitting in Hillier's office with the assistant commissioner and Stephenson Deacon had to do with the monetary compensation that Zaynab Bourne had mentioned. Feverishly, she went back over her conversation with the solicitor – held in the corridor outside of Yukio Matsumoto's room – and she recognised there was an element of that conversation that Bourne had not taken into account prior to speaking to the press.

She said, 'Mrs Bourne is exaggerating, sir.' She spoke to Hillier. 'We had a conversation about what led up to Mr Matsumoto's injuries, but that was the extent of it. I no more agreed to her assessment of the circumstances than I offered to slash my wrists in front of the television cameras.' She winced inwardly as soon as she'd spoken. Bad choice of visual image, she thought. From the expression on the assistant commissioner's face, she reckoned that he would have been only too happy had she slashed her wrists or any other part of her body for that matter. She said, 'The two of us talked alone as well,' and she hoped they'd fill in the blanks from there so that she would not have to do so: there were no witnesses to their conversation. It mattered little what Zaynab Bourne said. The Met could simply deny it.

Hillier looked at Deacon. Deacon raised an eyebrow. Deacon looked at Isabelle. Isabelle went on.

'Beyond that,' she said, 'there's the not inconsiderable matter of public safety to be considered.'

'Explain.' Hillier was the one to speak. He glanced at the phone messages fanned out on the table. Isabelle assumed they were from Bourne, the media and Hillier's own superior officer.

'There were hundreds of people in Covent Garden when Mr Matsumoto bolted,' Isabelle said. 'It's true we gave chase and Mrs Bourne can certainly argue that we did so despite knowing the man is a paranoid schizophrenic. But we can counter that claim with the weightier claim that we gave chase for *precisely* that reason. We knew he was unstable, but we also knew he was involved in a murder. His own brother had identified him from the e-fit in the newspapers. Beyond that, we had hairs on the body that we *knew* were Oriental in origin and that, in conjunction with a description of this very man running from the scene of a violent murder, clothing dishevelled . . .' She let the remainder of the sentence dangle for a moment. It seemed to her that the rest was implicit: what option had the police possessed other than to give chase? 'We had no idea if he was armed,' she concluded. 'He might very well have struck again.'

Hillier looked at Deacon another time. They communicated wordlessly. It was then that it came to Isabelle that something had already been decided between them, and she was in the room to hear that decision rather than to defend what had happened out in the street. Hillier finally spoke. 'The press isn't stupid, Isabelle. They're fully capable of working on your timeline and using it against you and, by extension, against the Met.'

'Sir?' She frowned.

Deacon leaned towards her. His voice was patient. 'We try not to operate like our American cousins, my dear,' he said. 'Shoot first and ask questions later? That's not quite our style.'

At his patronising tone, she felt hairs rise on the back of her neck. 'I don't see how—'

'Then let me clarify,' Deacon interrupted. 'When you gave chase, you had no idea the hairs from the body belonged to an Oriental, let alone to Mr Matsumoto. You had less idea that he was indeed the person who'd been fleeing the crime scene.'

'That turned out to be—'

'Well, yes, it did. And isn't that a relief. But the problem is the chase itself and your admission of culpability for it.'

'As I said, there were no witnesses to my conversation with—'

'And that's what you would have me declare to the press? It's our word against hers and so *there*? That's the best response you have to offer?'

'Sir.' This she said to Hillier. 'I had little choice in the matter at the hospital. We had Yukio Matsumoto conscious. We had his brother and his sister willing to let me talk to him. *And* we had him talking as well. We ended up with two e-fits, and if I hadn't made a deal with the solicitor, we'd not have anything more than we had yesterday.'

'Ah, yes, the e-fits.' Deacon was the one to speak, and he opened the manila folder he'd brought with him. Isabelle saw he'd come to Hillier's office armed: he'd already managed to get copies of the e-fits. He looked at them, then at her. He handed the e-fits over to Hillier. Hillier examined them. He took his time. He tapped the tips of his fingers together as he made his assessment of what Isabelle's deal making with Zaynab Bourne had – and had not – gained them. He was no more a fool than she was herself, than Deacon was, than any of the investigating officers were. He drew his conclusion, but he didn't speak it. He didn't need to. Instead, he raised his eyes to her. Blue, soulless. Were they also regretful? And if they were, what did he regret?

'Two days to finish this up,' he told her. 'After that, I believe we can assume that your time with us has come to an end.'

Lynley found the house without too much difficulty despite its being south of the river, where a single wrong turn could easily put one on the road to Brighton instead of, perhaps, the road to Kent or the road to Cambridgeshire. But in this case his clue to location was that, according to the *A to Z*, the street he wanted lay squarely between Wandsworth Prison and Wandsworth Cemetery. *Insalubrious*, his wife would have called it. *Darling, the place has everything to recommend it to the suicidal or the permanently depressed.*

Helen wouldn't have been wrong, especially with regard to

the structure in which Isabelle Ardery had established her digs. The house itself wasn't entirely bad – despite the dying tree in front of it and the concrete pad that surrounded the dying tree and made it a dying tree in the first place – but Isabelle had taken the basement flat and as the house faced north, the place was like a pit. It put Lynley immediately in mind of Welsh miners, and that was before he'd even got inside.

He saw Isabelle's car in the street, so he knew she was at home. But she didn't answer the door when he knocked. So he knocked again and then he banged. He called out her name and when that didn't do it, he tried the knob and found that she hadn't locked herself in, a foolhardy move. He entered.

There was little light, as would be the case in any basement flat. Dim illumination came through a crusty kitchen window, but that was supposed to provide daylight for not only the kitchen but the room that opened off it, which appeared to be the living room. This was furnished cheaply, with pieces suggesting a single hasty trip to Ikea: settee, chair, coffee table, floor lamp, a rug intended to hide the occupant's household sins.

There was nothing personal anywhere, Lynley saw, save for one photograph, which he picked up from a shelf above the electric fire. This was a framed picture of Isabelle kneeling between two boys, her arms round their waists. She was obviously dressed for work, while they wore school uniforms, with their caps set jauntily on their heads, their arms slung round their mother's shoulders. All three of them were grinning. First day at school? Lynley wondered. The age of the twins seemed right for it.

He put the picture back on the shelf. He looked round and wondered at Isabelle's choice of habitation. He couldn't imagine bringing the boys to live in this place, and he wondered why Isabelle had chosen it. Housing was expensive in London, but surely there had to be something better, a place where the boys could, if nothing else, see the sky when they looked out of a window. And where were they meant to sleep? he wondered. He went in search of bedrooms.

There was one, its door standing open. It was situated at the back of the flat, its window looking out on a tiny walled area from which, he supposed, access to the garden might be gained, if there was a garden. The window was closed and it looked as if it hadn't been washed since the construction of the house itself. But the illumination it provided was enough to highlight a chair, a chest of drawers and a bed. Upon this bed, Isabelle Ardery sprawled. She was breathing deeply, in the manner of someone who hasn't had a good night's sleep in days. He was loath to awaken her, and he considered writing a note and leaving her in peace. But when he walked round the bed to ease open the window in order to give the poor woman a bit of fresh air, he saw the glint of a bottle on the floor, and he understood from this that she was not asleep at all as one would think of sleep. Rather, she was drunk.

'Christ,' he muttered. 'Damn fool woman.' He sat on the bed. He heaved her upward.

She groaned. Her eyes fluttered open, then closed.

'Isabelle,' he said. '*Isabelle.*'

'How'd you ge' in, eh?' She squinted at him, then closed her eyes again. '*Hey,* 'm a po*l*ice officer, you.' Her head flopped against him. 'I'll ring some . . . someone . . . I'll do . . . 'f you don't leave.'

'Get up,' Lynley told her. 'Isabelle, get up. I must speak with you.'

'Done speaking wi' anyone.' Her hand reached up to pat his cheek although she didn't look at him, so she missed her mark and hit his ear instead. 'Finished. He said anyways and . . .' She seemed to fall back into a stupor.

Lynley blew out a breath. He tried to remember when he'd last seen anyone as drunk as this, but he couldn't. She needed a purgative of some sort, or a pot of coffee, or *something*. But first she needed to be conscious enough to swallow, and there seemed to be only one way to manage that.

He pulled her to her feet. It was impossible, he knew, for him to carry her from the room in the fashion of a cinematic hero. She was virtually his own size, she was dead weight, and there was not enough room to manoeuvre her into position anyway, even if he'd been able to load her fireman-style over his shoulder. So he had to drag her ingloriously from the bed and just as ingloriously into the bathroom. There he found no tub but only a narrow stall shower, which was fine by him. He propped her into this fully clothed and turned on the water. Despite the age of the house, the water pressure was excellent and the spray hit Isabelle directly in the face.

She shrieked. She flailed her arms. 'Wha' the *hell* . . .' she cried out and then seemed to see him and recognise him for the first time. 'My God!' She clutched her arms round her body as if in the expectation that she would find herself naked. Finding herself instead fully clothed – down to her shoes – she said, 'Oh nooooo!'

'I see I have your attention at last,' Lynley told her dryly. 'Stay in here till you sober up sufficiently to speak in coherent sentences. I'm going to make some coffee.'

He left her. He went back to the kitchen and began a search. He found a coffee press along with an electric kettle and everything else he needed. He spooned a copious amount of coffee into the press and filled the kettle with water. He plugged it in. By the time the coffee was ready and he'd put mugs, milk and sugar on the table – along with two pieces of toast which he buttered and cut into neat triangles – Isabelle had emerged from the bathroom. Her sodden clothing removed, she was wearing a towelling dressing gown, her feet were bare and her hair clung wetly to her skull. She stood at the door to the kitchen and observed him.

'My shoes,' she said, 'are ruined.'

'Hmm,' he replied. 'I dare say they are.'

'My watch wasn't waterproof either, Thomas.'

'An unfortunate oversight when it was purchased.'

'How did you get in?'

'Your door was unlocked. Also an unfortunate oversight, by the way. Are you sober, Isabelle?'

'More or less.'

'Coffee, then. And toast.' He went to the doorway and took her arm.

She shook him off. 'I can bloody walk,' she snapped.

'We've made progress, then,' he said.

She moved with some care to the table, where she sat. He poured coffee into both the mugs and pushed hers towards her, along with the toast. She made a moue of distaste at the food and shook her head. He said, 'Refusal is not an option. Consider it medicinal.'

'I'll be sick.' She was speaking with the same kind of care she'd used in moving from the doorway to the table. She was fairly good at feigning sobriety, Lynley saw, but he reckoned she'd had years of practice.

'Have some coffee,' he told her.

She acquiesced and took a few sips. 'It wasn't the entire bottle,' she declared, apropos of what he'd found on the floor of her bedroom. 'I just drank what was left of it. That's hardly a crime. I wasn't planning on *driving* anywhere. I wasn't planning to leave the flat. It's no one's business but my own. And I *deserved* it, Thomas. There's no need to make such an issue out of it.'

'Yes,' he said. 'I do see your point. You could be right.'

She eyed him. He kept his face perfectly bland. 'What are you doing here?' she demanded. 'Who the hell sent you?'

'No one.'

'Not Hillier wanting to know how I was coping with my defeat, eh?'

'Sir David and I are hardly on those kinds of terms,' Lynley said. 'What's happened?'

She told him about her meeting with the assistant commissioner and the head of the press office. She appeared to feel there was no point obfuscating because she told him everything: from her bargain with Zaynab Bourne in order to maintain access to Yukio Matsumoto, through her acknowledgment that the e-fits they'd had from Matsumoto were completely useless despite what she'd said to the team in the incident room, to Stephenson Deacon's thinly disguised condescension – 'He actually called me *my dear,* if you can believe it, and what's worse is that I didn't smack his smug face' – to the end of it all, which was Hillier's dismissal of her.

'Two days,' she said. 'And then I'm finished.' Her eyes brightened, but she shrugged off the emotion. 'Well, John Stewart will be delighted, won't he?' She gave a weak chuckle. 'I forgot him in my office, Thomas. He's probably still waiting there. D'you think he'll spend the night? God, I need another drink.' She looked round the kitchen as if preparing to rise and fetch another bottle of vodka. Lynley wondered where she kept her supplies. They needed to be poured down the drain. She'd only get more, but at least her immediate desire for oblivion would be thwarted.

'I've made a dog's dinner of this,' she said. 'You wouldn't have done. Malcolm Webberly wouldn't have done. Even that blasted Stewart wouldn't have done.' She crossed her arms on the table and put her head upon them. 'I'm completely useless and hopeless and buggered and—'

'Self-pitying as well,' Lynley put in. Her head jerked up and he added pleasantly, 'With all due respect, guv.'

'Is that remark part of being his ermine-clad lordship or just part of being a judgmental arse?'

Lynley made a show of thinking about this. 'As wearing ermine gives me nettle-rash, I suspect the latter.'

'Just as I thought. You're out of order. If I want to say I'm useless, hopeless and buggered, I'm damn well going to say it, all right?'

He added coffee to her mug. 'Isabelle,' he said, 'it's time to buck up. You'll get no argument from me that Hillier's a nightmare to work for or that Deacon would sell his own sister to a New York pimp if it meant keeping the Met looking good. But that's hardly the point just now. We've got a killer to arrest and a case against that killer to build for the CPS. Neither is going to happen if you don't pull yourself together.'

She picked up her mug of coffee and Lynley wondered briefly if she intended to throw it at him. But she drank from it and looked at him over the rim as she did so. She finally seemed to realise that he'd never answered her question about his presence in her flat because she said, 'What the hell are you doing here, Thomas? Why did you come? This isn't exactly your part of town, so I dare say you weren't just passing. And how'd you find out where I live, anyway? Did someone tell you? Did that Judi MacIntosh overhear . . . ? Did she send you? I wouldn't put it past her to listen in at doorways. There's something about her . . .'

'Control your paranoia for five minutes,' Lynley said. 'I said from the first that I wanted to talk to you. I waited more than an hour in the incident room. Dee Harriman finally told me you'd gone home. All right?'

'Talk to me about what?' she asked.

'Frazer Chaplin.'

'What about him?'

'I've had most of the day to think about this from every angle. I reckon Frazer's our man.'

She waited for Lynley's explanation. She drank more coffee and decided to make an attempt with the toast. Her stomach didn't recoil altogether at the thought of food, so she lifted one of the triangles Lynley had made for her, and she took a bite. She wondered if this was the extent of the inspector's culinary talents. She thought it likely. He'd used far too much butter.

As he'd done earlier in the incident room, Lynley spoke of a magazine he'd had from Deborah St James. Frazer Chaplin was in one of the pictures. That could indicate several things, he told her: Paolo di Fazio had been claiming from the first that Jemima had been involved with Frazer, despite the household rules that Mrs McHaggis had put up for all her tenants to see. Abbott Langer had said much to support this claim and Yolanda – at a stretch, Lynley admitted – had also indicated an involvement of some kind on Jemima's part with a dark man.

So we're going to listen to a *psychic* now? Isabelle wailed.

Just hang on, Lynley told her. They knew Jemima's involvement wasn't with di Fazio since she'd asked Yolanda repeatedly about whether her *new* lover returned her affections and she'd hardly be asking that about di Fazio after she'd ended her relationship with him. So wasn't it safe to assume that Frazer Chaplin – his denials to the contrary – was the man they were looking for?

How the hell did that follow? Isabelle demanded. Even if he *was* involved with Jemima, that hardly meant he'd murdered her.

Wait, Lynley told her. If she would just hear him out please?

Oh bloody all *right*. Isabelle was weary. She waved at him to continue.

Let's assume a few things, he said. First, let's assume that prior to her death Jemima was indeed involved romantically with Frazer Chaplin.

Fine. Let's assume, Isabelle said.

Good. Next, let's assume her possession of a gold coin and a carved carnelian are indications not that she carried a good luck charm or is sentimental about her father's belongings or anything of the like. Let's assume from these items that a Roman treasure hoard has been found. Then, let's assume that she and Gordon Jossie are the individuals who found that hoard and they found it on their holding in Hampshire. Finally, let's assume that prior to reporting that hoard – which must be done by law – something occurred between Jemima and Jossie that brought their relationship to a precipitate halt. She decamped to London, but all the time she knew there was a treasure to be had and that treasure was worth a fortune.

'What on earth brought their relationship to such a halt that she actually went into *hiding* from him?' Isabelle asked.

'We don't know that yet,' Lynley admitted.

'Wonderful,' Isabelle muttered. 'I can hardly wait to let Hillier know. For God's sake, Thomas, this is too much assuming. What sort of arrest d'you expect we can manage from all this speculation?'

'No arrest at all,' Lynley said. 'Not yet. There are pieces missing. But if you think about it for a moment, Isabelle, motive isn't one of them.'

Isabelle considered this: Jemima Hastings, Gordon Jossie and a buried treasure. She said, 'Jossie has a motive, Thomas. I don't see how Frazer Chaplin has.'

'Of course he has. If there's a buried treasure and if Jemima Hastings told him about it.'

'Why would she have done?'

'Why wouldn't she? If she's in love with him, if she hopes he's "the one", there's a good possibility that she told him about the treasure to make sure he stayed "the one".'

'All right. Fine. So. She told him about the treasure. Doesn't it stand to reason that he'd want to get rid of Gordon Jossie and not Jemima Hastings?'

'That would secure him the treasure only if he could hold onto Jemima's affections. Her various visits to the psychic indicate she may well have been having second thoughts about Frazer. Why else keep asking if he was "the one"? Suppose he knew she was having doubts. Suppose he saw the writing on the wall. Lose Jemima and he loses the fortune. The only way to prevent this would be to get rid of them both – Jemima *and* Jossie – and then he doesn't have to worry about anything.'

Isabelle considered this. Lynley rose from the table and went to the sink. He leaned against it and was silent, watching her and waiting.

She finally said, 'It's such a leap, Thomas. There's too much to account for. He's been alibied—'

'McHaggis could be lying. She could also be mistaken. She *says* he was home taking a shower but that's what he always did, didn't he? She was asked days later, Isabelle, and she could well want to protect him anyway.'

'Why?'

'She's a woman.'

'Oh, for God's sake, what's that supposed to—'

'Everyone agrees he has a way with women. Why not with Bella McHaggis as well?'

'What, then? He's *sleeping* with her? With her, with Jemima, with . . . who else, Thomas?'

'With Gina Dickens, I dare say.'

She stared at him. 'Gina Dickens?'

'Think about it. There she is in the magazine pictures of the Portrait Gallery's opening show. If Frazer was there – and we know he was – how impossible is it to believe he met Gina Dickens that night? How impossible is it to believe that, meeting Gina Dickens, he fell for her? Wanted to add her to his list of conquests? Ultimately decided to replace Jemima with her? Sent her down to Hampshire to get herself involved with Jossie so that—'

'D'you realise how many things are unaccounted for in all of this?' She put her head in her hands. Her brain felt sodden. 'We can suppose this and suppose that, Thomas, but we have no evidence that anything you're saying actually happened, so what's the point?'

Lynley went on, seeming undeterred. They did have evidence, he pointed out, but he reckoned they hadn't been putting it together correctly.

'What, for example?'

'The handbag and the bloodstained shirt from the Oxfam bin, just to begin,' he said. 'We've assumed someone planted them there to implicate one of the inhabitants of Bella McHaggis's house. We haven't considered that, knowing the bin wasn't emptied regularly, one of the inhabitants of the house put the items there merely to store them.'

'*Store* them?'

'Until they could be taken down to Hampshire, handed over to Gina Dickens and placed somewhere on Gordon Jossie's property.'

'God. This is madness. Why wouldn't he just—'

'Listen.' Lynley returned to the table and sat. He leaned across it and put his hand over her arm. 'Isabelle, it's not as mad as it seems. This crime depended upon two things. First, the killer had to have knowledge of Jemima's past, her present, and her intentions towards Gordon Jossie. Second, the killer couldn't have worked alone.'

'Whyever not?'

'Because he had to gather what evidence was going to be necessary to frame Gordon Jossie for this murder and that evidence was to be found in Hampshire: the murder weapon and a yellow shirt from Jossie's clothes cupboard, I expect. At the same time the killer had to know what Jemima was doing with regard to Jossie. If Frazer was indeed her lover, isn't it reasonable to assume that she showed him those postcards that Jossie had put up round the gallery in an attempt to locate her? Isn't it reasonable to conclude that, learning about these cards and already being involved with Gina Dickens, Frazer Chaplin began to see a way in which he could have everything: the treasure that he'd learned about, a means to get to that treasure, and Gina Dickens as well?'

Isabelle thought about this. She tried to see how it had been managed: a phone call made to the number on the postcard that would tell Gordon Jossie where to find Jemima; Jemima's decision to meet Jossie in a private location; someone in Hampshire to keep an eye on Jossie and monitor his movements and someone in London doing the same with Jemima and both of these someones intimately involved with Jossie and with Jemima, privy to the nature of the relationship they'd had with each other; both of these someones additionally in contact; both of these someones engaged in a delicate minuet of timing . . . ?

'It makes my head swim,' she finally said. 'It's impossible.'

'It isn't,' he said, 'especially if Gina Dickens and Frazer knew each other from the night of the gallery opening. And it would have worked, Isabelle. Carefully planned as it was, it would have worked perfectly. The only thing they didn't take into account was Yukio Matsumoto's presence in the cemetery that day. Frazer didn't know Matsumoto was being Jemima's guardian angel. Jemima likely didn't know it herself. So neither Frazer nor Gina Dickens took into account that someone would see Jemima meet Gordon Jossie and also see Gordon Jossie leave her, very much alive.'

'*If* that was Gordon Jossie at all.'

'I don't see how it could have been anyone else, do you?'

Isabelle considered this from every angle. All right, it could have happened that way. But there was a problem with everything Lynley had said, and she couldn't ignore it any more than he could. She said, 'Jemima left Hampshire ages ago, Thomas. If there's a Roman treasure hoard sitting down there on the property she shared with Gordon Jossie, why the hell in all that time did neither one of them – Jossie or Jemima – do a single thing about it?'

'That's what I'd like to find out,' he said. 'But I'd like to break Frazer's alibi first.'

Still in her dressing gown, she walked outside with him. She didn't look much better than when he dumped her into the shower, but it seemed to Lynley that her spirits were raised enough that she was unlikely to drink again that evening. He was reassured by this thought. He didn't like to think why.

She came as far as the narrow stairs that led from her basement flat up to the street. He'd mounted the first two steps when she said his name. He turned. She stood beneath him with one hand on the rail as if she intended to follow him up and the other hand at her throat, holding her dressing gown closed.

She said, 'All of this could have waited till morning, couldn't it.'

He thought for a moment before he said, 'I suppose it could.'

'Why, then?'

'Why now instead of the morning, d'you mean?'

'Yes.' She tilted her head towards the flat, the door standing open but no lights on within. 'Did you suspect?'

'What?'

'You know.'

'I thought there was a chance.'

'Why bother, then?'

'To sober you up? I wanted to toss round ideas with you, and I could hardly do that if you were in a stupor.'

'Why?'

'I like the give and take of a partnership. It's how I work, Isabelle. It's how I've always worked.'

'You were meant to do this.' She touched her fingers to her chest, seeming to indicate with this gesture that she was referring to the superintendent's job. 'I wasn't,' she added. 'That's clear enough now.'

'I wouldn't say that. You made the point yourself: the case is complicated. You've been handed something with a learning curve steeper than any curve I've had to travel.'

'I don't believe that, Thomas. But thank you for saying it. You're a very good man.'

'Often, I think the opposite.'

'You're thinking nonsense then.' Her eyes held his. 'Thomas,' she said, 'I . . .' but then she seemed to lose courage to say anything more. This seemed uncharacteristic of her, so he waited to hear what she wanted to conclude with. He came down one step. She was directly below him, no longer virtually eye-to-eye with him but instead her head reaching just beneath his lips.

The silence between them stretched too long. It evolved from quiet into tension. It moved from tension into desire. The most natural thing in the world became the simple movement to kiss her, and when her mouth opened beneath his, that was as natural as the kiss itself. Her arms slipped round him and his round her. His hands slid beneath the dressing gown's folds to touch her cool soft skin.

'I want you,' she murmured at last, 'to make love to me.'

'I don't think that's wise, Isabelle,' he said.

'I don't care in the least,' she replied.

30

G ordon hadn't phoned the Scotland Yard detective when Gina returned home on the previous night. He wanted instead to watch her. He had to learn exactly what she was doing here in Hampshire. He had to know what she knew.

He was rotten at acting, but that couldn't be helped. She'd realised something was wrong the moment she'd come onto the property and found him sitting in the front garden at the table in the darkness. She was very late, and he was grateful for this. He let her think that the hour of her return was the reason for his silence and his observation of her.

She said she'd got caught up in things, but she was vague when it came to what those things were. She'd lost track of time, she said, and there she was in a meeting with a social worker from Winchester and another from Southampton, and there was a very, *very* good chance that from a special programme established for immigrant girls, funding could be diverted for the use of . . . On and on she chatted. Gordon wondered how he hadn't seen earlier that words came far too easily to Gina.

They'd got through the rest of the evening and then to bed. She'd spooned against him closely in the darkness and her hips moved rhythmically against his bum. He was meant to turn and take her, and he did his part. They coupled in a furious silence meant to pose as wild desire. They were slick with sweat when the act was done.

She murmured, 'Wonderful, darling,' and she cradled him as she fell into sleep. He remained awake, with despair rising in him. Which way to turn was his only concern.

In the morning she was wanton, as she'd been so often: her

eyelids fluttering open, her long slow smile, her stretching of limbs, the dance of her body as she eased beneath the sheet to find him with her mouth.

He pulled himself away abruptly. He swung out of bed. He didn't shower but dressed in what he'd worn on the previous day and he went downstairs to the kitchen where he made himself coffee. She joined him there.

She hesitated at the doorway. He was at the table, beneath the shelf where Jemima had displayed a row of her childhood plastic ponies, a minor representation of one of her many collections of items she couldn't bear to part with. He couldn't remember where he'd put those plastic ponies now, and this concerned him. His memory didn't generally give him any problems.

Gina cocked her head at him, and her expression was soft. 'You're worried about something. What's happened?'

He shook his head. He wasn't yet ready. Speaking wasn't the difficult part for him. It was listening that he didn't want to face.

'You didn't sleep, did you?' she asked. 'What's wrong? Will you tell me? Is it that man again?' She indicated the out-of-doors.

The driveway onto the property was just outside the kitchen window, so he assumed she was talking about Whiting and wondering if there'd been another visit from him while she'd been gone from home. There hadn't, but Gordon knew there would be. Whiting had not yet got what he wanted.

Gina went to the fridge. She poured an orange juice. She was wearing a linen dressing gown, naked beneath it, and the morning sunlight made of her body a voluptuous silhouette. She was, he thought, a real man's woman. She knew the power of the sensual. She knew that when it came to men, the sensual always overwhelmed the sensible.

She stood at the sink, looking out of the window. She said something about the morning. It was not yet hot, but it would be. Was it more difficult, she wanted to know, working with reeds when the day was so hot?

It didn't seem to bother her when he didn't reply. She bent forward as if something outside had caught her attention. Then she said, 'I can help you with clearing the rest of the paddock now the horses are gone.'

Horses. He wondered for the first time at the word, at the fact that she called them horses instead of what they were, which was ponies. She'd called them horses from the first, and he hadn't corrected her because . . . Why? he wondered. What had she represented to him that he hadn't wondered about all the things that had told him from the first there was something wrong?

She continued. 'I'm happy to do it. I could use the exercise and I've nothing on for today anyway. They think it'll take a week or so for the money to come through, less if I'm lucky.'

'What money?'

'For the programme, silly.' She turned to look at him. 'Have you forgotten already? I told you last night. Gordon, what's *wrong*?'

'D'you mean the west paddock?' he asked her.

She looked puzzled before she apparently twigged how his line of thought of was zigzagging. 'Helping you clear the rest of the west paddock?' she clarified. 'Yes. I c'n work on that overgrown bit by the old section of fence. Like I said, the exercise would be—'

'Leave the paddock alone,' he said abruptly. 'I want it left the way it is.'

She seemed taken aback. But she collected herself enough to curve her lips in a smile and say, 'Darling, of course. I was only trying to—'

'That detective was here,' he told her. 'That woman who came before with the black.'

'The Scotland Yard woman?' she asked. 'I can't remember her name.'

'Havers,' he said. He reached beneath a holder for paper napkins that stood on the table, and he brought out the card that DS Havers had given him.

'What did she want?' Gina asked.

'She wanted to talk about thatching tools. Crooks, especially. She was interested in crooks.'

'Whatever for?'

'I think she could be considering a new line of work.'

She touched her throat. 'You're joking, of course. Gordon, darling, what are you talking about? You don't look at all well. Can I do something . . . ?'

Her words drifted off and she was left gazing upon him, as if waiting for inspiration. He said, 'You knew her, didn't you?'

'I've never seen her before in my life. How would I know her?'

'I'm not talking about the detective,' he said. 'I'm talking about Jemima.'

Her eyes widened. '*Jemima*? How on earth could I have known Jemima?'

'From London,' he said. 'That's why you call them horses, isn't it? You're not from round here. You're not even from Winchester, and you're not from the countryside. It's to do with their size but you wouldn't know that, would you? You knew her from London.'

'Gordon! This is rubbish. Did that detective *tell* you—'

'Showed me.'

'What? *What*?'

He told her then about the magazine spread, the society pictures and her own among them. At the National Portrait Gallery, he told her. There she was in the background at the galley show where Jemima's photo had been hung.

Her posture altered as her body stiffened. 'That,' she said, 'is absolute rubbish. The National Portrait Gallery, Gordon? I was no more there than I was in Oz. And when was I supposed to have been there?'

'The night the show opened.'

'My God.' She shook her head, her eyes fixed on him. She placed her orange juice on the work top. The *click* made by the glass against the tiles sounded so sharp he expected the glass to shatter, but it did not. 'And what else am I supposed to have done? Killed Jemima as well? Is that what you think?' She didn't wait for a reply. She strode to the table and said, 'Give me that card. What's her name again? Where is she, Gordon?'

'Havers,' he said. 'Sergeant Havers. I don't know where she's gone.'

She snatched the card from him and grabbed up the phone. She punched in the numbers. She waited for the call to go through. She said at last, 'Is this Sergeant Havers? Thank you . . . Please confirm that for Gordon Jossie, Sergeant.' She extended the phone to him. She said, 'I'd like you to be sure I've phoned her, Gordon, and not someone else.'

He took the phone. He said, 'Sergeant—'

Her unmistakable London working class voice said, 'Bloody hell. D'you know what time . . . ? What's going on? Is that Gina Dickens? You were s'posed to ring me when she came home, Mr Jossie.'

Gordon handed the phone back to Gina, who said to him archly, 'Satisfied, darling?' And then into the phone, 'Sergeant Havers, where are you? Sway? Thank you. Please wait for me there. I shall be half an hour, all right? No, no. Please don't. I'll come to you. I want to see this magazine photo you've shown to Gordon. There's a dining room in the hotel, isn't there? I'll meet you there.'

She hung up the phone, then turned back to him. She looked at him the way one might view road kill. She said, 'It's extraordinary to me.'

His lips felt dry. 'What?'

'That it never occurred to you that it might only be someone who resembled me, Gordon. How completely pathetic you and I have become.'

After a night in which Michele Daugherty's paranoia had entirely robbed her of sleep, Meredith Powell had departed her parents' house in Cadnam, leaving a note to tell her mother that she'd gone into Ringwood earlier than usual to deal with a massive pile of work. After the previous day's lecture from Mr Hudson, Meredith knew she couldn't afford any sort of cock-up without putting her job in jeopardy, but she also knew there was no way she'd be able to apply herself creatively to graphic designs if she didn't sort out the enigma that was Gina Dickens. So at five in the morning, she'd given up on the idea of sleep and she'd brought herself down to Gordon Jossie's holding, where she'd found a suitable place to park her car in the rutted entrance to a farmer's field a short distance down the lane. She reversed into this spot and settled down to gaze upon Gordon's cottage, itself hidden by the hedge at the edge of the property.

She spent a good deal of time trying to go over everything that Gina Dickens had said to her from the moment they'd met. She found, however, that there was simply so much information that it was difficult to keep everything straight. But that had likely been Gina's intention from the first, she concluded. The more details Gina Dickens threw out, the more difficult it would prove for Meredith to sort through them all and get to the truth. She just hadn't counted on Meredith hiring Michele Daugherty to do the sorting for her.

Because of the way things were developing, Meredith reckoned they were all in cahoots: Chief Superintendent Whiting, Gina Dickens and Gordon Jossie. She wasn't sure how the partnership among them worked, but she was certain at this point that each of them had played a part in what had happened to Jemima.

It was just after seven in the morning when Gina reversed her shiny red Mini Cooper into the lane. She headed in the general direction of Mount Pleasant and, beyond it, the Southampton Road. Meredith waited a moment and followed her. There weren't so many lanes in the area that she was likely to lose her, and she didn't want to risk being seen.

Gina drove casually, the sunlight glinting off her hair

because, as before, the top was down on her Mini Cooper. She drove like someone out for a day in the countryside, with her right arm resting on the upper ledge of the door when it wasn't raised to finger her wind-ruffled hair. She wound through Mount Pleasant's narrow byways, taking care to honk as a warning to potential oncoming cars when she rounded a curve, and finally when she came to the Southampton Road, she turned in the direction of Lymington.

Had the hour been later, Meredith would have assumed Gina Dickens meant to do her shopping. Indeed, when she drifted across the roundabout and headed into Marsh Lane, Meredith briefly considered that Gina might actually be getting a very early start on things by parking somewhere near the High Street and perhaps having a morning coffee at a café that she knew would be open. But in advance of the High Street, Gina made another turn, which took her over the river, and for a moment that chilled her with its implication of flight, Meredith was certain Gina Dickens meant to catch the ferry that would take her to the Isle of Wight.

Here again Meredith was wrong, albeit relieved. Gina went in the opposite direction when she reached the other side of the river, setting a course towards the north. In very short order she was on the straight towards Hatchet Pond.

Meredith dropped back to remain unseen. She worried she might lose Gina at the junction just beyond Hatchet Pond, and she peered ahead through the windscreen, grateful for the bright sun and the way in which it winked on the chrome bits of Gina's car, allowing them to act as a guide.

As the pond loomed ahead, Meredith gave thought to the fact that Gina Dickens might be meeting someone there, much as she herself had met Gina a few days earlier. But here again, Gina kept going and Meredith saw her make the turn east towards Beaulieu's Georgian red-brick cottages, but instead of driving into the village, Gina went north west at the triangular junction above Hatchet Pond, and in less than two miles she turned into North Lane.

Yes! was Meredith's thought. North Lane was an absolute treasure trove of meeting places. While it was true that Gina had taken a completely mad route to get to the area, what couldn't be denied was that its woodlands and its enclosures provided the kind of seclusion that someone like Gina – who was bloody well up to *something*, Meredith reckoned – would require.

North Lane followed the Beaulieu River, which disappeared from sight off to the left beneath the trees and Meredith dropped back once again. She was familiar with this area as it ultimately brought one to the Marchwood Bypass, which was the route to her own home in Cadnam. And when Gina led her directly to this bypass instead of stopping anywhere at all along North Lane, Meredith's first assumption was that the other woman had spotted her following and intended to drive to Meredith's house, where she would park, get out of her car, and wait for Meredith to come sheepishly upon her.

But again she was wrong. Gina did indeed take them to Cadnam, but she made no stop there any more than she'd stopped anywhere else along the way. Instead she now headed south towards Lyndhurst, and while Meredith gave fleeting thought to the Mad Hatter Tea Rooms and Gina Dickens' bedsit, it made absolutely no sense to her that Gina would drive to Lyndhurst by this circuitous route.

Thus, Meredith could hardly call herself surprised when Gina cruised even farther south, kept up the pace through Brockenhurst, and finally dipped onto the road towards Sway. Sway, of course, was not her destination and Meredith had twigged this long before Gina made no turn towards that village. Instead, she ended up back at Gordon Jossie's holding where she had begun her wild ride, like Mr Toad in his new motorcar, as if out for a morning cruise to waste petrol and time.

Meredith cursed: for being a fool, for putting her employment at risk and for being seen as she *must* have been seen for Gina to have driven so uselessly round the countryside.

She also cursed Gina for being wily, more than a match for Meredith and likely more than a match for everyone else.

Still, she paused for a moment instead of admitting defeat and heading to Ringwood with a ready excuse to give to Mr Hudson as to the lateness of her arrival.

She pulled back into the spot she'd earlier chosen to keep watch on Gordon Jossie's house, and she thought about her own consideration of Gina's lengthy drive round the New Forest. Wasting petrol and time, she'd concluded just a moment earlier, and she realised there was something *to* this simple conclusion and that something was the wasting of time. *Killing time* was the expression she wanted. If Gina Dickens hadn't spotted Meredith, wasn't it possible that that was what she had been doing?

As Meredith weighed this possibility and the reasons for it, the likeliest was the most obvious as well: she was killing time so that Gordon Jossie would leave the property for his own work, allowing Gina to return.

This did actually seem to be the reason, Meredith saw, for from her place of hiding she heard the slam of the Mini Cooper's door, followed by a second door slam coming from the cottage as Gina went inside. Meredith left the Polo then, and she sought a vantage point where roaming animals had munched a spy hole in the hedge along Gordon's property. From here, Meredith could see both the cottage and the west paddock and, as she observed them, Gina emerged from the cottage again.

She'd changed her clothes. Where before she'd worn a summer sundress, now she'd donned jeans and a T-shirt, and she'd covered her blonde head with a baseball cap. She strode over to the barn, disappeared within, and a few moments later came out trundling a wheelbarrow from which the handles of various tools stuck out. She wheeled this over to the west paddock. There she opened the gate and went inside. Considering the wheelbarrow and the tools, Meredith first concluded that, now the ponies were gone, Gina intended to shovel up their manure and cart it off to a compost heap for future use. It seemed a mad sort of employment for someone like Gina, but at this point Meredith was beginning to reckon that pretty much anything was possible.

Gina, however, began gardening, of all bloody things. Not taking up or putting down manure, but rather clipping madly away an overgrown area at the far side of the paddock, where Gordon Jossie had not made much progress in his rehabilitation of the fencing. Bracken, weeds and brambles grew here. They formed a mound that Gina was attacking with some considerable vigour. Reluctantly, Meredith had to admire the energy that the young woman was putting into the activity. She herself could have lasted no more than five minutes given the strength and the fury of Gina's progress. She clipped, she threw, she dug, she clipped. She threw, she dug. She clipped again. The casual nature of her drive round the countryside appeared to be cast aside. She was completely single-minded of purpose. Meredith wondered what the purpose was.

She had no time to dwell on possibilities, however. As she watched, a car pulled into the holding's driveway, having come to Gordon Jossie's property from the direction beyond where Meredith was standing. She waited to see what would happen next, and somehow she was not the least surprised when Chief Superintendent Whiting looked round for a moment as if for watchers just like Meredith, and then walked over and into the paddock to speak to Gina Dickens.

When, after a forty-minute wait, Gina Dickens had still not shown up at the Forest Heath Hotel in Sway, Barbara Havers reckoned that she was not coming. Sway was less than a ten-minute drive from Gordon Jossie's holding, and it was inconceivable that Gina had somehow got lost between the two locations. Barbara rang Gordon Jossie's mobile phone in an attempt to locate her, only to be told by Jossie that Gina had departed not fifteen minutes after phoning Barbara.

'She says it's not her in that magazine picture,' he added.

Yeah, right was Barbara's mental reply. She rang off and shoved her mobile into her bag. There was always the unlikely possibility that Gina Dickens had run herself off the road somewhere along the route to Sway, so she thought a quick recce of the area wouldn't be entirely amiss.

It took Barbara little enough time to accomplish this. The entire journey from Sway to Jossie's holding required exactly two turns, and the most complicated part was making a quick jig when one came to Birchy Hill Road. This was hardly a complex manoeuvre. Nonetheless Barbara slowed to a crawl and peered round just in case there was a car upended into a hedge or catapulted into the sitting room of one of the nearby cottages.

There was nothing of the like, and nothing at all the entire way to Gordon Jossie's property. When Barbara arrived, she found the place deserted. Jossie had gone off to work, she reckoned, and she'd caught him on a rooftop when she'd rung his mobile. As for Gina Dickens, who the hell knew where she'd taken herself off to? What was interesting, though, was what her disappearing act implied.

Barbara had a look round the property to make sure that Gina's car was not hidden away somewhere, with Gina herself cowering behind the cottage curtains. Finding no other car but Jemima Hastings' Figaro in its usual place, Barbara returned to her Mini and revved up. Burley, she thought, was her next stop.

Her mobile rang midway to the village, at a point where she'd pulled to the side of the road to have a look at her map in order to make sense of the myriad lanes she was finding herself in. She flipped it open, assuming that she was finally hearing from Gina Dickens – no doubt with a ready excuse as to how she managed to get lost on the way to Barbara's hotel – but she found it was DI Lynley ringing her.

Superintendent Ardery, he informed her, was more or less on board with Barbara's unauthorised trip to Hampshire, but Barbara needed to make it a quick one and she needed to bring back some sort of result.

'What's that mean, exactly?' Barbara asked him. It was the *more or less* part she questioned.

'I assume it means she has a lot on her plate, and she'll deal with you later.'

'Ah. That's bloody reassuring,' Barbara said.

'She's getting rather a lot of pressure from Hillier and from the Directorate of Public affairs,' he told her. 'It's to do with Matsumoto. She's come up with two e-fits, but I'm afraid they're not much use, and the manner in which she got them turned out to be questionable, so Hillier's had her on the carpet. He's given her two days to bring the case to a close. If she doesn't, she's finished. There's a chance she's finished regardless, as well.'

'Lord. And she *told* the team this? That'll bloody well inspire confidence among the foot soldiers, eh?'

There was a pause. 'No. Actually, the team haven't been told. I found out yesterday evening.'

'*Hillier* told you? Christ. Why? He wants you back on, leading the team?'

Another pause. 'No. Isabelle told me.' Lynley went on quickly, saying something about John Stewart and a confrontation, but what Barbara had heard served to block her awareness of anything else. *Isabelle told me.*

Isabelle? she thought. *Isabelle?*

'When was this?' she finally asked him.

'At the briefing yesterday afternoon,' he said. 'I'm afraid it was one of John's typical—'

'I don't mean her face-off with Stewart,' Barbara said. 'I mean when did she tell you? *Why* did she tell you?'

'I did say yesterday evening.'

'Where?'

'Barbara, what does this have to do with anything? And, by the way, I'm telling you in confidence. I probably shouldn't be telling you at all. I hope you can keep the information to yourself.'

She felt chilled at this, and she didn't particularly want to consider what lay behind his remark. She said politely, 'So why are you telling me, sir?'

'To bring you into the picture. So you understand the need . . . the need to . . . well, I suppose the best way to put it is the need to . . . to lasso information and bring it back as quickly as possible.'

At this, Barbara was utterly gobsmacked. She had no words with which to frame a reply. Hearing Lynley stumble round in such a manner . . . Lynley of all people . . . Lynley who'd learned what he knew on the previous evening from *Isabelle* . . . Barbara didn't want to venture another inch closer to the subject that she was inferring from his remarks, his tone and his awkward language. She also didn't want to think about why she didn't want to venture into that subject.

She said briskly, 'Well. Right. C'n you get those e-fits down to me? C'n you ask Dee Harriman to send them by fax? I expect the hotel has a machine and you c'n ask Dee to ring them for the number. Forest Heath Hotel. They've probably got a computer as well if email's better. D'you think there's any chance that one of the e-fits could be a woman? Disguised as a man?'

Lynley seemed relieved at this change in direction. He matched her briskness when he said, 'Truth to tell, I think anything's possible. We're relying on descriptions supplied by a man who's drawn seven foot tall angels on the walls of his bed-sitting room.'

'Bloody hell,' Barbara murmured.

'Quite.'

She brought him up to date on Gordon Jossie, his crooks, and whether they matched up with the sort of crook that was used by the killer, his reaction to the photo of Gina Dickens, and the phone call she'd had from that same woman. She told him she was heading to Burley for another conversation with Rob Hastings as well. Crooks and blacksmithing would be among her topics, she said. What, she asked Lynley, was on for him?

Frazer Chaplin, he told her, and an earnest attempt at alibi breaking.

Didn't he think that was akin to spitting in the wind? she enquired.

When in doubt, go back to the beginning, he replied. He said something about ending up in the beginning at the end of a journey and knowing the place for the first time, but she reckoned this was some sort of mad quote come into his mind so she said, 'Yes. Well. Right. Whatever,' and rang off to go about her business. Going about her business, she decided, was the best balm for the disturbance she was feeling towards whatever business was going on with Lynley.

She found Rob Hastings at home. He was doing some kind of major cleaning of his Land Rover, for he seemed to have it stripped of everything it could be stripped of without removing its engine, tyres, steering wheel and seats. What had been inside of it now lay on the ground round the vehicle and he was sorting through it. He didn't exactly keep a pin-neat Land Rover. From the amount of clobber, it looked to Barbara as if the bloke used it as a mobile home.

'Late spring cleaning?' she asked him.

'Something like.' His Weimaraner had come loping round the side of the house at the sound of Barbara's Mini, and he told the dog to sit, which it did at once, although it panted and looked pleased to have a visitor on the property.

Barbara asked Hastings if he would show her his blacksmith's equipment, and logically Hastings asked her why. She thought about deflecting his question, but she decided his reaction to the truth might be more revealing. She said that the weapon used upon his sister had likely been handmade by a blacksmith, although she didn't tell him what the weapon was.

At this, he didn't move. His gaze fixed on her. He said, 'D'you think I killed my own sister now?'

'We're looking for someone with access to blacksmith's equipment or to tools made by blacksmith's equipment,' Barbara told him. 'Everyone who fits the bill and knew Jemima is going to be examined. I can't think you'd want it any other way.'

Hastings dropped his gaze. He admitted that he wouldn't.

She could see, however, when he showed her the equipment, that it hadn't been used in years. She knew little enough about the workings of a smithy, but everything he owned that was related to his training and time as a blacksmith suggested that neither he nor anyone else had interfered with so much as its placement since it had first been deposited in the outbuilding where he kept it now. Everything was shoved and piled together with no room to move among it. A heavy bench held most of the equipment: tongs, preens, chisels, forks and punches. Wrought iron bars lay disused to one side of this in a hotchpotch pile and two anvils were upended against the front of the bench as well. There were several old tubs, three vices, and what looked like a grinder. There was, tellingly however, no forge. Even had this last not been the case, the unmolested dust upon everything bore not a mark of having been disturbed in ages. Barbara saw all this at once but still took her time with an examination of everything there. She finally nodded and thanked the agister. She said, 'I'm sorry. It had to be done.'

'What was used to kill her, then?' Hastings sounded numb.

Barbara said, 'I'm sorry, Mr Hastings, but I can't—'

'It was a thatching tool, wasn't it?' he said. 'It has to be. It *was* a thatching tool.'

'Why?'

'Because of him.' Hastings looked towards the broad doorway through which they'd entered the old building in which his equipment was stored. His face hardened. His thinking was obvious.

Barbara said, to head him off, 'Mr Hastings, Gordon Jossie's not the only thatcher we've spoken to in the investigation. He has thatching equipment, indeed. No doubt. But so does a bloke called Ringo Heath.'

Hastings thought about this. 'Heath trained Jossie.'

'Yes. We've spoken to him. My point is that every connection we make has to be tracked down and ticked off the list. Jossie's not the only—'

'What about Whiting?' he asked. 'What about *that* connection?'

'Between him and Jossie? We know there's something, but that's all at this point. We're still working on it.'

'As well you might. It's taken Whiting to Jossie's holding to have more than one heart-to-heart with the bloke.' Hastings told Barbara about Jemima's old friend and schoolmate Meredith Powell, about what Meredith Powell had revealed to him about Whiting's trips to see Jossie. She had the information from Gina Dickens, he said, and he ended with, 'And Jossie was in London on the day Jemima died. Or isn't that one of the connections you've made? Gina Dickens found the rail tickets. She got her hands on the hotel receipt.'

Barbara felt her eyes widen, and her breath hissed in. 'How long have you known this? You had my card. Why didn't you ring me in London, Mr Hastings? Or DS Nkata. You had his card as well. Either one of us—'

'Because Whiting said it was all in hand. He told Meredith the information had been sent up to London. To you lot. To New Scotland Yard.'

A dirty cop. So that was it. She wasn't surprised. Barbara had known from the first that something was off with Zachary Whiting, right from the moment he'd looked at those forged letters in praise of Gordon Jossie's performance as a student at Winchester Technical College II. He'd slipped up there, with his remark about the apprenticeship, and now she and the good chief superintendent were going to have a little chat about it.

Praise God, she saw as she looked feverishly at her map of the New Forest. She had only to retrace her route from Honey Lane back through Burley village. From there it was a straight route to Lyndhurst. Possibly, she thought, the only bloody straight route in all of Hampshire.

She set off. Her mind was spinning. Gordon Jossie in London on the day of Jemima's death. Zachary Whiting paying calls upon him. Ringo Heath in possession of thatching tools. Gina Dickens giving information to the chief superintendent. And now Meredith Powell, whom they'd have tracked down earlier had that bloody stupid Isabelle Ardery not ordered them precipitately back to London. Isabelle Ardery. *Isabelle told me.* Which took Barbara back to considering Lynley – that last place she wanted to be – so she forced herself again to Whiting.

Disguise. That was it. She'd been thinking that the baseball cap and sunglasses comprised the disguise because it seemed so obviously one. But what about the other? Dark clothes, dark hair. God, Whiting was bald as a newborn but putting his mitts on a wig would have been child's play for him, wouldn't it?

Her mind tumbling from point to point, she paid scant attention to the road. There was a **Y** she hadn't taken note of on the map, and she veered left when she came to it, at the Queen's Head pub, on the edge of Burley village. She saw her error at once as the road began to narrow – she'd been meant to veer right – and she zipped into the broad car park behind the pub to turn round. She began to negotiate her way past the tour coaches, and that was when her mobile rang.

She excavated it and barked, 'Havers,' when she finally got it open.

'Drinks tonight, luv?' a man's voice asked her.

'What the bloody hell?

'Drinks tonight, luv?' He sounded extremely intense.

'Drinks? Who the hell . . . ? This is DS Barbara Havers. Who is this?'

'I realise that. *Drinks* tonight, luv?' He spoke as if through gritted teeth. 'Drinks, drinks, drinks?'

At this, Barbara twigged. It was Norman Whatisname from the Home Office, her own official snout, brought to her courtesy of Dorothea Harriman and her friend Stephanie Thompson-Smythe. He was giving her the code words and they were meant to meet at the Barclay's cash point machine in Victoria Street and he had something for her and—

'Bloody hell,' she said. 'Norman. I'm in Hampshire. Tell me on the phone.'

'Can't do, darling,' he said breezily. 'Absolutely crushed with work at the moment. But drinks tonight would be the ticket. How about our regular watering hole? C'n I talk you into a gin and tonic? At the regular place?'

She thought frantically. She said, 'Norman, listen. I c'n get someone there in . . . let's say an hour? It'll be a bloke. He'll say *gin and tonic*, all right? That's how you'll know him. In an hour, Norman. At the cash point machine in Victoria Street. Gin and tonic, Norman. Someone'll be there.'

In the UK 'detention at the pleasure of the reigning Monarch' – a euphemism for imprisonment for life – is the only sentence that can be given to someone who is convicted of murder. But that is the law as it is applied to murderers over twenty-one years old. In the case of John Dresser, the killers were children. This, as well as the sensational nature of the crime, could not but have had an impact on Mr Justice Anthony Cameron as he considered what recommendations he would make upon intoning the required sentence.

The climate that surrounded the trial was hostile, with an undercurrent of hysteria that could be seen most often in the reaction of those gathered outside the Royal Courts of Justice. Whereas within the courtroom, there was tension but no overt display of aggression towards the three boys, outside the courtroom, this was not the case. Initial displays of rage towards the three defendants – characterised first by the mob-like gatherings at their homes and then by repeated attempts to attack the armed vans in which they daily travelled to and from their trial – segued into organised demonstrations and culminated in what became known as the Silent March for Justice, a noiseless gathering of an astonishing twenty thousand people who walked the distance from the Barriers to the Dawkins building site, where they were led in candlelit prayer and where they listened to Alan Dresser's broken eulogy for his little boy. 'John's passing cannot go unmarked' – Alan Dresser's words of conclusion – became the watchword for public sentiment.

One can only imagine how Mr Justice Cameron wrestled with his decision regarding whatever recommendation he would make. It was not for nothing that he'd long been known as 'Maximum Tony' for his propensity to let stand the maximum sentence at the conclusion of trials in his courtroom. But he'd never been faced with ten- and eleven-year-old criminals before, and he could not have been blind to all the ways in which the perpetrators of this horrible deed were themselves only children. His brief, however, demanded he consider only what would be appropriate for both retribution and deterrence. His recommendation was a custodial sentence of eight years, a punishment that, in the eyes of the public and the tabloid press, was deemed akin to walking away scot-free. Thus a series of heretofore unprecedented legal manoeuvres were made: within a week, the Lord Chief Justice reviewed the case and increased the sentence to ten years, but within six months the Dressers had amassed a petition of 500,000 signatures demanding that the killers be jailed for life.

This was a story that refused to die. The tabloids had seized hold of John Dresser's parents and of John himself and had made his death a *cause célèbre*. Once the verdicts were handed down in the trial of his killers, their identities and photographs could be revealed to the public as could salient details of his murder. The monstrous nature of his killing became a rallying point for those who deemed punishment the *only* appropriate response to such a crime. Thus the Home Secretary became involved, increasing the sentence to an unheard of twenty years in order, he said, 'To assure the public that their confidence in the judicial system is not misplaced, to allow them to see that crime *will* be punished, no matter the age of the perpetrator.' There the sentence remained until it went before the European Court in Luxembourg where it was successfully argued by the boys' lawyers that their rights were being infringed by the fact that a politician – who would perforce be influenced by public opinion – was allowed to set the terms of their imprisonment.

When the boys' prison term was reduced back to ten years, the tabloids flung themselves once again into the fray. Those who loathed the entire idea of European unification, seeing it as the root of all evils in the country, used the Luxembourg decision as an example of outside intrusion into the internal affairs of British society. What would come next? they pondered. Would it be Luxembourg forcing the Euro upon us? What about a declaration that the monarchy would have to be abolished? Those who supported unification saw the wisdom in making no comment at all. For any agreement with Luxembourg's decision was a dangerous position to take, somehow implying that a mere decade was suitable punishment for the torture and death of an innocent baby.

No one could possibly envy the officials – elected or not – who had to make the decisions about the fate of Michael Spargo, Reggie Arnold and Ian Barker. The nature of the crime has always suggested that the three boys were deeply disturbed, social victims themselves. There can be no doubt that their family circumstances were wretched, but there can also be no doubt that other children grow up in circumstances just as wretched or worse and they do not kill small children in reaction.

Perhaps the truth is that on their own as *individuals* the boys would not have committed an act of violence such as this one. Perhaps the truth is that it was a confluence of events that day that led to the abduction and the death of John Dresser. As an enlightened society, surely we must admit that something at some level was wrong with Michael Spargo, Reggie Arnold and Ian Barker, and equally as an enlightened society, surely we owed those three boys relief in the form of direct intervention long before the crime ever occurred or at the very least therapeutic assistance once they were taken from their homes and held for trial. Can we not say that in failing to provide either intervention or assistance we as a society failed Michael Spargo, Reggie Arnold and Ian Barker just as surely as we failed to protect young John Dresser from their attack upon him?

It's a simple matter to declare the boys evil but even as we do so, we must keep in mind that at the time of the crime's commission, they were children. And we must ask what purpose is served by putting children on public display for a criminal trial rather than by immediately providing them with the help they need.

31

She'd said afterwards, 'I'm not in love with you. It's just something that happened.'

He'd replied, 'Of course. I understand completely.'

She'd gone on with, 'No one can know about this.'

He'd said, 'I think that might be the most obvious point.'

She'd said, 'Why? Are there others?'

'What?'

'Obvious points. Other than I'm a woman, and you're a man, and these things sometimes happen.'

Of course there were other points, he'd thought. Aside from raw animal instinct, there was his motivation to consider. Hers as well. There was also what now, what next, and what do we do when the ground has shifted beneath our feet.

'Regret, I suppose,' he'd told her.

'And do you? Because I don't. As I said, these things happen. You can't say they haven't happened to you, of all people. I won't believe that.'

He wasn't quite as she seemed to think him, but he didn't disagree with her. He swung himself out of her bed, sat on the edge and considered her question. The answer was yes and it was also no, but he didn't speak either.

He'd felt her hand on his back, then. It was cool, and her voice had altered when she said his name. No longer clipped and professional, her voice was . . . Was it *maternal*? God, no. She was not in the least a maternal sort of woman.

She'd said, 'Thomas, if we're to be lovers—'

'I can't just now,' had been his reply. Not that he couldn't conceive of himself as the lover of Isabelle Ardery, but that he could conceive of it only too well, and that frightened him for all it implied. 'I ought to leave,' he said.

'We'll speak later,' she had responded.

He'd arrived home quite late. He'd slept very little. In the morning he spoke by mobile to Barbara Havers, a conversation he'd have preferred to avoid. As soon as he was able afterwards, he set upon the work of Frazer Chaplin and his alibi.

DragonFly Tonics had its offices in a mews behind Brompton Oratory and Holy Trinity Church. It faced the churchyard, although a wall, a hedge and a path separated the two. Across the alley from the establishment, he saw that two Vespas were parked. One bright orange and the other fuchsia, each bore transfers with DragonFly Tonics printed upon them, much like those he'd seen on Frazer Chaplin's motor scooter outside Duke's Hotel.

Lynley parked the Healey Elliott directly in front of the building. He paused to look at the array of goods that were displayed in its front window. These consisted of bottles of substances with names like Wake Up Peach, Detox Lemon, and Sharpen-up Orange. He inspected these and thought wryly of the one he'd choose had they only manufactured it: Show Some Sense Strawberry came to mind. So did Get a Grip Grapefruit. He could have used two of those, he reckoned.

He went inside. The office was quite spare. Aside from some cardboard boxes with the DragonFly Tonics logo printed on the side, there was only a reception desk with a middle aged woman sitting behind it. She wore a man's seersucker suit. At least it looked like a man's since its jacket hung loosely round her. It was a size that would have fitted Churchill.

She was stuffing brochures into envelopes, and she continued with this as she said, 'Help you?' She sounded surprised. It seemed that her day was rarely interrupted by someone wandering in off the street.

Lynley asked her about their method of advertising, and she jumped to the conclusion that he meant to cover the Healey Elliott – visible through the window from within the reception area – with DragonFly Tonics transfers. He shuddered inwardly at the thought of such a desecration. He wanted to demand in outrage, 'Are you quite mad, woman?' but instead he maintained an expression of interest. She pulled from her desk a crisp manila folder, from which she slid what appeared to be a contract. She spoke of rates paid for the size and number of transfers applied and the typical mileage expected from the driver of the vehicle. Obviously, she noted, black cabs received the most money, followed quite closely by motorcycle and motor scooter couriers. What sort of driving did he do? she asked Lynley.

This prompted him to correct her notion. He showed her his identification, and he asked her about the records kept of people who had vehicles of one sort or another decorated – and he used that term loosely – with the transfers from DragonFly Tonics. She told him that, of course, there were records because how else were people meant to be paid for swanning round London and regions beyond with advertising plastered to their vehicles?

Lynley was hoping to discover that there was no Frazer Chaplin with a contract to advertise DragonFly Tonics at all. From this, he had decided, it could be assumed that the Vespa Frazer had shown to Lynley outside Duke's Hotel was not his, but one produced on a moment's inspiration and declared to be a Chaplin possession. He gave the receptionist Frazer's name and asked if she could produce his contract.

Unfortunately, she did just that, and all of it was as Frazer had avowed. The Vespa was his. It was lime green. To it, transfers had been applied. They were, in fact, applied professionally in Shepherd's Bush since DragonFly Tonics hardly wanted a slapdash job done with them. They were put on to last, not to be easily removed, and when they *were* removed at the end of the contract, the vehicle would be repainted.

Lynley sighed when he saw this. Unless Frazer had used a different vehicle to get up to Stoke Newington, they were back to any and all CCTV films from the area and the possibility that one of them had recorded his Vespa in the vicinity of the cemetery. They were also back to the door-to-door slog – which was going on anyway per Isabelle's instructions – and the hope that someone had seen the scooter. Or, he reckoned, they were down to Frazer using someone else's scooter or motorcycle to get there, because with ninety minutes to do what needed to be done and to get to Duke's Hotel on time afterwards, he would have had to go to north London by that means. There was simply no other way that he could have managed the traffic.

Lynley was considering all this when his eyes lit upon the date of the contract: one week before Jemima died. This prompted him to dwell on dates in general, which made him realise there was a detail he had overlooked. There was indeed another way the murder of Jemima Hastings could have been managed, he thought.

He was getting into his car when Havers rang. He said, 'Lynley,' whereupon the sergeant began babbling – there was no other word for it – about Victoria Street, a cash point machine, the Home Office and having a gin and tonic.

He thought at first that was what she'd done – had a gin and tonic or two or three – but then in the midst of her frantic monologue he picked up the word *snout* and from this he finally was able to decipher that she was asking him to meet someone at a cash point in Victoria Street, although he still wasn't sure why he was meant to do this.

As she finally drew breath, he said, 'Havers, what's this got to do with—'

'He was in London. The day she died. Jossie. And Whiting's known it all along.'

That got his attention. 'Who's given you that information?'

'Hastings. The brother.' And then she banged on about Gina Dickens and someone called Meredith Powell, as well as tickets, receipts, Gordon Jossie's habit of wearing dark glasses and a baseball cap and wasn't *that* exactly how Yukio Matsumoto had described the man that he'd seen in the cemetery and please, please, get down to Victoria Street to that cash point because whatever Norman Whatisname knows he isn't spilling it on the phone and they need to know what it is. She herself was going to beard Whiting in his den or whatever the proper term was but before she could do that she needed to know what Norman had to say so they were back to Norman and Lynley *had* to get to Victoria Street and where was he, anyway?

She took another breath which gave Lynley the chance to tell her he was in Ennismore Gardens Mews, behind Brompton Oratory and Holy Trinity Church. He was working on the Frazer Chaplin end of things, and he reckoned—

'Sod Frazer Chaplin for a lark,' was her reply. 'This is hot, this is Whiting, and this is the trail. For God's sake, Inspector, I need you to do this.'

'What about Winston? Where is he?'

'It has to be you. Look, Winnie's doing those CCTV films, isn't he? The Stoke Newington films? And anyway, if Norman Whoever . . . God, why can't I remember his bloody name . . . He's a public school bloke. He wears pink shirts. He's got that *voice*. He says every sentence so far back in his throat that you practically need to perform a tonsillectomy just to excavate the words. If Winnie shows up at the cash point machine and starts talking to him . . . Winnie of all people . . . Sir, think it *through*.'

'All right,' Lynley said. 'Havers, all right.'

'Thank you, *thank* you,' she intoned. 'This thing's all a tangle, but I think we're getting it sorted.'

He wasn't so sure. For every time he made that his consideration, further facts seemed only to complicate matters.

He made good time over to Victoria Street by carving a route that took him ultimately through Belgrave Square. He parked in the underground car park at the Met and walked back over to Victoria Street, where he found the Barclay's cash point machine closest to Broadway, next to a Ryman's stationery shop.

Havers' snout was a case of by-his-clothes-shalt-thee-know-him. His shirt wasn't pink. It was bright fuchsia, and his tie featured ducklings. He clearly wasn't cut out for a life of intrigue since he was pacing the pavement and pausing to peer into the window of Ryman's as if studying which kind of filing tray he wished to purchase.

Lynley felt inordinately foolish, but he approached the man and said, 'Norman?' When the other started, he said to him affably, 'Barbara Havers thought I might interest you in a gin and tonic.'

Norman cast a look left and right. He said, 'Christ, for a moment I thought you were one of them.'

'One of whom?'

'Look. We can't talk here.' He looked at this watch, one of those multi-dial affairs useful for diving and, one presumed, going to the moon as well. He said as he did so, 'Act like you're asking me the time please. Reset your own watch or something . . . Christ, you carry a *pocket* watch? I've not seen one of those in—'

'Family heirloom.' Lynley looked at the time as Norman made much of showing him the face of his own piece. Lynley wasn't sure which one of the dials he was meant to look at but he nodded cooperatively.

'We can't talk here,' Norman said when they'd completed this part of the charade.

'Whyever—'

'CCTV,' Norman murmured. 'We've got to go somewhere else. They're going to pick us up on film and I'm dead if they do.'

This seemed wildly dramatic until Lynley realised Norman was talking about losing his job and not his life. He said, 'I think that's a bit of a problem, don't you? There're cameras everywhere.'

'Look, go up to the cash machine. Get some money. I'm going into Ryman's to make a purchase. You do the same.'

'Norman, Ryman's will most likely have a camera too.'

'Just bloody *do* it,' Norman said through his teeth.

It came to Lynley that the man was honestly afraid, not just playing at spies and spy masters. So he fished out his bank card and went to the cash point machine cooperatively. He withdrew some money, ducked into Ryman's, and found Norman looking at a display of sticky pads. He didn't join him there, assuming that proximity would unnerve the man. Instead, he went to the greeting cards and studied them, picking up one then another, a man intent upon finding something appropriate. When he saw Norman at last approach the till, he chose a card at random and did likewise. It was there they had their extremely brief tête-à-tête, spoken in a fashion that Norman seemed intent upon making look as casual as possible, if such was even conceivable, considering he spoke out of the side of his mouth.

He said, 'There's something of a palaver over there.'

'At the Home Office? What's going on?'

'It's definitely to do with Hampshire,' he said. 'It's something big, something serious, and they're moving dead fast to deal with it before word gets out.'

Isabelle Ardery had spent a good number of years putting the details of her life into separate compartments. Thus, she had no difficulty doing just that on the day following Thomas Lynley's visit. There was DI Lynley on her team, and there was Thomas Lynley in her bed. She had no intention of confusing the two. Besides, she was not stupid enough to consider their encounter as anything other than sex: mutually satisfying and potentially duplicable. Beyond that, her daytime dilemma at the Met did not allow for even a moment of recollection about anything, and especially about her previous night with Lynley. For this was Day One in the End of Days scenario that Assistant Commissioner Hillier had spelled out for her, and if she was going to be shown the door at New Scotland Yard, then it was her intention to go out of that door with a case sewn up behind her.

This was her thinking when Lynley arrived in her office. She felt a disagreeable jump of her heart at the sight of him, so she said briskly, 'What is it, Thomas?' and she rose from her desk, brushed past him, and called into the corridor, 'Dorothea? What're we hearing from the Stoke Newington door-to-door? And where's Winston got to with that CCTV footage?'

She got no reply and shouted, 'Dorothea! Where the hell . . . !' and then said, 'Damn it,' and returned to her desk where again she said, 'What *is* it, Thomas?' but this time remained standing.

He started to close the door. She said, 'Leave it open, please.'

He turned. 'This isn't personal,' he said. Nonetheless, he left the door as it was.

She felt herself flush. 'All right. Go on. What's happened?'

It was a mix of information from which she ultimately sorted that DS Havers – who seemed to have a bloody-minded bent for doing whatever the hell she felt like doing when it came to a murder investigation – had unearthed someone within the Home Office to do some digging on the topic of a policeman in Hampshire. He'd not got far, this snout of Havers', when he was called into the office of a significantly placed higher up civil servant whose proximity to the Home Secretary was rather more than disturbing. Why was Zachary Whiting on the mind of a Home Office underling? was the enquiry that was made of Norman.

'Norman did some fancy footwork to save his own skin,' Lynley said. 'But he's managed to come up with something we might find useful.'

'Which is what?'

'Whiting's apparently been given the task of protecting someone extremely important to the Home Office.'

'Someone in Hampshire?'

'Someone in Hampshire. It's the highest level protection. The sort of level that causes bells and whistles to go off everywhere when anyone gets remotely close to it. The bells and whistles, Norman gave me to understand, go off directly within the Home Secretary's office.'

Isabelle lowered herself into her chair. She nodded at a second chair, and Lynley sat. 'What d'you expect we're dealing with, Thomas?' She considered the options and saw the likeliest: 'Someone who's infiltrated a terrorist cell?'

'With the informer being protected now? That's highly possible,' Lynley said.

'But there're other possibilities as well, aren't there?'

'Not as many as you'd think.' he said. 'Not with the Home Secretary involved. There's terrorism, as you've said. There's protection for a witness set to testify in a high profile case coming to court. Like an organised crime case, a sensitive murder case where the repercussions—'

'A Stephen Lawrence thing.'

'Indeed. There's also protection from hired killers—'

'A *fatwa*.'

'Or the Russian mafia. Or Albanian gangsters. But whatever it is, it's something big, it's something important—'

'And Whiting knows exactly what it is.'

'Right. Because whoever it is the Home Office is protecting, this person's on Whiting's patch.'

'In a safe house?'

'Maybe. But he might also be living under a new identity.'

She looked at him. He looked at her. They were both silent, both evaluating the possibilities and comparing those possibilities to everything else they knew. 'Gordon Jossie,' Isabelle said at last. 'Protecting Jossie is the only explanation for Whiting's behaviour. Those forged letters of recommendation from Winchester Technical College? Whiting's knowledge of an apprenticeship for Jossie when Barbara showed those letters to him . . . ?'

Lynley agreed. 'Havers is on the trail of something else,

Isabelle: she's fairly certain Jossie was in London the day that Jemima Hastings was murdered.' He told her more about his phone call with Havers, her report to him on the subject of her conversation with Rob Hastings, Hastings' revelation about the train tickets and the hotel receipt and Whiting's assurances given to a woman called Meredith Powell that this information had been sent to London.

She said, 'She's called Meredith Powell? Why've we not heard about her before now? And why, frankly, is Sergeant Havers reporting to you and not to me?'

Lynley hesitated. His frank gaze shifted from her to the window behind her. It came to her that he'd occupied this office himself only a short time ago, and she wondered if he wanted it back now that she was done for. He was certainly in line to have it back if he so desired, and he could have little doubt that he was better equipped to have it back as well.

She said sharply, 'Thomas, why is Barbara reporting to you and why've we not heard about this Meredith Powell before now?'

He returned his gaze to her. He answered only the second of her questions although an answer to the first was implied when he said, 'You wanted Havers and Nkata to return to London.' He didn't say it as an accusation. It was hardly his style to mention what a cock-up she'd made of things. But then, he didn't need to when everything was so obvious now.

She swung her chair to the window. 'God,' she murmured. 'I've been wrong from the first about everything.'

'I wouldn't say—'

'Oh, please.' She turned back to him. 'Let's not go easy on me, Thomas.'

'It's not that. It's a matter of—'

'Guv?' At the doorway, Philip Hale was standing. He had a slip of paper in his hand. 'Found Matt Jones,' he told her. '*The* Matt Jones.'

'Are we sure of that?'

'Pieces seem to fit.'

'And?'

'Mercenary. Soldier of fortune. Whatever. Works for a group called Hangtower, most of the time in the Middle East.'

'Is anyone telling us what sort of work?'

'Just that it's top secret.'

'For which we can read assassinations?'

'Probably.'

'Thank you, Philip,' Isabelle said. He nodded and left them, casting a glance at Lynley that needed no translation, so clearly did it telegraph Hale's own conclusion about how their superintendent had deployed him in the investigation. Had she left him where he'd belonged, they'd have sorted out Matt Jones and everyone else days ago. Instead she'd forced him to remain at St Thomas' Hospital. It had been a punitive measure, she thought now, showing the worst kind of leadership. She said, 'I can hear Hillier already.'

Lynley said, 'Isabelle, don't worry about Hillier. Nothing that we've learned so far today—'

'Why? Are you operating from the "what's done is done" school of thought with that bit of advice? Or is this a case of things about to get worse?' She eyed him and read on his face that there was something else that he hadn't told her.

His mouth curved in a half-smile, a fond sort of expression that she didn't much like.

She said, '*What*?'

'Last evening,' he began.

'We *aren't* going to talk about that,' she said fiercely.

'Last evening,' he repeated firmly, 'we'd worked it all out and it came down to Frazer Chaplin, Isabelle. Nothing we've learned today changes that. Indeed, what Barbara's managed to come up with reinforces the direction we're heading in.' And as she was about to question this, he said, 'Hear me out. If Whiting's charge is to protect Gordon Jossie for whatever reason, we know two things that were stymieing us last evening.'

She saw where he was going. 'The Roman treasure,' she said. '*If* there is one.'

'Let's assume there is. We were asking ourselves why Jossie wouldn't have immediately reported what he'd found, as he was meant to do, and now we know. Consider his position: if he digs up a Roman hoard or even part of a Roman hoard and phones the authorities, the next thing is that a pack of journalists show up to talk to him about the whys and the wherefores of what he's found. This sort of thing can't be kept under his hat. Not if it's a hoard remotely like the Mildenhall or the Hoxne treasures. In very short order, the police turn up to cordon off the area, archaeologists arrive, experts from the BM show up. I dare say the BBC show up as well and there he is on the morning news. He's supposed to be in hiding, and the gaffe is irredeemably blown. Isabelle, it's the last thing he could have wanted.'

She said thoughtfully, 'But Jemima Hastings doesn't know that, does she, because she doesn't know he's being protected.'

'Exactly. He hasn't told her. He hasn't seen the need or perhaps he doesn't *want* to tell her.'

'Perhaps she was with him when he found the treasure,' Isabelle said. 'Or perhaps he brought something into their house because he himself didn't yet know what he had. He cleans it off. He shows it to her. They return to the spot where he's found it and—'

'And they find more,' Lynley finished. 'Jemima knows it has to be reported. Or at least she assumes they're supposed to do *something* besides dig it up, clean it off and display it on the mantelpiece.'

'And they can hardly spend it, can they?' Isabelle said. 'They'd want to do something with it. So she'd need to find out – anyone would – what one actually does with such a find.'

'This,' Lynley noted, 'puts Jossie in the worst possible position. He can't allow his discovery to be publicly known, so—'

'He kills her, Thomas.' Isabelle felt deflated. 'Be reasonable. He's the only one with motive.'

Lynley shook his head. 'Isabelle, he's practically the only

one *without* a motive. The last thing on earth he wants is to have *anyone's* attention focused on him, and it's going to be focused on him intensely should he kill her because she lives with him. If he's in hiding, he's going to be desperate to remain in hiding, isn't he? If Jemima is insistent upon dealing with the treasure appropriately – and why wouldn't she be since selling it on the open market will bring them a fortune? – then the only way to stop this and to keep himself out of the public eye isn't to kill her at all.'

'My God,' Isabelle murmured. Her glance locked on his. 'It's to tell her the truth. And that's why she left him. Thomas, she knew who he was. He had to tell her.'

'And that's why he came looking for her in London.'

'Because he was worried that she might tell someone else?' Isabelle saw the pieces click neatly into place. 'Which was what she did. She told Frazer Chaplin. Not at first, of course. But once she saw those postcards of her photo from the Portrait Gallery, with Gordon Jossie's mobile number on them. But why? *Why* tell Frazer? Is she afraid of Jossie for some reason?'

'If she's left him, I think we can assume she either wanted nothing more to do with him or she wanted time to consider what she was going to do. She's afraid, she's repulsed, she's worried, she's staggered, she's concerned, she's greedy for the treasure, she's had her life fall to pieces, she knows that to continue living with him puts her in danger . . . It could be any number of things that send her to London. It could be one reason that morphed into another.'

'She runs away first. She meets Frazer second.'

'They become involved. She tells him the truth. So you see, it comes back to Frazer.'

Isabelle said, 'Why doesn't it come back to Paolo di Fazio, since she's been lovers with him and he's seen the postcards? Or Abbott Langer, for that matter, or—'

'She ended her relationship with Paolo prior to the postcards and Langer never saw them.'

'—Jayson Druther if it comes down to it. Frazer has a bloody alibi, Thomas.'

'Let's break it, then. Let's do it now.'

First, Lynley told her, they needed to stop in Chelsea for another call upon Deborah and Simon St James. It was on the route they were going to take anyway, he said, and he reckoned the St Jameses had in their possession something that might prove quite useful.

A pause in the incident room brought forth information from Winston Nkata that the CCTV tapes were showing nothing more than they had showed before, which was also nothing. Specifically, there was documented on film no lime coloured Vespa belonging to Frazer Chaplin and shouting advertisements for DragonFly Tonics. Hardly a surprise, Isabelle thought.

She also discovered that, like Lynley, DS Nkata had spoken to the maddening Barbara Havers that morning. 'According to Barb, the tip of the thatcher's crook shows who made it,' he said. 'But she says to cross the brother off the list. Robert Hastings's got blacksmith clobber on his property, she says, but it's not been used. 'N the other hand, Jossie's got three kinds of crooks and *one* of the kinds's like our weapon. She wants to know 'bout the e-fits 's well.'

'I've asked Dee to send them down to her,' Lynley told him.

Isabelle told Nkata to carry on, and she followed Lynley to the car park.

At the St James house, they found the couple at home. St James himself came to the door with the family dachshund barking frantically round his ankles. He admitted Isabelle and Lynley and admonished the dog, who blithely ignored him and continued barking until Deborah called out, 'Good Lord, Simon! *Do* something about her!' from a room to the right of the staircase. This turned out to be the dining room, a formal affair of the sort one found in creaking old Victorian houses. It was decorated as such as well, at least as far as the furniture went. There was, mercifully, no plethora of knickknacks and no William Morris wallpaper although the dining table was heavy and dark and a sideboard held a mass of English pottery.

When they joined her, Deborah St James was apparently using the table to examine photographs, which she quickly gathered up as they entered. Lynley said to her, 'Ah. No?' in some sort of reference to these.

Deborah said, 'Really, Tommy. I'd be far happier if you read me less easily.'

'Teatime not being . . . ?'

'My cup of tea. Right.'

'That's disappointing,' Lynley said. 'But I did think afternoon tea might not be . . . hmm . . . shall I say a strong enough vignette to display your talents?'

'Very amusing. Simon, are you going to allow him to make fun or do you plan to rise to my defence?'

'I thought I'd wait to discover how far the two of you could carry an appalling pun.' St James had come only to the doorway, and he was leaning there against the jamb.

'You're as merciless as he is.' Deborah said hello to Isabelle – calling her Superintendent Ardery – and excused herself 'to throw this wretched stuff' into the rubbish. Over her shoulder as she went out of the room, she asked if they wanted a coffee. She admitted that it had been sitting on the hot plate in the kitchen for hours but with the addition of milk and 'several tablespoons of sugar' she reckoned it would be drinkable. 'Or I could make fresh,' she offered.

'We've not got time,' Lynley said. 'We were hoping to have a word with you, Deb.'

Isabelle heard this with some surprise as she'd concluded they'd come to Chelsea not to pay a call on Deborah St James but rather on her husband. Deborah seemed as surprised as Isabelle, but she said, 'In here, then. It's much more hospitable.'

In here was a library of sorts, Isabelle reckoned as she and Lynley entered. It was situated where one would normally expect to find a sitting room, with its window overlooking the street. There were masses of books – on shelves, on tables and upon the floor – along with comfortable chairs, a fireplace and an ancient desk. There were newspapers as well, piles of them. It looked to Isabelle as if the St Jameses subscribed to every broadsheet in London. As a woman who liked to travel light and live unencumbered, Isabelle found the place overwhelming. Deborah appeared to note her reaction because she said, 'It's Simon. He's always been like this, Superintendent. You c'n ask Tommy. They were at school together, and Simon was the despair of their housemaster. He's not improved in the least since. Please just shove something to the floor and sit. And it's not usually *this* bad. Well, you know that, Tommy, don't you?' She glanced at Lynley as she said this last. Then her gaze went back to Isabelle, and she smiled quickly. It was not in amusement or friendliness, Isabelle realised, but to cover something.

Isabelle found a spot that required the least amount of removal. She said, 'Please. It's Isabelle, not Superintendent,' and again that quick smile in return from Deborah followed by her glance at Lynley. She was reading something directly off him, Isabelle reckoned. She also reckoned that Deborah St James knew Thomas far better than her airiness suggested.

'Isabelle, then,' Deborah said. And then to Lynley, 'He's got to have it tidied up by next week at any rate. He's promised.'

'Your mother's paying a visit, I take it?' Lynley said to St James.

All of them laughed.

It came to Isabelle once again that the group of them spoke some form of shorthand. She wanted to say, 'Yes, well, let's get *on*,' but something held her back and she didn't like what that *something* told her: either about herself or about her feelings. She didn't *have* feelings in this matter.

Lynley brought them round to the purpose of their call. He asked Deborah St James about the National Portrait

Gallery show that featured her photo of Jemima Hastings. Might he have another copy of the magazine with pictures taken on the opening night? Deborah said of course and went to one of the stacks of periodicals where she dug down to unearth a magazine. She handed this over. Then she found another – a different one – and handed that to Lynley as well. She said, 'Really, I didn't *buy* them all, Tommy. Simon's brothers and his sister . . . And then Dad was rather proud . . .' Her face had coloured.

Lynley said solemnly, 'In your position I'd have done exactly the same.'

'She's claiming her fifteen minutes,' St James said to Lynley.

'You're both impossible,' Deborah said, and to Isabelle, 'They like to tease me.'

St James asked, not unreasonably, what Lynley wanted with the magazine. What was happening? he wanted to know. This had to do with case, hadn't it?

Indeed, Lynley told him. They had an alibi to break, and he reckoned the photos of the gallery opening were going to be helpful in breaking it.

With the magazines in their possession, they were ready to set out on the next phase of their journey. Isabelle couldn't see how a set of society photographs was going to be useful, and that was what she told Lynley once they were out on the pavement again. They got into the Healey Elliott before he replied. He handed the magazines to her. He leaned over when she found the photos of the National Portrait Gallery's opening show, and he pointed to one of them. Frazer Chaplin, he said. The fact that he was at the opening was going to serve as the wedge they needed.

'For what?'

'To separate a lie from the truth.'

She turned to him. He was, of a sudden, disturbingly close. He seemed to know this because he looked as if he was about to say something else or, worse, do something that both of them would come to regret.

She said, 'And exactly what truth would that be?'

He moved away. He turned on the ignition. He said, 'When I thought about it, the date on his contract didn't mean anything.'

'What date? What contract?'

'The contract with DragonFly Tonics: Frazer Chaplin's agreement to use his Vespa to advertise the product. The contract called for a bright colour of paint; it designated the number of transfers required. His signature makes it appear as if he went straight out and had the work done.'

'He didn't,' she said, understanding now. 'Winston's watching those films for a lime green Vespa with transfers. The house-to-house is asking about a lime green Vespa with transfers.'

'Something likely to be seen and remembered.'

'When he didn't use a lime green Vespa with transfers to get up to Stoke Newington at all.'

He nodded. 'I rang the paint shop in Shepherd's Bush after I spoke to Barbara about meeting her snout. Frazer Chaplin indeed went there to have the Vespa painted and the transfers applied. But he did it the day after Jemima died.'

Bella McHaggis was wrestling a new worm composting bin from her car when Scotland Yard arrived. Her visitors were the two officers she'd spoken to at the Met, on the day when she'd found poor Jemima's handbag. They parked across the street from Bella's house in an antique motorcar, which was how she noticed them at first, because of the car. The appearance of such a vehicle in Oxford Road – or any road, she reckoned – was going to draw attention. It spoke of indulgence, money by the bucketful, and petrol swallowed down willy-nilly. *Where* was conservation? she wondered. Where was good sense? She couldn't remember their names, but she nodded a greeting as they came across the street towards her.

The man – he politely reintroduced himself as DI Lynley

and his companion as Superintendent Ardery – took over the removal of the composting bin from Bella's car. He had manners. There was no doubt about it. Somebody had brought him up correctly, which was more than one could say about most people under the age of forty these days.

Obviously, they hadn't come to Putney to help her with her worm composting, so Bella asked them into the house. The inspector needed to put the bin into the back garden anyway, and since the only way to get there was through the house, once they were inside Bella did the proper thing and offered them a cup of tea.

They demurred, but they did say – this was the woman, Superintendent Ardery – that they'd like a word. Bella said of course, of course, and she added stoutly that she *hoped* they'd come to tell her an arrest had been made in this terrible affair of Jemima's death.

They were close, DI Lynley said.

They'd come to talk to her about Frazer Chaplin, the super-intendent added.

She said it kindly, and the kindness made Bella's antennae go up. She said, '*Frazer*? What's this about Frazer? Haven't you done *anything* at all about that psychic?'

'Mrs McHaggis.' It was Lynley now. He sounded . . . Bella didn't like the way he sounded, which was unaccountably regretful. Still less did she like his expression because it suggested to her an element of . . . Was it *pity*? She felt her spine stiffen.

'What?' she barked. She felt like showing them the door. She wondered how many more times she was going to have to direct these stupid people where they *needed* directing, which was onto Yolanda the Flipping Psychic.

Lynley again. He began an explanation of sorts. It had to do with Jemima's mobile and calls made to it on the day of her death and calls made to it *after* her death and pinging towers, whatever *they* were. Frazer had rung her within the time frame of her death, it seemed, but he had not rung her afterwards which, apparently, was suggesting to the coppers that Frazer thus had murdered the poor girl! If there was ever anything more nonsensical than that, Bella McHaggis did not know what it was.

Then the woman copper chimed in. Her explanation had to do with Frazer's motorbike. She banged on about its colour, the transfers he had put upon it to raise a bit of needed money, and how transporting oneself on a scooter like Frazer's made getting round town a rather simple thing.

Bella said, 'Hang on a minute,' because she wasn't as thick as they seemed to think and she suddenly understood where this was heading. She pointed out that if it was scooters they were interested in, had they thought about the fact that the scooter they were yammering about was an *Italian* scooter and *Italian* scooters could be hired for the day and she had an *Italian* living right there in her house, one who'd been thick-as-you-know-what with Jemima before Jemima had ended things between them? And didn't *that* damn well suggest that they ought to be looking at Paolo di Fazio if they were so intent upon pinning this crime on someone in Bella's house?

'Mrs McHaggis.' Lynley again. Those soulful eyes. Brown. Why did the man have hair so blond and yet eyes so brown to go with it?

Bella didn't want to listen and she certainly didn't want to hear. She reminded them that nothing of what they were saying mattered because Frazer hadn't been anywhere close to Stoke Newington on the day of Jemima Hastings' death. He'd been exactly where he always was between his work at the ice rink and his job at Duke's Hotel. He'd been here in this house, showering and changing. She'd told them that, she'd bloody well told them, how many more times was she going to have to—

'Has he seduced you, Mrs McHaggis?' It was the woman who asked the question and she asked it baldly. They were all sitting at the kitchen table and there was a set of condiment containers on it and Bella wanted to hurl them at the woman or perhaps at the wall, but she didn't do so. She said instead, 'How dare you!' which, she realised, was an antique remark that betrayed her age more than anything else she might have said. Young people – people like these two officers – talked about this sort of thing all the time. They didn't use the word *seduce* either, when they talked about it among themselves, and they thought nothing of what it meant to invade someone's privacy in such a way—

'It's what he does, Mrs McHaggis,' the superintendent said. 'We already have confirmation on this from—'

'This house has rules,' Bella told them stiffly. '*And* I'm not that sort of woman. To suggest . . . even to *think* . . . even to *begin* to think . . .' She was sputtering, and she knew it. She expected this made her seem a perfect fool in their eyes, an old bag who'd somehow fallen victim to a smooth talking Lothario come to remove her from her money when she *had* no money in the first place so why would he have even bothered with the likes of her? She gathered her wits. She gathered what dignity she had left. She said, 'I know my lodgers. I make a habit of knowing my lodgers because I'm sharing a bloody *house* with them, and I'm not very likely to want to share my house with a murderer, am I?' She didn't wait for them to reply to this question, which was largely rhetorical. She said, 'So you listen to me, because I'm not going to repeat myself: Frazer Chaplin's been here in this house from the first week I started letting rooms, and I think I'd have sorted out that he was . . . *whatever* you seem to think he is . . . a bloody long time before now, don't you?'

The two cops exchanged a look. It was the man who picked up the conversation next. He said, 'You're right. That wasn't a particularly helpful direction. I think the superintendent merely meant that Frazer's got something of an appeal for women.'

'What if he does?' she demanded. 'It's hardly his fault.'

'I wouldn't disagree.' Lynley went on to ask could they just go back over what she'd told them about Frazer's whereabouts on the day that Jemima Hastings died?

She said she'd *told* them. She'd told them and told them and telling them again was not going change things. Frazer had done what he always did—

Which turned out to be their point. If one day looked exactly like another in the life of Frazer Chaplin, was there a possibility that she was mistaken, that she was merely telling them what she *thought* he'd done, that he had perhaps done or said something later on to make her believe or assume he'd been home during that time when he was usually home, while the truth of the matter was that he wasn't at home at all? Did she always see him when he came home to shower and change between his two jobs? Did she always hear him? Was she always, in fact, here at that time? Did she sometimes go to the shops? Putter round the back garden? Meet a friend? Go out for a coffee? Become caught up in a phone conversation or a television programme or a commitment to something that took her out of the house or even to another part of the house, resulting in the possibility that she didn't actually know, couldn't swear to, hadn't seen, couldn't confirm . . .

Bella felt dizzy. They were spinning her round and round with all their possibilities. The truth of the matter was that Frazer was a good boy and they couldn't see this because they were cops and she knew about cops, she did. Didn't they all? Didn't they *all* know that what cops did was find a supposed killer and then massage the facts to pin guilt upon him? And hadn't the newspapers shown that to the public time after time with the Met putting supposed IRA blokes away for years on spurious evidence and God, God, Frazer was *Irish*, God he was Irish and didn't that make him guilty in their eyes?

Then Lynley started talking about the National Portrait Gallery. He mentioned Jemima and Jemima's picture and Bella understood from this that the topic had changed, moving from Frazer to society photos and, frankly, she was only too happy to look at them.

'. . . something too coincidental for our liking,' Lynley was saying. He mentioned someone by the name of Dickens and he connected that person to Hampshire for some reason and then he said something more about Frazer and then Jemima and then it didn't matter at all because 'What's *she* doing there?' Bella demanded. She went quite lightheaded, and her hands got icy.

'Who?' Lynley asked.

'Her. *Her*,' and Bella used her icy finger to point at the picture that was bringing reality home. It was coming at her fast, an express train from the truth. Its whistle blew *fool, fool, fool* and the sound was deafening as the train screamed towards her.

'That's the woman we're talking about,' the superintendent told her, leaning over to have a look at the woman in the photograph. 'That's Gina Dickens, Mrs McHaggis. We're assuming that Frazer met her that night—'

'Gina Dickens?' Bella said. 'You're both mad. That's Georgina Francis large as life. I tossed her out last year for breaking one of my rules.'

'Which rule?' the superintendent asked.

'The rule about . . .' *Fool, fool, fool.*

'Yes?' the detective inspector urged her.

'Frazer. Her,' Bella said. *Fool, fool, fool, fool.* 'He said she was gone. He said he never saw her once she left. He said *she* was the one who wanted *him* . . . but he didn't want it at all . . . Not with her.'

'Ah. I expect he lied to you,' Lynley told her. 'May we talk again about what you remember of the day that Jemima Hastings died?'

32

She was in big trouble, no doubt about it. She was already so late for work that Meredith knew she was going to have to come up with an excuse for her absence that was akin to an alien abduction. Anything less was unlikely to result in her continued employment.

And it *was* going to be absence at this point, not mere tardiness. That was certain. For once she saw Zachary Whiting in conversation with Gina Dickens, Meredith felt afire to take action, and the action she felt afire to take had nothing to do with driving over to Ringwood and sitting obediently within her cubicle at Gerber & Hudson Graphic Design.

Still, she didn't ring Mr Hudson. She knew she ought, but she couldn't bring herself to do it. He was going to be livid, and she reckoned if she could somehow sort out Gina Dickens, Zachary Whiting, Gordon Jossie and Jemima's death by the end of the day, emerging as a heroine who wrestles villains into submission would bring her enough glory to translate into a chance that she wouldn't lose her job.

She felt a bit like a headless chicken at first, seeing the chief superintendent chatting with Gina Dickens. She hadn't known what to do, what to think, or where to go. She crept back to her car and started off in the direction of Lyndhurst because that was where the police station was and one was meant to rely on the police. Only what was the point in going there, when the head of the Lyndhurst police was *here*, and he was obviously thick as thieves with Gina Dickens?

Meredith pulled to the side of the road, and she tried to sort through what she'd heard from Gina Dickens, what she'd discovered about her during her own investigation, and what she'd learned about her from Michele Daugherty. She tried to remember every statement made to her and from these statements she tried to sort out who Gina Dickens really was. What she ended up with was the decision that there had to be something *somewhere* about Gina, a piece of truth about her that Gina herself had not realised she was revealing. Meredith needed to find that truth because it would tell her exactly what to do.

The problem, of course, was the where of it. Where was she supposed to find this piece of truth? If Gina Dickens did not actually exist, then what was Meredith Powell supposed to do to sort out who she really was and why she was in cahoots with Chief Superintendent Whiting in the matter of . . . *what*? What, exactly, was the reason for their partnership?

It seemed to Meredith that any information about Gina, her purpose in Hampshire, and her true identity was information that Gina herself would keep quite close. She would keep it secreted on her person, or in her bag, or in her car, perhaps.

Except, Meredith thought, that didn't make sense. Gina Dickens couldn't risk it. For Gordon Jossie might well stumble upon it if she kept it nearby, and Gina would know that, so she'd want some place far more secure to keep the key to who she really was and what she was up to.

Meredith grasped the steering wheel tightly as she realised the obvious answer. There *was* one spot where Gina could be freely who she really was: within the four walls of her own bed-sitting room. For while Meredith had searched that room from top to bottom, she hadn't looked everywhere, had she? She hadn't looked between the mattress and the box springs on the bed, for instance. Nor had she removed drawers to look for anything that might be taped beneath them. Or behind pictures for that matter.

That damn bed-sitting room had to hold all the answers, Meredith reckoned, because when it came down to it, it had never made sense that Gina would be living with Gordon while maintaining her own digs, did it? Why go to the expense of doing that? So the answers to every riddle about Gina Dickens were in Lyndhurst where they had always been. For not only was Lyndhurst the site of Gina's room, but it was also the location of Whiting's police station. And how bloody convenient was *that*?

Despite all of this delicate thinking and supposing, Meredith knew she was perilously close to being completely out of her depth in the situation. Murder, police malfeasance, false identities . . . None of this was exactly up her alley. Still, she knew she had to get to the bottom of everything because there seemed to be no one else who was interested in doing so.

Although . . . Of *course*, Meredith thought. She took out her mobile and punched in Rob Hastings' number.

He was – as wonderful luck would have it – actually *in* Lyndhurst! He was – as less than wonderful luck would have it – just stepping into a meeting of all the agisters, which was likely to go on for more than ninety minutes and closer to two hours.

She said to him in a rush, 'Rob, it's Gina Dickens and that chief superintendent. It's them together. And there's *no* Gina Dickens at all anyway. *And* Chief Superintendent Whiting told Michele Daugherty that she had to stop looking into Gordon Jossie but she hadn't even started the process of looking into him yet and—'

'Hang on. What're you banging on about?' Rob asked. 'Merry, what the hell . . . ? Who's Michele Daugherty?'

She said, 'I'm going to her rooms in Lyndhurst.'

'Michele Daugherty's rooms?'

'*Gina's* rooms. She's got a bedsit over the Mad Hatter, Rob. On the High Street. You know where it is? The tea rooms over the road from—'

''Course I know,' he said. 'But—'

'There's got to be something there, something I overlooked the last time. Will you meet me there? It's important because I saw them together. On Gordon's property. Rob, he drove right up and got out and went into the paddock and they stood there talking—'

'Whiting?'

'Yes, yes. Who else? That's what I've been trying to *tell* you.'

He said, 'Scotland Yard's back, Merry. It's a woman called Havers. You need to ring her about this. I've got her number.'

'Scotland Yard? Rob, how c'n we trust *them* if we can't trust Whiting? They're all cops. And what do we tell them? That Whiting's talking to Gina Dickens who isn't really Gina Dickens anyway except we don't know who she is? No, no. We've got to—'

'Merry! For God's sake, listen. I told this woman, this Havers, everything. What you told me about Whiting. How you gave him the information. How he said it was all in hand. She'll want to hear whatever else you know. I expect she'll want to see that bedsit as well. Listen to me.'

That was when he told her he was heading into the agisters' meeting. He couldn't skip it because among other things, he had to . . . Oh, never mind, he said, he just had to be there. And *she* had to ring the detective from Scotland Yard.

'Oh no,' she cried. 'Oh no, oh no. If I do that, there's no way she'll agree to break into Gina's room. You know that.'

'Break in?' he said. '*Break in*? Merry, what've you got planned?' He went on to ask could she wait for him. He would meet her at the Mad Hatter immediately after his meeting. He would be there as soon as he could. 'Don't do anything mad,' he told her. 'Promise me, Merry. If something happens to you . . .' He stopped.

At first she said nothing. Then she promised and quickly rang off. She intended to keep her promise and to wait for Rob Hastings, but when she got to Lyndhurst, she knew that waiting was out of the question. She *couldn't* wait. Whatever was up there in Gina's room was something she intended to get her hands on now.

She parked by the New Forest Museum and hoofed up the High Street to the Mad Hatter Tea Rooms. At that time of morning, the tea rooms were open and doing a brisk business, so no one took notice of Meredith as she went through the doorway set at an angle to the tea rooms themselves.

She dashed quickly up the stairs. At the top, she was stealthy about her movements. She listened at the doorway of the room opposite Gina's. No sound from within. She tapped upon it just to make sure. No one answered. Good. Once again there would be no witness to what she was about to do.

She fished in her bag for her bank card. Her hands felt slick, but she reckoned it was nerves. There was more menace about breaking into Gina's room than there had been the last time she'd done so. Then her suspicions had driven her. Now she had certain knowledge.

She fumbled with the card and dropped it twice before she finally managed to get the door open. A final time, she looked round the corridor. She stepped inside the room.

There was sudden movement to her left. A rush of air and a blur of darkness. The door shut behind her and she heard an inner bolt driven home. She swung round and found herself face to face with an utter stranger. A man. For a moment, and it was just a single moment, her mind said ridiculously and in rapid succession that she'd got the wrong room, that the room had been let out to someone else, that Gina's room had never been here above the Mad Hatter in the first place. And then her mind said she was in real danger, for the man grabbed her arm, swung her round, clamped his hand brutally over her mouth. She felt something press into her neck. It felt wickedly sharp.

'Now what have we here?' he whispered in her ear. 'And what are we going to do about it?'

Once he received the phone call from the Scotland Yard sergeant, Gordon Jossie knew he'd reached the absolute end game with Gina. There had been a moment in the kitchen that morning when Gina's denials about Jemima had nearly convinced him she was speaking the truth, but after DS Havers phoned him wondering why Gina had not shown up at her hotel in Sway, he understood that being convinced by Gina had more to do with how he wanted things to be than how things actually were. That, indeed, served as a good description of his entire adult life, he thought morosely. There had been at least two years of that life – those years after he'd first met Jemima and become enmeshed with her – when he'd developed a fantasy future. It had seemed as if the fantasy could be turned into reality because of Jemima herself and because she'd seemed to need him so. She'd appeared to need him the way a plant needs decent soil and adequate water, and he'd reckoned that that kind of need would make the mere fact of having a man in her life more important than who the man was. She'd seemed exactly what he'd been looking for, although he hadn't been looking at all. There had been no sense in looking, he'd decided. Not when the world he had constructed for himself – or better said, the world that had been constructed for him – could come crashing down round his ears at any time. And then, suddenly, there she had been on Longslade Bottom with her brother and his dog. And there he had been with Tess. And she had been the one to make 'the first move', as it was called. An invitation to her brother's house, which was her own house, an invitation for drinks on a Sunday afternoon although he didn't drink, couldn't and wouldn't ever risk a drink.

He'd gone because of her eyes. Ridiculous now to think that's why he'd driven to Burley to see her again but that was it. He'd never seen anyone with two entirely different coloured eyes, and he'd liked studying them, or at least that was what he'd told himself. So he'd gone. And the rest of it . . . ? What did it matter? The rest had brought him to where he was now.

Her hair was longer those months later when he saw her in London after she'd left him. It seemed a bit lighter as well, but that could have been a trick of memory. As to the remainder of the package that was Jemima: she was all the same.

He hadn't understood at first why she'd chosen the cemetery in Stoke Newington for their meeting, but when he saw the place with its winding paths, ruined monuments and unrestrained growth of vegetation he realised her choice had had to do with not being seen in his company. This should have reassured him about her intentions but still he'd wanted to hear it from her lips. He'd also wanted both the coin and the stone returned to him. Those he was determined to have. He had to have them because if she kept them in her possession, there was no telling what she'd do with them.

She'd said, 'So how did you find me? I know about the postcards. But how . . . ? Who . . . ?'

He said he didn't know who'd phoned him, just that it was a bloke's voice, telling him about the cigar shop in Covent Garden.

She'd said, 'A man,' to herself, not to him. She seemed to be going over in her mind the various possibilities. There would, he knew, most likely be many. Jemima had never gone in for friendship with other women in a big way, but men she had sought, men who somehow completed her in ways that friendship with women never could. He wondered if that was why Jemima had died. Perhaps a man had misunderstood the nature of her need, wanting something from her that far exceeded what she wanted from him. It explained in some ways the phone call he'd received, which itself could be described as a betrayal, a tit for tat as it were, you take my man and I turn you over to . . . well, to whoever seems to be looking for you because I don't care who it is, I only want to balance the scales in which you and I do harm to each other.

He'd said, 'Have you told anyone?'

'*That's* why you've been looking for me?'

'Jemima, have you told anyone?'

'Do you actually think I'd *want* anyone to know?'

He could see her point although he felt it like a wound she was inflicting upon him instead of merely an answer to his question. Still, there was something in the way she said it that made him doubt her. He knew her too well.

'D'you have a new bloke?' he asked her abruptly, not because he really wanted to know but because of what it could mean if she had.

'I don't see that's any business of yours.'

'*Do* you?'

'Why?'

'You know.'

'I most certainly do *not* know.'

He said, 'If you've told . . . Jemima, just tell me if you've told someone.'

'Why? Worried, are you? Yes, I suppose you would be. I'd be worried as well. So let me ask you this, Gordon: have you thought how *I'd* feel if other people knew? Have you considered the wreck *my* life could become? "Just please give us an interview, Miss Hastings. Just a word about what it's been like for you. Did you never suspect? Did you not recognise . . . ? What sort of woman wouldn't know there was something terribly wrong here?" D'you actually think I'd want that, Gordon? My picture smeared on the front of some tabloid along with yours?'

'They'd pay,' he said. 'They'd pay you a lot for an interview. They'd pay you a fortune.'

She'd backed off, white faced. 'You're mad,' she said. 'If it's even possible, you're actually madder than you were—'

'All right,' he'd said fiercely. Then, 'What've you done with the coin? Where is it? Where's the stone?'

'Why?' she asked. 'How's *that* your business?'

'I mean to take them back to Hampshire, obviously.'

'Do you indeed?'

'You know I do. They must go back, Jemima. It's the only way.'

'No. There's another way entirely.'

'What way is that?'

'I think you might already know. Especially as you've been looking for me.'

That was the moment when he knew she did indeed have someone else. That was when he understood, despite her declarations to the contrary, how likely it was that the darkest part of his soul was going to be revealed to someone, if it had not already been revealed. His only hope – his guarantee of her silence and the silence of whoever else knew the truth – lay in complying with whatever she was about to ask of him.

He knew she was about to ask something because he knew Jemima. And his curse for the rest of his life was going to be the knowledge that once again he and no one else had put himself into a place of complete destruction. He'd wanted to return the coin and the stone to the earth in which they'd lain buried for more than a thousand years. More than that, he'd wanted to know that Jemima would keep his secret safe. So he'd put up those cards and in doing so he'd forced her hand. And now she was going to play it.

She'd said, 'We need the money.'

'What money? Who's *we*?'

'You know what money. We have plans, Gordon, and that money—'

'That's what this is about, then? That's why you left? Not because of me, but because you want to sell whatever's dug up from the ground and then . . . what?'

But no, that hadn't been it at all, not at first. Money was fine but money had not driven Jemima. Money bought things but what it didn't buy, could never buy, had never bought was what she needed most.

He said, understanding things further, 'It's the bloke. He's the one, isn't he? He wants it. For whatever your *plans* are.'

He'd known he'd hit upon the truth. He'd seen as much in the high colour that swept across her cheeks. Indeed, she had left him to get away from the truth of who he was, but she'd met another man in her inimitable fashion and it was to this other man that she'd told his secrets.

He said, 'Why did it take you so long, then? All these months? Why'd you not tell him at once?'

After a moment in which she'd looked away from him, she said, 'Those postcards,' and he'd seen how his own fear of discovery, his own need for reassurance which was unlike her need and yet ironically identical to it, had brought about this very meeting between them. Any new lover would have asked why someone was trying to find her. Where she could have lied, she had told the truth.

He said to her, 'What do you want then, Jemima?'

'I've already told you.'

To which he'd said, 'I'll need to think.'

'About what?'

'How to make it happen.'

'What do you mean?'

'It's obvious, isn't it? If you mean to dig the lot up, I have to disappear. If I don't . . . Or is it that you want me found out as well? Perhaps you want me dead? I mean, we *were* something to each other for a while, weren't we?'

She was silent at this. The day around them was bright and hot and clear, and the sounds of the birds intensified suddenly. She finally said, 'I don't want you dead. I don't even want you harmed, Gordon. I just want to forget about it. About us. I want a new life. We're going to emigrate and open a business and to do that . . . And it's your own fault. If you hadn't put up those cards. If you hadn't. I was in a state, and he wanted to know, so I told him. He asked – well, anyone would – how I'd come to find out because he reckoned it'd be the last thing you'd tell anyone. So I told him that part as well.'

'About the paddock.'

'Not the paddock itself but what you'd found there. How I expected we'd use it or sell it or whatever one does, how you hadn't wanted to, and then . . . well, yes. Why. I had to tell him why.'

'Had to?'

'Of course. Don't you see? There aren't supposed to be secrets between people who love each other.'

'And he loves you.'

'He *does*.'

Yet Gordon could see her doubts, and he understood how the existence of her doubts had also played a role in what was happening. She wanted to secure him, whoever he was. He wanted money. These desires combined to produce betrayal.

'When?' he asked her.

'What?'

'When did you decide to do this, Jemima?'

'I'm not *doing* anything. You asked to see me. I didn't ask to see you. You looked for me, I didn't look for you. If you hadn't done any of that, there'd have been no need to tell anyone about you.'

'And when money had come up between you? What then?'

'It never *did* come up, till I told him why . . .' Her voice drifted off at that point, and he could tell that she was reasoning something out on her own, determining the possibility of something that he himself was only too able to see.

He said, 'It's the money. He wants the money. Not you. You see that, don't you?'

She said, 'No. That's not true.'

He said, 'And I expect you've had your doubts all along.'

'He loves me.'

'If that's how you see it.'

'You're a rotten person.'

'I suppose I am.'

He'd said that he would cooperate with her plan to return to the holding and stake her claim. He would be gone but it would take time to effect the sort of disappearance that was required. She asked how long and he said he wasn't sure. He would have to speak to certain people and then he would let her know. She could, naturally, ring up the media in the meantime and make some additional cash that way. He said this last bitterly before he'd walked off. What a mess he'd made of everything, he thought.

And now Gina. Or whoever the hell she was. He told himself that if he hadn't decided to replace the bloody fence of the bloody paddock, none of this would have happened. But the truth of the matter was that the first event that had brought him ultimately to this moment had occurred in a crowded McDonald's when *let's jus' take him* had led to *let's make him cry* had led to *shut him up! how we to shut him up?*

When Zachary Whiting showed up at the Royal Oak Pub a few hours after his arrival at the work site, Gordon was up on the roof's ridge. He saw the familiar vehicle pull into the car park, but he felt neither nervous nor afraid. He'd prepared himself for Whiting's eventual appearance. Since they'd been interrupted during their last encounter, Gordon knew the chief superintendent was probably unwilling to let that moment between them go uncompleted.

The cop signalled him down from the roof. Cliff was handing a bundle of straw up to him, so Gordon told him to take a break. The day was as hot as every day that had preceded it, so he said, 'Have a cider,' and he said the cider would be on him. 'Enjoy,' he told him. 'I'll be along directly.'

Cliff was happy to comply although he muttered, 'Anything wrong, mate?' as Whiting approached. He didn't know who Whiting was, but he could sense the man's menace. Whiting wore it like skin.

'Not a bit,' was Gordon's reply. 'Take your time in there,' he added, with a nod to the doorway. And he repeated, 'I'll be along.'

With Cliff out of the way, he waited for Whiting. The chief superintendent stopped in front of him. He did his usual, getting in too close, but Gordon didn't pull away from the man.

'You're out of here,' Whiting said.

'What?'

'You heard. You're being moved. Home Office orders. You've an hour. Let's go. Leave the pickup. You won't be needing it.'

'My dog's in—'

'Fuck the dog. The dog stays. The pickup stays. This—' with a jerk of his head towards the pub, by which Gordon reckoned he meant the thatching, the job he was doing, his source of employment. 'This's done for. Get in the car.'

'Where are they sending me?'

'No bloody idea and even less interest. Get in the fucking car. We don't want a scene. *You* don't want a scene.'

Gordon wasn't about to cooperate without more information. He wasn't about to get into that car unprepared. There were any number of isolated lanes between this spot and his holding near Sway, and the unfinished business between him and this man suggested that he wouldn't be driven home directly, no matter what Whiting was claiming. He had no way to be sure the cop was even telling the truth although Jemima's death and the presence of New Scotland Yard in Hampshire suggested that it was likely.

Still, he said, 'I'm not leaving that dog here. I go, she goes.'

Whiting took off the clip-on sunglasses and polished them on the front of his shirt. It was clinging to him where he was sweating. Heat of the day or anticipation. Gordon reckoned it could be either. Whiting said, 'Do you think you can *negotiate* with me?'

'I'm not negotiating. I'm stating a fact.'

'Are you now, laddie.'

'I expect your brief is to take me somewhere and hand me over. I expect you've got a deadline. I expect you've been told not to cock it up, not to cause a scene, not to make it look like anything other than two blokes having a chat right here, with me climbing into your car at the end of it. Anything else and it's likely to attract notice, eh? Like notice of those people in the beer garden over there. You and I have a dust-up and someone's likely to ring the cops and if it's a proper dust-up – a head banging sort of dust-up – then it gets even more attention and someone wonders how you managed to made such a mess out of something so simple as—'

'Fetch the sodding dog,' Whiting said. 'I want you out of Hampshire. You pollute the air.'

Gordon smiled thinly. The truth of the matter was that

sweat was dripping down his sides and pouring like a water-fall along his spine. His words were hard but there was nothing behind them except the only means he had to protect himself. He went to the pickup.

Tess was within, thank God, dozing across the length of the seat. Her lead was looped through the steering wheel, and he took it up swiftly and dropped it on the floor where it was safe to fumble round. Tess awakened, blinked, and yawned widely, exhaling a cloud of dog breath. She began to rise. He told her to stay and climbed inside. With one hand he attached the lead to her collar while with the other, he made himself ready. He had a windcheater, so he donned it. He flipped down the sun visors. He opened and closed the glove box. He heard Whiting approaching across the gravel car park, and he said, 'I expect you don't want me to go into the pub. Cliff'll need a note,' and he was thankful he had the presence of mind to say that much.

Whiting said, 'Hurry it up then,' and returned to his car. He didn't get inside but rather lit a cigarette and watched and waited.

His note was brief, *This is yours till I need it, mate.* Cliff didn't need to know anything else. If Gordon had a chance later to get the vehicle back, he'd do so. If not, at least it wouldn't fall into Whiting's hands.

He'd left the keys in the ignition, which was his habit. He removed the cottage key from the ring, told Tess to come, and climbed out of the truck. The whole procedure had taken less than two minutes. Less than two minutes to alter the course of his life once again.

'I'm ready,' he said to Whiting as he and the dog – wagging her tail as always, as if the wanker in front of them was just another someone who might pat her damn head – approached the man.

'Oh, I expect you are,' was Whiting's reply.

33

Later Barbara Havers would think with some astonishment that everything ultimately had come down to the fact that Lyndhurst had a one-way traffic system in the heart of the village. It formed a nearly perfect triangle, and the direction from which she was travelling forced her to follow the triangle's northern side. This put her into the High Street where, midway down the street and just beyond the half-timbered front of the Crown Hotel, she was meant to turn into the Romsey Road, which would take her to the police station. Because of the traffic lights at the Romsey Road junction, a tailback formed during most hours of the day. This was the case when Barbara followed the curve round the expanse of lawn and thatched cottages comprising Swan Green and set her course into and through the village.

She found herself caught behind a lorry belching a hideous amount of exhaust fumes through her open windows. She reckoned she might as well have a smoke as she waited for the light to change. No point in avoiding an opportunity to add to the pollution that was blackening her lungs, she thought.

She was reaching for her bag when she saw Frazer Chaplin. He came out of a building just ahead of her, and there was no mistaking the bloke. She was quite close to the left-hand kerb in preparation for her turn into the Romsey Road, and the building in question – its sign identified it as the Mad Hatter Tea Rooms – was on the left side of the street. She thought briefly, What the bloody hell . . . And then she clocked the woman with him. They came onto the pavement in the unmistakable manner of lovers in post-trysting mode, but there was something about Frazer's two-handed hold upon his companion that wasn't quite right. He had his right arm tightly round her waist. He had his left arm across his own body to grip her left arm above the elbow. They paused for a moment in front of the tea room windows, and he said something to her. Then he kissed her cheek and gave her a look that was soulful, admiring and love struck. Had it not been for that grip and a decided stiffness about the woman's body, Barbara might have thought Frazer was up to what she'd quickly concluded he was apt to get up to the only time she'd met him: that wide-legged posture of his when he was sitting, that look-what-I've-got-for-you-here-baybee expression in the eyes, and the rest was history. But the woman with him — who the hell *was* she, Barbara wondered — did not appear to be floating somewhere in the aftermath of sexual rapture. Instead she appeared to be . . . well, *captive* seemed a fairly good description.

They headed in the same direction Barbara was taking. A few cars ahead of her, however, they crossed the road. They continued down the pavement and, within a few yards, disappeared into an alley on the right. Barbara muttered, 'Damn, damn, *damn*,' and waited in mounting agitation for the lights at the junction to begin their change from red to amber to green. She saw that the alley on the right was marked with that universal white P on a square blue background, indicating that there was a car park somewhere behind the buildings in the High Street. She reckoned it stood to reason that Frazer was taking the woman to it.

She said, 'Come on, come on, come on,' to the lights and they finally cooperated. The traffic began to move. She had thirty yards to go to get to that alley.

It felt like forever till she made the turn and zoomed between the buildings, where she saw that the car park was not only for shoppers come to do their weekly business in the village. It also served the New Forest Museum and the public facilities as well. So it was massed with cars, and for a moment Barbara thought she'd lost Frazer and his companion somewhere within the rows of vehicles. But then she saw him some distance away at the side of a Polo and if before she *might* have given idle thought to this being the end of a romantic tryst between Frazer Chaplin and his companion, the manner in which they got into the vehicle put the matter to rest.

The woman entered the passenger's side as one would expect, but Frazer kept his grip upon her and climbed right in behind her. From there Barbara couldn't see the action, but it seemed fairly clear that Frazer's goal was to force his companion into moving over to the driver's side, and he had no intention of losing his grip upon her while she did so.

A horn honked suddenly. Barbara looked into her rear view mirror. Naturally, she thought, this *would* be the moment that someone else would come into the car park. She couldn't wave them round her, for the passage was far too narrow.

She turned into one of the rows of cars and blasted up it and down another. By the time she had herself back into a position where she could see the vehicle into which Frazer had climbed, it had pulled back from the bay where it had been parked and it was heading in the direction of the exit.

Barbara followed, hoping for twofold luck: that no one would come along and keep her from catching Frazer up; that traffic in the High Street would allow her to slip in behind him at least relatively easily and unseen. For it was obvious to her that she had to follow. Her intention to confront Chief Superintendent Whiting at the police station had to be set aside for the moment because if Frazer Chaplin had come to the New Forest, he hadn't done so to take pictures of the ponies.

The only question was the identity of the young woman with him. She'd been tall, thin and decked out in something that looked like an African nightdress. It covered her from shoulders to toes. She was either in costume or protecting herself from the summer sun but in either case, Barbara felt sure she'd not seen her before these moments in Lyndhurst.

From what she'd learned earlier from Rob Hastings, Barbara concluded that it had to be Meredith Powell. If, indeed, Meredith Powell had been conducting some sort of mad investigation on her own – as, according to Hastings, it seemed she had done – then it stood to reason that somehow she'd stumbled upon Frazer Chaplin whose presence here in Hampshire suggested he was into things up to his neck as well. And the body language between them told a tale, didn't it: Meredith – if that was who it was and who else *could* it be if it wasn't Meredith? – didn't want to be in Frazer's company while Frazer had no intention of allowing her to set off somewhere on her own.

At the bottom of the High Street, they headed due south into another leg of the Lyndhurst one-way system. Barbara followed. The signs, she saw, indicated Brockenhurst, and at yet another point of this traffic triangle, they turned into the A337. There they dipped almost immediately into a vast area of woodland. Everywhere was green and lush, and the traffic flowed well but with an eye for the animals. As the road was arrow-straight for some distance, Barbara dropped back, the Polo well within her sight. There were very few options for turning when one came to Brockenhurst, and Barbara had a fairly good idea which one they intended to take.

She was unsurprised when they took it a few minutes later: the route to Lymington. This, she knew, was going to put them within range of Gordon Jossie's holding. She reckoned that was where they were heading. She meant to know why.

She received at least a partial answer to this question when her mobile sounded 'Peggy Sue'. Since she'd dumped her shoulder bag's contents onto the passenger seat when looking for a fag, the mobile was easy enough to snatch up. She barked 'Havers' into it and added, 'Be quick. I can't pull over. Who is this?'

'Frazer—'

'What the *hell*?' No *way* could he have her number, Barbara thought. Her mind was wrestling with all the possibilities of how he'd managed to get it as she demanded, 'Who's that with you in the bloody car? What're you—'

'Barbara?'

She realised it was DI Lynley. She said, 'Damn. Sorry. I thought you were . . . Where are you? Are you here?'

'Where?'

'Hampshire. Where else? Listen, I'm following—'

'We've broken his alibi.'

'Whose?'

'Frazer Chaplin's. He wasn't at home the day she died, not that Bella McHaggis can actually verify. She assumed he was there because he'd always come home between his jobs, and he encouraged her to think he'd done his usual thing that day. And the woman in the picture from the Portrait Gallery—' He stopped as someone in the background spoke to him. He said, 'Yes. Right,' to that person and then, 'She's called Georgina Francis, Barbara, not Gina Dickens. Bella McHaggis identified her.' Someone spoke to him again in the background. He then said, 'As to Whiting . . .'

'What about Whiting?' Barbara asked. 'Who's Georgina Francis? Who're you talking to anyway?' She reckoned she knew the answer to this last, but she wanted to hear it from Lynley's own lips.

'The superintendent,' he said. He went rapidly on to tell her how Georgina Francis fitted into the picture: former lodger at the home of Bella McHaggis, tossed out on her ear for violating the McHaggis dictum against fraternisation among those living beneath her roof. Frazer Chaplin had been the man involved.

'What the hell was she doing at the Portrait Gallery?' Barbara asked. 'That's some bloody coincidence, isn't it?'

'Not if she was there to check out the competition. Not if she was there because she was and is still involved with Frazer Chaplin. Why would their relationship have ended just because she had to find other lodgings? We reckon—'

'Who?' She couldn't help herself although she hated herself the moment she said it.

'What?'

'Who reckons?'

'Barbara, for God's sake.' He was not a fool.

'All right. Sorry. Go on.'

'We've spoken to Mrs McHaggis at some length.' He banged on then about DragonFly Tonics, transfers, Frazer's lime green Vespa, Winston Nkata's viewing of the CCTV films in the area, the two e-fits, and the yellow shirt and Jemima's handbag found within the Oxfam bin about which, he concluded, 'We reckon his intention was to hand them over to Georgina Francis to plant somewhere on Gordon Jossie's holding. But he didn't have the time to do it. Once Bella saw the story in the paper about the body, she called the police and you turned up. There was too much risk at that point for him to do anything but sit tight and wait for a better opportunity.'

'He's here. In Hampshire. Sir, he's here.'

'Who?'

'Frazer Chaplin. I'm following him just now. He's got a woman with him and we're heading—'

'She's got Frazer Chaplin in sight,' Lynley said to his companion on the other end of the conversation. The superintendent said something quite sharply. Lynley said to Havers, 'Phone for back-up, Barbara. That's not from me. That's from Isabelle.'

Isabelle, Barbara thought. Bloody *Isabelle*. She said, 'I don't know where we are or where we're going, so I don't know where to ask back-up to go, sir.' She was playing fast and loose for reasons she didn't want to explore.

Lynley said, 'Get close enough for the number plates if you can. And you can tell the make of car, can't you? You can see the colour.'

'Just the colour,' she said. 'I'll have to follow—'

'God damn it, Barbara. Then phone for back-up, explain the situation, and give your own bloody number plates and a description of your own car. I don't have to tell you this bloke's dangerous. If he's got someone with him—'

'He's not going to hurt her while she's driving, sir. I'll phone for back-up when we get where we're going. What about Whiting?'

'Barbara, if nothing else, you're putting yourself in danger. This is not the time for you to—'

'What've you learned, sir? What did Norman tell you?'

There was more talk from Ardery at his end. Lynley said to the superintendent, 'She thinks—'

Barbara cut in airily with, 'I'm going to have to ring off, sir. Terrible traffic and I think I'm losing the connection anyway and—'

'Whiting,' he said. She knew he did it to get her attention. Typical of him. She was forced to listen to a catalogue of facts: Whiting charged by the Home Office with the highest level of protection of someone; Lynley and Ardery were concluding the person was Jossie; it was the only explanation for why Whiting hadn't turned over to New Scotland Yard the evidence of Jossie's trip to London; Whiting knew the Met would focus on Jossie because of it; that couldn't be allowed to happen.

'Even if the evidence made it look like Jossie killed someone?' Barbara demanded. 'Bloody hell, sir. What kind of high level protection asks for *that*? Who is this guy?'

They didn't know but it didn't actually matter at the moment because Frazer Chaplin was the one they were after and since Barbara had Frazer Chaplin in view . . .

Blah, blah, blah, Barbara thought. She said, 'Right. Right. Got it. Oh damn, I think I'm losing you, sir . . . bad connection here . . . I'm getting out of range.'

'Phone for back-up and do it at once!' were the last words she heard. She was not out of range, but ahead of her the car she was following had made a sharp turn into a secondary road on the edge of Brockenhurst village. She couldn't be bothered arguing with Lynley at that point. She put her foot down to catch up and veered right just ahead of an oncoming removals van, where a sign pointed to Sway.

Her mind was swarming with a horde of details: facts, names, faces and possibilities. She reckoned she could pause, sort through it all, and phone for the back-up Lynley was insisting upon, or she could get to wherever they were going first, suss out the situation, and make her decisions accordingly.

She chose the second option.

Tess rode in the back seat of Whiting's vehicle. Dumb as the poor dog was, she was dead delighted to be going for a ride in the midst of a workday since she usually had to hang about waiting for Gordon to finish up before she was able to do anything other than lie in the shade and hope for the diversion of a squirrel to chase or a magpie to bark at. Now, though, the windows were open, her ears were flopping, and her nose was catching the delightful smells of high summer. Gordon realised that, come what was likely to come, the retriever wasn't going to be able to help him.

What was going to come soon became apparent. Instead of heading in the direction of Fritham – the first enclave of cottages they should have come to on the route to Gordon's holding – Whiting drove in the direction of Eyeworth Pond. There was a track in advance of the pond that they could have taken to get over to Roger Penny Way and another road that still would have made quick work of reaching Gordon's cottage, but Whiting passed this by and went on to the pond where he parked on the upper level of the two terraces of the roughly hewn car park. It overlooked the water.

This delighted Tess no end, as the dog clearly expected a walk in the woods that edged the pond and stretched out to encompass a vast acreage of trees, hills and enclosures. She barked, wagged her tail and looked meaningfully out of the open window. Whiting said, 'Either shut the dog up or open the door and get it out of here.'

Gordon said, 'Aren't we—'

'Shut the dog up.'

From this Gordon understood that whatever was to happen was going to happen right there in the car. And this made sense, didn't it, when one considered the time of day, the season, and the fact that they were not alone. For not only were there vehicles in the lower section of the car park at this very moment, there were also two families feeding ducks on the distant pond, a group of cyclists setting off into the woods, an elderly couple in deckchairs having a picnic beneath one of the distant willow trees, and a woman taking a pack of six corgis on a midday stroll.

Gordon turned to his retriever. He said, 'Down, Tess. Later,' and he prayed that she would obey. He knew the dog would run into the trees if Whiting forced him to open the door. He also knew how unlikely it was that the cop would allow him fetch her once she'd done so. Suddenly Tess was more important to him than anything else in his pathetic excuse for a life. Her affection for him, in the way of all dogs, was unconditional. He was going to need that in the days to come.

The dog lowered herself to the seat with great reluctance. Before she did so, she cast a soulful look from the outdoors to him. 'Later,' he told her. 'Good dog.'

Whiting chuckled. He moved his seat back and adjusted its position. He said, 'Very nice. Very, very nice. Didn't know you had such a way with animals. Amazing to learn something new about you when I reckoned I already knew it all.' He made himself more comfortable then, and he said, 'Now. We've some unfinished business, you and I.'

Gordon said nothing in reply. He saw the genius in what Whiting had planned and how well the cop had been able to read him from the first. Their last interaction had been interrupted but it had gone on long enough for Gordon to know where every future interaction would lead. Whiting understood that Gordon would never again see him both alone and unprepared to defend himself. But defending himself against Whiting in a public place would lead to an exposure he could not afford. He was caught again. He was caught on all sides. And it was always going to be that way.

Whiting lowered the zip on his trousers. He said, 'Consider

it this way, laddie. I reckon you've taken it in the arse but I don't fancy that. The other will do. Come along and be a good boy, eh? Then we'll call it quits, you and I. Off you'll go with no one the wiser.'

Gordon knew he could end it: now, in this moment, and forever. He was ready. But the aftermath of doing so would end him as well, and his cowardice was that he could not cope with that. He simply lacked the bottle.

How long would it take and what would it cost him to perform for Whiting? Surely, he thought, he could live through this when he'd lived through everything else.

He turned in his seat. He glanced back at Tess. Her head was on her paws, her eyes gazed at him mournfully, her tail wagged slowly. He said to Whiting, 'The dog goes with me.'

'Whatever you like.' Whiting smiled.

Meredith's hands were slick on the steering wheel. Her heart was pounding. She couldn't catch her breath. The bloke had something poked into her side – something sharp that he'd likely been holding in readiness when she'd stupidly broken into Gina Dickens' bed-sitting room – and he murmured, 'How d'you reckon it feels when it pierces the flesh?' in reference to it.

She hadn't a clue who he was. But he, evidently, knew exactly who she was because he called her by name. He'd said within moments and into her ear, 'And *this* must be Meredith Powell, who pinched my pretty gold coin. I've been hearing about you, Meredith. But sure I didn't expect we'd ever get the chance to become acquainted.'

She'd said, 'Who *are* you?' and even as she'd said it, she knew there was something familiar about him.

'That,' he said, 'is one of those need-to-know kinds of questions, Meredith. And you, as it happens, don't need to know.'

The voice. She'd heard enough at that point to connect him to the phone call she'd intercepted in Gina's bed-sitting room.

She'd thought at the time it was Chief Superintendent Whiting – *when* she'd thought at all, she concluded bitterly – but this had to be the man who'd placed that phone call. The voice seemed right.

'Your arrival changes the nature of things a wee bit,' he'd said to her.

So they had gone to her car. Her mind began racing when he forced her into the driver's seat. He said she was to take them to Gordon Jossie's property, so first she concluded that *here* was the answer: this bloke and Gordon in cahoots and Jemima dying because she'd discovered it. That, however, brought up the question of Gina Dickens and how she fitted in, which forced Meredith to decide that it was *Gina* and this bloke who were in cahoots. But that brought up the question of who Gina was, which brought up the question of who Gordon was, which brought up the question of where Chief Superintendent Whiting fitted in since according to Michele Daugherty, it was Jossie's name that had brought Whiting to her office making whatever threats he'd made. And *that* brought up the question of whether Michele Daugherty herself was involved because perhaps she was a liar as well since it seemed they all were liars.

Oh God, oh God, oh God, Meredith thought. She should have gone into work at Gerber & Hudson that day.

She considered driving wildly round Hampshire instead of heading to Gordon's holding when the man told her to take him there. She reckoned if she drove fast enough and wildly enough, there was a chance that she could attract the attention of someone – a policeman out on patrol definitely wouldn't have gone amiss – and save herself that way. But there was that thing poking into her side and the suggestion it made of a slow and painful entry somewhere in the vicinity of . . . what? Was it her liver down there? Where were her kidneys, exactly? And how much did it hurt to be stabbed? Was she enough of a heroine to undergo . . . and if she did . . . but would he really stab her if she was driving the car . . . and what if she drove erratically and he told her to stop and then he marched her into the woods . . . into one of hundreds upon hundreds of woods . . . How long would it take someone to find her while she slowly bled to death? Like Jemima had done. Oh God oh God oh God.

'You killed her!' She blurted it out. She hadn't intended to. She'd intended to remain calm. Sigourney Weaver in that old film about the space creature. Even older, *ancient* even: telly shows featuring Diana Rigg in her high-heeled boots kicking bad guys in the teeth. What would they do in this situation? she wondered ridiculously. What would Sigourney and Diana do? Easy for them because it was all in the script, and the alien, the bad guy, the monster, whatever . . . It always dies at the end, doesn't it? Only Jemima was already dead and, 'You killed her! You killed her!' Meredith shouted.

The deadly point of his weapon pressed harder against her. 'Drive,' he said. 'Killing, I've found, is rather easier than I thought it would be.'

She thought of Cammie. Her vision went blurry. She got a grip. She would do what was asked and what was necessary in order to get back to Cammie.

She said, 'I've a little girl. She's five years old. Do you have children?'

He said, 'Drive.'

'What I mean is you have to let me go. Cammie doesn't have another parent. Please. You don't want to do this to my little girl.'

She glanced at him. He was dark like a Spaniard, and his face was pockmarked. His eyes were brown. They were fixed on her. They held nothing. They were, she realised, like gazing at a blackboard.

She looked away and kept her attention on the road, then. She began to pray.

Barbara reckoned that if the other car was heading to Gordon Jossie's holding – as it apparently was since she could come up with no other reason that it had turned towards Sway – Gina Dickens had to be there. Or Georgina Francis. Or whoever the bloody hell she was. In the middle of the day, they wouldn't be taking a trek out to Jossie's property in order to meet Jossie himself, who would be at work. Instead, they were on their way to meet someone else, and that person had to be Gina/Georgina. All Barbara needed to do was to follow at a safe distance, to make certain they ended up where she suspected they would, and then to ring for back-up if it looked as though she wasn't going to be able to deal with them by herself.

If she moved too soon against Frazer Chaplin, then it stood to reason Georgina Francis would get away. In this part of the country that would not be difficult. Reaching the Isle of Wight took only a ferry ride. Reaching its airport from Yarmouth would not be difficult. Southampton was no great distance, either. Nor was Southampton's airport. So she had to be cautious. The last thing she wanted was to play her hand too soon.

Her mobile rang again. *I love you, Peggy Sue.* She glanced at the phone's screen and saw it was Lynley, no doubt ringing because he assumed they'd been cut off earlier. She let her voicemail take the message as she kept driving.

The Polo ahead of her made a turn into the first of the narrow lanes that led in the end to Gordon Jossie's cottage. They were less than two minutes from their destination now, and when they reached it and the car ahead turned into Gordon Jossie's driveway, Barbara was unsurprised.

She zipped past, just another car in the lane as far as *they* were concerned, she hoped, and she found a spot farther along the way where she crammed her Mini into an opening provided by the access into a local farm's field. There she parked, grabbed up her mobile phone in a bow to cooperating with her superior officers – although she was careful to switch it off – and hurried back in the direction from which she'd come.

She reached Jossie's cottage first, not his drive. The hawthorn hedge hid the dwelling from the lane, but it also provided her with a shelter. She crept along it far enough to gain a view of the driveway and at least part of the west paddock beyond it. She saw that Frazer Chaplin and his companion had entered that paddock and were crossing it. They passed out of her field of vision, though, within ten yards.

She went back along the hedge. She didn't fancy clawing her way through it. It was thickly grown and for all practical purposes impassable, so she needed another way to get onto Jossie's property. She found this way where the hedge made an angle and headed inwards to run along part of the property's east boundary. There, she discovered, it gave onto another paddock defined by the same wire fencing that was used elsewhere on Jossie's land. This was easier to climb through, and she did so. Now what stood between her and the west paddock and Frazer Chaplin within that paddock was the barn in which Jossie kept Jemima's car and his thatching equipment. If she circled that barn, she knew she would arrive at the north side of the west paddock, where Frazer Chaplin had taken the woman who was with him.

There was no immediate sign of Gina Dickens, but as Barbara slunk in the direction of the barn and towards its rear, she could see Gina's well-kept Mini Cooper in the drive. Now was the moment to phone for back-up, but before she did that, she had to make certain that the shiny red vehicle did indeed indicate the presence of its owner.

She gained the rear of the barn. Behind it, some fifty yards away, the woods began, edged thickly with chestnuts and crowned with oaks. They could have afforded her excellent refuge, a place of hiding from which she could observe what was going on in the paddock. But from that distance, there was no way to hear what was being said and, even if she'd had the means to hear, getting to the woods without being seen from the paddock itself was impossible. Even low crawling wouldn't do it, for the paddock was fenced in wire, not in stone, and the area between paddock and woods afforded only the protection of occasional gorse. Anyone on the outside was going to be easily seen by anyone on the inside.

That worked both ways, though. For from the edge of the barn, Barbara could see within the paddock easily enough. And what she saw when she eased her head round to have a peek was Frazer Chaplin with his fist clenching a weapon and that weapon held to the neck of Meredith Powell. His other arm gripped Meredith round her waist. If she moved, what Frazer held – and it had to be a thatcher's crook, Barbara reckoned, considering where they were – was going to pierce Meredith Powell's carotid artery, just as another crook had pierced Jemima's artery in Abney Park Cemetery.

Back-up was utterly useless, Barbara realised. By the time the cops from Lyndhurst arrived, Meredith Powell would be severely injured or dead. If that was to be avoided, Barbara was going to have to come up with the way.

He called her George. Meredith thought, stupidly, What sort of name is that for a woman? until she understood it was short for Georgina. For her part, Gina called him Frazer. And she wasn't exactly pleased to see him.

They'd interrupted her in the midst of what looked like a spate of gardening in the paddock where Gordon kept ponies off the forest when they needed special care. She'd been clearing out a mass of growth on the northwest edge of the paddock and she'd uncovered an old stone trough that had likely been there for two hundred years.

She'd said, '*What* the hell are you . . .' when she'd turned from what she was doing and spied Meredith being frog-marched in her direction. She'd added, 'Oh, Christ, Fraze. What in God's name happened?'

To which he answered, 'A surprise, I'm afraid.'

She cast a hurried look at Meredith before she said to him, 'And did you have to . . .'

'Couldn't leave her there now, could I, George?'

'Well, this is just grand. What in God's name're we supposed to *do* with her?' She gestured towards her gardening project. 'It's got to be here. There's nowhere else. We *don't* have time to mess about with any more problems than we already have.'

'That can't be helped.' Frazer sounded quite philosophical. 'I didn't meet her in the street, did I. She broke into your bedsit. She's got to be dealt with and there's an end to it. And it makes more sense to deal with her here than anywhere else.'

Got to be dealt with. Meredith felt her bowels loosen. She said, 'You mean to blame Gordon, don't you? That's what you did from the first.'

'So as you see . . . ?' Frazer said to Gina. He had a meaningful tone to his voice.

It didn't take genius to work out what he meant: *the bloody cow has got to the bottom of things and now she's got to die.* They would kill her the same way that they killed Jemima. Then they would plant her body – that was the word for it, wasn't it? – on Gordon's holding. Perhaps she'd lie undiscovered for a day or a week or a month or a year. But *when* she was discovered, Gordon would take the blame because the two of them would be long gone. But why? Meredith wondered. 'Why?'

She hadn't realised she'd spoken till Frazer's arm tightened round her waist and the tip of his weapon dipped into her skin. She felt the skin break and she whimpered and he murmured 'Just a taste,' and 'Shut the fuck up.' And then he said to Gina, 'We need a grave.' He gave a rough laugh as he noted, 'Hell, you were going to dig anyway. It'll just be a two-for-one deal.'

'Right here in the paddock?' Gina asked. 'Why the hell would anyone *ever* believe that he'd bury her here?'

'We don't have the luxury of answering that question, do we,' he noted. 'Start digging, Georgina.'

'We don't have the *time.*'

'We don't have a choice. It doesn't have to be deep. Just enough to cover her body. Get a better shovel. There has to be one in the barn.'

'I don't want to—'

'Fine. Shut your God damn eyes when it comes down to it. But just *get* the fucking shovel and start digging her sodding grave because I can't fucking kill her till we've got a place where she can bleed out.'

Meredith whimpered again. 'Please. I've a little girl. You can't.'

'Oh, *that's* where you're very much mistaken,' Frazer said.

They rode in silence. Whiting occasionally broke it with a lilting tune that he whistled in some merriment. Tess occasionally broke it with a long whine that told Gordon the dog understood something was wrong.

The journey took no longer than it would ever have taken to bridge the distance between Fritham and Sway in the middle of the day. It felt as if they were crawling, though. It seemed to him he'd be trapped forever in the passenger seat of Whiting's car.

When they finally turned into Paul's Lane, Whiting gave him his instructions: one suitcase and he had to pack it in a quarter of an hour. As to Gordon's question of what would be done with the rest of his belongings . . . He would have to take that up with whatever authority came to fetch him since the matter was of no interest to Whiting.

The chief superintendent made a gun of his thumb and index finger and used his next statement as the trigger which he cocked while saying, 'Consider yourself lucky I didn't pull the plug on you when I first got told about that little trip of yours up to London. Could have done it then, you know,' he said. 'Consider yourself bloody well lucky.'

Gordon saw how it had worked in Whiting's mind and understood how his trip to London – revealed to Whiting by Gina, there could be no doubt of that – had obliterated whatever caution Whiting might have felt in dealing with him in the past. Before that trip to London, Whiting had merely lurked on the periphery of his life, showing up to make sure he was 'keeping the snout clean', as he'd put it time and again, intimidating him, but not crossing any lines other than those defined by common or garden bullying. Learning he'd been to London, however, and connecting that knowledge to Jemima's death, had opened the floodgates that had previously held back the waters of the chief superintendent's loathing. One word from him to the Home Office and Gordon Jossie went back inside, a violator of the conditions of his release, and always a danger to society. The Home Office would remove his liberty first and ask questions later. Gordon had known how it would play out and this knowledge had kept him cooperative.

And now . . . At this point Whiting could hardly tell the Home Office about Gordon's journey up to London on the day that Jemima had died. Questions would arise concerning Whiting's possession of this knowledge. Gina could step forward and disclose exactly when she'd passed the information along. Whiting would be forced to explain Gordon's continued liberty, then, and the chief superintendent wouldn't want to do that. Better to have his final bit of fun at Eyeworth Pond and then hand Gordon over to whoever was coming to fetch him.

He said to Whiting, 'It doesn't actually matter to you that she's dead, does it?'

Whiting glanced at him. Behind his dark glasses, his eyes were shielded. But his lips moved with distaste. He said, 'You want to yammer about someone's *dying*, do you? I don't think so.'

Gordon said nothing.

'Ah. Yes. I shouldn't think that's a conversation the likes of you would ever want to have. But we c'n have it if you like, you and I. I'm not averse, you know. Far from it.'

Gordon looked out of the window. He understood that it would always come down to this in the end. Not only between himself and Whiting, but also between himself and anyone.

That would, eternally, be the measure of his life, and he'd been mad to think otherwise, even for a moment and especially in the moment those years ago when he'd accepted Jemima Hastings' invitation for drinks at her brother's house. He wondered what he'd been thinking in deciding he could have a normal life. Half mad and three-quarters lonely, he'd thought. That was him in a tablespoon. The companionship of a dog was not enough.

When they came to his holding, he immediately saw the cars in the driveway. He recognised both. Gina was at home, but Meredith Powell was also there for some reason. He said to Whiting, 'How d'you want to manage this, then?' as the chief superintendent pulled past the cottage and parked in front of the hedge. 'Can't exactly call it an arrest, can you? All things considered.'

Whiting looked at his watch. Gordon reckoned the chief superintendent was thinking about the wheres and the whens: where he was supposed to hand Gordon over to the Home Office and at what time. He was likely also considering how much time had already passed since the Home Office had told him to collect Gordon, time accounted for by their interlude together at Eyeworth Pond. The clock was ticking, so they could hardly come back later for his belongings, once Gina and Meredith were off the holding.

He reckoned Whiting would tell him he'd have to leave without the previously allowed single suitcase. He worked it out that Whiting would tell him his things – such as they were – would be sent along later. But instead, Whiting said with a smile, 'Oh, I expect you'll come up with something interesting to tell them, my dear,' and Gordon realised that the chief super-intendent saw this as part of the overall fun he intended to have at Gordon's expense. First Eyeworth Pond and now this: Gordon packing and having to come up with a reason that would explain to Gina why he was about to disappear.

Whiting said, 'Quarter of an hour. I wouldn't waste a second of it chatting with the ladies, me. But you c'n use it as you like. The dog stays here, by the way. To make certain. You know. Call it insurance.'

'Tess won't like it,' Gordon said.

'She will if you tell her. You've a way with the ladies, don't you, my love?'

At that, Gordon realised it was actually to his benefit to have the retriever remain in the car. If Tess bounded out, she would no doubt set out to find Gina, thus betraying his own presence. Without her, he might be able to get into the cottage by the front door, make his way quietly upstairs, do what he needed to do, and leave unseen. No explanation required. No conversation at all.

He nodded at Whiting, told the dog to stay and got out of the car. He reckoned Gina and Meredith were inside the cottage, probably in the kitchen, but in any case not upstairs in the bed-room. If he went in the front door, he *could* ease up the stairs without being seen. The floors creaked like hell, but that couldn't be helped. He'd do what he could to be quiet and he'd hope that whatever conversation they were having would be sufficient to cover his noise. As to why Meredith was there on the property . . . He didn't see how working out the answer to that was going to get him anywhere. He also couldn't see that it mattered.

Once in the front door, he listened for their voices. But the cottage was silent. He moved quietly for the stairs. The only sound was from his weight upon them as he climbed.

He went to the bedroom. A single suitcase and a quarter of an hour. Gordon knew that Whiting would be as good as his word. One minute more and he'd come sauntering onto the property, leaving Gordon to explain why he was being carted off or perhaps doing the honours himself.

Gordon fetched his suitcase from beneath the bed. He went to the chest of drawers and slid the top one open. The chest of drawers was next to the window, and he was careful with his movement here, trying to keep out of sight. For if Gina and Meredith were outside and looked up . . . He gave a glance to make sure.

He saw them at once. The window overlooked the drive and part of the west paddock, empty now of the ponies he'd used to keep Gina from going inside the enclosure. She was inside the paddock now, and so was Meredith. But with them was a man he didn't recognise. He was standing behind Meredith and he was gripping her round the waist in a manner that suggested she wasn't a willing participant in what was going on. And what was going on was a spate of digging. Gina had one of the shovels from the barn and she was frantically applying it to a rectangle of earth just beyond the old horse trough. She'd cleared away a mass of vegetation, he saw. She must have been working like mad since she'd returned from wherever she'd gone that morning.

At first he thought what an excellent job he'd done. Things looked exactly as he hoped they would look. Then he realised that he owed Jemima a debt of gratitude for this moment. She clearly had revealed some of the truth but she had, for some reason, not told it all. Perverse loyalty to him? Suspicion of the other? He wouldn't ever know.

He started to move from the window, knowing that the three of them would dig all the way to China before they found what they were looking for. But Meredith made a sudden move – as if she was trying to escape the hold the strange bloke had on her – and in doing so, she swung round and he swung with her so that they were no longer facing Gina and her digging but rather the cottage.

Gordon saw the bloke held something to Meredith's neck, and his glance went from the couple to Gina. He clocked what Gina was actually doing, the size and the shape of it, and he whispered a curse. She was digging a grave.

So these were Jemima's killers, he thought. He'd been sleeping with one of them. She *was* the woman from London that the Scotland Yard detective had declared was in the pictures of that photo show. She'd come to Hampshire in order to snare him and, eternal fool that he was, he'd walked right into her arms.

He saw how he'd helped them by placing those bloody post-cards round. *Have you seen this woman?* and of course they had. Jemima had confided in the bloke. The bloke had confided in Gina. They'd set the rest up from there: one of them in London and one of them in Hampshire and when the time was right, the rest was child's play. A phone call to Hampshire, made by the bloke. *This is where she is. This is where you can find her.* And then the wait to see what he would do.

And now this moment, outside, in the paddock. This was meant to be as well. There was going to be another body. But this one on his very own property.

He didn't know how they'd managed to pick up Meredith Powell and get her here. He didn't know why they'd done so. But as he watched, he saw what they intended as clearly as if the plan had been his own. The conclusion to it all was written out before him.

He headed for the stairs.

Once Gina Dickens began to dig in earnest, Barbara phoned nine, nine, nine. She reckoned Frazer was going to wait to dispatch his captive till he had a place to put her body. The only way to make it look as if Gordon Jossie had killed her was to plant her somewhere and hope to avoid detection till she'd been in the ground long enough to make the exact time of death – and hence Jossie's alibi – somewhat uncertain. This required a grave.

To her credit Meredith Powell wasn't cooperatively waiting for the blow that would kill her. She struggled as best she could. When she did so, though, Frazer applied the crook to her neck. She was bleeding profusely down the front of her body, but he'd so far avoided making the blow fatal. Just enough to settle her, Barbara thought. What a piece of work he was.

When her call went through, Barbara identified herself in a whisper. She knew the emergency operator could be anywhere in Hampshire and this, in combination with her own inability to make perfectly specific her exact location, meant that timely intervention was unlikely. But she reckoned Chief Superintendent Whiting knew where Gordon Jossie lived, so that was the information she passed along: ring the Lyndhurst station, tell Chief Superintendent Whiting to send back-up at once to Gordon Jossie's holding outside of Sway, he knows where it is, I'm on the property, a woman's life hangs in the balance, for God's sake hurry, send an armed response team and do it now.

Then she turned off her mobile. She had no weapon, but the odds were even. She was fully capable of bluffing with the best of them and, if she had nothing else on her side, she still had surprise. It was time to use it.

She headed towards the far side of the barn.

Meredith couldn't cry out. The pointed thing was inside her flesh for the third time. He'd pierced her neck once, twice and now again, a different spot each time. The blood was seeping down her bony chest and between her breasts, but she didn't look to see it for fear she would faint. She was faint enough already.

'Why?' was the only word that escaped her. She knew that *please* was out of the question. And the *why* referred to Jemima, not to her. There were any number of whys that dealt with Jemima. She couldn't work out why they had killed her friend. She saw that they had likely done it in a way that would lead the police to Gordon. She concluded from this that they wanted both Jemima *and* Gordon out of the way, but she could not come up with a reason for this. And then it didn't matter, did it, because she was going to die as well. Just like Jemima and for what for what and *what* would become of Cammie. Without a dad. Without a mum. Growing up without knowing how much she . . . And who would find her? They would bury and then and then and afterwards and God.

She tried to be calm. She tried to think. She tried to plan. It was possible. It was. She could. She needed. And then. There was the pain again. Tears seeped though she didn't want to cry. They came with the blood. She could no more produce a way to save herself from this than she could . . . what? She didn't know.

So bloody stupid. Her whole *life* was a shining example of just how stupid one person could be. No brains, girl. Completely utterly maddeningly incapable of reading a person for what he was. For what she was. For what *anyone* was. And now here . . . So what are you waiting for? she asked herself. Are you waiting for what you've always been waiting for? Rescue from where you've placed yourself for being so bloody-minded since the day you were born that—

'This is where it stops.'

Everything halted. The world spun but then it was not the world at all but the man who held her who was spinning round and she went with him and there was Gordon.

He'd come into the paddock. He was coming forward. He held a pistol, of all things, a *pistol* and where in God's name had Gordon got himself a pistol . . . and had he always had a pistol and why and –

She felt weak with relief. She wet herself. Hot urine splashed down her leg. It was over, over, over. But the bloke didn't release her. Nor did he ease his grip.

He said to Gina, 'Ah. I see we'll need to make it deeper, George,' every bit as if he wasn't the least bit fazed by what Gordon Jossie was holding.

Gordon said, unaccountably, 'And it's not there, Gina,' with a nod to where she'd been clearing the paddock. 'That why you killed her, though, isn't it?' And to the stranger, 'You heard me. This stops here. Let her go.'

'Or what?' the man said. 'You'll shoot me? Be the hero? Have your picture on the front of all the papers? On the evening news? On the morning chat shows? Tsk, tsk, Ian. You can't want that. Keep digging, George.'

'She told you, then,' Gordon said in reply.

'Well, of course she did. One asks, you know. After all, she didn't want you to find her. She was . . . well, I don't mean to offend, but she was rather repelled once she knew who you are. Then when she saw those postcards . . . She came home in a panic and . . . One *asks* when one's lover – sorry, George, but we're even on that score aren't we, darling – one does ask. She loathed you just enough to tell me. You should have left well alone, you know, once she'd taken herself off to London. Why didn't you, Ian?'

'Don't call me that.'

'It's who you are, isn't it? George, darling, it *is* Ian Barker, isn't it? Not one of the other two. Not Michael or Reggie. But he talks about them when he's dreaming, right?'

'Nightmares,' Gina said. 'Such nightmares. You can't imagine.'

'Let her go.' Gordon gestured with the pistol.

The man tightened his grip. 'Can't, won't,' he said. 'Not so close to the finish. Sorry, lad.'

'I'm going to shoot you, whoever you are.'

'Frazer Chaplin, at your service,' he said. He sounded quite cheery. He gave a little twist to what he held at Meredith's neck. She cried out. He said, 'So yes indeed, she saw those postcards, Ian, my friend. She panicked. She ran hither and yon talking nonsense about how this bloke in Hampshire mustn't ever find her. So one asked why. Well one *would* do. And out it all tumbled. Nasty little boy, weren't you? There's lots out there who'd like to find you. People don't forget. Not that kind of crime. Which is why, of course, you're not going to shoot me. Aside from the fact that you'd likely miss and hit poor little Meredith right in the head.'

'Not a problem, as I see it,' Gordon said. He swung the gun towards Gina. 'She's the one to be shot. Throw the shovel down, Gina. This business is finished. The hoard's not there, Meredith's not dying, and I don't bloody care who knows my name.'

Meredith whimpered. She had no idea what they were talking about, but she tried to extend a hand of thanks to

Gordon. He'd sacrificed something. She didn't know what. She didn't know why. But what it meant was—

Pain ripped into her. Fire and ice. It shot upward into her head and through her eyes. She felt something bursting and something else releasing. She toppled, unstrung, to the ground.

Barbara had gained the southeast corner of the barn when she heard the gunshot. She'd been moving stealthily but she froze in place. Only for an instant, however. A second shot went off and she charged round to the front. She gained the paddock and threw herself inside. She heard noise behind her, heavy footsteps running in her direction and a man's harsh yelling of *Drop that fucking gun!*

She took it all in like a frozen tableau. Meredith Powell on the ground with a rusty crook sticking out of her neck. Frazer Chaplin sprawled not five feet from Gordon Jossie. Gina Dickens backed into the wire fence with her hand clasped over her mouth. Jossie himself with the pistol held stiffly, still in position from the second shot he'd fired straight into the air.

'Barker!' It was a roar, not a voice from Chief Superintendent Whiting. He was storming up the driveway. 'Lay that God damn gun on the ground. Do it now. Now! You heard me. Now!'

And then, passing Whiting, the dog, of all things. Bounding forward. Howling. Running circles.

'Drop it, Barker!'

'You've shot him! You've killed him!' Gina Dickens at last. Screaming, running to Frazer Chaplin, throwing herself on him.

'Back-up's coming, Mr Jossie,' Barbara said. 'Put the gun—'

'Stop him! He'll kill me next!'

The dog barked and barked.

'See to Meredith,' Jossie said. 'Someone God damn see to Meredith.'

'Drop the bloody gun first.'

'I told you—'

'Want her to die as well? Just like the boy? You get off on death, Ian?'

Jossie turned the gun then. He pointed it at Whiting. 'Some deaths,' he said. 'Some God damn deaths.'

The dog barked. The dog howled.

'Don't shoot!' Barbara cried. 'Don't do it, Mr Jossie.' She dashed to the crumpled figure of Meredith. The crook was planted to its halfway point, but not into the jugular vein. She was conscious but overcome by shock. Time was crucial. Jossie needed to know it. She said, 'She's alive. Mr Jossie, she's alive. Put the gun down. Let us get her out of here. There's *nothing* else you need to do at this point.'

'You're wrong. There is,' Jossie said. He fired again.

Michael Spargo, Reggie Arnold and Ian Barker went into 'secure units' for the first part of their custodial sentences. For obvious reasons, they remained separated, and units in different parts of the country were used to house them. The purpose of the secure unit is education and – frequently, but not always, and generally 'dependent upon the cooperation of the detainee' – therapy. Information as to how well the boys did in these units is unavailable to the public, but what is known is that at the age of fifteen, their time in these secure units ended, whereupon they were moved to a 'youth facility', which has always been a euphemism for *prison for young offenders*. At eighteen, they were moved from their separate youth facilities and sent on to different maximum security prisons where they served the remainder of the term determined by the Luxembourg courts. Ten years.

That time has, of course, long since passed. All three of the boys, men now, were returned to the community. As was the case for such notorious child criminals as Mary Bell, Jon Venables and Robert Thompson, the boys were given new identities. Where each was released remains a closely guarded secret, and whether they are contributing members of society is also unknown. Alan Dresser has vowed to hunt them down and 'give them a taste of what they did to John', but because they are protected by law from even having a photograph of them published, it's unlikely Mr Dresser or anyone else will be able to find them.

Was justice served? This is a question nearly impossible to answer. To do so requires one to see Michael Spargo, Reggie Arnold and Ian Barker either as hardened criminals or as utter victims, but the truth lies somewhere in between.

Excerpted from '*Psychopathology, Guilt and Innocence in the Matter of John Dresser*'

by Dorcas Galbraith, PhD

(presented to the EU Convention on Juvenile Justice at the request of the Right Honourable Howard Jenkins-Thomas, MP)

34

Judi MacIntosh told Lynley to go right in. The assistant commissioner was waiting for him, she said. Did he want a coffee? Tea? She sounded grave. As she would do, Lynley thought. Word, as always and especially when it had to do with death, had travelled quickly.

He demurred politely. He wouldn't actually have minded a cup of tea, but he hoped he wouldn't be spending long enough in Hillier's office to drink it down.

The assistant commissioner rose to meet him. He joined Lynley at the conference table. He dropped into a chair and said, 'What a bloody cock-up. Do we a least know how the hell he got his hands on a gun?'

'Not yet,' Lynley said. 'Barbara's working on that.'

'And the woman?'

'Meredith Powell? She's in hospital. The wound was very bad but not fatal. It came close to the spinal cord, so she could have been crippled. She was lucky.'

'And the other?'

'Georgina Francis? In custody. All in all, it wasn't exactly textbook, sir, but it was a good result.'

Hillier shot him a look. 'A woman murdered in a public park, another woman seriously injured, two men dead, a paranoid schizophrenic in hospital, a lawsuit hanging over our heads . . . What part of this is actually a good result, Inspector?'

'We've got the killer.'

'Who is himself a corpse.'

'We've got his accomplice.'

'Who may not ever go to trial. What do we know about this Georgina Francis that we can take into court? She once lived in the same house as the killer. She once was at a Portrait Gallery show for some reason. She was the killer's lover. She was the killer's *killer's* lover. She may have done this, and she may have done that, and there's an end to it. Give that information to the CPS and watch them roar.' Hillier raised his eyes heavenward in an uncharacteristic indication of seeking divine guidance. When he apparently had it, he said, 'She's finished. She had a decent opportunity to demonstrate her leadership abilities, and she failed to do so. She alienated members of the team she was working with, she assigned officers inappropriately and without regard for their expertise, she made judgement calls that put the Met into the worst possible position, she undermined confidence in here and out there . . . Be so good as to tell me Tommy: where's the result?'

Lynley said, 'I think we can agree that she was hobbled, sir.'

'Oh, can we? Hobbled by what?'

'By what the Home Office knew and couldn't – or wouldn't – tell her.' Lynley paused to let his point sink in. There was little enough to use in defence of both Isabelle Ardery and her performance as acting detective superintendent, but he owed it to her to try. He said, 'Did you know who he was, sir?'

'Jossie?' Hillier shook his head.

'Did you know he was being protected, then?'

Hillier's eyes met his. He said nothing, and in that Lynley had his answer. At some point during the investigation, Hillier had been brought into the picture. He may not have been told that Gordon Jossie was one of the three boys responsible for little John Dresser's terrible murder all those years ago, but he'd known he was someone into whose life no one else was supposed to delve.

Lynley said, 'I think she should have been told. Not necessarily who he was but that he was being protected by the Home Office.'

'Do you.' Hillier looked away. He steepled his fingers beneath his chin. 'And why is that?'

'It could have led to Jemima Hastings' killer.'

'Could it indeed.'

'Sir. Yes.'

Hillier observed him. 'I take it you're arguing on her behalf, then. Is this noblesse oblige, Tommy, or have you, perhaps, another reason?'

Lynley didn't look away. He'd certainly considered this point before coming up to the AC's office, but he hadn't been able to get to what felt like the whole truth of the matter as far as his intentions were concerned. He was going on instinct alone, and he had to hope that the instinct he was operating under was the lofty instinct for justice. It was, after all, so easy to lie to oneself when it came to sex.

He said evenly, 'It's neither, sir. She's had a rough transition with little time to adjust to the job before she was thrust into the middle of an investigation. In addition to that, inquiries into murder beg for facts. She never had them all. And that, with respect, can't be attributed to her.'

'Are you suggesting—'

'I'm not suggesting it can be attributed to you, either, sir. Your hands were tied as well, I suspect.'

'Then . . . ?'

'It's because of this that she needs – I think – another opportunity. That's all. I'm not saying she should be given the position permanently. I'm not saying that you should even consider giving her the position permanently. I'm merely saying that, based upon what I saw during these past days and based upon what you yourself asked me to do with respect to her being here, she should have another go.'

Hillier's lips curved. It was not a smile so much as it was acknowledgement of a point well made and a point perhaps reluctantly taken. He said, 'A compromise, then?'

'Sir?' Lynley said.

'Your presence. Here.' Hillier chuckled, but it seemed self-directed. It declared itself as *Who could have thought I would end up here?*

'Back at work at the Met, you mean,' Lynley noted.

'That would be the deal on offer.'

Lynley nodded slowly in comprehension. The assistant commissioner would always, he thought, play a very decent game of chess. They hadn't come to checkmate yet, but they were close. 'May I think about it, sir, before I commit myself?' he asked.

'You absolutely may not,' Hillier said.

Isabelle was on the phone with Chief Superintendent Whiting out of the operational command unit at the Lyndhurst station. The gun in question, he told her, belonged to one of the agisters. He didn't explain what an agister was and she didn't ask. She did ask *who* the agister was and how Gordon Jossie had come to have his weapon. The agister turned out to be the brother of their original victim, and he'd reported his gun missing only that morning. He didn't tell the police, however, not at first and not that it would have helped had he done so. He told the head agister during a meeting, which set the wheels in motion, which was, of course, too late. Jossie, Whiting continued, apparently had the gun upon his person, either in his windcheater's pocket or tucked into his trousers with the windcheater covering it. Or, Whiting went on as if to test the waters of another theory, he could have been keeping it in the cottage as he'd gone inside to pack. The first theory seemed likeliest, Whiting said. But he gave no cogent reason why.

'There's a chance a treasure hoard's involved in all this,' Isabelle told him. 'You'll want to keep an eye out for that.'

A *what*? Whiting wanted to know. Treasure? he asked. *Treasure*? What the hell?

'A Roman treasure,' Isabelle told him. 'We reckon that's behind what's gone on. We reckon Jossie was doing something on the property – likely some kind of work – and he came across the first of it. He was able to sort out what he'd come upon but so was Jemima.'

And then what? Whiting asked.

'She probably wanted to report it. It would be valuable and the law requires that. Considering who he was, though, he probably wanted to keep it buried. He'd have had to tell her why eventually because keeping it buried would've made no sense. Once he told her . . . Well, there she was, living with one of the most notorious child killers we've ever locked away. That must have been a rather staggering piece of information for her to process.'

Whiting made a sound of agreement.

'So is there anything on the property to indicate he'd been doing some work? I mean, doing some work during which he might have stumbled upon evidence of a treasure hoard?'

There was, Whiting told her in a meditative tone: part of a paddock had been re-fenced while the other part had been left as it was. When everything was blown to hell a short time earlier that day, the woman – Gina Dickens – had been working in part of the paddock that hadn't yet been seen to. Perhaps that was why . . . ?

Isabelle thought about this. 'It would be the other part,' she noted. 'The newer section. The part already worked on. Because it stands to reason that Jossie would have discovered something where he himself had been digging. Any digging that's gone on there? Anything new in that spot? Anything unusual?'

New fence posts, new wire fencing, new trough, Whiting said. Bloody huge trough if it came down to it. Must've weighed half a tonne.

'There you have it,' Isabelle told him. 'You know, second thought on this: I'm going to set things in motion myself. From this end. On that score. The treasure. We'll get the authorities to come out there. You likely have enough on your plate.' She looked up at a movement in her office doorway. Lynley was standing there. She held up a finger, a gesture that asked him to wait. He came inside and took the seat that angled from her desk. He looked relaxed. She wondered if anything ever ruffled the man.

She completed her phone call. The duty press officer from Lyndhurst would be identifying Gordon Jossie as Ian Barker. While this would undoubtedly drag forth all the details of John Dresser's inhuman murder once again, the Home Office wanted it known that one of the three killers of the toddler was now dead himself, at his own hand.

Isabelle wondered at this. Was it supposed to be a cautionary tale? Something to give the Dresser family peace at last? Something to strike fear into Michael Spargo and Reggie Arnold, wherever they were? She didn't see how releasing Gordon Jossie's true identity would serve to do any of that. But she had no say in the matter.

When she and Whiting rang off, she and Lynley sat in silence for a moment. Outside of her office, the sounds of a day ending were unmistakable. She badly wanted a drink but more badly did she want to know about Lynley's meeting with Sir David Hillier. She knew that was where he'd disappeared to.

She said, 'It's a form of blackmail.'

He drew his eyebrows together. His lips parted as if he would speak, but he said nothing. He had a faint scar, she noted for the first time, on his upper lip. It looked like quite an old one. She wondered how he'd come to have it.

'What he's said is that he'll keep it under wraps as long as the boys stay in Kent with him and Sandra. He says, "You don't want a custody battle over them, Isabelle. You don't want to end up in court. You know what will come to light and you don't want that." So I'm stuffed. He can destroy my career. And even if he didn't have that power, I'd lose custody permanently if we went to court. He knows that.'

Lynley was silent at first. He regarded her, and she couldn't tell what he was thinking although she reckoned it had to do with how to tell her that her career was over anyway, despite her efforts to save it.

When he spoke, however, it was just to say, 'Alcoholism.'

She said, 'I'm not an alcoholic, Tommy. I drink a bit much occasionally. Most people do. That's all.'

'Isabelle . . .' He sounded disappointed.

She said, 'It's the truth. I'm no more an alcoholic than . . . than you are. Than Barbara Havers is. Where is she, by the way? How the hell long does it take someone to drive from Hampshire to London?'

He wasn't to be diverted. He said, 'There are cures. There are programmes. There are . . . You don't have to live—'

'It was stress,' she said. 'How you found me the other night. That's all it was. For God's sake, Tommy. You told me yourself that you drank heavily when your wife was murdered.'

He said nothing. But his eyes narrowed the way one's eyes would do when something is thrown. Sand, a handful of earth, an unkindness.

She said, 'Forgive me.'

He stirred in his chair. 'He keeps the boys, then?'

'He keeps the boys. I can have . . . He calls it supervised visits. What he means is that I go to Kent to see them, they don't come here, and *when* I see them, he and Sandra or he *or* Sandra is present.'

'And that's how it stands? Till when?'

'Till he decides otherwise. Till he decides what I must do to redeem myself. Till . . . I don't know.' She didn't want talk any more about it. She couldn't think why she'd told him as much as she had. It indicated an opening where she couldn't afford one and didn't want one. She was tired, she thought.

He said, 'You stay.'

She didn't understand at first that he'd switched the topic. 'Stay?'

'I don't know how long. He agrees this wasn't the best test of your skills.'

'Ah.' She had to admit that she was surprised. 'But he did say . . . Because with Stephenson Deacon . . . They told me—'

'That was before the Home Office business came to light.'

'Tommy, you and I both know my mistakes had nothing to do with the Home Office and whatever mad secrets they were keeping over there.'

He nodded. 'It was useful, nonetheless. Had everything been straightforward from the first, the ending to this story would be different, I dare say.'

She was still astonished. But astonishment slowly gave way to realisation. The assistant commissioner, at the end of the day, would hardly have granted her a stay of professional execution merely because the Home Office hadn't told her the real identity of Gordon Jossie. There was more involved, and she had a very good idea that the additional bargaining to keep her in place had to do with promises made by Lynley. She said, 'Exactly what did you agree to, Tommy?'

He smiled. 'You see? You're learning quickly.'

'*What* did you agree to?'

'Something I was going to do anyway.'

'You're coming back permanently.'

'For my sins. Yes.'

'Why?'

'As I said, I was—'

'No. I mean why did you do this for me?'

He fixed his eyes on her. She didn't look away. 'I'm not sure,' he finally said.

They sat in silence for another moment, observing one another. At last, she opened the centre drawer of her desk. She took out a metal ring that she'd placed there earlier in the day. From this dangled a single key. She'd had it made but hadn't been sure and she still wasn't sure, if the truth be told. But she'd long been adept at avoiding truths, so she did so now.

She slid the ring across her desk to him. He looked from it to her.

'There can never be more between us than there is just now,' she told him. 'We need to understand that from the first. I want you, but I'm not in love with you, Tommy, and I never will be.'

He looked at the key. Then her. Then the key again.

She waited for him to make his decision, telling herself it didn't matter, knowing that the truth was it always would.

Finally, he reached for what she'd offered. 'I understand,' he said.

The loose ends took hours, so Barbara Havers didn't arrive back in London till quite late. She'd considered staying the night in Hampshire, but at the last moment she decided that home was more appealing despite the fact that her bungalow was likely to be the temperature of a sauna after being closed up in the heat for two days. On the drive back, she replayed what had occurred in the paddock, and she looked at it from every angle, wondering if any other ending had been possible.

At first, she hadn't recognised the name. She'd been a young teenager at the time of John Dresser's murder and while the name Ian Barker was not completely unfamiliar to her, she had not immediately connected it with that death in the Midlands and with the man standing in the paddock with a gun in his hand. Her more immediate concern had been Meredith Powell's injury, Frazer Chaplin's condition, and the distinct possibility that Gordon Jossie was going to shoot someone else.

She hadn't expected him to turn the gun on himself. Afterwards, however, his reason for doing so was more than clear. He was, at that point, hemmed in on all sides. There would be no escaping the public revelation of his identity in one way or another. When that occurred, the incomprehensible evil act of his childhood would be once more dissected before a public who always, eternally and understandably, demanded payment.

With the dog barking, herself shouting, Whiting roaring and Georgina Francis screaming, he'd put the gun in his mouth and pulled the trigger. And then utter silence. The poor damn dog crawled on its belly then, like a soldier in battle. She reached her master, whimpering, while the rest of them raced to look to the injured.

A helicopter came from the Air Support Unit near Lee-on-Solent to take Meredith to hospital. Officers arrived from the Lyndhurst station. Hot on their heels, as always, came the journalists, and to attend to them the duty press officer manned a position at the end of Paul's Lane. Georgina Francis was taken off to the custody suite at the Lyndhurst station, while everyone waited two hours for the forensic pathologist to arrive. Eventually, matters came to a close as far as Barbara's participation was concerned. She spent some time on her mobile with Lynley in London, some time with Whiting going over the situation in Hampshire, and then she was finished. Time to stay the night or time to go. She chose to go.

She was completely done in by the time she arrived in London. She was surprised to see that lights were still on inside the ground floor flat of the yellow house as she trudged through the gate, but she didn't give much thought to it.

She saw the note on her door as she used her key in the lock. It was too dark outside to read it, but she could see her name written in Hadiyyah's hand, with four exclamation marks after it.

She opened the door and flipped on the lights. She half-expected another fashion offering to be laid out on the daybed. There was nothing, however. She slung her shoulder bag on the table and she saw the message light on her answer phone was blinking. She went for the phone as she unfolded Hadiyyah's note to her. Both contained the same communication: *Come to see us, Barbara! No matter what time!!*

Barbara was knackered. She didn't much feel like socialising but, as it was Hadiyyah making the request, she thought she could survive a few minutes of conversation.

She returned the way she'd come. As she was crossing the patch of lawn to the French doors that served as entrance to Taymullah Azhar's flat, one of those doors opened. Mrs Silver emerged, calling back over her shoulder, 'Delighted. Truly,' with a happy wave. She saw Barbara, then, and said, 'Really *quite* charming,' and she patted her turbanned head and went on her way to the front steps of the house.

Barbara thought What the hell . . . ? as she approached the door. She reached it at the same moment that Taymullah Azhar was about to close it.

He saw her. He said, 'Ah. Barbara.' And then he called back over his shoulder, 'Hadiyyah. *Khushi*. Here is Barbara.'

'Oh yes, yes, yes!' Hadiyyah cried. She appeared beneath her father's arm, beaming so much that her face alone could have lit a room. 'Come see! Come see!' she called out to Barbara. 'It's the surprise!'

Then a woman's voice from within the flat and Barbara knew who it was before she appeared: 'I've never been called a surprise before. Introduce me, darling. But at least call me Mummy.'

Barbara knew her name. Angelina. She'd never seen a photograph of her, but she'd allowed herself to imagine what she might look like. She hadn't been far wrong. The same height as Azhar and thin like him. Translucent skin, blue eyes, dark brows and lashes, fashionably cut hair. Slim trousers, crisp blouse, narrow feet in heelless shoes. They were the sort of shoes a woman wore when she didn't want to be taller than her partner.

'Barbara Havers,' Barbara said to Angelina. 'You're Haddiyah's mum. I've heard volumes about you.'

'She has!' Hadiyyah crowed. 'Mummy, I've told her *lots* about you. You'll be *such* friends.'

'I hope we will.' Angelina put her arm round her daughter's shoulders. Hadiyyah put her arm round her mother's waist. 'Will you come in, Barbara?' Angelina asked. 'I've been hearing volumes about you as well.' She turned to Azhar. 'Hari, do we have—'

'Dead knackered,' Barbara cut in. Hari. No. She couldn't take part in the moment. 'I only just got back from work. Rain check? Tomorrow? Whatever? That okay with you, kiddo?' to Haddiyah.

Hadiyyah hung from her mother's waist and gazed up at her. She spoke to Barbara but looked at her mother. 'Oh yes, oh yes, oh yes,' she declared. 'We've lots of time tomorrow, don't we, Mummy?'

Angelina replied, 'Lots and lots of time.'

Barbara said goodnight. She gave a mad little salute to them all. She was far too done in to process all this. Tomorrow would be time enough to do so.

She was heading for her bungalow when he called her name. She paused on the path at the side of the house. She didn't want to have this conversation, but she reckoned there wasn't much hope of avoiding it.

'This is,' Azhar began, but Barbara stopped him.

'You'll never get her to sleep tonight,' she said cheerfully. 'I expect she'll be dancing round till dawn.'

'Yes. I expect so.' He looked back the way he had come and then at Barbara. 'She wanted to tell you earlier, but I thought it best that she wait until . . .' He hesitated. There was an entire relationship between him and Hadiyyah's mother that rested in the pause.

'Absolutely,' Barbara said, to rescue him.

'If she did not return, you see, as she said she would do, I didn't wish Hadiyyah then to have to explain. It would make her disappointment that much worse.'

'Absolutely,' Barbara said.

'So you see.'

'Clear as anything.'

'Hadiyyah always believed.'

'She did. She always said.'

'I don't know why.'

'Well, it's her mum after all. There's a bond. She'd know that. She'd feel it.'

'You don't quite . . .' Azhar felt in his pockets. Barbara knew what he was looking for, but she'd come without her cigarettes. He found his own packet and offered her one. She shook her head. He lit up himself. 'Why she returned,' he said.

'What?'

'The truth behind why she returned is what I do not yet know.'

'Oh. Well.' Barbara didn't know what to say. The subject of exactly why Angelina had left Azhar and her daughter in the first place was something that had never come up. The euphemism had long been a trip to Canada. While Barbara had reckoned it stood for something other than a tour round that country – if that was even where Angelina had been – she had never pressed for more information. Hadiyyah, she assumed, would not have it and Azhar would not be willing to give it.

'I suspect it wasn't quite what Angelina thought it might be,' Azhar said. 'Living with him.'

Barbara nodded. 'Right. Well. That's usually the story, isn't it,' she said. 'The bloom fades, and at the end of the day people's knickers start showing no matter how they try to hide them, eh?'

'You knew there was another, then?'

'Another bloke?' Barbara shook her head. 'I wondered why she left and where she really was, but I didn't know there was someone else involved.' She looked towards the front of the house when she went on. ''F I'm honest with you, Azhar . . . ? It always seemed dead mad to me that she'd leave the two of you. Especially Hadiyyah. I mean, men and women have their troubles, and I get that, but I never got her leaving Hadiyyah.'

'So you understand.' He drew in on his cigarette. The lighting was dim along the path on the side of the house and, in the darkness, Barbara could barely see his face. But the tip of his cigarette glowed fire with how deeply he drew upon it. She recalled that Angelina didn't like his smoking. She wondered if he would now give it up.

'Understand what?' she asked him.

'That she will take Hadiyyah, Barbara. Next time. She will take her. And that is something . . . I cannot lose Hadiyyah. I will not lose Hadiyyah.'

He sounded so fierce and, if it was possible, at the same time so bleak that Barbara felt something give way within her, a crack in a surface she would have preferred to keep forever solid. She said, 'Azhar, you're doing the right thing here. I'd do the same. Anyone would.'

For he had no choice and she well knew it. He was caught in circumstances of his own devising, having left his wife and two children for Angelina, having never divorced, having never remarried. It was a nightmare situation that would end up in court if Angelina so chose and he'd be the loser and what he'd be the loser of was the only person in his shattered life who mattered to him.

'I must do what I can to keep her here,' he said.

'I completely agree,' Barbara said.

And she meant those words despite the fact that they changed her world as much as they changed the world of the man who stood in the darkness with her.

35

Twelve days went by before Rob Hastings could bring himself to call upon Meredith. During that time, he rang the hospital daily till she was at last released into the care of her parents, but he found he could do no more than merely ask for information about her condition. What he gathered from these phone calls was little enough, and he knew he could have learned more had he gone in person. He could, indeed, have seen her for himself. But it was too much for him and even if it hadn't been, he found he had no clear idea how to talk to her any longer.

In those twelve days, he discovered who had taken the pistol from his Land Rover and what had been done with that gun. It had since been returned to him, but it was a black mark on his career that he'd managed to have the weapon taken in the first place. Two people were dead because of this, and had he not been a Hastings with the Hastings history of service to the New Forest behind him, he'd likely have been given the sack.

The news was bursting with the story of Ian Barker: the wicked child killer of a toddler, a bloke who'd managed to keep his identity secret for the ten years since his release from wherever he and his murderous mates had been held. Reporters from every media source in the country had at first sought out everyone whose life had touched on Gordon Jossie's, no matter how remotely. There was, it seemed, a hideous kind of romance to the story that the tabloids especially wanted to feature. It was the story of The Notorious Child Killer Who Killed Again, with a minor headline indicating that this time he'd done it to save a woman in danger, before going on to kill himself. This didn't actually appear to be the case, according to Meredith Powell and Chief Superintendent Zachary Whiting, since the truth of the matter according to them was that Frazer Chaplin had charged towards Jossie and only then did Jossie shoot him, but that wasn't as symbolic an act of redemption as was the idea that Jossie had saved someone prior to ridding the world of his presence, so it was that story and not the other that got the most ink from the tabloids. Ian Barker's childhood photo was printed every day for a week, along with Gordon Jossie's more recent visage. Some of the tabloids demanded how people in Hampshire had possibly failed to recognise the bloke, but really, why would they have recognised in a quiet thatcher a long-ago child who, they suspected, had cloven hooves and horns beneath his schoolboy cap? No one was looking for Ian Barker to be hidden away in Hampshire, anyway, leading an unassuming life.

Neighbours along Paul's Lane were interviewed. *Never suspected* and *I'll keep my doors locked from now on, I will* were the general comments. Both Zachary Whiting and a Home Office spokesman made a few statements about the duty of the local police in matters of new identities, and for several days sightings of both Michael Spargo and Reggie Arnold were reported. But finally, the story faded away as these stories do, when a member of the royal family got into an unfortunate struggle with a paparazzo in front of a nightclub at 3.45 a.m in Mayfair.

Rob Hastings had managed to weather all this without speaking to any of the journalists. He let his phone take the messages, but he returned no calls. He had no desire to discuss how the former Ian Barker had come into his life. He had less desire to talk about how his sister had taken up with the bloke. He understood now why Jemima had left the New Forest. He did not understand why she had not confided in him, however.

He spent days pondering this question and trying to work out what it meant that his sister had not told him what had driven her from Hampshire. He was not a man prone to violence, and she surely had known that, so she could hardly have expected him to accost Jossie and do damage to him for deceiving Jemima. What would have been the point of that, anyway? He could also keep a secret, and Jemima had to have known that as well. Beyond that, he would have only too happily welcomed his sister home without question had she wanted to come back to Honey Lane.

He was left considering what all of this said about him. But the only answer he was able to come up with was the one that asked another question: *What would have been the point of your knowing the truth, Robbie?* And that question led to the next: *What kind of action would you have taken, you who have been always so fearful about taking action in the first place?*

The why of that fear was what he couldn't cope with in the aftermath of all the revelations and the deaths. The why of that fear led directly to the heart of who and what he was, of who and what he had been for years. Solitary not out of choice. Solitary not out of necessity. Solitary not out of inclination. The sad truth was that he and his sister had long been, in fact, much the same sort of people. It was only the manner in which they'd muddled through their lives that was different.

Understanding this at the end of days and days upon horseback in the Forest was what finally prompted Robbie to go to Cadnam. He went at mid-afternoon, with the hope that Meredith might be alone at her parents' home at that time of day so he could speak to her without anyone being there.

This was not to be. Her mother was in. So was Cammie. They answered the door together.

He'd not seen Janet Powell in ages, he realised. In the early years of the girls' friendship, he and Meredith's mother had met now and again when the act of fetching Meredith and Jemima from this place or that had been called for. But he'd not seen the woman once the girls had each been old enough to have a driving licence, which put an end to the adults in their lives having to ferry them here and there. He recognised her, though.

He said by way of introduction, 'Missus Powell. Afternoon. I'm—'

'Well, hullo, Robert,' she broke in kindly. 'What a nice surprise it is to see you. Do come in.'

He didn't know quite how to react to the welcome. What he thought was *Well, of course, she would remember him.* He had a rather unforgettable face.

He'd worn his baseball cap as was his habit, but he removed this as he stepped into the house. He glanced at Cammie as he tucked the cap into the back pocket of his jeans. She dodged at once behind her grandmother's legs, and she peered out at him with rounded eyes. He offered the little girl a smile. He said, ''Spect Cammie doesn't remember me, eh? Been donkey's years since I've seen her. Must've been only two years old last time. Maybe less. She won't know who I am.'

'Bit shy with strangers, she is.' Janet Powell put her hand on Cammie's shoulder and drew her forward, cuddling her to her hip. 'This's Mr Hastings, luv,' she said. 'You say hullo to Mr Hastings.'

'It's Rob,' he said. 'Or Robbie. Want to shake a hand here, Cammie?'

She shook her head, and she took a step backward. 'Gran . . .' she said. She hid her face in her grandmother's skirt.

'Ah, it's no matter,' Robbie said. He added with a wink, 'Present something of a sight, I do, this toothy old face, eh?' But the wink was forced and he saw that Janet Powell knew this.

She said, 'You come right in, Robbie. I've a lemon cake in the kitchen that's begging to be eaten. Will you?'

'Oh, ta, but no. I was on my way to . . . Actually, I just come to . . . I was hoping Meredith was . . .' He drew in a calming breath. It was the fact that the little girl was hiding and he knew she was hiding because of him. He didn't know how to put her at ease, and he wanted to do so. He said to Mrs Powell, 'I was wondering if Meredith . . . ?'

'Of course,' Janet Powell said. 'You've come to check on

Meredith, haven't you. Terrible thing. To think I had that young woman here in the house for a night. She might have . . . well, you know . . .' She cast a glance at Cammie. 'She could have m-u-r-d-e-r-e-d us all in our beds. Meredith's just in the garden with the dog. Cammie, luv, will you take this nice gentleman out to see Mummy?'

Cammie scratched one ankle with the toes of her other bare foot. She seemed to hesitate. She kept her gaze on the floor. When her grandmother said her name again, the little girl murmured, 'Mummy's been in hospital.'

'Aye,' Robbie said. 'That's why I've come. To say hullo and to see how she's feeling. Bet you were bit worried about her, weren't you?'

Cammie nodded. She said to the floor, 'That dog's taking care of her, though.' And then looking up, 'Hospitals're like where the hedgehogs go.'

'Really?' Robbie said. 'You like hedgehogs, do you, Cammie?'

'They got a hospital for them. Gran told me. She said we c'n go there an' see them.'

'I 'spect they'll like that, the hedgehogs.'

'She says not yet, though. She says when I'm older. 'Cos we're meant to spend the night when we go. 'Cos it's far.'

'Right. That makes sense. I 'spect she wants to make sure you don't miss your mum if you spend the night,' Rob said.

Cammie frowned and looked away. 'How'd you know that?' she asked.

'What? The bit about missing your mum?' And when she nodded, 'I had a little sister once.'

'Like me?' she asked.

'Just like you,' he said.

That appeared to put her at ease. She stepped away from her grandmother and said to him quietly, 'We got to go through the kitchen to get to the garden. The dog might bark, but she's quite nice.' And she took him outside.

Meredith was sitting on a lounge chair in the only shade there was: on the far side of a garden shed. The rest of the area was given to rose bushes, and they filled the air with a fragrance so intense that Robbie imagined he could feel it move like a silk scarf against his skin.

'Mummy,' Cammie called as she led him along a gravel path. 'Are you still resting like you're meant to? Are you asleep? 'Cos there's someone to see you.'

Meredith wasn't asleep. She had been drawing, Robbie saw. She had a large sketch pad spread on her knees and she'd used coloured pencils upon it. She created squares of patterns, he saw. Fabric designs, he reckoned. She still held on to her original dream. At the side of the lounge chair lay Gordon Jossie's dog. Tess raised her head, then lowered it to her paws. Her tail swished twice on the ground in greeting.

Meredith closed her sketch pad and set it to one side. She said, 'Why, hullo, Rob.' And as Cammie made to climb into her lap, she said, 'Not yet, darling. Still a bit too much for me,' but she moved to one side and patted the seat.

Cammie managed to squeeze in next to her, squirming round to make her little bottom fit the space. Meredith smiled, rolled her eyes at Robbie, but kissed the top of her daughter's head. 'She was worried,' she said in explanation, nodding at the little girl. 'I've never been in hospital before, far as she's concerned. Didn't know what to think.'

He wondered what Meredith's daughter had been told about what had happened to her mother on Gordon Jossie's holding that day. Very little, he expected. She didn't need to know. At least not now and maybe never.

He said, with a nod at the Golden Retriever, 'How'd you come by her?'

'I asked Mum to fetch her. It seemed like . . . poor thing. I couldn't bear the thought . . . you know.'

'Aye. Good for you, Merry.' He looked round and spied a wooden folding chair leaning against the garden shed. He said to Meredith, 'Mind if I . . . ?' with a gesture towards it.

She said, colouring, 'Oh, of course. I'm sorry. Do sit. Don't know what I was . . . Only, it's so nice to see you, Rob. I'm glad you've come. They told me at the hospital you'd phoned.'

'I wanted to see how you were coping,' he said.

'Oh.' She touched her fingers to the bandage on her neck, doubtless a much smaller one than what she'd had wrapping her wound originally. The gesture seemed an unconscious one to him, but apparently not because she said with a humourless laugh, 'Well, I'll look like Frankenstein's wife when this comes off, I s'pose.'

'Who's that?' Cammie asked her.

'Frankenstein's wife? Just someone from a story,' Meredith said.

'Means she'll have a bit of a scar,' Robbie told her. 'It'll give her distinction, that will.'

'What's distinction?'

'Something making one person look different from everyone else,' Robbie said.

'Oh,' Cammie said. 'Like you. You look different. I never saw anyone looks like you.'

'Cammie!' Meredith cried, aghast. Her hand went down automatically to cover her daughter's mouth.

''T's all right,' Robbie said although he felt himself go red in the face. 'Not like I don't know that—'

'But Mummy . . .' Cammie had wiggled from beneath her mother's grasp. 'He *does* look different. 'Cos his—'

'Camille! Stop that this instant!'

Silence. Into it, cars from the road in front of the house *swooshed* by, a dog barked, Tess lifted her head and growled, the motor of lawn mower sputtered. Suffer the little children, Robbie thought bleakly. Didn't they always tell the truth.

He felt all thumbs and elbows then. He might as well have been a two-headed bull. He looked round and wondered how long he had to remain in the garden in order not to seem rude by running off at once.

Meredith said in a low voice, 'I'm sorry, Rob. She doesn't mean anything by it.'

He managed a chuckle. 'Well, it's not like she's saying something we don't all know, is it, Cammie.' He offered the little girl a smile.

'Still and all,' Meredith said. 'Cammie, you know better than that.'

Cammie looked up at her mother, then back at Rob. She frowned. Then she said quite reasonably, 'But I never ever saw two colours of eyes before, Mummy. Did you?'

Meredith's lips parted. Then closed. Then she rested her head against the back of her chair. She said, 'Oh Lord.' And then to Cammie, 'Only once before, Cam. You're completely right.' She looked away.

And Robbie saw, to his surprise, that Meredith was deeply embarrassed. Not by her daughter, but by her own reaction, by what she'd assumed. Yet all she had done was reach the same conclusion that he himself had reached, hearing Cammie's words: he was truly ugly and all three of them knew it, but only two of them had thought the matter worthy of comment. Cammie certainly hadn't.

He sought a way to smooth the moment. But he could come up with nothing that didn't draw further attention to it, so he finally just said to the little girl, 'So it's hedgehogs, is it, Cammie?'

She said, not illogically, 'What's hedgehogs?'

'I mean what you like. Hedgehogs? That's it? What about ponies? D'you like ponies as well?'

Cammie looked up at her mother, as if to see if she was meant to answer or to hold her tongue. Meredith looked down at her, fondled her rumpled hair, and nodded. 'How *do* you feel about ponies?' she asked her.

'I like 'em best when they're babies,' Cammie said frankly. 'But I know I'm not meant to get too close.'

'Why's that?' Robbie asked her.

''Cos they're skittish.'

'What's that mean, then?'

'Means they're . . .' Cammie's brow wrinkled as she thought

about this. 'Means they're scared easy. An' if they're scared easy, you've got to be careful. Mummy says you always've got to be careful round anyone scares too easy.'

'Why?'

'Oh, 'cos they misunderstand, I expect. Sort of . . . like if you move too fast round them, they c'n think the wrong thing about you. So you got to be quiet and you got to be still. Or move real slow. Or something like that.' She wriggled round again, better to look up at her mother's face. 'That's right, isn't it, Mummy? That's what you do?'

'That's exactly right,' Meredith said. 'Very good, Cam. You take care when you know something's scared.' She kissed the top of her daughter's head. She didn't look at Rob.

Then there seemed to be nothing else to say. Or at least that was what Robbie Hastings told himself. He decided he had done his duty and, all things considered, it was time for him to leave. He stirred on his chair. He said 'So . . .' just as Meredith said, 'Rob . . .'

Their eyes met. He felt himself colouring once again, but he saw that she, too, was red in the face.

She said, 'Cammie, darling. Will you ask Gran if her lemon cake's ready? I'd like a piece and I expect you would as well, hmm?'

'Oh yes,' Cammie said. 'I *love* lemon cake, Mummy.' She clambered out of the lounge chair and ran off, calling to her grandmother. In a moment, a door slammed shut behind her.

Rob slapped his hands on his thighs. Clearly, she'd given the signal for him to take himself off. He said, 'Well. Dead happy you're all right now, Merry.'

She said, 'Ta.' And then, 'Funny, that, Rob.'

He hesitated. 'What?'

'No one else calls me Merry. No one ever has but you.'

He didn't know what to say to this. He didn't know what to make of it either.

'I quite like it,' she said. 'Makes me feel special.'

'You are,' he said. 'Special, that is.'

'You too, Rob. You always have been.'

Here was the moment, and he saw it clearly. More clearly than he'd seen anything ever. Her voice was quiet and she hadn't moved an inch, but he felt her nearness and, feeling this, he also felt the air go dead cold round him.

He cleared his throat.

She didn't speak.

Then on the roof of the garden shed, a bird's feet skittered.

He finally said, 'Merry,' as she herself said, 'Will you stay for a piece of lemon cake with me, Rob?'

And ultimately, he saw, the reply was simple. 'I will,' he replied. 'I'd like that very much.'